IN THE COURTS OF THE SUN

ALSO BY BRIAN D'AMATO

Beauty

IN THE COURTS OF THE SUN

Brian D'Amato

DUTTON

DUTTON
Published by Penguin Group (USA) Inc.
375 Hudson Street, New York, New York 10014, U.S.A.
Penguin Group (Canada), 90 Eglinton Avenue East, Suite 700, Toronto, Ontario M4P 2Y3, Canada (a division
of Pearson Penguin Canada Inc.); Penguin Books Ltd, 80 Strand, London WC2R 0RL, England; Penguin Ireland,
25 St Stephen's Green, Dublin 2, Ireland (a division of Penguin Books Ltd); Penguin Group (Australia), 250 Camberwell
Road, Camberwell, Victoria 3124, Australia (a division of Pearson Australia Group Pty Ltd); Penguin Books India
Pvt Ltd, 11 Community Centre, Panchsheel Park, New Delhi—110 017, India; Penguin Group (NZ),
67 Apollo Drive, Rosedale, North Shore 0632, New Zealand (a division of Pearson New Zealand Ltd);
Penguin Books (South Africa) (Pty) Ltd, 24 Sturdee Avenue, Rosebank, Johannesburg 2196, South Africa

Penguin Books Ltd, Registered Offices: 80 Strand, London WC2R 0RL, England
Published by Dutton, a member of Penguin Group (USA) Inc.

First printing, March 2009
1   3   5   7   9   10   8   6   4   2

REGISTERED TRADEMARK—MARCA REGISTRADA

LIBRARY OF CONGRESS CATALOGING-IN-PUBLICATION DATA
D'Amato, Brian.
In the courts of the sun / Brian D'Amato.
p. cm.
ISBN-13: 978-0-525-95051-6
I. Title.
PS3554.A467515 2009
813'.54—dc22   2008020986

Printed in the United States of America
Set in Kepler Light
Designed by Amy Hill

PUBLISHER'S NOTE
This book is a work of fiction. Names, characters, places, and incidents either are the product
of the author's imagination or are used fictitiously, and any resemblance to actual persons,
living or dead, business establishments, events, or locales is entirely coincidental.

Dedicated to Anthony D'Amato,
author of *Jurisprudence: A Descriptive and Normative Analysis of Law*
and many other writings in law and philosophy
and composer of *RSVP Broadway*
and many other musical works

A percentage of the author's after-tax profits
from this series is donated to various Maya-related
educational, social, and environmental projects.
For more information please see
www.briandamato.com

A NOTE ON PRONUNCIATION

Most Mayan words in this book are spelled according to the current orthography adopted by the Academía de Lenguas Mayas in Guatemala. However, I've retained older spellings for a few words—for instance, the text uses *uay* instead of the now-preferred *way* in order to distinguish the word from the English *way*. Specialists may also notice that some words are spelled to be pronounced in Ch'olan, which usually means a *ch* takes the place of a *k*. I've italicized Mayan and most Spanish words on the first use and dropped the italics after that.

Vowels in Mayan languages are pronounced roughly like those in Spanish. *Ay* in Maya, *uay* etc., is pronounced like the *I* in "I am." *J* is pronounced like the Spanish *j*, that is, a guttural *h* with the tongue farther back than in English. *X* is like the English *sh*. *Tz* is like the English *ts* in "pots." Otherwise, consonants are pronounced as in English. An apostrophe indicates a glottal stop, which is like the *tt* in the Scottish or Brooklynese pronunciation of "bottle." All Mayan words are stressed on the last syllable, but Mayan languages are less stressed than English. Mayan is somewhat tonal, and its prosody tends to emphasize short couplets. There's a certain lilt to it which in some places I've tried to convey with dactyls, although readers may differ on whether this is successful.

Words in the language of Teotihuacan are stressed, like the name of the city, on the penultimate syllable.

MESOAMERICA

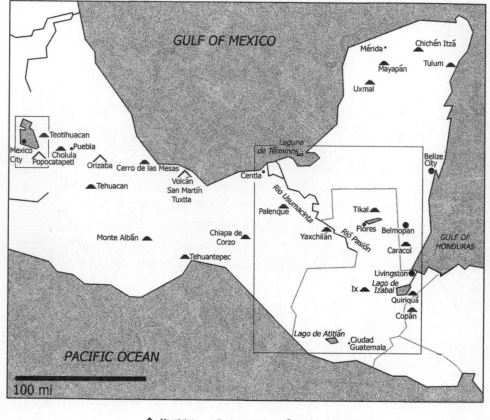

GULF OF MEXICO

Mérida •

Chichén Itzá

Mayapán

Tulum

Uxmal

Teotihuacan

Puebla

Mexico City

Cholula

Popocatapetl

Orizaba

Cerro de las Mesas

Volcán San Martín Tuxtla

Tehuacan

Centla

Laguna de Términos

Belize City

Río Usumacinta

Palenque

Tikal

Flores

Belmopan

Yaxchilán

Río Pasión

Caracol

GULF OF HONDURAS

Monte Albán

Chiapa de Corzo

Tehuantepec

Livingston

Ix

Lago de Izabal

Quiriguá

Copán

Lago de Atitlán

Ciudad Guatemala

PACIFIC OCEAN

100 mi

ᐱ Mountains   ▲ Ancient cities   ● Modern cities and towns

Note: This map shows only sites mentioned in the text

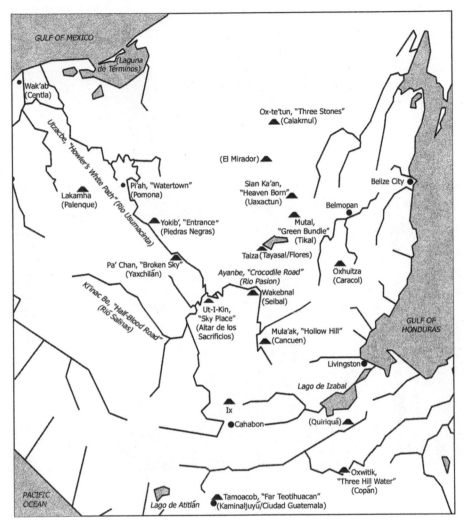

GULF OF MEXICO

(Laguna de Términos)

Wak'ab (Centla)

Utzacbe "Howler's White Path" (Río Usumacinta)

Lakamha (Palenque)

Pi'ah, "Watertown" (Pomona)

Yokib', "Entrance" (Piedras Negras)

Pa' Chan, "Broken Sky" (Yaxchilán)

K'inac Be, "Half-Blood Road" (Río Salinas)

Ut-I-Kin, "Sky Place" (Altar de los Sacrificios)

Ox-te'tun, "Three Stones" (Calakmul)

(El Mirador)

Sian Ka'an, "Heaven Born" (Uaxactun)

Mutal, "Green Bundle" (Tikal)

Taiza (Tayasal/Flores)

Ayanbe, "Crocodile Road" (Río Pasion)

Wakebnal (Seibal)

Mula'ak, "Hollow Hill" (Cancuen)

Belize City

Belmopan

Oxhuitza (Caracol)

GULF OF HONDURAS

Livingston

Lago de Izabal

Ix

Cahabon

(Quiriguá)

Oxwitik, "Three Hill Water" (Copán)

PACIFIC OCEAN

Lago de Atitlán

Tamoacob, "Far Teotihuacan" (Kaminaljuyú/Ciudad Guatemala)

Detail

▲ Ancient cities   ● Modern cities and towns   (Modern names in parentheses)

Please note: This map shows only sites mentioned in the text

ZERO

(0)

The first thing I saw was a red dot on a turquoise field. Then another dot appeared above it and to the left, and a third bloomed close below that one, and then there was another and another, five and then nine and then thirteen. The dots grew and spread, and where they touched they merged and flowed together, and I realized they were drops of my own blood, falling out of my tongue onto blue offering paper.

It worked, I thought. Holy *mierditas*.

It isn't 2012. It's 664. And it's March 20. Or in Maya reckoning, it's 3 Earth Rattler, 5 Rainfrog, in the eleventh *uinal* of the eleventh *tun* of the eleventh *k'atun* of the tenth *b'ak'tun*. And it's about 4:48 A.M. Sunday.

Hmm.

I guess it was like any other big life-mode change; you can only comprehend it after a drawn-out, unfunny double-take, like, oh my God, I'm actually being arrested, I've been stabbed, I'm getting married, I have a child, I'm really having a triple bypass, those buildings are really collapsing—and each time it feels like nothing remotely this serious has ever happened to you or to anyone else. *Hijo de puta,* I thought. I looked up and focused through the tiny trapezoidal doorway. The sky was violet now but somehow I could still see more stars than I ever had before, drifts and spatters of stars down to the fourth magnitude. They'd shifted, of course, but Taro had timed the download so that the tip of One Ocelot's cigar—Algenib, in Pegasus—was nearly in the same position in the trapezoid as before, framed just right of center. There was a new star to its left, halfway to Homam, that would have been bright enough to be listed as Gamma Andromedae. It must be within a hundred years or so of flaming out. Otherwise al-Khawarzimi would have named it.

Unbefarfreakingoutlieveable, I thought. They actually got it right. New bat time, same bat place. Not that I was actually in the same place in the universe, of course, if that even means anything. The solar system moves a lot in 1,347 years. But I was in the same spot on earth. I was still in a tiny room near the apex of the tallest pyramid in the city of Ix, in what would later be called Alta Verapaz, in central Guatemala. But now the sanctuary was orange with torchlight, and the columns of scarabesque glyphs on the walls were smooth and unpitted and polychromed in black, blue, and cochineal carmine. And now the city was alive. I could hear the crowds outside, or maybe, rather, I could feel their chanting through the stone. The point is that from my POV, I hadn't moved in space. But I had—

Hmm. I almost said I'd been sent back in time. But I wouldn't want to start out by dumbing down.

The sad fact is that time travel is impossible. Into the past, that is. If you want to go faster into the future you can just freeze yourself. But going backward is absolutely, unequivocally, and forever unworkable, for a number of well-known reasons. One is the grandfather paradox, meaning you could always go back in time and kill your grandfather, and then you'd presumably never have existed in the first place. Another is that even if you went back and did nothing, you'd almost certainly have some of the same molecules your younger self had been using incorporated into your body. And so the same molecule would be in two different places at once. And that can't happen. The third reason is just a mechanical problem. The only way into the past that anyone knows of is the famous wormhole route. But putting matter through a wormhole is like putting a Meissen vase through a pasta machine. Anything going through it is going to come out the other end crushed and scrambled and no good for anything.

But—but, but, but—there is a workaround.

The Warren Lab's insight was that even if you can't send matter into the past, that still doesn't rule out every possibility. If you can't send anything, that should mean that you can send nothing. And nothing, roughly speaking, includes electromagnetism. They developed a way to send bursts of energy through a tiny, artificially created Krasnikovian tube. They figured the pattern of energy bursts might be able to carry some information. In fact, it could carry a lot of information. The signal they sent back encoded a lifetime of distilled memories, basically everything that creates the illusion called a sense of self. In this case my self.

Of course, the next problem is that there has to be a receiver and storage

on the other end. And in the era we were interested in, there weren't any radar dishes or disk drives or silicon chips or IF antennas or even a crystal radio. Circa 664 there was only one existing object that could receive and store
that much information. A brain.

I began to be able to move my eyeballs. I started to make out how my right
hand, the one holding the thorn rope, was broad and beefy and heavily cal-
lused on the palm heel. Its nails were long and sharpened and inlaid with T-
shaped carnelian studs, and the fingers were tattooed with red and black
bands like coral snakes'. A jade-scale bracelet stretched from the wrist
almost to the elbow. Like the section I could see of my naked chest and my
cauliflowerish left knee, it was crusted with bright blue clay.

Score one for the Freaky Friday Team, I thought. I really was in another
person's body. Specifically, I was in the brain of someone named 9 Fanged
Hummingbird.

We—that is, we at the Warren Project—knew a little about him. He was
the patriarch of the Ocelot Clan and the *ahau*—that is, the king or overlord or
warlord—of the city of Ix and of the roughly two thousand towns and villages
in Ix's orbit. He was the son of the twelfth ahau, 22 Burning Forest, and Lady
Cyclone. Today he was forty-eight years and sixty-one days old. He'd been sitting in here, fasting, for about forty-two straight hours. And he was about to
emerge, at dawn, to be reenthroned for a second twenty-year period as the
ahau.

There was a bowl of hot embers five inches to the north of my left knee,
and without thinking about it I peeled the rectangle of blood-soaked paper
off the reed mat and held it over the heat. For a moment the light of the coals
glowed through the sheet and I could see glyphs on the other side, the phrase
Watch over us, protect us, and then the profile of an eagle:

More specifically, it was a harpy eagle, *Thrasyaetus harpyia*. In Spanish it
was *arpía* and in Mayan it was *hunk'uk*, "gold ripper." And the Aztecs called it
the Wolf with Wings. It was the emblem of a clan, my clan—that is, the clan
of the person whose brain I'd commandeered. The paper was a letter, my
clan's petition to One Ocelot, at the womb of the sky. Automatically, I folded

the sticky sheet into a triangular bundle—it was a complicated set of motions, like making an origami crane, but I, or rather my body's previous owner, must have rehearsed it a hundred times—and set the paper down in the bowl. It must have been soaked in some kind of copper salts, because it sizzled and then sputtered into green flame.

My tongue throbbed. I pulled it in—no, wait. I pulled—

Huh. Nothing happened.

I tried to swallow and then just to close my mouth over my tongue. It was like my face was frozen. Nothing moved.

M'AX ECHE? I thought, in Ch'olan Mayan. Who are you?

No, wait.

I hadn't thought it. It was from somewhere else.

It was as though I'd heard a voice, but I knew I hadn't actually heard anything except the hum of the throng in the plaza below and the swallowed booms of cedar-trunk slit-drums, throbbing in an odd 5/4 beat. Maybe it was more like I'd read it, on some kind of news crawl across my eyes. And even though it was silent it was as though it was loud, or rather forceful, as though it was written in upper case. It was like I'd thought it, but without think—

M'AX ECHE?

Oh, hell.

I wasn't alone in this body.

I was alone in the room, but not in my brain.

Oh, *coño Dios.*

The thing is, the first part of the Freaky Friday process had been supposed to erase the target's memories, to give my consciousness a clean slate to work on, as it were. But evidently that part hadn't worked, or at least not very well. He still thought he was him.

M'AX ECHE?

My name is Jed DeLanda, I thought back.

B'A'AX UKA'AJ CHOK B'OLECH TEN? Roughly, "WHY HAVE YOU POSESSED ME?"

I'm not possessing you, I thought. That is, I'm inside, I mean, my consciousness is inside you because, because we sent it into you—

T'ECHE HUN BALAMAC? ARE YOU ONE OCELOT?

No, I thought back, too quickly. I mean—

Damn it. Stupid.

Come on, Jed, I thought. It's like Winston says, when somebody asks if you're a god, you say yes. Got it? Okay.

Here goes.

Yes! I thought at him, more consciously. I *am* One Ocelot. Ocelot the Oce-tarian. I am Ocelot, the great and power—

MA-I'IJ TEC. NO, YOU ARE NOT.

No, I am, I thought, I—oh, *demonio.* It's not easy to lie to this guy. And no wonder. He's hearing everything I think. And even though he only spoke old Ch'olan and I was thinking in my usual mix of Spanish, English, and late, de-generate Ch'olan, we still understood each other completely. In fact, it felt less like talking with someone else than it felt like arguing with yourself, thinking, Jed, maybe you should do this, and no, Jed, you should do that, except that one side of the internal dialogue was effortless and self-assured, and the other side—my side—was having trouble getting its points together.

WHY HAVE YOU INFECTED ME, POSSESSED ME?

What? I said, or rather thought. I came to learn to play the Sacrifice Game. It was the truth.

WHY?

Well, because—because I come from the last days of the world, from the thirteenth b'ak'tun. Because my world is in big, big trouble and we need to learn the Game to see if we can save it.

GET OUT, he thought.

I can't.

GET OUT.

Sorry. I really, really can't. You're the one who—

IM OT' XEN. GET OUT OF MY SKIN.

I can't do that, I thought back. But, listen, how about this, I can—

THEN **HIDE,** he thought. STAY DOWN, STAY STILL, STAY SILENT.

I shut up. I was getting a bad feeling about this.

My hand rose to my open mouth and closed on a barbed cord, basically a rope of thorns, that ran through a hole in the center of my tongue. I yanked on it. Five thorn-knots squeezed down through the hole, spattering blood, before the rope popped out. Hmm, painful, I thought vaguely. Actually, it was enough to have made my former body scream for an hour, but now I didn't even squirm. More oddly than that, I didn't feel the Fear, the old hæmophili-ac's fear of bleeding out that I'd never gotten rid of when I was Jed. I coiled the rope into the bowl, as automatically as an ejected fighter pilot wadding up his parachute. It blackened and curled, and blood smoke filled the room with a coppery tang.

I swallowed a big gob of blood. Tasty. The chanting outside had grown louder and I found I could pick out the words, and that even though the Ch'olan was more different from our twenty-first-century reconstructed version than I would have thought possible, I could still understand them:

"Uuk ahau k'alomte yaxoc . . ."

"Overlord, greatfather,
Grandfather-grandmother
Jade Sun, Jade Ocelot,

Captor of 25 Duelist of Three Hill Lake,
Captor of 1,000 Strangler of Broken Sky . . ."

Our legs uncrossed. Our hands straightened our headdress—it felt like a tall stiff pillow tufted with cat fur—but didn't wipe the blood off our face.

"Captor of 17 Sandstorm of Scorched Mountain,

Nurturer, watchkeeper,
Jade 9 Fanged Hummingbird:

When will you next
Reemerge from your sky cave
To hear us, to look on us?"

We crept forward to the tiny door, keeping our head down, and crouched through, out into the wide air. There was a sudden silence from the throngs in the plazas and then a collective gasp, breath rushing into so many lungs that I thought I could feel the drop in pressure. We stood up. Jade scales and spiny-oyster beads clattered over our skin. It seemed like whatever little blood we had left had drained out of our head, and I suppose on any normal day even this body would have fainted, but now some higher hormone held him together and we didn't even wobble on our high platform sandals, which were really more like stilts, with soles at least eight inches thick. I could feel I was smaller than Jed had been. And lighter and stronger. I definitely didn't feel forty-eight years old. I felt about sixteen. Odd. I looked up. Ix spread out below us and covered the world.

Our eyes only sucked it in for two and a half seconds before they looked up again at Algenib. But it was enough time to see that not one of us in 2012—or, for that matter, in any of the preceding five centuries—had had the slightest notion of what this place had actually looked like.

We were worse than wrong, I thought. We were dull. It was as though we'd been walking through the desert and found five bleached bones out of the 206 or so bones that make up your basic skeleton, and instead of just working out the dead person's sex and age and genetic heritage and whatever else you can legitimately get from a few ribs and vertebrae and just stopping there, we'd spun out this whole scenario about what her life was like, her clothes, her hobbies, her children's names, whatever, and then we'd gone on to write a full biographical textbook about her, complete with beige pie graphs and anemic illustrations in scruffy gouache. And now that I was actually meeting the living person, not only did she have very little physical resemblance to the reconstruction, but her personality and life story and place in the universe were utterly different from our pedestrian guesswork.

The scraps of granular ruins that had survived into the twenty-first century had been less than 5 percent of the story, just the stone underframes of a city that hadn't been built so much as woven and plaited and knotted and laced out of reeds and lath and swamp cane, a wickerwork metropolis so unlike what I'd imagined that I couldn't even pick out the monuments I knew. We faced due east across the river, toward Cerro San Enero, the highest peak of the cordillera that ringed the valley of Ix. Now it was erupting, spewing a fan of black ash against the mauve predawn . . . no, wait, I thought. No way, it's not a volcano. They must have built a rubberwood bonfire up there—but the other hills were wrong too, they'd been forested before and now they were all denuded, carved into terraces and nested plazas cascading down the slopes like waterfall pools, and they were crested with headdresses of canework spikes that radiated like liberty crowns. Shoals of spots or flecks or something bobbed above and in front of the hills and towers, and, for the first half of the second I had to look at the city, I thought the spots were an illusion of my own new eyes, migraine flashers, maybe, or some kind of iridescent nematodes swimming in my aqueous humor, but at the next beat I realized they were hundreds of human-size featherwork kites, all either round or pentagonal and all in target patterns of black, white, and magenta, floating on the hot breath of the crowd, reflecting the city like a lake in the air.

The crowd started a new chant, in a new key:

"Hun k'in, ka k'inob, ox k'inob . . ."

"One sun, then two suns, then three suns . . ."

De todos modos, I thought. Focus. Get oriented.

Find some landmarks. Where was the river? I had an impression that it had been widened into a lake, but I couldn't see any actual water. Instead there was a plane tessellated with what must have been rushwork rafts and giant canoes, with bright-yellow veins between the boats that might have been millions of floating marigold heads. I had an impression of tiers within tiers of interlocking compounds on the opposite shore, stegosaurus-backed longhouses and buttressed towers with gravity-disregarding overhangs that seemed so structurally unsound they had to be featherlight, maybe made out of lattice and corn paste . . . but like I said, it was just an impression, because every facet, every horizontal or vertical surface, from the hilltops to the plaza just below us, seethed with life. Serried ranks of the *ajche'ejob*, the Laughing People, that is, the Ixians, carpeted the squares and clung to poles and scaffolds and façades in a pulsing mass, like the layer of polyps that ripples over the skeleton of a thousand-year-old reef, straining gorgonians out of the sea. The only unpopulated surfaces were the steep-angled shoulder planes of the four great *mulob*, the subordinate pyramids, rising out of the turbulence like step-cut chunks of lab-grown carborundum. And even those didn't show a single patch of their stone cores; everything was stuccoed over and dyed and oiled and petal-tufted, striated in layers of turquoise, yellow, and black, hard-edged and mischievous, an array of poisoned pastry. Each *mul* wore a gigantic fletched roof comb and spewed smoke from hidden vents. How many thousands of people were there? Fifty? Seventy? I could only see a fraction of them. Say there are two thousand in the Ocelots' plaza, that's about two and a half acres, then suppose there are thirty plazas that size in all—never mind. Stick to the mission. *De todos modos.* Where was 9 Fanged Hummingbird? Got to try to find him—

"Wak k'inob, wuk k'inob . . ."

"Six suns, then seven suns . . ."

Upa. Uh-oh.

Something was wrong.

That is, besides the way this guy was still in his head. There was something else wrong. Very ghastlyly wrong. What was it?

I tried to listen to his thoughts, the way he listened to mine. And I did hear something, and I got flashes of images, wrinkled toothless farmers' faces, naked, goitred children waddling out of twig huts, bloody footsmears on yellow sunlit pavement, big, heavy flaming rubber balls lobbing through violet air, arcing toward me, streaking away from me . . . well, they weren't the memories of a king. Somehow a sense of his sense of his identity percolated through, and I realized I knew his name: Chacal.

Not 9 Fanged Hummingbird. Chacal.

And he's not the ahau. No. I'm—he's—he's a hipball player.

Yep. Wrong. Something had gone really, seriously wrong.

This guy's *dressed* as the ahau, and he's up here in the ahau's special chamber, but he's not . . .

"Bolon k'inob, lahun k'inob," the crowd chanted.

"Nine suns, then ten suns,
Eleven suns, twelve suns . . ."

It was a countdown. Although they were counting up, to nineteen.

Okay, what the hell's going on with this guy? He's not the ahau, but he's going, he's playing . . .

The certainty descended around me like lead rain. He's taking 9 Fanged Hummingbird's place.

And this isn't a reenthronement, I thought. It's an offering. He's a sacrifice. A willing, happy sacrifice. They were counting up to a liftoff, or rather a jump-off. After nineteen, the count would go back to zero. And I'd go down.

Oh, cripes.

Stupid. Should've thought of that. Obvious possibility.

In fact, come to think of it, I even remembered reading something about this kind of thing. It was in an article in *JPCS* called "Royal Auto-Sacrifice by Proxy in Pre-Columbian America." The theory was that in the old days—that is, the really really old days even before this one—the ahau would only have been put in charge for one k'atun. A k'atun is a vicennium, a period of about twenty years. And then, before the ahau got old and feeble and spread that weakness to the body politic, he would have turned the town over to a younger heir and then committed suicide. But at some point some genius ahau had decided he could make it all a little easier on himself and still keep up the formalities. So he'd put on a big ceremony where he'd transfer his name and regalia to somebody else—not even a look-alike or an impersonator but just a captive or volunteer or whatever—and that person would take on his identity and act as the ahau for five days. And when the five days were up, he'd sacrifice himself. It was like burning someone in effigy. A living effigy. And then when that was over the old ahau would have another ritual where he'd give himself a new name, and he'd stay in charge for another k'atun.

Well, great. At least I know what's going on. What's going on is I'm all the hell up here in this unfamiliar body, I'm utterly alone—in fact, nobody I know has even been born yet—and now it turns out I'm supposed to kill myself. What next?

Okay. Don't freak. You can still pull this off. So you're not in the right guy. *Ve al grano.* It's still just a minor setback. Right? Luckily, we have some contingency plans just in case of little glitches like this.

Along with the Chocula Team and the Freaky Friday Team—and I realize this is throwing a lot of jargon at once—Warren had also put together a linguistic research group called the Connecticut Yankee Team. Its job had been to create a menu of things for me to say and/or do when/if I came up against this sort of problem or something like it. They'd trained me to the point where I knew every one of them as well as I knew the lyrics to "Happy Birthday." The appropriate action for this contingency was called the Volcano Speech. Okay. I ran through it a couple times in my side of my mind, adapting the words to the surprisingly unfamiliar version of Ch'olan. *Bueno.* Got it. No problem.

Ready? Just shout it out. "I am the blinder," et cetera. They'll hear the prediction, they'll wait to see if it's true, and then, when the sucker erupts, I'll be too valuable to kill. In fact, they'll probably set me up with my own shop. A modest fifty-room palace, three or four hundred nubile concubines, maybe a pyramid or two. Or maybe they'll even make me the ahau. It'll be like Lord Jungle Jim crashing his plane in the jungle. Just flick your Zippo and the cannibals'll pull you out of the stew pot and call you Bwana White. No sweat. Right? Right.

Estas bien. Deep breath. Go.

Go.

Nothing.

Okay. Go.

Nothing.

Again. Go. Shout. Now!

Frozen.

Oh, hell.

Come on, Jed, you know what to say. Spit it out. *I am the blinder of the coming sun.* Come on. Open the mouth. Open mouth. All I have to do is open my—

MY MOUTH.

Oh hell oh hell. *¡Ni mierditas!*

Okay, come on, guy, come on—nnnnnNNN*NN*Nh!!!

I strained to pry my jaws apart but the only physical effect was a distant ache, like somewhere I was biting a rock.

Oh Christ, oh Christ. This can't be happening. Chacal *cannot* be in control of this body. It's mine. Come on. Move. Anything. Just *squirm*, for crying out loud. Raise hand.

Nothing.

Raise hand.

Nothing.

Raise hand, raise hand! *Raise* finger—

Hell.

We screwed up, we screwed up. Stupid, stupid, stupid, stupid.

We took five formal steps toward the lip of the staircase. I strained against his body. There was no effect. It felt as though I was strapped into an industrial robot, maybe like the one in *Aliens,* and it was just marching along preprogrammedly while I couldn't even find the controls. We stopped. Our toes projected just slightly out into the void.

I knew that we were exactly 116½ vertical feet above the surface of the Ocelots' plaza, or 389 diagonal feet by way of the two hundred and sixty steps. But it seemed twice as high now, and not just because I was smaller than I'd been. We looked down into the vortex of the receding planes. Vertigo pulled at us. The turquoise stairs glistened with pink suds, a mixture of maguey beer and the blood of previous sacrifices. The steps were edged with triangular stones that made them look serrated, like hacksaw blades. Architecture as weapon.

The idea was that I'd leap down the stairs, with as much grace as possible, and by the time I got to the bottom I'd be in several different pieces. And they'd all grab up my parts and then, probably, mix me into tamale meat and distribute me throughout the tri-pyramid area.

Well, hell. That's some really bad luck. Maybe I'd been expecting too much.

I'd thought I'd just cruise back here and be all set, curled up in a nice clean brain inside the big chalupa of the whole place, and that since I was in charge I could do roughly whatever I wanted, I'd have a decent chance at getting the dirt on the Game, I'd build my tomb just the way I wanted, I'd live it up a little, no problem. If that had—

Stop it, I thought. Stick to the reality. The reality was that I was simply *not* in control of Chacal's motor neurons. I was just along for the ride, just hanging out somewhere in his prefrontal cortex. And he was totally, reverently, imbecilically determined to kill himself—in spectacular and heroic fashion—in only a few seconds.

"Fourteen suns, fifteen suns . . ."

The pitch of the chanting rose higher. They were cheering me, egging me on, and I felt the urge to leap, floating higher on the wave of their expectation. They were so hopeful, so eager, and they only wanted one little thing from me. It felt like anybody in this position might jump just because he was caught up in the excitement. Maybe it is the right thing to do—

No. Squelch that thought. Come on, Jed. Just push this doofus out of the driver's seat, grab the wheel, and turn the damn car around. The locals'll fall right into line. No sweat—

MA! Chacal snarled around me. NO!

I felt a constriction tightening on my thoughts, a kind of mental lockjaw, and for an indeterminate amount of time I was all just the plain panic of claustrophobia and suffocation. At one point I thought I started to scream, and then I noticed my lips weren't opening, my lungs weren't pumping, nothing was happening. I was just standing there, looking cute, flipping up inside, just sheer terror, repeating myself, oh God, oh God, oh God, and then I thought I could hear or sense Chacal's consciousness laughing, almost cheering, almost, in fact, orgasming.

Well, this is it. Old Jed's last moment before the click of oblivion, which in fact was seeming more and more attractive.

Estoy jodido. I'm fucked. This is it, this is what it's like, death—

Waitwaitwait. Snap out of it. Get back on track. *Think!*

En todos modos. Bad break. Regroup. New tactic.

What we need to do here is . . . uh . . . what we have to do is get old Chacal here on our side.

Right. Okay.

Chacal? I thought at him. Let's just cool out for a second. *Prenez un chill pill.* You don't have to do this.

Silence. That is, mental silence.

Chac man? *Compadre?*

Let me tell you something. Okay? Okay. All this around here isn't everything. There's a whole lot more to the world. Just take a peek in my memories. You can see in there, right? Check it out, Europe, Asia, computers, marshmallows . . . you see how relative everything is? Look into my memories. Bet you didn't know the earth was ball-shaped. Cool, huh? And there's other stuff. Doesn't this maybe provoke a few tiny second thoughts?

YOU ARE A SCAB CASTER'S MAGGOT-*UAY* AND THESE ARE YOUR USUAL LIES, Chacal thought.

Huh? I thought back. I didn't get all that. At least we've got a dialogue going, though. That's good. Okay. Chacal? Listen. You *know* I'm not lying. We're a team now. We're in this together. And I, for one, am just fine with that. What do you think? I think we'll do very well together. Chacal?

YOU ARE POLLUTED AND YOU ARE AFRAID. I WILL NOT LET YOU DEFILE THIS PUREST OF PLACES.

Fine, I thought. Whatever. Look, come on, Chaco dude. Wake up. You're being used.

IT IS TOO LATE FOR YOU. I HAVE MADE THE DUTIFUL DECISION.

Oh. Okay. Well, good, I respect that. At least you do realize there isn't any One Ocelot, right? Not in any Womb of the Sky or anywhere else. That's just propaganda. You know what propaganda is? Anyway, the thing is, even if it was the right decision at the time, the right thing to do now, even in terms of helping out your family, say, may be to at least see what I have to offer and then—

SILENCE FROM THE MAGGOT-UAY.

"Seventeen suns, eighteen suns . . ."

Okay, look, Chaco, let's just give it a shot, why don't you let me just say what I have to say and then see what happens. I promise that for both of us, things will improve dramatically—

NO MORE FROM YOU.

One second. I really have some ideas here. A few days and you'll be in charge. Crush your enemies, reward your friends. Live it up. I have magic. I'll just say a few really powerful—

NO!

It was his last word on the matter.

There was another constriction around me, tighter. Can't breathe. Can't think, even.

Nnn.

Come on. Resist. Have to get him to say the thing, one way or another. Think of something.

Nnnnn.

Okay. Come on, Jed. It's still quite possible that you can control this guy's movements. Maybe he's not really the dominant consciousness. Maybe he just thinks he is. It's probably just a matter of point of view. It's all about strength of character. Taking charge. Be a mensch for once.

Come on. Just show him you're tougher than he is. Say it! *I am the blinder of the coming sun.* Say it. Come *on*, Jed, assert your *chingado* self for once. *I am the blinder of the coming sun.* Come on, *TWIST THE WHEEL!* Get it out. *I am the blinder of the coming . . .*

Nnnnt.

"Nineteen suns . . ."

Come on, Jed old guy. Resist this jerk. Resistance is *not* useless. I strained. Nnnnnnnn.

Jed! Hey! **Now!**

You *must* do something. Talk, scream, grunt, anything . . .

NnnnnmmmmNNNzzznnkk. Fuck! It was like being hopelessly constipated, straining and squeezing and getting nothing, nothing coming out, nothing—

"Zero suns."

Come on, Jed. Save the Project, save the planet, save your ass, come on, just this one time, got to do something, something, come on do something clev—

ONE

The Qarafa of Megacon

(1)

B ut hold on a second. Maybe we're getting a little too cute here.
Maybe I'm throwing too much out at once. Maybe we need to answer some basic questions. After all, this is a deposition of a kind. I have a whistle to blow. So maybe I should take it a little seriously and not get coy, and briefly run through how the hell I got here. Maybe you can't escape at least a smidgen of backstory any more than you can escape, say, the future.

My full name is Joaquín Carlos Xul Mixoc DeLanda. Unlike most Maya Indians I was born in a real hospital, in a small city called San Cristobal Verapaz, in the Alta Verapaz area of southeastern Guatemala and thirty miles west of the Gulf of Honduras. SCV is about ninety miles northeast of CG, that's Ciudad Guatemala, or Guatemala City, and ten miles west of T'ozal, the village, or really the hamlet, where I grew up. My naming day, which is more important than my birthday, was three days later, on November 2, 1974, or, in our reckoning, 11 Howler, 4 Whiteness, in the fifth uinal of the first *tun* of the eighteenth k'atun of the thirteenth and last b'ak'tun. This was exactly one million eight hundred and fifty-eight thousand and seventy-one *k'inob*—suns, or lights, or days—since the first day of the Long Count calendar on 4 Overlord, 8 Dark Egg, 0.0.0.0.0, or August 11, 3113 BCE. And it was a mere thirteen thousand nine hundred and twenty-eight days before the last sun, on 4 Overlord, 3 Yellowribs, on the last day of the last k'atun of the thirteenth b'ak'tun. That is, before December 21, AD 2012. Which, as you probably already have heard, is the day they say time stops.

My father was a half-Hispanic K'ekchi speaker and something of an intellectual by local standards. He'd gone to the Santiago Indigenous Institute in Guate City and ran the area's rudimentary school system. My mother spoke Ch'olan, which, of all the living Mayan dialects, is the closest to the ancient southern Maya language. Her family had been displaced from Chiapas in the 1930s and was now part of a small Ch'olan enclave south of their main concentration. I learned more than most of the local kids did about who we were and the history of the country and whatever. But I still didn't know much. I knew that in the old days we had been architects and kings, but that now we were poor. Still, I didn't know our culture was dying. I thought our *akal,* that is, a house with cinder-block walls and a thatched roof, and—Jesus, I grew up under a *thatched roof,* for God's sake, it's like I'm Grout of the Cave Sloth Clan, I can hardly believe it myself sometimes—and our *jon-ka'il,* the town plaza, was the center of a very small universe. When I look back on it, it seems pretty benighted. But really I suppose I didn't know much less about history than the average U.S. public-school kid does today. Most people probably have an idea there are all these odd-looking ruined pyramids somewhere down south. A smaller group would be able to tell you there were ancient people down there called the Aztecs, the Toltecs, the Inca, and the Maya. A lot of people might have seen the Maya in the Mel Gibson movie about them, or they might have been to Mexico City and seen the ruins of Teotihuacan. But it would be unusual to just run into someone in the U.S. who could tell you, say, what the differences were between the Aztecs and the Toltecs, or who would know that there were a lot of other equally accomplished but less famous people, like the Mixtecs and Zapotecs and Tarascans, in the area from Central Mexico to Honduras that we now prefer to call Mesoamerica, or that the Inca lived thousands of miles to the southwest, on a whole other continent, so that as far as we Maya were concerned, they might as well have been on Neptune.

There are also huge stretches of time between the flowerings of these different civilizations. The Toltecs hit their peak around 1100. Teotihuacan was largely abandoned sometime between 650 and 700. What they call the Maya's Late Classic Period lasted from about AD 600 to 850, and by the time the Aztecs were getting started, about six hundred years later, the Maya were in an advanced state of political decline. The old saw in introductory Mesoamerican studies is that if the Maya were like the ancient Greeks, the Toltecs and Aztecs were like the Romans. Except that the only thing the Maya really had in common with the Greeks was genius.

Now, of course, these days you have to say each culture or whatever is outstanding in its own way. When I was in school there was a day when they went around and changed all the labels in the university art museum so that instead of reading, say, "Dung Fetish, Ookaboolakonga Tribe, Nineteenth

Century," they'd read "Dung Fetish, Ookaboolakonga Civilization, Nineteenth Century." Like five huts and a woodcarver and it's a civilization. But the sad fact is that cultures are like artists: Only a few of them are real geniuses. And of all the world's genius cultures the Maya seem most to have bloomed out of the blue. Phonetic writing was only invented three times: once in China, once in Mesopotamia, once by the ancestors of the Maya. Zero was only invented twice: once near what's now Pakistan, and once, before that, by the Maya. The Maya were and are special, and that's all you need to know.

Not so many people know even this much, probably for two reasons. One is plain prejudice. The other is that it's probably fair to say that probably no other civilization, and certainly no other literate civilization, has ever been so thoroughly eradicated. But there are more than six million living speakers of Maya languages left, more than half of whom live in Guatemala, and a lot of us still know something about the old days.

My mother, especially, knew something. But I had no sense there was anything remarkable about her, beyond being the most important person in the world. And I suppose you could say there wasn't, except for one little thing she taught me about in 1981, during the rains—when I got sick, as our padre charmingly put it, "unto death."

(2)

I got what they now think was dengue fever. It was more dangerous than it is these days, and on top of that I was hemorrhaging in my lungs and sneezing up blood because of what turned out to be a factor-8 deficiency, that is, hæmophilia B. I spent three months lying rolled up behind the hearth, counting the bright red stitches in my cotton blanket and listening to the dogs. My mother mouth-fed me corn gruel and Incaparina milk substitute and told stories in our quiet singsong style, sometimes in Spanish and sometimes in Ch'olan. Everyone else, even my youngest sister, was working down in the fincas, in the lowlands. One evening I was lying on my side, trying not to vomit, and I noticed a tree snail crawling up a wet patch on the cinder-block wall. It was a blue-green balled cone, like a plumb bob, striped with orange and black, a *Liguus fasciaticus bourboni,* as I learned much later. My mother told me the snail was my second *chanul,* a *"chanul de brujo,"* that is, a warlock's familiar.

All traditional Maya have a chanul—or, to use the Classic Mayan word, a uay. It's generally outside your body, but it's also one of your souls. If you're hungry, it gets hungry, and if someone kills it, you die. Some people are closer to their uays than others, and a few can morph their own body into the body of their uay and prowl around as an animal. It's a bit like the animal familiars in the *His Dark Materials* books, except it's more part of you. I already had a normal uay—a *sa'bin-'och,* which is sort of like a hedgehog—but according to my mother the snail was going to be just as important. It's an unusual uay to have and seemingly not very powerful. But a lot of *brujos'* uays are small and secretive.

Around this same time my mother started playing a counting game with me. At first, I guess, it was just to teach me numbers. Pretty soon we played it every afternoon. She used to roll the rush mat aside from next to where I was lying. Underneath she'd spooned twenty-five little holes out of the clay floor, in a cross shape. The idea is to visualize the cross as though it were in the sky and you were lying supine on the ground, with your head at the sun's current azimuth in the southeast:

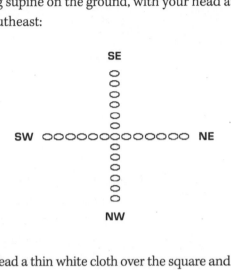

She used to spread a thin white cloth over the square and push it down a bit into each of the depressions, and chew up a bit of tobacco and smear some of the juice on the inside of her left thigh. When I learned to do it, she had me rub it on my right thigh. Peeling open one of her prized Tupperware containers, she'd take out her *grandeza*—which is a pouch of amulets and stones and things—and pour out a mound of red *tz'ite* beans, which are really these hard seeds from a coral tree—and set out her quartz pebbles, which I would hold up to my eye and look for bouncing lights inside. I never understood why she did this next bit— she'd smear a line of wet black across her face, starting from the crown of her left ear, running under her left eye, across her upper lip, and down her right cheek to the right mandibular angle. The routine was that we'd each take a random handful of seeds out of the mound and empty it out on the margins of the cloth, to the east and west of the depressions, while we each asked for help from the protector of the day. Then she'd tap the ground five times and say,

> "*Hatz-kab ik,*
> *Ixpaayeen b'aje'laj . . .*"

That is,

> "Now may I borrow
> The breath of the sun

Of today, now I borrow
The breath of tomorrow's.

Now I am rooting
And now I am centering,
Scattering black seeds
And scattering yellow seeds,
Adding up white skulls
And adding up red skulls,
Counting the blue-green suns,
Counting the brown-gray suns."

In Ch'olan the word for "skull" is also a word for "corn kernel." Next we'd take turns counting out the seeds into the bins in groups of four and use the beans to mark today's date on top of that. Then she would bring out a single thumbnail-size crystal of carnelian quartz. This was the runner.

Just like the pieces in Parcheesi, the runners move through the game board based on a randomizer. Instead of dice we use corn kernels that have a black dot on one side. You throw them up and count how many land with the black side up. Unlike Parcheesi, though, the number of kernels you throw varies on the basis of where you are in the Game. There were different counting protocols applied, like if your last group had three counters in it you'd sometimes break it up into two and one and count it as one even number and one odd one.

And the Game is complicated in other ways. There's a whole set of question-and-answer jingles, starting with one for each of the two hundred and sixty day-name-and-number combinations in the ritual calendar. Each of those names intersected with another three hundred and sixty names for the solar days. Combinations had their own attached proverbs and their own shades of meaning, depending on other aspects of the position. So—a little like in the *I Ching* or in Yoruban Ifa—the Game generates little phrases, which you could read as sentences. And because there are so many possible combinations, it can seem like it's conversing with you in a pretty unpredictable way. Usually my mother said it was Santa Teresa, who was something like the goddess of the Game, interpreting for us. When something bad came up, though, she said it was Saint Simón who was talking. He was a bearded man who sat at the crossroads, at the center of the Game, and whom some people still called Maximón.

So anyway, the Game is like a combination of a map, an abacus, and a perpetual calendar. Movements of the quartz pebble, the "runner" piece, give you variables depending on how far ahead you want to read and how much you want to rely on intuition. Sometimes out of two reasonable moves one just looks better. There's also a special way to press intuition into service. My mother taught me to sit still and wait for *tzam lic*, that is, "blood lightning." It's a kind of a twitch or fluttering feeling under the skin, maybe some kind of a miniature muscle spasm. I guess you could call it a frisson. When it came, its intensity and its location and direction on your body told you things about the move in question. For instance, if it were on the inner edge of your left thigh, where the tobacco stain was, it might mean a male relative was coming to see you from the northeast, and if it were the same feeling but on the outside of the thigh, it might suggest that the visitor was a woman. Usually my mother would try to find out—I don't want to say "predict"—just basic things, most often about the crops, like whether the squash beetles were getting ready for another attack. Nearly as often it was about the weather, with the red runner representing the sun and the others standing in for clouds or marking mountains. Sometimes she'd use the runner to represent relatives or neighbors, to try to help them with big events in their lives like marriages or, if they were sick, to find out when they'd get better. One time I remember I'd asked her to play for my maternal cousin's paternal grandmother, who had a bad stomach worm, and my mother stopped the Game in the middle. Much later on I got wise to the fact that it was because she'd seen that the old woman wasn't going to recover.

As my mother said, the Game didn't work so well for little things. There were times when I said I wanted to guess when my father was coming home that day. She'd resist it at first because it was too trivial, but finally she'd let me move the quartz pebble around as a stand-in for Tata, and she'd kind of play against him. So my counter had to stay ahead of my mother's seeds as they came after me. If at the end she finally trapped my counter in, say, the northwest bin, that would mean he was coming home to us very late, by way of the town northwest of us. If he fell in the south bin, that meant he was still at the school. If he ended up in the center bin, that meant he was just about to come home. And he always did. Within a few minutes he'd crouch through the door.

None of this seemed at all like fortune telling or astrology or any of that *disparate*. It was more like the Game—or just for continuity, let's call it, prematurely, the Sacrifice Game, although I realize I haven't properly introduced this idea yet—it was like the Sacrifice Game was helping you realize things consciously that your mind had already noticed. One time one of my uncles said that in the old days the original people had owls' eyes and could see up through the shell of the sky and through mountains into the caves of the dead and the unborn. If someone was sick you could look through his skin and into his organs to find the problem. You could see your birth behind you and your death in front of you. But since then our eyes had become clouded and we could only see a tiny fraction of the world, just what was on the surface. I practiced a lot. On the first day of my twelfth *tz'olk'in*—that is, when I was about eight and a half years old—my mother initiated me into life as a *h'men*.

The word's been translated as "daykeeper," "timekeeper," "sun keeper," and even "time accountant." Most literally, in Ch'olan it would be "sun totaler" or "sun adder-upper," or let's say "sun adder." A sun adder is basically the village shaman, a pagan alternative to the Catholic priest. We figure out whether a client is sick because some dead relative is hassling her, and if so what little offerings she should make to him to shut him up and which herbs to hang around her house for a faster recovery. When should you burn off your *milpa*, that is, your family cornfield? Is this a good day to take a bus trip to the capital? What would be a lucky day to have the christening? It's all blended up with Catholicism, so we also use bits of liturgy. If you wanted to be a bastard about it, you could say we're the local witch doctors. The reason we're called sun adders is that our main job is to keep track of the traditional ritual calendar. All the little ritual offerings that we do, even all the Sacrifice Game stuff— which, if you wanted to be a bitch about it, you could call fortune telling—is pretty secondary.

For the Ch'olan, things come in pairs, especially bad things. Two years after I got my adder bundle, that's how it happened with us.

One thing about places like Guatemala is that the Conquest is still going on. In Guatemala—just for the barest smidge of history—things had settled down for most of us indigenes in the late nineteenth and early twentieth centuries, and by the early fifties, things weren't all that bad. But in the summer of 1954 the CIA, at the behest of the United Fruit Company—the Chiquita banana folks—engineered a coup against the elected president and set up Carlos Castillo Armas as a puppet dictator. Besides doing everything the Pulpo—that is, the Octopus, as we called the UFC—wanted, he immediately began an unofficial ethnic cleansing policy against the Maya. UN estimates list about two hundred thousand Maya massacred or disappeared from 1958 to 1985, which gives Guatemala the lowest human rights rating in the Western Hemisphere. For us it was the worst period since the Spanish invasion in the sixteenth century.

The U.S. Congress stopped official aid to the government in 1982, but the Reagan administration kept it going secretly, sending weapons and training Guate army officers in counterinsurgency techniques at the School of the Americas in Fort Benning. Maybe a few of them were sincere anti-Communists who actually thought the guerrillas were a threat, but 97 percent of everything is real estate and by '83, when the genocide peaked at around fourteen aborigines per day, the war wasn't anything but a real-estate grab. They'd roll in, say, "You're all guerrillas," and that'd be it. A year later any producing fields would be occupied by Ladinos.

In the U.S. most people seem to think of the CIA as some kind of sleek, efficient secret society with good-looking employees and futuristic gadgets. Latin Americans know it as just another cartel, big, bumbling, but better financed than most, running errands for the big drug wholesalers and shaking down the small ones. In the seventies and eighties the military built thousands of little airstrips all over rural Guatemala, supposedly to help us disadvantaged types move products to nonlocal markets but actually so they could drop in anywhere, anytime they needed to goose a deadbeat. There were more than a couple around T'ozal. One of my father's many uncles-in-law, a *parcelista* named Generoso Xul, marked out and burned off a few milpas on common land that turned out to be a bit too close to one of them. By late July Generoso was missing, and my father and a few others went out looking for him. On the second day they found his shoes tied up and hanging in a eucalyptus tree, which is a kind of sleeps-with-the-fishes warning sign.

My father talked to this person he knew from the local resistance, who was a Subcomandante Marcos–like figure called Teniente Xac, or as we called him, Uncle Xac. Tío Xac said he guessed that the Soreanos *"habian dado agua al Tío G,"* that is, that they'd killed him. After that my father got all these kids and parcelistas and their kids to watch for the airplanes and write down their registration codes on cigarette papers and bring them to him, and he compiled a pretty long list. A friend in CG checked them with the AeroTransport Data Bank—Guatemala was so much these people's backyard that they hardly ever even bothered to change the numbers—and it turned out a bunch of them were operated out of Texas and Florida by Skyways Aircraft Leasing, which, it came out much later, was a shell corporation, and had flown out of John Hull's estate in Costa Rica. Hull—and this could sound a little conspiracykookish if it weren't well documented in, for instance, the 1988 Kerry Congressional Subcommittee paper " 'Private Assistance' and the Contras: A Staff Report" of 10/14/86, easily available at the Ronald Reagan Presidential Library, 40 Presidential Drive, Simi Valley, California, under "White House Legal Task Force: Records, Box 92768"—was a U.S. citizen who laundered money and shipped uncut cocaine for Oliver North's crew. Most of the money went to the contras in El Salvador, but the North cartel, the Bush cronies, and the Ríos Montt group—Montt was the puppet president of Guatemala at the time—all took home millions. My guess is that Uncle Xac was hoping to go wide with the list at some point, either just to focus some attention on the Soreanos, who were a big local family whom everybody hated, or to try to discredit the generals in the next election, which shows you how naïve he was.

On Christmas Day of 1982 I had another episode of pneumonia following blood loss and my parents took me to the Sisters of Charity Hospital at San Cristóbal. Supposedly I was ranting and raving. There was one of the younger nuns, Sor Elena, who kind of looked after me and kept asking how I was doing, and I thought she was really great. I'm sure I've thought about her every day since then, maybe even every hour, at least when I'm not in one of my fugue states. *Todo por mi culpa,* all my fault. Four days after I got there, on *la fiesta de la Sagrada Familia*, December 29, 1982, Sor Elena told me that government troops had surrounded T'ozal and were interrogating the Cofradias, that is, "cargo bearers" or "charge holders," who are a kind of rotating committee of village elders. Later I found out more. It had been a market day, when almost everybody had come into the village. A white-and-blue Iroquois helicopter with loudspeakers materialized and circled around and around like a big kingfisher, telling everyone to assemble in the plaza for a town meeting, where they were going to give out assignments for the next year's civilian patrols. By this time the soldiers had already marched in on two barely used dirt roads. According to my friend José Xiloch—or, as we called him, No Way—who saw some of it from a distance, hardly anybody tried to run or hide. Most of the soldiers were half-Maya recruits from Suchitepéquez, but there were two tall men with sandy hair and USMC-issue boots along with them, and the squad was commanded, unusually, by a major, Antonio García Torres.

Only two people got shot to death in the plaza that day. My parents and six of their friends got loaded into a truck and taken to the army base at Coban. That evening the troops burned down the community center with eleven of the more resistant citizens alive inside it, which at that time was the terror tactic of choice. It was also the last time anyone I know of saw either of my brothers, although it's not clear what happened to them. Much later I found out that my sister had eventually made it to a refugee settlement in Mexico. The troops spent two days forcing the citizens to level the village and then loaded them onto trucks for relocation.

T'ozal is one of the four hundred and forty villages the Guatemalan government now officially lists as destroyed. The final count names thirty-eight people as confirmed dead and twenty-six disappeared. I figure it's about 90 percent certain that my parents would have been tortured by what they call the *submarino,* suffocation in water, and probably kept in these tall barrels they have where all you can do is squat *(todo por mi culpa)* and look up at the sky. One witness said that my father died when they were trying to make him talk by putting an insecticide-soaked hood over his head. Whether this was what killed him, or whether it even really happened, is still not clear. My mother, supposedly, was, like most of the women, forced to drink gasoline. Their bodies were almost certainly dumped in one of the eight known trench grave sites in Alta Verapaz, but so far the Center of Maya Documentation and Investigation hasn't matched any remains to my DNA.

Retardedly enough, it took me years to start wondering whether my parents might have sent me away because they guessed there'd be trouble. Maybe it was just my mother's idea. She'd used the Game before to find out whether there was any current danger from the G2, that is, the secret police. Maybe she saw something.

A week later the nuns got an order to ship me and four other kids from T'ozal—including "No Way" José, who became my oldest remaining friend—to *la capital,* that is, Ciudad Guate, where, eventually, we'd be sent on to relocation camps. I barely remember the Catholic orphanage because I escaped the first day, although it wasn't much of an escape since I just walked out the door. I found my way across town to a much better-funded children's hospital called AYUDA that was administered by the LDS, the Church of Jesus Christ of Latter-Day Saints, or, as they don't like to be called, the Mormons. There was a rumor they were sending kids from there to the U.S., which at the time I visualized as a garden of earthly delights with french-fry bushes and rivers of dry-ice-cold Squirt. There was a hugely tall woman with bright hair at the back door who hesitated for a minute and then, against regulations, let me in. I only saw her a couple times after that and didn't learn her name, but I still think about her when I see that shade of chrome-yellow hair. Later, when I was listed as a probable orphan, they transferred me to something called the LDS Paradise Valley Plantation School, outside of town.

It took a long time for me to get any idea of what had happened to my family, and in fact I still don't know. There wasn't any one moment when I knew my parents were dead, just an endlessly swelling blob of revolting acceptance. Saturdays at the PVPS were free and relatives, if any, were allowed to visit with inmates in a back classroom, and every Saturday morning I'd borrow a math book from the upper grades and go in there and just lurk in the back in the cool hug of two pea-green cinder-block walls and a pea-green linoleum floor and just keep an eye on things. Nobody ever showed up trying to find me. *La mara,* the gang, made fun of me about it but I was already getting oblivious. I still have trouble with Saturdays, in fact; I get antsy and catch myself looking out the window a lot or rechecking my e-mail ten times an hour.

I was at PVPS for nearly two years before I got into their Native American Placement Program—which is partly a refugee-adoption foundation—and, just after my sixteenth tz'olk'in nameday, that is, when I was eleven, a family called the Ødegârds, with a little financial help from the Church, flew me to Utah.

To give the devils their due, the LDS actually do a lot of good things for Native Americans. For instance, they helped the Zuni win the biggest settlement against the U.S. government that any Indian nation has ever gotten. And they run all these charities all over Latin America, and this is all despite the fact that the Church was still officially white supremacist until 1978. They believe that some Native Americans—the light-skinned ones—are descendants of a Hebrew patriarch named Nephi, who's a main character in the Book of Mormon. But who cares what their motives are, right? They looked after me and many others. I couldn't believe how rich the Ødegârds were. Running water was one thing, but they even had an unlimited supply of *angelitos,* that is, marshmallows, in both the semisolid and the semiliquid forms. I kind of thought the U.S. had conquered us and I was a captive being raised in a luxurious prison in the imperial capital. It took a long time for me to learn that by U.S. standards they were lower middle class. I mean, these are people who say *supper* instead of *dinner* and even *dinner* instead of *lunch,* and who have a wall plaque in the kitchen with a recipe for "Baby Jesus's Butter 'n' Love Sugar Cookies," with ingredients like "a dollop of understanding" and "a pinch of discipline." And out there they're considered intellectuals. So it's taken some work for me to become the jaded sophisto I pretend to be today.

Still, Mr. and Mrs. Ø were nice, or rather they wanted to be nice, but they had to put so much energy into retaining their delusions that there wasn't a lot of time for each individual child. Also, my stepbrothers were horrible— deprived of mainstream TV and video games, they'd relax by torturing small animals—but of course the parents thought they were God's chosen cherubs.

Needless to say, I never converted to the LDS. Or got "helped to under-stand," as they put it. That is, made to realize that one had been a Latter-Day Saint all along. According to the program they weren't supposed to do that to you until you were a little bit older, and by then I was beginning to realize that baptizing your long-dead ancestors and laying on hands and wearing Ma-sonic long johns wasn't entirely normal behavior, even in El Norte. They even took me to a Catholic church once or twice, but it didn't have the right smell or the right saints in it or offering bottles all over the floor, like in Guatemala, so I said don't bother. They were cool enough about it, in their way. In fact I still call Ma and Pa Ø every once in a while, even though I can't bear them. When I ask about my stepbrothers they've always each just sired another brace of twins. What with the combination of ideology and fertility drugs down there, they multiply like brine shrimp.

As an alternative to becoming a living saint, I got steered onto the extra-curricular-activities track. I started with the Chess Team and the Monopoly Team. The folks at Nephi K–12 forced me to play the cello, the orchestra's most humiliating instrument. I wasn't good. I thought music was math dumbed down. I hid in the library a lot, taking mental pictures of dictionary pages for later retrieval. I learned to read English by memorizing H. P. Love-craft, and now people say I talk that way. I politely refused to bob for apples at the school Halloween party—well, actually I dashed crying out of the mul-tipurpose room—because I thought I was about to get waterboarded. I got involved with the Programming Team, the Computer Games Team, and the Strategy Games Team. You'd think that someone on that many teams would have had to talk with the other students, but I didn't. Most of the time I got to stay out of real PE because of the hæmo thing. Instead they made me and the other cripples sit on mats and pretend to stretch and lift weights. The only sport I was ever really good at was target shooting. The family were all gun nuts and I went along with it. I joined the Math Team, even though I thought it was silly to think of math as a team sport. It's like having a masturbation team. One time my math coach gave me a stack of topology quizzes and was surprised that I aced them. He and another teacher tested me a bit and said

I was a calendrical savant and that I calculated each date at the time, unlike some who memorized them, although I could have just told them that myself. It's not really a marketable skill, though. It's something about one in ten thousand people can do, like being able to lick your own genitals. Around that same time I got involved with the Tropical Fish Team. I built my first few tank systems out of garden hoses and old Tupperware. I decided that when I grew up I'd be a professional chess player. I wore my skateboard helmet on the bus. I decided that when I grew up I'd be a professional Sonic the Hedgehog player. I appeared, as "J," in a study in *Medical Hypotheses* called "Hypernumeric Savant Skills in Juvenile PTS Patients." I decided that instead of learning to play the cello, I'd learn to *build* cellos. I listened to the Cocteau Twins instead of Mötley Crüe. I made my first thousand buying and selling Magic cards. I acquired a hillbilly nickname. I did Ecstasy alone.

New treatments got my hæmophilia under control, but in the meantime I'd been diagnosed as having "posttraumatic-stress-disorder-related emotional-development issues," along with "sporadic eidetic memory." Supposedly PTSD can present like Asperger's. But I wasn't autistic in all the usual ways, like for instance, I liked learning new languages and I didn't mind "exploratory placement in novel pedagogic situations." One doctor in Salt Lake told me that PTSD was a blanket term that didn't really cover whatever I had, or didn't have. I figured that meant I wouldn't get any scholarship money out of it.

In September of 1988 an anthropology grad student from BYU, Brigham Young University, came to speak at our junior high school and redirected my life. She showed videos of old kivas and Zuni corn dances, and just as I was falling asleep she started showing Maya pyramids, and I sat up. I got my nerve up and asked some questions. She asked me to tell where I was from. I told the class. A few days later they let me and the other redskins out of school to go to a Native American Placement Program scholarship conference that she was chairing in Salt Lake. It was in a gym at the high school and included things like flint knapping and freestyle face painting with Liquitex acrylics. A student teacher introduced me to another professor named June Sexton and when I told her where I came from she started talking to me in pretty good Yukateko, which really blew me away. At some point she asked whether I'd ever played *el juego del mundo,* and when I didn't know what she meant she said it was also called *"alka' kalab'eeraj,"* the "Sacrifice Game," which was close to a word my mother had used. I said yes and she brought out an Altoids box full of curiously red tz'ite-tree seeds. I couldn't play at first because I was having something that I might identify as nostalgia, or the poor second cousin of nostalgia, but when I got it back together we played through a few dry rounds. She said a mathematician colleague of hers was working on a study of Maya divination and would love it if I could teach him my version. Sure, I said, thinking quickly, but I couldn't do it after school hours. Anything to get out of PE.

Incredibly, a week later a green van from a place called FARMS—the Foundation for Ancient Research and Mormon Studies—actually did pick me up right before lunch period and drove me north into the mountains, to BYU in Provo. June babe led me into a forgettable building and introduced me to Professor Taro Mora. He seemed to me like a wise old sage, like Pat Morita in the *Karate Kid* saga, even though he was only forty. His office was totally plain, with a wall of books and journals on Go—which is that Asian board game played with the black and white pebbles—and another wall of stuff on probability and game theory. He worked in catastrophe modeling. He said he'd collected versions of the Sacrifice Game from all over Central America, but that the variant I'd learned was one that only a couple of his informants had even heard of and that differed from the usual game in a few important ways. First of all, in most places the client just comes in and says, "Please ask the skull/seeds this for me," and the sun adder does everything else. But the way my mother did it, the client played *against* the adder. Second, she'd made a board in the shape of a cross, while almost all other adders just sorted the seeds into a single row of piles on a flat cloth. The third and most tantalizing thing was simply that I'd learned the Game from a woman.

This was almost unheard of. Throughout 98 percent of the Maya region, adders were invariably men. Taro said he wasn't an anthropologist but that he guessed my mother might have represented a survival of some Ch'olan tradition of female secret societies that had otherwise disappeared soon after the Conquest.

Taro met with me twice a week until the end of the semester, when he went back to New Haven. By that time I'd found out that he was the head researcher of something called the "Parcheesi Project" and that he and the graduate students in his lab had a theory that all or almost all modern games are descended from a single ancestor, an ur-game. They'd started out trying to reconstruct it by collecting tribal games in Central Asia, but pretty soon the research had led them to the Americas.

A lot of anthropologists at the time tore down the idea. And it did sound a bit like another Thor Von Danekovsky cult-archaeology crock-pot contact theory. But Taro was really a mathematician and didn't care. He was a pure researcher and one of only a few people working on the overlap between catastrophe theory, the physics of complex systems, and recombinant game theory, or RGT. RGT is basically the theory of games like chess and Go, where the pieces form different units of force in space. Economists and generals and whoever have been using classical game theory—which is mainly about gambling—since World War Two, but applied RGT only really got going in the 1990s. Taro's idea was that using a reconstructed version of the Sacrifice Game as a human interface could significantly improve performance in strategic modeling, like simulations of economics, of battles, or maybe even of weather. He'd had some experimental success with it before he even met me, but he said he wanted even more spectacular results before he published anything. His lab had worked up dozens of different reconstructions of what the original game board might have looked like. We all put in hundreds of hours, both before and after I went to college, trying to dope it out. But the thing that kept stopping us was that even if we'd been sure about the design of the board, there was no way to know what the exact counting protocol had been in the old days or how many seeds or pebbles or whatever they'd used. So Taro decided to try another approach. He brought in brain scanners.

I still had my five quartz pebbles from Guatemala. In fact, they were the only things from there I still had, since the tz'ite seeds had eroded to pink powder and had been replaced with Skittles. I'd only scattered—that is, played the Sacrifice Game—a few times since I'd been in the States. But when I started again, sitting all wired up in a Ganzfeld chamber in the basement in Provo, it seemed like I'd been a beneficiary of the particular sort of improvement that comes from not practicing. At first they had people in a room on the other side of the building acting out different scenarios, and I'd try to predict those. I did pretty well. Then we found it worked better when the experimenters were actually losing money, or getting hurt, or something real. After a few months we started working on events in the real world, the spread of the AIDS virus or the first oil war or whatever, which was a lot harder to set up controls for. We kept beating the odds and getting better and better but still on an agonizingly gentle curve. He said my calendrical savant thing was helping me play faster but that so far I wasn't really playing deeper. That is, I wasn't focusing enough. I was like, well, I'm a teenager, how should I be able to focus at all? Anyway, five years later, when I started working with

Taro again at Yale, he'd given up the isolation tests and was back to trying to crack the design of the original game board. By the time I left we were using two runners and playing on a game board that worked better but which he still didn't think was the original layout. It made the Game more flexible but also easier to play, even though it was more complicated than my mother's design:

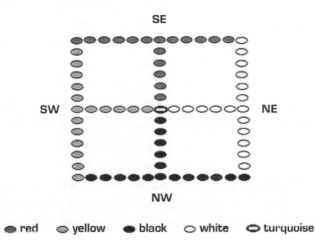

red   yellow   black   white   turquoise

My break with Taro was over something stupid. I'd thought my tuition was getting paid by the Berlencamp Fund and by his lab at Yale, but it turned out the money had come from FARMS, the same lunatics he'd been working for back in Provo. I'd known for a while that the foundation was a Mormon soft-think tank dedicated to proving, among other things, that American Indians are the descendants of the Tribe of Joseph. When I got into my angry Pan-Maya Coalition phase it started to really bother me and I grilled him about it. There's no pleasing some people, right? What an ingrate I was. Am. Anyway, he said that FARMS wasn't even the original source, and actually their account came from the same people who were funding the lab. He said he couldn't tell me who it was. I got cranky and walked out. At best the whole thing's commercial, I thought, just a bunch of mercenary economics grads looking for ways to beat the market.

And there were other changes going on. Before Taro left Utah, he'd hooked me up with a group at the University of Texas that was working on therapies for some of the lack-of-emotional-affect problems I was supposedly having. He made sure I wasn't in the control group and that I got the whole course. By the time I'd (barely) graduated and gotten the hell out of New Haven, I'd acquired something like real emotions. I started learning new things about humans. Like for the first time I got clued into the whole secret about facial expressions and what they meant, and how people try to hide their emotions or fake ones they don't have. Weird stuff. A whole shadow-world of interpersonal politics lurked out there, affectations and masks and subtexts and just plain lies. I became sensitive to my personal appearance, or, rather, learned I *had* an appearance. I lost thirty pounds and kept it off. I read a book called *How to Pick Up Chicks for Dummies.* I did 182,520 abs crunches. I moved to Grand Avenue in Los Angeles. I picked up some chicks for dummies. I decided to be an ornithologist. I started using the Game to research investments. I made some money right away, maybe just by luck. I had some motivation, because in those days prophylactic treatment for hæmophilia B cost about $300K per year, but without it you spent all your time worrying about getting bruised or cut and then plugging leaks like Super Mario. I gave up ornithology because I found out that really, people already know about everything there is to know about birds. I decided to go professional with the chess thing. I worked my FIDE rating up to 2,380. On May 11, 1997, when Deep Blue beat Kasparov, I gave up the idea of being a chess player. What was the point? It was like being a Dial-A-Matic adding machine. I decided I was going to move to Seoul and study to be a professional Go player. I learned some Korean. Then it turned out you had to learn some Chinese to learn Korean, so I learned some Chinese. I gave up the idea of being a professional Go player because it turned out they don't have *empanadas de achiote* in Asia. I decided to be a marine biologist. I left L.A. and moved to Miami. I gave up the idea of being a marine biologist because it was too depressing to go through water samples, logging all the different vintages of toxic waste. I decided I'd study biology and specialize in chemosensation. I gave up building cellos because of all the lacquer and varnish and glue. I decided I'd study olfactology. Then I gave up being a chemist at all because the field had become so industrialized that at the rate things were going I'd have been lucky to come up with even one decent molecule. I decided to get out of the sciences and write a novel. I moved to Williamsburg, Brooklyn. I wrote a few articles on computer games and whatever for magazines like *Wired* and *Artforum* and even *Harper's Bazaar.* The editor there told me a jaunty, irreverent tone was mandatory. I went around drinking single malts and picking up chicks for dummies. The phase didn't last long. I started trading commodities online. I gave up the idea of being a novelist because, as I learned more about the field, it turned out that even in this day and age novelists are expected to

cover a pretty narrow range of subjects. You're supposed to be interested in
certain things, things like, say, emotion, motivation, self-expression, relationships, families, love, loss, love and loss, gender, race, redemption, women,
men, women and men, identity, politics, identity politics, writers, Brooklyn,
writers who live in Brooklyn, readers who wish they were writers who live in
Brooklyn, the Self, the Other, the Self versus the Other, academia, postcolo-
nialism, growing up, the suburbs, the 1970s, the 1980s, the 1990s, growing up
in the suburbs in the 1970s, 1980s, or 1990s, personhood, places, people, people who need people, character, characters, the inner lives of the characters,
life, death, society, the human condition, and probably Ireland. And of course,
I have exactly zero interest in any of these things. Who wants to hear about
the characters' inner lives? I'm not even interested in my own inner life. I
decided I'd become a professional Hold 'Em player. I moved to Reno, Nevada.
In those days there were so many fish at the tables that almost anyone who
could count could make money. I made some money. I did some math for
Indian-reservation casinos in Utah, Arizona, and Florida, coming up with
new ways to fleece the white man. I made some more money. I gave up the
idea of staying on the pro poker circuit because I was already making more
money in commodities than I could at online or even real-world tables, and
with a lot less interaction. I kept up my column at *Strategy* magazine just out of
sentiment. I made some more money.

Money. Right. I suppose I should mention that.

By '01 I had enough cash to do what I wanted if I didn't mind wearing off-
the-rack jackets. I looked up No Way, my *cuate viejo* from T'ozal—who was
still with the Enero 31 resistance group, which had gone underground after
the cease-fire of '96—and I spent four years in Guatemala. I worked for his
friends in the CPRs, that is, the Communities of Population in Resistance,
and I quietly tried to find out what *(todo por mi culpa)* had happened to my
parents. And I went around and asked a lot of old sun adders about the Game.
I decided Taro's team had been right, that there had been a complete and
complex version of the Sacrifice Game, but that now it was just a dim collective memory. Most of the old *h'menob'* used the same much-abridged version
and even then worked mainly by instinct, like Alzheimer's patients who can't
play duplicate bridge anymore but who still enjoy a few hands of Go Fish.

I never did track down any more complete versions of the Sacrifice Game.
But my secret objective got me into enough trouble that as of 2011 the National Police still had an arrest warrant out for me. García-Torres was, in
typical Guate fashion, still in the army and now a general. No Way and I

worked up a profile of him—what his habits were, how his different houses were laid out, which cockfighting pits he went to and when, where his personal bodyguards lived, the whole thing, but I must not have done a very good job because one night No Way—who had a coyote uay and could get around silently in the dark—snuck in the back way and said he'd heard the G2 was onto me. My choice, he said, was either to clear out before morning or, probably, vanish. I cleared out. I moved to Indiantown, which is a Maya émigré settlement on Lake Okeechobee about twenty miles inland from Florida's Atlantic Coast.

In Florida word had gotten around about some good results I'd had with the Sacrifice Game, and I couldn't get out of taking on a few clients. I could never really be a really great community sun adder, though. One problem is that, in a traditional village at least, an adder has to do a lot of drinking, and alcohol's never really plugged my wound. As far as I'm concerned, C_2H_6O's a poor man's drug no matter how much you tart it up. Another problem is that a lot of the craft is just being a good listener, a relentlessly traditionalist pillar of the community, and a repository of local lore. And what fun is that? You also ought to be an intuitive psychiatrist, a Person Who Deals with People. And most adders, frankly, also do a lot of plain fakery—cold reading, behind-the-scenes research, stooge planting, and even sleight of hand.

And I can't do the religious stuff with conviction, and I hate leading people on like some TV medium. It's just too depressing to see how desperate and gullible they are. I've been told more than once that I'm kind of touchy about the adder thing because it sounds like it could be a scam. When they do surveys of most- and least-admired professions, "fortune teller" is usually second from the bottom, right above "telemarketer."

Which brings up the personal question: "If he can do what he says he can, why is Jed not rich?"

Well, the simple answer to that is that, as a matter of fact, I am.

(3)

I hate my autobiography. One hates all autobiography. Autobiography is the world's second-most-loathsome literary genre, just above haikus in English. The last time I went into a real bookstore—it was just to get a cannabispresso, by the way—I picked up an autobio by Ava Gardner while I was waiting, and the first sentence was "In Johnston County, North Carolina, you couldn't be any kind of farmer at all without a mule." It's like, uh-huh, that's sweet, Ava, but frankly, if you're not in bed with Howard Hughes, Frank Sinatra, Johnny Stompanato, Artie Shaw, Mickey Rooney, or some combination of the above by the bottom of this very page—or unless you're leading up to a comparison of the mule's genitalia to Frank's—your book is taking a header back into the remainders bin. Autobiographies are all alike, it's always "Okay, just because I've attracted a certain amount of attention I'm going to drag you through everything that ever happened to me even though 99 and $^{44}/_{100}$ percent of it is the exact same *basura* that happened to everyone else." So if you get anything out of this it shouldn't be about me, even if I do figure in it a bit. It's not about me. It's just about the Game.

Oh, right. We were going to treat, briefly, the Game as Gold Mine issue. Well, let's skip ahead a bit.

In the fourth watchfire of 4 Owl, 4 Yellowness, 12.19.18.17.16—or, in the newfangled reckoning, at 4:30 A.M. on Friday, December 23, 2011—the Nikkei closed up 1.2 percent and sent my estimated combined portfolios just north of the five-million-dollars U.S. mark. I was splayed out on the floor—I like hanging out on stone or cement floors—blinking up at a big screen on the low ceiling of my so-called house, which was a bit west of Indiantown and only one vacant block from Lake Okeechobee, Home of the Estrogenically Hermaphrodized Bullfrog. The house wasn't really a house but rather a bankrupt tropical-fish store, Lenny's Reefin' Stall, that I'd picked up for debt plus fixtures and was now converting into a 450,000-cubic-foot experiment in one-room mixed-phylum living. The only light in the room was an actinic blue glow from a 440-gallon cylindrical tank of Baja nudibranchs, which are basically sort of gaudy sea snails with the shell on the inside.

Damn, I thought, blinking up at the screen. After years of *vagar*, screwing around, I had finally worked out a way to use the Sacrifice Game to make real money. The Game won't work in casinos, of course, because it takes too long. It didn't help much with lotteries, because they're too close to truly random. The Game needs to work on something you already know about. Basically, it helps you notice things. Which isn't the same as predicting the future, but it beats just flailing around in the dark like most people. Anyway, the Sacrifice Game did work, slightly, with horses and sports books, especially with basketball, but I'd have to learn everything I could about the posted horses and the track, and by the time I'd played it all out a few times I could barely get the bet in before the bell. So I needed something that came at me a little slower. I started getting serious about stocks. But they were randomer than I'd thought, and I'd almost given up when I tried my hand at corn futures.

The advantage with commodities was that the harvest cycle was slow. Also, there weren't many players in the field. So I worked up histories of most of the big individual investors and started treating them as absent players in a giant Sacrifice Game. Usually I ran about twenty long-range climate simulations and then bought straddles on stuff that looked unclear. Pretty soon I had a slight but definite edge. Six months ago I'd banked my first half-million, and now I was heading into private-plane territory. Speaking of which, I thought, I'll lock up a little cash right now. Good idea. SELL 3350 DECEMBER CONTRACTS at 223.00 at MARKET to OPEN, I clicked. Hah. I hit COMPLETE TRANSACTION, counted the zeroes twice, and lay back on the floor.

Hot spit, I thought. Yes! I am KING of the FUCKIVERSE! ¡¡DOMINO EL MUNDO!! I RULE THE WASTELAND!!! Finally. I'm an eater, not an eaten. It was like the eyes that had been on either side of my head had migrated to the front and given me binocular vision. Predator, not prey. Dang. Next thing you know old Jed's a thrillionaire.

Hmm, what to do next? Well, I thought, with great power comes great responsibility. I must use my abilities for the cause of good.

I called Todd Rosenthal at Naples Motorsports. He was an early owl and he picked up his business line.

"Okay, I'll take the 'Cuda," I said. It was a Metalflake Aztec Red 1970 hemi collapsible hardtop, 383 block, all-original metal, new electronics, numbers-matching monster that I'd had my eye on for a while, and I'd dickered it down to only $290K. He said he'd have it and the papers trucked over by 9:00 A.M. so that I wouldn't have time for second thoughts. Click.

Ahhhhh. That's the ticket. Doing my bit to make the world a better place. Wouldn't want to let some cracker show monkey get his hooks on a work of art like that. I already had a '73 Road Runner parked outside, and another Barracuda in the Villanuevas' garage, but I hadn't quite reached Plymouth saturation. I have kind of bad taste. It's more fun than the other kind. Okay, now what? Maybe a little oceanfront property. Just a medium-size island, a loaf of bread, a jug of Squirt, a twenty-thousand-gallon reef tank, a five-thousand-gallon Jacuzzi, a couple of J-porn starlets, and a Vatnajökull Glacier of pure Colombian rock. Simple pleasures. Oriental vixens desire liquidity. *No problemo.*

Naturally, the rush didn't last. Two hours later I was still in my special spot on the floor, blinking up at the overhead screens, doing a reading for a client—one of the few I'd never had the heart to blow off—named Mother Flor de Mayo, from the Grace Rural School. She was wondering whether to finally retire this year.

"*¿Podré caminar después de la operación?*" her old voice asked over the speakerphone.

"*Déme un momento,*" I said. I was having some trouble because her surgery was scheduled for the morning, and for some reason the Game had always seemed to work better on things that happened later in the day. "*Estoy dispersando estas semillas amarillas y las semillas negras—*"

Codex. The word had popped up in the high-priority Google Search window on my trading screen. I clicked it up. Usually if anything comes in it's from a pretty obscure post, like the Foundation for Ancient Mesoamerican Research or the Cyberslugs Webring, but this was an article in *Time*:

An Ancient Book . . .

Whoa. Tzam lic.
That is, that sheet lightning under the skin.

An Ancient Book with Modern Relevance
Comes to Light in Germany

> The "Codex Nurnberg"—an eighty-page Mayan book
> that has been gathering dust and speculation in that
> city's Germanisches Nationalmuseum since the
> 1850s—has, finally, been read.

The lead photo showed the top half of a page from a Maya codex, a delicate drawing of what they call Waterlily Jaguar sitting in a field of Classic-period-style glyphs. That is, the forms were pre-900 AD.

Ni modos. No way, I thought.

"¿Joaquinito? ¿Está allí?" Mother Flor's voice asked.

"¿Madre? Perdóneme," I said. *"No estoy teniendo mucha suerte con las calaveras esta noche. ¿Usted piensa que podría venir mañana y la intentaremos otra vez?"*

She said of course, dear. I said thanks and clicked off.

En todos modos.

I blew up the picture of the Codex—which, since the release of that pinnacle of human achievement called the Logitech laser mouse, I could do just by waving a finger—and zoomed in on the number glyphs. Hmm. The calligraphy looked a little post-Classic to me. It didn't look like a forgery, though. Forgeries are usually either way bad or way too good. And from what I'd heard the Nurnberg book had a pretty clear provenance. People had been coming up with schemes for reading it for at least fifty years. Maybe it was a post-Classic copy of a Classic text—

Huh.

One of the date groups looked a little unsettling. I blew it up and enhanced it. It was fuzzy, but it seemed to be 7 Quetzal, 7 Snatch-bat, 12.19.17.7.7, that is, June 2, 2010 AD, which was the date of the particle accelerator implosion at the Universidad Tecnológica de la Mixteca in Oaxaca. Two members of a Tzotzil Zapatista group had gone to prison for sabotage, for supposedly somehow causing the thing, although I and every other right-thinking person thought they weren't guilty. Aerial views of the blast site showed a shallowly scooped-out area over a half-mile across, lined with sand that had been fused into dark-green obsidian.

Hmm . . .

> After it arrived in Europe from the New World, the
> fig-tree-bark pages of the book—possibly written more
> than a thousand years ago—fused together over the

centuries into what amounts to one solid brick. Researchers were unable, until now, to separate the accordion-folded pages due to the Mayan technique of priming the pages with gluelike compounds made from animal hides. The solution: the Scanning Tunneling Acoustic Microscope, or STAM, which "sees" ink through stuck pages.

"This is the biggest thing in our field since the discovery of the palaces at Cancuen in 2000," gushed Professor Michael Weiner, a researcher in Mesoamerican Studies at the University of Central Florida and director of the decipherment project. "Only a few scraps of Mayan literature survived the Conquest," he said, referring to the Spanish invasion of America that started around AD 1500.

Oh, *that* conquest of America.

The Codex (much of the contents of which will be published next year in the prestigious *Journal of Ethnographic Science*) is one of only four other Mayan "books" known to have survived the hands of Catholic religious authorities.

Weiner and his research team so far remain silent as to the exact content of the book's glyphic text. However, rumors have spread through the tight-knit community of Mayan scholars that the book contains a drawing of a cross-shaped "divination layout," a sort of game used to predict the future, and a string of eerily accurate predictions of actual catastrophic events, many of which occurred centuries after the book was written.

The Mayans, who flourished in Central America between AD 200 and their mysterious downfall around AD 900, were a highly advanced civilization with a complex writing system and a mastery of mathematics, astronomy, architecture, and engineering, as evidenced by the massive pyramids they built from

Honduras to Mexico's Yucatán Peninsula, now a chic vacation destination. More mysterious and unsettling was their unique spiritual life, which involved bloodletting rituals and human sacrifice, as well as an intricate system of interlocking calendars, which tracked starry events and predicted earthly ones far into the future. At least one of these dates has long been familiar to Mayan scholars and, in the last few years, has become known to many nonspecialists as well: December 21, 2012, or, as it is more popularly known, Four *Ahau.*

They meant *Kan Ahau, Ox K'ank'in,* or 4 Overlord, 3 Yellowness, 13.0.0.0.0. The old End of the World *bolazo* again. Dolts.

Maybe I should mention that I'd had a pretty big attitude problem about that date since about the seventh grade. People always asked me about it and I had to keep explaining that saying it's a doomsday thing was a huge, huge overinterpretation. The twenty-first was an important day, no question, but not necessarily the end of anything, let alone everything. It's only a big deal because there are a lot of deeply spiritual cretins out there, and they're disappointed by the lack of disasters at the turn of the Christian millennium and the fact that 9/11 took their gurus completely by surprise. So they're looking for another convenient deadline. Any time the world's going to end, church pledges go up. Because, you know, why save? It's an old scam ever young.

If you happen to be even one-eighth Native American, you already know how these airheads keep coming up to you and acting like you've got some kind of spiritual aura. If there's an Indian character in a movie, chances are twenty to one that he's got ESP at least, and probably telekinesis, hands of healing, and, somewhere, a third eye. And the 2012 thing is the worst. Everybody's got a different interpretation, and the only common denominator between them is that they're all wrong. The Maya tracked an asteroid that's going to crash into the earth on that date. The Maya left their cities and flew to Venus and that's the ETA of their return flight. The Maya knew that on that date there'd be a major earthquake, a volcanic eruption, a plague, a flash ice age, a drop in the sea level, or all five. They knew that on that date the earth's poles would reverse. On that date our yellow sun's going to go out and a blue sun will take its place. Quetzalcoatl is going to reemerge out of the transdimensional vortex in a jade-green flying saucer. The all-flowering oneness of the universal sea-sky-earth-goddess-truth is going to autopropagate through the cosmic oom. Time will get back in its bottle. Aurochs and mastodons will stampede down I-95. The Lost Continent of Mu will rise up out of the Galápagos Fracture Zone. The true Madhi, Joseph Smith Jr., will appear on the Golan Heights wearing a U2 T-shirt. Shirley MacLaine will shed her human form and reveal herself as Minona/Minerva/Mama Cocha/Yoko/Mori/Mariammar/Mbabamuwana/Minihaha. Scarlett Johansson will give birth to a snow-white bison. The NASDAQ will hit 3,000. Pigs will fly, beggars will ride, boys will be boys . . .

Although, on the other hand, you had to admit that the exactness of the date, 12/21/12, does have a sinister specificity about it that gives you a queasy feeling. I mean, it's not like Nostradamus, where it's so vague you can make up anything and it seems to fit. Of course, we, I mean, we Maya, had always been pretty sure of ourselves.

> This is the long-awaited last date of the Long Count, the Mayans' astonishingly accurate ritual calendar, which can be precisely correlated to days in the Christian one. A year from now, on this date, the current cycle of Mayan time comes to an end.
>
> Weiner is dismissive of doomsday scenarios. "We weren't planning to release this until a year or so from now, after the twenty-first," he says. "People can get ridiculous, and besides, we wanted to finish the research." However, he says, "With all the speculation about the comet, we thought we'd release some of the interesting Ixchel-related findings."
>
> Could the Mayans have timed their calendar to the appearances of Comet Ixchel? Its discoverers at Swinburne University, in New South Wales, who named their find after a Mayan goddess, clearly think so. Soon to be visible to the naked eye, Ixchel has a 5,125-year periodicity—or orbit—around the sun, meaning it was last seen in 3011 BC—Year One of the Mayan long-count calendar. If any ancient people

could have honed in on its return, that people were the Mayans. Determined doomsayers will need to find some other threat: The ball of rock and frozen gases will miss the earth by at least fifty thousand miles.

For the 2.3 million Mayans still living in Central America, the date betokens something nearer home: The twenty-first has also been set as a limit for talks in the renewed treaty effort between the small Central American state of Belize, a British protectorate, and the Republic of Guatemala, which in 2010, for the fourth time in a hundred years of disagreement, again claimed Belize as its twenty-third state, or *departamento.*

If the opportunity passes, the day might bring another era of disaster to the Mayans—but a resolution could begin a new era of peace in the troubled region.

U.S. efforts to aid the peace process have been complicated by the fact that the Mexican government has blamed a 2010 accelerator explosion in the Oaxacan city of Huajapan de León—in which over 30,000 people were killed—on Zapatistist indigenous-rights groups, Indian revolutionaries operating out of Guatemala and Belize. But if the region is not stabilized, there's also media trouble ahead: Many observers fear that the International Olympic Committee might favor other sites than Belize for the 2020 Summer Games.

What clues are there in the Codex Nurnberg? Along with the astronomical data usual to Mayan texts, the book is said to mention both the date of the accelerator blast and a celestial event that could well be Comet Ixchel. Predicting the future based on images of "year-bearers" in the images of rabbits, centipedes . . .

Whoa.

The old squirt of tzam lic under my left thigh. Something wasn't right about that last word. *Centipedes.*

I couldn't get a grip on what it was, though, and of course the harder I tried the more it slipped away. Come back to that one later.

> . . . centipedes, blue deer, and green jaguars may seem a bit far-fetched. Interpretation will be, to say the least, a long and difficult process.
>
> Aside from the Codex, does the divination game itself have anything to teach us? Professor Taro Mora, a physicist and specialist in prediction models who has been studying Mayan games with Weiner's help, clearly thinks so. Mora, a spry sixty-eight-year-old who spends most of his eighteen-hour days "teaching computers to teach themselves," waxes enthusiastic over its potential.
>
> "There is much to learn from ancient approaches to science," Mora says. "Just as we are using Go [an ancient Japanese strategy game] to help computers develop basic consciousness, we may use other games to teach them other things."

Way to go, Tar babe. That's the way to wax, if you want to wax at all.

> Asked whether the game held any insights about the world's eventual end, Mora joked, "No, but if the universe does disappear, at least we will know the Maya were on to something."
>
> Could the End Date foretell an unhappy event for the Mayan region, or even for the entire world? And if so, what should we do about it?
>
> Many people's answer seems to be, "When on Mayan time, do as the Mayans do." Thousands of visitors from all over the world, and from all walks of life, are already planning trips to Chichén Itzá and other popular Mayan sites, waiting to salute the comet, greet the dawn, and ask the old gods for another five

thousand–plus years for humanity. And while most of
us wouldn't go that far, we should be willing to enter-
tain the possibility that the mysterious Mayans had
far-reaching spiritual insights into their future—and,
possibly, our own.

Pendejos, I thought. Morons.

No, wait. *I'm* the moron.

The minute—well, the decade—that I leave Taro alone, he comes up with
the goods. I felt like I'd held a stock for thirty years and sold it just before it
took off.

Well, I thought, I certainly can't just wait until you decide to publish. I
need to see that game board this minute. This second. This picosecond.

I searched up Taro's page. It said he was at the University of Central Florida, and that the lab was now being sponsored by grants from the UCF Corporate Exchange Program. And funding for the UCFCEP—as I found with
only minimal snooping—had come from the catastrophe modeling team of
the Simulated Trades Division of the Warren Investment Group. I remembered the company because it was a big employer in Salt Lake, and I'd seen in
Barron's that it had had some ethics problems with an alternate-energy thing
a few years ago. Well, whatever.

I tried Taro's old filter password. It still worked and got me into his personal box. I couldn't come up with some other excuse for writing, so I just
wrote that I'd seen the article and wondered if I could come by soon, like, say,
later today. "Send," I said. It sent.

Estas bien. I switched the screens to tank monitor mode. It said the Gulf
tank was low on calcium, but I didn't have the energy to deal with it. Maybe
he won't write back, I thought. No, he would. One of the good things about
now is how you can lose track of someone for years and then get back in
touch in a trice. Or even a half a trice. Except you also need to come up with
more excuses.

Hmm. 4 Ahau. 12/21/12. So it's a big deal again.

Well, just wait until the twenty-second. Nothing gets old faster than an
apocalypse that didn't happen.

Right?

(4)

The Barracuda had a new live windshield, and on the drive up to Orlando I checked out Taro's new sponsor, the Warren Group. It turned out the chairman and CEO was Lindsay Warren, this big developer and philanthropist in Salt Lake City who'd built the stadia for the Winter Olympics in 2002. I used to go to hospitals named after him. He'd probably been funding Taro's work since back in the FARMS days. "The Warren Family of Companies" was definitely one of the fastest-growing conglomerates in the U.S. Four years ago, though, they'd been close to bankruptcy, and from what I could find it wasn't clear exactly what had bailed them out. Maybe they'd gotten huge so fast by using the Game.

Warren had its tentacles in all sorts of fields, from the esoteric to the stiflingly mundane. They made sports equipment and memorabilia. They developed motivational tools, human resource management systems, "beliefspace software," and interactive entertainment, anything and everything for a whole new centuryful of consumers with a whole lot of free time. Right now they were pushing this thing they called "Sleekers," which seemed to be some kind of low-friction wheelless shoe/skate that glided on specially treated asphalt. They also did aerospace and research contracting. In '08 one of their commercial labs had made headlines with the announcement that they had created a so-called desktop wormhole. The trendiest thing they mentioned was something called Consciousness Transfer Protocol, which people said was going to be bigger than the Human Genome Project but which was at least a decade off. Still, in their last annual report it looked as though their cash cow was entertainment construction—halls of fame, the eXtreme ParX franchise, and what they called socioimagineering. "The Warren Group is the leading developer of Intentional Communities ('ICs')," their site said. Apparently the division had started out on the reenactments circuit, people endlessly fighting the Civil War, and then they produced a lot of those Renaissance fair things, and then they got the contract to build the year-round *Star Trek* community, and now just a decade later they'd just reached 95 percent occupancy (or "communityship") on a ten-square-mile development called Erewhynn, about fifty miles north of Orlando. It was supposed to be like an eighteenth-century Cotswolds village. The citizens went to classes on handcrafts and Scottish dialects, and they put on Michaelmas and Maying festivals and the whole shitterie. Then there was another big IC called Blue Lagoon Reef, on its own island in the Bahamas. There was a new feudal Japan spread in northern California. And there were big plans brewing in Latin America and the Far East. A site called Warren Sucks said that the company wanted to develop boutique countries with their own currencies and constitutions, that it was piggybacking on the retribalization movement to get into politics and indoctritainment and rewire our brains, and that, basically, it sucked.

The lab was on the UCF campus in a new hacienda-style nerd ghetto. You could still see the grid lines in the new St. Augustine grass sod. Even though it was the day after Christmas, everybody seemed to be working. There were private security primates all over. They kept talking to each other, and eventually to Taro, over those Bluetooth ear thingies that make people look like processed livestock. Well, here I am, crawling back, I thought. Was he still mad at me? Maybe just ask him. Hey, are you still mad at me? No, don't. Don't embarrass him. Or yourself. He probably figures you've seen the error of your ways. Maybe he's right. I knew I'd decided Taro was just another mercenary, and I'd felt pretty disgusted, but now I didn't remember why exactly I'd felt that way.

Taro met me at the third door in. He didn't so much look older, but I'd been remembering him as a jovial Hotei sort of character, and now he was more of a Hsun Tzu, drier and grave. Like all Japanese people he only looked half-Japanese. He still wore his old powder-blue Tokyo University lab coat.

"It is nice to see you," he said. He held my hand for a second. For him it was like licking my face. His hand was smooth, dry, brittle, and delicately ridged, like the shell of a paper nautilus.

"It is nice to see you," I said. He seemed like it was actually nice to see me. Well, he's a guileless sort, I thought. If he said it was nice, it was nice. There was hug potential, but instead I shook his dry hand. Neither of us was a very demonstrative type. I'm not Latino in that way. I'm an Injun. Like, Chief Stone Face him no show any heap big emotions.

"Thanks for having me over," I mumbled. "You know, I feel kind of bad showing up after all this, whatever."

"No, not to worry," he said. He didn't have an accent—I mean, he had a bit of an Oxbridge accent but no Japanese one—but he spoke in that precise way that tells you an East Asian language is still lurking in there. "I understand that things sometimes are difficult." Despite myself I got a floodlet of that warm 'n' fuzzy feeling like you're a scoop of ice cream and somebody's pouring hot butterscotch over you. I hate it when that happens. Teacher/pupil has got to be one of the weirdest possible relationships. Well, maybe he'd guessed I might contact him as soon as I saw that *Time* article.

"Let us check in on the patient," he said.

"Great," I said. Come down to the lab, I thought. And see what's on the suh-luh-*AAAB*!

We went through another two sets of doors and into a keyed elevator. Brrr. Freezing in here. We went down three floors to the sub-subbasement. Taro's cold room was at the end of a long hall. I got the sense the complex was mainly industrial R&D. There were doors with lab names like HAPTIC FEEDBACK and LOW-FRICTION MATERIALS. Taro held his hand over a scanner and a door hissed open.

The room looked like it was about forty-one and a half feet square with an eighteen-foot ceiling, all done in your basic morgue white with bone accents and a hundred thousand lumens of shadowless fluorescent lighting. Its only remarkable feature was the computer in the center of the room: a clear Lucite tank about the size of a Ford Explorer van stood on its end. LEON, which they said stood for Learning Engine 1.9, was suspended inside the tank, a black thing like a big grandfather clock. Skeins and ratkings of cords and hoses curled out from the bottom of the tank and stretched across the white epoxied floor to a mound of chillers and Eheim pumps and Acer 6000 storage drives, all pushed against one of the windowless cinder-block walls. Four genderless perpetual graduate students huddled at workstations in the corners of the room, tapping and mumbling to themselves in HLASM.

"We replaced most of the silicon chips with doped germanium," Taro was saying. "But the thermal dissipation is still nearly three hundred watts. So for now we are refrigerating him like an antique Cray. The coolant is the same type of plasma they use for synthetic blood transfusions."

He led me over to the tank like I was a tourist at the Big Chunk of Rock National Monument. I squinted into it. Up close you could see that the black thing wasn't solid, but rather a tall stack of paper-thin black circuit boards, each about three feet square and a quarter-inch apart. Whorls of heat distortion spewed out of different layers through the clear liquid like diffraction waves over a summer highway.

"Huh. Nifty," I said. *Demonio,* this really was a cold room. About sixty f-ing degrees. I'm going to need a damn baby blanket, I thought. Or like, two shots of Tres Años. Brrrrrrrrrrrrrrrrrrrrr.

"Of course this is just the CPU," he said. "The drives are in another building. And the storage is . . . well, I do not know where all the storage is. Much of it is in Korea."

"How fast is it?" I asked.

"Right now he is close to six petaflops."

"Wow." Sounds expensive, I thought.

"At the moment LEON is running two hundred and fifty-six simulated worlds about ten minutes ahead of the real one. And for each of those he is playing through more than five million branches of the Sacrifice Game tree simultaneously. Each one is a three-stone game."

"How many simulated trades do you run?" I asked.

"Around twenty thousand a day," he said. "I don't know about the actual trades."

"Huh," I said. That's one of the great things about Taro, I thought. Most other people would have gotten all cagey and said something like "Where'd you hear we were running any trades?" But he just didn't have it in him.

"Would you like to play a game against him?" Taro asked.

I said I'd love to.

"Have you played with three stones?"

I said I had. As I think I said, this means that you use three runners, that is, the stone that represents what actually happens and that runs away from the hunting stones, which represent different potentials. The thing is, it wasn't three times harder than playing with one stone. It was 3^3 times, that is, twenty-seven times harder. It's sort of like how a mate-in-three chess problem is many, many times harder than a mate-in-two. So anyway, usually I used two stones. But I'd been working on playing with three. I figured I could handle it, against a machine, anyway. Really, computers still can't play the Game for shit.

Taro got a wobbly shop stool and I sat down in front of an old NEC 3-D monitor. He hoisted himself onto the Formica work surface and started tapping on a touchpad.

"You know how the average human brain runs about two billion operations per second?" he said, over the tappitty-tap-tap-taps.

"Well, it takes a lot of work to be average," I said.

"And then after that we should budget in another six or eight billion of our own operations just to compile out the parallelism." I nodded, as though I could easily have worked that out myself. "Then we must double that for record keeping and fail-safe. And then we have got about twenty billion ops per second. So as long as it goes through at normal speed and we do not have to store anything in LEON himself, that should be just enough."

"Great," I said. Enough for what? I wondered. To create a new master race of all-knowing nonorganic superbeings? Well, at least then I'll have someone to talk to. Yep, in the final showdown between man and machine, I know which side *I'll* be on—

"But I do not think it will ever surpass a human player," he said. "Even if LEON becomes as large, computationally, as a human brain—even if he becomes as smart as a human brain—this does not mean he will be as intuitive as a human brain."

The Sacrifice Game was like Go, and unlike chess, in that people could still play it much better than computers. A low-intermediate human player can still beat the world's best Go program. And Go's a very describable game, close to what programmers call a clean environment. The Sacrifice Game's a lot more anecdotal, more connected to the world, so it's at least a few million times messier.

"Well, don't sell yourself short," I said, "at least, not to any grant committees—"

"They guess that already," he said. "That is why we have so . . . gone corporate. At any rate, at this stage LEON is primarily of value as an assistant." He led me over to a bank of OLED monitors. "It helps improve the performance of novice adders. Like advanced chess." That is, what chess players call it when they play in consultation with two computers. I nodded.

He sat. I sat.

"We are working with five student players," he said. "Two of them learned the Game in Maya communities, and the others have trained here. One of them is very promising. He was not an adder before, though." I waited for him to say "Still, he cannot hold a candle to you, you ace," but he didn't. Instead he showed me some charts and pointed out where the spikes were on what, for want of an elegant term, we'd called the "worldwide event space." Basically, it confirmed that the Game did best at guessing what groups of people will do in crisis situations. "This is, of course, still very useful," Taro said, "and over time it could be immensely profitable." But it wasn't the sort of prediction his backers wanted. For instance, it didn't do a good job of predicting the markets per se, but just what people will do in the markets. You'd think this would be the same thing, because markets depend on psychology. But in fact there are still all these nonhuman factors going on in market fluctuations, too, industrial lag, capital flow, weather, and on and on, and getting that stuff together with the psychology requires interpretation. It's one of those things that is very hard, or maybe impossible, to teach a computer.

So Taro was having roughly the same problems I was . . . but still, I thought . . . hmm. Suppose their simulated trades average, say, 0.02 percent over industry standard, then that's still enough for a company that size to make a few million a minute. These days, even less of an edge could turn whoever had it into a market-devouring monster. The Warren Group could be on their way to being the richest company in the world. Although you'd think they'd be bigger already. Maybe they're just spending a lot more than they're reporting. Which might also explain why they're being so secretive about the Game thing. They'd be bragging about their investment results all over the place unless there were some specific reason not to. People don't dismiss game studies out of hand anymore. If anything, they're all trying to get a piece of it. Everybody wants to hire the next Johnny von Neumann.

Or maybe they don't want to manage other people's money, they want to grow their own. Maybe Lindsay Warren and some of the board members want to buy back the public shares before any word gets out. Or maybe they're afraid that if the government finds out they have something militarily interesting, they'll take them over. Maybe that's even something to be a little uneasy about, isn't it? Suppose Warren or somebody else does take the Game to the next level, then what? Maybe they're going to end up owning everything and just take over the world? It's like if Taro'd been running the Manhattan Project, except instead of working for the War Department he was sponsored by Marvel.

Maybe I should just post whatever I know about the Game. Maybe even later today. I'd been thinking about doing it for a while and I had most of it written up. Then at least everybody'd have it. I'd kept putting it off because—well, a few reasons. I felt like I hadn't figured it all out yet. It was still tough to learn and harder to master. Also, I had a few things I wanted to take care of with it myself before I attracted any attention. Well, frankly—I wasn't going to mention this, but maybe I should level with you, now that we know each other a little better—the truth is I was saving up to sponsor a blind-contract hit on García-Torres. It's not an easy thing to do these days, since the people you hire tend to turn you in even if they actually do the job. Still, I thought . . . but still, the other thing was, it wasn't even clear that putting the Game out in the world would be the best thing. Maybe it would be like with nukes; it's bad enough that some crook politicians have them, but it's still better than giving one to every nut on the planet. Hmm, mmm, mmm . . .

Except, the thing is, if Warren was trying to keep a lid on, why'd they let Taro talk to *Time*? If they couldn't keep the Codex from getting published, because too many Mayanists knew about it, they might have asked him to say something lukewarm—

"Would you like to see the current game board?" Taro asked.

I said sure.

"I should not be showing it to you because it is absolutely secret, but of course you helped develop it and I know we can trust you."

I said thanks. Damn, I thought. I'd been a real *pisado*. It was all choking me up a bit, actually.

Taro clicked it up on the screen:

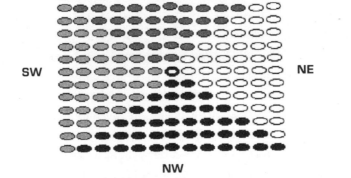

Whoa, I thought. Simple. Elegant. Sometimes you look at something and it's just obvious it's right.

Damn. Why hadn't I thought of that?

"Huh," I said. "And, uh, this one's based on the Codex, uh, Nymphenberg?"

He said largely, yes.

I spent about half an hour clicking around the board, trying different calendrical assignments and getting used to the interface. It wasn't so hard to adapt to as I'd have thought. One tends to think of game boards as always being the same size, like 9 squares for tic-tac-toe or 64 squares for chess. But that's not really true. Some people teach chess to newbies on a 36-square board. Shogi, or Japanese chess, has 81 squares. A standard Go board has 361 points, but even serious players sometimes play quick games on boards with only 81. Serious tic-tac-toe people play on larger or multidimensional boards. In feudal Japan, generals and courtiers used to play shogi on 625-square boards filled with all sorts of wacky pieces like blue dragons, evil wolves, and drunken elephants. And of course, in episodes 1-2, 1-3, 1-20, and 3-14, Kirk and Spock played chess on that trilevel board that you can now get a replica of from the Franklin Mint. So the Sacrifice Game is the same way; you can play on a larger or smaller board without changing the rules or even changing the strategy all that much. But it can take a long time to get really good at playing on a new scale. I could do nothing but kid around with this for ten years. Damn it, this is the right stuff, I thought. If I'd been using this version I'd have made billions by now, not just millions. Taro's company *must* be picking trades with this thing. If they're not, they're insane. Well, don't worry about it. Focus.

"I think I'm ready to try it out," I said.

"All right," Taro said, "I have the first question."

I fished my packet of chaw out of my watch pocket. *"Ajpaayeen b'aje'laj k'in ik' . . . ,"* I said. ("I'm borrowing the breath of today.") I tapped the screen five times, cast some so-called virtual seeds over the board, and snuck a look behind me, at LEON. Ripples rolled up through the fluid as the thing started to really think. I nodded that I was ready.

Taro threw me a few softballs and then started asking tougher questions. Suddenly the new board seemed bigger than I'd thought, as though my runners could get lost out in the wasteland and not get back until sometime after the Big Crunch. And LEON was a bear. Right away it felt like one of the best players I'd met. And it was certainly the fastest. But for a first shot I didn't do as badly as I might have. The Game was the one area of life I wasn't underconfident about.

"Our good student is on his way over," Taro said, after about two hours. "Would you like to play a real-time prediction?"

I said sure. I got a little flutter, though. Competition was never my long suit.

"The IRs are downstairs," Taro said. He meant isolation rooms. I said great.

What's going on? I wondered.

I took a break. I went upstairs, got four vending-machine espressi and a baglet of Jelly Bellies, and came back. Taro led me down to an even more sub-subbasement, through a cold hallway, and into a small conference room.

"This feels kind of like a test," I said.

"Well, you know I like testing everything," Taro said.

"If I do really well, do I get to see the Codex?"

"We would have to call Marena Park and ask her," he said. At first I thought he was talking about a place. "She is the big boss."

I said okay.

"Tony has been practicing with this layout for over a month," Taro said. "So I do not expect you to outplay him." I nodded like, *Neither do I, since I am but a humble disciple.* "But I know you do better under the stress of competition."

"Right," I said. Thanks, I thought. Yeah, I just need a little motivation. You know, I do even better with a xenon headlamp shining in my face and electrodes clipped to my scrotum. I was beginning to remember why I'd dropped out of the project.

There was a raplet on the door. Two people breezed in. One was a stocky Southeast Asian girl with glasses whom Taro introduced as Ashley Thieu, and the other, a demi-Maya-looking guy, was Tony Sic. We said hello in English and then Sic said in Yukateko that he understood I was from Alta Verapaz. I said yes. He had a really tight crew cut but he didn't seem like an army type. He said he'd just come from playing soccer. He was wearing shorts and old Diadora RTX 18s, which, if I remembered right, was a pretty serious professional shoe, and you could smell his fresh manly sweat. I breathed through my mouth.

"Is that your green car out there?" he asked in English.

"Yes," I said.

"Nice."

"Thanks. It's not green in terms of mileage, though."

"My older brother had one of those, in Mérida. Except it was composed out of many wrecked ones, like the Frankenstein."

I told him how I'd worked at the museum in Mérida for two months. He asked if I meant the one on Calle 48 and I said no, it's on 58, and he smiled.

We went out through another door into a bare hallway. The walls, floor, and ceiling were all bare DuraStone block, which was supposed to make it hard to hide any wires or transmitters that might let you fake a test. Sic opened a solid steel door and went alone into his room. They put me in one four doors down. There was nothing in the concrete room except a bare fluorescent bulb in the ceiling, an old LCD monitor, an uncomfy chair, a battery-operated, transmitter-free video camera, an EEG recorder, and a Formica task surface with a touch-screen board already set up.

Damn, I thought, they're taking this seriously. They must be having some kind of problem. And they need to call in the expert. Right? Right.

Ashley glued the EEG 'trodes to my head—she had some trouble with all the hair—and said, "Okay, we're going to leave you." She meant "leave you in here all alone." I'm not claustrophobic, I was going to say, but instead I just mumbled as usual. Sic and I were going to play against the exact same data at the same time, and Taro was going to run the exam and watch us both on video. Otherwise there was no connection between the two rooms, so there was no chance one of us could influence the other. Sic and I weren't exactly playing against each other, but just racing, both treating Taro as an ordinary client and playing, as usual, on his behalf against an absent god.

I got out my tobacco, rubbed it in, and rooted myself. In his own isolation room Sic did the same.

"Are we all ready?" Taro asked over the speaker. His voice had been converted to a synthesized one so that he couldn't give us any information through vocal clues. Sic must have said yes. I said yes. So, I thought, I'll just blow away this character on the first round. No sweat.

The test-case video came up on the screen.

(5)

It was a live streaming feed taken from a security camera placed above a square or plaza in what was evidently an Islamic or largely Islamic country. It was already night there, but the place was lit with harsh blue light, I guessed from military searchlights. A big crowd of men in dirty white tunics filled the lower half of the screen. Blood from self-inflicted head cuts ran down their necks in lines, like black enamel. In the middle there was a high chain-link fence with ten or fifteen soldiers standing behind it. The soldiers had mustaches, khakis, and what looked like SA-120s, but I couldn't see any insignia. They had that stiff look of trying not to look nervous. Then behind the soldiers there was what looked like a government building, maybe an embassy, white with white pilasters and a pair of dark Victorian-looking wood doors. There were signs on it, but they were too blurry to read. The sound was off and blue rectangles flickered over the bottom and top right corners of the screen, blocking out whatever crawls the news service had put in. And although a few people in the crowd were holding up homemade signs, either they were turned the other way or the writing was being pixelated out. Damn, I should have done my homework, I thought. Somebody who knew a little more about Islamic-world men's fashion and facial-hair styles could probably key this right down—still, okay, just think, where the hell is it? Well, it looks like there's no sunlight left there at all and assuming we're in real time, which I bet, that makes it probably too late to be the Middle East, since it's still daylight all the way to longitude seventy degrees, so I'm guessing we're looking at northern India. In fact, I'd bet it's in or near Bangladesh, since that's the hot spot right now. Okay. And their heads are bashed because . . . well, so there's no Islamic holiday, no Hindu holiday that I know of . . . so they're protesting something specific.

Let's see, I'm also guessing this isn't one of the big cities . . . so say this is the town hall, not an embassy. And the fierce Muslim hordes want—what do they want? They don't just want to trash the place . . . no, *pues,* they want to be let into the building. Right? Maybe because they're afraid that when the war starts the Hindu majority is going to lynch them.

Something like that. Not that any of this gave me a whole lot of insight into what they were going to do.

We watched, memorizing the scene. One minute later the screen went blank.

"All right," the voice with Taro's words said. "We would like each of you to answer three questions. One: Will the mob climb the fence and attack the structure? Two: If this will happen, when? And three: If this happens, will they be successful and take the building? You each have thirty minutes. Do either of you have any questions?"

Uh, yeah, I thought, is a brown Crayola the same as a number-2 pencil, or—

"All right, no questions," he said. "Please begin." I scattered my virtual seeds over the board. They bounced a little high, but it wouldn't really matter. The point was that there was randomness in the subject of the query, that is, the event in Asia, and there was also randomness on the board. Of course, Taro's team would also be running conventional software on the video and whatever other data they could get from the site. They'd use the same crowd-pattern catastrophe-modeling programs the DHS uses for riot response, and also anything the LEON project had cooked up. Still, I could do better. Right? I set my running stone in the center bin.

Basically, the object of the Sacrifice Game is to catch the runner. If you're playing a one-runner game, that means that one person only gets one piece, and his opponent gets many. This strikes some people as odd, even though there's a whole class of board games that are still played in the twenty-first century that are very similar. Some of the most popular ones are called Hare and Hounds, or Goat and Wolves, or that sort of thing. They're a bigger deal in Asia. Anyway, they're all classified as highly asymmetric games. And in all of them one person plays with a few fast or powerful pieces and the other plays with a whole lot of slower or weaker pursuers. If you're the runner—or the prey, or the quarry, or however you'd translate it—your object is to get away from the hunters, or "capturers." In Hare and Hounds, which is played on a checkers grid, this can mean just getting to the other side of the board. In the Sacrifice Game you begin on the starting date, at the center of the board, and to win you need to get to one of the four escape squares, which are at the corners. But doing that isn't easy, not just because of all the hunters, but because your movements are partly controlled by a randomizer. Also, in the Game, the runner leaves a record of where it's been. Every time it rests on a square, or rather a point, you leave a stone there to mark the spot. That trail is like real history, as opposed to the rest of the board, which is like an oceanic maze of possibility. Each time you move, it marks a date. So in a way the board is like one of those perpetual calendars they used to have with the four rings and all the pegs, like there were seven pegs for each day of the week and thirty-one pegs for the days of the month and whatever. So each time you move in space, you're also leaving a trail in represented time. And if you can read along that trail and extrapolate it and guess the next move, you're thinking into the future.

Any great game creates its own sort of trancelike state in serious players, and the Sacrifice Game has a particular flavor to it that's hard to describe. Maybe when you were little you played Parcheesi, or one of its slightly streamlined proprietary versions like Sorry! or Aggravation. And maybe you remember how exciting it was, shaking the dice and moving the little pegs or marbles out of your home base and into the circuit, how it felt finally bouncing your last man toward home just a few spaces ahead of your opponent, and how there was nothing in the world more frustrating than getting knocked back to base just when you were coming to the end of your long odyssey, and how the only thing that made that bearable was that it paled next to the pleasure of doing the same thing to someone else. And there was no question of stopping the Game or even of leaving the room for a moment. The Game was the essential reality. And even though Parcheesi, the way it's played in the West, is a kid's game, it's still the core of a huge number of adult games, for instance backgammon. And of course Monopoly, which is still the most popular branded board game in the world, is a form of Parcheesi. Anyway, there's a basic excitement in those constructions that's hard to pin down and harder to resist.

I think what happens is that the Game brings you right up against the rush of chaos. You're surfing the wave of probability itself, where the two sides of the universe, the determined and the random, crash together and crest, but in this little world it's almost manageable, you've just got the two dice making the different waves, the basic roll-frequency wave with the peak at seven, and then the hit-odds wave with a cliff at two and a peak at twelve. Even to someone who doesn't know a thing about the math, it's a hypnotic motion, like you felt when you were little and you stared at an old barber pole, wondering where the stripes went when they left the cylinder, or, if you're of a certain age, the pulsing label on a Vertigo LP.

Taro's voice came over the speaker again.

"Time," he said.

I looked at the board. My runner was two points from the northwest corner. It didn't look good for him. That is, in the short run. There was something farther out, a sense that the whole scene was hurrying toward a deadline, but I just couldn't fix on it. Damn.

"The protesters are going to break through the fence roughly two and a half hours from now," I said. "They will try to take the building but they won't succeed. A lot of them, I'll say more than fifty, are going to get killed or seriously wounded."

Taro said all right. I unplugged my head before Ashley could get in and walked out into the conference area.

The protest march was on the wall screen, this time with the sound on, and they were all watching it. It turned out that it was going on in some town north of Calcutta, and the building was an office of the Assam Rifles, that is, the northeastern counterinsurgency force, and the crowd of *mohajirs,* that is, Muslim refugees, was actually trying to rescue some leader of theirs who was being held inside. I wasn't crazy about missing that angle. But there were, supposedly, Hindu mobs threatening them somewhere offscreen.

Sic came in with Taro. They sat at the table. It was an awkward moment.

"Well, what did you come up with?" Sic asked me.

I said what I thought. He said he'd guessed that they were going to rush the building in less than half an hour and that they were going to take it successfully. I said "Mmmm" with as much professional friendliness as I could bring to the line.

Taro said that the conventional professional assessments from both the NSA observer and his own software both indicated that the demonstrators would disperse before there were any casualties. We all nodded. Ashley Thieu got up and brought back a tray with hot chocolate, Mint Milanos, and a selection of cheap, faggy herbal teas. On the screen the only major change so far was that somebody had climbed up on something and was speechifying in Urdu. We all sat around like a bunch of undergraduates watching election results. In fact it felt specifically like the presidential election of 2000, when it just didn't ever end and every time you wanted to go and crash, another sprig of hope sprouted up, and you just kept watching and biting your nails and hoping and hoping even though somehow you knew in your heart that it was going to end in a disaster.

Twenty minutes later, one of the men climbed the fence. A guard fired his carbine into the air with an impotent-sounding pop. Two seconds later the fence was covered with people and there were a few more pops. Someone fell off the fence, but you couldn't tell whether he'd been shot or just slipped. It wasn't easy to see what went on after that, since the fence covered two-thirds of the screen, but less than five minutes later, someone draped a homemade flag, with white Arabic writing on a black field, out of a second-floor window.

They were in. I was screwed. Sic had got it right. I'd messed up. I couldn't even look at Taro. I was about to leave and see if I could throw up, but nobody else seemed to be moving. I picked at a coral burn on my left index finger. It wasn't healing. Goddamn *Millepora alcicornis*. I should just rip those shits out of the tank and let them suffocate. I said I was going outside to get a little hot air.

"Let's keep watching," Sic said. "It's not over yet."

I said I would and linked my phone to the room system. It took me a minute to find the elevator again, and by the time I got outside I was ultraventilating.

The steambathish air revived me a little. How do people stand all that air-conditioning? I'd understand it if they were all from Finland or wherever, but they're not. Sic's a tropical person and he seemed fine.

Damn. Sic. Bastard.

Well, what do I do now? I was in the middle of about a square mile of would-be-tasteful cheap bricky campus architecture with lots of handicapped access and indigenous shrubs. I sat on a brick thing. The sky had smogged up to a gray-green greasy color, about Web-Safe #6699CC, and it gave the sprawl-scape a sinister look, as though it had been translated into German. Bleak-ness, I thought. Bleak. Bleak. I couldn't resist peeking at my phone. It looked like it had gotten tuned to a dead channel, but when I looked a little closer at the screen I could tell that the field of pinkish gray was a cloud of dust. People were yelling, and the commentator said he didn't know what was going on. I watched. After a while some of the dust blew away, and I could just see that a lot of the building wasn't there anymore. The commentator's voice was saying that it "appeared" the building had been blown up. He didn't say who'd done it, but even I—and I don't know a whole lot about explosives—even I could tell that the blast was too big for one of the men to have carried the explosive in. Somebody inside the police station must have set the charge before the mob broke through and then detonated it when he thought it would hurt them the most.

So what if I was off on the timing, I thought. Sic was way further off than that. Successful indeed. Hah! Gotcha, Sicko. I am de KING de la RING! I'm . . .

Cool it, Jed. *Pisado.* People are dying out there. Now, if you squinted at the rubble, you could see what had to be two curled-up bodies at the bottom of the screen. They looked sculpted out of the same gray plasticine as everything else. Damn, I'm a clod. Hell. I hate it when you come up against your own character and find yourself, as usual, wanting. You wish you were more upset because that would make you a good person. Although maybe just wishing you were more upset is almost as good as actually being more upset.

Isn't it?

(6)

About two hours later—well, okay, at exactly 4:32:29 P.M., according to the windshield—I pulled up in front of the Warren Entertainment offices, on the west side of Lake Tohopekaliga, just south of Orlando. My big win against Sic had gotten me an interview with Marena Park, who was Taro's boss and also the head of their Interactive Division. I'd Googled her on the drive over and it turned out she was new at Warren. She'd been the creative director of Disney's Game World complex at Epcot until two years ago. Then Warren had hired her away to work on Neo-Teo, which was pretty much my favorite first-person shooter. Most hard-core Go people or poker people or whatever won't even call computer games like that "games," and really, strictly speaking, they're not so much games as simulations, but I like some of them anyway for blowing off my toxic steam. Neo-Teo was basically a dumbed-down consumer version of Maya mythology, where you'd sneak through pseudo-Puuc-style palaces grabbing trinkets of power and gutting jaguar demons with a spear. So there were a lot of inaccuracies and a cheesiness that drove me crazy at first, but there was something fiendishly addictive about it, and now if I wasn't totally dependent I was definitely a user. And the look of it, which Ms. Park had designed, was actually pretty great. She'd definitely gotten those smoky coils and hook-and-barb lines like on the Classic Maya pots. Then she'd won an Oscar for production design on the movie version. Which all made one wonder, again, what someone like her was doing in charge of Taro's project. She wasn't a scientist. What was the connection? Except maybe I guess now all business is show business.

There was a big sort of studio gate and I had to tell the security-hub thugs who I was. From the way they checked I got the feeling Ms. Park was a pretty big deal. The guard gave me a live badge and I clipped it onto my right wrist.

I drove in and parked where he'd said. The complex was a menacingly tasteful scattering of low Dryvited buildings in a treesy office park with a giant green sculpture of three linked rings reflecting in a big reniform pond. The main building was six stories, higher than the others. Glass veils parted and I walked into heavily processed air. The big lobby had an overhanging clerestory of conference and exercise rooms and a giant potted Douglas fir with spherical video-display ornaments playing happy faces of Children of Many Lands. A woman greeter with hair greeted me by mispronounced name and steered me in around a sort of atrium that had a Healthy Gourmet Café and a big stone pizza hearth. A cruft of Generation Yuzz techies stroked around us, some on Segways and some on what I guessed were Sleekers.

"It's up here," she said with a beckoning motion, like, "Come on, it'll be fun, you'll see."

"Right," I said. "Thanks." I squeaked after her. Imagine what it would be like having a job, I thought. Next thing I'd be showering. Just kidding. I shower. Sometimes.

"So Professor Mora tells me you're one of the Mayans," she said at me. She pronounced it to rhyme with *paeans*.

"Uh, Ch'olan Maya, yes," I said. And by the way, I thought for the ten-to-the-nth time, the plural of *Maya* is *Maya. Mayan* is the language group. You speak *in* May*an to* the May*a about* May*a* stuff.

"I think all that is absolutely *fasc*inating," she said. She was tall with a lot of blond wool and, I suppose, pretty in an ovine way.

"It is?" I asked.

"Being from South America and everything."

"Central America."

"'Scuse me?"

"We're not from South America," I said, "we're from Central America. Like, north of Panama?"

"Oh, inter-*est*ing." She laughed. We went up a ramp to the second floor, past a vacant retro-thirties screening room. "You know what?" Whatsherhair asked. "Two weekends ago I went to an initiation workshop with Halach M'en."

"Oh?"

"He taught us how to make Mayan dreamcatchers."

"Oh, great. What do they do?"

"He said the Mayans were very spiritually advanced."

"We were?"

"We're here," she said. She led us into a waiting area with a black floor and green Djinn sofas, like a negative of the scene in *2001*. From there the receptionist took us into a trading-floor-like space with apparently happy workers in heavily personalized glass cubicles and snack-and-coffee stations with little condiment bars and Capresso machines and dwarf Sub-Zeros with notes on them like AMARANTH MILK IN HERE. We passed into a carpeted zone and she peeked around an ajar door. The occupant must have waved, because she guided me in.

Marena Park sat cross-legged on top of her desk, looking at a big green screen in her lap. It was the new trendy kind that can sense its owner's hands from across the room, because she was drawing something with her finger in the air next to it. She was smaller than she looked in photographs, at least a head shorter than I was, which made her teensy. Her face seemed flatter and more Korean than it had looked all made up, but I actually thought it was more attractive this way, "a face like a full moon," as they say in *The Thousand and One Nights*. She was wearing a sort of Issey Miyake pleated gray polyamide in-line skating costume, like she was from a luxurious and athletic future. She held up her one-moment finger. I blinked around the room. There was a wall-inset 125-gallon tank of the new Monsanto glow-flashing oranda goldfish. I tried not to sneer at them visibly. The immune systems on those things are totally for shit; they're so inbred they get hole-in-the-head septicæmia if you tap on the glass twice. There was a thick bias-cut katsura-wood Go board on the floor next to her desk, with old mulberry bowls that probably held a set of thick pink extinct-clam Go stones. If they did, the set would have to be worth at least a hundred thousand dollars U.S. The window behind the desk faced northwest, and you could just see the Epcot Buckyfullersphere floating on pea-green foliage like an old soccer ball in a duckweed-choked pond. She looked up.

"Hi, hang on a tick," she said. She had a little voice but not a high voice, like a male jockey's. There was a pause. "So just Babel fish it into Sanskrit or whatevertheshit they speak over there, what's the probs?" It took me a second to realize she had a phone somewhere in one of her ears. I didn't sit down. I realized my heart was coshing against my rib cage. I tethered my hands in my pockets and eased over to check out a big tchotchke shelf on the east wall. The largest and most imposing item on it was a brass skeleton clock that looked like it had been made sometime in the 1950s. It had five rotating wheels, with four of them grinding through the Maya calendar and the outer and largest one slowly ticking off Gregorian dates, all the way from 3113 BC to December 21, 2012. There was also a ring of portrait glyphs, but it didn't seem to make sense. Maybe it was just something somebody made up. There was another clock next to it, a smaller one with a triangular Masonic dial—it said "Waltham/17 Jewels/Love Your Fellow Man" and that it was trowel minutes from mallet o'clock—and the other things on the shelf were all trophies, little silver cups for Go and rock climbing, a couple of Webbys, a World Shareware Award, a bunch of E3 Game Critics Awards, two skinny glass pyramids from the Academy of Interactive Entertainment Arts and Sciences, a lot of things for stuff nobody'd ever heard of, and near the back, like she didn't want to look like she cared about it, an Oscar statuette dressed in a one-sixth-scale costume from Neo-Teo, standing like Jesus in a crowd of adoring Nephites. You really like me? I thought. Little me, king of the world? I wish I had someone to thank. Well, I guess I'll just thank Satan, who allowed me to trade this moment for my soul. On the wall over the shelf there was a child's drawing of Santa Claus holding a big universal remote and driving a team of robot reindeer, taped over and partly obscuring a framed Cibachrome of Ms. Park, who evidently had prehensile toes, dangling upside down from a yellow-granite overhang. A caption over it read, *Solo Ascent "Chocolate Swastika," E7 6c, Hallam View Buttress, Gritstone, 14/9/09.* Next to that there was a tiny-by-comparison framed snapshot in the exaggerated blues and russets of 1950s Kodak, an eager-faced young Korean in a USN flight jacket standing arm-in-arm with a familiar-looking five-star general in front of a dusty B-29 with a seven-up pair of dice, a chesty brunette, and the words *Double or Nothing* painted on its nose. A hand-scribbled note in the top left of the photograph read, *To Pak Jung—Thanks Always for Service "Above and Beyond"—S.C.A.P. Gnl. Douglas C. MacArthur, Kadena 12/27/51.*

"Yep," she said into the void. Pause. "Byebyeonara." Her eyes focused on me. "Hi."

She didn't get up. Usually it's a blessing the way people hardly shake hands anymore, but in this case I wouldn't have minded a little skin contact. I said hi. I wondered if I should say who I was, even though she knew. I didn't.

"Taro really thinks you're the greatest," Ms. Park said.

"That's very gratifying."

"I bet you play Go, right?"

I nodded. Maybe she'd seen me looking at the board. It's weird how people can tell stuff about me. I've always felt like I'm on the Planet of the Telepaths. Of course, it's supposed to be something to do with my putative PTSD.

"How strong are you?" she asked.

"Uh, six *dan*. Amateur."

"That's *godless*," she said. "I'm a five. Maybe we should play sometime."

"Great," I said. Five *dan* is actually pretty impressive, especially since most people in the entertainment industry would have trouble getting through a game of Cootie. Go is considered a martial art in Asia, and a *dan* is a belt. So a six-*dan* is like a sixth-degree black belt. I was still nothing next to a professional player, though. Anyway, a six-*dan* spots a five-*dan* one stone, which still gives you a really good game. She and I would be playing far into the night in the tatami room of her thrillingly minimalist sky-high doorman quadruplex loft to the romantic strains of vintage Jello Biafra, and as I apologized for clobbering her again by seventy and one-half points she'd push the board aside and grab me by the—

"Please, *Setzen Sie sich*," she said.

I sat. The chair had looked solid, but it yielded under me and conformed to my body type, so my feet flailed for a second. Doofus. "Hey, I'm a big fan," I said. "I play your game all the time."

"Oh? Thanks. What shell are you on?"

"Uh, thirty-two."

"That's very excellent."

"Thanks." Even though it was her product, I was embarrassed to admit I'd spent so much geek time on the thing.

"The thing is," she said, "even though it's my product I really don't know anything about the ancient Maya." No kidding, I thought. "Or maybe you can tell that from the game," she said, beating me to it.

"Well . . ."

"It's okay, it's just a fantasy. I know it's not historically accurate."

"Sure," I said. I realized I hadn't taken my hat off. Damn. I have this thing where it's weird to have my head uncovered, and I still forget to peel off my headpiece indoors. Better take it off now, I thought. No. It's too late. But she's got to think I'm pretty weird with the hat thing, right? No, don't do it. That's my look. The Hat Look. Better just be comfortable. Right? *Bueno*. Señor Hat stays.

"You grew up speaking Mayan, right?" Marena asked.

"Yes." I took my hat off. "Actually, the language where I'm from is called Ch'olan."

"Taro says you're from Alta Verapaz."

"Yes."

"Did you ever hear anything about any ruins down there, around, um, Kabon?"

"Sorry? Where, like the Río Cahabón?"

"That's it. Michael said something about an oxbow area."

"Downstream of T'ozal?"

"That sounds right."

"There are ruins all over around there," I said. "People know the hills aren't natural. My uncles used to tell us the hunchbacks built them, before the Flood."

"What hunchbacks?"

"Just, you know, magic mud dwarfs or boulder babies or trolls or whatever. I kind of pictured them as big chunky gravelly guys with, like, huge heads."

"Oh, okay."

"Why? Do you know the area?"

"Just on the map. But Michael's been trying to get a permit to excavate the royal tombs. Before this dam goes in and trashes the place."

"Well, that's good—"

"You know, maybe I shouldn't say this, but you don't look that much like a Native American."

"No, it's okay, I get that. Maya don't look much like the Navajo or whatever anyway. Sometimes we even get mistaken for Southeast Asians."

"You don't look Asian. Or Latin American." She smiled to give it all a flirty spin, like she was afraid of seeming racist. But it was true, I don't really look like much of anything. The Maya tend to be short 'n' chunky, but I was half Ladino, and because of all the calcium I'd gotten in Utah—atypically, I wasn't lactose-intolerant, and I'd landed on a planet where milk is practically the only approved beverage—I'd shot up to a towering five nine, more than a head taller than anyone else in my original family. Currently I was around 135 pounds, so I couldn't really shop in the Husky Department, and that seemed to have thinned my face out. A pure Maya usually has a wide face that looks like a hawk from the side and an owl from the front. But I just look vaguely tropical. Sometimes, when people hear my last name, they ask if I'm from the Philippines. Sylvana, that is, my sort of ex, used to say that my long hair made me look like a bad-looking version of Keanu Reeves in *Little Buddha*. I thought about saying all this to Marena and then decided to chill. Have a little mystery, for God's sake.

When I didn't say anything, she maybe got a little concerned. "You don't find the Ix game offensive, do you?" she asked.

"Oh, no—"

"I was afraid we might be making the Mayan dudes a little too, you know, uh . . ."

"Savage?"

"That's it."

"Well . . . ," I said, "at least you didn't make them cute."

"No."

"Anyway, I'm sure things were rough in those days."

"Yeah, people getting their hearts yanked out and whatevs."

"Actually, the Maya didn't do that," I said. "I mean, not so far as anybody knows."

"Really?"

"Maybe later on, like in the fourteen hundreds. Not in the Classic period. The hearts are more of a Mexican thing."

"Oh. Sorry. Still, they were really into cannibalism and everything, right?"

"I don't know," I said, "maybe that was just Spanish propaganda. They certainly sacrificed a few people sometimes. It's not that clear whether they ate them."

"Oh. Sorry."

"And anyway, what's the big deal with that? I mean, at this point cannibalism's so mainstream, it's like golf."

"Heh. Rather."

"You know, there was medicinal cannibalism in England into the nineteenth century."

"Like mummy dust and stuff?"

"Yeah, and, like, for instance they thought that the blood from somebody who died violently could cure epilepsy, so, like, at Lincoln's Inn Fields the pharmacists used to bleed people who'd just been hanged, and they'd reduce the blood down and mix it with alcohol, and you could buy it at Harris Apothecary."

"Neat."

"Yeah, and now there's some sort of, uh, Christianized consensual-cannibalism sect somewhere, it's called like the Church of the Overly Literal Communion or something."

"Oh, so so so, I did hear about that. Well, maybe it's just another weight-loss fad."

"Maybe."

"But I guess you're right, it's not a big deal. I mean, I ate my placenta."

That stopped me.

"Sorry, did that gross you out?" she asked.

"Well—"

"Hey," she said, "Taro also says you do astronomy tricks."

"Really?"

"Yep."

"Did he tell you how I can catch Frisbees in my mouth?"

"Oh, come on. Indulge me."

"Okay, pick a date."

"A date when?" she asked.

"Whenever."

"Okay, uh, February twenty-ninth, um, 2594."

"That's not a leap year."

"Okay, how about February twenty-eighth?"

"That's a Friday," I said.

"You're gonking me."

"It's true."

"Really?"

"Yeah. However, I can also tell you that sunrise on that day—assuming there is one—will be at about six fifty A.M. Eastern, and then sunset's at roughly six twenty-four."

"Sure," she said. "And I'm Anastasia Romanov."

"Wait, there's more. On that date Venus is going to rise at eight fifty-seven A.M.—although you wouldn't see that, of course—and set at nine fifty-six P.M. I mean, if you're around here. And Saturn's going to set at four thirty-four A.M."

"Bullshit."

"Google it."

"Never mind," she said. She had a big smile. "That's *godless*." Evidently *godless* was the new *awesome*. "So how many people can do that?"

"I don't know of anybody else. There are people who can do other things—"

"Hmm." She half giggled. Yeah, I thought, I've got a beautiful mind, all right. I'll unscramble your old Rubik's Cubes, I'll solve the undone pages in your Sudoku books, I'll do your taxes in base sixteen, just show me the book—

"Is it true that you speak twelve languages?" she asked.

"Oh, no, no way," I said. "I only really speak three. Unless you count the different Mayan languages. I can speak most of those."

"So you speak English, Spanish, and Mayan."

"Right. I can understand a few others. Like, to read. Maybe I could speak them well enough to buy tomatoes."

"Like which?"

"Just usual stuff, German, French, Greek, Nahuatl, uh, Mixteca, Otomi—"

"So, look," she said, "what do you think about the world ending? You think that's going to happen?"

"Um . . . well . . ."

I hesitated. We have a little problem here, I thought. On the one hand I was a little nervous about it despite myself. On the other hand I didn't have a single solid fact. And of course I wanted to say that there was a problem and that I could help her with it, but then again I was already getting a sense that Ms. Park might be a tad harder to snow than your average *chica alegre*.

"Um . . . well," I said, "no, not on the basis of anything I know. Why, are people around here nervous about it?"

"Some people are, and then, then I guess Taro said it might only apply to the Maya . . . not that that's not important, of course."

"Oh, sure, no, don't worry," I said.

"Seriously, though, what do you think?"

"Well, it's definitely an important date," I said. "In the old days they would have at least had a big festival. And they would have gotten all the wise old scribes or whatever together and worked out what to do next. Maybe they'd have constructed a new calendar."

"So no big giant whatever."

"I don't think so."

"Huh," she said. She almost sounded disappointed. "So is it true that the Maya, like, worshipped time?"

"Well, that's a little strong . . . it might be fair to say that no other culture has ever been so, so *obsessed* with time."

"But they did come up with all these impossibly complicated dates with the names and the weird numbers."

"Actually, if you teach kids Maya numbers, they say they're easier than Arabic ones. They're like dominoes; they're just spots and lines."

"Well, okay, but Taro was trying to tell me about the dates one time and I got totally lost. And I'm a code monkey."

"That's a great clock," I said.

"Thanks. Yeah, that used to belong to John Huston, you know, the film director, like *The Treasure of the Sierra Madre*?"

"Cool."

"And then the Neo-Teo team gave it to me after the AIE thing."

"It's great."

"But like I say, I haven't figured it out yet. Although they say it's running."

"Well, it's not really that hard," I said.

"You mean, like, the Mayan calendar isn't that hard."

"Yeah. There are some tricksomenesses to it but the basic idea is simple, if—well, look, don't think of it like a clock, think of it like an odometer, you know, in a car, I mean an old car, before they were electric."

"Okay."

"Well, so each place value in the mileage is on a gear, right? And when one gear turns over once the one to the left of it turns thirty degrees. One twelfth. Except with the Maya dates, most of the gears are in base twenty, like twenty teeth. Except for one that has eighteen. And then there's another important gear with thirteen teeth, that's the ritual calendar, and that one has the names on it. So every thirteen-times-twenty days, the same name-and-number combination comes up. Like say it's a Zero Bat day like today, then two hundred and sixty days from now there's another Zero Bat. So it's a big day when a lot of the cycles come up at the same time, like—"

"Like when the odometer's going to turn over another hundred thousand miles and the kids in the backseat all get really excited and lean over to watch."

"Right," I said. "Except each time it'll be in a different tun, that is, like, a bundle of three hundred and sixty days. And then a k'atun is twenty tuns, and then twenty k'atuns make a b'ak'tun. And eighteen of those—"

"Okay, I get that."

"Okay. And that's it, except there are other counts for Venus and other astronomical things, and for anniversaries, and for supernatural beings, like each day has a different set of protectors and threateners. It's kind of like how the Catholic saints all have days, except—"

"Except it's vastly more complicated."

"Well . . . except you have that kind of thing today, right? Like the Olympics and presidential elections are every four years, and then senatorial elections are every six years, but they're staggered, and then there's, like, economic cycles and five-year plans, and there's seventeen-year locusts and hundred-and-thirty-year bamboo. Uh, John Travolta makes a big comeback every fifteen and a half years—"

"Okay, I get it."

"Anyway, the only ones you really have to know are the solar cycle. That's

360 days, and the tz'olk'in, and that's in bunches of twenties and thirteens, and that makes up the ba'k'tuns. Those are about 256 years. The tz'olk'in sets the cycle seat and the main—"

"What's the cycle seat?"

"Oh, that's, that's like a temporary capital. Like they'd trade off, like, they'd decide on one city or, like, temple district, that would be the place where all the kings met and decided international policy and when the festivals would be or whatever. And then at the end of twenty years that temple district would get ritually killed. Like they'd cancel the inscriptions and the royal family would leave and they'd knock down the monuments and whatever. And then that area would be kind of taboo, and for the next twenty years the capital would be somewhere else."

"So is that the reason the Maya just left all those cities?"

"Well, yeah, it's possibly one reason that some of the ceremonial centers were abandoned, but—"

"So anyway," she said, "I understand you use a Sacrifice Game system to pick stocks."

"Commodities."

"Right. And you do it by hand, correct?" She meant not on computer.

"Well, I still have Taro's old software," I said, "but, yes, mainly."

"Do you have, like, a pouch of little pebbles or whatevs?"

"A grandeza," I said. "Yes."

"Do you have it with you?"

"Uh, yeah."

She didn't ask to see it. Too innuendoish, maybe.

"But you know," I said, "I'm not an astrologer or anything. It doesn't have anything to do with the supernatural." Hey, I thought, how about you show me the book and I'll show you my rocks?

"But, still, the Game really does let you predict things. Yes?"

"Well, a prediction sounds like a, like something a fortune teller would do."

"Huh." She paused. Don't be so honest, Jed, I thought. If she doesn't think you're special, she's not going to show you anything. Right? On the other hand, there is the theory of the soft sell. Anyway, you're not trying to get a date with her. Even if she is kind of hot. All you need right now is for her to show you the Codex. Right?

"So," she said, "so you're saying the old Maya dudes weren't really making prophecies?"

"Well, no, they—look, I guess what I'm saying is that they wouldn't have thought of them as prophecies. It's more like they were permanent, like flavors, or, say, like personalities, that each day naturally had. It's like a, a *Farmers' Almanac* that says there'll be snow that day, except it's saying there'll be disease or war or something. And then the flavors would develop over time, like if there were a big battle on that day, that would add a violent taste to the day from then on. Just like how a royal birthday is a lucky day. I mean even these days."

"Gotcha."

"But the real point is that the Game is *not*, like, giving you visions of the future. It just improves your guessing."

"How?"

"Well, to oversimplify, I guess I'd say it speeds up your brain somehow. Or allows it to focus better, and that feels like the same thing. It makes playtime. So like—"

"Wait, what's playtime, you mean, like, in nursery school?"

"No, well, that's just jargon from StrategyNet. But they use it to mean how each game generates its own kind of alternate time. Like, you know, a turn-based strategy game uses a different measurement of time that's not based on the wall time, or on duration, but on the events of the game itself. Right?"

"Right."

"Basically a game is measured in tempi. That is, moves. So if a player makes a move that achieves nothing, you've just lost a tempo. The clock time is just a convenience that has nothing to do with the dynamics of an actual game."

She nodded.

"And if your move doesn't keep up in the context of the game—if it doesn't jump out far enough or develop your pieces fast enough or whatever—it's still too slow."

She nodded.

"So playtime is like time measured in state changes. Without measuring duration."

She nodded.

"It also just means how, you know how when you're playing a game everything around you seems to be moving more slowly?"

She nodded.

This time I shut up.

"So anyway," she said, "you're saying all you're doing is just reading ahead."

In Go *reading* means working out the next sequence of moves. Professional Go players can read a hundred moves ahead.

"Right," I said. "Exactly." *Yes*, I thought. Bond! Game Bond! Brotherhood of gamesters! Now, naturally you'll want to show me the damn book. Right? Right.

The thing is, those of us who play a serious game—and by *serious* I mean what mathematicians call a nontrivial game, like Go, chess, shogi, bridge, poker, the Sacrifice Game, or one of the few important computer games like the Sim games—know, or feel we know, that there's a different and more purposeful world out there, one tuned to a more powerful wave. But this knowledge makes us exiles. And, of course, that makes us feel superior to everybody else—despite everybody else's somehow being healthier, happier, and more socioeconomically successful—and so we become intolerable.

"Still," she said, "reading ahead is enough for some good investing."

"I guess."

"I understand you've been making some good trades."

"May I ask according to whom?"

"The *firm*," she said, giving the word an ominous Grishamish inflection.

"Hmm."

"Don't worry."

"Okay."

"So anyway—look, you haven't seen any dooming—I mean, looming doom a year from now? Have you?"

"You mean the 4 Ahau date? The end of the calendar?"

"Right. Twelve twenty-one twelve."

"No, I haven't," I said. "Not yet, anyway."

"I guess that's good." I was getting that feeling that we were approaching the end of our conversation, like the sound of a bottle filling up. Come on, Jed. How do you make yourself indispensable to this woman? Come up with some persuasive, spectacular, façade-shattering . . . no, don't even try. Just ask something.

"Hey, I have a question," I said.

"Go for it."

"Why is an entertainment division sponsoring Taro's research? I mean, it's not exactly entertainment."

"Everything's entertainment now," she said.

"Right." Just show me the book, I thought. Show book to me. Show *me—book. Book—me.*

"Anyway, Lindsay's always been good at leveraging entertainment with whatever other things—you know, that's why the studio did the remake of *Silent Running,* because he bought Botania—that's a closed-system hydroponics company?"

"Right."

"And it tied in with that."

"Mmm." Great, I thought. Survivalism. More Mormon moronities. Stocking up for the Tribulation. You wouldn't want to have to meet Jesus on an empty stomach.

"It's got that survivalist thing going on," she said. Evidently she'd seen what I was thinking. Damn it, I thought. I hate psychics.

"Right," I said. "Yeah, I grew up in Utah—"

"Oh, right—"

"—so I know a little about that stuff."

"Right."

"Right."

"I mean, it's true, Lindsay's a major Saint and everything. He's just been elected to the Seventy."

"Gee." The Council of Seventy was the governing body of the Latter-Day Saints, kind of like the College of Cardinals.

"But *I* barely speak to those people. You know."

"Yeah."

"They're scary," she said.

"Right." Well, I thought, it's nice of her to try to put me at ease. Not that—

"But Lindsay's a lot more enlightened than the rest of them . . . anyway, those guys fund stuff nobody else'll touch."

"Like cold fusion?"

"Well, yeah, sure," she said, "but there are a thousand other things. It's not all O-rings."

"Right." For the benefit of those lucky enough not to have lived and/or worked in the Salt Lake region, the events Marena and I were referring to here were, first, the University of Utah's erroneous announcement, in 1989, that they'd successfully produced cold fusion, and, second, the *Challenger* space shuttle scandal, when it turned out that Mormon congressmen had steered construction of the shuttle to Morton-Thiokol, which skimmed millions of dollars off the project and, as some may remember, delivered an iffy product. And those were only two things out of many. It was kind of a joke, in fact, all the crackpot research the Saints kept paying for. Among science types in the Southwest, anyway. Mormon organizations spend millions every year on spirit detection, genetic memory, DNA-assisted genealogical research, cult archaeology, TEOTWAWKI retreats, free bug-out bags, and a dozen other pseudologies. Actually, the low point was probably in 1998, when a couple of researchers at the Layton Institute for Applied Physics said they'd jazzed the quantum foam and created a bubble universe. That is, for probably the first time since the big bang, a duplicate universe was now forming inside the usual one. They'd added that the two universes would be identical at the moment of fission, but that because of subatomic randomness they'd start diverging pretty fast. When an interviewer from CNN asked the senior guy where the new universe was, he'd said, "We're in it." Unsurprisingly, their results were not replicated.

"Anyway," Marena Park said, "it's easier to get it in the report on my budget because I already have Mayan-related stuff going on."

"Right," I said.

There was another pause. Well, great, I thought. I guess this means you don't need me for anything. I'll just slink out of here with my tail between my legs and—

"So you can read Mayan writing, right?" she asked.

"Well, yeah. I'm okay at it. But you know, it's not quite like regular reading, they're usually not really in sentences, and there's a lot of interpretation."

"Right. So, I guess you want to look at the Koh Codex, right?"

"Well, sure, of course I would," I said. YES!!! I thought.

"The thing is, it's still unpublished, so I'm not supposed to let it out yet. It's the biggest secret since Natalie Portman's nose job."

"Oh." Pause.

"But I don't know," she said, "maybe if you want to work with Taro again, maybe you could come in when he starts the next testing phase . . . that won't be for a while, though."

"Oh, uh-huh." Sure, thanks for the brush-off. You're a loser, Jedface. My hand tightened on the chair arm, inadvertently triggering it to self-adjust up a notch. I was getting a wave of molecular-level disappointment like the G-force reversal at the zenith of the Superman Tower of Power ride at Six Flags over Texas. Well, screw it anyway, this is just probably all part of the hype. They're trying to turn this thing into another Dead Sea Scrolls and maybe they don't really have anything, maybe the Codex is just another bunch of Venus tables, a few old names, maybe a recipe for guacamole—

"You want to look at the End Date page?" Marena asked. "I bet I can show you just that one without getting in trouble."

"Uh, sure." *Oh, God our GOD om NI potent REIGN eth! HaaleLUjah! HalleLU-jah! Ha-LE-E-loo-YAH—*

"Okay." She reached down behind her and without looking took a large-screen phone out of a drawer and tapped on it for a few seconds. I scooted my chair over but not too far over. Hot spit.

"Would you like me to sign a release or anything?" I asked.

"Well, you could leave a hostage."

"I am a hostage."

She put the phone on the desk, turned it around, and slid it over to me. It had a new OLED-3D display without a trace of a distinguishable pixel, just the high, narrow page lying in three dimensions just under the Zeonex film. Since the gessoed fig-bark paper hadn't seen the sun for centuries, its original fugitive dyes had been preserved, and the hyperspectral imaging had deepened them a little more, so that they throbbed between the dark outlines like old stained glass.

(7)

The game board was in the middle of the page, flanked by two figures. An overlord in jaguar-lineage regalia sat on the left, arms folded. According to Michael Weiner's notes, which floated annoyingly over the image, he was probably an ahau named 9 Fanged Hummingbird, who ruled from 644 to roughly 666 in a city in Alta Verapaz that Weiner's team had identified as Ixnich'i-Sotz—or, as the locals now called the ruins, just Ix. The portrait glyph above the other figure, who sat facing the future on the southwestern side of the board, seemed to read as something along the lines of Ahau-Na Hun Koh, that is, "Lady 1 Tooth":

The bottom right of her face was painted black, and so was her right hand, which also, maybe through a *lapsus peniculus*, seemed to have seven fingers. Her clothing seemed to be partly in the style of Teotihuacan, the then-capital of highland Mexico. There was a Muwan Bird and a double-headed serpent bar over the figure, and, underneath them the creature Mayanists call the Cauac Monster—a stocky, crusty character somewhere between an alligator and a toad—opened its jaws, ready to swallow the scene whole. A row of glyphs at the top said the Game was played on 9 Overlord, 13 Gathering, 9.11.6.16.0, that is, Thursday, July 28, AD 659. A second row at the bottom gave the starting date of the Mesoamerican calendar, and then on the lower half of the page there was a block of ten glyphs:

It was definitely part of a warning table. That is, it was an interpreter's catalog of major dates, with key astronomical events and notes on the historic and hypothetical future events on those dates. Some of the numbers were written with formal head variants and some were in bar-and-dot notation. Time-wise, they were all over the place.

Hmm. On the other hand, if you just looked at the verbs, it seemed like the whole thing was conceived of as a record—or "score," as we call it in chess—of a hipball game. That is, the terminology was similar to what the Maya used in their sacramental ball game, which I guess you could say was something between handball, volleyball, and soccer, but with a solid rubber ball the size of a basketball and you bounced it off, mainly, your hips. Anyway, whatever its oddities were, if this was only one page out of eighty the book was a bonanza.

The biggest problem for Maya epigraphers is that so few texts in the old script have survived. For a lot of words there's only a single glyphic example—

Marena must have said something again, and I must not have answered.

"Jed?" she asked.

"Huh? Sorry. I got distracted. To me it's kind of a big deal to see this."

"Can I call you Jed?"

"Hmm? Oh. Sure. I mean, it's the States, people I've never even met call me Jed."

"Yeah. So what do you think?"

"Well, uh . . . ," I went, "well, the language, that's definitely lowland Classic period. But the graphology, I mean, the style of the drawing, that looks a little post-Classic to me. Like AD 1100 to 1300. Just offhand." Is this a test? I wondered. Maybe if I don't come up with something I don't get another peek?

"That's right," Marena said. "Michael said it was a copy from seven or eight hundred years later. But still it's, uh, pre-Contact."

"Did Michael Weiner say this Lady Koh character was definitely from the Maya zone? Or was she from Teotihuacan?"

"I don't know," she said. "He didn't say. Is that really how you pronounce it?"

"What? Oh, yeah," I said. "Tay-oh-tee-*hwha*-cun."

"Damn, I produced a whole game about it and I've been pronouncing it wrong all this time."

"Well, I wouldn't worry about it," I said. "Nobody knows a lot about the place. Including what its actual name was."

"Really?"

"Yeah. It's a mysterious place." It was true. Nobody knows what language they spoke, or what they called themselves, or who their descendants were. But the main thing nobody knows, or rather, the main puzzle about the place, was how their city had sustained itself longer than any other city in the Americas and had flourished as the center of Mesoamerica for eight hundred years. And even after its destruction, the general location seemed to retain its power. Seven hundred years later, under the Aztecs, it was the site of the largest city in the Western Hemisphere, and now five hundred years after that, it is again.

"So what else strikes you about the page?" Marena asked.

"Well, otherwise the dates look pretty straightforward," I said. "But some of the verbs here are on the tricky side. I'd bet a lot of them are pretty much unique variants. I'd have to spend some time going through this with my dictionaries."

"Touch something and it'll give you Michael Weiner's translation," she said.

I did. The Mayan line grayed out and English glosses came up over it in blue. From the look of it Weiner had been able to solve almost 90 percent of the text.

"Hmm," I said. Just offhand, I didn't see any blunders. I'd always thought that Michael Weiner was a bit of a doofus, but maybe he wasn't. Anyway, I didn't know him. I'd just seen him a few times on *Secrets of the Ancient Ones*. He was a big, basso-voiced New Zealander with a beard who'd somehow gotten into New World archaeology, and the Discovery Channel was trying to position him as a kind of Mesoamerican-studies equivalent of Steve Irwin. He'd always be, say, walking through the market square at Teotihuacan, and he'd go, like, "This was the Rodeo Drive of ancient Mexico." Like, great line, mate. And you're the Benny Hill of archaeology.

Still, I thought, he'd sure gotten a lot out of this page. All the known Maya texts are frustratingly terse. This was the most narrative glyphic Maya writing I'd seen, and it was still pretty spare. The first phrase, *b'olon tan*, meant "ninth goal," suggesting that there had been eight goals, or captures, already, on pages I wasn't seeing. This meant that the Game had been played with nine separate runners—and you could also translate *runner* as "quarry" or even "ball"—instead of just one. This would have made the Game 260^9—that is, 1,411,670,956,537,760,000,000,000 times as hard to play as the one-stone version Taro and I had worked with. Anyway, it looked as though each time a runner had been captured it had been on a different intersection on the board, and each of those intersections corresponded to a unique date in the Maya calendar. Then, on the facing page, each of those dates—which Weiner had correlated on the overlay with Common Era ones—had a column of glyphs below it that said something about something that had happened, or was going to happen, on that day. A lot of these were celestial events, but near the bottom of the columns they started getting into historical ones. The first line of glyphs next to the twelfth goal started with 3 Tooth, 15 Jeweled Vulture, 10.14.3.9.12, a date Weiner had converted, correctly, to August 30, 1109. In his gloss Weiner had written, "Chichén abandoned?" As any tour guide will tell you, Chichén Itzá was the biggest Maya polity of that period. The next date was May 14, 1430. The gloss was "Mexican warriors take Champotón." At that time, Champotón, in Campeche, had been what they called the "seat of the k'atun"—that is, the closest thing to an international Maya capital. It sounded way too specific to me, but when I clicked on the pop-up it said that

Weiner had gotten geographical data for the site out of the astronomical numbers. Specifically, he'd given each of the events a latitude. And when I clicked on the astronomical glyphs, it did seem to work out. Each cluster gave a generic "place of" phrase followed by a separate date for the first solar zenith, that is, the first day in the spring when the sun is directly overhead, which, of course, gets later as you move farther north.

"Do you happen to know anything about this latitude business?" I asked Marena.

"Sorry?"

"I've never seen any Maya inscription where they specifically make a point of the latitude. I mean, I can see how you can derive it, but it's definitely a new wrinkle."

"Huh."

"Can I possibly look at the other pages?"

"Hmm . . . well, okay," she said. "Don't tell anybody." She looked down and scribbled at a big touch-screen. I flipped forward to the next page. It didn't have any pictures, but it said the next event was in AD 1498, in Mayapán, and it said something about how the "Laughing People," that is, the Ixians, were going to be eaten by "carnelians," that is, rubies or, metaphorically, pustules. Weiner had noted it as "Smallpox arrives from Hispaniola?" The fifteenth goal was February 20, 1524. The Codex had marked it with the phrase "Tears [under the] copper giant," and under that Weiner had written "Last significant Maya resistance surrenders to Pedro de Alvarado at the Battle of Xelaju." The next one was a date I knew as well as if it were tattooed on my wrist: 10 Razor, 16 Dark Egg, 11.17.2.17.18, or July 12, 1562. Weiner had marked it "auto-da-fé, Mani." It was the day Fra Diego de Landa burned all the remaining Maya libraries in the Yucatán. I'd always hoped I wasn't related to the bastard.

I was getting a funny feeling about this. It's got to be a fake, I thought again. Except the book just didn't look like forgeries usually look. It was too weird. Good forgers tend to be pretty conservative. And it wasn't just weird in what it said, it was that too many of the glyphs were unfamiliar forms, the sort of thing you'd only expect if you found a bunch of new texts from a city that was a little off the track. Which I suppose a really brilliant forger could just make up . . . except there was also this sense of rightness about it. It had the discordant ring of truth.

"Did Taro mention how many stones he thought they were using?" I asked.

"Sorry?" Marena asked.

"Uh, the number of runners. That they used when they played the Game."

"I don't know what that is," she said.

"Never mind, I'll ask him later," I said.

At the seventeenth goal, March 13, 1697, Martín de Ursúa y Arizmendi captured the Ahau Kan Ek', the king of Nojpetén at Tayasal, on Lake Petén Itzá, the last holdout of traditional Maya culture. It was the last place they still kept the Long Count. After that there was July 29, 1773, the day of the earthquake in Antigua Ciudad Guatemala, when they decided to move the capital to where it is now, and then May 4, 1901, the day General Bravo occupied Chan Santa Cruz, the last stronghold of the Maya rebels in the Yucatán. The third-from-last date was November 9, 1954. In a freeish translation, the full gloss would read:

> Last b'ak'tun,
> Seventeenth k'atun
>
> First tun
> Zeroth uinal
> And thirteenth sun,
>
> Six Cane, Four Whiteness,
> Kaminaljuyu,
> Not Kaminaljuyu:
>
> Enough are deceived
> By a far-off ahau
> And we shoulder the blame.
>
> We scamper away
> From the shit-stinking men.
>
> We hide in the bushes
> Like monkeys, like rats.
> We prepare for the grayness.

It was the date Castillo Armas marched into Guate City during the CIA coup, when, like I think I said, things started going really bad. And there were only three dates after that. The first was the one I'd seen in the *Time* article, the date of the explosion in Oaxaca:

Last b'ak'tun,

Nineteenth k'atun
Sixteenth tun,

Seventh uinal,
Zeroth sun,

Four Overlord
Eighteen Stag

Now,
Underneath Choula
Our names are unmade

In a fresh lake of knives
And we shoulder the blame

The last date was the big one. It was a little under a year from today: *Kan Ahau, Ox K'ank'in*, that is, 4 Overlord, 3 Yellowribs, 13.0.0.0.0, or December 21, 2012, the last day of the Maya calendar and the date that people who were both credulous and gloomy said would be the end of time.

Last b'ak'tun,
Last k'atun,
Last tun,
Last uinal,

Last sun,
Last watchfire,

Four Overlord,
Three Yellowness:

With smokeless eyes
Flesh Dropper sees

Four hundred Boys
And what they say.

They are more than before,
And yet there are none.

They beg him to give them
A thing the Flesh Dropper
Can only deny them.

Total the suns
Of their festivals,

Total the suns
Of their tortures:

One total wins easily.

Look for the place
Of denial, betrayal:
You still will not see it.

Look everywhere
For the Flesh Dropper: still
You can catch him and yet
You will not see his face.

Suns with no names,
Names with no suns:

Take two from twelve:
And it totals the Prankster,

The Sovereign One Ocelot.

Hmm, I thought.
Not too clear about all that. Need to put some thought in on it.
En todos modos, what's the really close one again?

I skipped back to the second-to-last date: 9 Imix, 9 K'ank'in, 12.19.19.0.1, or Wednesday, December 28, 2011. Five days from today. The gloss, roughly, was:

> The last b'ak'tun,
> In its nineteenth k'atun,
>
> The nineteenth tun,
> Zeroth uinal, first sun,
>
> On 9 Sea Rattler and 9 Yellowness:
>
> Now some fled northward
> And into the city
> Of pilgrims in daylight.
> It ends on the Zeroth sun
> As a warlock sprays fire
> From razors, from flint,
> And we shoulder the blame.

Weiner had also given a more literal translation of three glyphs from the middle of the last stanza:

Zero sun   it ends   place of daylight pilgrimages   precious stair-place

It was true that the glyph at the far left, a head with a hand on its chin, could mean zero, but it could also mean completion or beginning. The hand meant the dude was about to have his jaw torn off, which was supposedly one of my ancestors' favorite methods of cruel and usual punishment. But I guess it was a good thing if you owned the hand. But the second glyph, the hand reaching for a bauble and not grasping it, definitely meant "ending." The travel or pilgrimage glyph was pretty straightforward . . . but the second element of the fourth glyph, the one with the temples at the four sides, wasn't something I'd seen before.

Hmm . . . well, there's always the possibility that, you know, maybe this Lady Koh person, or whoever had worked all this out, hadn't seen this one very clearly either. Maybe she'd had a few loose thoughts and just tacked them together. I'd just had the same thing happen to me in Taro's lab. You get these notions or floating images, but you can't tie them onto a time or a place or even an agent. And often, if they pan out later, it's usually not in a way you'd thought of.

Otherwise . . . hmm. The astronomical data seemed good, but the latitude business wasn't too clear. It was confused, something about "beyond the overhead sun," which Weiner had interpreted as meaning just above the Tropic of Cancer. He'd written "Monterrey, Mexico?" as the probable location of the event. What else is—

Wait a second, I thought. Oh, hell. *No mames.* That is, very no way. *No* way. You've got to be kidding me—

"Are you looking at the twenty-eighth?" Marena asked.

"Uh, yeah."

"What do you think?"

"Well, it does look odd." I didn't mention that I'd been getting some funky results around that date myself. I don't like sounding like a café psychic.

"So it's a really bad day?"

"Well, that would depend on who you are. You know how, like, it's an ill wind—"

"Okay, okay. Look, what do you think of what Michael says about it?"

"Well . . . hmm. First of all I think the main thing is I think the first glyph here is a place name. It's not just the word *city*, the way Weiner has it. It means a specific city."

"Okay, what city is that?"

"Well, look." I turned the phone back around and slid it over to her. She bent forward a little and her hair almost brushed my forehead. "The infix has a, uh—"

"What's an infix?"

"Like, something you add to the middle of the word. Or in this case the middle of a glyph. Like English has prefixes and suffixes but no infixes."

"Okay. Wait, what about *fucking*?"

"Sorry?" I asked.

"You know, like in, like, *specfuckingtacular.*"

"Oh. Yeah, uh . . . huh, you're right. Maybe that's the only one."

"Anyway, *mian hamnida,* please go on."

"Right, um, the toponym, that's the pictogram in the middle one—that's the cross shape with the four sort of little pyramids?"

"Yes."

"Weiner doesn't really deal with that. But it's different from a lot of other city glyphs. It's a cosmogram that looks a lot like the Sacrifice Game board. You know about Taro's research with the Game, right?"

"I know a little about it."

"Well, you know how the game board has five directions?"

"Not four directions?"

"Four compass directions and then the center."

"So so so."

"But the point is, each direction's a different color. Right?"

"Right. Actually, all Native Americans and also a lot of Asians visualize the directions that way."

"We do?"

"Well, anyway, did Taro tell you about, like, the whole Jaipur thing?"

"What?" she asked. "No."

"You know about, like, the city of Jaipur, in India?"

"Aniyo." She shook her head a little so that non-Korean speakers could tell it meant no.

"Okay, well ... look, you know how, how the whole deal with Taro's research is that he postulates that a version of the Sacrifice Game was the ancestor of most modern games? Or maybe all games. You know, even chess and Go used to have quadrilateral symmetry, I mean, they were both originally games for four players. And certainly games like mah-jongg and bridge and backgammon all—"

"I thought he said it was like Parcheesi," she said.

"Right," I said. "Exactly, the, the closest descendant of it that people still play is Parcheesi. Parcheesi was the Brahman holy game. And there are hundreds of living versions of that all over the world. And the Parcheesi board is also a *thanka,* right? You know, a mandala. Like for meditation and stuff."

"You know, I'm feeling a little stupid because I design games and now it's like I guess I don't know a lot about them."

"Well, it's fairly esoteric stuff."

"Right."

"Anyway, what I'm getting at is that mandalas weren't just to stare at. They got played. Or they got walked around in. Like Southeast Asian pagodas were built on the plan of a mandala. Or you might say on the plan of a Parcheesi board. You know, the same way cathedrals are built in a cross shape. And all through Asia you get all these stupas and temples and wats—"

"Oh my."

"—and the whole city of Jaipur is laid out in the shape of a Parcheesi board."

"Ah, narohodo," she said. It meant "I understand." She exaggerated the Asian breathiness. One of the good things about being ethnic is that there's at least one accent you can mock without fear.

"But there's also a whole bunch of Native American versions of the same game. Not just the Sacrifice Game. The Aztec version was called *patolli.* Montezuma played it with Cortés. It's just like in Asia, it wasn't just game boards that had that sort of design. Maya hipball courts and probably their pyramids and sometimes maybe whole cities were laid out that way. And like in Jaipur, they'd do processions and rituals and stuff going from one direction to another to mean one thing, and a different—well, you get the idea."

"I think I do, maybe."

"Each section of the board, or the city—that is, each direction—has a different ruling god, and different days and times of day and even different foods and whatever. And the southwest and the northwest are also sort of the earth and lower world, and the northeast and the southeast are like the sky and the stars. And then the center is like a fifth direction."

"Why not six directions, with, like, up and down?"

"Up and down are in a whole different ballpark. They're about, like, the other twenty-two layers of the universe. The center direction is just, like, You Are Here. Or . . . maybe I'm going on too much about this—"

"No, no, please," she said. "Rave on."

"The directions are associated with time too. The east is the future and the west is the past. And the northwest is kind of female, which they thought of as the hypothetical, and the southeast is kind of male. And they interpreted the southeast as sort of leading into the here-and-now in the center." Do I look confident? I wondered. Sit up a little straighter. Right. Not *that* straight—

"Sorry, I lost the thread," she said. "What's that got to do with the name of the place again?"

"Well, what I'm getting at is, it looks to me like the third glyph is just a sort of miniature stylized map of the center of a Maya-type city. They've got "precious stair-place" here, but that really just means, like, a temple zone."

"Okay."

"And the suffix means, it means something like 'the seat of the k'atun.' So whatever happens three days from now is going to happen in a city that's

roughly divided into four colors. Or five, counting the center. And its inhabitants would think of it as the center of the world. Or at least the center of
something important."

"So it's some old Maya site."

"No, no, I don't think so. My guess would be that they meant some ceremonial center that's active today. Not some old ruin or anything. Because
there's a mat glyph in the phrase that means 'the k'atun-seat.' "

"What's a cartoon again?"

"It's about a twenty-year period on the solar calendar."

"Oh, right."

"Okay. So the seat of the k'atun means they're talking about the most important city of the next two decades. Like the capital. Anyway, it would be a
very important city that's at its peak right about now."

"Okay, so they mean D.C. Whoa. That's a little scary."

"Well, maybe," I said. "But my guess is that Washington doesn't fit the bill."

"Why not?"

"I think D.C.'s too much of a normal city. This word really means more like
a temple district. A regal-ritual city, not a governmental city. People might
not even live there. You'd make pilgrimages there to get favors out of some
powerful dead person. And you'd do some marketing on the way, of course.
But the buildings and rooms and everything in the center of town would only
be occupied for special functions, during a big festival or something. Also,
Washington doesn't have specific colors or time associated with the different
quarters. And anyway D.C.'s way farther north than what, uh, Dr. Weiner
thinks the latitudinal coordinates seem to indicate."

"Okay okay," she said, "so, look, where do you think they mean?"

"Well, it would be someplace that has a lot of people from all over making
long trips to get there, maybe at a certain point in their lives, or a certain age.
And like I say, it would be someplace with a sort of holy zone, in that kind of
configuration. I mean, with quadrants coded to different directions. Each direction would be associated with a different color, and with a different period
of time."

"So come on, what's your guess?" she asked.

"Disney World."

(8)

"What?" Marena asked.

"I'm serious," I said.

"Dude, we're practically *standing* in Disney World. You can see Epcot from here."

"Yeah, I saw it—"

"I worked at the Rat for years. I still live practically on *top* of the place. Walt *built my house*."

"Sorry, I don't know what to say. Except I could be wrong, and the book could be wrong—"

"Anyway, the thing—look." Marena turned and looked out the window, toward Disney World, and slid off her desk. She was short but svelte. "Look, in Disney World the colors are different from what you said. Like Fantasyland is coded purple. And anyway, the color coding's not that visible, you know, you only see it on signage and staff stuff and in the tunnels and wherever. And also I don't quite get the time thing; I mean, I guess Adventureland and Frontierland, those are in the west, so I guess you're saying that's like the past, right?"

"Yes," I said. I stood up.

"And Tomorrowland's in the east. That's obvs. But then in the south it's just Main Street USA."

"Well, right," I said, "isn't that, like, the present? Or the very recent past?"

"Well, okay, but then what's Fantasyland? That's in the north. That's not any particular time."

"Maybe that's like the hypothetical," I said. "In the Maya system it's called the unrevealed."

"Hmm." There was a long pause. "Shit."

"Yeah."

She looked troubled, but I couldn't tell how seriously she was taking it. "Okay," she said. "Look, what, what do you think is going to happen?"

"Well . . . I don't know, I'm not sure about the gloss anyway, it's not—"

"What?"

"Well, one thing is—look, Weiner's got the event glyphs for that day translated as, uh, 'the warlocks spray fire from razors, from flint.' Right?"

"Okay."

"Which is okay, as far as it goes, but it doesn't give you the whole sense of it. I mean, he's translated it, but he hasn't interpreted it."

"So what do you think it means?"

"Well, I don't know," I said, "but, for instance, 'warlocks,' that's from an idiom in Mayan that means 'scab casters.'"

"Which are what?"

"Like people who throw scabs at you from a distance. Like they could make you sick by thinking it. Witches."

"Okay."

"But the thing is, this is a verbal form, so it's more like 'someone casts scabs.' That would be, like, somebody sends a misfortune or a disease."

"Okay."

"And then the part about spraying fire, that's more likely to be the subject. In my opinion. And 'fire' could be light or fire or daytime or whatever. And then he's just got 'flint,' and I'd guess it's more like 'the middle of a stone,' or 'inside a pebble,' or something like that."

"So what's it really say?"

"I'd say it's more like, uh, like 'The light casts its scabs from within, from the rock. And we carry the blame.'"

"Okay," she said.

Pause.

"That's it?" she asked.

"That's all I can think of."

"Does that tell us any more than we knew already?"

"Uh, maybe not. . . ." I trailed off. There was another pause, a grimmer one.

"I mean, that's not really specific enough, is it?" she asked. "You can't just tell people to watch out for whatevs."

I shook my head.

"Okay, look," she went on, "the thing . . . you know, I have no idea whether to be worried about this, or like panicked, or completely dismissive."

"I know what you mean," I said.

"Also, there must always be a lot of predictions out there."

"Yeah. Always." I didn't want to say, "And of course, there's also always the possibility that your book is just a really clever scam," but she could probably smell me thinking it.

"What do you really think? Personally."

"Well, I know the thing works, so I guess I'd take it seriously. But I could be wrong. I should play it through a few times."

"You mean with the Sacrifice Game."

"Right."

"Good idea," she said. She was pacing behind her desk in a figure eight. I didn't know where it was okay to pace, so I just stood behind my chair. "Also, we could get another opinion. Or a few."

"Yeah."

We stood for a few seconds. Well, this had certainly dampened the mood. Finally I said, "Maybe we should call Taro and see what he thinks."

"All right," Marena said, "you call him. I want to look around for a second."

I did. It was six P.M., getting toward the end of his nineteen-hour workday, but Taro was still at the lab. He said we should come over. I said I would, but I didn't know if Ms. Park would. She'd gotten on her EarSet and was giving orders.

"Just keep him under your toe," she said to someone. "Hang on. Check this out," she said to me. She swung a monitor around. It said that at this time of year, Orange County "hosted nearly a quarter of a million visitors per day" and showed a list of events on the twenty-eighth in the Greater Orlando area. There was a Jamaican street festival, a concept-car show, a vintage-car show, an air show, a parade for some retiring Magic coach, a Disney parade for *Snow White II,* a Winter Festival Tree relighting at Holidays Around the World, Late Grinchmas at Universal, and a special show of the Osbourne Family Spectacle of Lights at MGM Studios. There was a preopening ceremony for the Capital One Bowl, the Magic were playing an exhibition at the arena, there was a Buccaneers game at the Civic Center, a marines drill exhibition at CityWalk, and the Father/Son Golf Challenge at ChampionsGate. Mega-Con, the big comics-and-sci-fi/fantasy-and-gaming-and-toys-and-whatever thing, was two months earlier this year and would be in its third day at the new William Hendrix Harmony Hall. The International Council of Island States was in town, and there were twenty-eight lesser conventions, including orthodontists, virologists, real-estate appraisers, roofers, roofing suppliers,

web designers, erotic-toy manufacturers, and mortgage professionals. Else-
where in the state, there were navy exercises based in Fort Lauderdale, a big
regatta in Tampa, and a Fiesta Pan-Latino in Miami. Ordinarily, I would have
fallen asleep before even finishing the list, but now it looked almost scary
enough not to be boring.

"See anything?" she asked.

I said no and that I wouldn't expect to anyway because *cuaranderos* didn't
work that way. "I wish I were more of a psychic," I said, "but I'm not, I have to
sit down and—"

"Okay, forget it," she said, "look, what do you think we should do? Assuming you're right."

"Um—"

"Because, you know, if the two of us just start calling people and posting
stuff, not many people are going to take it that seriously."

"No." Despite everything else I found a moment to like the way she said
"the two of us."

"And even if Taro's lab does, they're not that—I mean, they've done some
work for a few government agencies, but most of the predictions they've
made are just economic, and they keep them in-house. It's not a fund, there's
no newsletter or shareholder's report on it or anything."

"I understand," I said.

"So it might mean a little more if they say something, but—I mean, look,
you've, we've got to get some more data here."

"Definitely."

She took what looked like an old green enamel Ronson cigarette case out
of a desk drawer, took out a filterless Camel, looked at it, put it back in the
case, and put the case back in the drawer.

"Okay," she said, "one good thing is, Lindsay has some unspeakable connections in the DHS," she said. I guess she meant the Department of Homeland Security. "Maybe if he can get them to say there's a problem, it'll be better
than if it comes from us."

"Definitely," I said. I was thinking that, yeah, that sounded okay, if it would
really happen, but that the other thing to do was to post everything I knew on
as many blogs as possible, everything about the Game, Taro's software, the
Codex, and everything. Somebody else out there might figure something out.

Marena looked at me. I got a brief but creepy feeling that she knew what I
was thinking. I had a weird notion to turn and run out the door, lock myself
in an empty office, and start typing in the post. *Cálmate*, Joaquín, I thought.

It's just *el paranoia de las repúblicas bananeras*. There is no goon squad about to grab you and take you back to—

"Why don't you go back to Taro's and I'll call in a while?" she asked. I started to answer but her secretary—sorry, assistant—called back through the open door that she had someone named Laurence Boyle on five.

"Okay, I'm getting put through to Lindsay," she said. She waved as though I were already out the door. It was like she was saying, "Sorry, I have a conference call on line two with Kim Jong Il, David Geffen, and the pope." I sort of oozed backward out the door.

Most of the office folk had left, but the Hair walked me out to my car. The offices were cool and bright and outside it was gray and stuffy, so there was that feeling like you'd just gone indoors instead of outdoors. I did my meds and factor VIII injection and drove back to Taro's. Well, she didn't tell me to keep my mouth shut, I thought. She probably figured if she did I wouldn't. Or maybe she'd just sized me up as a paranoiac the minute I walked in.

Taro and I talked for an hour. He said he wasn't sure about the Disney thing but that he'd treat it as a priority. He said that he thought the author of the Codex must have been playing with nine stones, that is, nine runners. "Even though that would seem to be impossible," he said. I said it sounded impossible to me too. A nine-stone game would have 9^9 more possible moves than a one-stone one. And a one-stone game has an average of 10^{24} moves. So then a nine-stoner would have more possible moves than there are electrons in the universe.

At around eight o'clock he sat me down in front of a monitor. I dug out my tobacco, rooted myself, and started thrashing around with three runners, looking for anything that reminded me of the Codex. It was difficult. One of Taro's students brought me some Vegan Vibe Hot Pockets. Tony Sic came in. Taro told him about my idea for the twenty-eighth. He went into an isolation room and started working on it. Two more adders-in-training came in later. They weren't Maya, just Korean or whatever gamer types, and I didn't know either of them. They sat down and started working like they were already experts.

Marena didn't call until ten P.M. She talked to Taro for a while and talked to me for about two minutes. Evidently she and some of her cohorts had had a meeting. She said Michael Weiner, the TV Mayanist, had pooh-poohed it, naturally. She said she and Laurence Boyle—whoever that was—had talked with some people at the Orlando mayor's office, but without anything specific to tell them nobody was sure how much of a fuss they should make. "I didn't want to even mention the Maya connection," she said. "It would sound like we were *In Search of Ancient Astronauts* or whatever." Instead they'd pitched it as a surprise result of Taro's simulation research, which had at least some academic credibility. At least Taro had backed me up. He'd told her that he didn't want to be an alarmist, but I'd "often been right before"—what do you mean "often," I'd thought. If you're talking about that 1992 World Series business, if you'll think back you'll remember I said wasn't comfortable making that call—"so maybe we should take his interpretation seriously," Taro said.

"I see the DHS guy in the morning," she said. "I'll tell you what happens."

I said great. I went back to the keyboard. I kept getting the feeling there was something Taro wasn't telling me. Well, whatever.

I rubbed in another shot of tobacco, even though my leg below the knee was already buzzing. It feels like your leg's waking up from being "asleep," as they call it up here. *Bueno. "Ajpaayeen b'aje'laj k'in ik,"*

Okay.

What's the question?

Well, to ask the right question, you have to know stuff. You can't guess about things without knowing what things there are. Sometimes you don't have to know so much as you'd think, but you have to know something. Usually it boils down to reading a lot of news. I clicked up **HEADLINES**.

Top stories at this hour, it read: *Jorge Pena's 89th Homer Marks New Off-Season High . . . Five Michigan State University Students Killed in Hoops Loss Riot . . . 2 Killed at Universal Studios Tower of Terror . . . Bangladesh Seeks Explanation for the Downing of Troop-Carrier Chopper . . . Bob Zemeckis's Epic Vanessa, Based on the Life of Artist Vanessa Bell, Hits Screens Today . . . Man Dies in Spitting Contest . . . Twister Outbreak in Heartlands . . .*

Hmm.

I assigned the hypothetical author of the hypothetical catastrophe—who we were calling Dr. X—to black. I assigned the mass of the population to yellow. I took red, as usual. And I kept white in reserve, as usual. And since we were only looking three days into the future, I was only going to use the three outer rows. Right. I assigned the suns.

Bueno.

I concentrated on my uay for a minute, long enough to feel myself shrinking. Like I think I said, it's a snail. But I imagine it as a sea slug so that I can move a little faster. I scattered and counted the seeds and started swimming toward the twenty-eighth—9 Sea Rattler, 9 Yellowness—edging along the line of uncertainty. Pretty soon I had to start jumping. I guess it's hard to think of a slug jumping. But if you watch them in the water they actually do; they jump from one rock slowly down to another. Anyway, I thought, it's going like this. Right. Now that way. No. Okay, now I think it's going to go this way. No, wait, it'd go this way. *Claro.* He goes, I go. Then he reacts. *Primero, segundo,* this happens, then they react to that. Okay. *Claro que sí.* Bueno. Wait. No.

Damn. I kept getting something, a sense of these things like, I don't know, shapes, milling around in a reddish fog, lumpy clusters of something gyrating to a slow, silent beat. But it wasn't anything you could hang a label on.

I played for four hours. I took a break. I played for another five hours. Around dawn all of us adders huddled together around the espresso machine and compared notes. We'd all gotten similar results. They all said they were worried about something in the area on that day, but the event was vague, and nobody would have put it at Disney World without getting that from the Codex first. I couldn't think to play anymore so I took a nap on the floor of an isolation room and drove home at noon on Christmas Eve.

I did maintenance on the skimmers. I got my Perpetual Refugee stuff ready in case anything happened tomorrow. I plugged a driveful of Taro's top secret software (He trusts me! I thought) into my own system and fired it up on the overhead screens. It took an hour to get it working and then when I started playing, I couldn't get any further than before. The period after the twenty-eighth was just a blank. Not that that meant the world was going to end ahead of schedule, but just that all the causes and effects were too hard to read. LEON hadn't come up with anything, either, not that any of us thought it would. It just didn't know enough, I thought. No matter how many data streams it read, it didn't really know what they meant. I don't care how many games it can play through at once. Speed isn't everything.

I don't celebrate Christmas. Or Easter, even though I'm supposed to when I'm doing *cuandero* stuff. Or birthdays, or weekends, or anything. But I especially didn't celebrate Christmas this time. I spent the day working on the game. Numbers like 84, 209, 210 and 124,030 kept coming up again and again, but I couldn't make anything out of them. Marena called at six. There were kid squeals in the background. She said the DHS was willing to bump up the threat level on the twenty-eighth to "Elevated" in Orange, Polk, Osceola, Hardee, DeSoto, and Highlands counties. They'd said that would mean police and fire departments would be on evacuation alert that day. I guess that meant they'd make it easier for people to clear out if anything went wrong. Or they'd just gum up the system, I thought. Well, anyway, that Marena lady came through, I guess. Should I do anything else? Or would anything else make it worse?

By the end of the twenty-seventh, nobody'd gotten any further. That is, nobody from Taro's lab, and not me either. The only thing I could think to work on was Michael Weiner's translation. A few things about it were still bothering me, especially the "scab casters" bit. As I think I said, the phrase usually means a witch or a warlock, but here it was being used more as a verb, like "witching," which I didn't think was a known usage in any Mayan language. Although of course the old language was different, but still . . . anyway, it didn't go anywhere. This is bullshit, I thought. You're overthinking it. Maybe the whole business was just me being a Nervous Nellie. I gave up at two minutes after the beginning of H-hour. Whatever was going to happen was.

The twenty-eighth was a nice day in Central Florida except for worse-than-average smog. The heightened DHS alert made the local news, but reporting on it seemed half-hearted. Folks are jaded these days. To get any sort of a rise out of them, a lot of people need to already be dead. Although to be fair you can't just clear everybody out because one catastrophe-modeling team—and Taro'd said he figured there were at least five other serious ones operating, by the way, including the DHS's own, which had hardware almost as sophisticated as LEON and which they were very proud of—had come up with a totally speculative, unspecific bad feeling about a populated place and a vague time. I watched news and raw news feeds and local chat rooms all day. Even though I was pretty far from Orlando, it felt like my foot was half out the door. Whenever I encountered an odd-looking phrase, my teeth almost started chattering. Still, the worst things to happen in the Park District were a few false fire alarms and a bunch of people getting food poisoning at the Pinocchio Village Haus. Not exactly anything apocalyptic. I lay down just after midnight.

I Dios. Tired.

I'd been awake for about twenty-eight hours—which actually wasn't that unusual for me. I have DSPS, delayed sleep phase syndrome, on top of whatever else—but I guess there was a little stress in the system. Okay. Just going to grab a twenty-second *pestaña.* There was a dog barking somewhere—not the Villanuevas' little Xoloitzcuintle, but some bigger individual I hadn't heard before—and it kept reminding me of the Desert Dog. Although I guess I haven't told that story yet. Although maybe that's just as well, because it's a bit of a downer. Except now I've mentioned it. Hell. Well, briefly, the Desert Dog was a kind of ugly yellow-and-gray terrier/hound/coyote sort of individual that Ezra, the middle one of my three stepbrothers, said had attacked him while he was mowing the golf course, although I didn't believe that. Anyway, there was a lot with a bunch of old sheep crates and chicken coops and whatever out across 15 toward the gypsum mill, and Ezra had the dog in one of them. When the brothers showed him to me he had no front paws. There were just two ragged stumps there. Maybe he'd been injured by something, or more likely he had gotten caught in a fence or a trap and gnawed them off. You'd think he might have bled to death, but instead the wounds were healing and he was scrambling around on the zinc floor of the crate, getting up and sliding down, and his eyes were big and terrified of us. They had him in there without any water or anything. I asked Ezra what—

"—*not* a drill. Jed? It's me. Pick up. I'm serious."

Huh?

I clicked on the front door speaker. "We don't sell fish anymore," I started to croak, but as I got to the word *sell* I realized I was still in bed and that it was the middle of the day. Evidently I'd zonked out.

"Jed?" the voice asked. "It's Marena."

Whoa, I thought. What exactly the hell was she doing in here? That is, in my bedroom. Or rather it wasn't even exactly a room, it was a Mitsubishi *capseru*, a capsule, that is, one of those soundproofed, climate-controlled fiberglass sleeping pods they make for cheap Japanese hotels.

"I mean it, this is urgent, pick up." Her voice was coming from my phone, which weirded me out a bit because I didn't remember giving her the emergency number.

"Hi," I said, checking whether I could still speak. I sounded like Jack Klugman. I tried again. "Hi!" Better. *Estas bien*. I found the gadget and hit TALK. "Hi," I said chipperly.

"Hi, good," she said, "you exist."

"Huh? Oh. Well, I wouldn't go that far—"

"So there's a little bit of a problem at Disney World. It's probably nothing, but, you know."

"Sorry? Balaam's ass?"

"What?"

"Um—oh, sorry, nothing." It must have been something to do with an interrupted dream, although I'd already forgotten it, but there was that sense of just having stopped moving through some huge, complicated space—

"Jed?"

"Hi." WTF? I wondered. Did I sleep a whole day? No way. If I had I wouldn't be feeling like *mierditas refritas.* I found the thingie and hit TIME. Big green laser characters scrolled across the ceiling: **2:55:02** P.M. . . . **29-12-11** . . . **2:55:05** P.M . . .

"Uh, what kind of a problem?" I asked.

"I don't know," her voice said. "There's only a little about it, but my friend at the old place says it's not food poisoning and it's like eighty people."

"Oh. Huh." People *what*? I wondered. Dead? Sick? Making noise?

"Anyway, we're on 441 and Orange Avenue," she said. "And now this came up so I thought we'd come by. Just in case."

"Come by here?" She was only about forty-five miles away.

"Yeah," she said.

"Uh, sure." No way, I thought, she can't show up here. There's dead snails and tarantula molts and stuff all over. If there's one thing I've learned about chicks, it's that they don't dig invertebrates. "Um, so, why are you coming this way? I mean, that's great, but, you know—"

"Because the wind's from the southeast," she said.

"Oh," I said. Uh-oh, I thought. Gas. Fuck. "Okay, great, um, you know where I am?" Of course she does, I thought. I'd been trying to get my address de-listed, but the days when you could really do that were long gone.

"Yeah, I see it, look, you want to, uh, you want to go out to U.S. 98 and meet me there? I'm in the car, we'll be there in about thirty-five minutes."

"Um—"

"Just a second. Sure, go ahead," she said to someone else in the car. "No, I'm on it. Bye. Sorry, Jed. Yeah, forty minutes, okay?"

"Uh, okay."

"Okay, I'll call you back."

"Okay," I said.

She started to say, "Bye," but clicked off, as people do, before she'd finished the word.

It's got to be nothing, I thought. Anyway, bad stuff happens every day. Every minute. So it's probably just a not very incredible coincidence.

She's probably just getting jumpy. Or she just wants to drop in and jump my bones. Heh. Maybe she's got a touch of scarlet fever. Plus my yellow variety equals the orange flame of passion. *Esta belleza,* she has the uay of a panther. Better shower.

I clicked on the overheads and hit HOME→NEWS→ LOCAL. *PARKS DISTRICT ADMISSIONS SUSPENDED,* it said.

Hell.

(9)

The story under the headline said that beginning around three P.M. yesterday, people had begun to vomit and "to complain of other symptoms, including erythema and vertigo," and that the story was developing. It didn't sound like much and it didn't say anything about gas. I searched the keywords out of the article but all I got was one thread on a parks workers' forum where they were talking about "why everyone is freaking out so bad" and "why it's a two hour wait in the ER." Nobody mentioned any gas. It really sounds like nothing, I thought. She's just getting jumpy. Well, whatevs. Anyway, you like her, right? It's a cheap date. Right. Get it together.

I decapsuled, staggered in and out of the still-institutional bathroom, toweled off with a PDI Super Sani-Cloth Germicidal Degradable Wipe™ instead of showering, rubbed some tooth towels over my teeth instead of brushing, visited the espresso machine, ate a scoop of Fluff, checked the meters, looked over the 'branchs. *Bueno.* Tank temperature, check. Protein skimmers, check. Feeders, check. Chem monitors, check. Home system to phone link, check. Nourishment, check. *Bueno.* Hair, breath, deodorant. Check. I got into a clean copy of my winter uniform, reset the automatic feeders, dosers, and alarms, got another spoonful of Fluff, and staggered out the back door. It was hot for December. *De todos modos.* Wallet, keys, money belt, passport, phone. Check. Smoke hood, check. Hemi kit, wipes, meds, check. Hat. Shoes, shirt, service—

Oops.

I went back inside, into Messy Zone Beta, found Lenny's old safe, got two ankle wallets—they were pretty heavy and bulky because each one had thirty Krugerrands, $10K in hundreds, and $2K in old premagnetic twenties—and strapped them on just in case things really did go all *Omega Man.* Okay. Alarms, check. Main lock, check. Bolt, check. We're off.

It was too hot for the jacket, but I kept it on. It was clear. Lake Okeechobee was calm but not shiny, like the ventral skin of a swordfish, and a manslaughter of crows were freaking out about something on the end of the jetty. Otherwise the 'hood seemed normal. Irretrievably banal, even. Just the way we like it. The 'cuda looked good snuggled up between the old Mini Cooper and the Dodge van in my private little ten-car parking lot. Got to get her out to the lot at the Colonial Gardens ghost mall and do a few power slides. Burn down those Geoffrey Holders and get some Pirelli 210s. I walked the three blocks west. Sr., Sra., and all the little Villanuevas were out working in their yard and they all said hi to me like I was Squire Stoutfellow. Should I warn them to get out of here? I wondered. No earthly reason, right? A pair of troop carriers, maybe C-17s, whined west at about ten thousand feet, heading to MacDill. It always gets me how far-freaking loud those things are, even though I already know they are. My phone throbbed. I screwed the ear thing into my ear and said hi. Marena said she was getting onto 710.

"Okay," I said, "if you get off at 76 there's a Baja Fresh and I can be in there."

"We're not getting off the highway."

Hmm. "Uh, okay, then, I'll be, I'll be about a hundred yards past—"

"Can you turn on a locator?"

"Oh, okay," I said. "Right." I found the function under "Communications—GPS" and clicked it.

"Okay, I see you," she said. No, I thought, you see a dot representing me. I stumbled up to the road and stood on the shoulder in the truck gusts. *La gran puta,* I thought. This already sucks. I got Local6.com on the screen and squinted at it in the solar radiation. Apparently it hadn't been just a few people but more like a hundred, and the police had hit them with some kind of Active Denial System, that is, some kind of pain ray. Still, it doesn't sound that serious, I thought. She's just on edge. Which one can understand. Can't one? Yeps.

Hmm. Erythema means, like, red skin, right? Can you get that from food poi—

A black Cherokee loomed up and ground to a grudging halt. I♥OTOWN, its license plate squealed. I guess ♥ was a letter now. The passenger door puffed open and I got a twinge of ingrained fear that I'd been tricked and was getting arrested. *Cálmate,* mano, I thought. If you're from anyplace where *disappear* is a transitive verb, it's normal to break into a sweat every time you see a big new dark car slow down next to you. But the States are pretty much still the States. Aren't they?

I sogged into the fauxskin. We said hi. The car smells, in descending order of magnitude, were vinyl, fruit juice, and something along the lines of Shiseido Zen. The car took off before the door shut. News6 was on in one corner of each of the twin dashboard screens, burbling at low volume:

"—is Anne-Marie García-McCarthy. Hello, Ron, nice to see you."

"Nice to see you, Anne-Marie, how are the kids?"

"They're doing great, thanks." Anne-Marie beamed.

"Well, that's just fine, hello, everyone," Ron said. He paused. "Well, the Magic and the Jaguars kicked off their—"

"Oh, Jed, this is Max," Marena said. "Max, Jed. Who I told you about?"

"Hi," a low-tweenage voice said.

I turned around and said hi. He looked like a little male Marena who'd had his hair curled and been dunked in weak tea. He was all strapped in, wearing Sony VRG goggles pushed up on his head and a big sweatshirt with a picture of Simba the Lion King eating Bambi. I guessed he was pushing nine. The backseat was drifted with healthful-snack-food wrappers. He looked at my hat, then at me, and then at my hat again. "It's nice to meet you," he remembered to say.

"Look at this," Marena said. She pointed to CURRENT SURROUNDING CONDITIONS on her dashscreen. "JACKKNIFED TRACTOR-TRAILER, RIGHT LANE," it said, flashing an orange dot a centimeter ahead of us on at Port Mayaca. "WAIT ESTIMATE 45 MINS."

"Where are we going?" I asked.

"South."

"Well, you could go back up a little and there's a gravel road where you can cross over to Beeline."

"Good idea," she said. She found a break in the median strip and swung the car left and around in a luxuriantly fluid U-turn, like a catamaran coming about. A soft alarm buzzed and big red warning letters came up on the windshield's heads-up display:

"WARNING, THIS ROUTE HAS BEEN DESIGNATED AS ILLEGAL/UNSAFE." Marena entered a twelve-character password into the steering-wheel keypad. The heads-up and dashscreens went dark, but the alarm kept beeping.

"Shi pyong shin, a shi!" she muttered, evidently cussing in Zergish.

"I can do it," Max said. He leaned over between the seat backs, thumbed at the keypad, and silenced the thing by switching the car to off-road mode.

"Thanks," Marena said as he settled back into his lair. "You have to put your seat belt back on." He did. "So how are you?" she asked me.

"I'm good, uh . . . I couldn't find out much about what's going on up there," I said.

"Well, we'll check again later," she said. Maybe she didn't want to talk about it in front of the kid.

"I'm good at programming cars," Max said to me. "I'm the car whisperer."

"Uh, yeah, evidently—"

"Check this out," he said. *"Nigechatta dame da!"*

Wind roared in around us, and then light. He'd opened the sunroof.

";Ay, muy listo!" I shouted back to him.

";De nada!" he said. All rich kids speak a little Spanish.

"That's good, but we want to be able to talk," Marena shouted. "Do you know how to close it?"

"Yeah, okay, watch," he said. *"Saite!"*

"That's really something," I said as quiet returned.

"Yeah," Max said. "Do you always wear that hat?"

"Sorry?" I asked. "Oh, I don't, no, I wear a few different ones."

"But do you always wear *a* hat?"

"Well," I said, "yes."

"But there isn't anything wrong with your head, is there?"

"Not that you can see, no, it's just, some groups of Indians don't feel right without a hat on."

"Do you have a hat with eagle feathers?"

"No, those are different Indians. Maybe we used to have hats like that. But a lot of our old hats had stuffed animal heads on them."

"Do you get visions?"

"Well, not yet," I said. "Sorry."

"Too bad," he said.

"Yeah."

"Do you play Neo-Teo?"

"Oh, yes. Sure, I love Neo-Teo." My thumb was itching to flick open my phone but I squelched it.

"What's your shell?" he asked.

"It's, uh, thirty-two."

He sort of sniffed. "I'm seventy."

"Wow," I said. "Hey, didn't your mom *make* Neo-Teo?"

"Yeah," he said. "What avatars do you have?"

"Uh, just a Macaw House Blood."

He sniffed again. "Hhhn. Wanna do a jade quest in the canyons?"

"Well, I'm not so good as—"

"I'll level you up."

"Well—"

"I don't think Jed really wants to play right now," Marena said.

"How about if we play a little later?" I asked Max.

"When?" Max asked.

"We'll see," Marena said.

"I hate 'we'll see,'" he said.

"If you move up a shell you can help Jed out even better when he comes in," Marena said.

Max made a huffing sound, plugged in his eyes and ears, and started making small purposeful movements with his joygloves. Every once in a while he puffed into the air in some direction or other, which meant he was using the blowgun function. At least he wasn't spitting.

"So, I bet you think I'm overreacting," Marena said.

"Well, no, any—"

"It's just, I'm a mom, so I'm a little jumpy, it was like, we got out of town on Monday, and now I'm like maybe we weren't far *enough* out of town, so it's— you know, it's like you get this protect-your-young hormone. Anybody who gets near my den and looks funny at my young gets one of my tusks in his carotid artery."

"I think you did the right thing," I said. Lame, I thought.

She switched the dashscreen to CNN Local. There was a stock shot of the flowerbed Mickey face at Disney World.

"Audio on," she said.

"*—is Anne-Marie García-McCarthy resorting—reporting* live *from Winter Haven,*" it went. "*I'll be back at six. Now back to you, Ron.*"

"*All right, Anne-Marie,*" Ron's voice went. "*Thanks for staying out there. We'll all look forward to seeing you then. Hello, I'm Ron Zugema in Orlando.*" He paused. "*Officials at the Orlando Parks District are reporting that over five hundred park visitors are receiving medical treatment for apparent food poisoning. Hospital officials are saying that eight patients* have *died as a result of the unknown* toxins." There was a tiny and almost nostalgic twinge of fear somewhere in my abdomen, that old friend not quite knocking at the door yet but just, say, texting you, letting you know he might want to come over sometime.

"There is also an unconfirmed report of several deaths as a result of the incident, but these are as yet unconfirmed. At this point in time, residents and visitors are being warned to avoid the central park area and be on the alert for medical vehicles. This is . . ."

Marena looked at me. This is not a hopeful development, her expression said.

No, it's not, I looked back. In fact it's—

She swung her eyes back to the road, cutting me off. Her driving style seemed a little casual to me, like maybe she trusted all the seat belts and airbags and newfangled whatevers to protect her. But I didn't say anything.

"This is Ron Zugema reporting," Ron was going on. *"Now over to you, Kristin."*

"Thanks, Ron," a blond head said. *"Just a tragic situation shaping up there. Hi, everyone, it's three forty-two P.M. here at WSVN TV. I'm Kristin Calvaldos. Well, it's Midwinter Madness time again for soccer fans as—"*

Marena clicked it off.

"What do you think?" she asked.

"I don't know," I said. "It doesn't sound like a big—I mean, when people get killed, it's always a—"

"I know," she said. "Yeah, things do happen."

"Yeah."

"Well, so, if it's nothing, then, sorry to drag you out."

"No, it's fine," I said. "I love driving. Passengering."

"I'm going to make some calls," she said.

"Right." I put in my own ear thing. Not to be outdone. I started calling and then e-mailing various friends. It turned out I didn't have that many. I started calling businesses and institutions, like the Community Center and the Grace Rural School. Almost everybody was out. I didn't know what to say, so I told them I just wanted to give them a heads-up and I'd call back. Meanwhile I tapped around on my phone, looking for anything fresh. The Net was sluggish and a lot of sites were 404. Finally I got onto a group called TomTomClub that's kind of a local unofficial or almost underground first-on-the-scene muckraking news service favored by Libertarians, embittered veterans, high-end conspiracy theorists, and the Legalize Everything movement. It's really just a couple of aging cracker hackers who monitor police and military-band communications, pick the best stuff, and put it up almost in real time, along with their own instant commentary. People were saying that whatever it was that actually happened at the park, there were a lot more deaths than were being reported. Emergency rooms were overloaded at Orlando Regional and Winter Park Memorial. Also, there was a fire in Kissimmee that might have been started by rioters. And supposedly people were trying to get out of Epcot and the guards weren't letting them leave.

"Okay, call me back," Marena said. She pulled out her earbud and rubbed her ear. "Everybody says the problems are all in Orange County," she said at me. "The best thing to do is keep going south."

I said something passive like how that sounded right to me or something.

"Jeep, show times to Miami," she said. A scroll came up on the dashscreen and said anything would take about twice as long as usual. I looked at her, but she looked ahead. From the side her face looked less cute and more regal. She took the exit onto 91 and cut in ahead of a huge Winnebago motor home. An odd-looking aircraft zwooshed over at less than two thousand feet. Max twisted under his seat belt. "What kind of plane is that?" he asked.

"I don't know," Marena said.

"It's a Grumman AEW Hawkeye," I said. "The scoopy thing is an air sampler."

"Godless," Max said. He was all the way turned around so he could see it out the back.

"Yeah," I agreed.

"Hey, check this out," Marena said in a lower voice. "The thing's been tracking on the Magic Kingdom for at least an hour." She touched two icons and satellite view came up on her dashscreen. "Passenger side," she said to the onboard. It came up on mine too. I was expecting some outdated Google Earth thing, but it was a site called 983724jh0017272.gov, and it was a realtime view, and it wasn't from one of those fuzzy NOAA feeds. It was military. 3-324CC6/92000 FT/W4450FT/ORLANDO CURRENT, it said. I recognized the profile of Lake Apopka on the left, but the view was too wide for me to see any landmarks.

"Hey, that's great," I said. "I can't get that."

"I bet you think I'm really working for the government."

"Well, you know, I think everybody—"

"You just need one line of code and you can get into it."

"That's great," I said. "Can we zoom this?"

"No, but it zooms itself every couple of minutes."

"That's great."

She swerved around a half-crushed marsh rabbit. Send that to the Szechuan Palace, I thought.

"So why is this happening today?" she asked. "Wasn't the problem supposed to be yesterday?"

"I don't know. Didn't a few people get sick yesterday?"

"I guess so."

"Yeah."

"You don't really think it's unrelated, do you?" she asked.

"Well, not really," I said. "Maybe it's more—I don't know, maybe whoever did it saw the Codex and had the same idea I did."

"Nobody's seen the damn Codex. I mean, you can count the people who have on one hand. It's just another diaperhead. I bet."

"I'm sure you're right."

Marena made about fifteen calls in five minutes, to CNN Local, Bloomberg Local, the Civilian Early Warning Project, the Orlando police, the State Police, and the Parks District police. From what I could hear, they sounded inconclusive. She called Max's grade school, the Warren offices in Orlando, and at least five friends, urging them all to get out of town. She made sure to add text to all the calls. She tried to call Taro, Taro's lab, and their phones. Nothing. That didn't bode well. Damn. I got inspired and texted No Way's Mexico City mailbox and asked him to call back. I got Sra. Villanueva on the phone and told her to get herself and the family and any other people she knew into the truck and head south. She kept asking *"¿Qué? ¿Por qué?"* and finally, I just said, *"Por favor,"* and let it go at that. I tried No Way again.

"I need to stop at an ATM," Marena said.

I asked whether she was talking to me. She was. "I have some cash," I said.

"No, I really ought to. I have like five cents."

"I'm serious. I brought my panic money, I really have, uh, a lot. You don't have to stop. Besides, the machines might not be working. Besides, I know you're good for it."

"What's a lot?" she asked. I told her. She said okay, she wouldn't stop. She seemed pretty relieved. There was a sort of generalized atmospheric feeling in the car that we were both too spooked to go back toward the Theme Park Capital of the World until after tomorrow, even if it was just a folie à deux.

"We are sorry," a woman's voice was saying on my phone. "The subscriber you are trying to reach is not available at this point in—"

"Are you having trouble with your phone?" Marena asked.

"Me?" I asked back. "Yeah."

". . . just fifty cents," the synthevoice was saying, "we can retry your call at convenient two-minute intervals—"

"I can't get anybody," Marena said. "I'm going to try your line, okay?"

I said all right and clicked off.

"Dial Jed DeLanda," Marena said to her phone. Stupidly I held mine up like that would make them connect better, even though the signal had to go to an antenna and then up into outer space and then come back to another antenna and back to here. Anyway, it didn't throb.

"Nothing," I said. "Sorry." Maybe they, whoever *they* were these days, had pulled the collective cellular plug.

I switched to Panaudio, which is a new service that runs through all the VoIPs and supposedly can reach anything. At least, the FBI uses it. Marena did the same thing, and we reached each other. It was a nice feeling. Outside the car, though, the communicationscape still seemed sketchy. I got through to a few people, but not my own phone, not anyone in Indiantown, and not No Way. Skype, UMA, and three of the other big VoIPs weren't functioning. Face it, Jed, your window of being able to warn anybody, or get help from anybody, or do much of anything, has closed.

I tilted my screen so Marena couldn't see it and clicked up Schwab. Disney had already suspended trading. Bad sign. I checked out after-hours options on the Chicago exchange. Corn was jagging upward. Damn, those bastards catch on fast. One of the nice things about grains is that they always go up after a crisis, even a little crisis. If the president stubs his toe, corn goes up. On the other hand, if we're heading into World Whatever Three, options aren't going to get filled. Cash might devalue. And even gold and palladium and whatever can actually go down in a real crash because a big economic shock shakes all the PMs out of the—

"Mom?" Max said near my ear. "Check it out, I got into the Ninth Hell! Mom!"

"I can't look at it right now," Marena said. "That's great, though."

"Yeah, that's impressive," I said.

"I'll look at it when we get there," Marena said. "Hey, look at those." She pointed out her window and up. A pair of Aeroscraft zeppelins were sliding overhead with their mooring ropes trailing like catfish barbels.

Max looked. He sat back down, reentered the gameverse, and descended into Bolgia Nono. Just like the rest of us. I checked the DHS Civilian Alert site on my phone. ". . . ADVISING PERSONS NOW IN TRANSIT TO HEAD SOUTH OR SOUTHWEST," the crawl said. Well, that was what we were doing. "OTHER PERSONS SHOULD REMAIN IN THEIR HOMES OR PLACES OF BUSINESS."

Hell.

I looked in on my home security system back in Indiantown. The doors were still locked, the generator was humming, and on the cameras everything looked okay. I checked the tank readouts. Damn. My gorgonian feeder farm was sick, sick, sick. The ammonia levels were way too high. For years I'd been tuning the place so that it could supposedly go on its own for a week, but in practice it never worked. Where the hell was Lenny? Three more days of this and it'll be Love Canal II in there. I checked in with my sort-of posse on StrategyNet. Only two people were online, and they were in Japan. *Please help me analyze data re. the current situation in Orlando area FL,* I typed in. *We are in the middle of it and I will forward any on-the-ground information. Urgent. Thanks. Jsonic.*

We fed onto 95 and headed south. Traffic on the eight-lane was heavier than usual, but not so bad as you'd think for the beginning of the end of the world. And the mood, whatever you could tell about it from the way they were driving, seemed pretty normal too.

Hmm. The thing to buy if it gets really hairy out there, I thought, is weapons. I went back to Schwab and put in an order for 3,000 shares each of Halliburton, Bechtel, and Raytheon. As an afterthought, I put a few hundred balls on GE. It looked like the trades went through, but then when I checked on my positions, it said trading had been suspended on all exchanges. Fuck. I folded back the little keyboard. It snapped shut with that Bondishly efficient clicking sound. I looked around. There was a sense of aircraft screaming overhead but I didn't want to roll down the window to hear better. Well, this is getting a little tense. Might be a clever moment to give Ms. Park a reassuring, manly touch on the shoulder. On the other hand, she might bite off my finger.

". . . it doesn't matter, that's fine," she was saying on the phone. "Just roll in a cot or whatever. Okay."

"Dude, over here," Max said to someone in the Neo-Teoverse. "Over here. Blister's down."

"So, the firm owns this hotel on Collins Avenue, the Roanoke?" Marena said. "They'll take care of us. Although they might give you a really small room."

I said that sounded great. Although at this rate it looked like about five more hours in the car. We passed a billboard advertising the Arthropod Experience at Parrot Jungle Island. It was looping a clip of a scolopendra centipede charging at the camera.

I thought of something. "Hey, I was thinking," I started to say, "the thing with—"

"Aigo jugeta!" Marena said, looking at her dash screen. The satellite view had zoomed in, like she said it would, but it still took me a minute to sort out what we were seeing. Places look different from above when you can see all the tacky tar roofs and there's all this foliage and everything. Finally I picked out Space Mountain and then the foreshortened towers of Cinderella's Castle. The thing had focused on the Magic Kingdom.

I froze the view, got the cursor on the center of the park—that is, the castle forecourt, at the north end of Main Street USA, or what they call the Hub. I zoomed and enhanced. Holy hell, I thought. They knew. Face it, they just bloody knew.

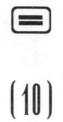

(10)

Six roads meet at the Hub, merging into a rotary. At its center, a circular bed of glads and poinsettias surround the "Partners" statue, the bronze figures of Walt and Mickey Mouse. There were drifts of what looked like big confetti all around the flowerbed and rotary and clumping under trees and kiosks. That is, if the trees were, say, HO-gauge ones in a model train set, then the confetti would be normal size. One clump in the center, at the statue's one o'clock, started looking weird and also familiar, and as the enhancement progressed it resolved itself into a big fuzzy costume of Mickey's dog Moloch, spread out supine on the polka-dot flagstones, with his black needley tail pointing west. It wasn't easy to tell, but it looked like there was still someone inside the suit. Then there was another costume, maybe the vizier from *Aladdin*, crumpled on the lower edge of the screen. I squinted at confetti. There were these white angled twisty things in between them, and then without any sense of sudden realization I knew they were bodies, in all sizes but especially in small. Oh, hell. I tried to block the sunlight with my hands and squinted closer at the screen. They were all contorted, holding on to each other, sheltering . . . oh Jesucristo, they were moving. Rolling, shivering. Hell. Holy hell. Kids. Several of those shapes are definitely kids. Jesus, Jesus. They're in really bad shape. Sometimes you can look at someone, even a mile away, and know they're not going to survive. And there were too many of them to survive. Where were the EMTs? Where were the police? Holy holy hell. What did this?

From the pattern of where they were lying I guessed they'd all gotten sick in other parts of the park and they'd made their way to this central location, and then couldn't go any farther. How long had it been going on? It can't have taken . . . I don't know, it had to—

"This is really bad," Marena said.

"That's not what happens," I said. "I mean, with food poisoning."

"No shit." She whipped her head around and checked on Max. He couldn't see the screen from there, but he was looking at us out of one eye, even though he was definitely still playing the game, bouncing a little and zapping beasties with invisible rays.

"It'd have to be something like VX," I said, "or some kind—"

"What's that?"

"It's a gas." Automatically, and to my internal mortification, I couldn't help thinking of the Buddy Love character in *The Nutty Professor*, when he delivers the same line. "It's some kind of fatal weaponized form—"

"Okay, okay. Don't say anything substantively horripilant, okay? He's just pretending he can't hear us."

"What?" I asked. "Oh. Right." It took me a second to get that she meant Max was listening and another two seconds to figure out that she'd used the antique word so that he wouldn't understand it. I'm a little slow sometimes.

"You know, because, these people didn't even start to get into the shelters, they're just—"

"Cool it, all right?" she said. Her hand darted in front of me and clicked off my screen. I looked over at her. She was facing forward. Her jaw was moving a little like maybe she was grinding her teeth. "Just don't say anything."

"Sorry." You idiot, Jed. Idiot. Quadruple idiot. Okay, get it together, I thought. Don't spook the offspring. Somebody in the Neo-Teoverse would probably tell him about all this pretty soon anyway. I got another shiver of that gross-out feeling that, as one gets older, increasingly substitutes for shock, sorrow, and rage. Damn. Kids. How many were there? Maybe it was just in the Magic Kingdom and not all over. Maybe a lot of them got out or weren't affected. Fuck. I tried not to imagine the sound of crying. That's the worst thing in the world. I'm not a big fan of human beings in general, but I guess one has a less-hard spot for the little dudes. Before they turn mean and discernibly stupid. Not that I'd want any around the house or anything, but still . . .

Damn it, I thought. I had an NBC mask, that is, a nuclear, biological, and chemical-rated gas mask, and I'd left it back in the house. Idiot. Sylvana's old Heckler & Koch P7 was in there, too, but I didn't have a carry permit so it wasn't a good idea for me to lug it around. Should've brought it anyway. At this—

The car hit a bump and I knocked my head on the hot padded dash thing. "Ow," I said. "I'm fine."

"Except, then, that's weird about the character suits," Marena said.

"The what?" I asked.

"Those big cartoon costumes, you know? They're all police now. They have gas masks and air-conditioning and metal-detecting goggles and radios and Tasers and everything in there."

"Huh. Maybe it came on too fast. Or it was something that got through the filters."

"Hmm," she went.

We crossed over the Hungryland Slough Canal. A sign said "Moroso Memorial Highway." And coming up, I thought, the River of Death and the Valley of Humiliation. Be sure to stop at the City of Destruction and pick up Mr. Despondency. "Okay, res me," Max said over his headphones to someone else in the Neo-Teoverse. "Next time, once she's down, we're going to switch all our DPS over to Jade Hag, and the reason we do Jade Hag last is because she has the thickest scales, so she dies really slow."

"Anyway, so you were right," Marena said.

"I don't know," I said. "No, I screwed up, I should've made—"

"Listen, Jed? I know I don't know you well enough to say this, but don't even start with that, okay?"

"Uh, okay." I'd been about to ask her something or tell her something or something and now I couldn't remember what it was.

"Anyway, if we'd prevented it, then the Codex would have been wrong."

"What—oh, no, no, it doesn't work that way," I said. "It's not some supernatural law, it's just a probability thing."

"Uh-huh."

"It's not seeing the future, it's just seeing what's out there and making a more informed guess."

She didn't respond. I shut up. Damn it, I thought. I should have just phoned in a bomb threat and done the time. All those kids were having, like, a great day, and they were all happy and shit, and then suddenly, everything got wrecked forever. It's not so much the suffering you can empathize with, with kids. It's the disappointment. Of course, just growing up is disappointing, but when it all happens at once, you know for a fact that there's no excuse for anything and it'd be a lot better if the world had never existed.

I clicked up the local news on my phone. "*. . . Orange County office of the State Police,*" that Kristin person's voice said on my earbud, "*now issuing a statement that earlier reports of a gas attack are unfounded. Ron?*"

"Thanks, Kristin. They're backed up on the freeways," that Ron character's voice said. *"On ramps, on access roads, even in suburban streets: vacationers and Florida natives fleeing the central part of the state, responding to uncon- firmed fears of chemical agents or military-style gas attack* in *Orlando, this de- spite new National Guard warnings telling citizens to remain in their homes, that the time for evacuation . . .* [dramatic pause] *has passed.* In *the vacation capital of the world, this is—"*

I killed the sound. Fuck, I thought. They don't know anything. Or it's just pure disinformation—

"So look, Jed?" Marena said.

I said yeah.

"So even if they say there's no point in clearing out, I think I want to keep going, okay?"

I said good.

"And the general consensus is that south equals safe, right? So I'm going to keep us on 95 for now."

"Sure," I said.

"Sorry to probably take you out of your way for no reason."

"Oh, no," I said. "No, thanks for saving me. If I'd just been sitting around, you know . . ."

"Don't mention it," she said.

"No way," Max said, "you can't play hipball against the Ninth Lord of the Night unless you're above a sixty-five."

I clicked the sound up in my ear. *". . . attack of unknown proportions,"* Ron's voice was saying, *"possibly some type* of *aerosol chemical weapon. By that they mean that the threat could be* in *the air and could reach a wide area. Because of the delayed symptoms, there is as yet no defined area where the casualties* are *occurring. We'll be back after this brief—"*

I switched to C-SPAN. There was a different doctory-looking person, talking to some committee. He was listing symptoms. The first things to look for were redness, itching, severe headaches, edemal swelling, and disorientation. Skin abrasions weren't healing. Victims at the Moffitt Cancer Center in Tampa had old herpes sores opening up, and even things like rosacea and acne had sud- denly become acute. I became reaware of a clamorous itch on the back of my neck, scratched it, vowed not to scratch it anymore, and clicked up YouTube. The first video had the head and shoulders of a large, puffy, ruddy-faced lady filling the window. Even on my phone's little screen you could see there were clusters of pink dots with red centers on her chin and left cheek. I hit the arrow. "We were at *Disney World*," she said. "We were here for *Christmas*." She kind of droned the words out in long, agonized croaks. "And now my husband is all . . . he's been, just, I can't even say it, it's just a, juuust a *horr*ror." She paused and sniffled. "I'm all bloated up. I can't lift my arms. They're all blown up. We were heeeere for a va*caaaa*tion! And this is at *Disney World, horrrrror, horrrrror—*"

Whoa. I clicked away. That doesn't sound right, I thought. I searched for information on VX. Every site I could find on it said the first effect would be nausea, but after that there'd be twitching or spasming, and then difficulty breathing. It didn't say anything about rashes or swelling. Maybe something more like tear gas? Except the victims didn't seem to have trouble seeing, either. And it definitely didn't sound like botulism or anthrax or ricin or any of that stuff. Hmm.

We were passing the North Palm Beach County General Aviation Airport. People and planes seemed to be milling around but nothing was taking off. Ahead of us the sun tumesced over brown loblolly pines.

I checked the news feeds again. There wasn't anything new, and there still wasn't anything about what we'd seen on the satellite. Bastards. They're all just state apparatchiks. I went through posts on unofficial news feeds. On some of those, at least, a few people had seen the satellite shot—and they were freaking out, of course—but nobody seemed to know anything. Damn it, I thought. You think how we're way, way into the Information Age, and then when something important happens, information seems oddly scarce. And you get a funny cut-loose feeling. Although, really, as you learn pretty quickly if you're doing stock trading or commodities or just if you actually know something about anything—anything except, say, pop stars or cats—information about what's really going on is always scarce.

"Did you tell anybody I don't know about?" Marena asked. "About the Codex thing?"

"No, I didn't," I said.

"Or about the dates in the Codex?"

"I didn't tell anybody," I said. "Come on, I'm a complete paranoid. I have twenty-three different passwords and I change each one of them every two days. I don't tell anybody anything. You and Taro are it. I didn't even tell my slugs."

"Okay, I believe you," she said. "Sorry." We fed onto 95.

"It's okay," I said. "That's what I was wondering about too." That is, whether anyone had seen or heard about the date in the Codex and then had decided it was up to them to make it happen. It could be like that Left Behinder guy in China who killed two thousand or whatever people with ricin in some reservoir and said he'd been trying to kill everybody because the Last Judgment was supposed to have happened two months before. These people always think God needs a lot of help.

We got past Lake Worth, Lantana, and Hypoluxo. Strip malls opened out on either side offering Gas, Food, Lodging, Burgers, Tacos, Sheila's Chichi Seashells from the Seashore, Cheeburger Cheeburger, Golf 'n' Flog S&M Country Club, Twistee Treat, Astrology, Tattoos, Taoist Massage, Alternative Pets, Piercings, Astrological Piercings, Electronics, Apparel, Thelemic Merchandise, Electronic Apparel, Pets, Porn, Pet Porn, Vegan Tattoos, and Thelemic Holistic Macrobiotic Vegan Genital Piercings and Burgers . . .

What I especially don't get, I thought, is what all this has to do with the Maya. Maybe just that there are a lot of us around here? Or maybe it's just that bit about how we shoulder the blame. Maybe some Maya guy's going to get blamed. Me, maybe. Damn. *Todo por mi culpa.* Even when it's not.

We breezed through Boca, but by Deerfield we were only averaging thirty-five mph. The orange sodium highway lamps came on. My brain, which I do not control well, kept dwelling on the Codex. Maybe that's why the Warren people waited until the eighteenth to let that story about the Codex out in *Time*, it thought. So that if anything did happen it would be too late to do anything about it. Or maybe somebody from the company knew about this earlier. Or maybe the company's behind the attack. No, that's just your paranoia again.

"I guess we should have gotten your opinion on the Codex thing earlier," Marena said.

"I don't know what to say to that," I said.

"Say whatever you're thinking."

"Well, you know, it does seem like a bit of a coincidence."

"What do you mean?"

"Nothing, just, you know, the book's been around for thirteen hundred and forty-eight years, and then three days before the second-to-last date . . . never mind."

"What are you trying to say?"

"Nothing," I said. "I'm just, you know—"

"What do you want me to tell you?" she asked. There was an edge in her voice like a razor blade in a taffy apple. "Okay, fine, Warren's a sinister, like, rogue corporation, kind of like, you know, SPECTRE, and *we* spread this stuff or whatever it is, and we forged that Maya book, and now we're, we're going to kill you. Except first we'll explain everything to you and then leave you somewhere in some diabolical trap that you can escape from. How does that sound?"

"It sounds very implausible," I said. "I was just—"

"Maybe it was both of us," she said. "Did you ever think about that? Maybe just by raising the alarm, we made it happen. Somebody saw the threat level was going to go up tomorrow so he decided to pull this today."

"Look," I said, "I'm sorry, let's just—"

"Let's just not speculate," she said.

"Okay, yeah, I—"

"Okay, stop talking. I'm serious."

My mouth closed. Damn, I thought. Now she hates me. I looked over at her. I wouldn't say her mouth was set in a grim line, but it was definitely set. Like I think I said, I have trouble reading emotions. She's not mad at you, Jed. Step back and think about it. What's really going on is, she's trying to be as cool as possible, but the fact is that she's absolutely terrified, and not for herself but for Max. She's a mom. And moms are not human. So, take that into consideration. You may not be able to understand it, but you should be able to take it into consideration.

We came up on the Miami River, where you can see the ocean for the first time. It looked deceptively inviting in the twilight. An ambulance crawled by in the center of the otherwise empty northbound lanes. ꟼƎMOTƎ COИTꞦOⱢⱢƎⱭ, it said. At least they weren't exposing government workers to hazard. At Cutler Ridge the traffic congealed to about forty mph. People must have gotten the gossip. There was a kind of uncertainty in the motion of the cars around us that I guessed came from fleeing a threat that they all hoped might still be imaginary. A V of F-18s shrieked over us, heading north, into the red zone. By Naranja we were just another log in the river, averaging under fifteen. Horns bleated around us. We got nudged a few times as people tried to cut in. Marena nudged back, harder. Crunch. Max thought it was great, like bumper cars. A gang of Puerto Rican kids passed us on Yamahas, weaving between the cars. Now that's the way to go, I thought. Steal one? Anything with a Confederate flag is fair game. We'd have to mug somebody. Could the three of us fit on a single motorcycle? No, forget it.

"I'm thirsty again," Max said.

"Isn't there another juice box back there?" Marena asked.

"I drank it."

"Could you just wait a little longer?" she asked. "If we have to stop before we get to the boat, then we'll find something around here."

He said okay.

I checked back in on the thread I'd started on StrategyNet. Amazingly, the gang had come through. There were fifty-eight posts, some with diagrams. Desiriseofnationsnerd said it sounded like some kind of LRAD noise gun, maybe like the thing the Israelis used in the Gaza incursion in '09. One efriend, a Go player from L.A. called Statisticsmaven, had plotted the outbreaks on one of his war-game maps and said that judging from the distribution and the timing, the "unknown agent" was obviously an airborne fast-acting poison, and that it must be quite a bit heavier than air because it wasn't spreading any farther. Some guy named Hell Rot agreed with him and said that he'd been wrong before but now he thought it looked more like radiation poisoning. Bourgeoise-ophobus was texting them both back furiously, saying that was unlikely:

> if watever it is got into there lungs/bloodstreams yes-terday and there alredy dying from it it wd have to be a COLOSSAL DOSE sayat lesat 10 SIEVERTS. U wd practcly hav to hold a ½-supercritical chunk of 239PU in each hand & bang them together. It took that Rus-sian spy 3 wks to die & hed ingested 10*+ microgrms of 210Po. NO WAY is this radiation. Get ur facts strait troll hell rot be4 u mouth off.

210, I thought. Number 84. *Idiota.* I got a twist of that particular sense of horror that feels like your lower intestine's a vacuum hose on high suction.

Okay. Chill. Just chill. Still. Chill.

I sat still, the way I used to do when I was, like, five. As always, it dissipated, eventually.

"It's polonium," I said.

"Sorry?" Marena asked.

Not very articulately, I explained. It took a while and she didn't sound entirely convinced, but at least she took it seriously.

"I'll text it in," she said. She meant she'd get it to Lindsay Warren, and from him to his unspeakable connection in the DHS.

She started thumbing on her phone, guiding the wheel with one finger of her left hand. Every once in a while she'd take a cursory glance at the road ahead. The hell of it is, I thought, after all this, we're going to get killed in an ordinary, avoidable traffic accident. Isn't that ironic? Well, actually, no, Alanis, it's not. It's just a bummer.

"How do you spell *polonium*?" she asked. I told her. She thumbed some more. I kept sneaking looks at her, trying to guess what encryption package she was using, but I couldn't. Of course, now the DHS'll think we did it, I thought. If they don't already. Not that we're supposed to care about that. Although I do.

She finished. She put the phone down on her thigh. Okay, I thought. Try to think. If it's polonium poisoning—well, that means there'd be a big spectrum of degrees of exposure: we might be okay, or we could all be hot as hell's hinges now and not know it yet. It could take months to see any symptoms and it'll still kill you sure as *scheisse*—well, let's not scream until we're—God damn it, I just don't get it, don't get it, don't get it . . .

Her phone beeped. She touched a button and listened to the text reading out in her ear.

"Okay, they assure me they're on it," she said after a minute.

I said great and asked her whether her Pentagon pals had given her any inside spook scoop on what we should be doing to stay alive.

"He just said to keep heading south and to let ES do its thing," she said.

"Right," I said. ES? I wondered. Did she mean—wait, maybe we should at least stop and get some iodine pills, just in . . . no, actually, don't mention it. Traffic's slowing down. One stop and we'll be in wherever forever.

We fetched up just south of Florida City. It was 7:14 P.M. Marena zoomed in on the GoogleTraffic map. It looked like we were only about ten car lengths down from the point where the highway changed from red to green. By now the horns were making an almost continuous tone as people just plain leaned on them, not even antagonistically but just to be part of the chorus of despair. On our left there was just that cheap-looking pink-and-turquoise horizon, like trimming on some ersatz Deco hotel on Ocean Drive. At least it looked like an appropriate place to die.

We sat for a minute. Marena fidgeted. On the CNN site they were saying that hundreds of cars had been torched in Winter Park and Altamonte Springs, and that there were at least a dozen out-of-control fires in Orange County alone. They put up a map of Belle Glade, which is a downscale town on the south end of Okeechobee, and said some kind of skinhead militia had raided an immigrant trailer town because they thought it was the headquarters of La Raza, which I guess they were blaming for the fires. Eighteen people had been killed. Crackers with torches, I thought. The Imperial Wizards ride again. Hell. The picture cut to a low-aerial shot of six corpses lying on asphalt.

"I hate dead people," Max said.

"Well, maybe you don't want to watch this," she said. She hit an icon and the screen switched to SpongeBob.

"Whatever happened to 'Viewer Discretion Advised'?" she asked me in a lower voice.

I said that maybe they couldn't find a one-syllable word for *discretion*.

"Are we going to get wiped?" Max asked.

"Nopes," Marena said. "The prob's too far away now. Let's watch this."

"Why wook, it's Wuidward!" SpongeBob said.

We sat. I tried calling the Indiantown Community Center. Nothing. I checked out TomTomClub. Somebody called BitterOldExGreenBeretCracker was saying it wasn't some Islamic outfit behind the attack, but rather a Native American group called White Buffalo. His reasons weren't too clear. Bourgeoiseophobus said it might be the Hawkingers, whoever they were. A poster called Gladheateher said he sure it was Nation of Islam. SpongeBob beat Squidward in a square-dance contest. Finally Marena couldn't stand it.

"I'm walking up there," she said.

"I'll check on it," I said. I started to get out.

"No, I want to deal with it." She scrummaged in her bag, took out a big video brooch with the Warren Borromean–rings logo, clicked it on, and pinned it to her sort of lapel.

"I want to get out too," Max said.

"No, sorry, you guys hang on here for a sec," she said. "I'm just going up there to see what's happening."

"Seriously," I said. "I can—"

"I know what I'm doing. I'll be fine. What was the name of that army base again?"

"The nearest one?" I asked. "Homestead Base."

"Right," she said. "Okay, look, you guys, don't let anyone in the car, no matter what they say or what uniform they're wearing. I've got my phone in and I'll keep the line open and you can watch it all on TV. I'll be back in about two minutes."

Max and I looked at each other and said okay.

She left the engine on, cracked open her door, and slid out into the gap between it and the left guardrail. The car took in a gulp of wet heat. I moved into the driver's seat. It was cramped and too high but I didn't dare touch the settings. Max bounced into the front seat and watched on the screen. I watched. I felt castrated. Oh, well, not the first time. Starting from the front of the pack the cars seemed to run out of breath and the horn drone died down. Marena's jiggly video view emerged in a small crowd of puffy human backsides.

"Excuse me, VIP," her voice said, echoing into her ear mike with a tone of authority. Amazingly, the clouds of adipose tissue parted to let her through. A few people grumbled but they didn't question her either. Morons. I got a glimpse of a little girl with bangled cornrows and one big bead hanging right between her eyes. "Do you have to potty?" a nasal woman's voice said somewhere. "Nathaniel!" she said. "If you need to potty this is *potty time right now.*"

"Sorry, VIP," Marena said. "Excuse me, thanks, VIP comin' through."

She pushed out into a narrow patch of road between the crowd and the front of a line of orange-and-silver-striped traffic barricades. A military police officer in a transparent bubble helmet was waddling back and forth waving a red light saber that spelled out DANGER in the air. From the point of view of Marena's chest, the long exit ramp leading down into Florida City was backed up solid. But behind the barricades a wide, clear scroll of seamless asphalt rolled south toward Cuba.

Marena walked up to the cop and half blocked his path.

"Hello, Officer?" she asked up into his helmet. "Could you tell me what we should do to help out here?"

"Yes, ma'am, just get back into your vehicle and wait your turn for the detour," he said in that slightly metallic voice. They probably tune the speakers' sound that way on purpose, just to make them more menacing.

"We've been told to head south past this point by the National Guard," she lied.

"I'm sorry, ma'am, but—"

"We could get over into the northbound lanes, but of course we don't want to go against federal orders—"

"Both routes are needed for emergency vehicles. Besides, there is no reason to try to leave the area. All of you must return to your homes or places of business." He turned around.

"Look, Officer Fuentes," she said, getting in front of him and using his name off his badge, "I bet you have kids, right? You know what's going on? The brass at Homestead put you up to this so they can get their own people out. And they're leaving you here to take the heat. You're going to get killed up here and your boss'll be sitting on a beach drinking tequila, you know what

I'm saying? So what I think we should do is move a few of these sawhorses and let these cars into the northbound lane at least. How does that sound?"

"A-four, copy?" he said into the microphone in his helmet. "Pedro? It's Bob in Zone Five. Hi. I have a situation here."

"Nathaniel, do you have to potty?" the woman's voice said again.

"You know I'm filming this whole thing, right?" Marena asked. "And if it turns out that these people die here today it's going to be all over the place. This is going to be one of those stories that catches the public eye, and you're going to turn into a, a symbol of what's wrong with this country, you're never going to be able to go anywhere without people pointing at you. You'll have to grow a beard and move back to San Juan."

"Yes, backup please, out," the officer said. "Ma'am, there *is* another squad car that will be here in a few moments to escort you to your vee-*hick*-le."

Marena stood and looked at him for a second or two. He looked back.

"Are you sure you don't have to potty?" Nasal Woman asked.

"What's that yellow thing on his shirt?" Max asked me.

"That's a nitrox tank," I said. "If the filters on his mask clog up, he can open that and get about fifty-two lungfuls of extra air."

"Oh," Max said. "Right. Cool."

Fuentes broke the stare-down first and turned. Marena spun around and faced the little crowd of thirty or so motorists who had braved the outdoors to see what was up. What happened on the screen next was confusing. But three seconds later we were looking down on them, from a different angle, and when she looked down at her feet we saw that she had climbed up on top of an old green SUV that was at the front of the line. Now she was standing with her feet on the chrome pipes between two sets of upside-down windsurfer boards, surveying the people. From what we could see through her bobbing wide-angle lens, they looked like just regular McFolks, the salt, sugar, and saturated fat of the earth, all white, for some reason. Git along, move 'em out.

"Okay, everybody?" she said to the crowd, projecting from her diaphragm. "I'm sorry to have to do this, but I think we may have a difference of opinion here and we'll need everyone's help, we should all get together, if we want to sort it out."

They just looked up at her. "Nathaniel," the woman went, "are you sure you don't have to potty?"

"My name is Marena Park. I'm a professional journalist, broadcaster, and mother, and I'm standing here at the intersection of U.S. 1 with 821, where a hasty barricade has been set up blocking all routes south. There's a pretty big group of us here who are concerned about how the authorities are handling this situation, and right now we're talking to the single officer who claims to be in charge. Now, I want to hear what *you* have to say. Officer Fuentes here has said that we will not be allowed to use either U.S. 1 or 997 to get away from the center of the attack, because the officers at Homestead Base want to use those routes themselves first."

"That isn't what I said," the cop's voice said at a distance. Marena ignored him. "And it's not true—"

"Now, Officer Fuentes here is wearing full protection against chemical agents, and we don't have anything. Also, my GPS unit shows both routes are clear of traffic all the way to the Keys. But listen, don't let me do all the talking, I'd like to hear what you think."

I imagined Marena's eyes darting from face to face. None of them said anything, except one of the younger women was murmuring something in a plaintive tone, like she was about to start freaking out.

"What do *you* think?" Marena's voice asked. It was clear she'd made eye contact with somebody, but we couldn't see who it was. "Do you think we're hearing the truth here, that we really should just sit tight, or is it all just more disinformation?"

"I understand what you're saying, dear," someone said. Max found who it was and zoomed in on her before I did. Marena had picked out this little old lady, about four feet five, ninety-five pounds, ninety-five years old, blue hair, blue-gray eyes, blue-white skin, the full deal.

"Thanks for your input," Marena said.

"You know," the old lady said, "ninety-five percent of everything you hear these days is complete bullshit."

There was a moment of silence. Even Potty Lady had shut up.

"My mom's always doing this kind of stuff," Max said in a confidential whisper.

"Your mom's very brave," I said.

"Okay, who else has an opinion?" Marena asked, apparently looking around.

"They need those roads for relief workers," somebody said. "They know what they're doing."

"Good, we've heard from the opposing side. Okay, how many—"

"I need to say something," Officer Fuentes said, but the helmet he was wearing evidently didn't have a loudspeaker on it because you couldn't hear him that well, and somebody else with a loud voice had spoken up instead. It was a dark, fortyish taxpayer with a brace of kids who, I guessed, he was taking back to their mother's house after a visiting-rights jaunt to the Magic Kingdom. ". . . don't give a damn about us," he was saying. "If we get south we may live and if we stay inland we're going to die, it's as simple as that. This guy has a goddamn space suit on and he's telling us—"

After that things got confusing again, audio-wise. The Murmuring Woman was now clearly shrieking, "We're gonna die, we're gonna die," over and over. More people had gotten out of their cars and come up, asking each other what the heck was going on. Officer Friendly said something about "necessary component of antiterrorist measures in this area at this point in time."

"Everybody?" Marena said above the din. "I think we're leaning toward *not* believing the local authorities on this one." There were a few revival-meeting yeahs and even an old-fashioned "Right on, sister!" Still, other people kept arguing. Nathaniel, I think, said something about how he didn't have to potty. I couldn't see Officer Fuentes anywhere, but I guessed he'd followed standard confronted-by-a-mob procedure and retreated to his squad car.

"All right, look, let's take a vote," Marena said. "Focus. If we don't get together on this, nothing's going to happen one way or the other. People? Come on, I need to hear what you guys are saying."

The competing voices died down but didn't stop.

"Okay," she said, "first, everybody who thinks the military police here have our best interests at heart and that we should all just go back in our cars and wait, please either honk your horn once or shout out the word *against*, okay? The word to wait is *against*. Everybody? One, two, three, shout."

There was a pretty big shout, in which the word *against* was often distinguishable.

"Great," Marena said. By now she seemed to have 95 percent of the crowd's attention. "Everybody who thinks that the troops here do *not* have our best interests at heart, in fact that they don't give a gosh-darn about us, everybody who wants to just drive through this thing, and remember they can't arrest all of us—in fact, I'm pretty sure that they won't arrest any of us, not even me— all those in favor of moving ahead, either sound your horn in short half-second bursts or please shout the word *for*. Okay? One, two, three—*FOR!*"

She got a lot of fors. "All *right*," she said.

The crowd didn't exactly surge, but it slumped forward, and there wasn't any cheer, just a scattering of *All right!*s and *Come on*s. Still, the point was made. Wow, I thought. Liberty leading the people. *À la Bastille!* The Divorced

Dad dragged the first barricade horse to the shoulder and a car pushed through before the others got cleared. Marena climbed down and was skirting around the crowd, trying to get to us without getting anywhere near anyone else. Someone called after her, but she ignored him. The cars around us started inching forward. *"Byong shina,"* she muttered.

"Mom? The cars are moving," Max said into her line.

"I'll be right there, big dude," her voice said.

She came into view in the real-life windshield. By now the cars, trucks, and RVs were roaring by her like they wanted to squash their deliverer. She got in, closed the door, and clicked into drive, in what I'm tempted to call a single fluid motion.

"I have to go to the bathroom," Max said.

"Can you hang on for another few minutes?" she asked.

He said okay. We inched past the tumbled sawhorses and then it felt like we'd been squirted forward out over the yellow Everglades.

"That was, that was really something," I said. "I wouldn't know how to do that. You're, like, a—"

"Joan of Arc?" she asked.

"How'd you know what I was going to say?"

"It's actually nothing, you know, we do a lot of human-resource management, there are a few button words . . ."

"No, no, really. How'd you know that lady was on your side?"

"Well, you can take a class in that stuff. People make little expressions when they agree with you, or not."

She accelerated for emphasis. It looked like we were skipping the Miami hotel idea.

"Gee."

"There's a Warren marina resort in Key West. It'll be easy to get a plane there."

"Great." If we get that far, I thought.

"And if we don't get that far," she said, "still, if we're near the water, they may be able to send a boat for us if we get stuck. I have pretty high KEP."

There was a short scream from a military jet speeding over us.

"I'm sorry," I said, "I don't know what that stands for."

"Key Employee Protection. Insurance. The company'll get ES to come bring me in."

"Oh. That's great."

"Max, stop doing that," she said.

"Why?" his voice asked.

"Because God wills it. You're making Baby Jesus cry."

"Okay, okay," he said. He must have stopped doing whatever it was. I checked CNN on my phone. The transcription scroll was saying how a few people with similar symptoms to the Disney World victims had turned up in Chicago, Seattle, and other cities as far away as Lima, but that most of them had gotten sick in airports and it was possible they were all vacationers who'd been in the Orlando area the day before. We cruised into Miami. For some reason it looked grungier than usual. I'd thought it would be a traffic nightmare already but we got through. Maybe everybody was at the beach. After you pass the city there's seven miles of swamp, and then you ride up onto the causeway, U.S. 1, over Blackwater Sound on Cross Key. In five miles you get onto Key Largo. I poked around the Net looking for White Buffalo. There was a Web site but it was just a logo, a few quotations from Leonard Peltier, and a password log-in strip. It looked like it might be a splinter group from AIM, that is, the American Indian Movement. On CNN they were saying that the Disney World Horror—as they were apparently now calling it—was officially a Mass Casualty Incident. Like, glad they got that straight. Drudge's links were saying that judging from medical radio reports the death cloud, whatever it was, hadn't been just in the Magic Kingdom but had affected an area extending south to Lake Tohopekaliga and west at least as far as downtown Orlando, with a long plume angling northwest at least to Lake Harris. Symptom clusters had been reported a lot farther out than that, but since people had moved around in the day or so since their exposure, it wasn't clear exactly how far the cloud had carried. And someone named Octavia Quentin, who they said was a risk diagnostician from the DHS, said that some of the symptoms were "consistent with heavy-metal poisoning and/or exposure to very high levels of ionizing radiation." Scab casters, I thought. Casting scabs. Out of the stone. Light out of a stone.

News6 was saying how reports of rioting were expanding out from the Parks District in a widening ring. "Panic is spreading because of panic," some purported expert's voice said. "It's what we technically call a self-sustaining reaction." FEMA's Orlando Area Emergency Evacuation Success Procedure had not been successful, and now all traffic in the central part of the state was stop-and-start. Airports in Kissimmee, Lakeland, Lake Wales, and Vero Beach weren't functioning. Hospitals as far as Tampa/St. Pete, Gainesville, and Fort Lauderdale had gotten so many patients by helicopter that they were already overloaded. State rescue workers were refusing to touch the glowbugs, that is, what they were calling people who might be contaminated. I guess it was sort of like that Japanese term for people affected by radiation at Nagasaki and Hiroshima. It's a word sort of like *hibachi* but I can't think of it right now. Police were scarce, either because they were working around the hospitals or because they just weren't showing up, and flash mobs were "engaging in organized looting," not just smashing store windows but loading whole electronics-store inventories onto trucks and driving fleets of cars out of dealers' lots.

Traffic thickened again at Fat Deer Key. Still, unlike almost anybody else in the state, we were still moving, since once you were out on the causeway, there were no more entrances from anywhere outside the Keys. On Marena's traffic site, it looked like just a few miles behind us nobody was moving. She really had done the right thing, cruising at the first hint of trouble. When paranoia pays off, it pays off big time. Max was looking out his window and up at the sky and I looked too. It was filled with planes, jumbles of military wingpower drawing a Gordian tangle of contrails, all shapes and sizes like a shark feeding frenzy, EF2000s like hammerheads, AV-8 Harriers like blues, Globemasters like great whites, Starfighters like bull sharks. Even, I think, a B-2 like a manta ray, the whole hellish crew. I tried my alarm system at home. They didn't pick up. I texted No Way's box again. Same story.

"Mom? I'm really hungry," Max's voice said.

"Did you finish that blondie already?" she asked. He said yes. She said to wait for half an hour, since we were on a top-secret commando mission now and had to make things last. I tried to sit back and chill. The best thing you can do right now, Jed, old bastard, is not infect the driver with your nervousness. We were over Islamorada, where you come into the real Keys. From here you can't see the line of the Florida peninsula anymore, just the causeway connecting the green coral dots of the islands and, on your right, the rusty old railroad trestle. On CNN it looked like we'd sleazed past Miami just in time. There was a riot in Pompano Beach, and in Hialeah a panicked crowd had rushed a line of soldiers who'd fired on them with that new goo gun thing that shoots oobleck or whatever. *Eh bueno,* I thought, at least we can still get incoming stuff online. No need for us to miss a minute of the agonizing holocaust. In the reality TV era, it's all good. We passed the Coast Guard station at the south end of Plantation Key. Oddly, it was deserted, with no boats in the slips or cars in the lot. Chains of aircraft hustled northwest overhead.

"Well, still, I guess that's it," Marena said.

"Sorry?"

"About casting the scabs. Right? These people, I mean, the victims, they have a lot of scabs."

"Yeah. I guess that's it."

"I guess you thought of that already."

"Yeah."

There was a long, bleak, gray, cheerless pause. Finally she looked over at me.

"Look," she said, "do you know any—"

(11)

At first I thought the sun had come out, because the line of reflective Botts' dots on the median glowed with this weird fuschia color and the pavement brightened into a too-cheerful yellow. But the sun had set a while back. Hadn't it? A moment after that there was a sort of slushy impact that seemed to jiggle the car's windows in their gaskets, and then it seemed like some time after that that I heard the sound, a rattle that rose into a sinners-in-the-hands-of-an-angry-god HRURWWRRWRSHHH and that finally terminated in the residue of what must have been the actual explosion, a single deep, merciless FWOMP. It felt like the car was sucked backward and to the right as air was rushing in toward the core of the blast.

"Sweetie!" Marena's mouth yelled silently. Her right arm shot back and grabbed for Max. One of Max's own little arms darted between the seats and toward the wheel, but she kept him from grabbing it and steered his hand down onto her thigh instead. I looked back at him. His head was wedged between the seats and his lips were drawn back, showing his teeth. Gravel snare-drummed over the Cherokee's steel membranes. Water hit the windshield, and I could see little bits of coral in it, and what seemed to be fish scales. The big wiper pushed one layer off and another formed. Oddly, the cars in our lane were still oozing along. You could feel an increased timidity in the motion, and almost see the drivers' expressions and hear them going, "What the fuck? What the fuck? Are we dead yet?" but the whole thing had happened too fast for many people to react.

"That was not a nuke," I said. "That was not a nuke. That was not a nuke." But of course Marena couldn't hear anything either. We were still in that quiet space, with that E-tone ring sloshing around in your cochlea and a feeling like recovering from a wound. Bovinely, I looked around. I didn't see any fire, but there was a widening white wedge at our five o'clock. It looked so unreal that it took me a minute to realize it was steam. How far away had it been? It had to have been at least a second between the flash and the sound. But now already I didn't remember. Five miles? No, closer than that. I looked back at Marena. The fingers of her left hand were still on the wheel, and they were so white I thought she was going to crush the thing. But I guess they make steering wheels pretty solid. Her lips were asking Max something like whether he was all right. This went on for what seemed like some time. Max's voice didn't say anything, and she asked again, and eventually, as some sound came back into focus, he said something like "I'm okay, I'm okay."

I noticed we were at mile marker 78, on the Indian Key Bridge just past Upper Matecumbe. At some point Marena asked me something, probably whether I was all right.

"That wasn't a nuke," I said. "Not a nuke."

"Are you okay?"

"That wasn't a nuke. Look, the windows are, they're not broken, so, so we're okay," I said. "It wasn't a nuke."

"No, are *you* okay?"

"Me?" I said. "I'm fine." Hints of a combustive smell were starting to snake their way through the car's air-processing system.

"Okay."

"That was not a nuke," I said.

"I know," she said.

"Are you and Max okay?" I asked. At some point, although I hadn't noticed, he'd climbed into her lap.

"Yes."

"Okay."

"Okay."

"I don't think it was munitions either," I said. By now the white wedge almost enveloped us, and it was darkening in the center.

"What?"

"I think that was a pipeline."

"Pipeline?"

"Like, natural gas," I said. A lot of the area behind us was already black. Oil smoke. "Except there's also fuel oil burning back there now." I realized my teeth were chattering.

By now the cars ahead of us had stopped. Be still, my teeth.

"Are we going to get wiped?" Max asked.

"No, we're very far from any problem," Marena said.

"Jed, are we going to get wiped?"

"No," I said, "we're in the best possible spot. We're over water, and the road won't burn."

"Okay," he said. Judging by his voice he seemed to be getting over being scared. I'd seen that sort of thing before, in the CPRs. Kids get spooked but then, if the adults seem calm, they can recover in a second. They don't yet know what's normal.

"Max, I need you to be tough right now and take care of us," Marena said. "Because you know about a lot of these things."

"It might blow up again right here," he said.

"No, no, it shouldn't do that," I said. "There are valves in there. Any fuels ought to go back toward the break and burn out. Also the pipes aren't near the road, they're out in the Gulf somewhere."

"Okay," he said. Actually, I thought, I suppose there could still be another pipeline blast. Or did the whole line drain out if there was a fire in one section? That was something I didn't know.

I said I had to look around for a second and got out. It was hot but the day had already been hot and the direction of the blast only felt a little hotter than the rest of the air. There were far-off sirens and a farther-off bullhorn over the whine of aircraft. A few people in the cars around us started to get out too. I closed the car door and climbed up on the roof. I didn't see any nearby fires or serious accidents. But ahead and behind us dozens of cars were wedged together at different angles. Damn, I thought. That's it as far as forward motion was concerned. They're probably packed all the way down to Key West anyway, I thought. Right into Ernest Hemingway's bedroom. Crowding out the six-toed cats. Nobody was going anywhere for the foreseeable future. Although, come to think of it, the word *foreseeable* was losing some of its luster.

"Jed, get back in the car," Marena said through the outside speaker system.

I did. Underneath my jacket my pathetically once-stylish shirt was soaked, like I was entering a Wet Dork contest. Marena shut off the engine but kept the AC working off the battery.

She seemed almost okay again. All things considered, she'd actually gotten herself together pretty quickly. We sat. We listened. Low sun slanted in. Marena touched her dashscreen and tinted membranes slid over the windows on the car's starboard side. The soundscape seemed grim, but distantly so. Eventually, Max climbed back into the backseat. Marena started tapping on her phone. I flipped around on mine. Now CNN was saying some technicians from somewhere who'd been at Universal Studios, and who'd happened to be wearing dosimeters, had reported lethal radiation levels to the police yesterday afternoon, but apparently nothing had come of it. Although you'd think other people would have noticed it, I thought. Didn't the DHS people ever check their Geiger tubes? Also, that many rads would affect electrical meters and set off smoke alarms and burn out all the X-ray film in dentists' offices and a hundred other things. And nobody noticed? Although come to think of it I had heard something about smoke alarms yesterday. Hadn't I? Damn it, there's ten trillion pages on the Net and not one of them is—never mind. I checked out YouTube again. The top video was a long static shot of Interstate 75, somewhere north of Ocala. North-going cars had filled up all six lanes on both sides of the highway and then gotten backed up and frozen in place like plaque in a doomed artery. Four apparently endless files of pedestrians, one for each shoulder, trudged alongside the cars. People carried plump trash bags and gallon jugs of water balanced on bindle sticks. Two corpses, or maybe just tired people, lay neatly on the median strip. It was the kind of thing I'd seen a lot of when I was little, but now like everyone else around here lately I'd only seen it on TV after the latest everyday holocaust in Africa or Asia, and it felt almost as odd to me as it must to most native U.S. citizens to see it happening right the hell here. Except it wasn't exactly like other refugee trails because the people were walking with this weird sort of Brownian motion. At first I thought they were picking their way over difficult terrain or something, but then I guessed that they didn't want to get too close to each other. That is, each of the human particles thought it might get contaminated if it touched any of its neighbors, so they all kept halting and dodging and compensating and the whole thing oozed forward with a kind of paranoid jiggle.

Polonium particulates, I thought. Hell. Maybe we should change out of our clothes. If there's even a few grains of that shit on there they might blow up and get inhaled or whatever . . . hmm. Hell. Like an idiot I hadn't thought of it before. Also like an idiot, I immediately imagined Marena peeling off her garments and exposing about two square yards of taut, tempting skin. Should I ask her about it? Except any clothes we can get from anybody around here, we'd be more likely to pick up something from those. Definitely lice, anyway. Well, we can just be naked. Except that kid's back there. And also except maybe none of us were really anywhere near the hot zone, but then if there's any of the stuff around here, like all the people around us must have dragged

a few with them, then if we're naked the particles are more likely to get absorbed through the skin, right? Say the odds are ten thousand—well, no, say
they're like—oh, forget it. You'd have to be Enrico Fermi to figure this stuff out.
I decided not to mention it.

Outside, in the unfortunately real world, the last blue drained out of the
sky. The lamps didn't go on. Still, the night seemed brighter than the day had
been, with the high shell of smoke reflecting the butterscotchy burnt orange
of the fires.

"Well, that's one good thing, anyway," Marena said, maybe to herself.

I looked at her.

"Oh, I just got a text from ES," she said.

"Sorry," I said, "what's ES again?"

"Oh, that's Executive Solutions. It's our security contractor. They check
out our cars and negotiate with kidnappers and whatever."

"Okay. Wait, can you get a text through to them, if—"

"No, but they know where we are, the homing thing's not—they say they've
got our locator on the satellite. And the boat's on the way."

"That's great," I said. "Uh . . . are you sure the coast guard's going to let
them in this close?"

"I guess they think so."

We sat some more. On my side you could just see green firework chrysan-
themums popping over the mainland. Somebody on TomTomClub said it
was the Muslim community in Homestead celebrating the attack. Outside, a
few people jogged past us between the cars, heading south. On CNN they
were saying that the Feds had lost touch with the Miami Police Department,
among many others. Bad sign. When's the looting going to spread to here? I
wondered. I looked around out the window but everybody seemed to be sitting tight. Drudge had something about how army doctors were estimating
that at least one-fifth of the population of Greater Orlando already had some
signs of exposure, which meant that many times that number of people
would present symptoms within the next few weeks. There was an item about
how in Belle Glade, six out of ten people surveyed by phone said they thought
the glowbugs were zombies or somehow victims of witchcraft. One of them
said that in his neighborhood his homies had a posse to "take care of them,"
by which he meant kill and burn them. On StrategyNet they were talking
about how there wasn't a single government agency that had the math to
predict the course of the cascading panic. "It is a HIGHLY COMPLEX SYS-

TEM," Bourgeoiseophobus said. "And right now it's spreading OUTWARD from Ctrl Florida and it's getting magnified because it FEEDS ON ITSELF. And the more people you warn about it, the BIGGER IT IS GOING TO GET." He sounded right to me.

The Net went down. I restarted and tried it again. It came back. I looked around YouTube. There were videos of burning shopping malls, spreading skin lesions, and lines of refugees waiting to get on school buses. Puffy hunch-dwarfs in chrome responder suits and SCBA probosci set up a Reaganville of arc lights and blue plastic tents outside whatever was left of the Miami air-port. Night-feeding buzzards who would soon be dead themselves picked at a dead lady under one of the giant psilocybe mushrooms outside the Mad Tea Party ride, with a background glimpse of a desolate Fantasyland street and a pair of elephants suspended in flight, all in the grisly chiaroscuro of a single emergency light, like that scene in *Pinocchio* where Pleasure Island is all de-serted because the boys have gotten turned into donkeys. A lone old guy, apparently the only moving object for miles around, staggered past aban-doned cars on West Gore Street in downtown Orlando. A bunch of ancient women gathered fuel in a vacant lot, like . . . well, I don't know what they were like. A ten-year-old-ish girl waded through brown muck toward a flashing orange light.

"Jed?" Marena asked.

"Yeah."

"I've got to tell Max some stuff."

"Okay," I said. I guessed she meant some private stuff. "Do you have any big headphones? Or I can stick my head out the window so I can't hear."

"No, it's fine," she said. "I'm just mentioning it." Maybe she thought the kid might freak out less if he wanted to look brave in front of me. "Max?" she asked.

"Yeah," he said.

"We have to talk about a couple of things."

Max said okay. Damn it, I thought, I really, really don't want to hear this. Max was at that age where they want to be a big kid but might still have an old spit-stained Beanie bear in their backpack. And you don't want to hurt their feelings by seeing them cry. I put on a headset and maxed up the ambi-ent noise cancellation and scrunched down in my seat, but it didn't help. I tried to concentrate on the news just to give him some privacy, not real privacy, but that kind of Japanese-style pseudoprivacy when you can't stand listening to something so you try to tune out and not hear. But I could still hear everything.

"Listen, sweetie?" Marena asked in a very low voice. "You know there's a chance that I might get hurt today, right?"

He must have said "Mm-hmm."

"Okay. Now, suppose I fall over and fall asleep, or something knocks me unconscious or something."

"Is that going to happen?"

"No, it's just a tiny possibility. But if that happens you'll need to stay in the car with the door locked, even if I don't look good, okay? Don't get out and don't go anywhere with strangers. Jed'll take care of you and you need to do what he says. But if Jed gets sick, or if he's not here, then just stay in the car and wait. Don't do anything anybody tells you to do unless they're wearing a police uniform and a badge that looks real. Otherwise stay in the car with the door locked even if somebody's hammering on the window. If that happens the glass won't break, and there'll be police here, so don't worry. The only time to get out of the car is if there's fire or something happening around it, or if it's making smoke. Or if there are a lot of policemen with badges, you'll have to do what they say. Except never let go of your phone and keep your watch on. I've gotten in touch with ES and they'll have your transmitter on your phone so they'll be able to find you. But still, don't let go of your phone because they may not always be able to see your chip. Okay?"

"Okay."

"Okay. You know the company's sending a boat to pick us up? They'll iden-tify themselves as Executive Solutions, and they'll have identification. You should ask to see it. Don't ask them if that's what they are, though. They have to say the name themselves. You understand that, right?"

"Yep."

"Don't get on any boats you aren't sure about. You remember Ana Vergara? She'll probably be on the boat or on the phone. Ask to talk to her. I'm just tell-ing you this because I know you're a big brave kid so you can handle it."

Silence. Hmm, she sure didn't mention any father in all that, I thought. Maybe he was an eyedropper job.

"Sweetie?" she asked.

"Okay," he said, "but how tiny a possibility?"

"It's very unlikely, but we're still in a hazardous situation right now so I need to remind you of this stuff."

"If you start dying we'll get you to the cryogenics place, right?"

"Well, if an ambulance picks me up they'll do that, but you can't think about that. There may not be time for that, and there may not even be time for an ambulance. So you can't stay with me if I tell you to go, you have to go with Jed or whoever I tell you to go with."

Max scrunched down in his seat. I think he may have whimpered a little. I can't deal with this, I thought, this is one of the many compelling reasons not to have kids in the first place. It's too sad to watch them find out what the world is really like. Marena started to say something to me and then seemed to think better of it.

We waited. A growing stream of people walked south around us, threading through the packed cars, some carrying people on slings or pushing them in carts. A lot of them looked sketchy. Still, I thought, these were all people who'd left their own vehicles. And they want to get to Key West. They're in too much of a hurry to do any more than cursory looting. I was starting to suspect that Executive Solutions was just a wishful hallucination. Tomorrow might be a pretty grim day. I guess any time now we'll just devolve back to the Paleolithic Age and start fishing for shark using each other as bait.

"Jed?" Marena asked.

"Yeah," I said, whipping my head over to her. I'm here for you, babe, I got ready to say. Hey, what are you doing? Are you sure he's asleep? Mmmmm, that feels—

"What's an ADW?" She was watching the C-SPAN transcript.

"Oh, uh, they probably mean an Area Denial Weapon," I said. "Like a dirty bomb. Like to keep soldiers out of some city or whatever for a while, until the radiation—you know, like if the half-life is only a week or so, the—"

"Who'd do something like that? I mean around here."

"I don't know," I said, "maybe it's, I don't know, it's some sinister Dick Cheney-Carlisle-Halliburton-CIA-NSA-DIA-DHS crypto-sub-rosa-false-flag-invasion-pretext-conspiracy thing. Or at least, that's what I usually assume."

"What's DIA, you mean the airport?"

"That's the Defense—"

"So look," she interrupted, "if I got messed up or whatever . . . uh, you'll hang on to Max, right?"

"Of course I will," I said. "Jesus, what do you think I am, a complete lowlife? Don't answer that."

"And just keep my phone with you and the ES people'll come and get you when they can. And they'll know what to do and who else to call and everything."

"Okay. Is there a code word?"

"Sorry? Oh. No. They know about you. Just give them ID."

"Okay."

"Anyway, they may be here any minute. In the last message I got they said their ETA was nine twenty P.M."

"It's eleven now."

"I know."

I tried to think of something to say that was clever, mood-lightening, and relatively masculine, but I guess I'm not Bill Maher, because I couldn't. She went back to watching TV. I looked up polonium on CHEMnetBASE. It turned out that the half-life of the 210 isotope is only about 138.38 days, so it could presumably be used like an N-bomb, to clear people out of a base or a city that your army wanted to occupy later. 209 is less toxic, but it has a half-life of about a hundred and three years. So if you left a lot of it lying around someplace, nobody'd want to go there for a while. Okay, that's two numbers. What about the other one that kept coming up, 124,030?

Don't even think about it.

Cono. Dizzy. Fear. Fear—

The Net went down again.

Hell. I tried and retried. Nothing.

What's the point, anyway? We're probably all exposed to some degree. You just have to wait a while, just a very little while, and your legs will start feeling heavy, your hair will start to pull out when you comb it—

Dizzy. Okay. Sit.

The brain has chemical counterirritants to terror that, if you wait, will eventually kick in, and I think I got it back together without the wimmenfolk 'n' chilluns noticing.

By midnight it became clear that Max couldn't go another minute without food. There was some discussion about whether whatever we might stir up around here could be contaminated but the upshot was that I left the car to forage. About a quarter-mile behind us I found a still-occupied Dodge motor home and made the please-roll-down-your-window sign. The guy in the driver's seat shook his head. But he looked Mexican, which for me is good. I started telling him what I wanted, in lower-caste Spanish, and waving a thick wad of bills. Finally they decided I wouldn't go away. I made sure they were from Miami, and that they'd left from Miami, and that there wasn't anything in their truck from north of Miami. I bought one bag of Rancheritos, one of Pulparindos, and an armload of alternative beverages, all for eight hundred dollars.

Well, that worked okay, I thought as I walked back. The night was humid. You could smell the marine biomass starting to rot. Preview of coming repulsions. There were artilleryish rumblings on the landward side. Somewhere, pretty far away but not far enough, you could just hear shouting and breaking glass. Damn. I should have asked those guys if they had any old guns I could buy. Maybe I'll go back. Or look for a pickup with a bumper sticker that says IF YOU CAN READ THIS, YOU'RE IN RANGE. No problem.

By the time I got back to the Jeep I had a whole scenario planned. I'd find a truck with cleaning supplies in it, buy some duct tape, a mop handle, a cardboard tube, and a detergent bottle, tape them all together, and paint the thing with grease out of the axle so that it would pass for a twelve-gauge in the dark, and then I'd sit on the roof all night and when some gang of hoodla came up on the car I'd face them down with my stainless-steel gaze, and by morning Marena would be so in awe of my manliness that she'd be pawing at my *casa de pinga* practically in front of little Maxwell, and as soon—

"Jed, get in the car," Marena said through an inch of open window. She'd moved into the backseat and was holding Max. She popped open the passenger door. "I'm serious."

I got in. I handed over the loot. We waited. I let them convince me to have one Pulparindo and a little Inca Kola. No need to fill up. Defecation can be a big problem in situations like this, and one didn't want to get involved with it more than necessary, even if one was on a bridge. I said she should try to chill a bit because there was no way I was falling asleep, and in fact even on a normal day I wouldn't fall asleep at this hour and in this situation. She said okay. I went back to watching the dashscreen. At least we could still watch. Basically, no matter what's going on, most of the time all you could ever do was watch. But at least these days we can watch better. The CNN scroll said that the White House and the Defense Department were now considering the event to be a terrorist attack, "although as yet there are no credible claims of responsibility" and it was "not yet clear how the toxic material was dispersed." On CNN that same Dr. Quentin was responding to questions, saying how it was true that particles they'd found on samples from the No-Go Zone were isotopes of polonium, which was very rare and normally very expensive, "seemingly prohibitively expensive for a dispersal of this scale." Someone on the committee asked where the stuff had come from originally and she said they weren't sure yet but that it was likely that the isotopes were made in Russia before the collapse of the Soviet Union.

We sat.

Some people, of whom I am one, have brain chemistry that's gotten a little over-tweaked, and one side effect is that fear or anger or any large emotion comes and goes a little more abruptly, or jaggedly, than it does in neurotypi-cals. So I kept getting those unmotivated ups and downs in my fear level, in-tervals when your brain just shuts down on it and steers you toward something else. I'd catch myself thinking about the Codex or the Game or even just about the last nitrate reading in my Baja tank back home and then think how this couldn't be right, how I ought to be more upset than this, for others if not for myself, and then I'd go back to trying to calculate how long the natural gas in the generator tank could power the calcium skimmers. At some point I real-ized that Marena was singing to Max in Korean.

I listened. Hmm. This is actually kind of nice. *Chingalo*, I thought, I only met this woman once before today and already it felt like we'd been through more together than Lewis and Clark, Bonnie and Clyde, Kirk and Spock, and Siegfried and Roy, put together.

Max was quiet. I snuck a look back there. He'd curled up in his headware and, as children can, fallen asleep from stress. Marena's eyes were closed. I noticed she had a can of pepper spray in her left hand. Like that was going to do anything. Maybe I should move back there too. Offer a sturdy masculine shoulder. No, that's ridiculous.

I tried the Net again. Nothing. All we could get was radio off the aerial, like it was 1950. We'd been bombed back to the Milton Berle age. Still, news shows now had the benefit of nearly ubiquitous video recording, and people were still managing to get them to the stations. There were green grainy night-vision shots of feral kids prowling in flash packs, smashing store windows and torching cars and worse. A trio of well-brought-up, articulate children filmed themselves choking out good-byes in a burning house. There was a long video of a gang of Mexican kids partying in a Macy's in a deserted mall that had a really strange *Warriors*-like quality. Another popular piece of video—out of the few that made their way from blogs onto the networks—was one of a two-year-old girl trying to feed Milk Duds to her dead mother.

Somewhere outside, pretty far away—sound can carry for miles over the flat roads and shallow water—somebody was screaming in this unnatural, blood-curdlingly high voice, but luckily most normals can't do anything—even talk, or sleep, or watch their entire families and themselves die in agony—

without their favorite tunage in the background, so it was almost drowned out by the closer noise of two boom boxes, one playing Hip-Hop Countdown and the other looping that old stupid Pixies song about the monkey, *If man is five, if man is five,* over and over, *if man is five, then the Devil is six, then the Devil is six, then the Devil is six . . .*

(12)

The sky was the color of a TV set tuned to the Playboy Channel.

It's late, I thought. There'd been a banging sound somewhere.

What happened? I must have zoned out.

The boom boxes were still going. Seagulls squawked somewhere.

Okay. Get it together. Better—*BAMBAMBAMBAMBAMBAM*.

I jumped. My head sank up into the luxuriously padded roof. I swung around. A dark figure was knocking on the rear window. Marena was twisted around, too, holding her pathetic pepper-spray thing. Oh, hell, I thought. Looters. Rapists. Rednecks. *Deliverance*.

"What?" Marena yelled.

"Mom?" Max asked.

"I'm Major Ana Vergara from ES."

Slowly, the fear balloon in my abdomen started to deflate. Amazing, I thought. They actually showed up. You need a little more faith, Jed.

"We have to go," Marena said to Max. "Time to get you some breakfast."

We got together. We got out. The air smelled like rubber smoke.

"Do they have waffles on the boat?" Max asked.

The woman ignored him. "There are three of you, correct?" she asked. She was standing between the car and the railing, with her legs set apart in that officerish way. She was an unattractive Cynthia Rothrock type in a sort of SWAT-team-looking outfit with Wiley X sunglasses and deck boots, with a badge of some kind and a holstered Glock and a big ear-and-microphone rig. She didn't smile.

"That's right," Marena said.

I blinked around. There were buzzards drawing wide spirals about two hundred feet overhead. *Κυνεσσιν οιωνοισι,* I thought. Dogs and carrion birds. Farther up a few aircraft were still whining north. Out past the shallows to the southeast the sea had filled up with coast guard cutters and navy assets. On the landward side of the causeway, between us and the black pilings of the old railroad trestle, the water was almost calm and glazed with oil from the severed pipes. Well, that ought to kill what's left of the reefs in that direction, I thought. Still, the gulf was more beautiful than I'd ever seen it, maybe more beautiful at the moment of its death than it had ever been before, swirling with over- and underlapping skeins of wavy parallel lines in every color of an alien rainbow. All kinds of things were going by in the water that you didn't want to see any closer up, chunks of coral, boat hulls, house timbers, clumps of mangrove roots, tires, dead pelicans, two-by-fours, sections of vinyl siding, clusters of midscale lawn furniture, knots of sea grape, and then, without any special notice, I got a shiver of revulsion-slash-fear as a dead human floated into view, a fat lady, prone, with her head underwater and with her floral day dress pulled way up so that you could see these white support panties, which were only a little whiter than the flesh of her thighs. What happened? I wondered. Were they just throwing them into the water? Hell. I turned back to the ocean side. It was a little better, slicked with oil but with no corpses in evidence.

"Do any of you need immediate medical attention?" Vergara asked.

We said no. I noticed there were people milling around behind her. They were surprised, though. That is, she hadn't drawn a crowd. Somehow she'd come in on a motor launch and climbed up onto the causeway without attracting any attention. I turned around. People were coming toward us from the other direction, from downstream. They were almost jogging, like the zombies in *Dawn of the Dead,* except scarier because they weren't yet dead. Hmm. Better just go along with these guys, I thought. Better than hanging around here and getting barbecued by peckerwoods. I checked my stuff. Wallet, phone, passport. Ankle wallets. Jacket. Shoes. *Esta bien.*

Vergara herded us over to the guardrail. There was something attached to it with big aluminum hooks, like on a rope ladder. She looked around at the growing crowd. Already things had gotten a little bit tense. People were staring at us with narrowed eyes. A dried-up cowguy-looking character sidled over. He had a loose posse behind him who looked like they'd sleazed out of an S. E. Hinton novella.

"Hey, glowbug, where'd y'all get the duck boat?" he hissed.

"Back off, sir," Ms. Vergara said. "These people are being arrested. If you want to come along that can happen but we'll have to arrest and cuff you too. Understood?"

Cowguy seemed a little cowed. For a microsecond his eyes glanced at her gun. By the time he got it together to say something back, the moment had already passed. The thing on the railing turned out to be one of those collapsible chute rigs, like a preschool play tunnel, and we and our stuff all slid down right into the boat. It was an old twenty-foot GatorHide. There was just one guy at the tiller, idling the Yamaha silent motor. Up on the bridge Vergara detached the chute and rock-climbed down a piling into the launch. They put us into ballistic life jackets. We shoved off.

They motored us out to a forty-six-foot Bertram. Its bridge was done so that from a distance it would look like a coastal patrol boat. So this is how the top 0.01 percent evacuates, I thought. So to speak. I felt like Alphonse Rothschild clearing out of Vienna ahead of the Anschluss in a private train car. Apparently the boat had some sort of radio beacon coded to give it a pass, the same thing they use on diplomatic cars around the UN or getting senators out of bomb-threatened airports. It was like a Get Out of Hell Cheap card. I almost felt a little wrong about it. You know that the U.S. government is just another mafia, and that the Bush family's Saudi cronies all got spirited out after 9/11 and that after Khalid was arrested in Pakistan he got sprung out of prison and whisked to Guam by Blackwater thugs and whatever, but still, when you see the special treatment yourself, when you cash in on it, like we were doing, it still feels weird. Not to complain, though. We set off ESE for Andros.

The crew made sure I got out of my clothes and put them in a chromed boPET-film bag for analysis, decontamination, cleaning, pressing, and eventual return. They put me in a cabin with its own tiny shower and made sure I showered. I got into some oversized off-white and blue U.S. Naval Academy sweats, lay down on the narrow berth, and checked the Emergency Broadcast System on the little overhead screen. There was a map with dots and splotches scattered all over the Southeast and covering most of peninsular Florida. The voice-over was still just telling you where to go and what to do, without telling you why. I tried CNN.

". . . evacuated persons without vehicles are now being released from shelters and allowed to march," the voice-over was saying. A crawl at the top said the president had invoked the Insurrection Act, which gave military personnel domestic police powers, and that over five hundred thousand people had been displaced, and that they were estimating the death toll from rioting, fires, and explosions—of which our pipeline blast was only one of many—at 18,000. That sounds low, I thought. Then it said that the estimated number of all casualties from the Disney World Horror was over 30,000.

Hell, I thought. The thing is, all fortunate events are pretty much alike, but each big disaster is ghastly in its own way. This time there hadn't been any of the futuristic instantaneity of Oaxaca or the ancient blind rage of tsunamis or earthquakes. There wasn't any jaw-dropping pyrotechnic artistry like on 9/11. We—and I try not to use that pronoun, but I think we can justify it in this case—we'd thought we'd become connoisseurs of apocalypse, and then when a new thing actually happened, it's like everybody's totally unprepared. Blind-sided yet again.

Hell, I thought. I tried Bloomberg. The video area showed a warehouse floor with rows of bagged bodies covered with dry ice, so that there was this low-hanging fog all over like in some old Wolfman movie. The voice-over said emergency-room personnel were refusing to treat victims until they were able to do it in hazmat suits. Until then, some hospitals were opening up their supply rooms and trying to use teleconferencing to tell patients and their families how to treat themselves. At the bottom of the screen—you've got to love Bloomberg for this—the financials were still crawling along. U.S. trading was still suspended, but overseas, cyclic commodities were still jumping. I waited until corn came up. Hah. Another half a buck just today. Well, don't smirk about it, I thought. You're a carpetbagger, Jed. A terror profiteer. You should be ashamed of yourself . . .

I lost consciousness.

They woke me up in the harbor in Nichols Town. It was late afternoon. A Kiowa pontoon helicopter showed up and took us to a private airstrip at Fresh Creek, near the field station.

"How are you doing?" Marena asked over the earphones.

"I'm good," I said. "So, where are you going after this?"

"The firm—now they want to fly us down to the Stake, in Belize."

"What's the steak?" I asked.

"That's like a Mormon word."

"Oh, right. Stake." It meant a small missionary community, which, in the fullness of time, might grow into a Temple.

"It's mainly just a big sports resort Lindsay's working on," Marena said. "I think the religion thing's primarily for, like, taxes."

"Right."

"Anyway, speaking of that, I was thinking it would be really great if you came along."

"Oh . . . well, thanks." Damn it, I thought, I'm getting kidnapped. No, that's nonsense. Don't get paranoid.

"It'd be a good idea to keep up with what you're doing with Taro," she said. "Don't you think? I'm going to get this thing green-lighted."

"What thing?" I asked. "You're making another Maya movie?"

"No, no movie, I'm going to get Lindsay to give us more cash to research the Codex and, just, do whatever's necessary."

"You mean, like, necessary to save humanity and everything?"

"Well . . ."

"Why would Lindsay Warren want to do that? I mean . . . Look, I don't want to be difficult, and I don't want to put you guys down, but . . . I mean, don't big corporations usually *destroy* the planet? Or at least not save it?"

"Well, if he doesn't have a profit angle on something, he'll probably shift the funding to his personal foundation."

"Okay."

"But anyway, no, I think he thinks that saving the planet might be *immensely* profitable."

"Huh."

"Anyway, if you don't like it in Belize we'll fly you back. People are going to be coming back anyway."

Hmm. Quick decision time, I thought.

"Where is it in Belize?" I asked.

"It's, um, it's in the hills, it's west, I mean, southwest of uh, Belmopan."

"You know, I can't go into Guatemala," I said. "I have legal problems there."

"Who said anything about Guatemala?"

"Well . . ."

"Anyway, the border's closed, there's practically a war on between them and Belize."

"I know, but—look, it sounds like the place is very near the border, and, I mean, I don't want to be an ingrate and it's nice that you have confidence in me and all—"

"Don't do a soft sell on me," she said, "just try to get your lawyer on the phone and get her or him ready to look over the contract. Okay?"

"Okay, boss." Contract?

"See, that's the attitude we're looking for."

"Right, MP."

"Right."

There were two planes idling off on the grass. One was a chartered Cessna for Max. Somebody called Ashley$_3$—Marena's maid or executive domicile director or whatever—and this other guy who worked for her named José were on it to meet him. To me it all seemed a little lavish. Still, why ride alone? They were going to Kingston and then, if they were sure they wouldn't have a problem, back to the States. Max started climbing up the boarding stairs, stopped, came back, and handed something to me. "Here, you might need this," he said. It was a little blue fat robot figurine. It was sticky from his little hand.

"Oh, great," I said. "Gigantor. Thanks."

"No, it's Tetsujin 28."

"Oh. Right. Thanks."

"It's a purple laser pointer," he said.

"Oh. That's awesome, I've never owned one of these before."

They taxied around and took off. The other plane rolled up. It was a Piaggio Avanti, a twelve-seater double-prop with a canard foreplane on the nose that meant it had the uay of a hammerhead shark. It had a big Warren-logo wing flash and the letters WAS, for Warren AeroSpace, in a trademarked fluorescent green called Warren Emerald. This big gray craggy guy in a Don Ho shirt got out of it first and shook my hand. He didn't squeeze, but his hand felt like it knew exactly how to slide up your arm, give you a single debilitating finger chop to the axillary artery, and then twist your humerus out of its socket, and would prefer to.

"Jed, this is Grgur," Marena said.

"Nice to meet to you," he lied in what sounded like a Serbian accent without the humor.

I lied back that it was nice to meet to him too. Grr-Grr? I thought. What kind of cooked-up tough-guy moniker is that? His real name's probably Evander.

We climbed into the plane. I'd been picturing the cabin as a kind of a Led Zeppelin '74 tour Orgytrailer, but it was just a roomier cowhide-and-burled-elm-veneer version of any other plane, all done in bisque, greige, and mushroom with notes of ecru and off-taupe highlights. There were two other passengers already on the plane, a missionary-type guy with acne and a woman from Lotos Labs—which I guess the Warren Group also owned—

named Dr. Lisuarte. She was a little, dark, efficient lady with a fishing vest and hair that looked like it had been tied back in the same severe way since the twentieth century.

"I'm supposed to do a checkup on both of you," she said. I was about to object and then decided not to be a *cabrón*. What the hell. They strapped us in. They brought us food. We didn't talk. We took off. At three thousand feet the sun zapped up through the portholes for a minute or so and then it went down anyway. At eight thousand feet Lisuarte tapped me on the shoulder and took me back to what I guess was usually the galley. The plane had been done up for executive transport and not for emergencies, but they'd set up a whole little EMT facility in there, everything you'd have in an ambulance plus, it turned out, some extra stuff they'd loaded on just for me.

I sat down on a folding phlebotomy chair. Lisuarte did an embarrassingly full checkup that included going over my thyroid three times. The G-M tube she had was so sensitive that when she turned it vertically, it clicked at the smoke alarm in the ceiling and she had to reset it. I appeared to be clean. Well, that's one relief, I thought. Another hundred bits of good news like that and we'll be back in the game. She gave me potassium iodide tablets anyway, just in case. There was also a fluid-balance screen for edema and a bunch of heavy-metal tests, which normally you'd have to send to a special lab. I guess they'd moved a spectrometer onto the plane. And of course she insisted on running my arterial blood profile, too, probably just to show off her new self-guiding needle. When she put the analysis up on the screen it looked okay to me, but of course she wanted to tinker with it.

"We might as well bring your factor-eight up to twice normal," she said.

"Okay, um, thanks," I said.

"I've also got some O negative just in case. We'll have it in the fridge down at the Stake."

"Great," I said. "Or I can just drink it here."

"Say, you know, speaking of that, did you ever hear about the Lacandon blood profile?"

I shook my head.

"Well, we have a couple Lacandons on the animal relocation crew—you know, the Lacandon Indians? And they have this extra compound in their blood. It's a whole extra clotting factor nobody else has. Supposedly they used to define themselves partly by their ability to heal."

"Really?"

"Yes."

"Maybe I should try to mooch a few jars of the stuff."

"It doesn't work that way," she said.

"Hmm."

"I'm going to make up a special snakebite kit. And I want you to carry it on your person at all times." She started to explain to me about how rattlesnakes and Gila monsters and a few other critters have this stuff that makes you make extra thrombin, which is like the glue T-cells use, and how it can get in your brain and totally glog you up if you're already dosed up with extra clotting factors to begin with, but how on the other hand, if you're a bleeder and you overdo the antivenins you could turn into a human sponge and crash out, and it's a tricky balance. I kept nodding, trying to convey that I knew all that already.

"Anyway, why would I get bitten by anything?" I asked.

"It's still a construction site," she said. "There's still jungle around it. Last week a bunch of howler monkeys stole all the peanut butter out of the cafeteria. And a month ago a worker got a pretty bad snakebite."

"Like a *barba amarilla*?"

"Sorry?" she asked.

"A yellowbeard. A fer-de-lance. *Bothrops asperger,* uh, *asper.*"

"Oh. Yes, that's right. Hemorrhagic toxin."

"Yeah."

"Still," she said, "say you get tagged by a centipede or something exotic, I want you to ID it and reread the file and then run through the correct antigens in the kit, in order, before anyone even thinks about cutting the puncture. And if you do have to cut I want you to wait an hour and then quadruple the dose of the desmopressin. Of course, the main thing is for you to call me first if you can."

"Thanks," I mumbled, trying not to sound like an ingrate.

"You know not to take aspirin or anything."

"I don't even know what aspirin tastes like."

I started to go, but she made me sit back down. Just for a finishing touch, she jet-injected me with mefloquine, Ty21a, hepatitis A vaccine, and ten other kinds of snake oil, like I was setting out with Baron von Humboldt to find the source of the Amazon. When I got back to my seat my thighs ached like—like I don't know what. Something with very achy thighs. Like a Vegas hooker on the morning after the Fat Acceptance Movement Convention? Well, maybe, Jed. Work on it.

Complete physical indeed, I thought. Jed, you are such a pussy. Shoulda, coulda, and woulda just said no. *Chíngalo* insurance companies. Paranoids. Why don't they just seal me in a big polypropylene bubble and get it over with?

I looked out the porthole. Water. I looked over at Marena. She was sitting "next" to me, but the damn CEO-class seats were so spacious and plush and widely separated that it was like she was in a different time zone. Like me, she'd given up watching the same disaster coverage over and over, and now she was doodling on her phone. She looked back and asked if I was okay. I said yes.

"I guess you guys looked up my medical records," I said.

"Oh, yeah," she said. "Yeah, Lance did that. Sorry. I guess that's illegal."

"No, it's okay, I just, you know, it's not that easy to do. Is it?"

"For those guys that's nothing," she said. "If you asked them to find out Queen Elizabeth's IUD size they'd get it to you in ten minutes."

She went back to her drawing. I found a USB on the arm of my chair and plugged in my phone. A connection came up, but most of my friendly sites were down or unupdated. Bad sign, again. Bad sign. I put on—donned?—earphones and tried CNN.

"*. . . thanks, Alice. This is Alexander Marning at the CNN All-Media News Center in Atlanta, thanks for joining us,*" somebody whose name was Alexander Marning said. He paused. "*The Disney World Horror has certainly been the most difficult period in the Southeast for many decades and stirred emotions all over the world. But the disaster has taken an emotional toll not just on Florida residents . . . but also on the reporters covering the story. Brent Warshowsky joins us . . . with more. Brent?*"

Rather than meet Brent, I flipped to C-SPAN. DISNEY WORLD EVENT WAS SILENT "DIRTY BOMB," SAYS FEMA RESEARCHER, the caption said. That Octavia Quentin person was on again, testifying, in front of a Senate committee this time. She was moving up in the world.

"*. . . forensics that release time was roughly noon on the twenty-eighth,*" she said. "And it's true that for a while the particles were airborne, but they're very heavy and because of the special coating they are also fairly sticky. So despite the high radioactivity in the No-Go Zone, we project there will be very little windblown particles—very little in the way of windblown particles in the months to come."

"But there will be particles in water runoff, is that correct?" a voice that sounded like Dianne Feinstein's asked.

"Yes, that is correct," Quentin said, "as far as the lake watershed goes, there is widespread—"

This is bumming me out, I thought. I clicked off and risked another glance at Marena. She was still scribbling on her phone. I leaned over and snuck a peek at the screen. She was sketching on an elaborate architectural fantasia with reflecting pools and an ornate round pyramid in the background. After mapping the pyramid with red and pink stripes, she seemed to become frustrated and started on a line of naked pilgrims riding across the foreground on giant flightless birds like dyatrimas. She looked over at me.

"Sorry," I said. "I shouldn't snoop, I got—"

"It's okay," she said, a little too loudly. She pulled off her headphones.

"Your drawing skills are really great." Did that sound too flip for conditions? After a major tragedy, how long do you have to wait before you can smile? Other people seem to have an instinct for that sort of thing and I never do. It's like I'm always laughing at a funeral. Or dying at a party.

"Oh, thanks," Marena said in a shrugging tone.

"No, seriously. Is that a set for Neo-Teo II?"

"Yep."

"It's so weird that you're an actual artist."

"Why is that weird?"

"Well, no, it's not weird, it's just, you know—"

"What?"

"Just, how'd you get interested in this?"

"In what? In the Sacrifice Game stuff?"

"Yeah."

"I've always been into games."

"Hmm."

"And you know, Lindsay's been funding Taro forever," she said. "And then when Neo-Teo did well, Lindsay thought I should look at some of the other game-related stuff they were into."

"Okay, but, the Sacrifice Game is not entertainment."

"Well, no, but it could become part of something like entertainment. Or you might say, something like entertainment could be, it could become a way to implement—or, like realize, something like the Sacrifice Game."

"You're getting a little ahead of me," I said.

"Well, look," she said. "My feeling about it—history goes through different stages. Right? From the eighteenth century the world's dominant paradigm went from a religion thing to a science thing. Right? And now in the twenty-first century I think it's shifting to a game thing."

"Okay."

"Games are kind of a third category. They're between art and science. But they're not just a mixture of them either."

"That sounds right," I said. "I mean, I'm big on games myself—"

"Sure. But what I'm getting at is, there's all these people out there now, and they're playing games all the time. To the exclusion of almost anything else."

"Yeah, that's true. That's good for you guys, though, isn't it?"

"Oh, sure. But the thing is, I kind of think there's a reason for that."

"Like what?"

"Like—well, maybe this sounds kind of girly and spiritual . . ."

"No, no—"

"Just that, doesn't it seem to you that a lot of these people are playing these games almost, I don't know, desperately?"

"Like how?"

"Just, really intensely and with a big sense of urgency."

"I don't know. But I've always played a lot of games, so I may not be the right person to ask—"

"Just that they're all kind of looking for something," she said. "Or another way of putting it is that a lot of other things, other media or activities or jobs or whatever, they're all starting to seem obsolete. People intuitively know that the games are the future. In fact maybe they're going to be the whole future. The whole social future, anyway. The whole human future."

"Hmm. I'm not sure about that one."

"Okay, maybe not, but I feel like—I feel like all the stuff I design, even when it's kind of tacky and violent like Neo-Teo, I still think I'm at least heading in the right direction. I'm still in the Utopia business. Or is this not making any sense? Sorry, I'm just blathering—"

"No, no," I said, "no blather, no, it sounds good to me—"

"That's why Taro's stuff is exciting, it's, like, it's trying to find out what, just, what it is about games."

"Well, I guess so," I said. "That's great. Maybe you should learn to play the Sacrifice Game."

"I'd like to. Especially now that I have all this free time."

"Sorry? You do?"

"I'm kidding," she said.

"Well, I'll teach you anyway."

"Great, it's a date." She closed her phone and her eyes and leaned back.

Go ahead, my inner Cary Grant said. *Kiss her.*

I can't, I thought back at him. It's in bad taste. All these people just got dead.

Do it anyway, he said. *She wants it.*

Sorry, I thought. I just can't get it together.

You wuss, Cary said. He vanished in a puff of Lucky Strike smoke.

Hell.

Just to do something, I tried the camera backups in my house for the 192nd time. It shocked me a little when I got through.

The reactors and filters and protein skimmers had failed, one by one, between Wednesday and Thursday, but the cameras had kept running on their array of UPS backups. I watched them all suffocate and die: the *Nembrotha* colony I'd collected in Luzon and, tentatively, was planning to name if I proved it wasn't a *chamberlaini,* the *Chromodoris* with their emerald stripes along the notum and glowing orange highlights on their rabbity heads, and the Spanish shawls with their yellow and ultraviolet bands, locomoting like tiny concertinas over the dead-man's-fingers coral, all dissolved into shit-tan sludge. *Todo por mi culpa.* I'll admit it, I cried, but not so anybody could see or hear. Crying is cheap. Crying's what tween pop stars do on TV in the daytime. Through the porthole behind Marena's ear I could just see the Belize coastline, black against the blue, with double dots of headlights moving through the Southern Highway like bubbles through IV tubes.

(13)

We flew west over More Tomorrow and the Valley of Peace—both were hopefully named refugee resettlement zones—and then turned south, toward the Maya Mountains. Marena talked on her ear. I sulked.

"Hey, there is a scrap of good news," she said, finally, to me.

"Really?"

"Taro and Tony and Larry Boyle—well, you don't know Larry—but anyway they flew Taro down this morning and he's fine."

"That's great," I said.

The captain PAed that we were landing in two minutes. We came up on a big circular area dotted with electric lights and cooking fires.

Warren Development had built two compounds in a wide plateau. It was about fifteen miles south of the ruins of Caracol and only four miles from the Guatemalan border. The sports complex site was 2,010 and a half glorious acres of freshly leveled cloud forest, perfectly circular, with a gigantic one-mile-diameter racetrack—which Marena said had a convertible surface that could accommodate horses, feet, Sleekers, or automobiles—forming the outer boundary.

"So, look, why are we circling?" Marena asked.

"Sorry?" I asked. "Oh." She was talking to the pilot through her ear thing. She paused, listening.

"Ears off," she said. She turned to me. "He says the air traffic control observer is checking on us. Like we're a typhus ship."

"Hmm. Damn."

"Yeah."

We dropped down to two thousand feet. At the center of the circle the main stadium—or Hyperbowl, as they called it—rose out of the black jungle.

It was a gargantuan loaf of electrochromic glass that looked almost finished under its web of scaffolding, raked by halite floodlights and spangled with blue sparks from the arc welders.

"All this will have to be redone for the Paralympic Games," Marena said. She was chewing something. "You know, the Special Olympics? That's six years from now." *If the world even exists two years then,* we both thought. "It's more than just a lot of ramps, they have to build special courts and put in giant Siamese Port-O-Lets and whatever."

"I thought this whole planet was the Special Olympics."

She said the deal was that eight years ago, as part of Belize's bid for the XXXIIIrd Summer Olympiad, the Warren Group offered to build a self-contained facility sixty miles inland from the capital in order to avoid the city's poverty and transportation problems.

"The joke is that they had to let Belize host one because they never win anything and won't, until they make drinking rum an Olympic event," she said. "You want some nicotine gum?"

"Oh, no, thanks, I'll stick with Vicodin for now—"

"So after the games we're going to convert the field-event grounds to golf courses and take over running the complex as a destination resort and themed community featuring Maya-style motifs and Neo-Teo-related activities, with a jaguar habitat, a state-of-the-art geothermal plant with a volcano-like steam fountain, and a subsidized population of over ten thousand local Maya craftspersons."

"I bet you could say that backward," I said.

"No, but I bet you can."

"Well, yeah, I guess I can."

"Yeah? Show me."

"Snos, repst, farc, nayam," I said. "Um, lacold, nas—"

"Okay, you've made your point," she said. "There's the shop."

The pilot had turned and was flying low across a straight asphalted road that led to the Stake, or as I should say, the Stake™, a mile and a half outside the Olympics complex.

The tires engaged the earth. We slowed, turned, taxied, and stopped. We waited. The door opened. There was the usual slap of choking nostalgia as I sucked in the first lungfuls of Central American aeroplankton. Plus the heady aromas of horses and wet concrete, with maybe a top note of ozone. We disembarked. There were seven people waiting for us on the tarmac in the sharp white light.

Two of them were Warren security guards in green outfits, and there was a Belizean inspector in his white short-sleeved shirt who checked everyone's papers. Then there were two so-called Stake elders—who were only in their thirties—who seemed to be the place's official greeters. One of them wore a sweatshirt with a picture of a robed guy with a wizard staff silhouetted against a big setting sun. "Moroni, 421 BC," it said in Papyrus Bold. "Last of the Good Guys®." They asked if we were all right and if our "people" were all right. My people haven't been all right for over five hundred years, I wanted to say. They all crunched my hand. It's times like these, I thought, that make me glad I'm left-handed. Finally, we were introduced to two tall burly agents from the U.S. Department of Homeland Security.

Great, I thought. Here we go. Back to *el bote*. Did I mention how I'd been in jail for eight days in Guatemala, in '01? Amazingly, though, all the two big guys did was take a little extra time making sure who we were. One of them scanned our passports and took pictures of us with his phone and waited for a response from his demonic overlords in their secret crypt under the Pentagon. They asked us whether we were planning to leave the construction site and we said no. They asked us if we could check in by phone at noon. We said sure. It was like being on parole. They set up an appointment with Marena for the next morning. I just stood there the way I do when I'm pretending to be foggy on English. They looked at me funny, but everyone looks funny at me. They didn't tell us why they were keeping an eye on us, but of course we were Persons of Interest in the Disney World attack.

"Here, let me start you out on these," the elder elder, the one without the sweatshirt, said. He gave Marena a live badge and helped her clip it on her jacket. For a second it looked like he was giving her a corsage for the prom. He gave me one and let me put it on myself. It had a bright scrolling green dot and a toothy alligator clip. Unsettlingly, it already had my picture on it, the one from the *Strategy Magazine* Web site that I'd made them take down years ago. Next he gave each of us a phone card.

"There's also a password for the LAN on there," he said. "You can use your telephone or any handheld browsing device to find where you all are on the map, contact Stake personnel, access schedules of Stake activity, Freaky Friday timetable, meal times, and other useful information."

"Thanks," Marena said.

"However," he said, "if you remove the badge, your head will explode." Sorry, just kidding. He didn't really say that. All he said was "No problem."

They led us east, away from the sports complex. The officials walked back ahead of us in that clompy proud-to-be-a-robot way. On each step my heels sunk a few millimeters into the heat-retaining asphalt. Grgur asked to carry my backpack, but I said it was there to cover my hump, so he took Marena's two little bags and walked about fifty feet ahead of us. We followed through a cluster of Quonset huts and prefab hangars. Invisible moths brushed our ears on their way to cremation in the tungsten work-lights.

"Hey, Jed?" Marena asked.

"Yeah?"

"Do you know why those donkeys have that pink spooge all over their legs?"

"Uh, yeah."

"So, why?"

"Well, you see how skinny they are, right?"

"Yeah."

"The deal is that vampire bats go for the ankles," I said. "Or hocks or shanks or whatever. And they tend to attack the same victims night after night. So the burro's owners paint on that pink stuff, and it has an anticoagulant in it. And it's mainly the male bats who hunt. So the daddy bats drink all this blood with the goo in it, and then they fly back to their wives and children. And the women and baby bats all hang upside down together in this big cluster, like a bunch of grapes. Right?"

"Uh-huh."

"And the male bat hangs at the apex of the cluster and regurgitates the blood for them and they all drink it. And then the baby ones are really fragile and they hemorrhage from the anticoagulant and die."

"You know, I'm not just sorry I asked," she said. "I'm sorry I was ever born."

"Sorry."

The main compound had two eight-foot chain-link fences around it, with a twenty-foot space between them and a little corridor between the gates so we wouldn't have to deal with the dogs that patrolled the no-man's zone. A few of them came up to give us the evil eye. They were big Nazi Shepherds, half cyborgized with little head-mounted cameras and chrome teeth. On the other side of the fence we came into a big military-style quadrangle of wide one-story prefab buildings with floodlights mounted at each corner of their low-angled zinc roofs. Someone of vision had cut down a three-hundred-year-old Spanish cedar, trimmed it into a neat cone, stuck it in a hole full of concrete next to the flagpole in the center of the square, and wrapped it in a net of about ten thousand twinkling green and pink LEDs. It was the most tasteful thing in the place. A pair of missionaries sleazed by, walking their bicycles. Christianity, I thought. Eradicating more interesting religions for over two thousand years. Ahead of us, on the far side of the quadrangle, Elder Beaver had reached our building and was having trouble getting its door open. Grgur parked the suitcases and started giving him his opinion on how to sweep or swipe the keycard through the thingie.

"See, check this out," I said to Marena. I squeezed the WIDE button on Max's laser pointer and waved the beam up over the nearest floodlight. It carved a violet cross section of whorls of insect life and a few big flickering masses.

"Those are bats," I said. "I mean, insectivorous bats, not—"

Marena winced. "If I want to wake up screaming tonight I'll watch C-SPAN."

"Sorry." I narrowed the laser to a dot, brought it down the wall in front of us, and eased it into the center of the still-closed door, right across Grgur's field of vision. You could barely even see him duck and run; it was more like he just vanished behind the far corner of the building.

Damn, I thought. Those are some expensive reflexes you've got there. Spetsnaz training? I pretended not to notice and kept playing with the pointer, drawing a circle on the ground. He came back, breathing a little heavily and with his right hand behind his back. He hiked his pants as, out of our sight lines, he reholstered his piece.

"Are you okay?" Marena asked him.

"Yes," he gurgled. I tried to play dumb, looking at Marena to avoid Grgur's eyes, but of course he knew, and I knew he knew, and he knew I knew, et cetera. Good going, Jed. Now he really has it in for you. Brilliant.

The door opened and we went through into a rush of processed air product with notes of freon and fresh drywall. We passed a lockout/tagout station emblazoned with the legend PRECAUCIÓN/SE PROHIBE LA ENTRADA SIN PERMISO and squeaked down a long hallway with flickering fluorescent lighting and No Trax SuperScraper matting spotted with rusty red mud.

"... no, thanks," Marena was saying to A_1. "What I really need is to get in to see Lindsay for five minutes."

"He may be too devastated to talk right now," Elder Junior said. "He was glad you got here, though."

"And you know Taro Mora is here, right?" A_1 said. "And the SSC's running. And we got you your old room."

Marena said yes, thanks. Someone handed me a keycard and steered me into my cell. Sorry. Room. Marena said she'd call me in a few minutes. They closed the door on me. The room was done up as though it were a real would-be-upscale hotel room, with a single *Cypripedium* orchid in a glass tube and a folded cardboard wedge thingie that informed me that the hospitality services were administered by Marriott Corporate Retreats International, that the Finn's Café Restaurant was not yet operational but that breakfast would be served in the Food Court from seven to ten, that the entire area was smoke-free, and that a nurse and a spiritual advisor were on call twenty-four hours a day. Finally, it asked whether, instead of an ordinary wake-up call, I would like to be awakened by an inspirational message. Oh, no, thank you, I thought. I'd rather be awakened by André the Giant pouring a gallon of iced Clorox on my face and kneeing me in the gonads. I prowled around a bit the way one does in hotel rooms. There was a bathroom with lots of sham-luxury amenities but, of course, no condoms. There was the usual Book of Mormon in a drawer. There was a fan of travel brochures on the dresser top. The top one was headlined "Guatemalan Adventures" and featured a picture of a Maya babe in quaint native garb, with a hey-Joe-you-got-nylons expression, standing in front of Stela 16 from Tikal. *"You may choose to visit the Mayans in stone . . . or in person,"* the copy said. *"Visit Guatemala, Land of Mystery."* Sweet, I thought. You may choose to exterminate the Maya with stones . . . or in prisons. Visit Guatemala, Land of Sorrow. *Dominio de Desesperanza.*

I sat down on the bed, got my phone onto the LAN, and found the You Are Here map. I typed in MARENA PARK and a blue dot appeared not far from my own little red dot. I zoomed in. Just down the hall, it looked like. I left the room and followed the dot. There was televisionish sound coming from a bright but deserted-looking break room, and I went in. It smelled like an office, which is to say it smelled pretty much like Comme des Garçons Odeur 53 but without the glamour. Plus a dash of instant coffee. On my phone the blue dot was practically on top of the amber one. Hmm. There was a henge of upscale vending machines in the center of the room. I went up to one, swiped a debit card through the little vagina—wow, currency still works, I thought—and got two bags of Jelly Bellies.

". . . toll on the reporters covering the story," some guy on the TV said. I edged around the machines. On the other side, Marena, Taro, and a few other people were sitting or slouching around three sides of a big oval table, watching a big TV on a sort of easel. The white Formica tabletop was scattered with

snack food, cups of liquid, and an assortment of the latest personal communications technology.

Hi, come over, Marena waved.

I came over. *"Brent Warshowsky joins us . . . with more,"* the TV went on. *"Brent?"*

"Thanks, Alexander," Brent said. *"Reporters in crisis: Are they getting too* **close** *to their subject?"*

I walked past Taro and silently said hi to him. He grasped my arm for a minute, definitely actually glad to see me.

Setzen dich down here on my left, Marena pointed. I did.

"I'm talking with Anne-Marie García-McCarthy of Miami's WSVN TV," Brent went on. The crawl at the bottom of the screen said SPECIAL ACTION SEGMENT: HOW REPORTERS COPE WITH DISASTER. *"Earlier today, she conducted an emotional interview with a distraught man in Overtown . . . who lost his wife in the tragedy."*

"How are you doing, sir?" Anne-Marie asked. The guy said something but he was crying and I couldn't hear what it was.

"And where is your home?" she asked.

"It's gone, my wife and I were, and we try to get out, and, uh, and, uh, the fire came . . ."

"And who's with you now?"

"Nobody."

"And where is your wife now?"

"Nobody there."

"Where is your wife now?"

"She not here. She gone."

"You can't find your wife?"

"I, I tried, I tried to hold her hand, and she on fire, and it's too hot, in there, I can't hold her. She said go on, you take care of the kids. And the grandkids . . ."

"Okay, sir, what's your wife's name in case we can put this out there?"

"There no point, she gone."

"And what's your wife's name?"

"Lakerisha."

"And what's your name?"

"JC Calhoun."

"Well, just in case rescue workers find a Lakerisha Calhoun—"

"There no point, she gone. She all burned up. She was my little . . . she all burned up . . ."

"Reporters face a difficult and emotional balancing act," Brent's voice said. *"Anne-Marie, thanks for joining us tonight. Now, confronting situations like this—here just now we were watching you, Anne-Marie, out on the front lines, and—"*

"Could you kill the sound on that?" Marena said. Someone did. "Thanks."

We all looked at each other in the fresh silence.

"Sorry," I said. "I'm interrupting. I was just seeing if they had any Peeps yet."

"No, stick around," Marena said. "There's no news on the news anyway."

"Okay."

"You've met Laurence Boyle," she said, "right?"

He said hello. He was that elder from the airstrip. Probably she'd tried to introduce me to him and I'd somehow missed it, the way I do.

"Laurence is the VP of R and D for Warren Research," Marena said. "And you know Taro and Tony."

We all said hi and that it was good we were okay. Taro looked tired. Sic looked absurdly healthy.

"And this is Michael Weiner." She indicated a mountain of flesh on her right side.

"Good to meet you," he said in his deep New Zealander public-speaking-coached voice. They say TV adds twenty pounds, but in his case it seemed to have taken a hundred pounds off. He was huge. He looked like that new-age health guy, Andrew Weil, with that same sort of humungo beard and big shiny pate, like his head was upside down. Well, at least he has a look, I thought. He stretched his foreleg across Marena's chest and crushed my thankfully expendable hand.

"Okay," Marena said. "What were you saying, Taro?"

Taro usually paused for a moment before he spoke, and he did this time. But instead of waiting, Michael Weiner broke in ahead of him.

"Doom Soon," Michael Weiner said. "Crossbow effect."

(14)

"Right," Marena said.

"Sorry, I still don't get what those are," Laurence Boyle said.

"Taro was saying that—"

"Hang on," Boyle said. He was stylusing at his phone. "Listen, I'm going to start recording again for a transcript for Elder Lindsay. Just in case anybody thinks of something. Is that all right with everyone?"

Everybody nodded. "Okay, everybody please speak clearly. And I'll make sure he plays it into his good ear." As is the custom in the U.S., he laughed heartily at his own nonjoke. "And watch the profanity, okay?" He touched his phone. "All right, we're on. Okay. What was that about again?"

"The idea is that the crossbow effect enables the Doom Sooners—what do you guys call them?" Michael asked.

"Doomsters," Taro said.

"Right, and that whoever did it, he may have thought he was going to destroy the whole human species," Weiner said. "And the theory is that whoever engineered the polonium dispersal may not have been just one person, but they probably aren't a lot of people or they'd have already have been identified."

"Yeah," Marena said, "the doomster thing—the point is that there are more and more people like that."

"More and more people like what?" Boyle asked.

"That is, more and more people who have both a desire to cause a lot of damage and the means to cause a lot of damage," she said. "It's Taro's idea."

"No, thank you, but no," Taro said. "It is not my idea. The doomster issue is an increasingly common problem in the field of catastrophe modeling."

"Well, okay, then," Boyle said, watching the computer transcript read out on his phone. "Professor Mora, can you briefly tell us what it's about?"

Taro paused.

"Here, have this one," Marena whispered to me. "I haven't touched it." She slid a cardboard mug of stuff into my zone of the table.

"Well, a potential doomster," Taro said, "that is someone who would like to kill everyone on earth, including himself. An actual doomster would be one of these people who finds the means to do this."

"Okay," Boyle said, "but there can't be many people who are that crazy."

"Well, there have been similar attempts," Taro said. His voice was getting stronger as he went into lecture-hall mode. "In Pakistan, twice, and then in Oaxaca. And there were other incidents during the Cold War, and probably several we do not know about."

"Maybe," Boyle said.

"But the issue is not exactly whether there are, say, ten people who are that crazy, or ten thousand. The problem is that at some point, one of those people will acquire the means to carry out his desire. And according to the crossbow effect, this will happen sooner rather than later."

"You'd better explain that term again too," Marena said.

"Excuse me?" Taro asked.

"The crossbow effect."

"Oh," he said. "Yes. In, in I think 1139, the Lateran Council tried to outlaw crossbows because they said they'd lead to, say, the end of civilization. Because now an ordinary soldier could kill an armored knight on horseback."

"But then crossbows actually didn't cause much of anything," Marena said.

"No," Taro said. "And then later, in the 1960s, munitions manufacturers used to cite that example to say how people should not worry so much about nuclear weapons."

"Okay," Boyle said.

"However, crossbows only killed one person at a time," Taro said. "And per shot, they were quite expensive for the period. Nuclear weapons killed many people, with much less cost per death. Say a few dollars per person. But they were still quite expensive. Now, today, however, we have many types of weapons that are devastating and cheap. And easy to manufacture. This is what happened in Iraq. The war games the U.S. used to plan the occupation did not reckon with that technology, that is, plastic explosives, even dynamite was coming into the hands of so many people. The Pentagon was using older models, from the days when plastic explosives were expensive. And they were hard to get. But by the 2000s, C4 was very cheap and easily available. So a single attacker could kill many people and do millions of dollars of damage for a moderate cost. Another way you could put it is that the massive democratization of the technology intersected with a growing population of potential users. That is, suicide bombers."

"Okay, maybe," Boyle said. "But they never manage to destroy *everything*. And besides, there can't be many people who want to do something like that."

Taro paused. I sipped at the stuff in the mug. It was freeze-dried and flash-reanimated green tea with tapioca balls. Kiddie drinks. Whatevs.

"Almost anyone has experienced a moment in their life when they are angry enough to want to end everything," Taro said. "According to most current models, at some point in the near future, someone who is, say, a little less tightly wrapped, and a little more technically savvy, will feel that way, and he will bring it off."

"And when'll that be?" Boyle asked.

"Well, you can graph it," Taro said. He started sketching on his phone. "In fact, you can even simplify it to just three main vectors. Okay. The thick line, *a*, that is the spread of access to technology. This is derived from a basket of subvariables. Like the rate of growth of the Internet and the rate at which things like explosives or viral vaccine lab setups were declining in price. And then the thin line, *p*, is the number of people that you could consider under stress. That is, at risk of extreme personal radicalization. Doomsters. And the third is *e*. That is the dotted line. It represents growing prevention efforts by the DHS and other police and antiterrorism agencies worldwide."

He ported the drawing over to the other screens. Marena showed me hers:

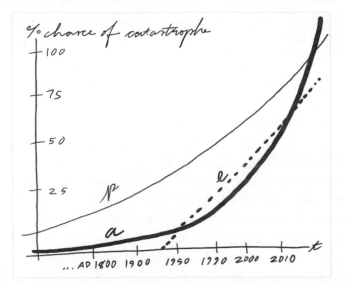

"This is a little mathy for me," Boyle said. Moron, I thought.

"One of the reasons p is so steep is because it includes internal feedback. Because of competition. You know how people who go into malls and offices and schools and wherever to shoot people, how lately they are competing with each other for larger and larger body counts? Of course, this is partly because now there are Web sites devoted to keeping score of this. But the point is that it creates a positive-feedback loop. People imitate former successes. And when they see something spectacular, say 9/11, they are inspired to try to top it. So you can chart the rate of growth of the doomster meme, if you like."

"So what you're saying is it's basically fashion," Marena said. "Like the way, you know, serial killer was the big power profession in the 1990s, and then the thing to be in the zeros was a terrorist, and now the big deal is to be a doomster and take everybody down with you."

"Wait a minute," Michael Weiner said. "How many people actually want to destroy everything?"

"That's right," Boyle said. "Do you really think people are capable of that?"

"Well, sure," Marena said, "plenty of people are."

"Many people have indeed expressed this wish," Taro said. "And not all of them are in mental institutions or in prison."

"Twenty years ago the cool thing was writing computer viruses," Marena said. "Now it's writing biological ones."

"So today anyone with even the equivalent of an undergraduate degree in biochemistry and a five-thousand-dollar home lab could probably create a system that could kill off all humans," Taro said. "And there are over fifty million people worldwide with that level of knowledge; at least a few of them will want to do just that."

"Well, screw me dead," Michael Weiner said.

"So the deal is, it used to take a mad scientist," Marena said. "Now you just need a mad biology major." She was feeding catchy phrases into the transcript so that Lindsay or whoever could use them at board meetings or whatever.

"You could say that," Taro said. "Or another way to look at it is, imagine that you gave every single person in the world a doomsday bomb. It is quite certain that somebody would set his off within a few minutes. In fact, many people would probably be rushing to do it because each of them would want to be sure to be the one. And even allowing for more uncertainty than is necessary, these curves still converge on a point close to now. Or even more probably in a few months from now—"

"And that's right around the Maya ending date," Marena said.

"Yes. Although it is approximate, of course, in terms of exactly when the event will happen. But it is utterly convincing statistically. That is, it will happen, and within a fairly short time."

"But there are people trying to stop these guys," Boyle said.

"Yes," Taro said, "that is the e curve. As you can see, it does not cross either of the others before they intersect."

"So what we need to do is raise the e curve," Marena said. She'd torn the sides of her paper teacup into a long, precisely spiraled coil on which the circular base bobbed gently up and down.

"We or somebody," Taro said. "Yes. Sharply."

No one said anything for a second. I tore open one of the Jelly Belly packs, THE ORIGINAL GOURMET JELLY BEAN, it said. TROPICAL FRUIT BLEND. I ate three Bellies, started feeling selfish, and dumped the rest of them out on the table. They were irregular spheroids in assorted jewel tones.

"Anyone want some?" I asked.

No one did.

"Well, thanks for your input," Boyle said. "But I need to just put in here, what everybody's going to say to this is, there's always been folks hollering about how the sky's falling. And they're always wrong. People are always saying it's the end of the world. They said the atomic bomb would be the end of the world. People said the year 2000 was going to be the end of the world. They said that accelerator blast in Mexico had created a, a little black hole at the center of the earth, and that *that* was going to be the end of the world."

He looked around the table. Nobody said anything.

Well, that was a little odd, I thought. I wouldn't have expected this Boyle guy to be the one to object, just because he was such a Peter Priesthood. Generally, LDS types are a pretty credulous lot. They always think the end of the world is right around the corner. Now the dude was getting all skeptical. Well, maybe I was stereotyping again. Marena opened her mouth and then stopped herself. I had the feeling she'd been about to say something along the lines of "Stuff it, hayseed, you're out of your depth." I decided to lighten the mood.

"Let's not use that term," I said. "It's derogatory. Let's just call it a 'hole of color.'"

Nobody laughed. Or smiled, or anything. I'm an idiot, I thought.

Taro spoke up. "Well, yes. Various people have been telling everyone how the world is about to end, for a long time. And so far, as far as we know the world has not ended. But that is the fallacy of induction. You cannot—"

"Could you explain that term?" Marena put in.

"That is, it is like Russell's chicken," he said. "You have simply to ignore an argument that—"

"Sorry, you'd better tell the record what the chicken is," Marena said.

"Oh," Taro said. "Yes. Bertrand Russell tells the story of a chicken who believes that the farmer is his friend. After all, the farmer has fed the chicken every day of his life and has never done him any harm. The chicken believes the farmer will go on doing what he has done in the past. However . . . one day the farmer comes in and instead of feeding him, he chops his head off. The point is that induction is often false logic."

"I'm not sure I or the board am going to get that," Boyle said.

There was a pause. I looked back at Marena. Her eyes caught mine for a second. *Dammit,* they said. *This Boyle bastard's trying to shoot us down. He doesn't want this project to go through, probably because it's taking budget away from his own bullshit division, so he tagged along and now he's trying to get us to say something stupid or too optimistic or whatever, and when we do, then he's going to go running back to Lindsay and spray poison in his ear.*

We looked back at Boyle. He started to say something, but Marena interrupted him.

"Look," she said. "There's always some nutcase who's been talking about how a big meteor's going to hit the earth like, tomorrow. And so far it hasn't happened. Lately. But if you looked up and saw a big giant meteor coming down, you wouldn't say it couldn't hit us just because all those nutcases jumped the gun. Right?"

"Correct," Taro said. "We need to evaluate the current world situation based only on its merits and not on what other people have said over the years. For instance, another piece of evidence is that we do not find any sign of extraterrestrial civilizations, despite odds in favor of their developing. Quite probably, they all blow themselves up when they get to roughly this stage of technological development."

Another icky pause manifested itself.

"Hey, look at what you did," Marena said. I realized she was talking to me.

"What?" I asked.

"They're all organized." She tapped on the table. "Check this out," she said to everybody but me.

I looked down. It was true, I'd arranged the Jelly Bellies in a wide grid, lining them up by color and pattern and, in the case of duplicates, by size.

"Oh, my heck," Boyle said.

"Oh. Yeah," I said. "They were messy. They were bugging me." I swept the shits off the table and into my hand. "Sorry."

"And one of the best arguments in favor of Doom Soon," Taro said—going on with his thoughts, as he did—"is simply that we are not encountering any time travelers from the future."

"Isn't that because of the Novikov thing?" Boyle asked.

"Well, maybe tha—" Marena broke in.

"No," Taro said, stopping Marena in midword. "No, that does not apply to us in the present anyway. The most likely reason that there are no visitors from the future is simply because there is no future."

(15)

Eleven hours later LEON was back online—it wasn't quite clear who was protecting the facility at UCF, or whether it had its own generator, or whatever, but he was back—and Taro, Taro's assistant Ashley₂, Tony Sic, three of Taro's other student adders-in-training, and I were all in Taro's make-shift lab at the Stake. It was really just a collection of brand-new Knoll open-plan cubicles, eye-popping new Sony monitors, and spanking-new Aeron ergosphere chairs, many of them still at least half stretch-wrapped, all hastily clustered in a big basement rehearsal hall under the Stake's Tabernacle Audi-torium Complex. In the sound of the keys clicking you could almost hear the panic.

Laurence Boyle had wanted us to put all our energy into finding "Dr. X," the presumed mastermind behind the Disney World Horror. "If you track them down, we'll get a lot more funding for the next phase," he'd said, al-though it wasn't clear to me what the next phase was. But Taro and I guessed some other people behind the scenes had convinced Boyle that the best play-ers should move right to the Doomster—that is, to whoever was going to create whatever was going to happen on December 21.

At this point Taro had said—he'd even given a little pep talk, in his under-stated way—we had to assume the Codex was correct. There would be what he called a "dire event" on the twenty-first, and if preventing it was even pos-sible, we had to move now. We needed to be detectives ahead of the fact. It felt to me like we'd somehow reached the absolute zero of the murder mys-tery genre—that is, we had to catch someone who hadn't done anything yet, who hadn't left any clues, and who could be anybody on the planet.

And not only that, but we couldn't just start looking for him—naturally, I thought of him as a him, although I tried to keep an open mind—without first working out a way of looking for him. To oversimplify, we basically had to write a program that would allow us to sift through the dataverse and, somehow, spot the Doomster.

All of us players were using Sacrifice Game 3.2, a new version of the software that had been updated with data from the Orlando attack. Each of us was trying to play through the second-to-last date, the Disney date, and get to the same final position, the one that ended 357 days from now, on 4 Ahau. We were trying to crunch massive strings of digital data—mainly lists of millions of names, addresses, and occupations—through the Game's 260-square grid. Each of us also had at least one other screen running. I had mine on Bloomberg—I like economic data more than the other kinds—and the crawl was saying that public dollar cost on the whole Disney World event was getting close to a trillion, and that didn't even count insurance settlements. It also said my last batch of corn contracts had nearly tripled up. Hot damn. Big bucks in bad news. Get used to it, Jed, you really are a rich old bastard. Too bad there's nothing to spend it on down here . . .

God, what am I thinking? There's also nothing to spend it on when you don't exist. Get back to work.

I called up LEON.

Okay, I thought. Quit stalling. Time to dive.

I got out my pouch of chawin' terbaccy and put a plug in my cheek.

I put in my passwords and challenged good ol' LEON to a four-stone game, ending on 4 Ahau. Naturally, he said yes, since he wasn't smart enough yet to be lazy.

I looked around. Nobody was watching me. I rubbed some tobacco juice into my thigh. It looks a little like one might be jerking off. I made my little offerings to the directions and scattered the stones and seeds.

I'd never even tried four stones before. There hadn't really been any point. It would be like a Go player deciding to play on a 29 x 29 board, or a chess player making a board with 144 squares and two kings per side. If you played it, it wouldn't even really be a game, just a higgledy-piggledy mishmosh of ignorant armies thrashing blindly in the wasteland. Well, even so, I thought. Do it—

Damn, I thought. Glare.

I cleared the screen, got up, and found Taro's assistant, Ashley$_2$.

"Do you think we could turn off some of the overhead lights?" I asked her. They were the usual ghastly, flattening fluorescents.

She said she'd ask around. I went back to my cubicle. Tony Sic passed me and said hi. I heard him jogging up the stairs behind me. Okay, here we are.

Cubicle.

Fuck.

No matter what happens, I still spend 97 percent of my time sitting in front of a screen and entering data. I make a fortune, cities collapse, cities rebuild, I lose a fortune, worlds revolve, I make another fortune, gods appear, gods die, universes turn inside out, it doesn't matter, I'll still just be entering data. Face it, Jed, you're a code monkey. Just pimp your cubicle, shut up, and enter that data—

About half of the lights flickered out. Ahh. That's better. I got back into playtime.

It started slowly, like icebergs building up in some places and falling down in others, and mistier, because the masses seem to congeal out of fog or deliquesce back into it. Each new runner takes into account the moves of all the previous ones. It's like it gathers up their strings of moves and collapses them into one, and when my fourth runner came out it was as though I'd jumped to a higher elevation and I could see for hundreds of miles in all directions, a whole Weddell Sea of false starts, detours, and dead ends, its outer rings compressed into shale by the curvature of the earth. Step, step. Step. Friday is dark, then two nothing days, then Monday is light. *De todos modos.* I was already at 1 Earth Rattler, 0 Mat, that is, April 2, 2012, closer to the end date than I'd ever gotten before without losing track. Wait. Step back. Okay, so the break was at 408. Try again. 948,389. Right. Looking clearer. The images started kicking in. They aren't visions or anything, just memories of pictures off the TV or wherever, but they do get activated by a sense that something similar might be coming up. A long line of refugees, like a convention of balloon-men with all their bunches of plastic bottles, scooped water out of a sinkhole. I scattered the seeds again, reducing the potentials. A few of the smokier paths vanished. A few of the longer ones caved in. Come on. Fewer and fewer. Now there were only a hundred or so primary scenarios, and now there were only twenty, good, wait, no, I'd gone too fast, I'd missed a path, many paths, I'd gone right past without noticing the branchings, those twenty scenarios were only a few out of millions, hell, hell, hell, things looked bad, very bad. Okay. Go back. Here it is. Try it. Blocked. Okay. Try that one. *Bloqueado.* That other one. *Bloqueado.* Hell, hell. *Desesperado.* The icebergs crushed together around me with a sound like ten thousand pit bulls gnawing ten thousand veal shanks. There's got to be a way to deal with this. This way. That way. Edge of a cliff. Sliding. Can't think. That way. No. Bad road. Bridge out. *Ninguna manera.* No way. Bad road. Bad road. All roads lead to doom. Rome. Doom. Roome. Dooooooooom . . .

Hell.

I clicked *resign.* On the screen, the board just winked out, but in my mind it was as though I'd tipped over the table and sent all the seeds and stones scattering over the linoleum floor. It said it was 4:33 P.M. I pushed back from the monitor, feeling physically bruised.

"Hi," Marena's voice said.

I turned around in my desk chair. It spun too far and I had to awkwardly brake it and get it facing her. Then I realized I should stand up because she was a female and everything, but she was already leaning against the wall of the cubicle and it seemed even more awkward, so I stayed where I was.

"Are you okay?" she asked.

"Hi," I said. "Oh, yeah. I'm good."

"I got a memo—" she started to say, "one of—oh, wait, hey, did your guy get that rider from Hammerhead, Mako, and White?"

"Oh. Yeah," I said. "Yeah, we're good." I forgot to mention that yesterday I'd finally gotten my business-law guy—Jerry Weir, from Grey, Timber, and Weir—on the phone. He was ready to work, even with Western civilization melting down. Jerry would go over a brief on his deathbed. From the grave, even. He'd taken his red pen to the contract and told me not to sign until they'd approved all his jottings. Astonishingly, they had. So now I was a part-time associate of the Warren Group, one of the world's fastest-growing and most progressive employers. And, as I was living proof of, a diverse workplace.

"I got a memo from Personnel and we still have to ask you a couple things," Marena said.

"Okay."

"Sorry. They wanted Dr. L to do it, but I said I'd do it. Unless you'd rather do it with her."

"Oh. No, no . . ."

"It's just for the insurance." She unfolded her phone.

"Fine," I said. "It's always prudent to have plenty of insurance."

"Yeah."

"Hey, speaking of that, do we have doomsday insurance?"

"Dude, I know it's all ridiculous," she said. "It's a *corporation.*"

"Right. Okay."

"Okay, the first thing is, on the hæmophilia thing, do you know whether any of those medications counteract any known psychiatric medications?"

"I'm told not," I said.

"Are you currently taking any medications that are not on the prescription list you gave us?"

"No."

"Any other drugs?"

"Caffeine."

"We don't have to put that in."

"Like, fifteen cups a day."

"Hmm. I'll leave it out anyway. But you really ought to ease up a little."

"Thanks, Mom."

"Right." She scribbled a notation on her screen. "Um, the other thing is there's another medical item. It says that when you got to the U.S., they classified you, um, they list you as having 'posttraumatic stress disorder presenting as similar to Asperger's.'"

"That's true," I said.

"Does that still affect your behavior?"

"Well, not in a dysfunctional way, as far as I'm concerned," I said. "Why, do I seem weird?"

"Not to me," she said, "no, but, you know, that's me."

"Hmm. Well, I can seem weird. So they tell me. They say I'm more interested in objects than people."

"Is that true?"

"I'm not interested in objects either."

"So what are you interested in?"

"Wait, what's the difference again? People are the things that move around and say stuff, right?"

"I'll just tell them I've asked you about it and you're okay," she said.

"Thanks."

"It's fine. I have a syndrome myself."

"Really?"

"Yeah, it's called Laurin-Sandrow syndrome."

"Is that serious?" I asked.

"No, it's a very mild instance. It's undetectable."

"Oh. Good."

"How are you guys doing?" Boyle's voice asked. We turned. He and Taro had come over.

"We're done," Marena said.

"Is Tony Sic around?"

"He's at that Care Space thing," she said.

"How are you doing with the four stones?" Taro asked me.

"Not so well," I said. Oops, I thought. Watch it. These are your employers, Jeddo. You're supposed to radiate an aura of cautious optimism. "I do have another idea, though," I started to say. "Maybe—"

"I am thinking that we would need to use five stones even to get a handle on the problem," Taro said.

"How can we get a what, a nine-stone game going?" Boyle asked.

"We would not even know where to start," Taro said. "Each stone—each new stone is like putting another wheel on the Enigma machine."

I didn't think Boyle got the reference. "We have to keep moving," he said to Taro, leading him toward the stairs. Marena went with them. "Text me when you're done down here," she said to me. I made a little wave.

I sat back down.

Hmm.

Something odd was going on. What was Tony Sic doing again? Oh, right. He was in the Care Space.

It sounded kind of familiar to me. Maybe I'd been to a Care Space at some point. It had to be some sort of children's hospital or outpatient center. One of Lindsay Warren's nonprofits. Back in Salt Lake, maybe? Except that didn't quite have the right ring to it. That is, I wasn't associating it with the hæmo thing.

Maybe it's the Stake's day care center. Does Sic have kids? He didn't say he didn't. Hmm.

Except that didn't ring right either. It felt like Care Space had to do with something else, something more abstract. Something mathematical.

I put another plug in my cheek. Say what you want about nicotine, but it does light a fire under a few gray cells.

The Care Space thing reminded me of something else. Two things. Something from last night that I didn't know and didn't check out. Freaky Friday? Somebody'd mentioned *Freaky Friday*. Which was what? It was just a dumb comedy movie that they remade as an even dumber comedy movie. Something that was going to happen on a Friday? Maybe that was just some local festival. Think about that one later. What else happened last night that was odd? Besides everything.

Well, it was a little odd when Taro brought up time travel at the end of that conversation. Or rather, it wasn't odd for Taro. Like a lot of math people, he and I had always talked about stuff like that. He gets speculative. But there had been something that seemed odd about it at the time. What was it? Taro said there wasn't any future. Because there weren't any time travelers. Okay. And then Boyle asked . . . right. He asked whether that wasn't because of Novikov.

Hmm. Well, the thing was, I happened to know what Novikov was. It was the Novikov self-consistency principle, which was a way to do time manipulations without the old and discredited many-universes theory. Basically it was a theorem about how time travel didn't necessarily cause physical contradictions. But how come Boyle knew about it? He wasn't a math person. He was kind of a dullard, in fact. And nobody questioned him on it either. And for that matter, why didn't somebody object that maybe time travel was impossible? Even that Michael Weiner guy let it go by. And he was looking for ways to put in his two cents.

And something else, some reference I didn't get and hadn't checked up on—

Care Space. No. *Kerr* space.

Roy Kerr.

Kerr space*time*.

Firefox, I clicked. *Kerr space*, I Googled. There were thousands of hits. I clicked the first one.

Kerr Black Holes as Wormholes, Wikipedia said. *Because of its two event horizons, it might be possible to avoid hitting the singularity of a spinning black hole, if the black hole had a Kerr metric.*

Dios perro, I thought. God dog.

No es posible, no es posible.

A little tingle started down in my lower back. It wasn't a tzam lic twinge, it was just the normal cold goose bumpy sizzle you get with a major revelation.

SSC, I thought, out of nowhere. A1 had said something like "The SSC was running."

What does *SSC* stand for? Okay. Secondary School Certificate, Societas Sanctae Crucis, Species Survival Commission, but, really . . .

Hah. Superconducting supercollider.

Holy shit, I thought.

That's it. That's it. Holy shit. Shit. It. It . . .

Taro wasn't just going off on some tangent of hypotheticals the way he does. He was continuing something. They'd been talking together about time travel before. *No es posible,* I thought.

I flicked my phone to the Stake map and hit TARO. His purple dot was nowhere in sight. How dare he turn off his dot? I wondered. Maybe he was in some secret, undottable part of the facility. Hell. I tried MARENA. Her blue dot came up in the dormitory-soon-to-be-hotel, probably in her room. So whatever Taro and Tony and Boyle were doing, she wasn't doing it with them. Hmm. I got up, walked, too fast, to the exit, ran up the stairs—the elevators weren't working yet—and dashed out into the sun, across the tarred lot, and into the dorm. The long hall was crowded with doughy, clean-cut Saints types bustling in and out of rooms with loads of unfashionable laundry. A planeload of them had landed this morning and more were coming in every hour. On the Stake LAN portal page—under "Other Important Information"—it had warned us not to call them refugees because they were Americans. I pushed through to Marena's door. I banged on it. No answer. I highlighted her dot and touched URGENT.

I waited. Her voice came on.

"What?" she asked.

"It's urgent," I panted.

"I'm in the shower."

"I'm serious. Really. Really."

"Hang on."

Two minutes later she opened the door. She was in a big tacky green Marriott Amenities bathrobe, with a green towel around her head like a feather headdress. Her face was wet. Any other time it would have been sexy enough to be distracting. I just said I had, had, had to talk to her, ultraprivately.

"Let's go outside," she said. Like me, and like a lot of Asians, and I guess more and more people these days, her instinct when she wanted privacy wasn't to go into some little room and shut the door, but rather to go outside where you could see nobody was listening. She led me past the break room and the laundry room and out the back side of the building, trailing the bottom six inches of her robe in the dust. We were in a shady sort of nook between the building's vinyl siding and a six-foot stack of rebar.

"Okay, what's the big deal?" she asked.

My lungs were stuttering, like I was back at Nephi K–12 calling Jessica Gunnison for a date. Okay, go for it, Jed. Say something.

"Well, I was thinking about this Kerr space business," I said.

"What about it?" she asked. At least she didn't pretend not to know about it.

"Just that, you know, if you really wanted to learn how the old guys played that game, you'd have to ask them."

"So how would you suggest we do that?" she asked. It was hard to hear her over the rasp of another turboprop coming in for a landing.

"Maybe you guys have a time machine," I said. Damn, I thought, that didn't really sound very casual. Not really.

"Are you kidding?" Marena asked. She peeled the towel off her hair. For a little person she really had a lot of hair, and now that it was swollen and spiked up she looked kind of like a cuter Troll doll. "Time machines don't work. Do they?"

"Doesn't that depend on what you do with them?"

"What do you mean?"

"It's not a—it's a *Freaky Friday* thing," I said.

"Who told you about Freaky Friday?"

"That means, they're not going to send any physical object."

She dropped the towel on the ground and ran her hands back through her hair, sculpting it into a big dangling flipper. She looked into my eyes. In her nearer eye the lower rim of the brown-and-gold iris was in direct sunlight, so you could see how it was a flattened torus over a dark hollow. I looked down into her pupil, hoping for a flicker or a dilation or something that would . . . but the thing is, people think that the eyes are windows into the soul, but actually they're just as mute and opaque as anything else.

Her phone buzzed somewhere. As her hand went into her pocket to turn it off, she broke the stare-down. "I said I'd call Max right now," she said.

"They're just sending a wave or whatever, the SSC makes a, a naked singularity or a wormhole or something, and then it's going to, you're going to rewire somebody's head back there."

"Hmm," she said. "Well . . . I guess you have cracked a physics book once or twice, haven't you?"

I said something or other, but it probably came out like mush because most of my head was busy tumbling into a swirlpool of expanded potential.

In one of the oldest Arthur stories Merlin had a chess set with pieces that moved by themselves and, even more impressively, never lost a game. These days, most of us who've lived to see such things have also seen them grow and mature, so it's no wonder we take them for granted. But one time, in 1998, I showed my old Excalibur 2400 to an eighty-plus-year-old chess-addicted

Maya sun adder in Santa Eulalia—which is way up in the Huehuetenango Highlands, totally the backside of beyond—and you could feel the full force of the onrush of technology in the fear and excitement in his eyes, and the way he kept playing and playing the thing, sitting on a Pemex Oil box outside the bodega, clicking it through one old Ruy López after another, losing game after game, way into the night. Finally I just left the thing with him, along with a year's supply of AAs. And now I was feeling that rush myself, that whole moon-landing, DNA-solving, radium-refining wonderment. Son of a bitch, I thought. Son of two bitches.

She'd turned and walked out of the little nook, past the rebar and into a canyon between a giant backhoe and a cement mixer in matching apotropaic stripes. I followed.

"And Tony Sic's going to go," I said.

"Go where?"

"Go back."

"Back to, like, olden times?"

"Yeah."

"That's not exactly—"

"Just loan me the thing for a minute," I said. "I promise I'll bring it back before I leave." Fuck Sic, I thought. Sick fuck. Fick suck. That smug outdoorsy bastard. He's going to see it. He's going to know what it was like. And I'm not. FUCK! People say that sex, greed, and fear are the three biggest motivators, but actually jealousy is. None of the others are even close.

"Listen," I said. "Seriously. I can do this *much* better than that guy. I *clobbered* him on three-stone, I know *infinitely* more than he does—you know, the stuff he has to study, I knew it cold when I was five."

There was a short, brutish pause. Another helicopter whipped by to the west, patrolling the border.

"Look," she said. She sat down on a plug of newly cast concrete, crossed one invisible leg over the other, and, with a Dietrichy set of motions, lit a Camel. I stood, trying not to pace in circles like I do. Come on, Jed, get it together. Have at least a drop of sangfroid. She knows you want it, but you don't have to let her know how much.

"It's not just me running this," she said. "Whatever's going to happen with Tony is already in the pipeline—"

"Also I know I can pick up *anything* about the Game," I said. I noticed my hands were waving around in front of my face and got them into my pockets. "No matter how complicated it turns out. Anything."

"You don't know what's involved. *I* don't know what's involved." She took a long drag. She exhaled. "Anyway, now I'm in trouble."

"I don't care what's *involved*," I said. *Involved* indeed. Please. "I've got a billion times the motivation to do it right. I've got more motivation than the, than the, I don't know, than the, than the whole Lee Strasberg Institute."

"I'm sure that's true."

"Yes, it is." In fact I'd give my right testicle, I thought. And my right arm, right eye, right leg, and right brain. All my nondominant—

"Anyway, now that I've told you, I have to commit seppuku." She dropped her cigarette and toed it into the gravel with a size-six bright-green complimentary-Crocs-shod foot. It was an eloquent old gesture and she did it with some assurance.

"Would it help if I begged you?" I asked. "I'll beg you. It's got to be me." So much for cool.

"Let's see what things look like in a few hours when we're not running on fumes," she said. She ran her hands up over her cheeks like she was rehearsing a facelift. "You know, it's not easy to get people to change their whole—"

"Please," I said. "It's got to be me."

(16)

On 9 Death's-head, 19 Whiteness, 11.14.18.12.6, or Friday, November 8, 1518, when the soi-disant Army of New Spain marched up the wide eastern causeway into Tenochtitlan, the Aztec capital was the fourth-largest city in the world, a canal city like a clean, gridded Venice in the center of the lake that then covered sixty square miles of central Mexico. In the best eyewitness account, Bernal Díaz, one of Cortés's lieutenants, said that the gleaming pastel palaces and pyramids rising out of the water "seemed like an enchanted vision from the realm of Amadis, and indeed some of our soldiers asked whether it was not all a dream."

Now, *The Tale of Amadis of Gaul* was a King Arthur knockoff written in 1508 by a mediocrity named García Ordoñez de Montalvo, and really, it's a pretty run-of-the-mill popular romance, the then-equivalent of Tom Clancy, and an easy target a long time before Cervantes spoofed it. And the fact that this mercenary twerp was thinking about something like that as he helped initiate the largest episode of genocide in the history of the planet is truly beyond revolting.

But the worst part, the real *chingo* of it, is that in fact it actually *was* like a fantastic romance. The Conquest, or at least the first part of it, really did partake of the period's fabulous epic tales of derring-do. The Spanish actually *did* voyage to this incredible place, penetrate a splendid and fierce empire, meet exotic people, torture them, triumph against overwhelming odds, and become vastly wealthy. They got to live their dream, and that was the problem. Humans have a way of actualizing their hallucinations, and the thing to really watch out for is when people take their passion and, as Irene Cara says, make it happen. Still, at that moment, when I realized—dimly, as it turned out—what they were going to do, I wasn't thinking about that sort of thing either.

I'd passed into the lands of Amadis, into the Dream Dimension of Unlimited Possibility where the galaxy reverses its polarity, Lolita whispers in your ear, and Moby Dick rises out of the sea.

Marena wouldn't tell me exactly what they were planning to do. But I figured it wasn't conventional sci-fi time travel, because I was pretty sure that was impossible. From the way she hemmed and hedged, it sounded like it would be some kind of remote viewing, which couldn't be very active or dangerous. I guess I imagined myself sitting comfortably in Taro's lab, enjoying a quintisensory VR feed from some counterpart in ancient Mayaland as he watched two adders playing the full nine-stone version of the Sacrifice Game. No problem.

Marena said that the idea of my trying out for Sic's position in what they called the Count Chocula Project—apparently all Warren black ops were named after breakfast cereals—had already occurred to her. She said she'd even mentioned me as a backup. But the Kerr-space people had said Sic had some advantages over me. I asked what they were. She said mental stability was probably one of them. Another was that he'd already conducted a few wct tests. She wouldn't give me any more details about what they were planning.

She said she'd talk to Taro about it and that I should either go back to work or take some Vicos and calm down. We talked again that day at 8:40 P.M., on the phone. She said she was having dinner at "Lindsay's compound," and that she'd put in a word for me. I said thanks. I took the Vicodin. Taro called at eleven. He said Marena had asked him about it and that he'd been thinking about it too. He said he couldn't tell me any more about the project. He said he'd put in a word for me.

I stayed up all night agonizing. I was back at the lab at 7:00 A.M. Sic wasn't there. I kept asking to challenge him to a game. A_2 said they—or They—didn't even want me to talk to him anymore. Maybe They were afraid I'd kill him. I managed to get back to work on the Game. But of course I couldn't focus.

The next day, the thirty-first, Marena told me they'd got me a trial, which could get me into the candidate pool. That evening, the Stake's Morons, now over twenty thousand strong, gathered in the Hyperbowl to watch the current prophet give his fireside chat on a six-story video screen. Afterward, there was a sing-along with the Tabernacle Choir Road Show. I really, really wanted to go but somehow I just didn't make it. I stayed in and checked on the home front. Things in Indiantown weren't good. About half the people I knew from there were still unaccounted for. Instead of quartering the displaced in other cities, which had caused problems after Katrina, FEMA had built a single refugee center at Camp Blanding, which now had over two million inhabitants.

On the blogs, BitterOldExGreenBeretCracker was going on about how the Nation of Islam was behind the attacks because Wednesday had been predicted as the second coming of a mad scientist named Yakub, who I guess was sort of like their Antichrist. Hell Rot was saying that the polonium particles had been dispersed with some kind of smog-seeding system that was way too complicated for any independent hacker/terrorist/whatever to design, and that the attack had almost certainly been engineered by a big government, probably our own. He's probably a bit, somewhat, slightly right, I thought. The trouble with conspiracies isn't that there aren't any. There are plenty. But for every real conspiracy behind X situation there are a few thousand untrue theories, some of which are even started by the actual conspirators. There are so many half-truths camouflaging the real ones that even decades later there's almost no way to sort out what actually happened. Except maybe this time . . .

Testing started on the second. I'd thought it would be something that if I worked hard I could do better than someone else. Instead it turned out to be already out of my hands. That is, it was all about the way I was already. It started with six hours of medical and cardiovascular-fitness tests. We determined that aside from having a life-threatening disability I was in B+ shape, not because I wanted to be or because I liked exercise, but because if you're a bleeder you're either in decent shape or dead. There were fourteen hours of basic mental tests, including memory (easy), sequence and spatial puzzles (almost as easy), linguistic exams (still pretty easy), emotional sampling (which I assumed I failed as usual), and interpersonal skills like trying to tell if someone on video was lying or not (utterly incomprehensible). They did a new emotional-assessment sort of thing where they wired me up and played videos of sick children and gut-shot dogs, like I was Alex DeLarge. Then there were personalized tests, including a whole expanded-polygraph thing where, as far as I could tell, they were trying to determine how committed I was and what my motivations were. God knows what the results were on that one. I wasn't sure how honest I needed to be about my real motivation. I mean, my motivation aside from saving the day. Not that I didn't care about Doom Soon. I mean, who wouldn't? But that wasn't my personal reason. And neither was Marena. That is, of course I thought she was kind of hot, and it's a natural urge to want to be the hero. Right? Well, if she needed to go out with somebody major, fine, this was my way to be major, not just rich major but total hero major, absolute Dudley Do-Right major, so that anything else I ever did, no matter how rotten, wouldn't matter. But that wasn't my main motivation either.

The fact was, I already had my own agenda. And I'd had it practically since birth. Have you heard about those people who were one of a set of twins, and one was aborted or absorbed or eaten early in the pregnancy, and when they grow up, even if they don't know about it, they always say they feel they're missing someone? I don't have that, but I've always had this feeling that I'm looking for something I've lost. I figure about three-fifths of my dreams are about running around looking for something. Or someplace, rather. It's not something small. It's somewhere that ought to be around the corner but never is. And now I was finally drawing a bead on the little gray personal demons I'd been swatting at for my whole glum-ass life. I wanted the books back, I wanted my beaten, maimed, raped, infected, abandoned, and all-but-deceased culture back, and I wanted it right the hell now. Corny but true. Suppose you were a child exile from some trashed place, say Atlantis or the Warsaw Ghetto or Krypton or Bosnia or Guatemala or wherever, and before your parents sent you away they gave you—as a kind of γνωρισματων, that is, a birth token—a couple of pieces out of an old wooden jigsaw puzzle. They're worn around the edges, but the colors of their cryptic bits of picture are still deep and festive. And you've carried them with you through your whole life, but as much as you'd stared at them you only had vague guesses about what the image they were part of might be. And now you heard that somebody had the picture, or at least some of it. What would you do? What would Jesus do? What would anybody do?

Well, what I was going to do was, I was going to get myself chosen over Sic, I was going to go through the Kerr-space thing. I was going to deal with whatever I had to deal with. And I was going to bring back my whole goddamn civilization, all soaked up in the little 1,534-cubic-centimeter sponge of my own brain.

(17)

On Wednesday the fourth, Marena called and said to be ready early on Friday morning to meet the great man. It was the final hurdle. One would have thought he'd have wanted to sign off on me, or not, before they'd gone through the effort and expense of the testing. But Lindsay Warren was one of those people who'd be wasting his time if he stooped to pick up dropped thousand-dollar bills. Clearing me on everything else first was just standard procedure, the way they used to make dinner for Louis XIV in each of his hunting lodges every day, just in case he stopped by.

Marena confided that as of now, the plan was still for Sic to go. Stability and social skills beat brilliance every time. And Sic had model looks. Well, Patagonia-catalog-model looks. Still, there were three people who still had to vote on me-versus-Sic: Lindsay, somebody named Snow, and somebody named Ezra Hatch. They'd tip the result one way or another. I didn't know how Boyle or Michael Weiner had voted. Or Marena, for that matter. Although she liked me, I thought. And Taro . . . well, Taro thought—okay, fine, he *knew*—that I was a bit of a flake. But he'd probably come through. But Boyle hated me. And Weinershitzel hated me. So it was probably two against two so far. Well, Lindsay probably really had eight votes anyway. The thing was—and if there are any kids out there, please at least consider this bit of duffery wisdom—nothing ever happens just on the merits. Even when you're talking about something like, say, last-ditch doomsday-aversion, it's still mainly about whether they like you or not, how good-looking you are, what secret societies you weren't in back in New Haven, and whether or not your name ends in a vowel. The usual.

I spent two days agonizing. On Friday morning, Laurence Boyle met Marena and me in a low, wide, blank room in the Stake's R&D Temporary Facility #4, a bunkerish building under the stadium. He was all put together at 7:06 A.M., with a tab-closure collar that made his head look like it was being squoze out of a tube and a dark last-of-the-three-piece-suits. We scuffed past rows of cubicles, each with a cubicle trog keying away. A few of them were playing eXtreme Foosball at a break area in the center. They stared at Marena like she was Queen Amygdala.

"These rooms go down two more levels?" Boyle asked or said. "It's all programming and testing for the Battlefield Air Targeting System?"

"That's a UAV, right?" Marena asked without the sense of really caring.

"Yep," Boyle said. He hosted us into a big glass-lined elevator with a green-suited guard in it.

"Right now we're right under the west sideline of the multipurpose play field," Boyle said to me. Dutifully, I nodded and glanced at my you-are-here map:

BELIZE OLYMPIC HYPERBOWL

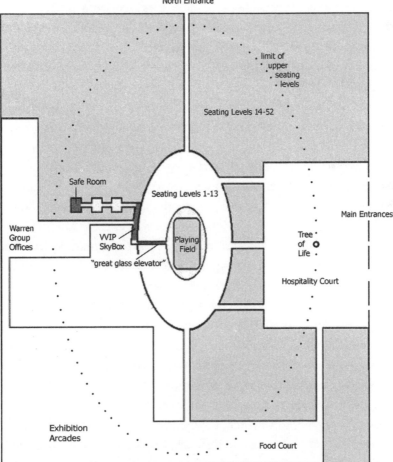

"Good morning," Julie Andrews chirped. Stupidly, I looked around. *"Please grasp one of the padded safety handrails as we begin our ascent."* I realized it was the elevator talking, in a voice fleshy enough to fool a blind vocal coach.

"Sir?" Marena asked the Elevator Goon. "Do you think you could please, uh, shut that woman the heck off? Thanks." Her voice sounded dulled. Over breakfast, or I should say between gulps of espresso, she'd said she'd just found out her friend Yu Shih had died in a fire in Vero Beach.

We began our ascent. It was dark outside the glass and then light fell around us as we rose out of the ground into the interior of a titanic inverted ellipsoid cone. I was very reluctantly impressed.

"We are now entering the Hyperbowl Stadium Seating Area," Julie said. There was an odd perspectival effect as our transparent box oozed up toward the directrix, as though the rows of stairs above us were both advancing and receding. Despite myself I actually did grasp one of the padded safety handrails. On the far side of the SofTurf field four tall athletes in Day-Glo green sweats were kicking around an illuminated soccer ball. My nose grazed the window and left a little spotted smudge.

"That's Mohammed Mâzandar right down there," the guard dude said. I figured out, a little on the late side, that he was talking to me.

"Who?" I asked.

"The *forward*," he said like I was a two-year-old.

I must have given him a blank look.

"The *basketball player*," he said. He pointed down at the far-off red giants.

"Oh," I said. "Great." *Chinga tu madre,* I thought. What's with this automatic assumption between guy types that all anybody with a Y chromosome is going to be even remotely interested in is team sports? Do I come up to you, a total stranger, and say, "Hey, buddy, can you *believe* Natalia Zhukova won that EEC Interzonal yesterday? Seventeen g takes f5, g takes f5, eighteen h-Rook to g1? *Un*believable!"

Although maybe I wouldn't feel that way if I'd been even remotely jocked out in school instead of being a flash-bruising little redskin geek—

"We are now at the first seating level," Mary Poppins said.

"Sorry, I'm trying to turn this down," the lease-a-cop said, messing with the control screen. For a second I thought I saw it say that one of the functions was SELF CLEAN.

"When completed, the Belize Hyperbowl will seat over a hundred and eighty-five thousand fans, making it the third-largest sports spectatorship facility on the globe." That's progress, I thought. I guess if you build it, they'll show up. Unless it's the set for *Waterworld*.

"So look," Marena said, "you know not to use cuss words around Elder Lindsay, right?"

"Oh, sure," I said. And I'll take that especially seriously coming from Ms. Cloacamouth. "You know, I grew up around these people. I mean, the LDS."

"He's a bit of a holy roller," she said. "Supposedly when he was an archdeacon he converted more people than anybody else, ever."

"Great." I was getting the feeling that this meeting was going to be a little more decisive than she'd let on.

"We are now at Level Fourteen," the Sound of Muzak said as we came to what was actually Level Thirteen or, in another system, Bolgia One.

"Welcome to the VVIP SkyBox."

We oozed to a stop. There was a pause, and more pause. Finally there was an A-flat synthesound and the box's north wall slid open with a powerfully understated and probably unnecessary hiss.

The rest of the ring-shaped building was still in the last phase of construction, but this room was all ready for the cover of *Interior Design*, done up in brass and blond wood like a press box at a classy 1930s racetrack. On our left a seamless sweep of glass looked out into the field, and the receding rings of tens of thousands of desolate green seats generated a sort of vertigo that made me want to pitch myself through the bulletproof Perspex and roll all the way down to the end zone. Below the window an angled desk topped with a single long plasma touch screen ran the length of the room, with at least fifty windows streaming away on it, stocks, commodities, football games, surveillance cameras, shots of construction at other parts of the site, *Good Morning America,* a Special Miss Universe Pageant, and a shot of one of the riots in India, which had grown from the one I'd handicapped back at Taro's lab into region-wide chaos. One of the windows had the sound on and Anne-Marie Chippertwit's voice bubbled out of it: *"Orlando,"* she said. *"The Aftermath. A city searches for meaning."*

There wasn't anyone around. It was one of those odd limbo moments. Marena drifted toward the far end. I followed. The elevator guy stayed at the door. Behind him, the elevator doors shut slowly, paused, as such doors do, before closing completely, and then sucked together into an airtight seal.

I looked away from the window and tried to focus on the shelves. Wow, I thought. I'd pictured Lindsay Warren as kind of a corncob Bond villain. But the thing is, at least in the movies Ken Adams worked on, the Bond villains all had really good taste. Dr. No had a Goya, Scalamanga had a yellow-jade Teotihuacan mask in his foyer . . . but the decor in Lindsay's offices was so tacky it made Carl Varney look like Palladio. Most of it was sports memorabilia, autographed footballs and hurleys and jerseys and balls and bats and pucks. I noticed a pair of little old cracked brown mittens signed "Jack Dempsey," with a framed photo of the infamous Long Count leaning behind them. There was a plaque on the wall that said all the wood in here was salvaged from old shipwrecks in the Gulf of Honduras, and a plaque on the floor that said its pink granite tiles had been retrieved from the lobby of One Liberty Plaza after it burned down on 9/11. We fetched up at the north end of the room, at what seemed to be Lindsay Warren's personal desk, although it couldn't have been his main one since it was too low-tech and uncluttered, or rather all the clutter was more mementi. There was a model of an F-17 Hornet, an ancient gold plastic Nabisco two-in-one compass and magnifying glass, and a cut-Lucite trophy—a pyramid embedment, as they call it in the trade—with the words Dᕈᒐᕈᒐ ᏘᎣᏞᏏᎩᏅᎵ ᏫᏒᎾ ᏮᎭ ᏮᎭᏈ etched on it and a little flock of real honeybees suspended inside. Next to that there was a Rawlings baseball encased in a beveled-glass pyramid. MARK MCGWIRE #70, the pyramid screamed in Bradley Hand Bold. It was that *cagado* three-million-dollar baseball. *For the price of this baseball, you can save thirty thousand AIDS babies.* The wall treatment ran toward humanitarian awards and honorary degrees and framed articles from the *Financial Times*. One showed a giant family portrait, a huge clan of happy, healthy all-American types with teeth, all ranked in front of a façade I recognized. *"With Huge Gift, Utah Researchers to Study Neural Diseases,"* the headline said. I read the caption under the photo:

> Lindsay R. Warren, a Salt Lake City businessman and son of Korean War ace Ephraim "Stick" Warren, who gave $1.5 billion for research on Alzheimer's and other pathologies of the nervous system, is seen here with his family. Mr. Warren is at right, holding three of his eighteen grandchildren, next to his wife, Miriam. His family gathered in front of the Salt Lake City hospital that bears his name.

There were pictures of Lindsay Warren with Gerald Ford, Michael Jordan, Bush I, Bush II, Tiger Woods, the Osmond Family, Gladys Knight, James Woolsey, and Bono. There was even one of a young him standing in front of a USO truck with John Wayne, Vicki Carr, and Ronald Reagan. You almost expected to see him in a group shot with J. Edgar Hoover, Jesus Christ, and the five original Marx Brothers. Below the photos there was a shelf crowded with Colt Peacemakers and old 1911s and other patriotic handguns. All but one of them were dutifully fitted with trigger locks. The exception was a Beeman/FWB C8822-CO_2 rapid-fire air pistol, nestled on aqua velvet in an open cryptomeria-wood box. It had a gold Olympics medallion inset in the grip, with a pyrographed inscription: *In Grateful Appreciation from His Excellency Juan Antonio Samaranch 24/2/02.* I looked back down the long room toward the door we'd come in and, yep, there was a metal-and-plasticine trap-target hung on the wall with a close group of 0.177-caliber holes edging into the bull's-eye. Cowboys. Rednecks from Planet Kolob. Who even cares about marksmanship anymore? These days even squirt guns have laser sights.

"They're in the videoconference facility," a woman's voice said. It came from a sort of hostess or secretary who'd materialized from somewhere and who turned out to be Ashley$_1$. She led Marena, Boyle, and me around the desk and through a door on the left into a paneled hallway. It led away from the field and into the depths of the Hyperdoughnut around it. A single door was open at the far end and we tromped through into a big, dimly lit cube-shaped conference room, windowless but with big white velvet curtains all over. There were clear plastic drop cloths over the eggshell wall-to-wall. We squeaked across to the far door.

"Sorry about the mess," Laurence said. "When we get it cleaned up and bring in the hospitality team . . . well, it's gonna be pretty special." He opened the door and led us into a second meeting cube bigger than the first. It was covered with badly painted murals of Pleistocene life, fruited plains teeming with megatheria, glyptodonts, phororhaci, and nuclear families of suspiciously Caucasoid early hominids. The far wall also featured an olde-timey-looking map of the Western Hemisphere, with a line in gold enamel that I guessed represented the route of the Jaredites, winding from Chesapeake Bay down into Central America. We all squeaked across the room to yet another door. It led directly into a third conference cube.

This one was smaller than the others, only about a thousand square feet.

Something's weird about this place. Oh. I see. Yeah. The walls, the ceiling, the padded floor, the square conference table, and even the mostly empty Aerons all seemed to be slightly translucent, like they were made out of the same dark frosted glass. I guessed the stuff was some kind of wraparound video cell-film, so that if you put a specially modified VR program on the giant seamless plasma screens that made up the walls, ceiling, and floor, the surfaces of the furniture would key themselves to it and practically vanish so that you could feel like you were floating goggleless through a desert sunset or an underwater ice cave or a beloved episode of *Dawson's Creek* or whatever. Right now three of the walls were running what must have been meant to be a soothing screensaver, misty ripples of blue-gray smoke over dark green, and there were just four scattered windows open on the wall facing us. The smallest and leftmost was running another news shot of troubles on the subcontinent. The second, bigger window showed a rotating computer-rendered image of a Sleeker, an advanced-looking sport shoe with oddly fat, tractionless soles. The biggest window was a sort of digital 3-D diorama. It looked like a real window facing out on an unnaturally still woodland landscape. Two glowy angels floated between the trees in the upstage left, and down center a man in black knelt with his back to the picture plane: the prophet, Joseph Smith.

Four post-middle-age Caucasian males sat at the near side of the table, pecking at nearly untouched plates of bran muffins and fruit cubes. There were also pots and mugs of what was undoubtedly herbal tea, and a chocolate layer cake, also apparently untouched, skewered with a single burnt-out sparkler. One of the men's heads was bald, one was silver, one was not quite bald and had an unemphatic goatee, and the fourth and youngest, which was talking, had a thin coating of short tan setae.

"... the main thing with Sleekers is you don't need ice," Tan Head was saying in an avuncular voice. "They move like in-lines. On almost any smooth surface. But they're lighter and they brake better. So you've got your speed, but you can also dig in deep and really launch that ball."

"And the kids are, they're already taking to this?" Bald asked.

"Oh, yeah," Tan said. "In fact, it'll feel like it started out as an underground sport. Like snowboarding. A real homegrown trend with a high-octane mixture of team spirit and individualism. I visualize the game as having the one-for-all feeling of football plus the zany characters of pro wrestling."

"But it's not going to be fixed like wrestling?"

"No, of course not," Tan said. "It's a real, demanding sport."

"Hold up a second," Bald said. He stood up and slowly turned thirty degrees to look at us. The other three men swung their chairs around and, as one, struggled up onto their hind legs.

"Don't get up," Marena said. "Please. Okay, never mind." She edged around the table, sort of hugged the Tan Head Guy, and half-hugged or shook hands with the others. Laurence did the same, minus the hugging. I took my hat off. I still forgot to take it off indoors sometimes. I was still wearing the jacket I'd had on during the attack, newly dry-cleaned in the Stake's on-premises plant, and I even had on a tie, an ancient J. C. Penney *funèbrerie* on loan from the family of Saints next door at the motel, so I felt marginally respectable. But to these people I still probably looked like the Frito Bandito.

Marena steered me into the group and introduced me to Bald first. His name was Elder Snow and he was totally hairless down to the lack of eyebrows and lashes. I wasn't even sure he had fingernails. He shook my hand with a pretty strong grip, for a wraith. The next one was about sixty and named Ezra Hatch. He had the creepy Tenexed helmet of silver hair and a sort of peachy Palm Beachy resorty sport jacket and slacks. And under that, probably, Jesus jammies. He gooshed my hand like we were old roommates at business school. The goatee guy was named Orson something. He was in a Warren sweatshirt. They were all pretty friendly. Wait. Let's be more specific: One felt that their default position was the usual overfamiliar joviality—which is what people in the U.S. have instead of manners—but it was hampered by current events. We were still in that awkward period after a big disaster when everyone feels like he's supposed to be sympathetic and grave but just doesn't feel it.

Lindsay Warren was the tan-headed one, the one who'd been speaking. He also turned out to be the tallest. He took three steps toward us, limping badly from what I'd bet five to one was a football injury. It was practically an obligatory accessory for middle-age Utah businessmen. Walk a few blocks down Temple Street on a Sunday and I guarantee that at least three not-yet-old Longjohn Silvers will hobble past you on their way to salvation. He was wearing Warren-green cross trainers and a UNICEF warm-up suit printed with colorful drawings of Children of Many Lands. All he needed to complete the look was orange hair and a tomato nose. He had one of those ruggedly good-looking Anglo-Saxon outdoorsy faces, with supraorbital wrinkles like twin engravings of the Delicate Arch National Monument. Was he around fifty? Did he dye his bristles? He fixed me with an Ancient Mariner gaze and treated me to the firmest and driest of all old-boy handshakes, numbing out what was left of my carpal nerves. Shaking hands is always awkward for me anyway, and I rated my performance on this one at about four.

"Real glad to meet you," he said.

(18)

"It's nice to meet you," I said. "I spent some time in one of your hospitals."

"Oh, yeah? Salt Lake Central?" he asked. I nodded. "That's real gratifying to hear, Missus Warren and I are real proud o' that one . . . and you're feelin' better now, I suppose?"

"So they tell me," I said.

"Hey, what's this cake about?" Marena asked.

"It's my birthday," Lindsay said. "I'm fifty-darn-two."

"Full of grace," I said.

"What?" he asked.

"Tuesday's child," I said. "Is, you know, full of grace. Sorry."

"Oh. No, no, you're right," he said. He smiled. "I was born on a Tuesday."

"You should see the other stuff he can do," Marena said. "He's like Rain Man."

Thanks a lot, I thought.

"Without all the problems," she backtracked.

"Very interesting," Lindsay said.

"Would either of you like a slice?" Ashley₁ asked. We said no, thanks.

"How about some jasmine tea?"

"Oh, thanks, uh, a coffee would be great," I said.

"Oh, sorry, no, there's no coffee, there's, there's hot chocolate, I can do a Snelgrove's Smoothie, or—"

"Oh, okay, chocolate, sure, thanks," I said. *Jesu,* I thought. So these people are such by-the-books Saints, there's no caffeine up here anywhere.

"Just give me a sec," she said. She left through the door we'd come through. Maybe it was the only door.

"The gals had it all ready to celebrate," Lindsay said. "But then things in the wide world . . . we weren't feelin' very festive."

"Oh, yeah," Marena said. "No kidding. Still, congratulations anyway."

"Thanks." He looked at me again. "All righty. What's my Mayan horoscope?"

"What day were you named on?" I asked.

"The same day."

"So that's 2 Jaguar, 2 Growing," I said. "That's a royal-type day, like a king would have. Only, that's not exactly a horoscope. You'd have to ask for advice about a certain day."

"Well, good deal, then, what advice would you have for today?"

"Well, today's 3 Venus, 16 Growing. So for you it's a very good time to start a project, or go on a trip, or anything like that." I didn't mention how the night of today was ruled by the Heart of the Mountains, and how that could also mean betrayal of, or by, another jaguar. It sounded like a downer.

"Well, maybe we can start a project," he said. He turned to the other three men, who'd sat back down. "Just gimme two shakes."

"Here you go," Ashley₁ enthused. She handed me a brimming mug of foamy sweetness. One side sported the Warren logo and the legend "Warren. Works for Me.™" I said thanks.

"Y'know, I looked over Larry's report on that Mayan book," Lindsay said. "And it was a real good report. But I didn't quite get all those dates in it."

"What exactly about them?" Marena asked. She sat down, or rather she balanced on the back of a chair, with her feet on the seat. Boyle drifted toward the table but didn't sit. Hatch and Snow just sat where they were, looking out of their depth. Orson, at least, seemed fascinated.

"Just, why'd they pick out those dates and not others?" Lindsay asked. "There must have been a lot of dates that were just as wrong 'uns." He looked straight at me. "Why didn't it have 9/11, or Katrina, fr'instance?"

It was something Taro and I had been over a hundred times. But for a nonspecialist it was a good question.

"Well, they didn't write it for us," I said. "The book was probably commissioned by a single cat clan—"

"Cat clan?"

"Like a royal family."

"All righty."

"And they were probably only interested in what would happen to their descendants. Nine-eleven or Katrina didn't affect many Maya Indians. That's why—with the possible exception of the Orlando event—all the events in the book take place in or near the Maya area."

"Well, fair enough," he said. He eased one haunch onto the edge of the table. As friendly as he was, there was a sort of relaxed rich-guy aura around him, like he wasn't used to other people asking questions or choosing subjects of conversation. And he sure wasn't asking me to sit down.

"But then why do we think the last date, the one a year from now, why do you-all think that's going to mess up everybody? Maybe the last date just means their last *descendants*'ll die off this year."

"That's a clever thought," Boyle brown-nosed.

"Well, less because of the Codex and more because of other calculations," I said. "And also, when I play through scenarios with the Game, it feels like there's a real problem right around that date."

"So you think the whole world is way up a crick."

"Well . . . for what it's worth I am beginning to think it's very possible—or let's say it's probable. And of course, if it's the end for everybody it's the end for the Maya too—"

"But you're not sure."

"Personally, I'm quite sure, but I can't give many concrete reasons. Besides the Game records, I mean—"

"So then we might be reading too much into it," he said. "Right? Maybe there isn't really a problem."

"Well . . . personally, I'm now convinced there's a problem," I said. "A week ago I hadn't been. Playing through, I just don't see a way around it. But it is hard to describe and you might have to learn to play the Game to really see it for yourself." Damn, this guy's not an idiot, I thought. Unlike your average Saint, he seemed to have a skeptical streak. Most of those guys were always expecting the End Times to start about five seconds from now. Well, maybe they were right this time. Even an anosmic hog finds a truffle once in a while. No wonder they built this place up in the hills. Imagine the thousands of square feet of bunkers they must have under here. Fifty years' supply of freeze-dried meat loaf and sugar-free Tang. Just kill me now.

"All righty, then, tell me, Jed, then, what's it really feel like playin' that Game thing?"

"Well . . . when you start out it's called rooting yourself, like you're centering yourself on the world." I was starting to feel not just terrified but also really, really uncomfortable. Whenever I talk about the Game it comes out sounding insufferably zhuzhy-wooshy-newy-agey. And I don't know how to avoid it. "Then when you're looking for a move you wait for what we call blood lightning, that's a kind of fluttering feeling. A physical feeling."

"Where?"

"It can be in any part of your body, usually it feels like it's down near a bone . . . it's not easy to put into words. But then when you act on that, and you move through the game board, it starts to feel like you're traveling. You feel there are lots of paths ahead. Or in this case, you feel that past the end date, there are no paths."

"All righty, good enough," Lindsay said. "Let's move on. Suppose you folks do find out how to play the thing with—what is it, nine stones?"

"Yes."

"I'm not even going to ask what that's all about. Let's just say you do find out how to play it, and then that still doesn't help? What if it just says, yep, the world's had it, and you can't do anything about it?"

Another tough one, I thought. Had he asked Sic these same questions? I wondered. Or different ones? I should have asked Marena before we came here. Idiot. I'd almost gotten a response together when he answered himself.

"I s'pose then we won't need to worry anyway," he said. "Eh? We won't have lost anything."

"Well, no," I said. "But personally I don't think—the thing is, the way to avert whatever it is ought to be contained in *what* it is." Jed, that was totally incomprehensible, I thought. "Let me put that another way. The thing you have to understand is that they didn't think of them as prophecies. They thought of them as advance reportage. They're not supernatural events."

"All righty."

"And the ancient guys—they didn't think in terms of progress. In fact, they thought of history as a process of decay. And to keep the world running as long as possible you had to do certain things. Like for example, with the Maya, even a historical event like a war was a holy act. And you had to do it at certain times and in certain ways, and you had to be purified first, and Lord knows what else. And maybe that was less silly than it sounds. Maybe by sacrificing this or that person—for instance—or by starting a forest fire or whatever, they were actually tweaking history."

"Well, fair enough," he said. "But why's it always a fire or a war or murders . . . y'know, everything that happens in that book is *bad*."

"That's true," I said.

"Why is that?"

"Well, I think the Game was designed to focus on the negative. It helps you identify trouble spots."

"That's why the trading software version does best after crashes," Boyle put in. "Or with short funds."

Lindsay smiled. "Well, that's for sure the true bill," he said to Boyle. He turned back to me. "Y'know," he said in a confidential voice, "you might have heard how back in 2009, after the housing crash, we were almost in Chapter Eleven?"

"No, I hadn't," I said.

"Well, we were. And we kept the coyotes off the herd by starting to base our actual trades on your friend Taro's simulated trades. Back then it was only a half-point or so over our regular managers, but as of the first of this last year we were making nearly thirty-two percent per blessed annum."

"Wow," I said. Who the hell cares? I thought. It's *The Last Days of Pompeii* around here and you're worried about your margin? That's pretty cold. Although, come to think of it, an automatic 32 percent really is pretty—

"But like Larry says, that software did its best work right before bull markets."

"It did well at predicting meltdowns," Boyle said. "Almost every point of profit we made on Taro's work was from shorting major funds before a crisis."

"That sounds right to me," I said.

"You're involved with corn futures, right?" Boyle asked.

"Right," I said.

"Well, good," he said. "So you're in the same boat we are."

I kind of nodded.

"You know, though, some of Taro's work is proprietary."

"I'm aware of that," I said. "I'm not using any of Taro's work in my own trading." It wasn't entirely true, but on the other hand I'd never signed anything beyond the usual university research papers. And that was a long time ago, before we'd even changed the Game layout the first time. And also, Warren was definitely using some stuff I'd come up with, things I'd clued Taro in on years after the school gig.

"We were talking about the big problems, though," Lindsay said. "Let's get back to that. Everything in that Codex thing is bad. And it's all happened."

"That's true," I said. "But not everything you foresee with the Game on a day-to-day basis happens. With a lot of things, at least, so far, it's helped people stay out of trouble. Isn't that right?"

"Right," Lindsay said.

"So the hope is that the 4 Ahau date will be just like that," I said. "On a bigger scale. If the Game operates well, if it describes the event more specifically, then it shouldn't be anything unavertable." Was that a real word? I wondered. Never mind. Move on. "Especially since it's almost certainly going to be anthropogenic. I mean, since it's likely to be caused by people. It's just the last link in a chain."

"A chain of what?"

"Of cause and effect. That is—well, what we think it is, the Game is a reading-ahead of a web of catastrophe that spreads outward from the point in space-time where the Game was played."

"You're saying what you're calling a web, that these disasters, they have the same ultimate cause."

"That's right. It's not just that they have features in common. It's that they're part of a larger process. It's as though they were battles in a single continuing war. That's why there aren't any natural disasters in the Codex. And the Game doesn't work very well on natural events. On weather, it only does a little better than the programs that the Air Force Weather Agency uses. It's just about the human world."

"So if some really big asteroid had slammed into the earth or, or something of the sort, something unpredictable . . . then what?"

"I'd say that might have thrown the process off the track. And they wouldn't have foreseen that. But that didn't happen. Whatever process they identified is still going on."

"Got it."

"So the point is, it's not that they foresaw that there would be a Disney World. It's that they knew that a progression had been set in motion that would require that sort of a pilgrimage center to be roughly in that location at this particular time, in order to keep things together—"

"But still, that doesn't tell us what we need to know," Boyle said. Shut *up*, Boil Face, I thought. "What we need to know is whether a nine-stone version would really allow us to head off whatever's coming."

Lindsay's eyes were on Boyle for a second, so I glanced at Marena. She looked back like, yes, Boyle's a jerk, he'll stab us in the back in a second, in fact he'll shoot us in the back from a long distance and make it look like somebody else did it, and then—

"Well, it's just a hugely high percentage," Marena said. "There's no hundred-percent guarantee. But like the report should say, I've had Taro's math checked by two outside labs and they both said it seems pretty sound."

"Look at it this way," I said. "The four-stone version of the Game that we're playing now works pretty well on human events within, say, three days. A nine-runner game would work one thousand and twenty-four times better, so in terms of advance warning—"

"Let's just take that as a yes," Lindsay said.

There was a pause. Lindsay looked at Marena. I looked at Marena. She looked back at Lindsay. I looked back at Lindsay.

"So then they knew how to do all this back then, and we don't," he said.

I nodded. I took a sip of the hot chocolate. Ahh. Bland but still welcome.

"And that's a sockdolager of a skill set. Ain't it? Back then, your people had the bulge on everybody. The Maya back then, they could write their own ticket. Right?"

"Well, I guess," I said. Had I gotten any foam on my upper lip? I wondered. "They did very well for a very long time. But of course, it didn't go on forever." Marena's eyes caught mine. A little less soft sell, they said. Idiot.

"That's just what I'm drivin' at," Lindsay said. As quickly and discreetly as possible, I sort of wiped my upper lip with my lower one. "If the Maya knew so darn much, then why didn't they take over the whole world?"

"Maybe just knowing how isn't enough," I said. "Or maybe they would have, but for some reason they, they lost the knack."

"Why?"

"Maybe just because the Game was a specialized skill. Maybe they tried to keep it too secret."

"So they didn't let other people draw water from the well," he said.

"Very possibly," I said. "Anyway, you know, technologies fall out of use all the time. Like when the first people came to Tasmania like ten thousand years ago or whatever, they had pottery and seagoing canoes and fishing nets and a lot of other things. But by the time of their first contact with outsiders they'd forgotten how to make them. They'd even forgotten how to start fires. They had to wait for lightning to hit a tree and then they'd carry the coals around."

"So it's just like today, nobody knows how to make a real ice-cream soda anymore," Lindsay said. "Right?"

"Definitely," Boyle said.

"Also," I said, "the ancient Maya's priorities may not have been the same as ours. They may not have wanted to take over the world."

"Well, even today, not everybody wants to take over the world," Marena said. "For instance, I don't."

"Righty right," Lindsay said. He shot his left cuff back and looked at his watch, a silver Oyster Perpetual on a brown calfskin band. Like, instead of looking at the digital time readout, which was right there in a window on the live tabletop, and which like all computer timers these days was synchronized with the cesium-decay clock at the National Institute of Standards and Technology in Boulder, Colorado, which is accurate to within a picosecond a century, he had to go out of his way to read a vastly less precise time measurement off a mechanical movement that hasn't really changed since the eighteenth century. I watched the second hand sweeping from two to three. Finally, he decided what time it was.

"Well, it's about five of," he said. "We'd better be movin' out." He looked back at me. "Maybe we'll jaw about this all later on."

"Great," I said. I was about to try to say something either wishy-washy or stupid, but Marena saved me.

"Well, anyway, Jed, I have to justify my existence here for a few minutes," she said. One could tell that she meant they were going to vote on me right now. She started steering me toward the door.

"Hold your horses a sec," Lindsay said. "Jus' let me give you a copy of this thing. I'm handing 'em out like beechnuts these days, but I can't help myself. First-time-father's pride." He took a little pigskin case from the top of a short stack on the table and flipped it open. Inside was a dedicated e-book, which he signed across the screen with a sort of silver Swiss Army multithing with a stylus on it. He handed it to me.

"Oh, great, thanks," I said. His signature was in dark blue, with gold sparkles permanently coursing through it like bulbs in an old theater marquee, and it took me a second to read the title graphics underneath:

TEAM SPIRIT™:
COACHING SECRETS of MOSES, JESUS,
LOMBARDI, and JACKSON

The timeless teamwork wisdom that will give you that "Leg Up—"
Both on the competition and in your family and spiritual life

By International Entrepreneur Lindsay R. Warren

With an Introduction by Dr. Stephen Covey, Ph.D.

I started scrolling through the text to show how interested I was. "Harnessing the Power of Pain," one chapter heading said. Little ads kept popping up in the corners, for audiovisual versions of the book, children's versions, subliminal versions, related teaching materials, courses and seminars and spiritual resorts and corporate retreats and motivational posters and indium energy bracelets and a large selection of something called "incentives." Creeds for the credulous section, I thought. *Easy Answers for New People. Harnessing the Power of Self-Delusion—*

"God bless," Lindsay said.

We had to crush hands all around again before I could leave. I slunk back out through the empty rooms. Hell, I thought. They hate me. I looked like a *papisongo* in there. And I sounded like two *papisongos*. They're voting for Sic. Hell, hell, hell.

The SkyBox was empty. Anne-Marie's voice was still burbling out of a speaker somewhere, going on about how the once (presumably) happy-go-lucky city of Orlando was now all death and devastation. *"But the long-term social and economic effects . . . are only beginning,"* she said. I drifted over to the window. Sheesh, the place was frugging monstrous. You could drop two Salt Lake Cosmodomes in here and still have room left for the Taj Mahal and some pizza. The funicular track was even with the zero-yard line, and so from here the field was perfectly symmetrical, and some optical illusion made it seem like the enormous oval was tipping up toward you. I indulged in another slug of chocolate, put the mug down, and spread my hands on the desktop, trying to stay steady.

¿Y ahora que? Now what?

"Hi," Marena said behind me. And even before I turned around, just from the sound of her voice, I knew it was a go. I'm in, I thought. I'm going to get to see it. I'm *there*. I was that Dawn of Man Australopithecine Dude in *2001*, tossing up that Zarathustran femur. I was Marie Curie squinting down at that 0.0001-gram speck that was brighter than the sun. I was the New Prometheus. What a feeling.

I turned. She made a double thumbs-up.

(19)

ampeche, Mexico, is a yellow city in the Yucatán with the gulf on the wrong side. Calle 59 was narrow and hot with bus horns and a sewage smell. What they were now calling *rakjano* music—which I guess is basically Ozomatli at four hundred beats per minute—throbbed out of a likely-looking bodega. I went in and got four six-packs of Shasta Tamarindo, five bags of de la Rosa *malvaviscos*, that is, marshmallows, five big candles, and a carton of 555s, all in a real brown paper bag like in the old days. I walked back across the street and into a little door in the south side of the Iglesia de San Francisco. The façade and most of the nave had been built in 1694, but it had just been repainted, for what must have been at least the hundredth time, so that it looked like it had grown a new layer of birch bark. It had that cool stony waxy myrrh scent inside and before I could catch myself I dipped my hand in a font and crossed my heart. And hope to die, I thought. *My name's Jesus, Son o' God, take and suck, this is my cod. Peace!* Goddamn childhood conditioning. Padre Manuda was still standing at the altar, trying out a new sound system—bought with our money, I guessed—but he had the main amp too close under the hanging microphone and when he hit a high note it picked up the reverb off the pink-washed stone walls. He didn't look at me. I passed a pair of ancient nuns with cornets and big white bibs, two of few remaining members of the once numerous sisterhood of Poor Clares. From what I could gather, over the last few hundred years the order had driven itself almost out of business by refusing to compromise on the austerities issue. Supposedly they were pretty hard-core, and the nuns spent all their time not speaking, kneeling on stone floors, eating barley gruel, and fisting each other. The only other customers were two old Tzotzil women in wool scarves and cotton three-web *huipiles*, spanking white and embroidered with green and red toad-and-Earthlord patterns. Workday wear. Four mangy pigeons fluffered around the vault.

I walked up the nave to the second transept and stopped in front of a newish retablo dedicated to Saint Teresa of Ávila, who, as I think I mentioned, was a patroness of the Sacrifice Game. She's also the patron saint of chess and headaches, which must keep her pretty busy. I ground one of the candles onto a spike, lit it with No Way's Zippo, and laid the other four next to it. I turned into the right transept and went into a little side chapel.

The room was taken up by a cream-colored cracquelured casket, closed on the top but with windows on the sides: *"El mero ataúd della santísima Abadesa Soledad,"* as the priest had put it, "the very coffin of the blessed Abbess Soledad." It had turned out she was something of an off-the-books local saint. It was just the two of us in here. I crouched down, and even though I've had a real problem with nuns since my Sisters of Charity days, I had to resist the urge to kneel. The glass had sagged over the centuries, but you could still just see a little skully head like a five-year-old's, cupped in a web of opus araneum lace, with bisque skin like strudel dough pulling back from projecting gray teeth. The notion of chickening out crossed and recrossed my mind, but I did the what-the-fuck trick and got over it. Basically you just repeat "What the fuck, the world is shit" to yourself over and over, with conviction. You don't even have to do any special breathing.

I left. I walked around the chancel rail and up the other side, behind the altar. I really am being silly, I thought. They're not trying to put something over on me. Why would they bother? Especially with anything this elaborate. Still, it didn't hurt to be sure. This is just a dry run anyway, I thought. Controlled conditions. It's not a big deal. Don't be scared. *Guarde sus pantalones.*

Okay.

There was a little steel door at the end of the south transept, and, like I owned the place, I opened it and went into the old rectory hall. At the far end of the hall there was a courtyard and, on the far side of that, a wing that used to be Convento de la Orden de las Damas Pobres. I took a route I'd rehearsed a few times, up eighteen tiny zigzag stairs to the second floor, which was just a long low hall with five little doors on each side.

Grgur was slouching outside cell #4, poking at a military-looking laptop. He was wearing a polo shirt and seafoam-gray Ralph Lauren slacks, like he was the assistant manager of a cruise line. I waved. He nodded, glowering. I'm glad he's joined us, I thought. He really brightens up the place. The various gadgets spread out in the hall included two thirty-inch monitors, two boxes that looked like big speakers, a four-foot steel rod with a handle on it, and two things on tripods that looked like ordinary portable radar dishes, that is, shallow Plexiglas parabolas about thirty inches across, with big cylindrical sponge-covered boxes out in front where the microphone would be. I edged around Grgur into the tiny white room. The little window was open and letting in flies, but the place was still like a moldy sauna. There was a camp cot, a cheap new crucifix on the wall, an electrocardiogram reader, and an IV rig. Terror. Whoa. The combination of rig, cot, and whitewash triggered this flash from when I was six and in the hospital in San Cristóbal—

Squelch that.

The cell was also crowded with people. Taro and his Ashley, that is, the one they called Ashley$_2$, not, as I had first thought, Ashley Thieu, to distinguish her from the other Ashleys, were sitting on the floor messing with a workstation and Marena and Dr. Lisuarte were talking in the arch by the window. Hitch, the cameraman—we called him that because he was an aspiring director who looked a bit like a young, Hispanic Alfred Hitchcock—was gaffing a microphone to the top of the door frame. I offered my snacks around, but nobody wanted any. I fished out the last surviving box of Shasta. The thing had an autocooler on it— *"¡Está Frigorífica!"* it said—and I was worried that it was going to taste all defanged and updated, but . . . no!, it still had that bitter Cold War Apollo-era ultraviolet aftertang, the great taste of basic esters and aldehydes before the flavorists got too clever. Could you even get this stuff in the States anymore? Dr. L said we had to get going and this was as good a time as any.

I said okay.

Yikes, yikes. Okay. Chill. Be a mensch, for Christ's sake. I deshoed and sat cross-legged on the cot. Supposedly it was in the same orientation of the original pallet, and the crucifix was in the same spot as Sor Soledad's would have been when she died here. Of course, in a way it was overkill. We didn't really need to do this here. The point in real space—whatever that is—where this room had been in those days was millions of miles away by now, so theoretically I could have been back at the Stake, or in the lab in Orlando, or anywhere. But the feeling was that it would be less disorienting if I was in the same place now as I would be back then, with the same weight of mud brick and plaster all around me, the same courtyard outside, and the noises of the same city. Although of course back then there were more sheep and goats around here than people. And it would be the same time of day, but not the same time of the year.

"You don't mind if I'm here, do you?" Marena asked.

I said no and that I used to like watching my mom pluck chickens.

I don't think Marena really heard me, though. A menacing buzz arose, *re-pente*, behind my head. Dr. L didn't even start with scissors; she just drove into my hyacinthine locks with her clipper thing like it was a McCormick Harvester, which, I suppose, it was descended from.

"How'd it go with Padre Cual-es-su-nombre?" I asked.

"He's been a pain," Marena said. "We offered them enough cash to buy this whole shit town and they didn't want to take it."

"Well, they've about had it with worldly ambition around here," I said.

"No kidding, we had to call his boss and endow a school."

"You talked to God?"

"No, no, the bird guy, the, the cardinal," she said. "I bet God would have taken half that much. It's going to be called, like, the Sisters of the Blessed Immaculate Sacred Bleeding Technical Virgin K through Twelve or something."

"What a waste."

Dr. Lisuarte finished the left side.

"Yeah. And even then we had to throw in two cases of El Tesoro."

The whole thing took about two minutes. I felt weak, not like I was Samson to begin with or because I put that much faith, even unconsciously, into the whole Indian hair thing, but it was just that my ostrich-eggshell helmet was just way out there in the breeze.

"Done," Lisuarte said. I touched my forehead and moved tentatively up and over. My hand felt like the Lunik 3 moon probe. Into the farthest reaches of—

"Hey, that's a great look for you," Michael Weiner's voice said. I hadn't seen him come in, and of course he hadn't knocked or anything. I said thanks. He clapped me on the back. Ow. Schmuck. Too many warm bodies in here. Michael asked Taro how they were doing. Taro said they were ready. Dr. Lisuarte said ten minutes. This was already getting to be routine for them.

"Okay, well . . . just to review?" Michael said for the camera in his TV voice. "The good sister croaked at terce, that's about nine in the morning, on November 28, 1686."

Was that supposed to sound all jaunty and irreverent for TV? I wondered. *Ocho ochenta*, dork. This guy is a total stiff and always will be.

"She hadn't left this room for at least a month before that," he went on. Or let's say prattled on. "But she was conscious on the twenty-fourth because she signed her will on that date. Which had about three objects in it. Then it says she was able to take a last communion on the twenty-seventh. Otherwise there's not much to know about her, but I think if we go for one in the morning on the twenty-fifth we'll be fine."

Yeah, *we*, I thought. Egomaniac. You're not on the Pop Archaeology Channel anymore. Can it. "We'll go for between matins and vespers. That's when they were all supposed to be alone, so theoretically nobody else would have been in here."

"One hopes," Marena said.

"I'm going to palpate your cranium," Dr. Lisuarte said. I said it was fine as long as she didn't feel my skull. She did, though. It's weird to feel fingers on your scalp. Where no hand had gone before. Except for my mother's, I mean, my real mother's, when I was really tiny. I got a flash of myself sitting in her lap, her stroking a scratch on my forehead, rubbing white ashes into it to stop the bleeding. Lisuarte asked if it was okay to give me the injections and start the countdown. I said sure. Blast off, Flash. She unwrapped two syringes. The stuff didn't come in a hypospray. I tightened up. Like most hæmophiliacs I have a touch of aichmophobia, that is, fear of pointed objects.

"O-*kay*," she said, "how about if I start you out with forty mgs of Adderall?"

"Great," I said. I didn't tell her that for me that was about the equivalent of a demitasse of green tea.

She swabbed my right inner thigh and slid in the needle. Ow. Next I got 3.8 ccs of ProHance. It's a solution of a paramagnetic contrast medium called gadoteridol. It makes every tiny little microevent in your brain show up loud and clear on the screen, like the fissures in Angelina Jolie's lips.

"All right, lean back," she said. I did. The foam of a cheap institutional pillow gave and bounced under my delicate head. I was in borrowed CONCACAF sweat pants and a Neo-Teo T-shirt and already felt highly vulnerable all over. She asked if I was really ready to sit for six hours. I said yes. She asked if I wanted to go to the bathroom. No, I said. If I want to do that I'll tell you, I thought. In fact, I'll make you hold the jar. Nosy bitch. Clara Barton, she-wolf of the Red Cross.

"Okay," she said, "I'm going to glue on some positional 'trodes." There was a hiss and a tiny Boreas of solvent above my occiput.

"Do you want this?" Marena asked. She meant my hair, which she'd thoughtfully collected. I said I did, thanks, I wanted to knit a suicide voodoo doll out of it.

Lisuarte and A₂ squeezed my head into a kind of bathing cap—it was made out of that fabric that's spun out of old soda bottles, which I guess is invisible to electromagnetism—and opened a big Zero Halliburton case. Marena helped them lift out a portable magnetoencephalograph, that is, a thick enamel-coated metal ring about the size of a Vespa tire, with two thick cables coming out. We called it the Toilet, since you stuck your head in it and upchucked your brains. It didn't really look like much. In fact, not much of anything around here looked like a high-tech operation. One thing Taro had said that I was catching on to was how 90 percent of the technology they were using had been around since the 1970s and that they were just putting it together. They nestled the big ring into the pillow. I nudged my head up next to the opening. They twisted it down around my head and squnched the fabric up into the gap with slivers of foam, so that the bagel's lower lip was just over my eyebrows. Lisuarte asked if it was too snug. I said it was just exactly snug enough. She hooked it up and switched it on. There was a discreet hum from the electromagnets cruising around and around inside the ring at about 380 miles per hour. When I'd tried the thing on before, I was afraid it was going to find a sliver of steel in a sinus or somewhere and pull it out through my eyeball, but evidently I was shrapnel-free. A₂ rolled over a sandbagged tripod with a big monitor on a swing arm and positioned the big OLED screen just below the crucifix.

"Can you see the monitor?" she asked.

"A little closer," I said. She moved it toward me and angled it down. "Okay." My gray matter was all up there in layered translucencies like it was my carry-on bag in an airport scanner.

"Taro?" Marena asked. "Are you on?"

"We are already sending a leader signal," he said.

"How do you feel?" Lisuarte asked. She'd given me a combination of aripiprazole and lamotrigine a few hours before, supposedly just to get me thinking clearly but not obsessively. I wasn't sure it was working, but I said I felt tip-top.

"Okay, we're scanning," Lisuarte said.

I made a thumbs-up.

"You'll be fine," Marena said. "Remember, it's all about motivation."

"Yeah," I said.

"I'm betting my bra on you."

"Great." Hmm, I thought, well, that sounded at least a little suggestive.

Over the last few days it had felt like Marena and I were getting pretty close to the border of Intimacyland. Or at least it felt that way, but lately it had seemed more like we were approaching it asymptotically and might never get there. And also, to me, anyway, the fact that it hadn't either been crossed or definitively not crossed was becoming a bigger deal every day.

"I'm going to start the TMS on your left hemisphere," Lisuarte said. She meant transcranial magnetic stimulation, which confuses the electronic events in a selected part of the brain. This supposedly encourages other parts to work harder and fire more often, and that would make their structures more visible.

"Okay, let's have a little privacy here," Marena said. "Thanks."

Taro and everyone cleared out of the room. For the next few hours it would be just Marena, Lisuarte, and me in here. Although of course the others would all be outside watching on video, and probably providing wise-ass commentary.

"Okay," Marena said. "You want to start?" I said sure. I'd asked for her to read the cues instead of Lisuarte. The CTP team—that stood for Consciousness Transfer Protocol—had voted on it and decided it was all right because, as I think I said, all this was mainly for my benefit anyway. Although they did want to run the new field equipment once before the main event. But the thing was, of course, if it didn't work, that wouldn't really tell us anything. It might just mean that Sor Soledad was too sick to move or something. And if it didn't work, we'd just move on with the project anyway. However— according to Warren's team of crack shrinks—if it did work, the psychological benefits would be huge.

I sort of settled myself into the cot. Lisuarte put a thin blanket over me, I guess on the theory that it would relax me. Hmm. Actually, I was already feeling a little floaty. I focused on the crucifix, trying to get myself into a medieval mood. The plastic JC had a pretty big basket going on in his loincloth. Writhe for me, you hot, hot divinity. Take it up the rib cage. Take it up the metatarsus. Take that tree up your ass, you sacred slut. You've been a *bad* god. Suck my sponge, King of the Kikes. Ooooooh! My God, my God. The earth doth quake, and the graves do ope, and the dead saints' members do rise and swell! Oooh, I am rent in twain! Top to bottom! OOOO*OOOOH! OOO—*

"Okay, let's go," Marena said. She was chewing her nicotine gum, but she talked around it well enough not to be disgusting. "Can you tell us what you did yesterday?"

I told her.

"Okay. What's Samarkand the capital of?"

"Kazakhstan." On the screen a silent green snarl of anvil-crawler lightning flashed between the thunderheads of my ventromedial cortex.

"What time is it?"

"One eighteen."

"What's the date today?"

"March fifteenth, 2012. 7 Cane, 6 Dark Egg. In the Chinese calendar it's the twenty-third day of the second—"

"Okay, what's in the news today?"

"Well, the FBI arrested those Hijos de Kukulkan people. Which I guess takes care of the 'shoulder the blame' thing in the Codex." HDK was a new sort of pseudo-Zapatista group from Austin, sort of a Maya version of the Nation of Aztlán. Supposedly they'd claimed responsibility, in a rally, for the Disney World Horror. On the other hand—according to No Way—this guy Subcomandante Carlos, who was kind of the head of it and who used to be in Enero 31, had told him the HDK hadn't had anything to do with it.

"Yeah," Marena said. "What else?"

"Uh, a bunch of the glowb—I mean, about eight thousand persons who were exposed to polonium particles—have gotten out of the quarantine camps and they're camped outside D.C. And the White House is saying they're going to intercept the marchers and keep them from reaching the Great Lawn. Uh, let's see . . . they're saying that they estimate there's about five hundred pounds of polonium 210 in the No-Go Zone, so there's no way anyone's going in there for a long time without protection. Except there's this shortage of shielded responder suits because most of them are in Pakistan, and eighty percent of the suits that are still in the U.S. are defective. Uh . . . there's all this video of dead bodies coming out, and the government's trying to close down YouTube because they don't want people to see it, and the ACLU filed a suit yesterday to make all of it public. And some of it really is pretty . . . it's pretty gruesome." I was thinking of this one video of people at MegaCon. It was from the main display floor in this gigantic hall. Somebody'd cleared the booths out of an area in the center, and about two hundred of the conventioneers had died there together in this big sort of heap, because sick people tend to seek human contact. Like most of the bodies they were all contorted and open-mouthed or grimacing, but they were also, it seemed, uniformly overweight, and about half of them were still in costume as orcs or Hyperboreans or Klingons or whatever, and it all gave the whole thing a medieval feeling, like some mountain of slain foes that, say, Tamerlane would have left on the steppes, except it was all in that flat green fluorescent light, and then as the videobot waddled closer you could see that a lot of them were holding things in their hands like Harry Potter wands and Sith amulets and other sorts of talismanic trinkets, and then it got so close that you could see how puffed up they were, and you could see the flies on them and practically smell the putrefaction through the screen—

"What else?" Marena asked.

"Oh . . . well . . . a lot of victims' families, they're demanding that they get the corpses out, but the authorities and public opinion were sticking pretty firmly to the other side, that if they did it would spread polonium 209 around, and that they should send in some robot backhoes and maybe a few priests and whatever in Demron suits and bury all the bodies at some site inside the No-Go Zone."

I paused, but she didn't say anything, I guess because the people at the Stake were seeing enough new regions of my brain lighting up that they didn't want to put in a new stimulus.

"So, and then there were some whistleblowers at the EPA," I said. "And they were saying that even that would kick up too much dust and the best thing to do is leave the whole area unchanged, with all the buildings standing, as a monument, and then there was another faction that I guess wants to at least bulldoze the buildings and cut down all the trees because if there's another fire in there it'll spread more of the polonium, but I guess now the idea is to keep enough Forest Service planes on hand to put out any new fires. And with the bodies, now there's a bill in the Florida state legislature for what they're calling the Pompeian solution, which I guess is they're going to send in teams of EMTs in special suits, and they're going to plastinate the corpses with some kind of von Hagens process, and I guess spray them with gold paint or fix them up somehow and just leave them there, and then once there's no more particulates in the wind they want to take the families for flyover funerals in blimps. Although that sounds kind of ridiculous to me, but—"

"Okay, what else?" Marena asked.

"Uh, the Ayatollah Razib says the attack was, uh, foretold in the Koran. Ted Haggard says it was to punish us for the federal gay marriage thing. The official death toll on the combined poisoning and rioting and fires, it's getting close to forty-five thousand. About a third of the southeastern U.S. is still under martial law. A whole bunch of people got mugged for their blood last night in Tampa. I guess they woke up all pale and drained and everything, with—"

"I mean what else is in the news other than Disney World?"

"Oh. Uh, let's see . . . there's a civil war in Bangladesh. There's that terrorist, Hasani, that they caught last month, he's terminally ill, supposedly, and the public is asking for a torture sentence. Right? And today the president signed a waiver of the Geneva Convention, uh, protocols, so it could go forward. Right? And July corn contracts are up thirty percent, and spot gold's about sixteen hundred dollars an ounce. And—"

"That's fine. Good. I mean, that's not all good, but you're doing fine."

"Thanks."

"Right." She looked at her phone. "Okay, what's the square root of nineteen?"

"Four point, uh, hang on, uh, three five nine."

"I think it's so sexy that you can do that."

"Huh? Oh, thanks." Hmm, what was that about? I wondered. Was that a flirt? Huh. I wouldn't mind beaming into *her* transversable wormhole. Or was that part of the idea? Get me a little embarrassed, a little turned on? Probably. Gotta watch these people. They're tricky—

"What was Kiri-Kin Tha's first law of metaphysics?" she asked.

"What?" I asked.

"What was—"

"Wait a second," I said. "I remember, uh, nothing's not real. Or something."

"Nothing unreal exists," she said.

"That's it. Heh."

"I'm going to give you that series of nouns," Marena said, "and we want you to remember them and write them down when you're in place."

"Right, I know."

"Shoe . . . eraser . . . goldfish . . . skull . . . balloon . . . wheelbarrow."

"Got it," I said. I also had a message to myself in mind, something I'd just come up with, had never told anyone about, and had never even uttered aloud: Houdini's afterlife code, *Rosabelle, believe.*

"Okay," she said. "So, now we're going to turn off your view of yourself and show you some pictures.

"Okay, here's the first image," Marena said. A still of Ronald Reagan in *Stallion Road* came up on the screen in glorious organic-LED detail.

"That's scary stuff," I said. My amygdala was probably flashing DANGER DANGER DANGER.

"Now, just answer when I ask." The picture changed to a video of baby geese walking in a line behind their mother. "What color socks are you wearing?"

That one nearly stumped me, but I think I got it right. Not that getting it right mattered. In fact, you often get more flash, that is, you get more neuronal routines to fire, when you don't know the answer—

Whoa. On the screen a big brown weasel or stoat or something had slunk into the shot and had already torn apart four out of six goslings. The mother flapped around the little killing field, honking in despair. Hell.

"Okay," she said. "Let's go through the message one last time."

I said okay. For the hundredth time we went over what to write down, what to write it on, and where to leave it.

"Good," she said. "Okay. Tell me about the Desert Dog."

What? I thought.

Whoa. How'd she know about that? I'd never told anybody about it. Maybe I'd mumbled it in my sleep during one of those long EEG tests at the Stake. They'd probably dosed me with sodium ammitol or something. Bastards.

"Jed?"

"Sorry," I said, "I haven't, uh, that's not, uh—"

"I know," she said, "it's a surprise question; please answer it anyway."

There was a pause. Fine, I thought. I started to tell her how my stepbrothers had caught the dog, how he had no front paws, just scrappy stumps with strings of cartilage trailing out, how his eyes were bulgy with fear, and how when I'd been out there by his cage for a little while the fear had lessened, and how I'd tried to solve the combination padlock and couldn't do it, and then to jimmy it and couldn't do that, and then I'd tried to bend the thin bars back. Somehow I was going to get them together again so that my stepbrothers wouldn't know it had been me. But I was only eight and didn't know how to do anything mechanically serious, and the crate was some sort of heavy-duty industrial thing made for pigs or whatever. Desert Dog had known what I was doing, and he seemed to trust that I'd get him out. It wasn't easy at first, telling Marena about it, especially since I despise sentiment, and my voice was getting hoarse and monotonal, but maybe something in the pharmacocktail they'd given me loosened the tongue, because I kept going. I told her how I'd brought a can of Mountain Dew, and how I poured it into a little pool on the zinc and how he practically dove for it and lapped it up, resting on his elbows, and then looked at me with this grateful expression in those kind eyes dogs have, with almost even a dampness of hope in them, how I gave him a snack-sized bag of Rold Gold pretzels that I'd rubbed the salt off of, and how he'd loved those, and how he wagged his threadbare tail and shook his gold earflaps, and how I'd given him the rest of the Mountain Dew, and how happy he was getting it, looking at me with that doggy feeling of trust, how I could tell he thought that for sure I'd do the right thing, that I was powerful and would let him out when I wanted to, that he'd come along and be my lookout, that he was saying he could still get around fine even without his paws, that he'd come along with me and be a good friend, how soft his snout was when he licked my hand, with that compact sort of coziness in his doggy head, how his spongy nose was dry and hot but not so dry as it had been, how his tongue flicked over my bruised fingers as I tried this and tried that, I tried bending the ground plate with a piece of metal and couldn't do it, and how finally I just lay back crying, looking at my bloody hands and seeing I'd scratched my fingertips and knuckles in several places, and knowing that if I didn't get back to the house and get to work with my wound plasters I could bleed too much, and how I scratched Desert Dog under his soft flaps with my fingers and told him that I had to leave but I'd be back, you wait, you good dog, and how I walked back home across the vacant lots in the white highway lamplight, frustrated beyond the strength of the word *frustrated*, like I was biting on the rock of the universe. It was one of those moments when you see with just a sliver of clarity, just one little finger-melted dot on your frosted goggles, just how terrible existence is, how it's all just the disappointment of innocents, transmuting their hope into shit at a headlong rate, and how much the torturing just has to somehow stop. When I got home I could still hear Desert Dog crying across the highway, not so much in a canine whimper but more just sobbing, like a two-year-old human with an earache. And another—

"Uh, okay. Good," Marena said. Probably Lisuarte had told her over the headset that they'd finally gotten enough activity out of my limbic cortex. At last, Jed Mixoc de Spock shows some real feeling. "Now we're going to start some stims." She meant neuronal stimulations.

I said fine and closed my eyes. There were ten seconds of normalcy and then a flash of green light.

"I see green," I said.

"Good," she said. There were another few seconds of downtime and then the sound of raindrops.

"I hear rain," I said. I was also noticing that someone had lit a stick of sandalwood incense. Then I realized it was probably just one of the stims.

"Incense," I said.

"Right," Marena said.

Sounds, smells, and images flashed up and faded. I heard violins in G minor, a bar of Prokofiev's Piano Concerto no. 2. I smelled cinnamon and burning rubber—somebody's messing with my temporal lobes, I thought—and then, all at once, a sweet woodsy smell like wet old books. I saw Silvana's face. I felt itches on my chest and a jab in my ribs. I saw the faces of people I didn't remember but must have known. I saw my mother's face. She smiled. I saw a scary pattern of wood grain on the door of our room in the Ødegårds' house that I'd thought looked like a devilish goat in a bow tie. I remembered an orange Tonka backhoe I'd dug out of a landfill and played with for hours and days, thought about one of the first fish I had, a *Glossolepis incisus* I'd named Generoso, and how starting one morning it grew all spiky and belligerent and killed the other male rainbowfish and then the females and then died itself, about things that not only hadn't I thought about in years, but that I maybe hadn't thought about between the time they happened and today. Oddly, they all seemed to play out backward, and out of sequence with each other, and then later on they'd happen forward again, as though they were first being defragmented and then rewound and assigned to new positions on my hard drive, and then replayed, and a few times I was so out of it that I almost thought I might be the one, that is, the one of me who would find himself back there, stuck in the late seventeenth century, and here I was hoping and even praying to deities that were both evil and nonexistent that it wouldn't be me, let it not be me who goes, let me be the one who stays here, because if I were the other one, I wouldn't be coming back.

(20)

M aybe I should clarify that just a little.

You know how when, say, Kirk or Bones or whoever goes through the teleporter, he's copied and disintegrated here and then the information beam goes to wherever and he's reintegrated over there out of available local atoms, and you tend to think, wait, why disintegrate your captain when you don't have to? Why not just skip that step and integrate him over there anyway? Then there'd be two Kirks and one of them could stay on the bridge. In fact, who cares about teleportation when you've got duplication? Why not make a whole bunch of Kirks so every ship in the Starfleet Command could have one? Well, in a way you could say that the Kerr Space Project system made use of that very principle. That is, when I was lying on that cot with the thing on my head, it didn't disintegrate me, or zap me out of my head, or even put me to sleep, any more than taking a picture of me would have. Despite all the stims and whatever psychotropics I had in my system, I was awake and conscious and even thinking relatively clearly. I didn't feel a thing.

Or maybe it would be better to say that the "I" that happened to stay, the one who was still here after the picture was taken—that "I" didn't feel a thing. But the picture itself—a much less lucky version of Jed DeLanda—would be like the hypothetical second Kirk, the one who ended up down on the planet's surface and had to deal with the Romulans or whoever. The less lucky Jed would be trapped in the body of a withering, pustuled crone. Shit. Supposedly, dying of smallpox is pretty painful. Maybe they'd give her some opium. No, probably not. That other Jed is *so* screwed, I thought. Sorry, Other Jed. But we have to do this.

Of course, in the interim stage, that other Jed would just be a pattern, without any way to be aware of itself. It was just a code written with a special protocol, the P of CTP, which had originally been developed by the Human Cognome Project and which was in some ways similar to a high-level assembler. In fact, since the code was transmitted digitally, you could say that it was a number, a number with more than a trillion digits, but still just an integer like any other.

Over the course of six hours the EEG/MEG scanner would take a 3-D movie of the behavior of my brain in action, trillions of electrical and chemical events more or less triggered by the Q&A. Neurons generate voltage spikes at distinctive rates, and chemical reactions release measurable bursts of heat and infrared. Every one of these microevents would go through source-analysis software and get triangulated to a specific location. Then it would get tagged and sorted by location, strength, and time and—out in one of the boxes in the hall—it would be integrated into a mathematical space that would overlay the electrophysiologic signalling onto a matrix of biochemical and metabolic information. Finally, this-all would be coded into a data stream. The code, presumably, would represent everything that I thought of as myself, the Alps-size grab bag of memories and attitudes and habits of calculation and rationalizing and multiple and contradictory self-images and everything else that creates the illusion of selfhood—which is, take it from me, definitely no more than an illusion, and not always a convincing one. Then all those roughly two hundred trillion bits of information that made up my consciousness—or my id and ego, or let's just call it my SOS, my Sense of Self—all of that flowed through a pair of heavily shielded 2.4-gigahertz signal boosters—the things that looked like speakers—and over parallel fiber-optic cables through the hallway, up a little back stair, and out into a small transmission dish on the rectory roof. The dish bounced my SOS off a Spartacus Intercellular Communications satellite—retasked through unimaginable Pentagon connections—to a relay station near Mexico City. From there it went via ordinary data transmission satellites to the Very High Speed Superconducting Supercollider, a new accelerator ring with a 14.065-kilometer circumference, which, according to the briefing, was near CERN, on the French/Swiss border. The data went into a bank of hard drives in the collider compound, which together could store about six hundred trillion bits.

This was a lot less, though, than the total of roughly four hundred quadrillion bits that would come out of my head over six hours. So we'd run into the problem of storage. In fact, there wasn't yet enough computer memory on the planet to hold all the data. You'd need over twenty billion five-hundred-gig hard drives. Part of the problem was simply that it was digital and not analog. The only device with enough room was another human brain. And the brain we were interested in had shriveled into crumbs a long time ago. So we'd have to catch it when it was still working.

Now, as I'm sure you know, over the last century, and especially over the last decade or so, there's been an awful lot of loose talk about time travel. Maybe it's because people are getting used to certain long-percolating sci-fi forecasts finally coming true. With all the brilliant and personable computers, with all the space tourism, nanobot surgeons, with all the world's books, music, and video right in your pocket, with all the wet artificial life, invisibility panels, cryonics, teledildonics, and glow-in-the-dark Labradoodles, people assume that someone must also be close to cracking the time thing. It's no wonder there have been so many scientific frauds about it. It's like alchemy in the Middle Ages. Back then it was like, "Sure, give me a thousand copper Soldos and I'll turn them into 0.99 gold by Saint Whitlough's Day." Now it's "Give us another billion and we'll have Cleopatra in your office in time for your IPO."

Unfortunately, time's actually a bit of a tougher nut. Or rather, the past is. It's easy to go into the future, even with current cryonics. But going the other way you run up against two big problems.

The first one, of course, is the grandfather paradox. For a while, the main way people tried to get around it was by positing parallel universes. You could go into your past and do anything you wanted—even including killing your grandfather—and your future there would be different from the future you'd come from, and everybody'd be happy. But there are problems with this. For instance, if you have all those universes to choose from, why not just go to a parallel universe where everything is great—where, say, you bought Google in '04, milk chocolate has one calorie per ounce, and Bill O'Reilly never existed? But the biggest problem is it's not the case. That is, according to the best current theory and the best experimental evidence, there is not an infinite number of universes out there. And even if there were, you couldn't get to any of them. Energy from now that radiates out of black holes in the past comes out in our past, not in an infinite number of pasts. And even if this isn't the only universe, the number of actual universes is still probably rather small. Which still doesn't mean this one is special, of course. When we were going over this in one of the briefings, Marena said, "It's like how there was only one episode of *Chic Chesbro,* but it still wasn't any good." Although none of us, including me, got the reference. Taro put it a little better. He said that the line around physics departments was "Multiple universes: cheap on theory, expensive on universes." That is, when you can't get some equation to zero out, you can always just say, "Oh, the remainder must have just gone into some other universe." Not only is this a cop out, but eventually, somebody always solves those equations without it. So the polycosmic dream is fading.

The other big problem with time travel is that anything you send back runs about a 100-percent risk of spaghettification. More specifically, it's not too much of a problem finding or even making a black hole. And in a black hole, energy goes back in time all the time. Or more specifically, time's passage inside it isn't clearly related to how it passes for the rest of the universe, and in fact it tends to go backward, which is why black holes eventually evaporate. Right now there's energy from the distant future spewing out of singularities not all that far from earth. Not that it does us any good. But the point is that even though it's not prohibitively difficult to drop something into a black hole and have it automatically spew out at some point in our past, it will emerge hopelessly crushed at the atomic level, and often converted into pure energy. This means that ordinarily, you can't send information. You could drop in an encyclopedia, but all you'd get, back in the past, would be a lot of heat and light, signifying nothing.

However—however, however—you can send something that's nothing, that is, that doesn't have mass. You can send energy.

At the Superconducting Supercollider, the raw data stream of my SOS got processed into an information-rich wave map. This also compressed the signal, collapsing the distance between the waves, so that the information that was taking hours to download today would take less than forty seconds to blast out on the other end. A gamma gun shot a stream of energy based on the wave pattern into the Kerr space path, an imaginary perfect circle at the center of the collider's torus. The stream traveled around the ring about six hundred thousand times, accelerating to the point where its centrifugal force made it spin off from the ring and into the tangential tunnel, where there was a new electromagnetic installation specially designed to create and suspend miniature Krasnikovian wormholes.

It had already been four years since the gang at the Large Hadron Collider announced that they'd created a microscopic black hole. Creating a wormhole is a similar process, but in some ways it's easier. Black holes have event horizons, which are nothing but trouble. Wormholes don't. Wormholes have two mouths—and you need both of them—but black holes only have one. And to keep a black hole around for any decent amount of time, especially anywhere near the surface of earth, you'd need several sun's worths of energy.

The care and feeding of a wormhole is much easier. But even for an ordinary wormhole—if one can call it that—you still need advanced engineering and a lot of power. Your basic hole, say the Schwarzschild type, in a space-time $R^2 \times S^2$, looks something like $ds^2 = - (1 - r_s / r) \, dt^2 + (1 - r_s / r) - 1 \, dr^2 + r^2 \, d\Omega^2$, that is, when Ω is your density parameter and where $r_s = 2G M / c^2$, and $d\Omega^2 = d\theta^2 + \sin^2 d\varphi^2$. And of course M is the molecular mass, G is the gravitational constant, φ is the angle, r is the radius, and d is the distance. So anyway, if you tweak at it for a little while, you can see that its throat has huge tidal forces on it, and without a lot of opposing energy, it's going to collapse. Really it's just part of a black hole/white hole system. But the Krasnikov variety has a Kerr metric of $ds^2 = \Omega^2(\xi)[-d\tau^2 + d\xi^2 + K^2(\xi)(d\theta^2 + \sin^2\theta d\varphi^2)]$, where Ω and K are smooth positive even functions and $K = K0\cos\xi/L$ at $\xi\epsilon(-L, L)$, $K_0 \equiv K(0)$, and K is constant at large ξ. So it's very, very stable. It's static, it satisfies the weak energy condition, it doesn't need exotic matter, and it's spherically symmetric. In fact, at first it doesn't even look like a wormhole, but if you transform the coordinates as $r \equiv B^{-1}\Omega_0 \exp B\xi$, with $t \equiv B\tau r$, then you can make it as flat as you want by just increasing the size of r. And you can fold that into a usable wormhole with a length of $\Omega_0 L$ and a throat radius of $\min(\Omega K)$. Of course, to make it wide enough for, say, a space pod to get through, you'd still have to throw a few planets in the fusion stove. But a very tiny version doesn't take a huge amount of energy to make, or to hold onto—that is, to keep it from sinking into the core of earth. The narrowest point of our baby was only a bit wider than a hydrogen atom. But as long as it was a bit wider than a single photon, information could still get through. The pulsed gamma beams—although actually they were made of a lot of different wavelengths, some of them more in the spectrum of hard x-rays than gamma rays, but let's stick with calling them gamma beams because it sounds so retro–Cold War–space-operatic— would focus down into the wormhole's mouth, converge at its throat, and then spread out at an angle that would bathe Sor Soledad's little room in a movie of my mind.

But even with all that, just because of quantum fluctuations, it would take more energy than the SSC could muster to keep a hole that size open for longer than a few microseconds. So the lab's biggest insight was that you didn't have to do that. You could just create a new wormhole in the same "place," so to speak. Or, more specifically, along the same predictable curve on the Cauchy hypersurface. And then you'd make another and another. The gamma beams that would encode my consciousness would be phased to enter each of the series of holes, and when they came out the other end, they'd be lined up at the right point behind us on the space-time curve, that is, in the past.

Actually, the trickier part was the next stage, that is, working out the angles. A_2, who despite working for Taro had a degree in experimental physics from Pohang University of Science and Technology, said that it had taken more man-hours to get working than all the other elements of the Kerr space system put together.

If you just sit still, at the end of a minute you'll have moved about 85,000 miles from the point in the universe you started from. So if the beam encoding my SOS emerged in the past at the same place it started, it would come out in the middle of nowhere, somewhere roughly midway between the sun and Alpha Draconis. So a little tweaking was a must. Of course, our GPS sent our exact position to the Swiss team, so where we were now wasn't a problem. But they also had to extrapolate our location into the past, to identify the point in space-time where most or at least many of the atoms in this room would have been exactly 170,551,508 minutes ago.

This requires fine-tuning to about 1 part in 10^{32}. And of course the data on where earth was doesn't go back that far. Even using old eclipse records and whatever other astronomical archives they could find, the cone of accuracy for AD 664 was way, way too large. And of course the sun also moves. Just like the earth, it shrinks and inflates. It jiggles around its plasmic core. It gets buffeted by meteors and cosmic winds. So for beyond-astronomical precision they'd had to zero in the transmission largely by trial and error. They'd started by blasting energy into the center of a big block of freshly cut wood sitting on a lab table in a basement room. They'd angle the beam so that it would emerge five minutes ago—which is already in outer space, in fact a few thousand miles behind where it is now—and the gamma beams would shake up the carbon isotopes in the center of the block so that they'd decay just a little more quickly than the ones on the surface. When they'd gotten that right they started aiming for further back in the past and directing the beam at sections of well-dated historical buildings in old mining towns and abandoned pueblos around Bryce Canyon, blasting the conjectured position with enough radiation to turn the uranium 238 in the foundations halfway to lead, drilling out samples, testing them, usually coming up empty, and trying it again a few feet away on the building's foundation and a few million miles forward or back, in the path of earth through space. The calculations were fraught with tricksome variables. Even earth's internal motion, which you'd think wouldn't be a lot, had turned out to be a bitch. As you probably know, it's gooey down there, and that causes wobbles in the rotation that can be very close to random. And even if you had that licked you had to take into account things like continental drift, erosion, changes in absolute land level versus the core of earth, orbital slips caused by passing comets, and a hundred other things. And there were similar problems with the spin of the sun and the Milky Way galaxy. Still, over the last two years they'd drawn a tight picture of where our planet was in the past, extending an imaginary helical track from the surface of earth out into space, out of the solar system, out of the Milky Way galaxy, and far back toward the center of our expanding universe.

Luckily, the other end of our wormhole didn't have to travel that far. They didn't need to load it on a spaceship and truck it out to Vega or wherever. It could stay here, right on earth with us, and from here it could be angled so that the energy they put into it emerged in different positions in space, the same way it could come out at different positions in time. In fact, the whole project had originally gotten started, way back in 1988, as part of a NASA space-travel program. Since the nineties Warren had been continuing the research, working more on the time angle. As of today, the program—which was still housed at one of the big Ames Research Center servers in Mountain View, California—could tell you how to hit any given spot on earth's surface at an exact second centuries ago. It was like shooting an arrow into the air and hitting the eye of a Tralfamadorian wasp on the far side of Titan. But assuming it all worked, the stream of data would emerge at the right point in space at the right time in the past, in this case, in Sor Soledad's cell, three days before her death. Taro's assistant A_2 had done a whiteboard sketch of the concept for the last presentation to Boyle that made it all look pretty straightforward:

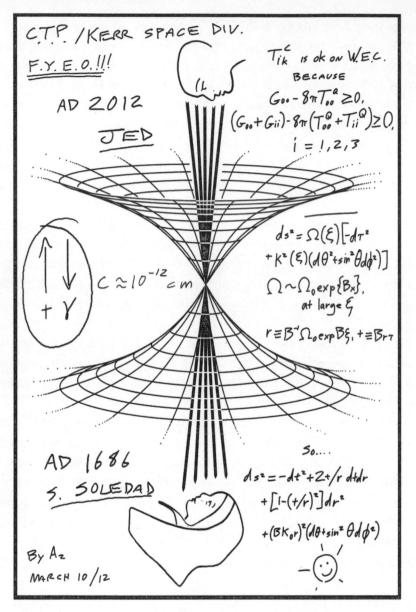

Like the Kerr space system, the Consciousness Transfer Protocol hadn't originally been developed for time projection. And it had also started from humble roots and grown slowly, over decades. In the 1980s it was still just planaria swimming through simple mazes at the University of Illinois in Champaign. One flatworm would learn the routine, and they'd record pulses from its little neural node and fire a repeating pattern of x-rays based on the recording into a second one, and the second would learn how to navigate the thing a little more quickly. The goal was to develop a surgical technique that could rewire parts of donor brains to make them easier to transplant. But by the early nineties the university was doing it with macaques, and in 2002 the Warren Research Group did their first human trials on terminally ill volunteers in India and Brazil. Two years ago they'd done what they said was their last real-time human trial—the first "wet test" that Marena had mentioned back at the Stake—and downloaded Tony Sic's SOS into the head of a sixty-one-year-old Honduran man who was dying of stomach cancer. There was no measurable loss of Sic's essential memories, cognitive ability, or personality. Or so they said.

I got the feeling, though, that they'd also done some other tests they weren't telling me about. Probably they'd done at least one test like this one and sent Sic's data into the mind of someone in the past. But I couldn't find out anything about it. "Some things are just so illegal nobody wants to know about them," Marena said, as though all the other shenanigans I'd found out about lately were just traffic violations.

And really, what we were doing wasn't nice. Before they started with my SOS, the Swiss team had sent a salvo of photons in a pattern designed to irreversibly confuse Soledad's mind, or, as A_2 put it, to "wipe down the target's gray matter." Obviously, her brain's so-called lower functions, like sensory and motor skills, had to be left intact. So what they called the "wash wave" wouldn't disturb what they call noetic memories, that is, semantic and spatial knowledge, things like how to speak the language or walk down stairs. But her episodic memories—that is, more contingent multiple copies. You could say that what we were doing was more along the lines of a photographic print, or rather a hologram. A holographic negative contains a 2-D record of the rates that light waves bounce off an object, and when you pass light back through the negative, it sculpts the waves back into position, as though the object were still there. And every bit of the hologram has a complete picture. That is, if you cut the negative in half and put light through it, you still see the whole image, still in 3-D, although with some loss of detail.

But you do need a human eye to read it. Like a hologram, the record of my consciousness was just a template. It was only useful as a way of rewriting another system, and like I think I said already, at this stage of technology the only system large and complex enough to work was another human brain.

The upside of this was that none of the content—that is, my SOS—had to be interpreted. Beyond making sure it was as complete as possible, none of the people or programs working on the transfer had to know anything about what pattern encoded which memory, or caused what thought or action, any more than a camera would have to know whether the face it was taking a picture of was smiling. As long as the intervals between each wave crest were precisely timed to mimic hippocampal output—most long-term memories go through the hippocampus—the cortices would think they were getting information in-house.

Of course, gamma photons have a lot of charge, and they can do a lot of damage. That's why the Gamma Knife is the hot tool in microsurgery. In this case, the host—as they liked to call her, as though she were inviting us in— would be exposed to nearly two sieverts of radiation, not an immediately terminal dose, but enough to get some tumors or personal things, like, say, what her father had looked like or what she'd worn to her first communion— dearticulated, and she would become an anterograde amnesiac.

So what we were doing wasn't much different from murder. No, let's be honest. It was murder.

According to Taro, who wasn't a neurobiologist but who in his polymathic way knew a lot about the research, the first tests had come out "spotty." Subjects picked up some, but not enough, or the induced memories got misinterpreted, or they got confused with unerased innate ones. Maybe the poor Honduran guy had wondered whether he was himself, or Tony Sic, or just crazy. In the last year, though, they'd found a solution to this: massive redundancy. Brains don't store a single memory or skill set or whatever in a single spot. It's distributed through different neural networks and sometimes even across different cortices. So we could send each gamma packet many, many times. If one of my memories didn't take hold in a given part of Soledad's brain, it still had a good shot at getting picked up by some other area on the next go-round. This strategy also took advantage of the fact that memory has a tendency not to overwrite. That is, when the neurons were in their confused, amnesiac state, right after the wash wave, they were especially eager to form new connections. But once a microregion of the brain had encoded a bit of memory, it was more or less set there, and the next induced memory would have to settle somewhere else.

Presumably, if the target brain was still healthy, everything that I needed to be me would be represented somewhere. Even though the old saw about how you use only 10 percent of your brain isn't at all true, there's still enough room in there for a lot of storage. Not that that would matter this time. Anyway, since the waves were spread out over hours, her brain wouldn't fry. Instead, it would experience something like a series of simple focal seizures—which are too localized to interrupt consciousness—and then would immediately begin to repair itself. It would form new attachments and run new routines. It would stabilize its EEG. And as it went on living—especially in the first few hours, but also for days afterward—it would start discarding duplicated memories in order to make room for new ones. It would react and learn and function normally. The same way your sleeping brain makes sense of random firings from sensory and motor nerves by converting the noise into a more or less coherent dream, the abadesa's brain would heal by building new memories that would correlate with mine, and would even construct a way of understanding the world that would be very much like mine, so much so that it would think of itself as me. But her rewired brain would never replicate mine exactly. It would be more as though she were watching a tremendously detailed movie of my life, and then, as she left the theater, she would find that she didn't remember her own life and would begin to think that instead, she'd lived mine.

In fact, if everything went well, she wouldn't even be aware of a difference. She'd be lying on her pallet staring at her crucifix, and she'd start to forget things. Her face would begin to feel hot from the increased blood flow through her vertebral and carotid arteries as millions of neurons fired over and over to the point of exhaustion. Technically, there'd be a short period of neural bursts and then a longer refractory period of suppression. Her breathing and digestion and everything would, presumably, cruise on as normal, but she'd slowly forget who she was, and where she was, and then even how to speak. But then, like muscles rebuilding themselves after heavy lifting, her neurons would put the new connections together, and in a very little while she'd have constructed a sense of identity that, if I were able to meet her, I would recognize as my own.

But of course I wouldn't meet her. Back in 1686, the abadesa would live two more days, do a few things—secret things that weren't yet represented in our historical record—and then she would die on schedule. She'd be laid out in the habit she died in, without being embalmed or even washed—in those days, the brides of Christ trusted that their sempiternal purity would keep them from putrefying—and cured for one year in a well-ventilated room in the *almacén*. Then she would have been moved to where she was now, and if she'd still been able to see with her deflated and shriveled eyes, the window in the casket would have let her see silhouettes in the chapel archway, her aging sisters hobbling in, praying, and rustling out, and then new sisters and priests, and then strangers, and then strangers in odd and immodest clothing, peering at her through boxes and not praying at all. One evening an oddly colored flood of unvarying light would spill in from the nave, and it would come back every evening after that. The offering candles that had lit her through most nights would dwindle but never quite stop. And then, on one of the nearly identical and almost innumerable afternoons, she would have seen Marena, Dr. Lisuarte, Grgur, Hitch, and me as we walked in, a little hesitantly, to desecrate her corpse.

"Can you go wake up that queen?" Marena asked Grgur, who was trailing behind with Hitch. "Thanks." She meant the priest.

They set up a halogen work light and turned it on the *retablo* and it squelched any touch of Gothic mood the scene otherwise would have had. Padre Panuda came in with a little sort of camp stool and sat in front of the casket. He got out his keys—there were about a hundred of them, on a loop of green twenty-pound fishing line—found the right one, teased open the old Yale padlock, and tried to pull up the dark oak lid. It stuck. He stood up and tugged. The coffin lifted up but the lid stayed on. Hitch found a kind of miniature pry bar in his kit and we tried that, but it was no good. Finally Grgur found a couple of old squarehead nails on the head and foot ends of the frame and yanked them out with a multitool. Padre Menudo jiggled the thing and pulled at the thing again and it croaked open. There was a cloud of vegetal smells, like basil and old roses. He peered in through the cloud and moved aside a couple of big corsages or nosegays or whatever. The petals shattered and the shards fluttered around.

"*Mejor hacemos nosotros esta cosa,*" Marena said in surprisingly decent Spanish. "We'd better do this part ourselves." The priest said okay, blessed the place again, and left. The three of us stood there for a minute, looking at the corpse.

"*Me da rabia,*" Hitch said. That is to say, "This is giving me rabies." Meaning, "It's bumming me out." I could hear his arm move like he was crossing himself.

"We were all going to hell anyway," I said.

"Hey, let's get Jed," Marena said, imitating the old Life cereal commercial. "He'll touch anything."

"It's okay, I trust you," I said.

"No, really, go ahead."

"I'm sure you don't have anything up your sleeve."

"I know, just—for crying out loud, just go for it. Really. I'm serious."

"Okay, fine," I said. I squatted down. Lisuarte had thought I was still a little speedy, so she'd given me a hypospray of noraephron, and now I was wobbling a little. I reached into the casket and started to peel back the layers of homespun wool and then muslinish cotton skirts from around the body's crotch level, but they were all sort of oily and crumbly and just broke where I folded them back. She was an air mummy, so underneath the fabric her skin was in pretty good condition, almost a dark green, dripping over this little delicate abstract Henry Moorish pelvis. I felt for the anterior iliac spine and then down at a forty-five-degree angle, pressed to find the pubic symphysis, and hooked two fingers up under it. There was all this hard, sharp skin in there and under it there was this sort of stringy greasy stuff. Grave wax. I found what felt like the right two flaps of skin, like dried jade-plant leaves, and moved my fingers up into the vagina, through clogs of crumbly adipocere. Poor lady. Of course, I'd done this with one or two shall-we-say mature women in my day, but this was a new record. Just relax, babe. My finger hit what I thought at first was the coccyx, but then I realized it was what I was looking for and got two fingertips around it. A flood of mixed relief and anxiety sort of inflated my blood vessels, to what felt like Michelin Man proportions. I pulled my hand out and rolled the thing around on my palm. It was a little hexagonal box, about the size of a large calcium-magnesium tablet, black now but I supposed made of copper. It was crusted with crumbs of grave wax and I scuffed them off with my thumbnail. It wasn't a locket. I guess it must have been a needle case or something. Lisuarte had laid out a little lightbox and magnifier on a towel on the floor, and I set the thing down and looked at it. Some of the goo on one end looked like it might be red sealing wax. After a minute of messing around with tweezers and a dental scraper I got the little lid off. There was a black roll inside. I tweezed it out and when I put it down on the plastic it seemed to be made of metal. I started unrolling it carefully, but then it turned out it was really a thin, triangular sheet of hammered silver foil, about the size and shape of a Cape of Good Hope stamp. Maybe she'd torn it off a pyx or something. Maybe I had, rather. At first it looked blank, but when I breathed on it you could see lines scratched on with a needle, in a twitchy mix of uncial script and my own five-thumbed southpaw handwriting:

[handwritten signature and scrawled text]

C X D X F Z C J J Z B A X A Z B H F X B E X B Z E G X A F X F Z A A X C A X D Z F
A X B H X I Z F B H X A D X B Z C X A X D Z P A D X A C X C Z C A J X F X H

Tonto—Did

That was all. Excuse me? I thought. Tonto did what? And I don't recognize those letters and numbers either. Huh. I couldn't tell whether I was disappointed or scared or confused, or what. I just felt like I'd jumped to a standing position after an hour of inversion therapy. Later on Marena told me she'd put her hands on my shoulders because she thought I'd fall over backward, but I didn't feel them.

"Wow, congratulations, all," she said after what I guessed later must have been a long silence.

I didn't say anything.

"Jed? You okay?"

"Yeah," I said.

"What's wrong?"

"It's all misspelled."

(21)

They slipped us in silently, very Zen, like eels. I have to admit it was a quality operation, not like the clunky sort of thing a regular military would do. I guess I haven't said much about the war so far. Maybe it's because, like all politics in Latin America, it's just the same old story. Briefly, three days after the Orlando attack, Guatemala had said that the U.S. was now a nonfunctioning state, that any agreements they'd made under pressure from the U.S. and NATO had to be renegotiated "in regard to the new political landscape," and had demanded that Belize allow their inspectors full police powers. Why the inspectors were there in the first place is a long story, but basically a lot of Guatemalan criminals/indigenous freedom fighters were now underground in Belize, and the Guates wanted to put some of them on trial. The trouble with this was that Guatemala had always considered Belize to be its twenty-third *departamento,* and every once in a while they tried to prove it.

Naturally the Belizeans had said no and jailed the inspectors. The Guatemalans had sent troops to the border. On January 29, a Belizean SSM armed with a vacuum explosive detonated near a Guatemalan village in Petén. The Belize government said the missile had killed five soldiers at a chemical weapons plant. The Guates said it had killed 142 civilians at a school. The Guate parliament had declared a state of war. Of course, a few weeks ago the U.S. would have gotten involved, but now they were battening down the hatches. By the day we'd set for the crossing—Saturday, March 17—the warlet had settled down into so-called "sporadic shelling" near Benque Viejo del Carmen. No big deal. Anyway, it meant that I wasn't the only person on the crew who didn't want to cross into Guatemala officially. Maybe if it hadn't been for me they'd have bluffed/forged/bribed their way through a checkpoint. But instead they'd decided to go old-school and hop the border. They'd be taking the five of us—Marena, Michael, Grgur, Hitch, and me—in first, and then they'd bring the others over tomorrow, by a different route, and we'd meet up outside of San Cristóbal Verapaz.

We were twenty-five miles south of the Stake, at a small site called Pusilha. Supposedly it had been an important town in the Late Classic period, but it didn't look like much now. We were sitting on tarpaulins in a Quonset hut that some archaeologists had built years ago. Oh, by *we* I mean the five of us mojados—illegal immigrants—plus Ana Vergara, who was the same girl–Green Beret type who'd extracted us in the Florida Keys, and her second-in-command, a Boy Commandoish–looking guy named . . . hmm, wait a second. Maybe we'll stick with our policy of not bothering to repeat the names of minor accessories to our crimes. We waited for dark. There were two tables, a stack of old screen frames, and a lot of brooms and brushes. Michael stretched his bulk out on a tarpaulin and appeared to go to sleep. Hitch sat and went through his gear. Marena chatted with Ana. Helicopters churred over us, *fuckfuckfuckfuckfuckfuckfuck*, north to south, following the border. Ana'd given me a big Tyvek envelope full of what she called my dead babies, and I was looking through them in the light of my phone. There was a well-worn U.S. passport and a pleasantly plump old trucker's wallet. The passport was real and undoctored, and belonged to one Martín Cruz, a real person—a travel journalist, in fact—who was now out of sight in Guate City and whose biography and assorted writings I'd spent a half day memorizing. I opened the wallet. It featured two $5K international scratch-off debit cards, an American Express Thulium card, a good Sunshine State driver's license in Martín Leon's name but with my new Warren mug shot on it, U.S. $1,155 in twenties and fives, and 2,400 Guatemalan quetzales—which was worth about two hundred dollars, although I don't understand how they can name such a worthless unit after such a valuable bird—and some well-worn miscellaneous Martín Cruz ID-establishing pocket litter, bills and taxi receipts, and even some bits of lint and scuzz. Finally, there was an international press card from *National Geographic* magazine. Uh-oh, I thought.

"Uh, Marena?" I asked.

"Yeah?" She kneed over and recrossed her legs.

"Uh, you know, *National Geographic*'s a CIA front."

"Sure, so?" she asked.

"So, I've got this press card here from them."

"Okay."

"And I just wonder sometimes, what's going on?"

"What do you mean?"

"I mean, who are we really working for?"

"We're working only for Lindsay," she said.

"And that's a personal guarantee?"

"Yes. As far as I know." There was a pause. "Look, I'm sure he called in some favors at the State Department on this, but, yeah, I can guarantee the spook squad knows nothing. Come on, use your head. If anybody big in D.C. did know about this, they'd close it down."

"I don't know," I said, "they do a lot of weird stuff these days."

"This is *way* too out there for *any* government agency."

"I'm just really, really allergic to those Agency guys, I mean, you know what happened, they're total thugs—"

"Fine," she said, "so fuck it, bail out. Renege."

"I'm not bailing out," I said. "I just want to know if you know for sure, you know—"

"I don't know anything for *sure,* except that you can't second-guess everything. Anyway, that card's only in case we get grabbed, and that won't happen anyway."

"No Way's going to bolt if he sees it."

"Well, that's his—look, you know, he's your friend, what can I tell you?"

"Okay, nothing," I said. "Never mind."

"Good."

"Except how about we all just don't mention *National Geographic* when No Way's around?"

"I will personally tell everybody never to speak the name," she said.

"Thanks."

We sat. She's probably right, I thought. Maybe they know what they're doing. I'd looked up Executive Solutions—as much as possible—and it seemed like even though they were incorporated in South Africa, most of their work lately was in Latin America, guarding oil rigs and so forth and also, I guessed, troubleshooting for antidrug outfits. On the other hand, they seemed to be a high-end outfit. Maybe Cruz even did write for *National Geo* sometimes, although I hadn't noticed it in his file. Anyway, most people who work for them are legitimate. Right? And anyway, my IDs probably really wouldn't be that important. Michael Weiner had the real goods. They'd shown me the document portfolio he was carrying. It was packed with letters and permits from different Guatemalan administrators, including the home secretary. I'd guessed that some were paid for and some were faked. ES was going to use just one four-person team to get us in. Then, just as a standard precaution, we'd take a little evasive action by going through a festival in San Cristóbal Verapaz. There'd be ES spotters there, looking for anyone who might be following us. We were supposed to spend a few minutes in the square, where the crowd would be thickest, and then walk out of town almost in the opposite direction from the way we came in. After that, once we were out in the bush, there'd be those four with us plus six different spotters watching our perimeter. So that's at least nineteen people on this detail, I thought. That I know about. Oh, plus No Way, my old homie from Enero 31 who I think I told you about, was the wild card. He'd be meeting us tonight and staying with me the whole time, kind of as my personal bodyguard. I'd insisted on it. That's twenty. Not exactly a skeleton-staff operation.

Oh, well. *Calmate que te calmo,* I thought. Just go with it for now. Accept the energy of the wave.

"Sorry," I said.

"It's fine," Marena said. She moved away, back to her former zone of tarp. Damn.

She looked good, I thought. I'd been at the Stake the whole time since we'd gotten back from the Saint test, training for what they were calling the Chocula Project, but Marena had just gotten back from three days with Max in Colorado, and she seemed freshened. She had on a little Jungle Jane vest and matching ensemble that turned one's thoughts to tree-housekeeping with Tantor and Cheeta.

We listened to the crickets. They had that soothing tone, but it felt like there was something missing from the general soundscape. Marena sighed. Reach out and touch her? No, don't. She's mad at you right now. Anyway, let the gal make the first move. If she doesn't go for it, there's no hope anyway—

"Okay, heads up," Ana said. "Let's check the communicators."

We screwed them into our ears. Supposedly the system was really high-end and it stegonographed its transmissions. That is, if anyone picked up our chatter it would sound like a stock recording of police broadcasts. Only receivers with a copy of our dedicated chip could dig out the real conversation.

"—hearing me?" Ana Vergara's voice was saying on the bud.

"Asuka here, check," Marena said.

"Pen-Pen here, sounds good," I said. Michael and the camera guy said they were here too. Christ, code names. *Pendejadas.* These people all acted like they were still trying to bump off Castro.

We left the hut and hiked a mile west toward the Rio Moho. Ana led and I went second. There was just enough of the moon left to see without goggles. The corn stubble and mullions gave way to scrub cedars. I started to get that good feeling you have walking at night, not alone. Even when the situation is a little tense, as it was now, there's something encouraging about it. The foot track narrowed until it was just a tapir path. Ana looked back at me a couple of times. Finally she stopped, turned, planted her feet, and got right in my face.

"Mr. DeLanda," she said. "There are no mines in this area."

Her tone sounded like she was about to add something along the lines of "You yellow-bellied faggot." She was right, though. I'd been looking down at my feet and stepping right where she'd just stepped.

"Okay, okay," I said. "Understood." *Sir,* I thought. She faced front again and marched. I picked up the pace. *Cerota.*

The path graded down between cecropia trees. Under our feet the ground turned to silt and dead reeds. Ahead of us the Moho was a black void about ten yards across. Ordinarily it was just a brook, but now, with the flooding, it was navigable for a long way upstream. Ana led us along the bank to where there was an eddy in the lee of an ox-bow. I could just see a stocky figure standing knee-deep in the water, and then a local-looking *lancha,* a wooden flat-bottomed boat, like an old duck skiff. Its stern was up on the bank and a Minn Kota silent electric trolling motor was tilted up on its stern. The six of us climbed in. I half twisted an ankle on one of the big batteries they had lined up in the bottom. Michael got in last and we dipped and rocked like he was going to sink us. The stocky guy pushed us off and jumped in himself over the gunwale. He had night-vision goggles with a heads-up GPS display, the military-standard kind that tell you where you are within a half-inch. He lowered the propeller and motored us upstream, across the phantasmal border. Supposedly there'd been a net stretched across, but somehow the advance people had pulled it aside without setting off the alarm. They must have a few people inside, I thought. I meant on the Guate side. Well, don't worry about it. A monkey roared up in the hills north of us. It felt odd moving so smoothly in the dark. More aircraft went over, none with lights, and none slowly enough to be looking for us. We fetched up a few times. They grew cardamom around here, and you could smell it. The glow of propane lights rose on the haze ahead of us. It was a village called Balam.

My earbud beeped. "Heads up, A Team," Ana's voice said over the earbuds. "Copy all."

"Kozo here, copy," Michael's voice said. We all said *copy*. The boat banked at a distinctive-looking gumbolimbo tree. Two figures scrabbled down the bank to meet us. One of them half hooked the boat with a branch and pointed to where we could step onto roots without sinking in the mud. We staggered up to a footpath and formed up. The ES people seemed to be looking us over with a these-are-the-new-recruits? sort of disdain, but it was probably my imagination. We all nodded at each other. Vergara reindicated the footpath—it looked like it followed the river—and signed "two hours' march or less" in ASL. We followed.

We walked two miles across old cornstalks and cover clover. Some kind of small jet rasped low over us, north to south, without any lights, momentarily rippling the water. It's not looking for us, I told myself. Supposedly they didn't do much observation from planes anymore. It was all about satellites now, or small drones that you could hardly ever see or hear. On the Guate side they also still used ground-based sonar and heat sensors, but there were so many pigs and deer and things around here that they were basically useless unless a whole army ran across at once. An east breeze came up, with a smell of horses. I remembered walking with my brother when I was little, on a similar night, and being afraid that the flesh droppers—that is, skeleton bandits who put on suits of flesh to disguise themselves during daylight—would come out of the cornrows and sneak up behind us. We hopped another fence and stumbled down a bank to Route 13. You could smell that it had been recently tarred. Vergara made us line up and stand and wait for two minutes. She walked north on the side of the road and signaled for us to follow. We followed. The moon had gone behind the trees, but there was still just enough glow to get around. A truck came up behind us with its dims on, scraping against low pine branches. It was a dark 1980s-vintage Ford Bronco, the preferred transport of discriminating migrant farm workers throughout Latin America. It had a homemade wood cab on the back painted with a Squirt logo. We moved aside. It passed us and paused ten yards ahead. The driver stayed in the cab. An ES person got out of the passenger side and another climbed out of the back. As the second guy's feet touched the ground I recognized No Way's silhouette, maybe from his stance or motion or something even more subtle. I almost ran up to him. He'd aged in that way people have of looking older without actually changing in any way you can identify, they just seem a little heavier or slower, like they're the exact same sculpture but cast out of a different alloy. Maybe it's just an expression you can't make when you're young. Still it was weird, or wild, seeing him again, especially here, and I felt that gush you get when you're thinking about bursting into tears or whatever you do, but it didn't seem like the right time.

"*¿Qué tal, vos?*" he asked. He gave me an *abrazo*. That is, a manly bear hug.

"*¡Cabron!*" I said. "*¿Qué onda, mano?*"

"*Sano como un pimpollo,*" he said. Literally, "Healthy as a sprout." He and I did an Enero 31 handshake. "*¿Y que onda, al fin compraste esa Barracuda?*"

"*Tengo dos. Podemos competir.*"

"Hey, *mucha, callenze!*" Ana's voice said on my bud. Quiet down. "*Zolamente ezenciales.*" For a second I thought she was lisping because she wanted to speak Castilian style and then I figured out that she was just doing it so the sibilants wouldn't carry. I held up a one-moment finger to No Way and said, "Thorry, underthtood, Keelorenz," trying to show that I was talking into my earbud. Just don't let me intrude on your GI Jane fantasy. *Voy aca loca.*

Ana took the shotgun seat. The rest of us, including the two ES guys, piled into the back. It was furnished with a whole lot of empty nylon corn sacks. I introduced No Way all around softly. Everybody said hello but nobody seemed chatty.

"*¿Pues, vos,*" I whispered in No Way's ear. "*¿Qué piensas de este?*"

"*Me da pena, vos,*" he said. "*¿Confías en estos cerotes?*"

"I don't know," I said, "do you trust anybody?"

"*Confío en que dios se cague en mi,*" he said. "I trust God to shit on me."

"*Es verdad.*"

"*Esa Ana, en los noventa trabajó para los embotelladores,*" he said. "In the nineties, Ana worked for the bottlers."

By "bottlers" he meant "the soft drink company," which was an old URNG slang term for COLA—that is, Chief of Operations, Latin America, at the U.S. State Department, and also before that, Covert Ops, Latin America, which was the old Bill Casey/John Hull/Oliver North group.

"Well, look," I said, "I didn't want to be here without you, but you should really just take off if something looks wrong."

He said no, though, that I'd paid in good faith and he was going to stick around. I reminded him that they'd paid me a lot. He said he was aware of that. I told him about the *National Geographic* thing. He said it figured.

"It's good to see you, though," I said. "Thanks."

I relaxed a bit. Having him around took some of the wind out of my paranoia. The thing was, I hadn't known any of these people for very long, except for Taro, of course, and I still wasn't entirely sure what I was getting into, and I really wanted at least one person around who was on my side, who wasn't connected to Warren.

"It's okay," he said. He stretched his arms up to the vinyl roof and pushed against it like he was testing how solid it was. I asked him how things were going at the CPRs. He said there hadn't been any sign of Tío Xac and by now everyone assumed he was dead.

"I saw Sylvana last year," he said. "In Tenosique."

"Oh. Mmm. How is she?"

"*Casada.*"

"*¿No con el pisado del ONU?*" I asked. "Not to that UN dweeb?"

"*Simon.*"

"*Mierda!*"

"*Me das lástima, mano . . .*"

"I can't think about it," I said. "*Si comienzo a pensar de él, me hago lata.*" "If I start thinking about it I'll make myself a can. I guess the idiom doesn't really translate." I started asking him about his contingency plans but he pointed to the ceiling, meaning we'd talk about it later. I guess he was right; for all we knew these people had nanomicrophones hidden in the rat turds.

"*Pues, vos, me voy a dormir,*" he said, and started up this kind of muffled snoring. He had that soldier's ability to fall asleep anywhere in a few seconds. Anyway, for him a covered cap in an air-conditioned pickup probably felt like the Tallyrand Suite at the Crillon. I looked over at Marena but couldn't see much. I half inflated a nylon pillow and leaned back on it. I kept wondering whether I should try to sort of cuddle over against her, or pretend to fall asleep on her shoulder, or maybe just ask her if it was okay if I did. No, don't do anything. Maybe she'll do something.

She didn't.

We slowed. A sign came up, lit with a single bulb. CAMPAMENTO MILITAR ALTA VERAPAZ, it said, with a painting of a rabid-looking commando and a shield with a black skull and crossbones over the words GUARDIA DE HONOR. Just before we passed it, we turned left onto a graveled road and bent back 130 degrees, toward the yellow direction, the southwest, the direction of the recent past.

(22)

We piled out of the truck a mile up the road from San Cristóbal Verapaz. It was just after sundown. You could hear a marimba band playing corridos, competing with loudspeakers blasting the old Ricardo Arjona version of "Time in a Bottle." The car turned around and left. We split into two groups to attract less attention, with me, Marena, No Way, Lisuarte, and Ana Vergara in one, and the others in the other. We walked.

I had some bad memories about the place. The hospital there was where I was when I learned about the massacre at T'ozal. But there was a little fiesta going on for San Anselmo, and the idea was that we'd take advantage of the crowd and go through town on foot. Like I said, four ES people were supposedly already there, and as we walked through, they'd look out for anyone following us, or eyeballing us, or whatever.

Our appearance was worrying me a little. Lisuarte had a big schlumpy hat and looked okay. Marena was going as a new-agey student, and she had it totally down, with strings of cheap turquoise beads around her throat and a beat-up North Face backpack with a FREE TIBET sticker. Grgur didn't fit in, though. Well, maybe he'd pass for a Turkish heroin dealer. Whatever. We passed some loose dogs and then pigs and then groups of Indians in twos and fours. Everybody said hello. Strangers got noticed around here, although also welcomed. Usually. I saw some faces I thought I knew, so I took my hat off. It felt very wrong. But nobody would recognize me with the bald head. They'd have to be my own mother. Damn it. I wondered about No Way, but I guessed he had his own ways of getting around without being spotted. Anyway, he'd said he hadn't been here in at least fifteen years. A thin old guy smiled at us with a mouthful of mainly silver teeth, the signature face of Central American dentistry. The mosquitoes were bad. Kids clustered around us, trying to sell us rockets.

"Heads up, A Team, proceed with caution," Ana's voice said in our ears. I could feel all of us tensing a little and then trying to walk as inconspicuously as possible. Headlights came up out of the valley at us and we stood aside and nodded to four blue-uniformed troops in a covered jeep. They roorshed past without acknowledging us. Yay. Just as I thought. It was hard for me to look at them and not imagine their heads blowing up in the crosshairs of a telescopic sight, though. Calm down. They're fresh conscripts, they weren't even around then. Breathe.

Tonto, I thought. Jeez. What the bleeding fizzuck had I meant by that? Tonto did what? Something bad, probably. *Ay gevaltarisco.* Maybe I'd been just sick and delirious back there. Maybe I just meant, "Rosabelle, believe— after all, Tonto did"? Did I mean *I* was Tonto? I hadn't been called that since I was ten, and even then it was just a popular slur, it wasn't like my nickname or anything. Did I mean "Befriend the White Man, Tonto Did?" Also, *tonto* is Spanish slang for "stupid." Stupid did what? What, what, what?

The road turned into the main east-west street. There were strings of dim little red and white Christmas lights hanging across along with the ropes of colored crepe paper, but the big lamp hanging above the crossroads was out, and since they were usually proud of those things around here I figured it meant the blackout was still officially in effect. Like, sure, the UK was about to launch a Falklands-strength air raid on a country that can't afford paper towels. Don't flatter yourselves. There were linked cinder-block house/stores on each side of the road, each house painted a different shade of turquoise, peach, lemon, or robin's-egg blue, with hand-painted renditions of the logos for Orange Crush, Jupiña Gaseosa de Piña, and Cerveza Gallo. The last one was an ice store now, but it used to be the United Fruit *oficina del comisariato*, that is, kind of the company store, and I got a burn of rage looking at it. Very B. Traven. *Mate el Pulpo.*

Hometowns are weird. You think they can't get any smaller or more squalorous, and then every time you go back they still seem more so. It's the Incredible Shrinking Past. And this wasn't even really my hometown. When I was little, coming here was like leaving your home in Far Rockaway and visiting Manhattan. *Ay yi yi.* The Sacred Heart Hospital was just two blocks south, if you could call them blocks. You could almost see it from here. I kept looking at a two-story building across the street. There was a green moldy water-stain on the pink wall under the eaves that was totally familiar. I realized it was the place where the soldiers had made me stand when they lined us up—

Oh, *mierditas*. Flashback trouble.

The G2—which is, or was, the Guate army's "counterterrorism" squad— had come in that morning to put on what they called a *"celebración."* They came in on big old U.S. Army trucks with big loudspeakers and assembled the whole available population, including me in my little white sack dress and all the other kids from the hospital who could more or less walk. They lined everyone up roughly according to height—I still don't know why—and made us stand in the sun while the commanding officer made a rambling two-hour speech about how the town council of T'ozal, and also of two other towns, had deceived us and how they were all Communists on Castro's personal payroll. He told us how lucky we were to have a free enterprise economy with all we could ever want if we weren't lazy, how the country was going to be different, not like under García, how the current government had always kept its promise to treat the Indians fairly, and how the prisoners they'd taken would be tried in a proper court of law. They'd played "Guatemala Feliz" on the loudspeakers over and over. Sixty-eight times, in fact. After every few plays they'd made us all do a pledge of allegiance modeled on the U.S. one, and then they'd play it again, *que tus aras no profane jamás el verdugo,* et cetera, et cetera, and then there'd be another speech. Finally they read us the list of relocations. It included everyone from my town. It was one of four they'd burned down that week for sheltering "Cubans," which was what they called anyone with even supposed sympathy for the rebels. They played the anthem again, and played recorded speeches, and played the anthem, and all of this went on over and over until the CO's own soldiers got so bored they started picking fights and then beating people up. Most of the three thousand or so Indians and Mestizos in the square didn't run away but just stood there, not out of passive resistance, but because if they ran they might get shot. Sister Elena—I was seeing her wide face again in too-too hi-def, with all its little pores and the hint of black down on her upper lip—and the other nuns managed to get us kids back into the hospital; I understood what had gone on, a little, and I was just a thrashing little ball of terror. What had happened to my parents?

So, unlike some of the kids in the 'hood, I didn't see our house get torched, and I didn't see my mother and sisters get raped and my father get interrogated and executed. I was away from home. I guess I didn't even imagine it until a long time after it had happened. In those days I couldn't imagine my mother being afraid of anything. Now I have this image of her with terror in her eyes and blood in her hair, and a big red can of gasoline in front of her, and I know it's correct. *Todo por mi culpa, todo—*

"*Más despacio, vos,*" No Way said in my ear. "Let's slow down a little bit." He didn't want us to look too purposeful.

We oozed into the square. It looked like about five hundred people had gotten up and out for the *procesion*. A loose herd of kids in parochial-school sailor suits, looking all Coca-Colonized with Bluetooth earbuds and Hello Kitty barrettes, milled around a squad of soccer players in blue jerseys who were strutting around looking all young, hung, and full of spung. We passed through a gauntlet of vendors with stalls of *roscos* and *buñuelos*. I got Marena a bag of *empanadas de achiote* and got two for myself. Four soldiers were playing dominoes on a folding table under a plastic ramada. They just glanced up at us, looking pimply and untrained with their gummy old L85A1s tented together. The clicking tiles triggered this flash of my father and uncles when I was tiny, sitting around a little table, stirring the mysterious spotted teeth as I fell asleep. We passed a few gringos hanging back at the periphery, one group of what I guessed were German tourists, and another group of three that I was pretty sure were evangelical missionaries. I didn't make out any of the ES spotters, but of course one wasn't supposed to—

Oops. Sorry. Out of nowhere a brace of Mormon missionaries had nearly bumped into us. I was afraid they might recognize Lisuarte, but they didn't seem to. They're probably not from the Belize Stake anyway. There's a whole army of those *huevos* bicycling all over Latin America, cutting weak-willed individuals out of the herd for further intellecticide. Somebody—

Oh, sorry. *Huevos.* Maybe I should explain the expression. *Huevos* are eggs or, figuratively, testicles. Around the Petén we call Mormons *huevos* because they're white, like eggs, and there are always two of them, like testicles. Of course, it sounds funnier when you've been picking coffee for fourteen hours.

Somebody killed the *tapa cuarenta* and the little band started up "O Salutaris." We followed the crowd's gaze up the north-south street, which sloped up into the hills. Thirteen *cofradores*, charge holders, old men in bright striped suits and big hats, were coming down from one of the high north shrines. Nine of them carried big green foliated crosses and the last four carried a palanquin with an old corn-paste statue of Anselmo. He had a bishop's miter, doleful eyes, and a green bifurcated beard.

I shifted from foot to foot. I looked ahead at No Way. He looked back. We watched the procession for another half-minute and then No Way eased his way out of the little crowd and moved on to the west. I followed. Marena, Lisuarte, and Ana followed me. At the third residential street we crossed, a group of four Quiché women—the Quiché are a Mayan language group that lives west of here—passed in front of us. They were carrying candles, bougainvillea flowers, and unopened packs of Marlboros, so I had a pretty good guess about whom they were going to visit. I hadn't seen him before in this town, but he'd be around. Hmm. I asked Marena whether she still had any of those Cohiba Pyramides. She said she had fifteen left and dug the box out of her backpack. I took six.

"Just give me a second," I said. "I'll be right back." I turned to follow the four women.

"Pen-Pen, what are you doing?" Ana's voice said in my ear. "Come in."

"I just need to do one thing," I mumbled.

"Not understood," she said. "Stay on the route."

"Just hang on for a second," I said. I thought she was going to run up and get in front of me, but No Way sort of happened to get between her and me, and by the time she got around him we were already at the open front of the cinder-block house. The four women were inside, kneeling and adding candles to the hundred or so that were already lit on the floor. The *cuandero* was sitting outside at a folding table. He looked familiar, but I didn't know his name and he definitely didn't recognize me. I nodded my bald head to him. He looked a little askance at it but nodded back, like, go ahead.

I turned to Marena. "This may strike you as silly," I said.

"Uh, no," she said nonplussedly.

The women finished and left. I picked my way in through the clusters of flowers and bottles and candles on the concrete floor. Marena followed. There was a little plastic stoup in there and I automatically dipped my hand in it and crossed myself and then got embarrassed about being still programmed after all these years. Marena glanced down into the water and for a terrible second I thought she was going to spit out her gum in it.

Maximón sat smoking and watching, as he does, in a shrine area at the back of the room, next to his empty coffin. He wore sunglasses, a wide black felt hat, a black suit, a red shirt, and dozens of offering scarves and ties around his neck and shoulders. He was larger than usual. Most of the time he was pretty scrappily constructed, but this cuandero had used an old shop-window mannequin for his body, and the hand that held the silver tip of his staff was feminine, with nails painted in an odd light red, or I guess orange-red, lacquer. His face looked like it had been recently painted, and his black mustache was glossy. His legs were widely spread and there was a tray on his lap with a bowl of twisted quetzales and bottles of Squirt soda and *aguadiente*.

I knelt and touched the ground.

"*Salud, Caballero Maximón,*" I said. "*Ahora bien, le encuentro bien.*" I stood up. "Every moment, every hour, every year, I thank you," I said in Spanish. "And I thank the saint of today, Saint Anselmo, and the cuandero of San Cristóbal, for bringing you here today. And I've brought you a few things, just to spoil you."

I knelt again and laid the cigars on an offering cloth. They'd been well-kept at high humidity, and even with all the smoke in here you could smell their tangy goodness that was filling the room. Maximón smirked as usual and, it almost seemed, nodded.

I stood up. "I thank you, señor," I said. "God big, God small, God medium. There is one larger, and one smaller, one who takes care of the earth and our feet and our hands. Please bless my grandeza. You count with us the red seeds, the black seeds. You count the stones and skulls along with us. East, north, west, and south, you watch at the crossroads. You watch us when the earthquakes come. You give us the night and you give us the power. All the dead who are dead have taught us how to take care of you, and we will teach the newborn and the unborn. Well, that's the way it is. We thank you, Sanita. Excuse me for turning my back. *Salud,* Don Maximón."

I turned, walked out, nodded again to the cuandero, put another five hundred quetzales—about sixty-five U.S. dollars—in a Gallo box near his table, "for the novenas," and left. We walked back to the main street. Ana gave me an angry glare. Well, still, better safe than sorry, I thought.

"Is that, like, a regular Catholic saint?" Marena asked.

"Well, he's kind of off the books," I said. "He's not really for good Catholics. He's for slightly bad Catholics."

"Huh."

"He goes back a long way, though. Supposedly."

We walked west out of town with the brown moon bouncing ahead of us—*wenn sie auf der Erde so wenig, wie auf dem Monde,* I thought, pretentiously—and down into the valley, onto one strand of the network of footpaths under the Cordillera de los Cuchumatanes. A mile out of town the path branched south down alongside the river. I could hear its white noise just out of sight, and I could smell cut reeds and mud, and then mold and something like fresh ginger, and then something else under all those, as faint as the hint of amber-gris that might still be evanescing from the dry residue at the bottom of an empty Guerlain Samsara flask that you might pick out of a dusty box at a flea market on a hot afternoon: the pheromone for home.

(23)

Sylvana's eyelash fluttered against my shoulder, the way it used to when she was dreaming, but it wasn't her, it was something else, scratch it. Thing! Live thing. Okay, got it, oops, now on the back of my hand, running up the arm, shake it off shakeoffoff. I spasmed with prelinguistic revulsion. The little brown lizard dropped casually off my wrist and padded away over the metalized-nylon groundcloth. *Qué jodedera.* Getting citified in my old age. Not used to critters and shit anymore. I looked at the time readout on my phone: 3:04 P.M. *La gran puta.* Late.

Okay. Where the hell was I? The light was an odd purple-blue shade. I blinked up at the ceiling. It was high and corbel-arched.

Oh, right. Ix Ruinas. Michael'd said this was one of the palaces.

I flayed the damp sleeping bag off my person and sat up. It looked like everybody else was outside. The room was a big old Maya *audiencia*, a receiving room, about fifty feet long by nine deep and twenty feet high at the apex, with a single high doorway in the center of the western long side. The door was covered with a purple-blue nylon tarpaulin. In the Classic period there'd been a big mural on the back wall, and there was still about 20 percent of it left. You could just make out a little figure on the left, walking up some stairs, and then, faintly, a temple on the right with Earthtoadess volutes streaming out, but lately, that is, in the last few decades, water had been seeping in and it had washed away most of the stucco there. Still, the room was pretty dry at this season. Ana's advance team had shoveled out the bat guano, but you could still smell it. They'd also prestashed most of the equipment in here, and the whole north third of the room was stacked with sections of oil-drilling rods, flexible conveyor tubes, boxes of drill bits, four Honda 90 hp motors, six

Volvo jacks, and a pair of big yellow cases that held two tunneling-and-sampling robots, courtesy of Schlumberger Oilfield Services, one of which had been rigged with lights and video. The place looked like a pre-Columbian chop shop. Closer to the sleeping zone there were two silent gas generators and a bevy of power conditioners, a skein of fat cables snaking out the door and north toward Mound A, two medium-size lab freezers, a vacuum box, a vacuum packaging machine, rolls of aluminum foil for carbon 14 samples, a thirty-inch glove box, an as-yet-unpacked air-line system, two water pumps, a pressurizer (all available from Lab Safety Supply), boxes that held two stone saws and their circular blades (also Schlumberger), and the usual archaeological stuff—shovels, spades, label printers, light boxes, rolls of bubble wrap, packing boxes, work lights, LED probe lights, brushes, brooms, and sifting trays—basically enough gear to keep a whole graduate-study and summer-internship program busy out here for a decade, not that any real scholarly research was actually going to happen. We'll never use half this stuff, I thought. Well, next time, don't do—

Wait.

TONTODID.

Hmm. *DON TOD IT . . .*

DON'T DO IT.

I'd tried to warn myself.

Hell.

Don't go back to the old days. Don't trust these people. Don't go through with this madness. Don't do it.

Hmm.

I lay there wondering, squinting at a tall trapezoid of blue light, a nylon tarpaulin stretched across the single door of the ancient room. My teeth chattered a little. Don't do it why? Couldn't I have been just a little more specific? Because it's an abomination before God? Because it's unpleasant? Because I'd be missing the season finale of *Gossip Girl*?

Good going, I thought. It takes my subconscious four days to solve one Junior Jumble. Could've done it on my phone in between four and six seconds.

And now tonight I've got my appointment with a dead guy.

Y ahora que, what can you do about it now? Bail out? Run off into the bush with No Way and sneak south into Honduras? Fake a nervous breakdown? Just say no?

No wonder Tony Sic hadn't seemed so upset when he found out I was going instead of him. I'd felt really sheepish about it, and then he'd seemed all
philosophical and unfazed. Maybe he'd been having second thoughts. Jed,
you're an idiot, idiot—

Squelch that. Unproductive.

Whew. Okay. Let's pick up the pieces. Time to Awaken the Giant Within.

I scratched my ankle, found a blue Patagonia Capilene sock that during
the night had crawled from the foot of my bag past my head and out onto
my inflatable mattressy thing. Inside the sock were five little rubber-
banded bundles of foil packets. I found the General Foods Espresso Vien-
nese, tore the thing open with my canine tooth, and poured a shower of
powder onto my tongue. Yuck. Okay. I washed it down with two marshmallows. I opened two big PDI Super Sani-Cloth Germicidal Wipes,
Proven Effective Against Tuberculosis, Salmonella, SARS, and HIV, and
ran them over as much of my face and body as I could reach without
spraining something. Next I found a packet that said No Need to Brush
in big ice-blue letters. I ToothToweled my thirty-one teeth and ran the
other side of the paste-impregnated paper over my wooly old tongue. The
fourth packet held a four-by-six-inch square of gauze soaked with Skin So
Soft, which neutralized the drying effects of the germicides. I tore a new
Hartz Advanced Care 3 in 1 Control Flea Collar out of its wrapper and
buckled it around my right knee. Arthropod bites and hæmophilia don't go
together too well. I bunched all the junk into a ball, put the ball in a pocket,
screwed my earbud into my left canal, and crawled through the tarpaulin's
lower right flap.

"Care for a cuppa?" Michael asked, mercifully not on the earbud. He, Lisuarte, and Boy Commando were sitting on a ground cloth, like it was a picnic.
I didn't see No Way, but he'd said he'd snoop around. I said thanks but I'd had
some. It sounded like an invitation, though, so I squatted next to them. We
were in the shade of a long building that had been the west side of an eighty-
yard quadrangle that Michael said was probably part of the Ixian Ocelot
Clan's men's palace. The other buildings were covered with shrubs and just
looked like small ridges, and the building we'd set up in wouldn't have been
noticeable, either, if the ES people hadn't cleared out the doorway. The area
that had been the courtyard looked like it had been planted with corn a few
years ago. But now it was overgrown with nettles and ferns. The whole compound was about halfway up a once-terraced mountainside, a quarter mile
uphill from the river and about a hundred yards south of the site's biggest

pyramid—which the great Sylvanus Morley had called Mound A and which we now, with better epigraphy, knew had been the Ocelots' mul. But with all the leafage you couldn't see either the river or the mul or, except in patches, the sky.

There was a big open OtterBox next to Michael, filled with packets of jellies and honey and juice boxes and corn chips and protein bars and stuff, and I picked out a Land O' Lakes TravelPak and a half-liter foil-covered paper brick of Undine, which I guess was the latest thing in positron-enriched all-sports superwater. My last Ziploc, the one with my many-hued meds 'n' vitamins, was still in my left hand, but I managed to peel the little Mylar tab off the box top. There was a puff-adder hiss as the little canister of CO_2 inside shot its wad and instantly cooled the liquid down to thirty-two filling-cracking degrees. I poured my pills into my mouth, started to drink, found that my left hand was stuck to the frozen condensate on the outside of the box, peeled it off, picked the box up again, got the now-congealing cluster of capsules down with two-thirds of the heavy water or light water or whatever it was. Michael's hand handed me something. It was a granola bar. I pushed it out of the wrapper and crunched into it. *Bring it!* the wrapper said,

> And that's what we did. We brought 50% more protein to the table than our traditional granola bars. This way, you won't have to worry about where you get your strength from, just where it will take you. At Bear Naked™ Granola, we believe true strength is seeing every finish line as the next starting point. So go ahead, set your sights a little higher. It's not important how far away your goal is—just that you're moving toward it. This is the granola that gets you there.

Excellent, I thought. I drank the remaining third of the box of water, crushed the box around the wrappers and the baggie, and dropped the wad in the Leave No Traces bag.

"Ow," Marena's voice said somewhere. "You *cunt.*" I looked a little more carefully out into the milpa. Ana and Marena were fighting out in the middle of the field. No, they were practicing hup kwon do or something. Ana was teaching Marena some new and devastating low-body shin kick. *America's Bloodiest Psycho Dyke Catfight Videos,* I thought. *El video mas sangriento de lucha-libre de marimachas. Spick Chix Kick Dix. Mistress Ana, She-Jackal of Abu Ghraib*—

"Cornstarch?" Michael asked.

Excuse me? I thought. "Excuse me?" I asked.

He pointed to an open box of Argo. I looked at it. Boy, the Corn Maiden had really slimmed down at some point over the last couple of decades.

"Why?" I asked.

"Oh, sometimes I give it to people who aren't used to hiking," he said. "They tend to get chafed about the tender bits."

"Oh," I said. "Right. Uh, no, thanks."

"Did you just eat that thing of butter?" Boy Commando asked me.

"Huh?" I asked. I looked down at the empty foil wrapper. "Oh . . . well . . ."

"Like, straight?" Boy asked. "You just eat plain butter?"

"Uh . . . I guess you can't take the Third World out of the Indian."

"Hey," he said, "I bet you can't tell me how many cigs I've got left in this pocket." He tapped his left breast.

"No, I can't," I said. "I'm not a remote viewer."

"We have two mung-sprout pita pockets left," Michael said.

I said no thanks again and asked where the designated *latrina* was. He pointed to the southern side of the field. I creaked upright and headed over.

"Cover your traces," Ana's voice said out of my ear. Thanks, I nodded. *Tortillera*. I don't care how many contras you blew away for Bill Casey. I scrubbled forward, slipping a bit. My guess about Ana was that she was one of probably a lot of women who'd been in the marines and wanted to run combat-level missions, and then when the U.S. wouldn't let them they'd quit in a huff and hired themselves out either to more swinging countries or to the private sector. Anyway, she sure had a big chip on each shoulder. Damn. I was having some trouble getting a second Wet One out of its packet. Shoulda just stood in sleeping bag. Person packet. Pick a peck of pita people packets—

My ear buzzed. "System on," I said. The system came on.

"It's Kozo," Michael said. "Good news, check this out."

I shuffled back and crouched into the *audiencia*. Hitch and Boy Commando were just inside the doorway, tinkering with audio stuff. Michael and Lisuarte were in the back, hunched over a monitor.

"We got a heads-up from the home office," Michael said. I sat down. "You know about the markings in the ahau's niche?" he asked.

"Yes," I said. I'd memorized them, as I was sure he knew.

"Right. Well, the recoronation, the k'atun-seating ritual, that was at dawn on the twentieth, right? In 664."

"Exactolutely," I said. At the downloading we'd be shooting for twenty minutes before sunrise, when 9 Fanged Hummingbird would be inside the niche, waiting to emerge and show himself to the assembly in the plaza.

"Remember the San Martín thing?" he asked.

"Yes," I said.

"Max says hi," Marena said. I hadn't seen her come in. We said hi back. She relayed the messages, signed off, and slid her phone—a new, clunkier, encrypted one, with a black case—into a little Velcro pocket on her sleeve.

"Sorry," Marena said. "What's San Martín again?"

"It's a volcano on the coast of Veracruz," Michael said. "There was an eruption there right around the target date."

"Oh, yeah," she said. "Right."

"Well—I was telling Jed—the dendrochronology couldn't really pin the date down," he said. "But the Connecticut Yankee Department just came through with something aces," he said. "Have a squiz at this." He spun the monitor around to face me. It showed the first line of a scan out of some English liturgical document:

kolendis cipriubus postridie qxxxxxx

I touched TRANSCRIPTION:

> kalendis aprilibus[,] postridie quinque panum
> multiplicationem [,] anno consecrationis
> praesulis nostri wilfredi[,] anno domini
> DCLXIV[,] indictione V . . .

Hmm. Okay, whatever. I hit ENGLISH TRANSLATION BY SRM/CFSU:

[Chronicles, Columcille (Abbey, Iona Island, Scottish Hebrides):]

> On the Kalends of April, the day after the multiplication of the five loaves, in the year of the consecration of our bishop Wilfred, the year of the Lord 664, the

5th indiction, the following envoyed to Oswiu Lord [of Northumbria]: We do petition in thy charity for relief from the burdens of our donative for the space of sixty days[,] as the Lord of Hosts has visited upon our flock warnings of the sins of the Earth and the coming apace of the Court of Judgment[,] as[:] First[,] that seven mornings ago, on the third Lord's Day after the imposition of ashes [i.e., March 24, 664 CE] our novices ending their devotions at matins [about 7:15 A.M.] were alarmed by thunderclaps as of a summer storm[,] although the vault was clear. Second[,] that the following day before prime [noon], Paulus pastor [of Iona] and also of other hamlets on the coast and [accompanying a number of] palmers [i.e., refugees] making on foot the long journey descended upon this Abbey in great terror and affliction applying for alms[,] only lamentations echoing their mouths as they thought themselves abandoned by our redeemer[,] as before matins [about 5 A.M.] a ferocious wave as of the trunk of Leviathan had descended upon all the strands of the West[,] followed by two further like [waves] and then uncounted [waves] of decreasing severity[,] such that the docks of both towns and all vessels of nets and trade were destroyed[,] four free burghers and nineteen souls [i.e., serfs] were drowned[,] and an unknown number starved and starving, and God's mercy be on them—

"Isn't that a kicker?" Michael asked. "That means we can date the eruption down to the hour."

"Uh—" I started to say.

"Great," Ana said, sounding unconvinced. She'd come over, too, and was reading over my shoulder. Out beyond the blue door-flap the day had darkened. There was a little grunt of thunder.

"How long does a wave take to get across the ocean?" Marena asked.

"Uh, Ireland's like, uh, five thousand miles from Veracruz, the wave would have gone about four hundred miles per hour," I said. "Right? So if—"

"They worked that out," Michael said. "The main eruption was at—hang on. It was at about four thirty A.M. on March twenty-second. Local time."

"That's really something," I said.

"Yeah, awesome," Marena said.

"Also, you know," Michael said, "Taro says the old guys didn't predict this thing before it happened. You know, the Sacrifice Game doesn't work well on natural events."

"Not unless the adder knows a lot about natural events," I said.

"Right."

"Did they say they were sure that people in Ix would feel it?" I asked.

"They say it was an eight point five," he said. "You would have felt it in Panama."

"Right."

"Also, you know, that eclipse is only a few weeks later."

"Right."

He meant a total eclipse of the sun that had been visible in the area on what we'd now call May 1, AD 664. It was also visible in Europe, and it's even in Bede. Of course, the Maya sun adders would have known about the eclipse. In fact, they'd probably calculated it to within an hour. But these days we knew it within a second, so that might give me an edge.

"Anyway, that's two predictions you can make good on," Michael said.

"That's great work," I said.

Michael laid a bigger monitor flat on the floor between us. "You ready to look at what we've got on the site?" he asked with the air of someone who'd been up early and working while some others of us had been asleep. I nodded. "Here's the latest subsurface map." A three-dimensional view of the reconstructed city of Ix came up on the screen. You could see layers of soil, rock, and water under the green wire-frame buildings. Marena and Ana sat down. No Way stood over us.

"The great thing about this software is you can select for density and some chemicals," Michael said. "So this'll show just the rock and not much else." He highlighted and deleted everything below 2.6 g/cm^3, which is roughly the density of limestone. What was left looked like a flat-topped abscessed sea sponge, sprinkled on top with the tumbled blocks of the temples and palaces, surrounded by clouds of specks and chips and shards. I'd already decided that maybe Michael had a little more to him than you'd think from just his TV personality, but now I was almost getting impressed.

"Right. Now, this is the current cavern system. Which we visualize by mapping all the subterranean open space as a solid body." He deleted everything with a density over 1.25 kg/m^3 or a temperature over sixty degrees. All that was left was a purple semitransparent structure like a many-holed scholar's rock. He started it rotating slowly.

"Was that all processed in the last two hours?" I asked.

"Yessir," he said. "Isn't that beaut?"

I said yes. It was pretty amazing, in a nerdy way. In the nineties, in the early days of ground-penetrating radar, you had to drag around a dish the size of a tire, but now one little antenna at the top of Mound A was giving us a bat's-ear view of the whole subterranean landscape out to nearly a two-mile radius. It made the best fish-finding sonar look like poking the water with a stick.

"Now, it seems that in the tenth bak'tun, the caves were more extensive," he said. "A lot of it's collapsed pretty recently. Geologically speaking. Within the last few hundred years. Then, all right, we're going to move farther west under the mountain. See? That's a chain of caves underneath. Apparently these lower ones are still active. That means they're wet and forming."

"I've actually done a little caving," I said.

"Oh. Great," he said. "Well, we can get this all a little more specific." He zoomed in and moved a bar in a window that read "Tunneling Acoustic Scanner." The wipe slowed down and began slicing virtual sections down into the rock. "Let's look for calcium."

He typed in BONE MODULE. The software started defining the view based on the difference between the average amount of calcium in limestone, which is almost pure $CaCO_3$, about 40 percent Ca—and in hydroxylapatite, which is about 33 percent. Bones are about 70 percent hydroxylapatite, and dental enamel is almost 97 percent. As it eliminated the limestone, the image faded into clusters of specks, like a frog's egg masses, strung out through the caves, and in wide drifts closer to the surface.

"A lot of this is prolly animal," Michael said. "But some of it's got to be burials. Especially under the main mounds or anywhere in the caves past the twilight zones. And these three dinguses—well, take a look." He highlighted three roughly rectangular globs under the west side of Mound A. "These are very bone-rich. And from the size profiles we can get down this low, it's not animals. It looks like about forty individuals. In fact, in terms of the stats, this one looks like a Roman catacomb."

"Huh," I said.

"So I think that the interior stairway prolly used to connect to these. They were part of the caves, and they were artificially enlarged, and then, sometime after the bones went in, they collapsed. Although of course we get decent dates without digging."

"Right."

"But what I'm getting at here is that I'm pretty sure these are the royal tombs. So we really hope you can get yourself into one of these three. I mean, this should be, you know. Where we're going to look, for, you know—"

"My corpse," I said.

"Uh, yes."

(24)

A pod of rain went by outside, drumming like bored defleshed fingers on the blue tarp. I picked my way over to the storage side of the room and sat down on a Cabela's inflatable between piles of gear. Over in the work area the gals were busying themselves with little camp-keeping projects, a bit ostentatiously, I thought. Boy Commando had put on a pair of antique Marantz water-filled earphones and was turning the knobs on a big Raytheon receiver with safecrackerish slowness, boring through layer after layer of the local electroscape, radar and radio and VHF and UHF and other more exotic bands, listening for increeping troops or snoops. I leaned back on a compressor case. The humidity was around 90 percent, but the cool stone made it seem okay, as though one were slowly and pleasantly turning into a frog. There was an irregularly placed T-shaped block in the wall over my head, about a foot below the corbeled arch, and I couldn't keep from looking at it.

No Way sidled over and dropped down next to me. He was wet. He didn't speak.

"So, what did you see out there?" I asked.

"There are at least five ES people out on the west side," he said. He got out a pack of filterless 555s. "On the east I'm not sure. But the mayor"—he used the word *alcalde*, which is really more like an unofficial mayor—"of the village sounds like he's on the payroll. He told everybody not to go out to any fields over here."

"So they know what they're doing, anyway," I said.

He made a *"supongo"* grunt and lit his cigarette with an old Zippo. I felt Ana glare at him from the other side of the room, like, sir, this is a smoke-free palace, but amazingly she didn't call him out on it.

"I really want to get on that thing with the hairy guy," I said. I meant that I wanted to start seriously planning the hit on García-Torres—the officer who'd been in charge when my parents were killed—who had a big beard.

No Way exhaled and glanced up at the ceiling, meaning he was sure that Executive Solutions was listening and in fact probably recording everything we did. Sonically, visually, and maybe biochemically. Smoke floated up and collected in the long channel of the corbeled arch, like mist over a canal.

"I don't care," I said. "I really need to make it happen."

"If you're still that worked up about it, why don't you just strap on an ECA and walk into his house?" No Way asked. By ECA, he meant *"explosivo combustible-aire,"* that is, a fuel-air explosive.

"Because, you know, I want to know it worked. And anyway I'm a rich coward now. It's time to start throwing some money at this problem."

"I'll see what I can find out."

"Anyway, I want it to hurt," I said. I'd decided a while ago that G-T had to know he was about to die. People who get blown up or shot in the back of the head or whatever barely even notice. So what's the point?

"Let's do one thing at a time," No Way said.

"Seriously, how much do you think it'll run?"

"Five dollars."

"Right."

"And, no, I'm not going to do it." He took a long drag, incinerating more than half of the shaft, and stubbed the rest of it out on the side of a hand-sized fire extinguisher.

"I don't want you to do it," I said, "I want you to stay healthy and help on the next one." And I just hope the world stays existent for more than another nine months, I thought. Just so I can exact my horrible revenge. After that, who cares?

Someone lit a lamp on the other side of the long room. I noticed the rain had gone by and it was getting dark outside. No Way leaned back and closed his eyes, as I remembered was his habit. I stood up and tottered over to the monitor area. The screens said it was T−5:49 hours. From when I lift off. I ought to be running through the drill, I thought.

Marena had come over.

"Let's take a walk," she said.

I said great. Ana materialized and whispered into Marena's ear, obviously telling her not to let me run off. I turned toward the door. "I'll keep an eye on him," I figured Marena answered.

I pushed out through the flap. Marena followed. Keeping a six-foot leash on me, I thought. As though I didn't have a locator on my ear anyway. As though I might sneak off. Well, you couldn't blame them. I was already the biggest investment any of them had ever made. Millions and millions of dollars just to run an electric comb through my frontal cortices.

Marena got in front of me and picked her way down the deer path toward the river. I was about to pull the flashlight out of the little ES-approved survival pack and then realized I could still see. The path ran through these thin, twisty *ixnich'i'zotz* trees, and it was easy to trip over their roots. Incidentally, *ixnich'i'zotz* means *palo de colmillos de murciélago,* that is, "bat fang wood," and they're called that because their little fruits have two fangy spines, and the ancient city—Ix for short—was named after them. The undergrowth was wet under my snake boots. ES had put an upside-down lancha in a crook of the riverbank where it would be hidden under foliage, and I sat down on it. It wasn't totally dark yet, but the water was black. It was only about ten yards across at this point, though, so it didn't look intimidating. The insect choir was out, but it still felt like there was something missing.

Marena sat down next to me but not right up against. Uncharacteristically, I almost didn't notice.

"Are you okay?" she asked.

"I'm fine, thanks," I said, but I probably sounded pretty distant and unsympathetic. She put her hand on my shoulder for about a half-second.

"You're hyperventilating," she said.

"Well, normally I infraventilate."

"Have you been in swimming yet?" she asked.

"No."

"I went in this morning, it's great. Also Michael certified it crocodile-free. And piranha-free."

"That makes sense," I said. "Piranhas live on a whole nother continent."

"Excellent." She was wearing a kind of a top and a bottom, and she wriggled out of them. Whoa. *Quieto neron.*

"Sorry, I don't mean to make you uncomfortable."

"Oh, no," I said, trying not to gawk but not to look away, either, because that's equally stupid. "I'm always uncomfortable."

"Just don't get any ideas." She balanced on one foot and pulled off a pair—well, "pair" is a little strong—of barely-there panties. Her body was sexy in an ethnic way, tiny, slightly chunky, and rounded off at the edges, and she wore it with that kind of Euro-aristocratic unconcern, like, oh, please, grow up, we're all adults here. Although of course we're not. She had very little pubic hair but it didn't look shaved, just, like, sparse.

"I've never had an idea in my life," I said. It was too late to turn around without giving the game away, so I put my Kleenex hand into my front pocket in order to nonchalantly wrench my mighty *verga* into its full upright position, but she'd already spotted the move.

"Don't be embarrassed, lots of guys tend to get erections when they see me naked." Her nipples were perky and inviting in the gray light, like miniature truffles from La Maison du Chocolat.

"I'm sure, I mean, one would hope so, it's biological . . . ly . . ."

She waded out on tiptoes and slid splashlessly under the surface. I took the opportunity to readjust myself. The guy thing is so embarrassing, it's like, after two hundred million years since we separated from arthropods there's only one hydraulic muscle left in the human body, in fact only half of all human bodies, and guess which it is. Just this automatic grasshopper ready to jump. Women are mammals and men are insects. Her head and shoulders bobbed up.

"Damn, this is refreshing stuff," her head said.

"The worst thing you have to worry about around here are the really big snapping turtles," I said. "Although you should also check for leeches."

"Bullshit," she said. "I dare you to come in."

"Well—"

"Oh, wait, we have to address the sexual-harassment issue. The fact is, you're an outside contractor and technically I'm not the one hiring you."

"Oh, right," I said, "don't worry about it—"

"Even so, you could get me fired, not that that seems like a big deal anymore, in fact if I could get it together to still worry about something like that I'd be happier than—"

"Please, you needn't give it another thought," I said. Hmm, I wondered, is this leading anywhere really interesting? I've been thinking about her for weeks and now I'm sort of flustering up at the moment of—

"Okay," she said, "great, come on, the water's, it's dark."

"Lovely, dark, and deep?"

"Yeah, like me, come on, don't be a felch."

"Hmm. Is it all right if I come in fully clothed?" It felt odd talking with this disembodied head in the deepening dark.

"No, you have to bare your body as you have your soul."

"What if Gulag shows up and kills me?"

"You mean Grgur?" she asked.

"Yeah. Sorry. Is that like, uh, Trog or Grout or some kind of, you know, cave dude name?"

"It's Croatian for Gregory."

"Oh. Cute."

"He's not going to show up," she said.

"Hmm."

"Okay," she said, "stop stalling or I'll think less of you."

I said okay. I yanked off my boots with concealed difficulty and dug my way out of my Menelaus—I mean, many layers—of fabric. I left the ear thing in. I waded out, imagining I was going to step on a not yet totally defleshed skull. Like a lot of river water in the tropics it was weirdly cold. The bottom was silt with the occasional pebble. Before I knew she was close, Marena got one hand on the top of my head and pushed it down under the water. I only swallowed a little of it and managed to get myself together before coming up.

"Your head feels so weird," she said, "you're like a new Chia Pig."

"Yeah." I felt soft human parts brushing against me underwater.

"So, listen," she said, "I want you to fuck me but I'm too stressed out right now to go through a whole foreplay thing or like any drippy cuddling around or anything. Okay?"

"Uh—right. Okay, great." *Oh my God,* I thought. *OMG OMG OMG—*

"You sure? You up for it?"

"Uh, sure," I said. Ridiculously, I was all high-school-dance achy-breaky dizzy. Wait, what about the STD Talk? I thought vaguely. Although of course, she'd seen my medical reports. And I wasn't about to look a gift tuna in the mouth. I'm sure she's fine. Right? Right. She has a kid, for God's sake, that makes her fine. Likely to be fine. Also, I was a little nervous that somebody might be listening, but I guess she figured we were out of range of any nosy parabolics Ana might have set up.

"Not to twist your arm."

"No," I said, "I mean, yeah, that's, great, this is quite romantic—"

"All this jungle and shit is romantic enough." She sort of rock-climbed up my front. She didn't weigh a lot anyway, and so in the water she felt like a ten-year-old. Why is this happening now? I wondered. Motive? Cheer me up? Release the sexual tension common among coworkers in stressful fields? Get me all relaxed and cozy before the big download? Because I'm about to die, sort of? Never mind, don't look a gift hearse—

"Don't worry, it's not just a pity fuck," she said, reading my mind again.

"Huh? Oh, no, pity's okay, I mean, I'll take it—"

"It's *not*, you're cute, I'm totally wet for you, I've just been a little preoccupied lately. Mommy stuff."

"Right," I said.

"Okay, come on." She dove under, popped up, shook her head like a Labrador retriever, and climbed out onto the bank. I followed. You could still just see outlines in the dark. She stood on the thin band of exposed silt between the reeds and the water, like a G-scale beach, whipped her hair around, whirled it into a helix, and wrung it out. I had it enough together to stand close to her, but I hesitated and before I could do anything to feel more in control of the situation she grabbed my—well, you know, my . . . hmm. What to call it? Tumescent manhood? Nine-Inch Nail? The Cat in the Hat? Anyway, she grabbed it and twisted it, like her hair.

"Okay, check this out," she said. "I'm beta-testing these things."

She knelt down, grabbled around in one of the pockets of her deflated shorts, and un-Ziplocked something that turned out to be one of these new kind of condoms that only go over the glans.

"Gird up your loins," she said.

I managed, barely, to don the device. It had some kind of nonpermanent Krazy Glue or whatever inside and it felt a little weird, but I guess still better than the old Hefty bags.

"Okay, come on," she said. "Just vadge, though, okay? I know it's retro but I don't have the engery for anal right now."

"No, that's great," I said. "Hang on, I'm just, uh, I'm screwing my courage to the sticking place—"

"Come on. You've got until the count of two. *Uno, . . . uno y medio . . .* nnh. Excellent." She grabbed me around the neck, pulled herself up to face level, wrapped her legs around me, and steered my whatever we decided on above into her—her yoni? Batcave? *Su Tusa? Concha? El Gallo?* Anyway, we were finally there.

"Whoa," I said.

"Yeah, how about that? You feel how tight I am?"

"Yeah, no kidding," I said. It was like I was trying to wriggle into a size-one halter dress.

"That's last year's vaginoplasty."

"I thought you said you had a C-section."

"I did, it's just, you know, the modern girl gets her unit taken in every once in a while, whatever. It's like having your teeth whitened."

"Great, that's, uh, very thoughtful of—"

"See, that's the scar of Max." She guided one or the other of my hands to her shall-we-say bikini line. I couldn't feel anything but fat-free skin but then I distinguished a long curved ridge, as delicate as an enamel pinstripe on my '73 Plymouth, whence the boy had emerged in 2004.

"They did a good job on that, huh?" she asked.

"Uh, yeah, I guess these days having a kid is as easy as, uh, getting a manicure."

"Rather. *Unnnnhh!*"

I didn't think I could stand up much longer, so I knelt down and eased her arched back down into the silt.

"Dude," she said. Dudette, I thought of saying, but instead I managed to kiss her. She kissed back, briefly. Her face had the bittersweet taste of diethyltoluamide from the Ultrathon, and mixed with sweat it made a kind of girl-flavor Shasta.

"You're kidding, nobody fucks missionary anymore," she said.

"Okay, wait—," I started to say.

"No, it's great," she said. "It's nostalgic. It's part of your whole retro-sixties thing."

"Mnff," I said. "Unh, unh." It sounded pretty stupid. I was trying to be halfway cool about this, but of course she liked to see me losing it. She flexed her rock-climber gluteus medius and whatever together and for some reason I got this image of myself being sucked into a sort of celestial car wash on textured conveyor belts with all these different kinds of foam brushes working me over. I noticed her bouldering finger was a few phalanges up my—hmm, *culo*? Servant's entrance? Moaning Myrtle?—anyway, she was way in there, not, so far as I could tell, out of technique, but just for a better grip, like I was a bowling ball. I started sneaking one hand down between us, but she pulled it away and repositioned it on her shoulder.

"I'll deal with the man in the kayak," she said, "you just better pump me like an oil rig. Okay?"

"You're so romantic."

"Romantic equals girly."

I followed instructions. She readjusted me so that we were both focusing on that same spot, that vertex of the delta. She released an inchoate sound. Ah, involuntary vocalization. My favorite.

"That's great," she said, "just stay with that angle." We clicked into a bit of a rhythm. I guess speed isn't usually considered a goal of contemporary erotic activity, but sometimes the hottest thing is just to get whatever it is the hell over with, especially at a time like this when I'd been building up all this fear and trembling over the last few weeks. In fact—and maybe I forgot to mention it—I really was pretty much absolutely terrified all the time now, with my teeth permanently on the verge of really, truly chattering. So instead of much of a pleasure event, what we really had here, on my end, anyway, was a long buildup of agony and a sudden and total, if transitory, release from it. "Okay, now!" she said. "*Rrrrrsh!* You *bitch!*" There was that familiar flash of the photo of the *Hindenberg* on the Led Zeppelin cover, oh, the humanity, and the crest-and-ebb of that old sound-beyond-sound:

nghnghnghnghnghbbbbBWOMP!!!zhwoooohzhngzhzhng . . .

Damn. Well, that was an orgasm, all right.

Ow. She bit my ear. "Ow," I said.

"Sorry," Marena said.

Little Elvis had left the building.

She pushed up on my chest with her super strength, rolled me out of the way—great, now we were both mud people—and peeled herself off me like an authoritarian school nurse yanking off a Band-Aid.

Whew. I'd been hosed down, soaped up, scrubbed, rubbed, brushed, dried, hot-waxed, hand-buffed, and towed to the lot and sold for 40 percent under list.

"Golly," she said, "I think I had a fallopian orgasm."

"Uh . . . yeah, I felt that," I said. Is there such a thing? I wondered. "Uh . . . that . . ." I trailed off. My overprobed brain felt like it had gotten a shot of about ten ccs of dopamine. "Sorry," I said finally. "I'm sneechless. Speechless."

"Okay, how about one more time?"

"Huh?"

"I've got a bag of super blues, we'll get you started again in two minutes."

"Well, okay." *Qué pistola,* I thought.

"Gimmie that." She pulled up the end of the newfangled male cleanliness device and twisted it, making a little balloonful of—*¿Qué debe llamarle? Leche? Néctar?* Pearl Jam? My whatever stretched until, just before we had a real injury to deal with, adhesive plastic separated from skin.

"Yeeowch," I said.

"Good," she said. "Ow." She swatted her back with an impressively flexible arm. "Damn." The mosquitoes were starting to find us.

"How do you get the glue off?" I asked "Is there—"

"Hang on," she said. I realized our earbuds were beeping.

"Heads up, full team, this is Keelorenz," Ana's voice said. "We're getting some movement on the GR that we don't like. Sound off and come in."

Boy Commando, Michael, Dr. Lisuarte, Grgur, and Hitch all said they were here. There was a pause and No Way's voice came on. "*Capisce*, Shigeru here," he said grudgingly.

"System on," I said. "Copy, Pen-Pen here."

"Copy, Asuka here," Marena said. "Please say specifics."

"They're on foot," Ana said. "It's ten to fifteen units. Patrol size. They're twenty clicks off, but I still want to move everything up three hours. So we hit Mound A now. Then if they do come through we'll still have time for step one. So everybody get back to base. Understood?"

"We copy," Marena said. "Give us two minutes. System off." She paused. "Let's rock 'n' road."

(25)

"I'd like to thank the Academy," Marena said, looking down the staircase toward her imaginary audience. "And thanks to Steven and James and Francis and Marty, and especially to the *circle*. The *trusted ones*." She raised her arms above her head in a born-to-win pose. "I'm *queen of the world*!"

"Somebody's going to see or hear you up there," Dr. Lisuarte said.

"Sorry," Marena said. She climbed down.

Lisuarte, Hitch, Michael, and I, and a few piles of Otter cases and transformers, receivers, monitors, and cameras, were all squatting on the lower landing of the Ocelot's pyramid, with the door of the ahau's niche behind us. We faced southeast across a shallow alluvial valley about two miles in diameter. You could just see a white squiggle of the river, segmented by tree trunks, and on the opposite bank, the outlines of a few of the closer hills, which had all once been mulob. Behind them the ring of natural hills rose up to the cleft peak of San Enero.

As I think I mentioned, the Ocelot's mul was the highest pyramid in this part of Guatemala. According to Morley's survey it had originally been gigantic, almost as large as the so-called Pyramid of the Moon at Teotihuacan. But locust trees had grown from between its stones, and the valley had silted up around it, and the temple at its peak—which would have been thirty feet above us—had been dismantled, so it wasn't the commanding hulk it once must have been.

Sun adders from the village had been burning copal and chocolate bars up here, and clumps of Ibarra wrappers and broken stoneware crunched under our feet.

"I'll be inside," Marena said. She went into the little doorway behind us.

"Okay, Jed, first we'd like you to orient yourself," Dr. Lisuarte said. "Visually."

"Right," I said. The nearly full moon was still low and yellowish. Bloody Rabbitess—the rabbit the Maya see in the moon, with its ears at Mare Fecunditatis and Mare Nectaris—was in her house, that is, there was a lunar halo, meaning rain was coming. But it cast enough light for me to follow instructions. I looked around for a minute.

"I think I'll remember where I am," I said.

"Okay, let's go," Lisuarte said.

I went in first. The trapezoidal doorway was just big enough for one small person to crouch through without using his/her hands. There was that bottomless smell of old stone, or rather, since most stone is pretty old, I should say that smell of stone that's been hanging out in the same place for a while. Marena was tapping at her workstation. Her face was lit blue on one side by a laptop screen and red on the other by the weak astronomy lamps that Hitch used for low-light-level video. The room was about nine feet deep and five feet wide, with a spacious five-foot ceiling. Three of the four main walls had been carved with glyphs, but about 60 percent of them were now unreadable. Michael had said they'd been in better shape the first time he'd been here, in 1994, but since then the acid rain had seeped in and given the limestone *cancer de piedra*. There was a sort of ambry or niche in the back wall, which, according to Michael, had been an entrance to the now rubble-filled interior stairs. With the three of us, and its tangle of boxes and cables, and the Toilet— that is, the head-scanner ring, which weighed about a hundred and ninety pounds and hung on a cable hoist screwed into anchors in the ceiling—it was a tight fit but not unbearable. Good thing there's no room for Michael, I thought. And it's a blessing Ogre isn't here. In fact, he wasn't up here at all, come to think of it. Maybe Marena'd gotten the message that he creeped me out. Anyway, supposedly he and Boy Commando and No Way were going to go out later and try to get a closer look at that in-marching patrol, or whatever they were.

Lisuarte took my head in her latex hands, eased me back into a reclining slump on an inflatable incline, and stuffed a sandbag under my neck so that I could see the sky through the door. I noticed that Hitch had mounted one of his tiny video cameras right above it, in the crook of the ceiling. She taped on the body electrodes and respiration gauges, clamped the blood-oxygen thingy on my right ring finger, slipped a blood-pressure cuff on my other hand, shot me full of a few drugs and tracking metals and whatever while I stared at the carved glyphs above the doorway. Some of the inscriptions went back to the early 500s, but the first one we were personally interested in was just to the right of the door. It was dated 11 Earth Rattler, 5 Quail, 9.10.11.9.17, that is, June 15, AD 644. The date followed a verbal phrase that Michael had interpreted as announcement of the death of 14 Fog Lizard, 9 Fanged Hummingbird's uncle and the previous ahau. Then, half out of my sight, there was a block of text dated one uinal after that, on July 5. It commemorated 9 Fanged Hummingbird's seating, or you might say enthronement or accession, at the age of twenty-four, as the patriarch of the Ocelot House and the ahau of Ix. The third inscription that concerned us was on the back wall, and I couldn't see it from here. But it was dated one k'atun—that is, about twenty years— after that, on 3 Earth Rattler, 5 Rainfrog, and it commemorated 9 Fanged Hummingbird's second seating, or reinstatement as K'alomte' Ixob and Ahau Pop Ixob, that is, Warlord of Ix and Lord of the Mat. In his first k'atun of rule he'd presided over Ix's second period of major expansion. He'd recorded victories over the sites known as Ixtutz and Sakajut and taken one of their ahaus captive. And, obviously, he'd stayed in power. Before his second seating, he would have held a vigil in this room, probably for at least two full days, before emerging at dawn on the twentieth—the day of the vernal equinox—to show himself to the people. This was the moment we were aiming for. Then there were two more dynastic inscriptions, also on the back wall. They were too damaged to reconstruct except for the dates. The first was 13 Sea Rattler, 9 Yellowness, 9.11.12.5.1, which was Saturday, November 19, AD 664. And the last was an 8 Hurricane, 10 Jeweled Owl date, probably May 13, AD 692. The only other readable part of the last inscription was the word *weave* or *weaving*, but it wasn't clear whether it was a verb or a name.

"Ikari, give us your status, please," Ana said.

"All his vitals are fine," Lisuarte's voice said. I supposed my nonvitals were the usual litany of disaster. "We're set."

"Okay, we're recording," Hitch said.

"Okay, up-top team, you're good to go," Ana's voice said. She and Boy Commando were somewhere near the base of the pyramid, probably lying in the mud and smearing their faces with camo paint.

"Let's roll," Michael's voice said.

Roll. Please. Roll your own, for God's sake. This whole thing seemed a lot more elaborate than it needed to be. From my POV, anyway. For that matter, this wasn't even the main event. And we didn't need to do it here. We could have run this whole download thing back at the Stake and it would have been a lot easier. Still, we needed to be out here anyway—since, the moment the downloading was over, we were going to start excavating those tombs. Really, we were here to dig. Still, like with the nun-snatch test, the idea was to put me in the same place in order to minimize my possible confusion on the other end.

Confusion, I thought. Let's hope that's my biggest problem.

"How are you?" Marena asked me.

"Pen-Pen is ready," I said. And scared phlegmless.

"Okay, Michael?" she said.

Don't do it.

"Righty right," Michael said over the earbuds in his TV voice. "Ohhh . . . KAY. Right now it's twelve oh two A.M., and we'll be narrowcasting for three hours and eighteen minutes. So all personnel, please take care of whatever personal matters you need to attend to." *Cállate el pico,* I thought. Shut up. Shutupshutup—

No, hold on there a second, Jed. Be nice. Remember, he's sixty, he's working hard, he's probably sweating all over . . .

"We'll be shooting for March twentieth, AD 664," Weiner went on. "Same bat-time, same bat-infested ahau's niche, and roughly just thirteen hundred and forty-seven years and eleven months and twenty-eight days and twenty-two hours and zero minutes back into the good ol' days."

Great, I thought, now, *SHUT . . . THE FUCK . . . UP . . . SHUT . . . FUCK . . . SHUCK . . . FUT—*

"You done?" Marena asked him.

"Go for it," Michael said. "Keep the f—"

"Okay, I'm cutting the GC channels," she said. My earphones clicked. Off the air at last. Thank God.

"Okay," Lisuarte said. "We've got about four minutes of system checks and then we'll start the Q and A."

"Right," I said.

Lisuarte crawled out the door so she could watch the rundown on the big monitor. Or maybe it was because somehow Marena let her get the message that we had a little thing going on. Girls chat.

Marena kneed over and kissed me.

"Hi," I said.

"How are you doing?" she asked.

"I'm good. No. I'm unstoppable."

"Godless."

"Yeah."

"Uh, you know to watch out for parasitic diseases, right?" she asked. "Try to just drink boiled water or at least really cold well water."

"Yeah, I know." I'd been over it a hundred times.

"They'll have some kind of tea from willow bark for quinine. Right? They'll have insect repellents. Uh, try to get more protein in your diet than the rest of them had. You can eat turkey bones."

"Thanks, Mom."

"Oh, and they'll have pine-bark tea for vitamin C, you should try to get a lot of that."

"I just hope that general wellness is my biggest problem."

"Right."

"Maybe they'll decide I'm a *brujo* and feed me to the catfish."

"Well, but, maybe they'll turn out to be great. The *living* Maya are the nicest people on the planet, right?"

"Yeah. Thanks." It's true, we're too nice, I thought. It's no wonder everyone's been taking advantage of us for five hundred years. We're always like, sure, come on in, sit down, have a tamale, rape my sister—

"Anyway, you're not going to pick any fights or anything, right?"

"I'll be good."

"Nothing grandiose either. Don't try to reform the system. No trying to take over the continent or anything."

"Well, that probably didn't happen anyway," I said. "As far as we know, nobody took over the continent during that period."

"Uh, right," she said. "Actually, I still don't get that. That Nabokov thing."

"Novikov." She meant the Novikov self-consistency principle.

"Right."

"Well, it just means that I'm not going to do anything that contradicts what we already know. About the past."

"Yeah, okay, but, the part I don't get is, you know, if you've already done everything you did back there, then, why don't we just dig up those caves now and skip sending you back?"

"Then I won't have done it. No Way asked me about that, too, and—"

"That's the part I don't get. I feel like, that we'd still have, you know, a grandfather problem."

"Well, it's like—hmm. It's like, as far as we're concerned, like, you and me here, the past is just a historical record. Right? So I can go back and do a lot of stuff back there, but nothing I do is going to change the history we know about now. Although luckily we don't know much about this city, or, really, this whole area anyway. So, you know, my range of activity isn't terribly constricted."

"Okay," she said, "but, so, like, say you go back and invent gunpowder. That'd change the record."

"No, no . . . I might do that. But if I did, gunpowder didn't really take off back there. Not enough for us to know about it, anyway. Maybe I did that, and then people used it for a while and forgot about it, and anything people wrote down about it got lost. That could happen. And then, suppose, tomorrow you find some twelve-hundred-year-old jar of gunpowder around here. That would be very possible."

"I don't know . . . that still doesn't, uh . . ."

"It's easier to understand if you just go through the equations," I said. "Explaining it in English . . . you know, it's like trying to fold an origami rhinoceros beetle out of a Post-it note."

"Well, okay, so I've got some homework to do."

"I wouldn't worry about it."

"I'm not worried, I'm just a little nervous."

"Well, thanks," I said.

"Yeah. You're my friend."

"Maybe I shouldn't mention this, but I'm feeling a little affectionate," I said.

"Well, we'll talk about that later."

"Right." Callous mask, I thought. Callous mask! Callous mask!

Like I said, I'd been in a constant state of terror a lot of the time lately, first during the Disney World Horror, of course, like everybody else, and then because of the 4 Ahau thing. And then when I got over that it was already time to worry about what kind of trouble I might get into back in Olde Mayaland. It was like there was this chunk of ice in my stomach that had been melting for more than a month but still never went away. But even so, for the last couple of weeks I'd also, contradictorily, been raging to just get on that luon beam and get it over with. I'd wanted to be Jed$_2$, that is, the one of me who ended up back there. And now I was starting to feel like I wanted to be the me who stayed here, in the twenty-first century, even if there wasn't a lot of future in it. Just because of Marena. Although really, come on, Jed, you're dreaming. What makes you think she's all that into you? She's a little red Corvette. Let things happen or not happen. Okay? Okay.

Lisuarte crouched back in the door. "Everything looks fine," she said.

"Cool," I said. Calm down, Jed.

"Okay." She and Marena levered the Toilet down onto the pile of sandbags behind my head. "Just ease back a bit. Lift up. Good." She guided my head into the ring and set it in place with her gobs of putty. "Is that too snug?"

"It's fine," I said. Just as snug as a rug in a jug. Slugbug shrug gl—

"Okay. Let's start going through this. You think you can concentrate?"

"Absolutely."

"Okay," Marena said. I'd requested that she do the Q&A again, and everybody agreed. She paused, listening to her earbud. "Taro says hi," she said. Back at the Stake he and the CTP team were feeding her the questions and evaluating the readouts of my responses.

I said hi.

"All right, it's T minus twenty seconds, let's start recording," Lisuarte said. She touched her phone and there was a discreet rising hum as the magnets zooming around my head accelerated to full speed. I focused on the equinoctal starscape through the dwarf-size doorway. You could just see Comet Ixchel, an unimpressive blue smear across Capricorn.

"Everything's go," Lisuarte said.

"Okay, Jed," Marena said. "First question. What's nine factorial?"

"Uh, hang on. 362,880."

"What day is this?"

"It's March twentieth, 2012," I said. Confusingly, even though we'd been referring to our D-Day today as Freaky Friday, it wasn't a Friday. "That's One Earthtoadess, 12 Dark Egg. And in—"

"Okay. What's in the news today?"

"Well . . . there's a big project where all the terminally ill people in Florida are all making farewell videos, and they're all going to be in this big sort of museum. And about eight thousand of them are like, children." Oops, I thought. She's a mom. Don't talk about dead children. Although Max is fine, but still. They worry. Except it was no wonder that slipped out, I'd watched a couple of the movies earlier in the day, out of a stupid sense of duty, I suppose, and they were still preying on my mind. I mean, it was the kind of thing that would break the heart of Joe Stalin himself. I changed the subject.

"The U.S., uh, it's basically slipping into a kind of Chinese-style totalitarianism," I said. "There's a checkpoint on, like, every corner. And there's the Operation Freedom Bill, which got passed yesterday, that centralizes control of the armed forces in the executive branch." She didn't say anything so I kept going. "The rationale behind this is that all these different divisions of the military were shooting at each other, and there were about five times as many fatalities just from that as there were from the attack itself, so . . . and it basically gets rid of habeas corpus, so, you know, one is planning to move to Sweden. And there's still a big waiting list for platelets so in Tampa and Miami there's a blood riot almost every night. And the No-Go Zone is now officially a national monument, so it's now the world's largest *qarafa*."

"What's that?" she asked.

"That's like, a city of the dead. A necropolis. Cancelled and made permanently taboo."

"Okay. What's Abuja the capital of?"

"Huh? Oh, uh . . . Nigeria?"

"Spell *kaleidoscope*."

"K, A, L," I said. "Uh, I, D, O, S, C, O, P, E."

Instead of telling me whether I was right or wrong—which didn't much matter anyway—she paused, listening to someone back at the Stake.

"Okay, they say that looks good," she said. Evidently all my little thoughtlets were coming through okay. And as of now they were already boring through quadrillions of Planck units of space-time at one foot per nanosecond. But of course, I hadn't and wouldn't feel anything or experience anything of the trip, any more than you feel anything when you make a phone call and a digital double of your voice shoots into outer space and caroms off two satellites and ends up on the other side of earth.

"Now, we're going to go through mission profile one more time," Marena said.

"Right." They wanted it to be the absolute last thing I'd forget, even if the tumors set in early. Oh, did I forget to mention that? The downloading had a problem side-effect: 9 Fanged Hummingbird's brain would absorb so much gamma radiation that it would develop some serious cancers in it within a year. We figured I'd have about eight months back there to learn the Game and get the information sent back to the twenty-first century. After that—

"Okay," she said. "Thirteen?"

(26)

"First, play along with their routine," I said.

"Right," Marena said.

The idea was that the most important thing, even if I was confused or disoriented when I took over 9 Fanged Hummingbird's body, was not to panic, and to let his automatics—his habits of movement and gesture and so on—take over. That should be enough to carry me through the rest of the reseating ceremony. Then, when I got back to the sweatbath or sleeping house—or harem, one hoped—or whatever, I'd have time to rest up and get my wits together.

"Twelve?"

"If you must, name the blast date and hype up yourself."

This meant that if I slipped up somewhere, or something else went wrong and I felt threatened, I'd deliver a speech that Michael and I had written forecasting the eruption of San Martín, sixteen hours after the seating. The speech also stressed that the audience was in dire danger and that I was the only person who'd be able to save them from the darkness once it happened. It was a decent piece of Ch'olan verse and we were pretty proud of it.

"Eleven."

"Just bond with your crew and it's easy livin'," I said. The idea behind this one was that the main thing I should do first, once the rituals were over and I went back to the daily business of ordering people around, was to bond with my staff. "You'll be like a mafia chief," Michael had said, "running things through a few key people. So even if you don't know what's going on, or what to say, you ought to be able to engage them enough to find out and relearn the behavior." We'd rehearsed a lot of phrases like "Tell me over you what you think about X," or, if they asked me about something, "What would you under me do about it if I were away?" That sort of thing.

"Ten."

"Learn the nine-stone Game and play through it again."

That is, I needed to learn how they managed to play the Game with nine runners, and then I also should try, if possible, to re-create the Game that had been recorded in the Codex Nurnburg. If I managed that, I might be able to work out what would happen on 12/21/12, and they—the Chocula team— wouldn't even have to get the Game working again. They'd just act on my notes.

This sounded a little ambitious to me, though. I was confident I could learn a lot more about the Game, and Michael and company were confident that the Game had been fairly common, even if it was an upper-class secret, like writing. But I wasn't sure how well I'd be able to play if I were using some-body else's gray matter.

When I'd gotten this job, I'd thought it was the motivation tests that had done it. But later, Taro had said it was the calendrical savant thing. According to Taro, the CTP lab said that that sort of skill could transfer to the host brain and give me an extra edge in picking up the nine-stone Game in a short time. It was a good thing for them that I'd shown up, I thought. Basically the CTP people had said that my consciousness should be able to work with almost whatever material it found. Supposedly, if the target brain was of at least nor-mal intelligence, he'd get enough mental architecture from me to be able to think effectively in all the ways I knew how to think. That is, he'd have some Game skills, some above-average memory, and might even be able to do some of my idiocomputo tricks. "And if the guy turns out to be a dummy," Lisuarte had said, "you'll probably just feel like you're always a little drowsy. But you should still be able to make good decisions, because you'll still be yourself with your own habits of thought." It seemed to me that she was projecting more confidence than they really had. Still, from the evidence we had, 9FH didn't sound like a dummy. And he sounded tough. Well, he was in for a sur-prise. And then oblivion. Poor bastard.

"Nine."

"Write down all you know and you're doing fine."

"Eight."

"Find a good dry spot for the message crate."

After a bit of study I had a pretty good map in my head of Alta Verapaz and, to a coarser level of detail, of all Mesoamerica. We'd singled out eighty-two areas on the map that were dry, diggable, and where there wouldn't be any development, mining, archaeological excavation, or even deep tillage—not in the rest of the pre-Colonial era or in the Colonial or modern ones. When I buried my notes, packed in wax, salt, and rubber, I could be pretty sure that nothing would disturb them for thirteen hundred years.

"Seven."

"Make a magnetite cross we can see up in heaven."

I'd be burying the notes in the center of an imaginary cross about five hundred feet wide. Each point of the cross would be a cluster of at least twenty pounds of magnetite or meteoric iron—lodestones—also sealed in wax. In a few hours—back here in 2012, that is, as soon as we'd finished the download—three data-mapping Spartacus satellites would go off-line for normal traffic and start scanning. For safety they'd look in a zone covering almost all of Mesoamerica, from the twenty-fifth parallel, which runs through Monterrey, Mexico, all the way down to the twelfth, which runs through Managua. When one of them spotted the electromagnetic signature of the cross pattern, an ES helicopter would take off with a crew of excavators to dig up the notes and bring them back to Michael's staff at the Stake. If it all went perfectly, they'd be looking at the stuff in less than twenty-four hours.

"Six," she said.

"Scope out a tomb with a ton of bricks."

This was the start of the second part of the operation, the Amber Tomb. In case the notes couldn't cover everything—that is, if it turned out that the Game was too much of a skill and not enough of a describable procedure—we still had another chance, although it was much more of a long shot. It was the reason we had all the stuff ready in the palace. If we were lucky, my brain would be coming back, carefully plasticized. And in order to protect it, I needed to find a burial chamber I could wall off from inside, so that rival kings or tomb robbers or whoever couldn't possibly get to it. Hence the phrase *ton of bricks*.

"Five."

"Find the eight gel components so you will revive."

I'd be preserving my brain, and incidentally my body—or, to be strict about it, 9 Fanged Hummingbird's body and brain, but my mind—in a quick-setting colloid. It was something Alcor had been working on for decades as an alternative to cryonics, but it was just in the last few years that they'd started getting good results. Back at the Stake we'd watched some rather un-PC videos of the procedure working on macaques. And I have to say, the critters seemed just fine, once they got used to their new bodies.

Anyway, Warren Labs had adapted the recipe to the sort of low-tech—well, let's say nontech—tools and ingredients I'd be able to find. We'd also made up a separate mnemonic rhyme for the eight ingredients—bitumen, beeswax, alcohol, copal resin, and a few other things—and another longer rhyme for the refining and mixing procedures. I guessed they'd make me go over that again later on. Anyway, in my last few days at the Stake I'd made the stuff from scratch four times and only screwed up one batch. I was the Iron Chef on the stuff. No problem.

"Four."

"Rig the counterweight bags to close off the door."

"Three."

"Seal your notes, rig the lid bags, and be sure to pee."

That is, just for safety I should leave a second copy of the Game notes in the tomb. The counterweight bags were to bring the stone lid slowly down over the casket. And the third item was there because we didn't want any fluids besides blood contaminating the colloid.

"Two."

"Heat the gel, poke the sandbags, and send off your crew."

"One."

"Just open two veins and you're nearly done."

I wasn't wild about this part.

"Zero."

"Get under the gel and you'll wake up a hero."

I wasn't crazy about this part either. I'd have to weight myself down with sandbags, including one tied to my head, lean back in the lukewarm goo, let my head fall under the surface, exhale, count backward from ten, and inhale.

"Good," Marena said. "All right, let's move on. Name three Fellini movies."

"Uh, *Satyricon, La Strada, Roma*—no, scratch the last one, I like *8½*—"

"Repeat this number backward: 9049345332."

"2335439409," I said.

"Very good."

"I'll take Zambian numismatics for ten thousand, Alex."

"I'm asking the questions here."

"Sorry."

"If you painted each side of a tetrahedron either red or blue, how many distinct color patterns could you make?"

"Um, five."

"So, can you tell us a little about your mother?"

Hell, I thought. I knew something like this was coming. Lisuarte had mentioned that when they were looking over the charts of the other download— that is, the one for the Soledad test—they'd decided they wanted to get a little more emotion out of me on the next round. Light up a few more layers of the old hippocampus. Well, whatevs. I started telling her how my mother had taught me about the Game, and how we got into trouble with the fincas, and maybe it was the drugs or the mood or something, but somehow I realized I was just babbling on and on about how I'd been in the hospital and I'd heard about how there'd been an arrest up in T'ozal, and how it was all my fault. *Todo por mi culpa.* All my fault, all my fault, damn it. Damn. It.

"Los Sorreanos están un grande calamidad," I'd said. I remember it was morning, because they'd given me white-bread toast. "The Sorreanos are in big trouble."

"Diciendo debido a Teniente Xac?" that nice Sor Elena asked, ever so casually. "You mean because of Lieutenant Xac?"

Of course, I was a dopey, eager seven-year-old. I guess I'd forgotten how I wasn't supposed to say . . . or maybe I was just too angry, or I just wanted the attention, or I wanted to be important. *"Mi padre y Tío Xac van a quemarse la casa Sorreano,"* I said. "My father's with Uncle Xac and they're going to burn the Sorreanos' house down."

Damn, damn, damn. *Todo por mi culpa.* I focused through the door at Homam, that is, Zeta Pegasus, which was just coming up through a little predawn glow in the lower left. It's not a bright star, but it's a nice yellow in that rather desolate part of the sky between Formalhaut and Vega. I realized I'd stopped talking. There was a pause.

"Okay," Marena said, maybe about two decibels more softly than usual. "Right. Please solve for x: x cubed times five over x squared plus seven x equals zero."

The Q&A went on for another hour. At three forty-five, Lisuarte suggested we take a one-minute break. Although we were still uploading, of course. Marena gave me a sip of Undine through a straw.

"Thanks," I said. "I guess I should . . . hmm."

It didn't make sense to say good-bye, since, as far as anyone around me could see, I'd be staying right here. After the Q&A I wouldn't even be going to sleep. I'd just pull my head out of this metal anus and climb down off this dirt pile. And the I that would stay here wouldn't notice anything.

But if I was the I that was going to find myself back there . . . hmm . . .

"I'd like to say good-bye on behalf of my identical twin," I said.

"Yeah," Marena said. "Break a leg, babe."

"Thanks."

"You're going to kill 'em."

"Thanks." I realized she was holding my hand. Yikes. Tenderness. Watch out for that shit.

"Okay," she said. "Let's move on. What was your first nudibranch?"

"It was a pair of *Hermissenda crassicornis.*" Dawn was coming up outside, and maybe because of the red lamp the sky looked greenish. Ixchel was still visible. It seemed almost orange, and larger. I coughed.

"Who was your first real girlfriend?"

"That would be Jessica Gunnison."

"Who was the voice of Mickey Mouse?"

"Hang on a second," I said. My tongue hurt. I kept looking at Ixchel. Now it was almost red, and for some reason Vega, which is above it and to the left, also looked red, and then a third red star became visible just below it, and then there were five and nine and then thirteen, and the dots grew and merged together, and I realized they were drops of blood, dripping out of my tongue onto our folded petition to One Ocelot, at the womb of the sky. The growls of giant mahogany-trunk rasps pulsed through the stone.

"Jed?" Marena's voice asked.

I'm okay, I tried to say, but my mouth was all full of pain and blood. There was something I'd forgotten. Don't worry, I tried to say, I actually feel pretty great. My body had that running-on-fumes quality of having been awake for a long time, but there was a compensating lightness to it. I inhaled a flood of resinous air. It was sticky with the full spectrum of the offering smoke, wild tobacco, geranium buds, burning skin, cilantro, rubber, bubbling crystals of copal amber, and something else underlying everything, something from before, something happy, oh, that's it, that's what it is, it's chocolate—

Wait.

There was something I'd forgotten, not—

TWO

The Opposite of Cinnamon

IX IN AD 664

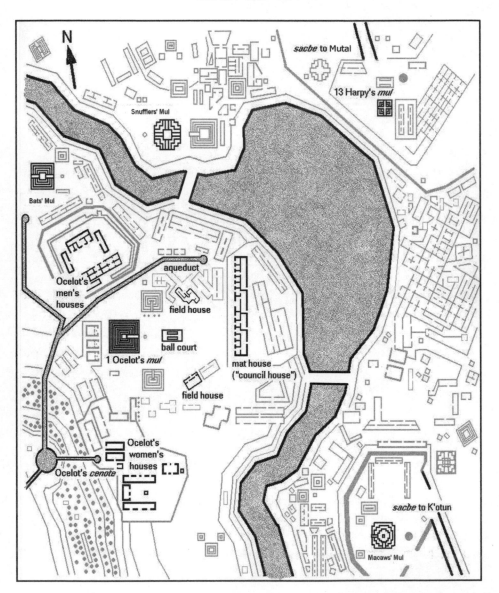

N

sacbe to Mutal

13 Harpy's *mul*

Snufflers' Mul

Bats' Mul

aqueduct

Ocelot's men's houses

field house

ball court

mat house ("council house")

1 Ocelot's *mul*

field house

Ocelot's women's houses

Ocelot's *cenote*

sacbe to K'otun

Macaws' Mul

(27)

We pulled the rope of thorns through our tongue, burned it, crawled out the door, took five steps, and stood at the lip of the great killing stairs. The Laughing People, the Ixians, strained up toward us and started the countdown, or rather count-up, pulsing to the numbers, spinning their featherwork parade shields from front to back so that the whole human field flashed from cold red to blue-green and back again and again.

Damn, I thought. We really had no clue.

I'd had a pretty clear idea of what the place would have looked like—and then the actual thing was so different that for a second I actually thought I was somehow in the wrong place, that the wave had missed Ix and I was in ancient Khmer, say, or Atlantis, or in the future, or on some other planet. Come on, Jed, orient yourself. That's the cleft peak, San Enero. Except it's all built and—damn. Things wobbled in and out of visibility through the gold whorls of offertory feathers. A domehead captive screamed somewhere below and trailed off into a kind of cackling gasp.

Holy shit, I thought. It had actually worked.

I tilted my head back and swallowed a mouthful of my own blood. *Es delicioso,* I thought, so many layered tastes, sweet-corn oil, copper, umami, seawater . . . it really is the best thing in the world, the way it shoots out of a dark-purple vein and then flashes instantly into scarlet, and then the way it slowly mellows to sienna and then skins over into black amethysts and finally puckers into those chewy nuggets that are just *packed* with tangy goodness . . .

M'AX ECHE? Who are you?

Are you one of the four four-hundreds?

What?

Huh.

What was that?

Are you one of the thirteen? Or one of the nine?

Was that me?

Get out of my skin.

Oh, hell. I wasn't in charge. The target had not been erased. I was trapped.

"Uuk ahau k'alomte' yaxoc . . ."

"Overlord, greatfather,
Grandfather-grandmother—
Zeroth sun, firstborn sun . . ."

Oh, hell.

Bad break, Jedface. Wrong place, wrong time. No, right time, roughly right place, definitely wrong body. *Coño coño coñocoño* fuckedy fuckedy fuck fark fook.

"Ahau's niche" indeed. Sure, it's called the ahau's niche, so naturally the ahau would be in it, right? *Malo.* Wrong.

This Chacal character is 9 Fanged Hummingbird's replacement. Royal autosacrifice by proxy. They're going to toss me to the human sharks, and then in a few days, 9 Fanged Hummingbird's going to come back from the grave, or rather the kitchen, and step right back into the saddle. Damn, we were dumb. Good going, guys. You too, Jed. Serves you right for trusting them. *¡Cutre!* Jerk, fool, moron—

Hold it.

Bad luck. Do something. Assess the damage. Regroup.

Oh, shit, *Dios te salve, María, ni modos,* no way, no way.

Phalange, eyelid, sphincter, whatever. Move. Move. Move.

Oh, *chíngalo,* oh fuck, oh God, oh fuck God.

Trapped. Frozen. *Helido.* Cast in epoxy. Lucite souvenir paperweight.

Focus, I thought. Move. Concentrate. Move. Open mouth. Say it!

Nada.

Claustropanic. Holyshitholyshit.

Está chupado, no sweat, so, let's all just shout it out, shall we? Stand and deliver.

Everybody does it, everybody's doin' it, birds do it, bees do it, even educated fleas do it, let's do it, let's cease to exist, oh God oh God.

And give these bastards a lethal dose of R-E-S-P-, et cetera. They'll be lining up to kiss our *culo*. Right?

No answer.

Jesu-bloodyfucking-*cristo*.

Last chance. Come on. Chacal? We're pals, right? *¿Compadre?* Don't do this. Listen. At least give it a hearing. Think about it. How often does this happen to someone? It's not an event to just shrug off. No matter what these hustlers tell you, if you just give this a try they'll all just fall into line. We can take over this whole place. Together. You and me. Chang and Eng. No sweat. Give me ten days and we'll have those Ocelot wankers wiping our *calabazo*. Nobody's going to think less of us. Come on. Say it. Say it.

Nothing.

Listen, I thought hard, if you can stop just enjoying the damn moment for a second I think I can get you out of this, but you've got to listen to me listen listen please listen a second listen listen please—

Silence. He wasn't buying it. It was like his concentric certainties were hugging me to death.

HEY, I thought at him. Think. Try to understand what I'm telling you. This is *not* the center of the universe, *por el amor de Dios,* it's just plain Central America, and if you could just let me set you straight on a couple basic things you won't want to die anymore, I can get us out of this out we can get out get out, get, get . . .

"Four suns, then five suns . . ."

Chacal's hearing was better than mine. It was like he could zero in on each individual voice and tell whether its owner was sick or healthy or young or old or had filed or unfiled teeth. And we could tell that each voice believed, that each one knew its presence was essential for the collective to conjure One Ocelot down from his sky cave.

"Eight suns . . ."

We were looking down. Deathward. Ropes of black rubber smoke scrolled up to us from twin-giant *incensarios* at the base of the stairs, at the eye of the vortex . . . God dog, those stairs. They were stairs that didn't go up. Just down. According to Michael's calculations, when someone the weight of an average Maya gent of the period—say, Chacal—took the big leap, he'd be at the bottom in about 2.9 seconds, that is, roughly the time it takes a bowling ball to roll down the alley and hit the pins, and in most cases he'd be in at least two main pieces. Yep, about a minute from now we'll be tamale filling, our head will be a ball in the cosmic soccer game, and not only will I be *fuqueteado* but everybody in 2013, and I really mean everybody, they, too, will be *fuqueteados—*

Come on, Joaquín, just grab the wheel. Just move his mouth, just find that synapse, *push* that button, *LIF' DAT BALE*. Come on. Wait. Did my left leg just quiver? I think so, I think so. Again.

Again.

Nothing.

A flake of skin ash scuttled across our forehead and I thought I could see Chacal's uay, that is, his animal self, fly out ahead of us, a gray owl. There was an instant of perfect balance. All 620 ± muscles of my body were at full tension. I thought I could see where I was heading, into a rush of egoless motion, a feeling like I was a chrome flying fish leaping over a green guilloché-enamel sea, and then that I wasn't just one fish but the whole school, and then a seawide army of them, all leaping in unison, swimming on the wind. We took a last breath.

Hell. Marena's going to wonder what happened. She'll think I screwed up.

Try. Again. MOVE!

Nothing.

"*Wuklahun tun . . .*"
"Nineteen suns . . ."

Last chance gone. Chances all used up.

Well, at least I got to see it, I thought. That's still a lot.

Ready.

Please. One more second. Please.

My feet shifted for purchase on the stone launching pad. They found the exact spot. I lowered my bejeweled body into a feline crouch, eager to spring out over the stairs. I'd make it, I thought. I'd never be enslaved by the Night Chewers. I wouldn't have to fight my way through the underwaterworld. The smokers would treat me as well as if I really were 9 Fanged Hummingbird himself. They'd convey me straight to the womb of the sky's thirteenth shell, right into the fire. Finally I'd be able to rest. I would achieve oblivion.

". . . Twenty-score twenty-score sheaves of suns,
This is the number we ask you to give to us,
One Ocelot, over us, come to us, grace us."

Silence. Somewhere, a rock dove cooed.

This is it, I thought. Really better think of something, something clev—

A single voice spoke, somewhere behind and above me. It wasn't a human voice. It's a macaw, I thought. No, it's a trained spider monkey. Or maybe it's some kind of scraper instrument, a stone *guira*, a bone ratchet, anything but a person—but then somewhere in the sea of my new memories I knew it was human, that it was a dwarf's voice, magnified by a giant megaphone and distorted by splintering off the city's thousand angled planes. It was a male, but it was above a countertenor, like the voice of Alessandro Moreschi, the Last Castrato. There was an odd blankness to it. Or maybe I should say there was a lack of doubt. It was as though the voice had never, ever been questioned. It wasn't that it was used to commanding, but rather that it had never said anything that wasn't an order by definition and that there had never been even a possibility in the mind of the voice's owner that it would ever be disobeyed. And in some fold of my new brain I could feel that Chacal knew whose voice it was, and then a moment later I also knew. It was the voice of the real 9 Fanged Hummingbird, the ahau and k'alomte' of Ix.

It said:

"Pitzom b'axb'äl!"

Which, roughly translated, meant:

"Play ball!"

That was it. Time to dive.

(28)

"*Ch'oopkintikeen k'in ox utak!*"

It was me. I'd shouted it out. *I DID IT!* I thought, *I CAN OVERRIDE CHACAL! YyyaaaAAAAYYY JED!!*

Silence. A green jay cackled somewhere.

Okay. Get out the rest. Verb difference. Remember the consonant shift. *Ch'opchin*, not *ch'oopkin*. Sub in that thing they call themselves, *ajche'ej winik*. Laughing People. Breathe from the diaphragm. Go.

"*Ch'oopchintikeen k'in ox utak!*" I said, trying to project without shrieking,

"I am the blinder
of the third sun hence:
Fourteenth k'atun,
on 12 Wind,
on 1 Toad,
The Northern Belcheress
will burst with ulcers
she'll rain her blackness
on the hills, the valleys,
And only I know how to lead you through it,
You laughing people, you need—"

WA'TAL WA'TAL WA'TALWA'TALWA'TALWA'TAL!!! STOP STOP STOP STOPSTOPSTOP!!! his mind shrieked around me. I choked up, sixty-one words before the end. Come on, damn it. Get it all out. Through the darkness, through the—

Nothing. *Mierda.* I was just barking airlessly like a lung-shot dog. A feeling, a very terrible feeling, like shame but deeper than shame, rose up around me like a tide of acid vomit. It soaked into my mind and filled me up with a single word:

AJSAT!

Like all important words it didn't quite translate. But there is an English word that's very close, especially if you imagine it used in a setting of high social pressure, say in an important kickball match in, say, fourth grade:

LOSER!

You've made me LOSE, you made me LOSE, LOSE, LOSE, I AM A LOSER BECAUSE OF YOU, LOSER, LLLLOOOOOOSSSZERRRR—

Chíngate, I thought, fuck you, I fucked you up. I tried to step back from the edge but my body had seized up again. Something rose out of the city, a collective intake of breath. What were they thinking? Somehow we seemed to tip forward without quite falling and I saw the frozen crowd rotating up over me and the chopper-steps rising to meet me, and as my eyes focused on the flint teeth of the third stair from the top, the one that was going to cleave into my face, time really did stand still.

I'm dead, I thought. That was the last thing I saw, and it's etched on what's left of my brain. Going to fade out slowly. *Na' na.* Mommy. Please. Hmm. Odd things were happening in the hinterlands of my vision. A sort of wicker beach ball floated past me on the left and bounced down the stairs. On its fourth bounce it shattered and iridescent green and magenta things exploded out of it. Feathers? No, too fast. One darted by us. Hummingbirds. Huh.

No, it's not subjective, I thought. We're not falling. We're really suspended somehow, or rather, somebody's holding us from behind. Hmm. A huge unfired-clay pot—it was at least as big as one of those man-size olive-oil jars *(pithoi?)* in the palace at Knossos—arced over my head, slowly settled on the seventh step, and smashed into a house-size puff of yellow and black. The puff grew and spread around us. They were bees. Other things fell around me, orchids, marigolds, bits of jade, stiff white tortillas Frisbeeing over the stairs, but now we'd already turned around, or rather we'd been turned around, our back was to the sun and we were facing the door of the sanctuary, a black lamprey's mouth in a giant cat-toad's face crowned with vegetable glory.

Don't let me fall backward, that would be just *too* undignified. Did I think that? Or was it Chacal?

I also realized we weren't breathing.

We die, we burst.

Well, *that* was Chacal. Hey, sorry I blew your big—

Zero, zero. Gak. Claustrophopanicaphobiofear. *Don't choke us, please, just breathe, just breathe in, breathin. Got. To. Suck. In. This. Sucks. Breathe. In.* Gkk.

Hands held me on either side and a giant live thing reared up in front of the doorway. At first, what they'd call the purely associational or prediagnostic or whatever part of my perception read it as a bird, and not just any bird, but a phororacoid, an eight-plus-foot flightless flesh-eating Miocene hellbutcher with nine-inch talons and an eyespotted cockscomb the size of yearling pigs. But the Chacal side of me—and it was a side of me, by this time—knew who it was. It was a greathouse, that is, an aristocrat, in his full ceremonial headdress. Although headdress isn't a strong enough word. It was a swollen prosthesis, a vegeto-mechanico Synthetic-Cubistic construct avant la lettre. One of the long plumes of its crest brushed my forehead and I saw that it was artificial, a composite of hundreds of red macaw feathers sewn onto a bamboo stalk. It extended a claw and held me by the chin. Under its bone-inlaid papier-mâché beak, deep down in its gizzard, I saw it had just swallowed someone else, there was a tiny head down there, as bald as a turtle's and wrinkled like brain coral, glistening red, glaring at me with burnt-orange vulturine eyes. I could feel that Chacal had known him personally, that in fact to Chacal he was both close and revered, and then I realized I knew he was the red *bacab*, the bacab of the east. It was 2 Jeweled Skull.

Kill me, Chacal thought. Absolve me. I have ruined us, I have ruined myself, kill me, renounce me.

Shame. God damn it, I tried to think, this is *not* about *me*. But Chacal and I shared emotions the way conjoined twins share a blood supply, and I thrashed along with him in that quicksand of cosmic embarrassment. It was an emotion I knew but hadn't felt since—well, I don't even know when. But I suppose anyone can bring back a whiff of it by remembering something from kidhood, like, maybe in the recess period following that kickball game the other kids ganged up on you and started pelting you with those big red shards of processed cedar bark, and if you could relive what it felt like to have everyone you knew laughing at you, how desperately you tried to will yourself to melt down into the ground, and how there was no contradiction between hating the teasers and still needing their acceptance . . . but then you'd have to add that for Chacal there wasn't even the hope of eventual refuge that you might have seen dimly on the horizon of the playground. There'd never be any parents to run home to, no sympathetic school nurse, no eventual growing up, nothing. There'd only ever been one exit for him and I'd just welded it shut. My vision tunneled in on 2 Jeweled Skull's arm, on the jade scutes around his wrist, on the exposed upper arm with a crust of cinnabar cracking into scales on his loosening skin, on a lone shoot of black hair sprouting out of the scales like an *Aporocactus* in the Mojave, I mean, epiphytic cacti, grow, usually . . . whoa. Dizzying out. By now we hadn't taken a breath in over a minute and I was getting that gray fuzz like the times when I was little, when I'd cut myself and nearly bled out. A vulturine voice I thought was 2 Jeweled Skull's pierced the carbon-dioxide buzz in our skull and I thought I caught the word *luk'kintik*, "defilement." There was something in the tone, something maybe even— apologetic? Pleading? Hot fingers wriggled into my mouth and even though I'd lost proprioception, there was still a sense of falling into the soft red dark. Am I finally rolling down? I wondered. Please let me fall, don't catch me, let me roll, it's what I want, it's what I want.

(29)

I realized I'd been aware of the dimensions of the box for a long time without seeing or feeling it. It was a bit too short to stretch out in and a bit too squat for me to sit up. Which was fine with me. I was thrilled just to curl.

Itchy. Eye itchy. Scratchme.

Can't. Hands tied somewhere.

Thirsty.

I tried to swallow and couldn't close my mouth. Finally I managed anyway but it was a dry swallow that just made it worse. Ouch. Shit.

I had a notion that I was in a fetal position on my left side, or, no, rather, on my right side. One arm was missing. Or, hmm, probably just pinned under me. Numb from the shoulder down. Right foot gone too. Or left. Easier to tell if I could see them. At any rate, pretty much the earthward half of my body was numb. And the upper side was a grab bag of aches and strains. Whatever.

Itchy. I noticed I was squirming, trying to scrunch my left eye onto the wall of the box to scratch it. Got it. Ah. Bliss.

Huh.

I thought I'd stopped wriggling, but there was a residue of motion. No, it wasn't me. The box is moving. Back and forth. No, it's swinging. I'm hanging up somewhere. How high? I ground my cheek into the wall again. It was nubbly and yielding. It's not a wood box, it's wicker. I'm in a basket. Basketcase.

Well, that makes sense. No edges to slice yourself on, no hard floor to crush your head against, basically a padded cell. They want to keep me alive. Roughly. No wonder I can't close my mouth. There's a wad of stuff in there so I can't bite my tongue off and bleed out. I uncurled a little and then rolled a little, pressing on the walls of the box. It was about one arm wide and two arms long—and somewhere in my jumbled head I noticed that I was already thinking in Maya arm lengths, that is, units of about twenty-six inches, and not in feet or meters—and, I thought I could sense, about one and a half arms high . . . that is, not high enough to stand up, not long enough to stretch out, not . . . oh hell oh hell. A chord of claustrophobia swelled up and I figured I was about to lose it but then maybe just because my new body was still so exhausted I managed to think, Chill, chill, *cálmate,* it's all right, Jed, you're alive, and it settled. Stay frosty. Fros-T-Freez. If you panic you're really done for.

Thirsty.

Maybe it was something about the air currents or the stored heat radiating off stone beneath me or the way a puppy was yipping somewhere behind stone walls, but I was pretty sure I was in a small enclosed courtyard and that it was late afternoon. I listened. There was a kind of creaking sound somewhere, and turkeys making that burbling-brook noise, and another dog, not the puppy, barking a long way away, and then, beyond all that, there was a distant but pervasive chorus of innumerable clicks, the nostalgic tearjerking sound of women making *waahob,* tortillas, tossing the corn dough from hand to hand. It was the same exact sound, it was going to stay unchanged until Jed's childhood, I mean my childhood. And then even beyond that—damn, I thought, these new ears really rock—I thought I could hear echoes of game calls and the mother's-heartbeat thunk of a rubber ball.

Whoa.

I'd gotten a visual flash of a game, that is, a hipball game, and it wasn't mine. That is, it was Chacal's. There was a forest and a strip of cleared dirt with a pile of logs and dirt on either side—the barest possible excuse for a hipball court—and two naked boys facing me, with a vague bunch of people behind them, standing around the end zone. One of the kids' faces was a sheet of blood, and I thought for a second that I was being punished. But then I heard or remembered something like cheering, and I understood that knocking the ball into his face had been a winning move, a big achievement. But that was all I saw of it before it somehow blended into Chacal's last so-called game, the one that had been an entirely staged event, a one-on-one against 9 Fanged Hummingbird, where the ahau played 7 Hunahpu, the hero twin, and Chacal impersonated the Ninth Lord of the Night. That is, Chacal was the bad guy. It was a night game, lit by hundreds of overhead torches. 9 Fanged Hummingbird had just stood there at the other end of the court, fully masked and in stiltlike platform sandals but still obviously an achondroplastic dwarf. Stagehands—or maybe "invisibles" would be a better term, like in Noh theater—maneuvered a hollow paper ball with two thin cords attached to long poles, swinging it back and forth like a bird in a marionette show. Of course, it hadn't fooled the audience, but it wasn't meant to. As far as the spiritual effect was concerned, going through the motions was as good as the real thing.

Two of the faces I was pretty sure were real were people I guessed were my teammates in the ball game, a smooth-faced guy whose revealed name, I thought, was Hun Xoc—that is, 1 Shark—and a stockier, flatter-faced kid named 2 Hand. But it was hard to find my way around, flipping through his memories, it was like—

Well, there's the same question again. What does it really feel like to be part of someone else? Like waking up in total darkness and finding you're in a large, unfamiliar house, crowded with furniture and *objets,* and having to work out how to get out? I'd thought that I was pretty hard-core Maya, deep down, but now I knew I'd been just another couthless clueless Yankee yuppie yob, that from this body, from this mind, the universe was truly another species. For instance, I still knew that the earth—or as we'd say, *mih k'ab',* "zero earth," or the zeroth shell of creation—was round, that is, globe-shaped. But if I didn't think about it I felt a different world around me, neither spherical nor flat, but more like a stack of tortillas. Each layer, or shell, was inside the other, kind of, maybe like skins in a squashed onion, but they were also alive.

Choke.

Come on. Breathe. Thing in mouth. A sponge, maybe. Open. Okay. Shut. Can't. Ouch. Acid reflux sores. I tried to pull a big slug of air into my cracked throat and my pain graph hit another peak, but I ignored it in a way I couldn't have as Jed. Chacal's body's pretty tough, no question. Not much good if I can't move, though. Thirsty. I have really just got to swallow. Get tongue involved. Where is it? Cut out? No, wait. Numb. Still there. Good tongue. Up, boy.

I got my tongue peeled off my palate, and I got my teeth together, although they didn't quite fit right, and I swallowed but it was all just dry, it hurt worse, ouch, ouch, wait. Wait a while. I pulled his tongue—*my* tongue, I thought, *pronoun trouble*—back into my cottony maw and twisted it, digging for liquid, and finally got some and started working around the sponge, painting the unfamiliar bumps and fissures of my mouth with thick sour goo. Hey, where's my flap? Oh, right. Gone. Hmm. Something wrong with my teeth. Not wrong. Just different. The two upper central incisors had been filed to sort of squat L shapes. That is, about one-third of each tooth, on the medial side, projected normally, but then to the left and right of those sort of spurs they were each missing a chunk. I hadn't realized how much I used to enjoy sliding my tongue around my old teeth. I was a total stranger to these pointy little suckers. I'd cut myself on them if I wasn't careful . . . whoa, what's this . . . hmm. There was a gap on the female side where it seemed like two molars were missing. Oh, right. I lost those in the One Cane game at 39 Courts, also against 2 Sidewinder, when I scored four and killed—

Or, I thought, not *I. Chacal*. That was *Chacal's* hipball career. Watch it.

Okay. Get those eyes open.

Ouch. Can't.

Going to sneeze.

La gran puta, I thought, what a *Schande* this turned out to be. Why did it have to be me back here? I should've been the one who stuck around in aught-twelve. The other me is probably in a sleeping bag with Marena right now. I mean, so to speak right now. Bastard. He doesn't know the half. Wait a second, now I'm getting jealous of myself. Stop obsessing. Keep it together.

Okay. Open eyes.

Nothing.

Well, this is great. A six-hundred-million-plus-dollar project and I end up in a basket like moldy pears from Harry & David. How long have I been in here? Days? Thirsty. What about the volcano? Could I have missed it? No, *ni modos*. I haven't been here three days. No way. Anyway, they said it wouldn't be possible to miss it, that even this far away it would still bruise your eardrums. And supposedly a day or two afterward, when the ash clouds got high enough, you'd be able to see the glow at night from anywhere in Mesoamerica.

Hmm. Maybe they're waiting to see if it happens like you said. Maybe you have a chance. And at least that Chacal character's gone. Or rather, I don't still half-think I'm Chacal. That's all it is, right? The self is something you think you are, not something real—

Ow. Itchy eyes a little too real, though. Scratchem. Okay. I flexed my—

CRACK.

Ouch.

I got the fingers of one hand going. Each one left a little trail of crackles and pops of welcomely focusing pain. Ow. Okay, get that other arm out from under there. Wait, where—

Shit, amputated! Panic.

I felt for what I thought was the stump with my other hand. Nothing. Shit. Wait. You're moving something, it's just the wrong hand in the wrong direction. Weird.

Huh. Maybe I've been reversed. I must be right-handed now.

Hmm.

Yeah, that's it. Okay. I worked on getting my working hand rubbing the numb one, but it kept slipping off. It was like trying to move a cursor around when the screen's unexpectedly shifted from landscape to portrait mode.

Get hands up to eyes. Ow. Hell. Do it again. Ow. My hands kept stopping before they got there. Oh, I get it. They'd been tied together in front of me and then tied by a longer rope to the roof of the box. Shit. I tried to pull myself up toward them but couldn't do that either. Maybe my chest was strapped to the bottom. Yeah, that's it. Damn. Thirsty.

I took another snort of air. For some reason that sort of icky sweet smell brought up a picture of Desert Dog. He had those big raw spots on his forearms. Yeah. It was ooze or pus or something, from an open sore, the scent of a skin disease. Damn. Probably on me. Hell.

Wait.

Listen.

The creaking that I think I mentioned had gotten louder, to the point where it definitely wasn't creaking. It was more like a sort of mewing. A cat, maybe? No, it's human. It's moaning.

My eyes tried to open and then gave up. A little kid? No, it's not, it's . . . oh. It's an old man.

The moaning finally pulled up a pic out of Chacal's hard drive: It was a line of eight or ten or so of the same big wicker boxes, hanging from a sort of bare arbor in front of a wall. The image even had very specific colors: That is, the two baskets on the far right were fresh and green, but the ones to the left of them were sun-bleached to gray. Maybe it was this same courtyard, where I was now, or maybe it was a place like it. But either way, I knew through Chacal that each of the baskets held a prisoner, and that I was in the one on the far right, and that the fluttering was the other captives breathing, and the oozy smell was their rotting skin slowly falling off their flesh, and the moaning was from one of the oldest baskets, and that the prisoner in it had been there for years, and years, and years.

You'll be in this box for a long, long time. Maybe a whole k'atun if you're unlucky, that is, twenty years, until the same deathday rolls around again. They'll get more pain out of you that way. More pain, more rain, more grain.

Hell. This is it. This is everything. This is the last thing I'll see. This is the last place I'll be. Ever. Ever. Forever. Oh God, oh God, oh God.

Deep panic isn't like a dream or a blackout, but it's still hard to remember. I suppose I thrashed around for a while, and probably screamed, or maybe one of the other prisoners screamed, and then I was trying to see again, got to get my eyes open, come on, have to see. Focus on eyes.

I flexed and strained. Nothing. There were orbital muscles there I didn't even know about. I flexed them again and again. Still no go. At some point I realized—either from the pain, or from the strength of the bond, or maybe because Chacal had seen it done to other people—that my eyelids had been sewn shut. Oh, Jes—

Wait.

Someone out there. Close by. Shouldn't have jiggled this thing. What are they doing? Watching me? Thirsty. No, don't ask. Don't let—

Off. I fell up. Something me hit. Ouch. Too bright, even just through eyelids. The eruption? Wait—

(30)

The side of the box slapped me and flipped me over. Someone held me, but not with hands. Maybe they were mittens. I felt cords being cut, but I didn't have a chance to pick up much detail. They were too professional about it, like policemen who can have you searched, cuffed, and into the cage seat in less than ten seconds. The box coughed me out into sunlight that felt like hot oil on my skin. The air tasted weirdly sweet. I was lying prone on the flagstones. Fresh blood crackled into my cold leg and smoldered around the bedsores on my back. A pair of ducks quacked overhead. This is definitely not the eruption, I thought. My hand, or rather, that is, my right hand, found a little elongated spur on the powdery stone and I got it under my forefinger, sort of holding on to it mentally, the way I guess you do sometimes when things aren't going right. You fasten on a random object as though it can help prove you exist. Or I do, anyway.

I'd been right that it was late afternoon, and without seeing the sun, just by feeling the low angle of the light on my side, Chacal's sense of direction oriented itself. I was facing south. But it was a different sort of south from Jed's south. That is, the whole sense of orientation was different. Like almost everybody in the twenty-first century I'd tended to think of north as up and south as down, and east as right and west as left, just because that's the way they have it on most maps. But for Chacal southeast was up and northwest was down. And the whole place, that is, the world, seemed to be on a sort of incline, tilting down to the west, with—

A throaty tenor voice half sang and half snarled at me:

"Into'on ho tuulo
Ta'änik-eech . . ."

"We five address you
One below us: who
Was it who shat you out,
Who bore you, pus-man?"

The voice's owner was about ten arms away. From the words he used I knew he was a Harpy sun adder, sort of like a family priest, and from the voice itself . . . yes, a fuzzy image of the person it came from flickered in Chacal's memories. Somehow he was messed up, physically, although he wasn't a dwarf . . . in fact I almost knew his revealed name, it was . . . hmm, what was it? I know I know his name—

"Offer him yellow water,
Red oil, red ale,
White water, shielding oil,
And blue-white ashes—"

It started raining. Hot rain, from all different directions. Oh, fuck, it's urine. I instinctively contracted into a ball, with my still numb leg just a big void tingling at the edges.

There were at least four people around me, and each one was relieving himself of a prodigious amount of waste liquid. Fuck this, I thought. Damn. Water sports. They don't mean it personally. It's purifying. Right? Maybe.

Somebody steered his stream into my face. I thought I heard a snicker but maybe I just imagined it. Don't get humiliated, I told myself. Anyway, what do you care? They don't know you. Still, it's hard to keep your equanimity when you're . . . Jesus, how do they hold this much? Put 'em away, guys, you've made your point. Bastards, bastards. Wait'll I'm in charge around here. I'll put you on lifetime latrine duty, and that means you'll *be* the latrine.

As is the way of things, the stuff petered out. A wave of something else hit me, cool slippery stinging stuff, some mixture of sour b'alche'—that is, lilac-tree beer, oil, and lye, with an evil-lemon smell of formic acid that, in these days before Janitor in a Drum, had to have been made out of crushed ants. The patches of raw skin on my back seemed to have caught on fire. As Jed I would have screamed like a stuck banshee, but Chacal had trained himself never to scream or squeal or even squirm. One of his earliest memories, and one of the most recurring, since it had already come up in my head more than once, was of lying naked and unoiled in high grass, letting a menagerie of insects nibble food mines in his skin, and seeing how long he could go without a twitch. I squinted harder and tried to clench my mouth around the gag but the cleanser wormed into my nostrils, and as I started to sneeze it sizzled into my throat.

"Ku'ti bin oc," a different voice said, in a different language from Ixian that I still seemed to understand. "Turn him over." There was a recoil in Chacal's nerves, as though I'd just tasted something his tongue didn't like. Something about the voice seemed small and low-rent, like a Maya version of Timothy the Circus Mouse. I guessed it pegged its owner as a member of some sort of untouchable caste.

They flipped me over and stretched me out. Wait, I need my piece of gravel. That was my special piece of gravel. Two more sluices of the stuff came down, and then for a few beats they let me just lie there writhing and dripping on the flagstones. Someone pulled the gag wad out of my mouth and poured in some cool drinking water. Wow. An indescribable blessing. I lapped at it like a dog at a lawn sprinkler. I noticed I was being messed with, but still not by hands. They're wearing deerskin mittens. Got to protect themselves from my uncleanness. They scraped me with what I supposed were shell strigils. They cleaned all the hard-to-reach areas, if you know what I mean. They dug what I guessed were the last flakes of sacrificial blue pigment from under my seven remaining fingernails. They rubbed, or rather Rolfed, me with some kind of oil. It had a slight fishy quality under essences of vanilla and geranium. Maybe it was from a porpoise. They oiled and brushed my hair, or what was left of it, and when their mittens touched the stump of what, before the not-quite-sacrifice, had been my queue or pigtail or whatever, another of those instinctive shame-gorges rose up in my throat. Bastards. Eventually I got dusted with something, evidently the "blue-white ashes" he'd talked about. I just lay there and let it happen, like a Linzer torte under a shower of powdered sugar. I tried to pretend I was getting a full-body treatment at Georgette Klinger at 980 Madison Avenue, but it didn't quite take in my mind.

They tied my hands in front of me with soft rope, leaving a lot of slack on each end, and tied another rope in two loops around my chest and neck, like a dog harness. Finally they hooked me under the arms and lifted me up. As I said, Chacal's body was used to abuse. I could feel it was strong in a different way from a modern athlete's body, not muscle-built or stretched out by aerobics, but thickened and somehow solidified, like you couldn't knock me over with a bus. At any rate, even after the fairly high blood loss and the days of fasting that had preceded the botched sacrifice, I, or it, didn't quite faint. They tried to march me along, and I actually tried to help, but my leg was still out of commission and they ended up carrying me vertically, with my feet dragging on the pavement.

From the shadows I felt crossing over me, I got the impression that we'd gone through a gap in the wall of the courtyard, and then from the way we moved we went up an inclined path. There was a breeze and a sense of space that might mean we were on the west face of a hill. After sixty steps we turned right and went into shadow and up eighteen stairs into a dark corridor. We twisted through a narrow switchbacked passage. There was a strong scent of high-quality tobacco, like we were inside a giant humidor, and maybe an underscent of vanilla. We paused. There was the sound of someone holding aside something like a bead curtain and we moved forward again into a stone-cool room.

Cerise light seeped into my buried eyes. They set me down on a stone floor with something thin and soft over it. Someone tucked my legs under me and sculpted me into a proper captive's squatting position. Everything stopped.

"He over us addresses you beneath him," the tenor voice chanted on my left. The room had a muffled echoless quality, like a recording studio.

There was another long pregnant-with-monster-quintuplets pause. At some point maybe someone gave an order, because two hands grabbed and held my head and two more did something—oh, shit, blinding me, oh, Christ, no, wait . . . no, they were cutting through the stitches in my eyes with a tiny blade. I would have struggled, of course, but Chacal's body didn't move. Finally I noticed I wasn't being held anymore and I creaked one eye open. The first thing I saw was my own hairless and unfamiliarly foreskinned genitalia hanging between my thighs.

Hmm, I thought, that's a new one. Most twenty-first-century Maya aren't circumcised, but I'd been born in a real hospital, where they had their own ideas. Next I noticed the big skanky cauliflowery ballplayer's calluses on my knees and then the bloody tears dripping onto my green thighs—green?— and then an old impact scar on my iliac arch where some ball must have smashed it, and then a dark violet glyph the size of a Zippo lighter tattooed on my chest. From somewhere in Chacal I recognized the tattoo as giving my nine-skull hipball-game rank. There was something reddish all over the floor, petals of something. Geraniums. But they weren't really red. They were something else. And my skin really did look green, and it wasn't the oil they'd rubbed into it. The color really was different. And it wasn't any sort of drug or the film of blood from the stitches. I'd suspected it up on the mul, but at the time I'd been pretty busy, and I guess I just shrugged it off.

Chacal's eyes were different. The colors were not the ones I'd known as Jed. My skin wasn't even exactly green. It was more like the false green you get by mixing yellow and black paint. But it wasn't even quite that. The color of the carpet of wild geranium petals over the floor, which ought to have been about a deep orange, was more like a fluorescent magenta. But that isn't quite it, either, the color I was seeing was north of that somehow . . . maybe Chacal's colorblind, in some weird way? Except I think I'm seeing *more* colors. Maybe he's a tetrachromat, that is, someone who can see four primary colors instead of just three. Yeah. Except supposedly the few documented cases of human tetrachromacy were all women. Huh—

Wait. Get back on track. Think about this some other time.

"2 Jeweled Skull
Addresses you
Beneath him captive.
Face him, hear him."

It was the tenor voice. I hoisted my head and focused into the red murk.

I was in the center of a high, square room about fifteen arms on a side. The walls seemed to be glowing crimson, or rather the color that Jed would have seen as crimson. Now it was a creepy underwater-flesh blue-red-whatever. The left and right walls sloped inward at about thirty degrees, so that the wall I was facing was a high isosceles triangle with its peak about thirty arms off the floor. There didn't seem to be any doors besides the one we'd come through, which was directly behind me. As things got clearer I could see the walls only looked lit from behind. Actually they were covered with tapestries or panels woven out of what might be the throat feathers of ruby trogons, knotted onto reed latticework, and they were reflecting indirect light that ricocheted down from a tiny oculus, burning with sunlight at the peak of the trapezoidal wall behind me.

There were six people in the room. Three of them were the guards who'd brought me in. Two crouched on either side of me, and I could feel the warmth of a third at my back. Each of them held a sort of club or mace, I guess so they could control me at more than arm's length, and as one of the mace heads floated near my face I could see it wasn't stone but some kind of pincushiony spiky thing. Then there was someone three arms in front of me and a bit to the left. He was a hunchback, nearly normal-sized but with a big wide head and all balled up, with a lopsided blue-striped face and a tufted conical hat that made him look like a blue macaw. I guess it sounds a little silly, but around here, or maybe in my new, preconditioned mind, it looked the opposite of silly, in fact it looked so deadly serious you could plotz.

And then, four arms directly in front of me but just now coming into visibility out of the gloom, 2 Jeweled Skull sat cross-legged on a wide double-headed jaguar bench, smoking a long green cigar through his left nostril.

His body was turned forty-five degrees away from me, and instead of looking at me he looked down at a couple of breadbox-sized dark gourds or wooden pots on the floor in front of him, each studded with green-white stones that spelled out the glyph *awal*, that is, "enemy." He wore a sort of skirt or kilt with a wide sash that nearly reached to his sternum, and I could just see the *profil perdu* of a shrunken head, sewn by the hair to the back of the sash so that it faced away from him, watching his back, as it were, with a petulant expression. Besides jade wristlets and anklets and rawhide sandals, his only other clothing was a complicated crownless turban with an artificial vanilla orchid—made, I thought, of bleached eagle feathers—at the peak of his forehead. A green-throated hummingbird—a real, well-taxidermized one with lifelike polished-jet eyes—hovered in front of the orchid on a nearly invisible stalk, as though time had stopped just as it was about to plunge its beak into the nectary. It confused me for a second, because during training we'd been so fixated on getting my head into 9 Fanged Hummingbird, who, as you may remember, was the ahau of the ruling family, the Ocelots, and the k'alomte'. But things around here were a little more involved than that. *9 Fanged Hummingbird* was just a name, one of the k'alom'te's many revealed and unrevealed names, and it didn't have anything to do with his totem or uay or whatever, any more than someone named "April Fish" would have to be born in April or be a fish. So the hummingbird on 2 Jeweled Skull's headgear didn't mean he had anything to do with hummingbirds—although it might mean, metaphorically speaking, that people liked vanilla. And in fact, I was half remembering that vanilla beans were somehow important to the Harpy House, maybe one of the main sources of their *nouveau richesse*.

Below the orchid his forehead swept down at a low angle and connected to a small wooden bridge that eliminated the indentation of his brow and brought it into line with the vulturine wedge of his nose. Spirals of blue tattooed dots scrolled up from the corners of his mouth to his blackened eyelids. In spite of his creased and sun-cured skin he didn't seem old . . . but he was old, I knew from Chacal's brain, at least he'd certainly had his second birth, that is, he was over fifty-two, and I thought I knew he was quite a bit older than that.

His eyes turned and looked at mine. People like to say that there's a certain blankness to the eyes of someone who's killed a lot of people. I don't think it's true. Some of the world's most bloodthirsty cats have the most convincingly expressive eyes around. But there was a certain chill factor in there, a habitual disdain like what pigs probably see in the eyes of slaughterhouse workers, and I did get that caught-in-the-police/NewsChannel-helicopter-floodlight feeling. Automatically my eyes teared up and I blinked and looked down at the gourds on the floor. They were moving, shuffling around on little hands, and it took me a few seconds to realize that they were armadillos, each with its shell studded with azurite plugs and tethered to the floor by a ribbon through one of its ears.

"Who is Mickey Mouse?" 2 Jeweled Skull asked.

My heart didn't quite skip a beat, but it did seem to contract into a tight little ball. He was speaking in English.

(31)

H e hadn't gotten all the vowels right, so it sounded more like "Meh-*kay*
Mah-*ohs*." But I hadn't misheard it. Had I? No, no way. My head got
weightless and then leadenly heavy.

"I underneath you answer you above me," I said automatically. Had I said
it in Ch'olan or English? Ch'olan, I think . . . damn, I'm going crazy. Okay. I'm
going to speak in English. Here goes.

"Mickey Mouse is not a living creature," I said in English. "He is a cartoon
character. A drawing."

Silence.

"Who is the ahau pop Ditz' ni?"

What? I wondered. Oh. Okay.

"The ahau Disney died two k'atunob' before my time," I said. "He was the
voice of Mickey Mouse." It wasn't easy talking to him without an honorific, so
I added an "I below you say."

"Is Mickey Mouse his uay?"

"No, Mickey is just an effigy. He's a . . . he's a puppet. A *b'axäl*."

"Is Jed-*kas* your uay?" 2 Jeweled Skull asked. You wouldn't think a voice so
high, almost squeaky, could be so commanding. But *commanding* was really
too weak a word. "Or is it Mickey?"

This isn't going well, I thought. -*kas*, the suffix he'd attached to my name,
meant something along the lines of "you thirteen steps beneath me." That is,
as far down the social pyramid as possible. It was the declension an ahau
would use to address a domehead, that is, a barbarian, someone who wasn't
even a proper Maya enemy but just a nonperson.

"No," I answered. "Neither of those things."

There was a pause. How the holy bloody hell had this happened? I wondered. He can't have just learned—

Oh, wait a second, I thought. I know how.

He must have been in there.

2 Jeweled Skull had been inside the King's Niche with me, up there on the mul. At least for part of the time, that is, part of the eight minutes or so of the download window. And when my consciousness got zapped into Chacal's, it must have gotten into 2 Jeweled Skull's head too. Holy shitzus.

"What did you come to steal?" he asked.

"We don't want to steal anything," I said.

There was a pause. He wants me to look at him, I realized. I lifted up my head, but my new body shied away again from making eye contact—you weren't supposed to eyeball your superiors around here—and instead I focused on the glyphs tattooed on his chest. They weren't any I'd seen before. Some kind of secret language. He had his cigar between his thumb and forefinger, and he set it down on a little stand with a sort of backhanded grace that reminded me of something, what the hell was it . . . oh, okay, it was a Japanese waiter serving tea—I think it was at Naoe, when I was there with Sylvana—and this old guy there had done the whole thing with the whisk for us, and he'd set down the wooden ladle on the mouth of the water jar in that special way. But 2 Jeweled Skull did it with a sort of heavy, brooding, haughty quality that wasn't at all Japanese, or Asian, or Navajo, or anything, but just totally Maya. I felt his eyes like a pair of stone blades sliding down my chest and along the veins of my arms to my quivering fingers and back up to my face, looking for tells or microexpressions that might give me away. Except if he's got my memories inside him, why doesn't he know everything I'm thinking? I wondered. Maybe his brain had gotten a smaller dose of me than Chacal's had. Or maybe he was tougher than Chacal, and he'd willed it away. Come on. Think. What the fizzizuck had happened up there? Well, 2 Jeweled Skull had donated Chacal to serve as 9 Fanged Hummingbird's proxy. Right? So at some point in the ceremony, probably as a kind of last farewell, 2 Jeweled Skull must have gone inside the King's Niche with Chacal. So he got at least a decent-size dose of my mind. But he seems to have retained his own mind in good condition. At least he's in control of his own body. Apparently.

Christ, what a bunch of fuckups we are. Although come to think of it, Taro had mentioned that there might be "scatter," as he put it. Of course, I'd pretty much shrugged it off. In fact, he said they'd even thought about coding my consciousness on a wider beam and maybe hitting a lot of people. But the sanctuary on the mul was the only structure in the area they had a solid date for, and the stone walls would help contain any scatter from the EPR beam, and anyway if they'd blasted me all over the place who knew what would happen. Having a lot of Jeds and semi-Jeds running around would probably be a recipe for trouble even in the twenty-first century.

"You came to learn how to play against the smokers," he said. From somewhere in Chacal I knew that by the "smokers" he meant what a so-called modern Westerner might misleadingly call "the gods." Is he talking about the Game? Got to be. Could he possibly even know how to play it? Maybe he was a sun adder. Maybe all the greathouse ajawob' were adders to some extent. At least I'd come to the right place. Should I ask him for a Game? How about best nine out of seventeen?

> "And will there be
> More like you coming?"

                              he asked in Ixian Ch'olan.
"No. Probably no more ever." Don't elaborate, I thought.

> You think you can
> Entomb yourself
> Alive,
> And pickle flesh
> Against thirteen
> Times thirteen hundred rains."

No, not exactly, I said—

> "You plan to hold
> Your body skyward
> In your b'ak'tun,
> In your k'atun,
> Again in your
> Abandoned skin."

"Body skyward" basically meant "alive." Around here the dead folks walked upside down, like reflections in water.

"You over me
Are in the light,"

I managed to say.

"And when we kill you,"

2 Jeweled Skull asked,

"Will your foul twin in me
Die in me too?"

What? I thought. Oh, shit. Maybe I'd better not answer that one directly.
Pause.
Suddenly, I had an idea.
"Jed?" I asked. "I'm Jed DeLanda, too, you know. You and I are like twins."
"I am not Jed."
Uh-oh, I thought.
"As you above—," I started to say, but 2 Jeweled Skull's right hand opened
and rotated slightly to the left, and from Chacal I knew it was a sign for "si-
lence," and my mouth snapped shut with Pavlovian speed. 2 Jeweled Skull
looked past me, toward the hunchback.

The guards on either side of me eased back a bit on their haunches. The
hunchback waddled toward me and stopped about three arms away. He
studied me. I tried not to flinch. Somewhere in Chacal I was sure I knew his
name. He had little stunted talonish arms like a T. rex's, with syndactyl fingers
on his right hand, and a permanently grinning mouth with jutting upper
teeth spaced nearly a tooth's width apart from each other. It's got to be some
kind of Morquio syndrome, I thought. How old is he? He looked old, but people don't live past forty with a case like that. Do they? Cripes, what the hell
was his name? It was 10 Smoking Caterpillar, or ½ Mock Turtle, or something. Oh, okay. Got it. It's 3 Blue Snail. He was an *ajway*, that is, sort of like a
family priest, only *priest* sounds like he's part of a big organization, and this
guy was a private contractor. Maybe *shaman*'s a little closer, except that it
sounds like some Siberian dude with antlers. How about *theurgist*? Or is that
too fancy? No, let's go with it. Okay. Anyway, I was pretty sure he—3 Blue
Snail, the Harpy theurgist—was the owner of the tenor voice. Yeah. Definitely.
I even pulled some images of him dancing around at a first-burning ceremony. At least I was starting to learn how to access Chacal's memories. The

trick seemed to be to think in Ch'olan, not the twenty-first-century variety but the current Ixian dialect, and then not to try too hard, just to let word association do the work—

3 Blue Snail set his fan of tobacco leaves down in a dish, picked up something else, stood up to his full height, and was still for a minute. No one seemed to breathe, least of all me, and I could hear the blood in my ears. I realized he was sniffing the air.

Something else is going on here, I thought. Not that I knew how these people behaved normally. But there was a definite sense that they were being cautious about something, and it was something other than me. It was like we were in someone else's house and didn't want to be overheard. But still, this is 2 Jeweled Skull's *audiencia* or throne room or whatever, isn't it? Or maybe not, maybe we're in some sort of temporary place . . . and anyway, my showing up when I did must have thrown everybody off their game a little.

From what I could get out of Chacal's head . . . well, it was tricky. But to oversimplify, if Ix were England in the 1450s, the Ocelots would be like the House of Lancaster. They were still in charge of everything, but they were unpopular and hemorrhaging wealth. 2JS's Harpies would be like the House of York, who had been subordinate for a long time but were gaining strength and making noises about taking over. Then there were also three other royal houses in Ix. Two of them favored the Harpies, but the other, the Vampire Bat House, was inseparably allied with the Ocelots.

So the Ocelots are probably using the botch-up on the mul as an excuse to come after the Harpies. Okay. Use that.

3 Blue Snail turned around in place, and turned around again, whirling, I guess, but very slowly, slower than a Sufi dervish, which is pretty slow. Each time he passed one of the four directional points—that is, AITISB, northeast, southwest, and so on—he tapped once on a sort of clay drum in his left hand, using a sort of thimble on his index finger. He was listening for echoes, I guess, or rather for hostile uayob who might be spying on us, animal doppelgängers or disembodied eyes or homunculi or whatever. His eyes searched the twelve corners of the room, moving independently from each other, which was pretty disconcerting. And it didn't seem like one was a wandering eye either. Instead it looked like he could actually control it and focus on two widely separated objects at once, like a chameleon. Finally he stopped, bent down, picked up a fresh tobacco leaf, and used it as a spoon to scoop up some kind of powder or ashes out of the dish. He threw one leaf full over his right shoulder, one over his head, behind, one over his left shoulder, and one in front.

There was another pause, and then he tapped the side of his drum with a sharp wakeuppy sound. Either from Chacal, or just because it was obvious, I knew it meant we were all clear and that I was expected to look back at 2 Jeweled Skull. I managed to do it. Focus on the thing on the bridge of his nose, I thought. Not on his eyes—

"Why did you choose me and not the sky-born k'alomte'?" 2 Jeweled Skull asked, in Ixian. He meant 9 Fanged Hummingbird. 2 Jeweled Skull and his peers were ahau popob, "lords of the mat," but, like I think I said, the k'alomte' was more like "emperor" or "warlord."

"We didn't," I said in Ixian. "We wanted—we were looking for 9 Fanged Hummingbird. It was—it was an *accident.*" I said the last word in English because there wasn't any Ixian word for "accident," or "chance," or any of those things.

"Why did you choose this sun?" he asked, meaning this date.

"We chose this time because we found it in a codex . . . that is, a Game record in a screenfold book."

Pause. He didn't say he didn't understand, but I had the feeling his English wasn't quite up to code. He had to have less of me inside him than I did. If that makes any sense. Maybe he just hadn't gotten the brain-wipe section of the program, the way Chacal had. He's still more himself. Not that even Chacal got wiped enough, of course. And maybe he'd only gotten a tiny bit of me after that. Although even that would probably be more than enough for most people. I said the sentence over again in Ixian.

"And have you crouched beneath ahau-na Koh?" he asked.

"What? Like, have I met her?" I asked. "No, no, we just read about her in the Codex."

Pause. I thought that next he was going to ask why we had chosen this particular city, instead of some other, but he didn't. Maybe as far as he was concerned, Ix was the center of the universe, and no one could want to be anywhere else. What's weird, I thought, is that he doesn't seem too surprised by all this. Or rather he seems violated and upset, natch . . . but it felt like the idea that I came from what we'd call the future wasn't a big deal to him. I guess around here the future was more like a place. In fact, I suppose uayob, or souls or whatever, from the future and the past turn up around here all the time—

"What will you recompense me for my ranking son?" he asked.

What? I wondered. I'm responsible for his son's death?

Hell. That didn't sound good.

Had they substituted 2 Jeweled Skull's son for me on the mul? That's got to be it. Damn. Good job, Jedediah. You're really getting these folks to like you. Rulers do tend to be touchy about their firstborn. Do I apologize? How? "I under you don't understand," I said.

"You disrespect me over you," he said.

"No, I great-respect you," I gurgled. "I apologize, but I don't understand." And I really, really don't, I thought. Fuck.

"I know things that can help us," I said. "Two lights from now there's going to be a firestorm in the northwest." I switched to English. "A volcanic eruption—"

"We above you all know this already," he said. "The Ocelots' adders warned against it twenty lights ago. You underneath me offer nothing."

Oh, I thought. Okay. Great. There goes my big prophet routine. So much for the Connecticut Yankee. Well, fine, *me caigo en la mar.* What else have we got to put on the table? Okay. Let's try another prepared Contingency Speech. I said:

"I underneath you
Will pay this debt somehow,
I can build you
A puppet that throws
Giant javelins,
Hipballs that
Burst into fire,
Or perfectly
Rounded pot—"

"We over you
Do not need help
From a reeking thing,"

2 Jeweled Skull said.

Evidently I was too polluted even to deal with.

I switched to English. "I can help us defend ourselves against the Ocelots," I said. "You can become the k'alomte'. Look in my memories. Look for 'gunpowder.' We can whip some up in a few days, just dig some guano out of those caves on the north side and leach out the nitrates—"

He tilted his head in a way that shut me up before I even knew it meant "You have our permission to be silent."

"You are talking with sand in your mouth," he said. "The overlords of this b'ak'tun will not allow those things."

What? I thought. Luddite alert. Wait, I started to say—

"X'imaleech t'ul k'ooch mix-b'a'al," he said. "You are walking as though there is nothing in your back-rack." It was one of those idioms you understand right away. Basically, it meant, "It seems you don't have anything to offer."

"I'll take your world to mine," I said, "and rebirth it there. I'll give your descendants their names again, their time, their history, everything."

"B'a'ax-ti'a'al chokoj upol?" he asked. "Why should I care about that?" It wasn't really a question.

"As you above me say," I said automatically. "But—"

"Then I allow you to take back your Jed."

Uh-oh.

He's got to know I can't do that, I thought. Doesn't he? Or maybe he really did only get a few bits of my mind. Or maybe his ego's just too big to accept it. Or does he even really know what I am? Maybe he really thinks I'm just some kind of creepy imp who snuck into his ear. Well . . .

"But you above me could learn from it," I said.

"Call your reflection out of my skin now," 2 Jeweled Skull said. Deep in his composed voice there was a sense of a stifled shudder. He's grossed out, I thought. He feels dirty. Having me in there disqualifies him. He thinks he's going to be kept out of the goddamn Celestial VIP Lodge or whatever. Oh cripes oh cripes. Should I just fess up that he's stuck with me? No, he'll just go even more bananashit. Time to lie like linoleum.

"I will, but it will take me time," I said.

Pain like a snapping banjo string shot from my stomach up to my left eye. It was something in Chacal's nervous system twisting out of alignment at the thought of keeping secrets from his greatfathermother. The idea of lying to this guy just wasn't in Chacal's gestalt. Hold still, for God's sake, don't twitch but don't hold your breath, either, just breathe, breathe . . .

"How soon will this be done?" 2 Jeweled Skull asked.

"It can't be done without the right preparations," I said, half in Ixian and half in English. "We have to offer to the right . . . I need to find a certain kind of herb." Yeah, eleven secret herbs and spices, I thought. He'll believe that, all right.

I felt his eyes palpating my skin, looking for a flutter, a shiver . . .

"What will you need?" he asked.

I said if he gave me paper and a brush I could sketch it out for him. Anything to stall, I thought. I'll draw a catapult too. Maybe a crossbow. Stranger engines for the brunt of war. Get him interested in those, and he'll forget about—

"Remove your uay worm from my stomach *now*. Finished."

"Finished" was what you said when you were done with a subject. It was like saying "full stop."

I hesitated. I repeated the lie. He looked at me.

When he was a child, Chacal had believed that 2 Jeweled Skull could smell his thoughts through dirt walls, that on moonless nights, in the shape of something like a harpy eagle, 2 Jeweled Skull would glide over their villages and scrutinize his thralls' sleeping bodies through the smoke vents in the roofs of their houses, guarding them, but also ready to swoop through the roof and scratch out a betrayer's eyes. And even now it wasn't like Chacal's mind quite disbelieved it. I felt like a career army sergeant trying to lie to a five-star general.

2 Jeweled Skull—or now that we know him a little better, why don't we just call him "2JS"—must have given some kind of a signal, because all at once there was another person in the room, a nondescript middle-aged man with a plain gray turban and no particular markings that I could read. He had a thin, junior-high-school physical-education teacher's face, like a Maya version of the elder George Bush. Somehow he'd just materialized out of the left-hand wall. I figured out that he'd crouched in from a hidden door through a slit in the feather tapestries. He squatted and set down a round tripedal tray on the floor an arm in front of me. There was a thing on the tray. He turned to 2 Jeweled Skull and held his right wrist on his left breast with his arm parallel to the floor. It was almost like an ancient Roman salute or the old French military salute. Maybe it was some sort of universal cultural constant. I stared at the thing in the tray. It was a steaming hot black wobbling bulbous shape, like a whole boiled eggplant.

"Oh, boy," I said in English. "Cajun fetus?"

I got zero reaction. Some people take themselves so seriously.

The new guy picked up the Thing with his free hand. It had some kind of tube-and-nozzle on it. There was an instant of disorientation, and before I realized that the guards had picked me up and bent me over into the Eternal Position, there was an electrosnake wriggling up my anus *EEEOOOWUUGHFFFFF!!!*

Eeeyah. Boofed on the first date.

I actually saw stars, and even in accurate constellations. There was Draco,

Scorpio, the Dumbbell Nebula was right over there . . . and then it was already over, except for the trickle of hot liquid between my legs and a heat spreading from my intestines out onto my skin.

Whoa. That'll put some hair on your eyeballs.

The guards let me collapse flat-out prone into the red sea.

"Thank you, sir, may I have another?" I said, my breath raising a puff of petals.

They waited. I waited. We didn't wait very long. Drug enemas work almost instantly. There'd been a vogue for taking K—which is a synthetic tranquilizer popular among vets that makes humans feel really, really perky—up the ass at gay clubs in the 1990s. I'd only done it a couple of times—okay, sixteen times—but it really was something; you went from blah to rah in under twenty seconds. Anyway, I could already feel gravity subsiding.

"And when you take your twin *ixnok'ol mak* out of my stomach," 2JS asked, "will the rot still burn through my head?"

It took me a minute to get what he meant. *Ixnok'ol mak* meant something like "malicious uay," or maybe "parasitic worm, intelligent variety of." Supposedly the idea of demonic possession is a cultural universal, so that wasn't so surprising. But by the rot in his head . . . well, not to put too fine a point on it, he meant cancer.

Damn. If he didn't pick up all of Jed's memories, why'd he have to get that one?

The deal was, as I may have mentioned, the downloading process wasn't entirely benign. Basically, the luon beams would have hit the target—that is, Chacal's brain—with around forty thousand mrads, about the equivalent of three hundred thousand current chest X-rays. Because their wavelength would be tuned to neuronal tissues, they wouldn't cause skin cancer or leukemia. But brain and possibly spinal tumors would start forming that same day. Dr. Lisuarte had said that within seven or eight months, even if the target wasn't predisposed to cancer, the growth would be severe enough to "inhibit normal functioning." The odds of my living more than a year would be under one in fifty. So I was already on a pretty tight clock. And 2JS—well, he wouldn't have gotten such a big dose, but he was probably still in trouble. He was going to die, maybe not in nine months, but not of old age either. I'd guess he'd have less than five years. Okay, what do I do, lie? No. Prevaricate.

"Jed's uay has been given to ours. To both of us. As a servant. And it will bring us huge advantages. Jed had to come here to protect us and our descendants."

Silence.

Damn, that was lame, I thought. I was feeling as swollen and sore as a big tourniqueted foot. I'd expected whatever they'd shot me up with to numb me into cretinism, but instead it was doing the opposite. It was a sensitizer. The petals under my thighs had hardened into stone chips, and the air currents curling over me felt like strips of sharkskin.

"Tell your xcarec-uay to stop wearing me."

"I will," I said, "but I can't do it right here right now. I don't have the right tools." Keep it simple, I thought. My good hand involuntarily slid over the petals on the floor and it felt like a herd of giant hissing cockroaches was stampeding under my palm.

"How?" he asked.

"It's a mental thing, there are procedures for it, but it takes training." Christ, I thought, now I'm trying to sell this guy on talk therapy.

"And then not what?" he asked. He meant what if that didn't work.

"Well, then, if I get my memories back to 2012, I'll be able to do it from there." I said it again in Ixian. He didn't answer. I rattled on a bit. "Just as you above me must see in Jed's uay, I need to be preserved in gel, that is, in a colloid, that is, a liquid that becomes hard, the way copal sap transfigures into crystals."

Silence. Darn.

"The bitumen suspension . . . will preserve the connections in my brain sufficiently for them to be copied," I quoted, in English, from Taro's project summary. "That is," I said in Ixian, "it will keep my souls from escaping. My b'olonob."

B'olan was actually one of three or four things people had here that you could call souls. It was the one you'd see in shadows and reflections, and the one that might have to make its way through Xib'alb'a and serve the landlords there, before someday being allowed to dissolve into nothing. The other souls were the uay, that is, your animal counterpart, and the *p'al*, like the name, which stayed with the remains of your body. There was also the *ch'al*, "breath," although it might be a stretch to call that a soul.

"And after that, my souls will help you, over me, they will, after . . ."

I trailed off. My bullshit muscles were locking up. And it wasn't just because I could feel in Chacal's body how much he revered 2 Jeweled Skull, how much Chacal thought he was semi-supernatural—although, strictly speaking, in this mindset nothing was really supernatural, it was just that—some beings were more natural than others—anyway, it was mainly just that he absolutely radiated authority and would have even if you had no idea who he was. Behind him the walls seemed to be flowing, like we were in a crystal box sinking into lava.

"This is while I above you wait for you to come back?" he asked. "And hope for you below me to come and call your twin?"

"You over me would not have to wait at all," I lied. "We can time it to the exact moment."

"And what will you send to take away your uay?"

"It's like a javelin of sunlight," I said, "a sort of lightning."

No answer. Maybe he's just not answering what he doesn't understand, I thought. I switched to Ixian:

"In my own k'atun I will send the right, the right message, through the passage I came through, and it will reach you here and erase me, pull me out of you."

Pause.

Maybe he's buying this, I thought. Wait, don't even think that way. That's not how to lie. Believe what you're saying. Don't change your story again. Be cool.

2JS looked at the nondescript new guy. I was getting the sense that I hadn't passed.

Suddenly I had an inspiration.

"Or we can go together," I said. "We can entomb the two of us, and then, and then your souls can get sent back."

He looked at me. My eyes scurried away and focused on the shrunken head on his belt. It was glowing with golden fuzz. All faces, even Native American ones, have this fine down all over them that you can barely see, but when a face gets concentrated to the size of a peach it gets that cute fluffy-stuffy toddlery flocking—

"You underneath me, you would like to trick me," he almost whispered.

"No," I said, "I wouldn't." Fear, like a self-cooling soda can, popped open in my small intestine. Oh, *chíngalo*. Chacal's nervous system might keep me from flinching, but my mind was Jed's, and Jed was a wimp, and I was afraid.

"PULL OUT YOUR PARASITE NOW OR LIVE IN PAIN!"

I started to say something and couldn't.

Oh, spooge and corruption. I'm going to die today. I'd never been much of an actor, and now what with the dope and the new bod and the tough audience—

The Bush-looking character, who I'd realized was a *b'et-yaj*, a "teaser"—
that is, a torturer—sat on my left side and walked his fingers up my cheek.
They were in sort of finger-cots made, I guessed, from intestines. When he
came to my left eye he held the lids apart, rather gently, and, with his other
hand, lifted the lid off a miniature *incensario*.

"Hun tzunumtub tz-ik-een yaj," the teaser chanted. He spoke in the women's
language and had a womanly voice. He held the censer underneath my eye. I
got a glimpse of pink embers and a curl of tan smoke.

Now, I generally like chilies. Poblano, serrano, rocoto, habañero, you pick
'em, peel 'em, cook 'em, serve 'em, and pay for 'em, I'll put 'em away. And at
first it didn't even seem so bad. Maybe they were using some special species,
or the reaction was delayed by the bufotenine or whatever it was that was
spreading through my bloodstream. But there was just a faint tingling at the
beginning, like someone across the room was peeling a single onion. The
teaser set down and covered the *incensario*. There was something in the way
he did it that triggered a flash of my real father putting down a Squirt bottle
with the same species of motion, and I bit my lip to stifle the nostalgia rush.
The teaser took a tobacco leaf and fanned away the smoke. I felt one of the
guards holding me stifle a cough, as though if he let it out he'd be demoted to
the ranks, which was probably close to the case. Dryness spread out from the
rims of my eyelids and around the balls, back toward what felt like the base
of my optic nerve, but I, or rather Chacal's warrior's body, didn't want to give
these guys the satisfaction of trying to wink.

"Take back your twin," 2 Jeweled Skull said.

"I'm going to," I said lockjawedly. "You have to let me start." Fluid swelled
in my nose and little dust devils whirled up under my lids. Probably everyone
who's not from a chili culture has had the experience of innocently munching
a slice of spic-flavor pizza and biting into a wayward level-ten green habañero. So this kind of pain ought to be easy to identify with. Except that's con-
fined to your mouth, and somehow this spread to my whole body. Now, as I
said, Chacal's body had this disconnect, this precious ability to distance itself
from major pain. But I could almost see the gap narrowing, closing like slow,
slow elevator doors. My orbital muscles contracted. I managed to keep my
other eye open and not twist my head, but then before I knew it I'd tried to
wink, and as his fingers pushed the lids wider the teaser turned to 2JS and
grinned, and 2JS looked back and it was like I could hear him chuckling even
though his face didn't move and he didn't make a sound. Now my eyeball was

rolling in onion zest and the tighter I squeezed my lids the more it swelled up like a red sun, and the more tears streamed around it the more desiccated it felt, and then everything crashed in as the capsaicin penetrated the liner cells around my eyeball and blasted the overload into my spinal cord. The priceless disconnect closed and evaporated. I screamed, almost but not quite silently, more like a sort of endless sputtering hiss like rain falling on a hot griddle, and even though I was more or less insane at that moment I felt that automatic shame rising out of Chacal's brain, that brown, crushing shame that the Oprah Syndrome had nearly wiped out of twenty-first-century emotional life. It was like his body knew that my weakness had disgraced it.

"How will you take it out?"

"I have to show you," I said.

"Take out your twin worm now."

Okay, I thought, or rationalized. Fine. Let's say we can't bullshit this guy. Come clean. Be a mensch. "I can't do that," I gasped out. "Look through Jed's memories, look for Taro Mora. You'll see I just don't have the ability to do that, I don't, I don't—"

"*Take it out*," 2 Jeweled Skull said again.

"I beneath you don't have the ability to do that," I said, trying not to scream. "I can't get me out of your head, because, for the same reason I can't get me out of my head."

Pause.

"But you above me and I can operate together," I said, "the Jeds in you and me could take care of the Ocelots in almost no time, and I think we will win, beat 'em, beat 'em . . ."

You're babbling, I realized. Shut up. But I couldn't. I heard myself trying to talk about fireworks and crop rotation, but it came out as near gibberish. Well, this is great, isn't it? I thought. "Mickey Mouse is gonna come get you for this," my voice was saying somewhere. "He's a very powerful demigod and he's a pal of mine besides, *eeeeyyh*, he's a friend who's made for you and *meeeyeeeehYYYAAAHHH* . . ."

He must have signaled again, because the teaser chanted, "*Hun tzunum-tub tz-ik-een yaj*" again and my orbital muscles automatically squeezed so tight I thought my eyeball would pop and I realized it was a Pavlovian thing, a little formula they say before each stroke of the lash, as it were. He gave me another shot of smoke. My eyeball sizzled like a frying egg. This is your eye on toast. Don't ask them to stop, I thought, then you're really in for it. It'll just make it worse. How could it be worse? Hmm, fair question. Still, they're pretty professional with this stuff. Let's figure they actually could make it worse. They could put on an Alicia Keys album, for instance—

"Then tell me how to force your twin to leave."

"I forced Chacal to leave me," I managed to say. "You can force Jed to leave you. I can't tell you how to do it. Just do it."

I almost added the word *Nike*, but we were speaking in Ixian so it didn't follow. There was a long pause. I guess you could say it was an uncomfortable pause, only at this point that probably sounds a little weak. Suddenly the teaser took his fingers away. My eye clamped shut. Tears actually squirted out of the lachrymal glands and I could hear them hitting the teaser on the chest. Something soft settled into my eye and the burning descended on a long arc, until it was almost just a pleasurable buzzing, like someone had stuffed a magic finger in the empty socket. Although of course it wasn't empty, it was still filled with an eyeball the size of a croquet ball. The teaser was still chanting to One Harpy in that soft maternal voice. A finger was buttering my eye, coating it with some kind of salve that smelled like oil of cloves, although there weren't any cloves in the New World. Were there? I guess you don't want the eye to burn out permanently, you want it to be all right in a while so you can do it again, and again, and again. Saltwater sprayed into my eye out of someone's mouth. The hands let go of my head and let me dog-shake it automatically, and then wiped it down with wet cloth mittens. It felt so great I got that stupid rush of pathetic gratitude.

"So you have killed me," 2 Jeweled Skull said.

I started to explain that he'd have gotten a lower dosage of luons.

"B'aax ka?" he asked. "How long?"

"More than two and fewer than seven rounds of the tz'olk'in."

"How long exactly?" he asked.

"That's as close as I know," I said. "Look in my head, it's not—"

"Hun tzunumtub tz-ik-een yaj," the teaser said. It felt like a timpani roll that you know is building up to a crash of cyclopean cymbals, like in "The Crusaders in Pskov," and you'll do anything to stop it. My body strained against the ropes, struggling to get a hand or a toe or something up to my eye, but everything was held down, and I passed into that absolutely insupportable pain of the frustrated imperative, the itching that demands to be scratched more than your body demands even, say, air. I'd thought I'd felt big pain before, as Jed, getting skewered by ten-thumbed nurses for arterial blood tests, for

instance. And I'd always felt I'd still prefer it to, say, eternal nothingness. But that was just ignorance. Death is a million times preferable to real pain. After an indeterminate while my eye—or rather the liner cells in the fatty tissue surrounding my eye—was feeling fine again, feeling kind of great, in fact, and there was my hand, there were the cool red petals on the floor—yeah, I was even seeing out of it. I looked up.

2JS crouched in front of me. Beads of sweat covered his face like the scales of a Gila monster. His hands were in big long sharkskin mittens that looked absurdly like something that Williams Sonoma would sell to suburban barbecue chefs. The thumbs were covered with chili paste. He took me by the head and shook me, like a dog killing a squirrel.

"TAKE OUT YOUR PARASITE!!!" he said. *"FINISHED!"*

I didn't even have a chance to answer before his thumbs dug into my eyes. This time I really screamed. I screamed for a long time, and then, as I gulped in air, I found I was breathing in chili fumes, that they were holding the censer under my mouth, I felt like—or in fact I somehow believed that—my body had been turned inside out and dipped in sulfuric acid.

At some point I realized, again, that I wasn't in pain anymore. A happy nectared breeze caressed my face. I noticed I was prone on the floor, and my head was on its side. I opened my good eye and saw something odd: a long, snouty, spiky-haired giant rat thing's blank black bead-eye staring into mine. It was one of the armadillos, and it was licking my eye. I recoiled with that absolute prehuman revulsion, but my body was still being held down, and all I really managed was to quiver.

"Hun tzunumtub tz-ik-een yaj," the teaser said.

Big pain stretches time, so I don't know how many times 2 Jeweled Skull said, "Take back your uay." Maybe ten, or a hundred. Finally his voice tapered off, and the teaser's voice took over, yelling things into my ear, using casting-out language, and I realized they weren't simply torturing me out of anger but trying to exorcise Jed from Chacal, I guess on the theory that if I left I might take my twin, the one in 2 Jeweled Skull, along with me. Once in a while the teaser would start the Salve Chant, *"Ukumil can . . . ,"* and I'd get this cooling blast of hope and longing, as though the waiter at the restaurant where you'd eaten the habañero was coming toward you with a big old mango milkshake, waving it under your nose . . . and then the teaser would stop without giving me anything, and it became not even so much about the pain, but about wanting the salve, and then they'd bring the chili out again. Three billion years later there was barely any me left, just a big ball of reptile panic, but at some point I had an unlocated feeling that they were giving up, and a little later I heard 2JS's voice say, *"Ch'an,"* "Enough."

"Xa' nänbäl-een ek chäk'an," 3 Blue Snail's voice said. "We'll see him to the course." Maybe it was just my messed-up perceptions, but I thought their voices had even more of a vibe of urgency than they'd had before, a looking-over-the-shoulder tension. Hmm.

The guards gathered me up and marched me outside, into vegetal humidity. I didn't need a blindfold this time, of course, but I could tell that night had fallen while I was away. They took me down a flight of forty rough stairs into a big wooden roundhouse and tied me down on a wood pallet in a pool of heat from two sputtering torches. I tried to relax my muscles to accept whatever pain they were going to dish out. A cold, purposeful tickling came up over my legs and arms and onto my chest.

What the shit's going on now? I wondered, not for the first time. They were tying thin-soled running sandals onto my feet, and a tight sash around my waist, and now there was a tightening around my head. It was some kind of leather cap with wooden inserts that they were fixing onto my skull with gum and wound gut cords, like they were hafting a spearhead. For a while I guess I kind of pretended to myself that it was still just Dr. Lisuarte gluing the 'trodes onto my head and that none of this had happened, but then one of the cold tickling things worked its way up to my neck, and as I involuntarily giggled and squirmed and got my good eye open I saw for a half-second that it was a long-bristled paintbrush, like a Chinese calligraphy brush. They were painting white glyphic dots on the tan field of my skin. I found myself looking at the pattern of tattooed zigzag stripes on the arm that was holding the paintbrush and instantly knowing from it, the way you'd know that a person in a black-and-white-striped shirt was a football referee, that its owner was an *ajjo'omsaj*. That is, he was a getting-readyer, or a dresser or valet, or maybe the best word would be "preparator." And then the fact that the zigzags were brown and not blue meant he was an *emsa'ajjo'omsa*, a "lower" preparator, a kind of untouchable who could handle dangerously unclean things. I tried to roll my head to either side to see what the others were doing but I couldn't turn it, there was some kind of big thing on it stopping its movement, a wide headdress with two pairs of branching stalks . . . maybe they were horns, I thought . . . no, not horns, I realized, they were antlers. They were dressing me up as a deer.

(32)

There was a sense of jostling motion and the air was hot and stale. I strained to get a hand to my face, but my arms were tight to my sides. I was rolled up in a grass blanket. Two people were carrying me, I thought. And it seemed like we were going uphill. I listened.

The motion stopped. They laid me down on turfy ground. I picked up a few words; it was 2JS saying something about how he'd invited all these people here as part of his penance and that he was offering a deer to the fastest among them, with more profuse apologies and plans for a more elaborate festival in the near future. Stupidly, I felt embarrassed for 2JS and the whole Harpy House, even though they were going to kill me. I flipped over four times as the blankets unrolled. Air. It was like diving into cool alcohol. I was on my back, on a canvas ground-cloth under bright torchlight. A wave of jeer/cheers rose up on all sides and cut off as though someone had given a sign. There were four beats of silence and then a chorus of "We far below you thank you over us," in the high aristocratic voices of thirty or forty young *k'iik'ob'*— literally, "bloods." A blood was any male who had been initiated into one of the warrior societies. So in practice the term had connotations of both "high-born" and "able-bodied," someone born or adopted into one of the great-houses, and usually under eighteen years old. Someone else held my mouth open and spat in a hot thick syrupy mixture of b'alche, honey, some kind of blood, and something else—one of their superduper secret ingredients, I guessed—that gave the stuff an epoxy undertaste. But my throat was so withered that I was like, yum, a delicious beverage, and I gurgled it down. A third pair of hands—also wearing those damn mittens—helped me get my eyes open. The left one was still too swollen to see much, but the right one was almost fine. Huh.

The three preparators and I were in the center of a circle, or rather a nonagon, about twenty arms wide, marked by nine short torches stuck into recently burned-over turf. We were on the bare crest of a wide hill, and not in a residential area. So we were at least a few miles away from the ceremonial district of Ix. There was a wider circle, marked by about fifty torches. But there was no moon and I couldn't see anything beyond it.

Bloods crowded around the circumference. I counted thirty-one of them—my new head couldn't count as fast as my Jed-head had, but I guess I could still count pretty fast—and then guessed there were forty, since they liked to do things by twenties around here. Each blood held a javelin a little taller than he was. Like most spears the javelins were in two parts, a long shaft and a two-foot ferrule that fit into it loosely enough to detach on impact, but instead of a flint blade they were tipped with blunt wooden plugs. The javelins were wrapped with fur around the shaft, jaguar for the Ocelots and monkey for the other clans. The bloods wore deerhide kilts and wide cotton sashes with two extra ferrules stuck in the back. They wore rubber-soled sandals, like mine, and their skins were oiled for night hunting with red-pigmented dog grease. Their hair was pulled into tight tails that sprouted from the whorl and curled back up over the head toward the face. More than half of them were on the fashionably portly side. As in India, if you could afford food, you wore it. Chacal's memories must have been kicking in pretty well by now, because even with the bewildering patterns of their kilts and body paint I could tell there were bloods from all five Ixian greathouses. The bloods from the ruling Ocelot House wore turquoise spots on their calves, and the bloods from the Vampire Bat House, who were closely related to the Ocelots but whose patron direction was the northwest, wore black and orange vertical stripes all the way up their legs. Then the Itz'un House, that is, the Snuffler House, from the northwest, wore white stripes all over, and the Macaw House, who represented the southwest and were the Harpies' biggest supporters, wore yellow spots. There were also bloods there from the Harpy House, in red and black stripes, and they seemed to be stretching their legs and swishing their javelins and getting ready along with everyone else. Great, I thought, even my own family's competing to waste me. I couldn't bring myself to look them in the eyes, but just from their voices I could tell that Chacal had known a few of them. There was a sort of formal jokey strutting going on, and while they swaggered and vogued they were sizing me up with an exaggeratedly professional air, like I was a racehorse in the paddock. *"Ymiltik ub'aj b'ak ij koh'ob, impek' ya'la,"* I heard somebody say. "I'll keep the antlers and the teeth, but my dogs get the rest." There was a lot of laughing. These are happy folk, I thought. Salt of the earth.

"No, *I* get the antlers, you can have the penis, and my dogs get the rest," somebody else said. Great, I thought, I'm back in junior high. Despite myself I looked up at the line of faces, trying to think of some searing riposte. The blood who'd come up with the remark, one of the younger Snufflers, bent down to my level, puffed out his cheeks, and crossed his eyes, making a face a lot like the Harpo Marx Gookie. Somehow I started laughing along with everybody else. It all seemed like the funniest thing in the world. Of course it was a bummer to be on the receiving end, but in another way it didn't matter. It all just meant you were alive. I made a mock-pouting face back and I got an even bigger laugh. Who cares what side you're on, the world can use a little more laughter, can't it? I turned around, scanning the circle. A few of the faces felt like old friends. Some of them smiled at me, genuinely approving. I smiled back. There was empathy there. But it was an empathy that didn't preclude what they were going to do to me, because they wouldn't ask for different treatment themselves.

The preparators stood me up, steadying me by the antlers. The head guy took up a shell blade and knelt down next to me. There was a moment of premature terror—I thought he was skinning me already—but he just scraped me lightly with the sawtoothed edge, etching faint parallel stripes down my legs. As I looked around, I saw that some of the hunters were doing the same thing to themselves. Next he sunk his mitt into a dish of powder that looked like pollen and slapped it into the cuts. Ouch. Little curls of heat crawled up my legs. My feet twitched, practically jumping on their own. The stuff was some kind of powdered nettle. Making me feisty and insensitive. Whatever. Outside the circle the bloods were slapping their legs with the same stuff, pumping themselves up and razzing each other. Finally the preparators let go of my appendages and backed out of the circle into the ring of bloods. I staggered but caught myself and managed to stay on my feet, my heavy head wobbling. A hail of hissing—the Mesoamerican equivalent of applause—blasted in at me on ale-soaked air.

The hunters settled down, exactly like third-graders when the teacher walks into the room, and drew apart, letting a tall elder-statesmanish character enter the circle. He came up to me with a bundle of something in his hand. Automatically I assumed the do-what-thou-wilt-with-me crouch. He squatted two arms in front of me and unrolled a strip of white deerskin. Inside there were four small but perfect jade celts, that is, smooth-ground ceremonial ax-heads, or "currency blades" as anthropologists call them. He rolled them back up and tied the skin on each end. Next he poured a little hill of sienna-brown cacao beans out of a conical basket and, with the efficiency of an old-time croupier sorting chips, counted out eighty of them into a deer-scrotum pouch and tied it shut. Just out of habit I couldn't keep myself from ransacking Chacal's memories to try to estimate what the roll was worth. Of course, the economy was so different that you couldn't really exchange it into 2012 money anyway. I mean, around here a good quetzal tailfeather was worth two decent male slaves. But as a rough figure I'd say I was getting about eight thousand dollars U.S. Just enough to get started in a new town. Forty acres and a mul. Cheapskates. He rolled the roll and the pouch in a larger strip of cotton and gave it to the preparators to tie onto the back of my sash. When that was done he backed away from me and waved his goad at the line of bloods. They parted, making a gap for me on the northwest edge of the nonagon.

"*Ch'een b'o'ol*," he said in a trilling, singsong voice like an old country auctioneer's. "Throw in your stakes." It was like saying, "*Faites vos jeux.*" Place your bets.

Beyond the gap the hilltop looked like a midnight garage sale at the Museum of Natural History. There were at least four hundred other people up here, all straining to get a look at me over the ring of hunters. There were bundles and packs and travois carts and dozens of green rush trading mats piled with all sorts of stuff, bolts of white cotton, bales of some kind of aromatic bark, bags of what I supposed were cacao beans, bouquets of spoonbill feathers, green-obsidian cores and currency blades, leashed bunches of live *kutzob'*—that is, neotropical ocellated turkeys—and piles of wooden and clay personal counters, which I guessed were like casino chips, representing gods know what. Officials of some kind in black-and-white capes and monkey headdresses, evidently managers or bookies, walked between the groups in pairs, keeping track of the bets with baskets of little paper chits. At the edge of the crowd I could just make out what looked suspiciously like two shiny skinned bodies hanging together from a tall tripod like a teepee frame. Warm-up victims, maybe. Don't think about it. I listened to the crowd, trying to sort out the betting. From what I could hear at first, it seemed like all the bets were on which hunter would catch me. Finally I heard a few people offering bets that I'd make it. It made me feel pretty good until it turned out they got odds of eight to one against me. There was a disagreement starting somewhere, on my left side, and it grew. For a minute I thought everybody might start fighting each other and I'd get away like in some Keystone Kops movie, but they resolved it by letting another person come into the circle and take a look at me. He was a short, scruffy-looking guy, and definitely an untouchable, but he must have been a popular oddsmaker because he put on a pair of those mittens and lifted up my arms and guided my legs apart, feeling for muscle tone. It was pretty degrading, but I went along with it. He announced something to the effect of how I was in pretty good shape and the odds against me shot down to a whoppingly optimistic five to one.

Looks bad, Jeddio, I thought. Pretty damn hopeless. Not fair. I mean, sure, there's a *chance* I'll make it. But, really, nobody gives odds like that except for a stunt. You're a point spread, babe.

"*Tz'o'kal, tz'o'ka,*" the adder said. "Final offerings." It was like saying, "*Les jeux sont faits.*"

The crowd quieted down. Some of the bloods took off bits of jewelry and handed them to their squires or whatever. Behind me someone blew a horn like a shofar. Everyone turned, looking to the northwest. I looked too. Out in the darkness, where the stars disappeared, bonfires lit up one after the other, tracing the undulating spine of the next ridge like a string of Christmas LEDs draped over a ragged hedge. How far away was it? About half a mile, looks like. I couldn't see what was in the valley I had to cross. Damn.

I knew through Chacal—although, of course, at this point anybody would have been able to figure it out—that if I made it safely across that line I'd be off the menu, free to go anywhere I wanted. Of course, I'd still be on the lam to some extent, and I was too tainted to be a blood again, just another homeless or, as we'd say in Ixian, hearthless nonentity skulking from one no-name town to another. I tried to conjure some sort of plan out of Chacal's foggy notion of local geography, but all I could come up with was that I'd have to get on the northern *sacbe*, that is, the sacred highway, and stay on it until I was in the ever-shifting borderlands between the zones controlled by Yaxchilán and its ancient enemy, Ti ak'al, whose empire was currently in a state of near collapse. I'd probably get robbed and eaten the first night. And even if I didn't, what good would it do? I had less than a year here anyway. Maybe I'll just sit here. Maybe I just don't feel like playing this game right now. Did they ever think of that? Reindeer games are a drag anyway. Although if you do stay here they'll just practice some more of their nefarious torture arts on you. Maybe the best thing is to just grab one of those spearheads and swallow it. Let the world go to hell thirteen hundred years from now. That's too far away to care about. Screw it.

There were four beats of silent waiting and then 2 Jeweled Skull's voice:
"Tz'on-keej b'axb'äl!"

I stepped out of the circle and, with as much dignity as possible, walked through the crowd of bloods and other Ixob' to the outer circle. I didn't look at any of them. They all drew back and gave me plenty of room, but the moment I crossed the line of firelight the bloods slid into a chorus:

> "Nine boys run down a big fat deer and say:
> 'Your head is light, your ass is heavy, Deer.'
> The deer's two ears become the ninth boy's spoons . . ."

It was a counting song, like eeny-meeny-mynie-moe, and Chacal and every other Ixian child had grown up with it. Nobody had to explain the rules to me for me to know that the instant they got to the last word—*ts'ipit*, that is, "ring"—the bloods could leave the outer circle, and I was fair game.

> "The deer's two antlers are the eighth boy's rakes . . ."

I dashed down down the terraced slope.

> "The deer's hooves are the seventh boy's four hammers,
> The deer's one back becomes the sixth boy's purse . . ."

Step. Step. Stepstep. Stepstep. Ditch. Over. Tree. Around. Chacal wasn't a hunter, but his feet still found safe steps in the undergrowth. The drilling whines of cicadas whipped past me and I smelled pine and horsemint. So what if I'm in a passel of trouble, I thought, I actually feel kind of great. I think I'll just jump over the next tree instead of going around it.

> "The deer's intestines are the fifth boy's necklace . . ."

No problem. They haven't even started yet. I bounded over the edge of the first terrace and for an instant of dislocation I thought I was somehow upside down, falling up into outer space. There were more stars below me than above—but they were flickering and drifting in amorphous constellations and for the next two seconds I thought I was running down into a lake, and then as I passed over the first few stars I realized the shoals of lights rippling below me were glowworms, armies of green-white elaterids raving and orgying over the ferns and jacarandas. We have to be east of Ix, I thought. On Harpy land, probably, somewhere in the folds of east-to-west limestone ridges that strung out of the Sierra de Chamá and slowly diminished toward the Lago de Izabal. Okay. Try to guess the distance. From hilltop to fireline was about half a mile as the laser flies. So how far will I have to actually run? Two miles? Maybe more like three. One uphill. So what, I'll handle it. Whoops. Shrub. Ground not burned over so recently here. I half slid down to the base of the hill and rolled over onto clover and marigolds. Up. Up. Hup. Can't see the Fire Ridge anymore. Forward. Zoom. Okay, we're back on track. The rhythm section was still jamming back at Home Base and I noticed my steps were syncing to it. The slope here was tufted with eucalyptus and ceiba trees, some were like gigantic umbrellas and others just saplings, some trunks leafless, some fallen, and some that were just decaying stumps. But they were all too regular and too widely spaced to be a natural forest. They'd either been planted or systematically thinned. In fact, if you ignored the way the trees were festooned with bundles of tobacco leaves tied with multicolored ribbons— offerings to the clan mate whose uay was lodged within each tree—and also the fact that there were fewer live trees than dead ones, you could almost imagine you were in some Capability Brown–style English park. Behind me the bloods' voices were rising as they neared the end of the chant:

"The deer's one jawbone makes the fourth boy's fork . . ."

Fast, fast. Moving well. Chacal's instincts were kicking in, the old adrenaline autopilot. You only have to operate the top cortex of your brain. Left.

Stepstep. Stepstep. Over. Tree, tree. Around. Over. More uneven ground here. Barriers. Steeplechase. I felt strangely light. It couldn't be just because Chacal's body was so young, or because it was so much stronger than mine had ever been, even after being wasted by presacrifice fasting. It had to be just that I was smaller now. It's why little kids have so much energy, it's not just because they don't know what a pit the world is, it's just that they don't have much to lift. How tall am I now? If I hadn't been a little preoccupied up there, I could have compared myself with what I knew was the four-foot-two-inch height of the lintel of the King's Niche. But the average height of an upper-class Maya male of the period was about five feet two, and I was only a bit above average. So say I'm five four. Jed was five nine. So if strength increases with the square of your height but weight increases with your height cubed, let's assume my G-drag is about—

Ouch. Pointy. Careful. Right. Stepstep. Stepstep. Don't get distracted. You're not home free yet—

"The deer's one nose becomes the third blood's pipe . . .
Deer's thirty teeth become the second's dice . . ."

I think I can I think I can I think I can I think I can. Wobbling. I got my hands up around my *cagado* antler-rack, maybe I can get this sucker off, no, glued on, I was just wrenching my scalp off like the thing really grew out of my skull. Forget it. Focus.

"The deer's one sphincter is the first boy's ring,
The deer's one sphincter is the first boy's *ring*!"

The word *b'aac*, "ring," stretched out into a long hissing cheer and the patter of evil little feet. *And* they're off and *run*ninggg. Don't look back. Ahead. Ahead.

Trees. Slalom between the trunks. Left. Right. No, left. Now right. Left again. Nearly halfway. Doing good.

Footsteps came down after me like a wall of light rain.

Fuck 'em. Left. Into the thicket. Don't get your antlers caught. Look down. Left hand shields eyes. Right arm front and over. Anticipate branches. Think, then run.

Still way ahead of them. No sweat. As I came into the valley between the two hills the ground leveled off, but it was full of twigs and crud. Watch it. Twigs and crud equal sound. Sound equals death. Silence = Life. I tip-ran forward. Still another mile, maybe. Largely uphill.

Ouch. Step. Ouch. Nettles. Pain twanged up through my legs. Forks in the road. Well, if it slows me down, it'll slow them down.

Stop. Listen.

Group getting closer. How many? Four? Maybe they split again. They're good trackers. Don't leave a trail. Run backward on footprints and then veer off? No, too difficult. Doesn't really work. Only foxes.

Forward. Quiet. Step. Step. This is actually a pretty good game. After all, *game* just means a victim you can eat—

"*Unf.*"

Chacal's body knew what it was, the grunt of someone throwing a javelin, and we dodged-and-ducked automatically. The spear whistled three feet or so overhead. And it really whistled, with a high-A fifth chord. There were tiny reed flutes attached to its shaft.

—*eeeeeeethdgdgdgt.*

Dag. Landed pretty close. Stuck in a tree or something. Ought to find it. No, no time. I skidded the rest of the way down into a dry gully between the two hills. Behind and above me the bloods whistled to each other in house hunting-codes. You could tell they were fanning out and advancing down the hill in pairs, covering the whole slope. Timeless classic hunting technique.

I paused. Go straight up? Yeah. Just go. Up the hill. Come on. I crouched up the slope.

Zhhhweeeee—

Another. *Duck!*

Thhgdg.

Damn. They couldn't see me through the trees, could they? They're throwing by sound. Just chipping. Don't worry. Stay out of kill range and you'll be fine. I veered right. Shit. Antlers caught. I could hear a couple of the fastest hunters panting up the hill after me. Potential puncture wounds tingled over my back. Pull. Branches. Pull them *out*. Pull. Vines. Ouch. Neck. Dammit.

Whzhhweee. Bkt!

There. Got my antlers free. Left. I hightailed it uphill and left. Up. Left. Left. Shit—

Whzeeeeeeeeeee . . .

Overhead. Down. Crouch. Down. Don't let them get a clear shot. Keep the trees between us, then get up to the torch line somewhere, find a hole. Damn. The place didn't offer cover like a natural forest. It was more like hiding behind pillars of a colonnade. You had to keep moving from trunk to trunk. Okay. Up. Antlers unbalancing me. Head heavy. Damn. I got an image of myself as one of those prehistoric Irish elks with the racks as wide and heavy as two Yamaha Road Stars. No wonder they didn't last. Gotta get these fuckers *off*. I dug my fingertips in under the leather straps around my head, but there was some sort of gum or resin under there, bonding to my skin. Never mind.

Quiet. Run silent, run deep. They're fast too. Just keep going.

Got to vomit. The thing is, if you really run faster than you can, you throw up. Gotta go. Gork. Uchg. Whew. I think I managed to do it quietly. Anyway, there wasn't much there. Keep going. Come on. Don't worry about where you're getting your strength from, just where it will take you. Hup. Hup.

I veered uphill and south. Can't take this abuse much longer. Such a knot of pain in my heart. Lung. Whatever.

It was quiet again. No more shouting. They were still coming after me, though. Listening. Slow down. You're too noisy.

Stealthy. Healthy and wise.

Hmm. The line's right up there. Just a little farther. Just go for it. No, wait.

I paused.

Oh, shit. Close behind me on the left. Damn. Twigs snapping. Better—

Wait. No. Making too much noise. Too showy. He wants to drive me forward into the others.

Think. What are they doing?

They're above you. Waiting for you. And the rest are spreading out. A few trackers were going to stay on my trail as I went up the slope, and the rest would fan out in front of me. And then they'd close in.

The hunters above me were settling in. Listening.

Stay put. You run for it, yousa goin' die.

You're going to have to go for the line from a different spot. From the left.

Okay. Back down. Retrace.

I padded backward as silently as my feet knew how, back toward the valley. The ground here was clear, but some of the eucalyptus branches drooped down to chest height. Watch it. I turned around and stumbled downhill. Now that I was facing southwest for the first time I saw a vague larger glow beyond the next ridge of the sierra, a glow that Chacal's brain knew very well, the temple watch fires of Ix.

De todos modos. Just curve west and try again. They probably expect you to go counterclockwise. Everything around here goes counterclockwise. Go clockwise.

I couldn't see the ridge, but the stars were like having a GPS. Judging by 9 Death's Head, that is, Regulus, it was right over there.

I figured it was about seventy difficult steps up the burnt turf from here to the torch line.

Bueno.

Go.

I headed up the hill in a wide curve, aiming to come out of the line of trees as far to the west as possible—

Close. Something. I threw myself on the ground without knowing why.

Cht-tzii—thkgk.

Shit. I jumped up, whoa, falling back, no, *grabbed*, damn, my neck, *coño Dios,* holy shit, a hand on my goddamn antlers. I wrenched my head forward but he had me by the main shaft of the right fork. I pulled left, no, too late, he had me, but then without thinking I arched my back and slammed my points back against him. There was a moment of resistance and a sharp exhalation of breath, and as I twisted forward again the hunter's hand released and I spun around facing him. His legs said he was from the Ocelot House, and he was twelve or fourteen at the most, but with tauntingly long hair, like, Hey, go ahead, grab it. He was holding his left hand over his right collarbone where a point of my antler had gone in. I repositioned myself and jumped frog-style at his face. The shock wave went from his skull to mine like we were a couple of pool balls. Eat horn, fathermotherfucker. Ty spikes the baseman. Fuck y'all. He grabbed my horns and twisted them, Theseus-and-the-Minotaur style. I let myself turn and fall, got a hand around the big knot at the front of his sash, and pulled my points up into his neck again. This time he stumbled back and when I arched my back again his hands let me go.

Ouch. Was my neck broken? No, then I wouldn't be moving. I stepped back and looked sideways up at the Ocelot. The right side of his head was shiny black in the starlight, blood from a gouge below his eye. He staggered toward me.

Don't worry, he's too messed up. I backed away from him.

He's losing blood, he's getting weaker. Just hold him off until he collapses and then pop him. On the other hand, maybe I should just run.

Or should I take the time to kill him so he won't give an alarm? That's ridiculous, just run. They can already hear where the hell I am. Speed. I ran. Just make it up there and you'll be free to leave. Free as a bee, free to bee, you and meeee—

Whoa. Who' hoppen?

I was prone on the ground again. I rolled over and sat up. My right leg was hot. Hmm. A javelin had hit it on the back of my thigh, two inches above the knee. Oh, hell, I'm hit. Shit doggy dog. Blunt or not, those things still do some damage. Not deep, but still. Bloody. Bloody hell. As I was checking out the cut I noticed the javelin was still in one piece and lying on the ground, and as I was looking at that, it slid away from me, backward through the grass like the tail of a snake. I grabbed it by the fur covering, just below the joint where the replaceable ferrule attached to the main shaft. Somebody tried to yank it away. I yanked back and looked up. It was the same Ocelot blood. Oh, Christ. Face it, dude, you're beat. We glared at each other but there wasn't any real communication there. Fine, I thought, just don't yell for backup. Save me all for yourself. I twisted the javelin against his thumbs, but he wouldn't let go. I lowered my antlers between us and got into a squat and managed to climb back onto my feet, still holding the spear shaft. Okay, Jed, just don't let go. I twisted behind the tree, still hanging on to the spearshaft, and I circled counterclockwise, keeping the roughly eight-inch-diameter trunk between us, using it as a fulcrum, going faster and faster. I took my right hand off the spear, swung it around the trunk, and got my hand onto a leather-and-jade band around his upper left arm, and I had him by both arms, with the tree between us. He seemed to recoil as my skin touched his and for a moment he was off-balance, his feet still on the ground while mine were already walking up the trunk. I tightened my grip on the leather band, leaned back, and straightened myself. There was a beautiful *thwotch* sound as his chest slammed into the trunk. The muscles of his wrists went slack for an instant, but he didn't let go of the spear shaft and I choked my left hand farther up on it, finally getting to his wrist cuff, and then grabbed that and pulled again. This time, even through the wood of the trunk, my feet could feel his mandible mashing into his upper jaw. Chew tree, scuzzface! Power to the dirty fighters! He shouted something, slurring badly, and then just went into a series of yelps to help everyone locate the direction of the sound. Fucker. He must have decided that he'd had it and he might as well turn me in. Shut up shutup shutupshutup, I thought, you are bumming me out and you are buttfucking dead. I twisted around the trunk to the right, got enough arm slack to move my right hand off the shoulder strap and up onto the back of his head, got a good grip on his beaded topknot, and pulled him into the trunk again, feeling the skull split somewhere, and from the way it shifted you could tell it had lost its rigidity, like an egg with a cracked shell that hasn't yet popped its membrane. The yelping stopped. You are *over*, I thought. Got that? I am the hottest shit known to man, I thought. Hah. Sure, I'm a little woozy, but none the worse for wear. I can handle this. Anyway, I'm armed now, right? *I've* got a *ja*velin, my mind singsonged, *I've* got a *ja*velin. I have the technology. Up. Firelight right up there. Not far at all. Come on.

There were weird sounds behind me. Oh, cripes.

Snuffling.

They're sniffing for my sweat. And blood. Damn. Damn.

Quiet.

Inhale. Hold. Exhale. Softer. Inhale. I synchronized my panting with the trills of a nearby cricket. Blend in. Think like a bush.

Still, they'll smell me. Better move out soon.

Now. No, wait.

Either the fear or just the whole situation or something was triggering

flashes from Chacal's memories, a snippet of his early training, a sort of character test when the pilomancers, that is, the hipball augurers, had led him
down into the Hipball Brethren's soul cave. They'd walked through the cav-
erns without torches, feeling their way by grooves in the floor, and laid him
naked in a stone sarcophagus. And then they'd gone away, supposedly. At the
time he'd believed he'd been there for days before the voices started. They
started as faraway whispers, *Who is this, I smell someone who shouldn't be here,
let's eat him, let's jawbone him.* They were the uayob of ancient disgraced hipball players coming to take him to Xib'alb'a, drawing closer and closer, demanding secret names that he'd sworn never to divulge, ordering him to leave
the casket and come with them, and when the voices nestled right in next to
him, so loud and close they seemed to be burrowing into him, he didn't know
whether he'd ended up shouting along with them in the hurricane of screams,
but he knew that he hadn't run away, that he hadn't told the name, that he
hadn't even moved. When they'd lifted him out the next day, the eight-year-
old who was going to be Chacal had passed the point of utter insane terror
into something else. And by the time he'd realized that it was only the pilomancers calling through tubes that fed into the vents of the casket, it didn't
make any difference. The boys who'd survived that and the other tests had
either been born with a flint core or had grown one. They were opaque to suffering. Twenty-first-century people would have said that the trauma of the
tests deadened their day-to-day emotions and seeded a rage that could blast
out with almost no provocation. Here it just meant they could become
bloods.

A leaf crinkled twenty feet behind me. Nothing else for it. Go. Gogogogogo.
I ran.

Oh, shit. Too soon.

There was a spear whistle on my left. I jumped left, rolled forward, and
pushed myself back upright with the javelin shaft. For a second I thought I'd
done everything right, but then my right leg slipped out from under me. Did
it get hit? I wondered. If so, why didn't I feel anything? Too much adrenaline,
or what? I caught myself enough to fall on my knees and spin around in a
squat. A Snuffler Clan blood was charging me, holding the headless shaft of
his javelin like a club. I stuck the butt of my javelin into the ground and braced
for a collision. Off to the right there were two hunters about three hundred
arms away, coming up with their javelins raised, ready to throw. One of them
was an Ocelot and the other was the Harpy kid with the sweet round face. I
knew his name, I thought, Chacal had played hipball with him, he was a new

initiate into the Harpy hipball team, I knew his name, *hah*, that's it: Hun Xoc.
1 Shark.

Okay, I thought, just get through these three stooges and you're in. I
snapped back to attention and angled my javelin up at the Snuffler. He dodged
the point and swung around my back, raising his shaft to brain me, and I
turned to try to parry it. For an instant, and for no reason that I could see, he
hesitated and took a half-step back, settling himself. Oh, I know, I thought.
I'm polluted. Superstitious dick. I spread my arms and lowered my head rack
and lunged at him. His shaft came down and knocked two points off my right
rack but only grazed my forehead. You've spoiled your trophy, dude. I shook
the dizziness out of my head, got my javelin in gear, and swung it in a wide arc
eight inches above the ground. Snuffler Dude jumped and got his left foot
clear, but the ferrule connected with his right one and snapped off the shaft.
He tipped over, hit the ground, and sat up on the grass. Without needing to
think I pulled back the javelin shaft for a thrust, and for an instant it was as
though his skin was so thin and tight in the starlight that I could see through
it. I zeroed in on where the exterior iliac artery was swelling and slackening,
right inside the crotch, and jabbed the splintered end of the headless javelin
in and around and dug for it. There was that gooey split-second resistance
and release as the wood made it through the skin and twanged off a ligament
and then I struck oil, an artery popped and I got that spurt of blood, *yeah*,
spurt, spurt, SPURT! Ha! Wow, I really am hot shit, I thought. The Snuffler
blood stayed silent and the only reaction in his face was maybe a flicker of
disappointment in the eyes. I rolled away from him, hanging on to my javelin
shaft, and wrenched myself upright.

I wobbled a bit. For some reason I thought of the number eight.

It doesn't take a long time to register a lot of things, as long as your mind
doesn't try to move them up to a verbal level. In the span of less than a second
I realized the Snuffler was dead, and I realized this was the first time I'd killed
anyone. People say that your first time can bring on waves of guilt and ela-
tion, that you might get a sympathetic reaction and hear the blood rushing in
your ears and get tunnel vision and faint, or you might get an adrenaline
spike that can lead to an orgasm, or a sympathetic reaction that can make
you faint, and then more guilt, and so on. And despite everything else that
was going on, some part of me was expecting at least some of those things.
But instead I felt something oddly familiar. It was the way I used to feel when
I was shopping, when I'd bought something expensive, like, say, that last
Plymouth Barracuda. Or even like I'd just clicked in a big bid on eBay in the

last five seconds of the auction. There was the same little peak of tension, and then a release and relief, and then a fading aftertaste that's a combination of buyer's remorse and the satisfaction of ownership. It was as though I owned the Snuffler. Or, rather, I'd separated his body from his uay, and now his uay was prowling and snuffling around me, ready to follow me wherever I went, and if I did the right things, I could keep it from taking revenge on me and instead make it my pet. Or, rather, my slave. But then mixed with that I was feeling something like guilt, but not guilt. It was more physical, a sense of defilement, like I'd stepped in dog vomit, say, or like I'd been playing with radioactive chemicals and gotten my arm hot and now I had to be decontaminated. It didn't feel like there was anything wrong with my character. It was just that I'd gotten close to death, and death is infectious. And finally, I realized that I was feeling these things, and not the things I'd expected, because this actually wasn't my first kill. I'd killed before. That is, Chacal had killed people before, seven of them, on the hipball court.

I wasn't feeling what I would feel, I thought. I mean, what Jed would feel. I was feeling what Chacal would feel. Yes, I was in control of his body, but my emotions were his. And no wonder, because 99 percent of his whole nervous system was still his. And then there was this thin little pattern wrapped around his frontal cortices that told him he was me and not himself. The self isn't some big cosmic force. It's flimsy.

Short Ocelot had come up on my right, yelling his capturing cry. I got up but there was no way I was going to get ahead of him, so I turned around. He had his javelin up like a lance, about to skewer me. I dove and rolled. He reacted quickly and got it together for another run, but he was close enough so I spat a big gout of blood at him and it hit him right in the chest, a big red mucousy splotch. *Take that*, I thought. *COOTIES!!!*

He recoiled. Behind him I could see the Harpy blood hanging back. Why? Maybe he's afraid of infection too. Or because he's still kind of on my side? No, it's just that they're all really scared of touching me. I'm unclean. Irrationally, I felt insulted. Oh, for God's sake. Just use it.

The short Ocelot was coming back. The torchlight from above me reflected in his eyes, and something in Chacal knew that if he was looking into the light he couldn't see me as well as I could see him. I dove low and deflected his javelin with my left hand and steered my spear handle up into his mouth. It caught and I felt something soft. Have a tonsillectomy, punk. I jumped back and twisted the shaft out through his cheek. He didn't make a sound and he didn't back up, that whole macho ethic, he just got his balance back and came forward again. I wound up and slashed and my shaft bounced on his javelin and slid up it into his fingers. There was a little crunch and his hand released the spear. Try to get it? No, too late. Time to boogie. Step. Step. Eight steps up the hill I heard the telltale rattle of shell jewelry as the Harpy blood adjusted his body, getting ready to throw. An easy shot.

Damn, I thought, you would have made it. I braced for the shock of flint on my spine, but the javelin hummed through the air to my left with this beautiful sort of lost sound. Two more hops. I heard the Harpy blood trip on something and fall. Weird. Incompetent clod. Maybe he missed me on purpose. Forget it. Just make it the bloody blue hell to the *chingado* fire-line. Details later.

Keep going. Listen.

They had a trick of panting silently, and they ran gingerly like foxes so you usually didn't hear their feet, but their ankle beads clicked against each other and air whistled over their gaudy earrings, and as they came up behind me on my right I even thought I could feel the heat of their bodies. How many were there? I didn't want to slow my limping run even enough to turn my head. Just listen. Listen between steps.

Three. Three close enough to intercept me. One close on the left. Two farther on the right. Others coming farther away. Don't worry about them. Just get down for a second and then make a break for it.

Get ready for a serious dash. The back of my thigh was still trickling, like a faucet turned down just to the point where the thread of water is about to break into individual drops. I felt a jab of the Fear, the old bleeding-out fear. I scooped up some dirt and pushed it into the puncture in my thigh. You need blood right now, I thought, deal with the germs later. No, there is no later. You have no later anymore.

I could feel that there were more than a few of them, on my right and probably on my left, watching the ridge from the trees. When I ran for it, at least a few of them would get within firing range.

I realized I was laughing, almost but not quite silently. Quiet, idiot. Or maybe I was whimpering. Not being very stoic about this. Chacal would *not* behave this way—

Wait. Who's that?

No one here. But—

Hmm.

I was sure that there was someone there, someone right next to me ... but there wasn't anyone. Someone inside me ...

Chacal?

Are you there?

Oh, Christ damn it, he's *here*, he's watching me, he's *enjoying* this, fuck—

Shh. They're coming. I got my feet under me and scrunched backward into a cluster of myrtle saplings. Come on, go for it, *maricones*, I'll bite your toes off. I chuckled. Shushup.

I squatted. Act like a pebble.

Time to come up with a plan. Right. Heh heh. Shh. Shh. Somewhere between me and the torch line someone sang again:

"Your head is light, your ass is heavy, Deer . . ."

My hands and feet were freezing from blood loss and my jaw was chattering. Stop it. Stop it. Don't let the teeth hit. Quiet. Quiet.

"The deer's two ears become the ninth boy's spoons . . ."

Shit, this isn't working out. Nope. I'm dead. I am Spam. Spam I am. I heard feet all around me. Four people. No, five. Eight. Hell. Okay, fine. I'm moving out. I crawled toward the light. Actually, it wasn't even crawling, it was creeping. In fact, it was scuttling. Like a horseshoe crab. A paraplegic horseshoe crab.

Face it, you're not going anywhere.

Too slow. Too slow.

"The deer's two antlers are the eighth boy's rakes,
The deer's hooves are the seventh boy's four hammers . . ."

Damn. Run to ground. I guess I'm dead I guess I'm dead I guess I'm dead.

"The deer's one back becomes the sixth boy's purse,
The deer's intestines are the fifth boy's necklace . . ."

Anyway, there's still the other version of me somewhere, right? Except that's not all that comforting when the only consciousness you're in is dying. I'm dead, this is it, this is really what it's like, this is going to be it . . .

Hmm. Well, what's the wait? It's—

(33)

Something was wrong. And not just with me.

Silence.

It wasn't anything I'd thought about—I'd been a little preoccupied—but of course all this time I was running for my life, the night had been so loud that it wasn't so much a matter of hearing the pursuer's footsteps as picking them out from the roiling ocean of night sounds. Now there was a rising all around, a universal whir and flutter like twenty thousand decks of cards simultaneously sprayed out of the hands of ten thousand show-off dealers. My mind, or maybe Chacal's, separated a few nearby flaps and flops out of the cacophony and realized what it was: It was the global rush of some huge and incalculable but definitely even number of wings, all the bats and birds in the world taking off at once. It was too big, wrong, and what was most wrong about it was that the birds didn't cry. Almost but not quite all at once, the stars went out. The invisible sky boiled and crackled, but in all of it the only vocalization was the automatic ultrashriek of the bats.

Pop.

Pressure on eardrums—

rrrrRRRRZZglglglglgl DDDDDDD*DDDDDDDDDDDD*!!!

The subway beast growled up at me and that inside-out elevator-falling jet-dropping last-stair-not-there inner-ear panic filled existence as the ground liquefied. I held on to the turf as though, even if the world disintegrated, I'd have a chunk of asteroid to cling to in outer space. At some point I noticed the shocks had faded and that the silhouette of one of the hunters was standing above me, watching me, holding a club or mace in his left hand.

It happened, I thought. It was Volcán San Martín.

Damn, they got it right. Taro, Marena, the Connecticut Yankee Department, even Michael Weiner, for once they knew what they were doing. I'd been near minor eruptions before in Guatemala and I'd felt one fairly serious earthquake, in San Pablo Villa de Mitla, in February of '08. But this was in a whole different league. Even the soft dirt under me was thrumming like the bottom skin of a snare drum. Four hundred miles to the volcano and it sounds like it's right over the hill. Well, eruptions are like—

Uh.

(34)

For about twenty-five seconds, and for the only time in my life, I believed there was life after death.

I tried to shout, but the heavy blunt head of the blood's mace had hit me in the abdomen and knocked out the air. I tried to grab his legs, but now a second person had gotten around me from behind and was holding my arms. I tried to kick but the first blood was sitting on my legs. I spat. He didn't react. I writhed. It didn't help. Panic. They're skinning me anyway, I thought, the eruption doesn't matter. They don't care, it doesn't matter, they're skinning me anyway, ohgodohgod. The blood—it was the Harpy blood, Hun Xoc—set down his mace and pushed my forehead down into the turf. Oddly, though, I didn't feel it. This can't be it, there's got to be more just give me a little more please this can't be totally it this can't be it. He pried my mouth open and gripped my lower jaw, his thumb over the central teeth and under the tongue. I still didn't feel anything. He wrenched it left and right, first out of one socket and then out of the other. The mandible tore off with sprays of blood and saliva. The tongue came off with the rest and lapped comically at the air. This is weird, I thought, that really ought to be pretty painful. I must be beyond pain . . . but also, it was as though I was watching it from outside, lying next to myself. There were four bloods standing around me now, all from the Harpy House. One of them, the squat one with a wide face, held a tiny torch, like a birthday candle, cupping the light in his hand. Another sliced down the undersides of my arms and disjointed the wrists, careful not to tear the skin so that the full hands would stay attached to the cured pelt. It was the most hopeful moment I'd ever experienced and probably ever would experience. I thought I was my freshly released astral body, just hanging out for a little while to observe the treatment of my husk before setting off for parts unknown.

Soon I realized that was just too silly to believe. For one thing, I was still in immense pain. I still felt my various injuries, the weight of the two bloods holding me, and even an ant or something crawling on one of the thistle stalks gouging into my back. And more importantly, even though the body they were dressing out had a truncated pigtail like mine, and a face, or what was left of one, that seemed about like mine, he wasn't quite the same. His forearm was hipball-impact toughened, but not so much as mine, and the calluses on his knees weren't nearly so big and impressive. Besides, the way I was watching the scene didn't seem right either. I wasn't floating in the air above it, the way ectoplasm is supposed to. I was still pinned to the ground, still blinking dust and blood out of my eyelids.

It isn't you, I thought. Face it. It's some other guy. Even though he's roughly the same size, age, and body type, and even though he has roughly the same deer-spots, he just isn't you—

Ouch. Damn it. What's wrong with my chest? I got my eyes down far enough to see. One of the bloods holding me had a tiny obsidian razor between two fingers, and he inserted it into my chest at the base of the sternum. He drew it up in a convex arc to the U of my clavicle and symmetrically back down again, making a mandorla shape. And this time he was really doing it to *me*, by the way, not the substitute me. He pinched the point of the patch of skin and peeled it upward. Ouch. Ouch. That really hurts. The beatings, the chilies, the enema, all that hurt a lot, but this, ow, yow, this really hurrrruuuiiiieeeeEEEEE—

A strip of integument about a half-inch wide and four inches long released with a little pop. For an instant he held it up with the suede side toward me, glistening with tiny globular fat cells, and the weak light shone through it just right, and I could make out the familiar column of blue glyphs running down the center, my nine-skull hipball-rank tattoo.

Did I blank out? I don't know. After all, blanking out is something you can only infer from its effects, like dark energy. At some point cotton felt blankets wrapped around me and contracted. Four hands flipped me over and I felt smothering again as they rolled me up. There were javelin shafts in the roll with me, I guess as camouflage. And by now, and despite Chacal's training, I was actually crying, whimpering an existential Nancy Kerrigan "Why, why, *WHYYYYY?!?!?*" crushed that I wasn't dead, that I wasn't a ghost, that I was still trapped here, that it wasn't me.

(35)

Ataste, or the memory of a taste, that I somehow recognized as mother's milk rose up first, and then other previsual memories that it took a while to realize weren't mine but Chacal's. I knew I had a body, because every square millimeter of its surface itched, it itched like I had Parsee-cake crumbs under my skin, and I couldn't scratch, I could barely wriggle against my fat-soaked wrappings. Got to scratch, got to scratch . . . and then the external itches would concentrate into my chest, where I'd lost what felt like about a square foot of skin, and then that would fade and for a long time my whole self would be in my throat, a vast furrowed Nazca salt desert, thirsty, thirsty, until finally, after centuries of zero precipitation, someone unwrapped my face into bright sunlight, squirted in a spray of salty corn gruel, and covered me back up. During the long descending curve of relief I became aware that I still had a tongue, swollen like a big dried-out dill pickle but still all there, and that my face was covered only by a thin layer of something like cheesecloth, and I could breathe almost normally. It seemed that it was afternoon, and that a team of porters was carrying the long, narrow bundle with me in it up zigzag hillside paths, eastward and upward, into the highlands, over rope bridges and alongside rushing streams.

Why'd they bother to save me?

The Harpies wanted to fool the other greathousers. That had to be it. They wanted everyone else in Ix to think I was dead. Well, so that's great, right? 2 Jeweled Skull's had a change of heart. He's decided you might be good for something. He wants to keep you alive.

Hmm. Maybe 2 Jeweled Skull had timed the hunt to wind down right around the time I'd predicted for the eruption.

Yeah. You know, now that I had a chance to think about it, really, it wouldn't have made sense for all those guys to be out playing protopaintball if they'd thought the sky was about to fall right then. They would have been back at home, crouched over their household icons, muttering pleas to their misbe-gotten gods.

So, what must have happened was that old 2JS figured my estimate of the time of the eruption would be more accurate than whatever their local geo-mancers had predicted. If they'd even predicted anything. Maybe he was just bullshitting me about that. Huh. Anyway, he'd figured the big bang was going to come ahead of schedule—and maybe the general population wasn't ex-pecting it to be such a big deal anyway, maybe they thought it would just be a couple of pops and sparkles on the horizon—and so he timed the deer hunt to be winding down right around then. So that would have been around four A.M. on the twenty-seventh. So maybe when it happened all the bloods in the hunting party got flipped out. Except the Harpies knew about it, and in the middle of the confusion the Harpies subbed in a proxy to get skinned instead of me. And that's why they took the strip of skin off my chest, the hipball tat-toos . . . that was something they couldn't fake. They'd sew it onto his skin and try to hide the seam.

Yeah. Okay. That makes sense. So I guess that Harpy blood, the one with the smooth sweet face, Hun Xoc, he really did miss me on purpose when he threw that javelin at me from like four steps away. And that's why those Har-pies were always so close on my tail without nailing me. They were following me all through the hunt, watching out for me . . . although what if somebody from one of the other clans had caught me anyway? Maybe they had some plan to switch me later on somehow . . . except probably not. Probably if that had happened they'd just have given me up.

Bastards. Well, anyway, they didn't.

So, I did get it right, didn't I? I called the eruption a hell of a lot better than their people did. Did that mean I'd gained any status around here?

The road was filled with traffic, long foot caravans with their dogs yapping ahead and behind and messengers dashing past us, rattling their warning maracas. Chacal's senses picked up something grim about the sound, like they were all rushing to get home. Refugees, almost. The jacanas and swifts were calling again, a bit warily, maybe confused by the eruption, but Chacal's mind could still tell from the calls that it was toward dusk. The going was slower here. A couple of times my bundle got passed from hand to hand to hand, like they were portaging a canoe. At some point they started carrying me upright, tied to a board, through a lot of shadow and little sunshine. It seemed more remote here, and the porters sang a sort of rosary song, listing their ancestors' unassuming names. But it wasn't a carefree little workday song. It had an apprehensive quality, like a charm against goblins. Every so often they'd squeeze me and listen to my breath to make sure I was respirating. Occasionally we'd stop and one of the dressers would unwrap the cheesecloth from my head, pry open my mouth, and pop out the wad of cotton. Then before I could even grunt, he'd spit in a spray of whatever knockout stuff they were giving me—it tasted like strong balche, but the effect was like Dilaudid—and then swab out my nose, restuff the cotton in my mouth, and replace the veil. Finally the bundle must have become too awkward for the terrain—or else we'd come to a private enough spot—because they put me down and unrolled me into the cool air. They peeled off my blindfold and I panted up at the sky.

It was a blue twilight. There were no clouds, no obvious effects from the eruptions out in the gulf, except for that hint of anxiety in the birdsongs. Hun Xoc's face looked down on me and before I could react, two pairs of arms hoisted me upright and helped me balance. None of them said anything. I didn't feel like I could say anything. I just panted. There was a big piece of ashy cotton wool stuck over the wound on my chest. Someone, maybe one of the untouchables, spat honey water into my mouth and I managed to swallow a few drops. I blinked around. We were on the south side of a ridge, on a narrow traverse near the top of a broad curved slope. On our left the incline rose at about forty-four degrees, dark serpentine boulders held in a natural net of yellow lianas. On our right the slope descended three or four hundred feet to a line of Montezuma pines. Behind them there were glimpses of a village, linked clusters of small houses, granaries, and half-open workshops, all built up from uncut mountain stones, sealed with dull red plaster and thatched with *xit*-palm fronds. The red and black stripes on the walls meant it was a Harpy town, but there were black-and-turquoise-dotted awnings stretched on the ramadas of some of the central buildings, which Chacal's brain understood to mean that members of the Ocelot House were also in residence. There weren't any mulob' or ritual structures that I could see. Maybe this was the profane town, and its sacred twin was somewhere else. There was a big, elaborate cistern, though, on a stepped platform in the center of town, and slaves with their short hair and strips of gray cloth through their earlobes and skin streaked with gray body paint, trudged to it and from it it with white rubberized baskets of water on their backs, like nurse ants carrying their pupae. Beyond the village there was a ridge that matched this one, and then, just slightly visible, another ridge beyond that. There wasn't any smoke haze over the valleys, meaning the burning season hadn't started yet. Maybe it had been postponed by the eruption. In front of us a hewn staircase, or rather more of a ladder, angled steeply down for at least seventy feet into a wide crevasse in the gray rock. They were probably going to tie a safety line onto me and see if I'd help them pass me down.

Hmm.

There were twenty people in the party. Four were Harpy bloods. Six were *liksajob*, or guards. That is to say, they were warriors from one of the Harpies' subordinate clans, who could never become full-scale bloods no matter how tough they were. The rest seemed to be untouchables and porters. I looked from face to face. They all stared back as though I were a Word Search puzzle. No one said anything. My focus skidded to a rest on Hun Xoc. He looked back with as much curiosity as the others but a little more sympathy. It was coming back to me. Hun Xoc. Right. Chacal had helped train him at what you might call the Little League division of the Hipball Society. He was dark and unusually wiry for a greathouse blood. Oddly enough, his name sounded almost the same translated into English: "1 Shark." A pair of chocolate-brown hairless hunting dogs swaggered up to sniff me. They were like Mexican Xolos, but larger, about the size of Dalmatians. A vic of lesser Canada geese honked by overhead, heading southeast at the wrong time of year. Away from the volcano.

Hun Xoc turned back to the rest of the group and started reordering them for the climb down the stairs. I realized I was being held only by a single mittened hand around each of my wrists.

Just the one lookout man ahead of me. One untouchable behind me. Then the dogs. Then the stairs.

The geese banked right, to the south. No better time. Now.

I twisted against the untouchable's thumbs, got free, butted my way past the surprised lookout, dove at the top step, and somersaulted out over the edge. Even before the rush in my ears and the release of weightlessness, the shame sloughed off me like a radiation-soaked lead suit. I giggled in midair and it was my Jed side giggling, too, feeling absolutely free for once, almost for the first time, and even though I'd realized it wasn't me, that Chacal had reasserted himself, all I could feel was the cocainesque exhilaration of—

My right shoulder exploded at the impact of a stone stair. I bounced once and turned over slowly in space. My left hip cracked down next, but the impact was mushy, somehow, not enough pain, not quite there. I should have been picking up speed but instead I was slowing down, there were hands all over me, they'd jumped down after me and they were clinging to my body, shielding me, digging their knees and elbows into the rocks. A few of them grunted, but no one screamed. I rolled over four more times, the center of a giant warm Loony Tunes snowball of shredding flesh, and then we ground to a stop with a swirl of gurgling sounds. Damn. I pushed the remaining air out of my lungs. Got to suffocate myself. No. Not me. Chacal. Chacal holding our breath. Shit. Can you really hold your breath until you die?

Chacal seemed to answer that he could do anything.

Things started to get all soft the way they do when you're blacking out, and then the limbs around me shifted. Someone yanked my head back by the hair and I thought, Finally, I *am* being beheaded, I under you thank you, fathermothers, take my head, it's what—

(36)

So, you were just lying low, I thought at Chacal. You were waiting for the first unsupervised moment to bounce up and off us both. Pretty lame.

Chacal didn't answer. I could tell he was there, though. I could feel him crouching sullenly in a cortex fold, knotting, clotting, coiling . . .

I know you're hearing this, I thought. You enjoyed watching me getting all terrified when we were being hunted down. That's big fun for you, feeling me be afraid. You're pathetic. Still, if you wanted to kill yourself, why didn't you just take over on the hunt?

No answer.

You could have just made us run our head into a rock. But you didn't. You didn't want to get captured, right? That's it, isn't it? You're okay with killing yourself, that's fine, but you didn't want to get humiliated by some Ocelot punkwad. Right?

Nothing.

Hmm. Well, if you want to sulk, fine.

Okay. Where was I this time?

Well, first of all, this time I really had been drugged. And it felt like a plain narcotic, maybe ololiuqui or some other morning-glory derivative. So there wasn't a lot to remember. I knew I'd been carried again for a long time, first horizontally and then vertically. And now I'd been laid down on a mat inside what smelled like a freshly built, or, as we say, freshly bound, reed hut. I still had a sponge gag in my mouth and some kind of sticky stuff over my eyes. My hands were tied in front of me—which seemed like a luxury at this point, compared to having them tied behind my back—and my feet seemed to be tied together, although there was too much throbbing and numbness down there to really tell. The antlers and, as far as I could feel, the other elements of the deer costume were gone. There was a rushing sound somewhere, maybe wind in bare branches, and a sense of water. Maybe there were birds, because I was pretty sure it was just after dawn.

Got to make sure I'm in charge, I thought. I wriggled a bit. Yeah, I think I'm running the show. For now, anyway. When Chacal's mind was in charge it felt more like—

Hmm. What was it like, really? That's a tough one. On a general level I guess it felt like . . . I don't know. It felt like the taste of salt. It felt like the sound of a viola. It felt like a four-dimensional sphere.

Something was different.

The rhythm of the people carrying us had slowed and deregularized, like they were coming to their destination. The air was different.

I know this place, Chacal thought all of a sudden. There was a feeling in him I hadn't felt before, not rage or panic but more of a creeping unease. Our arbor, he thought. The Place Where Our Clay Comes From.

We were near Bolocac, Chacal's village. I got an image of a forested defile, and the rushing sound resolved itself into a gurgle of rapids and beyond that the steady off-white noise of a waterfall.

Hmm. You seem a little upset, I thought at him.

He didn't answer, so to speak.

You know, I thought, I'm sure we can work out a time-share on this body. How about you can have it whenever we're eating or having sex, and the rest of the time I'll—

Air. I realized I wasn't breathing. I took a breath. Nothing. Oh, hell.

I found a connection to my body and sucked in. Stuffed up. Come on—

Got it. I snuffled my nose clear. The air trickling in carried that cool sweet reassuring clay smell and hints of other scents beyond it, roasting corn, something like creosote, a pinch of the rendering-works stink of burnt fat gone rancid. There was a smell of cardamom somewhere, or rather something that smelled almost like it. An orchid, maybe?

My smell, Chacal thought. Mine.

Gac. I choked again. Come on. Get control. *Grab* that neurosystem. It felt like we were playing that game where you and a similar-sized kindergarten friend sit on a teeter-totter and each one tries to keep his end down on the ground. The slightest lean backward or just a barely perceptible lowering of your body's center of gravity can make the difference between staying down or getting bounced up, and you each become so extrasensitive to the other's weight and position it starts to feel like you're conjoined twins.

Gkk. Suck in. Come on.

Now, despite what you may have heard, it actually isn't possible to kill yourself by swallowing your tongue. The most you can do in most suicide-restraint situations is bite off the tip of your tongue and maybe some of your lips, keep spitting the blood out, and hope that when you pass out you've lost enough to die. But even that's not a sure thing. In fact, a marine sergeant tried it in Iraq in '04, right after the Salat-al-Isha, and the rebels still found and revived him in the morning. And at any rate, so far the sponge gag in my/our mouth had kept Chacal from doing it. But there had been—or would be—cases of kidnapping victims getting stuffed up and choking to death in their gags, and this was what he was aiming for.

I swallowed a bubble of air. I'm *not* letting you choke us to death. I found a connection to my lungs and squeezed, gritting my arms and legs like teeth. I'm as tough as you are and I'm in charge—

Eastward our breath is stopped,
Northward it stops,
Our breath is dead,
It stops, it dies, it stops—

My breath, I thought, but there was no breath. I tensed and writhed but nothing came in. He was running the lungs. Oh, hell, I was just clucking, gargling, my ears were ringing like the locked groove at the end of the first cut of the original vinyl of *Metal Machine Music.* Heart racing upstairs. Thirteen flights. My tongue swelled to a lump the size of a tennis ball. Going green-gray—

It stops, it ends—

Let it out. Out. Hell. This isn't good. People who've nearly drowned say there's a moment when you have to let your breath out even though you know the water's going to come in and kill you. But Chacal had this willpower thing going on, in fact that was still too weak a word, and he was going to do it, he was going to drown us in our own carbon dioxide, and for a second I felt I was diving down to an ocean floor swirling with electric-ultramarine *Phyllidia varicosa* and ruby coral. Just let it happen. Just let yourself sink for one more mo—

Crock. Hkk. Slammed into.

Hhhhs. Hit in the stomach.

Gasp. Ha! Air. Involuntary reaction.

Mittened fingers held my teeth open, probed down into my mouth, and yanked out the gag like a stopper out of a drain. Air whistled in and my chest ballooned up. Sweetness. Pop. Jaw hinges cracked. So what. Thank frooging God. I was afraid you guys were asleep at the switch. Morons. About time. Someone jammed a stick of something into my mouth, propping it open, yes yes no no no no no *ononononononono*—

Shut *up,* I thought. They want to keep me alive. You got that?

Just die, let's simply die,
We die, we die—

They were holding me up and someone was sort of Heimliching my abdomen, but I was still graying out. Chacal can't just *will* me to die, can he? That's just not possible. They're keeping me alive, alive, alive—

Thump. I exhaled everything. Gak. The mittened hands sat me up again. I was breathing, somewhere. Good. Step in the right— .

Afraid, you're so afraid,
You're soiled, polluted,
You're afraid, afraid—

Fine, whatever, so what? I thought back. Stupidly, though, I still felt . . . well, I felt embarrassed. Of course I was frightened, and of course Chacal knew it, and he knew that I knew he knew it. There just wasn't a hell of a lot of privacy in this relationship. It's true, come to think of it, my strongest and most persistent emotion so far had been just plain embarrassment.

You're too ignorant to be frightened, I thought at him. You're just like everybody else, you believe whatever they told you when you were—

You're not from the thirteenth b'ak'tun, Chacal thought at me. You just made that up. You made up your whole life. Think about it, pictures shooting through the air, canoes that swim to the moon, a box the size of your tongue that knows more than you do, it's all a ridiculous lie.

Well, it does seem a little improbable, I thought. But, no, I didn't make it up. I couldn't have. Nobody could possibly make up the DNA spiral, or China, or Anna Nicole Smith. It happened.

B'aax? Really? Which is more likely, that there are such things, or that you are just a deluded cacodemon?

You have no curiosity, I thought at him. You'd actually be interested in where I come from if you were more interesting yourself. You're just like any other small-town bore.

Even as I thought it, I sounded wishy-washy, like I was sitting in an inter-rogation room with a Texas sheriff and trying to explain the difference be-tween Baroque and rococo. Besides, I was just being peevish. One thing in all this that had kind of disappointed me was that Chacal hadn't been more blown away by what I'd brought along. I'd have thought that the second he met me, if that's what to call it, he'd have been completely awestruck and it would just be like, Yessuh, massa Jed, suh. But he'd been totally unimpressed. He was all about contempt. I mean, I always had resentment and hatred and everything, too, but Chacal had true, pure, confident contempt. Classist, rac-ist, everythingist contempt. If you weren't a Harpy or an Ocelot, you were barely even fit to eat. I mean, like, to be eaten.

What a bastard, I thought. To know is definitely not to forgive. I could have killed him. But there was nowhere to go with that. Even if I could have bopped myself on the head or whatever, that was what Chacal wanted. Right?

On the other hand, he did have a point—the twenty-first century did seem a little improbable. From where I was writhing, anyway. Kind of arbitrary. Well, even if I had made up some of it—

Whoa. Wait. Hang on. That way lies madness.

Now the mittens were dipped in palm oil and they were massaging us, scraping us—

Ah cantzuc che, Chacal's mind shouted. You have the inner-eye dis-ease. That is, you're crazy. *Ah cantzuc che!!!*

I understand you're upset, I thought back, it's not every day your whole conception of the universe turns out to be totally bogus. Every other day, maybe. But still—

B'ukumil bin cu—

Cram it, I thought. *You're* the one nobody wants. 2 Jeweled Skull doesn't care about you. He wants to keep *me* around.

No.

Yes, he does, you know it's true.

He is keeping you just to torture you.

No, he's keeping me for something potentially profitable. You're out, loser.

Ah cantzuc che, ah cantzuc che . . .

Ouch. Shit. They were suturing up my chest. Although *suture* might be too grand a word, since it felt like they were using knitting needles and speaker wire. One million stitches later I felt them oiling us again, turning us over like we were a baby getting diapered. We felt them tie an embroidered breech-cloth around our groin and push wide-flaring spools through our distended earlobes. They brushed and redressed our stumpy hair. I guessed they were tying in extensions. It was like I was a shih tzu at a dog show. They fastened cuffs of stone scales onto our wrists and strapped an ornamental stone hip-ball celt to our right palm. We got some kind of rather heavy headdress and a ceremonial stone hipball yoke around our waist, much too heavy to use in a real game. Finally, they dusted us with a powder that Chacal knew from the smell was cinnabar and bone ash. With, of course, a hint of vanilla. I was sure we looked and smelled good enough for even a god to eat. However, that wasn't what we were here for.

The preparators stood us up, let Chacal get our balance—he was back in charge again, somehow, although right now he wasn't making trouble—and guided us out of the low door. We took nine steps into light. They set us down and positioned us on a stiff, smooth mat. The head preparator—who, I noticed, didn't use the mittens—peeled the sticky bandages or whatever they were off my eyes and licked the remaining goo out of them. They blinked open.

We were deep in a treesy gorge, facing east, twenty feet from the bank of a narrow stream. Everything was sheltered, cool green, and vertical, like the Hiroshige print of Fudo Falls. We could hear the water cascading in several stages from what seemed to be the crest of a limestone cliff about a hundred feet above us—even now, I or Chacal thought, at the end of the dry season—but we couldn't see it.

Around our mat a fifteen-arm square of turf had been burned down and covered with wild magnolias, like an artificial snowfall. It was dotted with shallow baskets of different sizes, each ostentatiously overflowing with a different commodity—coral beads, greenstone currency ax heads, cigars, rolls of undyed cotton flannel, vanilla beans, cacao beans, quite a little hoard for a guy like Chacal, who was, after all, just a prole from the provinces made good. Five men sat at the east side of the square. 2 Jeweled Skull was in the center, on a thick snakeweave state mat, wearing a harpy-eagle mask and headdress. He held a live red-tailed hawk on his right wrist, not hooded like in old-world falconry, but tied by its feet to a thick wooden bracelet. You could hardly see his skin under all the ropes of jade, and in the center of his chest there was a big oval mirror, like a Claude glass, ground out of a single chunk of pyrite.

Damn, he looked good.

Two representatives of the Harpy Hipball Brethren sat on his right. First there was Hun Xoc, the one with the smooth, amused face. He'd been Chacal's principal blocker, or backcourt man. Then there was a much older blood who looked like a smaller, scruffier version of Ben Grimm, the Thing from *The Fantastic Four*. I felt a sunbeam of affection for him pass through Chacal, despite or because of the dude's having beaten Chacal within inches of death on several occasions. His name and title clicked into my head: 3 Rolling, the yoke steward of the Harpy Hipball Society. The title basically meant he was the coach. He was Chacal's second uncle, and an adopted cousin of 2JS, and his nickname was 3 Balls, for the simple reason that he was a whole lot *más macho* than anybody. Before he'd become Chacal's mentor and first foster-father, he'd been a legendary blocker, never defeated but badly injured in his last game, eighteen war seasons ago. In that game he'd gotten pretty messed up on top of the extent to which he was already messed up, and now his left hand was frozen into a nonfunctional claw, and there were only two teeth and one eye poking out between the cauliflower folds of his wide face. But he still looked like if you got too close to him he might crush your neck in his good hand and rip your head off with his gums. Two local people sat on 2JS's female side, that is, on his left: first, a rustic gentleman in a tall blue cylindrical hat, the little hamlet's current burden-bearer. He was a roundhouser—that is, he was one of the class that lived in round huts instead of the squared-off houses the elite lived in—and he was way out of his social league in this group, but he still came off as dignified. Chacal knew him, of course, but he also gave me—I mean, me, Jed—the biggest rush of nostalgia I'd felt since I'd gotten here, since he looked 98 percent like Diego Xola, one of the *cofradios* from T'ozal, the village where I grew up. Things hadn't really changed that much, I thought, or wouldn't. Next to him—sitting on the ground, since he didn't rate a mat—was my, that is Chacal's, biological father. He was a coarse-looking and surprisingly young milpero, with bad teeth and a creased brow from carrying loads with a tumpline. His wide straw hat looked beachy and almost 1960s-moderne. His name was Wak Ch'o, that is, 6 Rat, a typical peasanty roundhouser name. Somewhere I knew that Chacal's mother was dead, not that she would have been allowed near here anyway, and not that it seemed to have made much of an impression on Chacal. But he had brothers, and they weren't around. Hmm. Anyway, you'd think seeing his father again would have brought up emotions like love and sadness and whatever in Chacal. Right? But if they did, I didn't feel it. All I felt from Chacal right now was shame. Or maybe his emotion was a little more specific than that, more like . . . hmm. Oh, I know. It was more like stage fright.

There were only two other people I could see from here. 3 Blue Snail, the hunchback with the throaty tenor, stood off by himself at the far right. He wore a blue feather cape and a short spiral headdress that made him look all head and mouth, like one of those deep-sea fish with the elastic stomachs. And then across the stream, about fifty arms away, a tall Harpy blood was standing in a little grove of spiny guava trees.

Then there were the three dressers behind us, I thought—counting everyone the way I do—and there was someone else, sitting close by on our right, who I wasn't supposed to look at. If there were any guards or porters around, they were out of our line of sight.

"Te'ex!"

3 Blue Snail shouted almost in my ear in his buzzy voice: "You!"

Chacal snapped to attention. To him it was like I'd felt once when I was fifteen and some cop just bullhorned me out of nowhere: "Hey, YOU! Pancho! You with the faggy hat! Freeze!"

"Te'ex m'a' ka' te!!" "You after-the-end shit-skin child!"

"Who were your mothers, and who were your fathers?
You don't know? Offal—fetus doesn't know."

2 Jeweled Skull held his hand out to us and turned his palm upward. It meant that if I—or rather Chacal, since he was pretty solidly in charge of our time-share body right now—had anything to say, we'd better say it now.

I screamed:

"Cal tumen hum pic hun, pic ti ku ti bin oc!"

that is,

"Fathermother, make me holy,
Give me death!"

Or rather, Chacal screamed it. Or maybe I should say he made us scream it. He couldn't move, of course, not because the voice was magic, but just because if you were a Harpy it was a voice you obeyed. But he knew what they were about to do, and he didn't want it. He wanted them to kill him, or us, in this body, his old body. He was fine with dying, of course, but he wanted to take me and his body with him.

2JS turned his hand palm down. Request declined. 3 Blue Snail took the cue and started coaxing us in his educated-baby singsong voice:

"You, One Chacal,
Great hipball striker, bone breaker,
You red one, you strong one,
Victor at Ix over 22 Sidewinder,
Over the Ocelots,
Victor at 20 Courts
Over Lord 18 Dead Rain
Of the Jaguars,
Why are you sitting there
Wearing that ugly skin?
Here is your real one.
All your three selves are here,
Here is your tree,
Here's your skin,
Here's your hawk-uay,
All to receive you.
They're all here,
Your fathers,
Your elder brothers,
Your younger brothers,
Your teammates . . ."

At the word *tree* our eyes focused across the stream, on the guava grove. Each of the trees had a few old offerings hanging from it, but one of them was absolutely festooned with new cotton streamers and strings of orange spondylus shells and wads of blood-spattered offering letters. Even if I hadn't had his memories to draw on, I would have guessed it was Chacal's *motz*, his root, that is, a tree that had been planted or at least dedicated when Chacal was born.

And 2JS had the hawk, of course. What about the skin?

Breaking form, Chacal strained our eyes to the right. Four arms away from us a naked teenage boy crouched on the flowers in a supplicant's position, smiling a slightly stupid beatific grin that I figured was the effect of presacrificial drugs. He was younger than Chacal, although since his hair said he'd passed his last initiation, he was officially at the same life-stage. Probably he had a similar birthday and name day, which were more important than his actual age. His face was only a bit like mine, that is, what I remembered through osmosis to be Chacal's. And I didn't even have a good idea of that, since around here mirrors were rare and water was underworldly and considered dangerous to stare at, and so Chacal had only seen his own reflection a few times. Still, his facial tattoos were the same as ours, double spirals of tiny dots emerging from the corner of his lips and spreading up onto the cheeks, and he had a fresh brand in the same spot above his hip where Chacal had the big hipball-impact scar.

Just what I need, I thought, another brain transplant. So I guess the other proxy, the one in the deer hunt, that was the fake proxy. This was the real proxy. Whatever.

"This is your garden,
Your dooryard, your hearthstones,
Your hammock. Here!
Over *here*! Leave that sack or
We'll all disrespect you, renounce you ..."

Well, hey, Chacal? I thought. This seems like a pretty clear choice to me. Come on, they've even got your stuff all packed. Take a hint, Clint.

He didn't respond, but he seemed to swell, like a clogged sinus on a depressurizing airplane. 3 Blue Snail halt-stepped over and crouched at my left side, like a hundred-pound newborn baby. He held a cylinder pot of something up to our mouth, and either because we were still parched or because Chacal couldn't help being at least physically obedient, we drank it down. Uk. I'd had some skanky cocktails around here already, but this one was a real puzzle. At first it seemed totally bland, just some kind of broth with a rusty undertone and a brainy texture like ground sweetbreads, but after it was down I started to get this gross chalky aftertaste. It reminded me of something— oh, yeah, I know. It was like this joke drink we used to make at school called a Phillips Screwdriver, that is, vodka and milk of magnesia. Now I felt like I'd had a dry sponge in my stomach that was puffing up to football, no, basketball, no, beach ball size. I noticed the residue in the cup was a periwinkle blue. Blue-corn syrup, maybe? Next 3BS took a stingray spine in one hand and two little clay cups in the other. He leaned forward and I felt his swollen fingers pinch my earlobe. He pushed the spine in and pulled it out with a little tearing sound.

Ears bleed a lot, and in less than a minute the cups were full. My two dressers kneed forward, took the cups, and, using sponges, started painting, or rather daubing, the proxy with my blood. When he was covered with red and already drying to brown, they moved back to me and my ball yoke. Inside me Chacal said something like No, no, no, but not in words. You're *over*, I thought. You're history. Take a hike, Ike. Meanwhile the dressers kept working on me. They plastered my earlobe and cleaned the extra blood off my chest. They cut off the wrist cuffs they'd just tied on. They unfastened my headdress. They took my loincloth, my stone toe rings, everything. When I was naked, they strapped all my regalia onto the poor teenager. He tottered under the weight. They came back and sharkskinned the blood-scroll tattoos off my cheeks. They rasped the huge hipball player's cauliflower calluses off my knees and elbows. I bet if my eyes had been different colors or anything else that would have identified me as Chacal, they would have dug those out too. It all hurt. I went through some changes.

By now 3BS was addressing the proxy, taking on the voices of Chacal's parents, grandparents, great-grandparents, and presumed founding ancestors, all of whom he named, and all of whom, it seemed, were presumed to be still living somewhere inside the grove of guava trees or the hills behind them. Each of the personae he took on begged Chacal to join them.

Sounds like a good deal, I thought at Chacal. If I were me I'd get out of this old body and into that kid right away. Out of the corner of our eye I watched the dressers cut a patch of skin out of the proxy's chest, like the one they'd stitched up on mine. Without interrupting his harangue, 3BS handed them something. It was the strip of glyphs they'd peeled off my chest on the deer course. It had been tanned, and now it was all supple and translucent. It was a little confusing, because I'd thought they'd used it on the skin of the other proxy, the one from the deer hunt. Maybe they'd forged a substitute in the meantime and switched it again. Or maybe the skin of the deer-hunt proxy wasn't still hanging up on display. Maybe they'd gotten to take it home. Whatever. Anyway, they started to sew it onto the proxy's chest with gut thread tied to an eyeless thorn needle.

"*K'aanic teech chaban,*" 3BS said. Roughly, "This is your last chance." He set a wide-flared bowl on the mat between my knees and picked up an ornate jade vomiting spatula, or rather vomicus, to use the scholarly word. Great, I thought. Will the real Chacal please throw up? He pulled down my lower jaw—for a second I got a stab of fear that he was going to tear it off—and then with the other hand he inserted the stick in my throat.

Ek—

The sinus burst, the pressure released, and I erupted. Three waves of sour yellow liquid vomit crashed through my throat and spattered into the bowl. I thought I'd turned inside out. I collapsed on the mat. I'm dead, I thought, they got me too. Out of the corner of my eye I saw the proxy take the bowl and drink it in one draft. When he was finished they poured a cup of balche into the bowl, swished that around, and made him drink that too. Across the stream the tall blood at the edge of the woods raised a big black steatite ax in a long handle, threatening to chop down Chacal's birth tree.

"I, Chacal beneath you, am happy in this vessel," the boy choked out as soon as he could talk. He'd been rehearsed, of course, but you could tell he believed it all. It was a big honor for him. Actually, that's putting it mildly. For him it was like a royal wedding. He was a regular little Lady Diana Spencer. Yeah, you're a lucky kid, all right—

Wait.

Chacal was gone.

It was true. I'd only just realized it, but he was gone.

The blood put down the ax.

I felt empty and stupid, like, along with whatever else, I'd just vomited out about twenty feet of intestines and two-thirds of my brain cells. But at least it was me doing the feeling. One of the dressers—a different one now, not an untouchable—reached into a bag and sifted a handful of white feathers, or actually I think it was eagle down, over my wet body.

Each of the nine guests of honor walked to the new Chacal, greeted him, and returned to his place. 2 Jeweled Skull was the last. He extended his foot and the new Chacal touched its underside. It was an unusual honor. When he got back to his mat, 2JS picked up a conch shell engraved with red blood-scroll clouds and blew it, like Triton. It had a feeble, apprehensive sound. We all waited.

There was a chunking sound of little clay bells, like a St. Lazarus rattle, behind us, to the northwest. I didn't look around, but soon enough the Harpy's *nacom,* that is, 2 Jeweled Skull's house sacrificer, walked slowly into view, like he owned all the time in the universe. His skin was blackened with carbon and he had a black turban bristling with black catbird feathers and a giant black bill-mask that made him look like Daffy Duck's evil twin. The neurons in Chacal's brain didn't want to look at him or think about him, but my mind found his name anyway: 18 Salamander. Two little boys followed him, twins about eight or nine years old and with carbonized skin like his.

"Fathermothers, make me holy, grant me death," the proxy—or maybe I should call him the new Chacal—whispered. The nacom's two assistants helped the poor kid stretch out on the mat and held his arms and legs as the sacrificer made a transverse incision across his abdomen. He reached into the cut and up under the rib cage, still holding the knife, using it to part the diaphragm and detach the heart from the aorta and vena cavae. It took him nearly twenty seconds or so, but finally he pulled the heart out, leaving the knife in its place, and set it on a dish of corn porridge. I wasn't supposed to be watching, but everyone seemed to have pretty much forgotten me, and I kept one eye cracked as I lay on the mat. It turns out that a heart can go on beating for a while after it's removed, and in fact this one even kept squirting pink mist for about fifteen beats until it started just pumping air, making little squeaks, and ran down. I watched sideways as the nacom's assistants lifted the new Chacal into a big basket, curled him up like a sleeping dog, and tied the wicker lid over him with four complicated hitch knots that spelled the glyphs for four hundred times four hundred, an idiom for eternity. Evidently they didn't want him to come creeping back. Even before they were done, 3 Blue Snail was standing over me, squinting at the sun in his eyes, his blue-clay body paint running in the heat, asking me to promise not to tell anyone my new inner name, that is, the name of my new uay. I promised. If anyone ever found out your real name, they could use it in a curse, and you'd be an easy target for whatever demonish critter they got to go after you. He bent down, whispered it in my bleeding ear, and told me to repeat it. I tried but it was hard to talk around a mouthful of what seemed to be either blood or vomit, so I swallowed what I could of it and the new dresser wiped the rest off my chin. 3 Blue Snail must have thought I was stalling, because he rapped me on the side of the head with his knuckle and made the dresser back off. I whispered the name. He made me repeat it twice before he stood back up and announced my new outer, or revealed, name. Like most names involving animals it had nothing to do with my uay:

"10 Skink," he said. "Finished."

Bummer, I thought. I always get the uncoolest names. Damn.

Behind me someone had lit the hut on fire. I guess it was just a one-use disposable item. I lifted my head and saw the nacamob's assistants hoist the big basket onto their shoulders and start off, followed by a line of porters with all the other tchotchkes. Chacal's father and the burden bearer followed them down the trail to the village, shaking maracas to keep away the Xib'alb'ans. I felt lonely. 2 Jeweled Skull untethered the hawk. It didn't move at first, so he shooed at it until it flapped grumpily up into the trees.

(37)

They hustled me a long way both uphill and downhill. I was still pretty weak from—well, from everything. When I fell asleep they carried me. They gave me hot water. Hun Xoc, who was running the operation, took a cone of salt out of his own traveling bag and let me lick it. At one point I noticed I was moving in a funny way. I'm swinging, I thought, I'm on the end of a rope. I mean, not figuratively. They were lowering me down horizontally, like a girder, out of the light, into a space full of echoing clicks and whispers and the smells of chocolate, urine, pine pitch, and wet stone. It was dark. Other hands took the bundle, unfastened it from the ropes, and carried it about forty paces, set it down, and unrolled me onto a drift of corn husks. When my eyes adapted, it turned out I was in a wide cavern that, after all my cooping up, seemed as large as the Hyperbowl. The pile of husks was near a storage niche braced with cedar logs and stacked with hills of unhusked cacao pods and tanned deerhides reeking of natural ammonia, as far as possible from a zone of green sunlight that sifted down from a ragged oculus thirty arms across and fifty arms overhead, fringed with what I first thought were exposed roots and then saw were stalactites. The space was filled with scaffolding, struts, and ropes and buttresses and drying racks, but the main feature was what had to be the world's largest rope ladder, a strip of about sixty twenty-to-ten-arm logs looped into thick braided cables and strung at a steep angle from our side of the floor to the far edge of the oculus. Five nearly naked workmen clambered around on the ladder like sailors on the shrouds of a square-rigged ship, guiding down a bundle of board-hard untanned deerskins. There were at least thirty other workers in the cave, and some of them must have been looking at us with too much curiosity because Hun Xoc, who'd already climbed down, barked at them to get back to what they were doing. They stood me up, but I still needed two people to help me walk, not because I was shaky from all the abuse—although it didn't help—but because with Chacal's consciousness gone, I was having to relearn how to control my new body. The worst thing was trying to turn left and turning right instead. We steered around a big natural impluvium in the floor and passed a male cook in women's clothing who was slapping the morning tortillas over three small hearthstones. I guessed he was what anthropologists would call a berdache, a sex straddler who could do women's work in a male space. A sort of woven-clay chimney rose over the hearth, almost like a stovepipe, and twisted up the side of the ladder to the outdoors. We had to duck under a rack with a brace of just-killed jabiru storks tied together by the necks and bunches of plucked Muscovy ducks—which, despite the name, do not come from Muscovy. I noticed how hungry I still was. Past the kitchen zone there was a raised wooden platform where a couple of old Harpy accountants in monkey headbands were counting out measures of seed corn and passing them to assistants, who poured the kernels into corn-husk packets and tied them up with colored thread. Rolls of rubberized canvas and banana bunches of fifty-gauge torpedo cigars were stacked on wicker sort-of pallets, away from the walls but out of the reach of the rain. No wonder the Harpies have been in charge of this town for three hundred years, I thought. They're survivalists.

They steered me out of the main room into a dark diagonal gash that led to a side passage, half-natural and half-hewn-out, with the most dangerous spicules ground away to a level just above our heads and an irregular floor sloping up at thirty degrees. Before we were quite in the dark zone, they stopped in the middle of a sort of antechamber and called back the dressers. We waited. The dressers showed up and cleaned me up again. At least you don't have to do your own toilette around here. When I was at school I went out for a while with this woman from India—in fact, she was once Miss India, although I don't expect you to believe that—and I was surprised to find out that she'd never washed her own hair, not once, in her entire life. It turned out that wasn't unusual in India, where the maids have maids, and they have maids. So around here, even a jailbird like me got a stylist. When that was done they stood me up and we went on into total blackness, feeling our way along a ridged path cut into the limestone floor. We spiraled deeper into the mountain. There was less ventilation here and less-healthful smells. My feet felt a floor leveled with clay and the passage widened into an L-shaped room with a dim fuzz of daylight. In here the walls had been cut into shelves and packed with unornamented jars and, above them, ranks of little clay ancestors looking squalid and ad hoc. One shelf held a row of these sort of pornographic wood statues of gargoyley old men groping young women. Each was kitschier than the last. Well, so they have lousy taste here too. Not everything from the past is great. One just tends to think it is because it's mainly the good stuff that gets saved, and the only time you do see how most of everything from the past was junk is when everything happens to get preserved all at once, like in Pompeii. Now, *that* was a tacky town. The Coconut Grove of ancient—

Whoops. They ducked-and-pulled me through a deerskin flap I hadn't seen and steered me thirty steps up a torchlit ramp to another flap, this one scaled with shell beads. There was an older Harpy blood sitting in front of it, and he and the captain of the porters exchanged a nonsense code greeting. The old blood stood up, lifting the flap, and flattened himself against the wall to let us pass. There was a cardamomy smell of wild allspice. Hun Xoc and I crouched into a small tertiary chamber the size of a refrigerator and then through another little door into a bubble-shaped room about the size of a one-car garage. There was no natural light, but there were two rushlights— reeds dipped in tallow—burning at the far end, and instead of the smoke's filling up the place it practically shot up into a crack in the far wall, caught in a steady cool breeze. Just from the air you could tell it was what spelunkers call a dry room, that is, a room sheltered from rain and above the flow of any running water, with nonporous walls that wouldn't mold. The far wall was artificial, made of cut blocks, but the side walls had been roughed out of the natural cave, and on our right two gray flowstone stalagmites had been left relatively untrashed. The largest was carved into an old-fashioned half-statue of a Harpy lord. His seating date was still readable as 9 Ahau, 3 Sip on the first day of the eighth b'ak'tun—that is, September 7, 41 AD, 244 days after the assassination of Caligula. There were old covered offering jars around its base, most of them broken. The rest of the library—or maybe I should say records room or *genizah*—was filled with neat stacks of breadbox-sized chests. Four of them were open and in one I could see a screenfold book half-buried in rock salt.

Including Hun Xoc and me, there were eight people in the room. 2 Jeweled Skull sat on a cushion at the far side, with his legs wrapped in a quilted cotton blanket. A big guard squatted on his right-hand side, facing down at the floor. He stiffened as we came in but didn't look up. He was about a head taller than and twice as heavy as anyone else, and he was older than the other guards I'd seen, which maybe meant he was trusted. He wore a light quilted padding on his shoulders and hips, and according to the tattoos on his calves, during his military career he'd offered eight captives to One Harpy. Two people squatted between me and the guard, also on the left side of the room. The first was a thin old man with a dark manta over his shoulders and with his head wrapped up in a kind of veil under a hat, like a pith helmet with mosquito netting. I couldn't see much of him, but he seemed familiar. There was something odd about his forearms, but I couldn't quite put my finger on what it was. Next, closest to me, there was the same monkey-costumed scribe who I'd seen before in the red-feathered room. He had a long, thin paintbrush tied to his index finger, and without looking at us he went on with what he was doing, copying tallies of something onto sheets of dried palm leaf in quick sloppy columns of dots and bars. In fact, the word *scribe* sounds a little grand and monastic for him. It might be less misleading to call him a combination stenographer and accountant. Or maybe we should just translate his title literally: "remembrancer."

Three other men sat against the right-hand wall. 2JS's grand-uncle 12 Unwinding was closest to me, and then there was 2JS's great-great-grandfather 40 Weasel, and finally someone else, whose wrappings were too old and crumbly for me to read, sat close to 2JS's left hand. They were dead, of course, and semimummified—that is, they were basically shrunken heads, probably stuffed with the allspice, sitting on top of bundles of a few key bones, ulnas and fibulas and so on, each on a little platform like an Indian tea table, all in a line on the left wall. Their skulls would be buried somewhere else for safety along with the rest of their bones and favorite wives and whatever. Present but not voting.

2JS spread his hands apart in a blossoming gesture, the Maya equivalent of a shrug.

Hun Xoc positioned me on a subordinate's mat. I turned down my eyes and automatically my right hand moved to my left shoulder. I heard Hun Xoc crouch out behind me. 2JS spoke:

"Again, take out your worm."

What the hell? I wondered. I thought we'd gone through this. By now, I'd caught on to the protocol around here enough to know that if I didn't have anything to say, I should just shut up. I looked down at the ground. Hell, I thought. He's still going to kill me. Hell, hell, hell.

"I knock you the ninth hipball," he said. It was like saying, "This is your last chance."

I looked up.

"Jed?" I asked. "Get out of there, okay? Or just stifle. Please. Take one for the team."

Naturally, there was a pause, and naturally, nothing happened. If the Jed in his head did anything special on hearing me, 2JS didn't say so.

"Will he ever listen to you?" 2JS asked finally.

I said I didn't know.

I suggested, delicately, that 2JS might be able to purge himself of me the way he'd had me purged of Chacal.

"What is the Jed inside you saying?" I asked.

"He is screaming," 2JS said.

I shuddered. Damn. Imagine that poor larval retarded me in there, writhing under the lashes of 2JS's indomitable will. Wow. That must really suck—

"I see it but don't know its names. In me,
Your life is like a pile of broken pots,"

he said, for the first time sounding almost uncertain.

Huh, I thought. Well, at least now we're talking. I was beginning to learn to trust Chacal's body's automatic responses, to worry about the big decisions and otherwise let his body do what it did instinctively. This time it knew the correct way of not responding, and without missing a beat I clicked my tongue and gestured, "As you above me say." Don't volunteer information, I thought. The more you tell him, the more expendable you become. Right? He needs you around to help him make sense of the alien mishmash in his head. Not that he couldn't just torture it all out of you anyway. But maybe he doesn't really want to torture you. Maybe he isn't really that bad, and he just got angry because he felt violated. Anybody would have. Right?

Damn. Now I was feeling irrationally guilty. Or maybe not that irrationally. After all, I was a cocephalic colonialist. Forget it, I thought, don't start feeling sorry for him. He'd kill you in a second.

"You underneath me
Have cost me a son
And have ruined our household,"

he said.

What? I thought. Son? Oh, right.

As I think I mentioned, I'd already guessed what had happened, that 2JS's son had been sacrificed in my place when I spoiled the ceremony on the mul. I didn't know whether to pretend I didn't know about it or not, so I asked for more information.

> "I underneath you
> Now beg absolution,
> But I underneath you
> Do not understand
> How I birthed this catastrophe,
> How it unfolded."

It was the closest thing to asking a direct question that I could manage, since the language made it almost impossible for an inferior to question a superior. And even this much wasn't exactly polite. Still, 2JS did answer. He told me—in a formal, accusative way—that two solar years ago he had been asked to give the ruling house, the Ocelots, a gift to commemorate the re-naming and reseating of their patriarch, 9 Fanged Hummingbird, as Lord of the Fertilizing Waters and k'alomte'—warlord—of Ix. The gift would either have had to be an absolution of debt—which I gathered he'd been unwilling to do—or one of his own sons, as a proxy to be used in 9 Fanged Humming-bird's mock autosacrifice. But since 2 Jeweled Skull only had two biological sons, he'd been able to negotiate a compromise: One of his adopted sons—the Harpy House's hipball champion, Chacal—would throw a high-ceremonial hipball game against 9 Fanged Hummingbird, and then, as the "new hipball," or the loser, throw himself down off the mul in place of 9 Fanged Humming-bird.

Then, during the ceremony, when Chacal had spoiled the whole thing by apparently freaking out, 2 Jeweled Skull had had Chacal wrapped up and saved for later—for an "excremental killing," as he put it—and sent a messen-ger down to his two primary sons, who had been standing in the Harpy House formation in the plaza at the base of the mul. The elder son, 23 Ash, immedi-ately climbed the stairs. The preparators had quickly painted him in the sac-rificial blue, and he dove.

2 Jeweled Skull paused.

Damn, I thought. No matter how cold-ass you are, losing a kid's got to hurt. *Here is the firestone and the wood, but where is the sheep for a burnt offering?* Do I apologize again? Somehow it didn't feel right. Instead I said I'd do whatever I could to make up for it.

He said,

> "You underneath me,"
> Would need to give more than your head,
> More than twenty times twenty *tunob'* of pain,
> More than your ancestors' children."

Sorry, I thought.
He said,

> "Also 8 Steaming's sons jawboned themselves,
> And 3 Far's son, the deer hunt's following sun."

What this meant—and it took me a minute to figure it out—was that the three bloods I'd beaten up during the hunt had been so humiliated that each of them had poked a hole through his platysma muscle—just behind his chin—pushed a rope up through the hole, pulled it out through his mouth, tied it, and then tied the rope onto a tree or whatever and fallen backward, yanking off his own jawbone.

And as if that weren't bad enough, he added that one Harpy blood had been killed and four were injured in my suicide attempt on the traverse. One of the injured bloods was crippled permanently and was asking to be killed.

There must have been porters hurt, too, I thought. But of course that wouldn't matter to him. I started to say that it wasn't I who'd leapt down the slope but Chacal, but I stopped. 2JS already knew that, and it didn't matter. I still held responsibility for the event.

And even all that was nothing, he said, next to what you might call the religiopolitical damage. People were saying that Chacal's scandalous screw-up on the mul had made the Earthtoadess sick and had turned what should have been a little coughing spell into a guts-vomiting seizure. Today, couriers had come in from the coast with accounts of how huge the eruption in San Martín really was. As always, gloomy types were saying it was the end of the world.

Well, gee, I thought, maybe taking credit for the eruption in my speech on the mul actually hadn't been such a brilliant idea. Oh, well, they can't all be gems, right?

"So," he said, coming to the end of his litany of woe, "what can you offer to to compensate?"

"I still know some things that are going to happen—"

"Like the Earthtoadess's seizure?" he asked.

I said yes.

"9 Fanged Hummingbird had already named that sun, two tunob ago."

Hell. Wasn't my prediction more accurate? I asked.

He said yes, and that he'd used it to time the deer hunt to wind down at the right time. What else did I know? he asked. What would happen to the Harpy House after his death?

I had to say that we didn't know, but that as far as we could tell, Ix would be abandoned within twenty-five years. Or, at least, much of the irrigated land in the area would return to an uncultivated state, occupational residues and trash deposits would drop to near zero, and there wouldn't be any further stone buildings or monuments.

"And what will happen to me after my death, in the next k'atun?" he asked.

What? Oh, he means his head and skeleton. I said I didn't know. He didn't move, and the tone of his voice didn't change, but somehow you could tell he was losing patience fast. Shouldn't he already know these things? I wondered. I snuck a glance up at his face and was a little surprised at something I thought I saw. There was something in there behind the poker eyes, something almost maybe feeble, or rather pained, or even despairing. He asked about his intended heir, 17 Jog. As it turned out, this wasn't his other son but a favorite nephew whom he'd sent away to Oxwitzá, that is, the site in Belize that in the twenty-first century would be called Caracol.

I said I didn't know, but I didn't recall the name turning up on any monuments. This isn't going well, I thought.

"And will our descendants suckle us on our lights?" he asked. He meant would they burn offerings to him and his family on their various anniversaries.

I started to talk about how there was still a generalized respect for the ancestors in what we would call traditional Maya communities, and how they do burn offerings on some of the same festivals, and whatever, but the more I said the less convincing it sounded. As far as specifics went, I started to say, your names—well, frankly, by the end of the next b'ak'tun your name will probably be forgotten even by your own descendants, and your inscriptions, if any, will be covered up for sixty k'atunob' until they get dusted off and mistranslated by a bunch of PhD'ed grave robbers. "That is, unless I get back," I said, thinking of what seemed like a clever segue. In fact, I told him, we could even write down all his accomplishments and the history of his whole dynasty, and I could take it back with me and make sure my people made a fuss over him—

He made an audible intake of breath. It was like saying, "You have our permission to shut up."

I did.

He asked what was going to happen over the remaining 256 lights of this current tun.

"10 Jade Smoke of K'an Ex will be seated on 4 Raining, 17 Ending," I said. "He'll capture 2 Sparkstriker of Lakamha 23 lights after that." [Note to self: too many confusing names. Go back and explain what the hell is going on. —Jed]

"And how much smoke does that send my way?" 2JS asked. That is, why should I care?

"Maybe no smoke," I said. Damn. I was running out of A material. Maybe I should just the hell ask him about the Game. No, don't. You're still on thin quicksand around here.

"What else?"

Hell. Come on, JD, think of something. Maybe just make something up. Then at least he won't have already seen it. Except, no, really, he's a pretty shrewd character. Don't try to fool somebody who's already proven himself to be sharper than you are. Just let him decide you can help out around the house. Okay.

"I can help Harpy House prevail in any fight," I said. My Ixian sounded a little stilted, but at least now I was yacking away in it without having to think too much first. "Look in Jed's memories for weapons."

"What weapons?" he asked.

I described explosions and said there had to be some in my memories. He seemed to understand. I explained how I could mix up gunpowder in less than twenty days of processing.

Instead of answering, 2 Jeweled Skull lit a cigar on a rushlight. He put a finger over one nostril and sucked in the smoke through the other.

"If anyone saw a weapon like that," he said, "if anyone even heard of it, they'd say we bought it from a scab caster."

Scab casters were people who could give you skin diseases by breathing on you from a distance. By extension the term meant any makers of esoteric mischief, that is, like witches or sorcerers. A scab caster might be human or not entirely human, and he or she might be alive or dead or not entirely either. But in any event, if you were one of the pillars of the community like 2JS, you didn't deal with them.

Maybe, I said, we—I mentally italicized the *we*—could just chef up a few longbows at first and train a squad of bloods to use them. Bows might be a novelty around here—which in itself was pretty odd, come to think of it, I thought—but nobody would think they were supernatural.

"I know what bows are," he said. "Forest domeheads shoot birds with them. They are not to be touched by fineheads." By *fineheads* he meant us Maya elite, who, as I think I mentioned, had acutely sloped forcheads. They were made by swaddling newborns in a sort of frame with a slanted board pressing on their face, and they were considered elegant and de rigueur. *Domeheads* could mean anybody who couldn't afford such things, either domestic thralls, foreigners, or, in this case, uncivilized tribes.

"But even without new weapons I can still help our house exalt itself," I said. "What I can do"—I tried to think of a word for *technology*—"the crafts I know are not just for building things. They are a different way of strategizing."

"You mean a better way," 2 Jeweled Skull said.

Not necessarily, I said. They might be worse. Tetchy bastard, I thought. Well, at least I've got him talking. Okay. What I've got to do here, is, I've got to make him think I can be the best consigliere since Karl Rove.

"Suppose some of our bloods were caught by a raider," I said. "If they shot to kill, in formation, instead of trying to take prisoners. They—"

He cut me off with a "Zzzzz!" sound, the equivalent of "Shhh."

"The Choppers are nearby," he half whispered, "in our household, around our hearthstones."

Choppers? I wondered. I didn't know what they were, except I had an automatic sense from Chacal's neurons that they were living people who were more powerful than we were.

"When you above me say Choppers," I asked, "do you mean the Ocel—"

"*ZZZZZZ!!*"

I shut up. I kept my eyes on the ground. There was silence, except for the sound of the monkey remembrancer's brush on the dry leaves. I snuck a look at him out of the corner of my left eye. He made a few more strokes and stopped. I realized he was taking notes on our conversation in some kind of shorthand. Hmm.

I counted another ten beats. I looked up at 2JS. His face was like wood behind the tobacco haze. His eyes had hardened. Stupid, Jed, I thought. Stupid, stupid.

"The Overlord of the Choppers has been seen prowling here, in his hunting skin," 2JS said. He must mean 9 Fanged Hummingbird, I thought. And they think that 9 Fanged Hummingbird can morph himself into an ocelot, and slink around his subordinates' towns at night, and listen to them through stone walls with his feline superhearing. And if I ever forget it, and I say anybody's actual name, it might alert his wandering uay. And I'll be in trouble. Right. Got it.

Still . . .

"You can't still believe that," I said. "Look in my memories, you know that can't be done."

2JS didn't answer. Instead, he took a long nose-puff and blew a chestful of smoke at me. At first I felt a zap of offendedness, and then I realized that he hadn't meant it as an insult. He was trying to purify the area against any lingering Jed-pollution. Even after going through every purging ritual in the book I was still Typhoid Marty. The smoke was a lot stronger than the twenty-first-century product. Wild tobacco, I thought. Yuck. Like I said, I chewed but I didn't smoke, except when I was making an offering, like to Maximón or whoever. But now . . . hmm. Oddly enough, I realized I wanted a cigar. I guess it was another of Chacal's hardwired habits. Yuck. Yum. Yuck and yum at the same time.

I sat. Okay, I thought, this time let him speak first. And don't try to convince him about stuff he's not going to get. Don't try to turn him on to the scientific worldview. If he still believes in warlocks and were-jaguars, let him.

And also, I was starting to understand that in this society, no one was ever alone. Even just the way 2JS had these other people here right now—the monkey, the guard, and the other character with the veil—while we were having a conversation that he wanted to keep secret—well, for him, this was like being alone. Around here, even if you didn't happen to have someone else's consciousness in your head, you were almost never alone physically. Nobody here slept alone, or even with one other person, but rather in the same small room with the whole family and, for the upper classes, servants and guards. No one ate alone. Nobody traveled alone, nobody worked a field alone, and nobody lived alone. When people did happen to get separated for a minute from the rest of the pack, they tended to get very nervous. So even in ordinary life, even if you were just an ordinary person, there was no opportunity for secrecy.

"So what shall I above you do with you?" he asked.

I decided to show a scrap of backbone.

"You over me must already have a purpose for me," I said, "or else why go to all this expense?"

After three beats I thought he might be smiling, not from his mouth but from a bunching of his cheeks. At least there's a grain of humor to this guy.

"What makes you under me think I have saved you for something pleasant?" he asked.

Uh-oh. I didn't know what to say.

"I still want you in the dark," he said. It was like saying, "I'm still furious at you."

I looked up, and despite myself, I looked into his eyes. There was a click-and-whir of unorthodox contact. Eyeballing was seldom if ever done around here. Still, I couldn't look away.

His eyes weren't friendly.

"Now, you underneath me," he said, "I owe you a dark debt." He paused. "I am going to do many things to you."

Oh, *chingalo*, I thought. Think of something.

I looked around frantically. I looked at the guard. He was still crouching, unmoving, two arms to 2JS's right, facing away from him and staring down at an empty spot on the red cotton groundcloth. I looked at the monkey remembrancer. He'd stopped writing and was cleaning his brush in a leather water cup. I looked at the stacks of baskets and bales. I looked at the old dude in the veil.

Huh. I realized what was odd about his arms. They were hairy.

As you probably know, Native Americans don't have a lot of body hair. I have exactly—I mean, my Jed body, which was probably relaxing with a piña colada about now—has exactly five chest hairs. And that body's more than a third Spanish. Around here, in these old days—well, I hadn't seen any body or facial hair at all yet. But I'd known it wasn't unheard of, since in the twenty-first century I'd seen more than a couple of old Maya figurines with beards. Maybe you had to be from some special family to grow them, or you had to be over seventy years old, or something. I looked at him more closely. He had a pebble in his hand. And from the way he held it—

He's a sun adder, I thought.

No wonder he'd been allowed to be here this whole time, to hear all this stuff . . . the more your adder knew about your business, the better. That is, the farther ahead he'd be able to read for you. Of course he has to be trusted, a total confidant. Like a confessor. This guy was probably only in-house. Maybe he was even a bit of a captive, since he'd know secrets.

I turned to the adder.

"I next to you request a Game," I said.

(38)

The adder's head tilted slightly under the veil.

"I don't own anything right now," I went on, "but what I can find to give, in this light or the next or the next, I will offer, to you and to Lady Turd, who is the Cradler of Tonight, 9 Darkness, 11 Rainfrog"—it was Monday, March 28, AD 664—"and to Mam and the Waiting Woman, the smokers of the Game."

Silence.

The veil twitched. I interpreted the motion to mean the head under it was turning to look at 2JS. I looked at 2JS. He looked back. There was that shock of eye contact again, and before I turned down again I thought I could see a sort of weary wisdom behind his yellowing lenses, not anything passive or placid but an amused awareness of what was possible and what wasn't.

2JS said

> "My adder underneath me, 7 Prong,
> Reads only for his chiefs,
> But he can play a bone-count duel against you."

Oh, hell, I thought. Duel. Great. 7 Prong, huh? Charming. I wondered whether they'd kill me if I lost. Probably, I thought—

Suddenly the guard whirled silently around and faced us, ready to lunge forward and strangle me. 2JS must have signaled him somehow. He signed to the guard in a language Chacal didn't know. I realized the guard was deaf. Probably he'd been deafened intentionally. And he'd been looking away, so he couldn't read our lips. I thought 2JS might be telling him to take me away and feed me to the armadillos or whatever they normally fed people to, but instead the guard crouched to the back of the room and, with a symphony of creaks and crackles, climbed up onto a stack of baskets. I looked back at 2JS and then at 7 Prong. He'd unwrapped his veil and taken off his hat. He was older than 2JS, and there were streaks of gray in his long pigtail, and his face would have been nondescript if he hadn't had a beard. But he did, and here, it was shocking. It wasn't thick, and it was four inches long or so, but it was respectable, and tied into a cylinder like those Egyptian pharaohs' beards, and I couldn't help staring at it. His body was thin and old, and without any tattoos, except a row of four penny-sized blue dots on his left shoulder. But it was hairy. His eyes were bleary and friendly. He touched his right hand to his left elbow, which was the closest thing to shaking hands or nodding or whatever that seemed to get done in these sorts of sit-downs. I did the same, except, since he was senior to me, I touched the arm just above my elbow. Hi, guy, I thought. Hi from one adder to another. Brotherhood of Gamers. No problem.

Without getting up 7 Prong turned so that he was facing me. I turned so that we were facing each other. He got out a pouch of tobacco, poured out a few leaves, and popped about half of them into his mouth. I took the rest. We chewed. Damn, this stuff is strong, I thought. He put a bowl of sand between us. I rubbed some of the tobacco juice into my thigh—there was no stain there on Chacal's thigh, I noticed, this was his first time—and spat the rest out into the sand bowl. A minute later he did the same and pushed the bowl away. Meanwhile the guard had come back with a two-arms-long roll of thick cloth. He set it down between us and unrolled it. It felt as though the Rockefeller Center Christmas tree had just sprung into being, fully lit, in the small, gloomy room.

It was a woven-feather game board. The time quadrants glowed carmine and buttery amber, and even the black quadrant was so glossy and Ethiopic that you felt you could fall into it. This was one of those freaks of artifice that you can't believe was made by human fingers, like Gobelin tapestries, say, or Rajshahi silk brocades, or that crystal-beaded Romeo Gigli snood that Kristin McMenamy wore on the cover of Italian *Vogue* in October of 1993. It was octagonal, instead of square, and instead of circular bins, like the boards we'd made from Taro's design, this one just had a tuft of quetzal-throat emerald at each of the 260 points. But I was still disappointed. I'd been hoping there'd be something new to me in the design, something that would help answer the questions I'd brought with me . . . but instead, no matter how gorgeous it was, it was pretty much like the layout Taro had worked out from the picture in the Codex.

Damn.

2JS slid off his cushion, kneed over to us, and turned the mat a few degrees counterclockwise so that the directions of the colors were correct. As it turned out—or, I suppose, intentionally—7 Prong was in the southeast, the Harpies' direction, and I was playing for the black northwest.

Like a good referee, 2JS ran through the rules. This version was a bit like the one-on-one Game I'd played a few rounds of with Tony Sic, but it was more similar to something my mother and I used to play. Although we hadn't had the big board, of course. Anyway, it's bit like Battleship, because you each have five points on the board corresponding to your throws, and you have to guess your opponent's points and keep him from guessing yours. But to "guess" you have to move your stone onto that point, so you can also block the other guy with your seeds, to some extent. But then you try to fake him out by blocking decoy points and whatever. Anyway, you couldn't lie—especially since 2JS knew what the points were anyway—but you could conceal and misdirect. I guess you could say it was also a little like Stratego—which is one of my favorite games—because there's almost no chance, but it's not perfect information either. Of course, it's different from the real Sacrifice Game that you'd use for reading out someone's days, but not entirely different. Maybe it's about as different as gin rummy is from poker.

The guard brought out a pot with a hole in the side. 7 Prong—who still hadn't spoken except in sign language—looked away. I put my hand in the hole. 2JS looked down into the pot. I had to choose any five numbers between 0 and 260. I tried to make my choices as random as possible—which isn't easy—and signed them to 2JS. I took my hand out of the pot. 2JS put his hand in, held the pot so I could see, and repeated my choices. He got them all right. Next I turned away and he did the same thing with 7 Prong. When they were done I turned back to the board. 2JS loaned me a quartz pebble and nine tz'ite-tree seeds. 7 Prong took out his own stone and seeds. We each touched our right hand to the ground at the side of the board. It was like the way you nod before you start a game of Go. Since he was senior to me, 7 Prong moved first. He scattered the seeds and moved his quartz pebble out to 11 Ahau.

De todos modos. I scattered the seeds. I moved. He moved.

Hmm. Okay. I think it's going to go this way, no, wait, it'd go this way. Okay, first this happens, then they react to it by this, okay—

Damn it. I couldn't think the way I would have in my Jed body. I moved anyway. 7 Prong moved.

Okay. Come on, Jed. Come on, Chacal's brain. Focus.

I thought. I was starting to sweat. Since we didn't have a clock, I figured 2JS would interrupt and demand a move if I took too long.

Okay. Come on. This way. That way. Here. There. At least Chacal had a high IQ, I thought. Imagine how bad it could have been. I might've gotten zapped into some idiot. Also, the Game's really just a way of opening logic up to insight. You don't have to be the greatest number-cruncher. Although it doesn't hurt. I moved. He moved. I moved. He moved.

Hmm.

I moved.

Correct, 7 Prong signed. Ha! I'd gotten one of his numbers.

Okay. I was starting to get the hang of using Chacal's head. At least my old skilz hadn't all been in the lower levels of my brain. Wherever they were, they'd made the trip along with my Jedditude. Taro had been right, as usual.

7 Prong got one of my numbers. I got another of his, and then another. On the hundred-ninety-second move, 7 Prong put both of his hands flat down on the mat, signaling that he resigned.

Damn, I thought. That's it?

I'd been disappointed before, but now—even though I supposed I should have been happy that I'd passed a test—I was crushed. *Mierda,* I thought, this guy doesn't know anything. Was he just a no-talent 2JS had brought in to discombobulate me? Or maybe they weren't any better at the Game back here than we were back there. Maybe this whole thing was a waste. Or maybe I'd just ended up in the wrong place. Great, I'm way out here in the boonies with a bunch of bush-league losers. Hell, hell, hell and prostration.

7 Prong signed something. 2JS signed back. I didn't catch what they were saying. 7 Prong signed, "Agreed." He took a fingerful of tobacco out of his pouch and popped it in his mouth.

"*T'aac a'an,*" 2JS said. "Rematch."

"Agreed," I clicked.

The guard handed 2JS a big clay bowl. It was full of salt. 2JS reached down into the salt, rummaged around, and pulled out two tiny clay bottles, each sealed with wax. He put the first bottle down on a small cotton cloth on the mat in front of him and folded the cloth over the bottle. The guard handed him a hammerstone. Delicately, 2JS crushed the bottle under the stone. He unfolded the cloth. An odd blue smell, something neither I nor Chacal had smelled before, grew in the room. 2JS stirred the bits of the bottle with his long black-lacquered and garnet-inlaid index fingernail. He picked out a tiny shriveled glob of what looked like brown wax—it was about the size of an

Advil tablet—and laid it on the red quadrant of the board in front of 7 Prong. The adder took the tobacco mud out of his mouth, kneaded it together with the little bead, and put the bolus back into his mouth between his teeth and his upper lip. He didn't chew it. 2JS broke open the second bottle. There was a pinch of coarse yellow powder inside. It looked like stale shredded Parmesan cheese. 2JS scooped up a tiny bit of the powder with the nail of his little finger and carefully held the finger out over the board. Slowly, 7 Prong leaned forward, got his nose into position, and snorted it up. He sat back. 2JS covered the remaining drugs with a pair of gourd bowls.

"My adder underneath me, 7 Prong, requests assistance from Old Salter," 2JS said.

It took me a minute to get what he meant, but basically Old Salter was one of the gods of the Game, and Old Salter, or Old Salter's dust, was also the name of the drug. The thing to remember was that around here everything was personified. You wouldn't say "rain is coming from the south," you'd say "Yellow Man Chac is coming." Corn was Fathermother 8 Bone and chocolate was Lord Kakaw. A dust devil was Little Hurukan and the fog was Lady Cowl. And they called the wind Mariah. Anyway, I signed "Agreed." We chose numbers again. It was my turn to move first. I scattered and moved out.

7 Prong hesitated a bit before his first move. He seemed normal, except that his eyes were unfocused, or I suppose it's more correct to say they were focused far away.

He moved. I moved. He moved. I moved. He hesitated and moved. Damn. He got my first number. I moved. He moved. I moved. He moved. He got my second number. I moved. He moved. I noticed there were lines of mucus trailing out of 7 Prong's nostrils and back over his cheeks, and snot's a characteristic side effect of most psychedelics. He didn't wipe them away and, oddly, I wasn't grossed out to look at them. On the fortieth move I only had one number left and he still had four. There wasn't any point. I resigned.

Damn. What is that stuff? Old Salter, huh?

The guard lit a new set of rushlights. Even though I knew I was being impolite, I sat back a bit and recrossed my legs. They were stiff, but they were used to staying crossed for long periods and somehow they knew how not to get numb. Maybe because there was no weather in the earth-temperature air and almost no indication of time, I wasn't tired or hungry and barely even thirsty, even though we'd been sitting here for what must have been at least three hours.

Okay, I thought. Tiebreaker.

I signed that I wanted to play another game.

2JS signed that it was all right with him. 7 Prong signed, "Challenge accepted."

I looked at the two upside-down bowls. I looked at 2JS.

He looked back, knowing what I was thinking.

Speak, he signed. I guessed you had to ask for the stuff.

"I under you beg to play with the assistance of Old Salter," I said.

2JS got a pinch of the brown powder out of his stash and dropped it on the board in front of me. It was less than half of the amount 7 Prong had gotten. I took some tobacco, chewed it up, scooped it out of my mouth, and kneaded it together with the powder. I was about to pop it into my mouth but 2JS caught me, putting his hand over mine.

Rub it into your thigh, he signaled.

Why? I wondered. 7 Prong did oral. Why can't I do oral? Maybe they're short-shrifting me here. Well, go along with it.

I rubbed it into my thigh.

"Old Salter is a hoary-green man," 2 Jeweled Skull said. "You can recognize him by the spots on his cheek and the pack on his back. If he comes in a canoe, he'll be sitting in the middle."

"Uh, right." I gestured. "I'll keep an eye out."

2JS put the first empty bowl down again and lifted up the other. I shivered a little for some reason. Even though the stuff hadn't gone into my mouth, I thought I could taste something, a sort of inhuman, synthetic flowery taste like you might remember from grape bubblegum or Shasta or Froot Loops or something. 2JS got some of the other stuff on his fingernail—only four or five grains, from what I could see in the rushlight, probably less than a tenth of the amount 7 Prong had snorted—and held it up to me. Oh, well. I huffed the stuff up—something at which I was an old pro—and sat back.

Nothing happened. I thought 2JS might give 7 Prong another blast, too, but maybe he was still flying on the same hit. Well, whatever.

It was 7 Prong's turn to go first. He scattered and moved. I scattered. I moved. He moved. I moved. He moved.

Hmm.

There was a salt taste at the corners of my mouth, and I realized that tickles of mucus were scrolling down on each of my cheeks. It's a common side effect of LSD and most other hallucinogens—that is, a running nose is—but whatever this stuff was, it didn't feel like a hallucinogen. In fact, it didn't feel like much of anything yet.

Yuck, I thought. Still, I didn't touch my face. I got the feeling that snot was a holy manifestation, a stigmata from the smokers of the Game. Maybe that's what some of those tattooed cheek scrolls meant. Snot, not blood. Hmm.

I realized that 7 Prong had moved a while ago. I looked down at the board. It was already pretty obvious where two of his three other numbers were. There was a wisp of something in the air between me and the board and I thought at first that it was a cobweb, but when I focused on it more closely I could see it was a shred of the smoke from 2JS's cigar, hanging motionless in the air. Better move, I thought. I picked up my pebble—except, no, my hand was still parked on my knee. I tried to move it and it didn't seem to budge, and for a moment I felt that terror of paralysis rising up in my stomach, but then I saw that my hand had moved, slightly, and was already an eighth of an inch or so off my knee, and was slowly edging toward the quartz pebble, which was about fifteen inches away on the right edge of my side of the board. I tried to move it faster, straining against what felt like gelled air, and it did pick up speed, traveling about an inch to the right in what seemed like about a minute and a half.

Huh.

Normally when you're playing a game, your own time slows down, so that you don't realize how long you've been there until, say, you notice it's dark outside. But now the time around me had slowed down. Or, rather, the Old Salter's dust was a chronolytic drug, something that sped up the synapses in the brain without giving you a seizure or making you confused or frantic or whatever. I blinked, and the brown darkness of my eyelids rolled down as slowly as a thick cloud front passing overhead. On the other hand, my thinking wasn't at all slower, in fact it seemed clearer. I did a few in-head calculations to check. Pretty soon I was sure about it, and not only that, but I was sure I had a huge amount of working memory available, more than I'd had as Jed, which was a lot. When I looked at the board and thought about all the dates and contingencies stretching into the future, it felt as though I was standing under a waterfall of dice, and there was plenty of time to look around and pick one out and read it, and in fact to focus on any and all of them, and to memorize the positions of all of them as they fell past you, and to calculate how each of them would finally land.

Maybe this is it, I thought. Got to get this stuff back to the team. Although when Taro finds out, he'll be disappointed. He'd wanted a mathematical answer, something he could teach LEON. Now it looks like it's more of an intuition thing. Well, score one for wetware.

Eventually, I completed my move, and 7 Prong moved—I watched one of his fingernails and it was like watching the moon fall across the sky—and I managed to move again, and he started to move again, although by now I already knew what he was going to do, and I was getting a little bored and looking around the room, rolling my eyeballs slowly around in their sockets. I watched a puff of smoke extrude out of 2JS's nose like a starfish painstakingly inching its way out of a coral crevice. I watched the hair curling out of 7 Prong's face like spring leaves budding on a tree-covered mountain. I watched the flame of a rushlight swaying back and forth as slowly as a Rasta woman at a grounation. On the nineteenth move I plunked my pebble down onto 7 Prong's last number. He didn't even have time to resign.

Hot damn. Just give me a few dime bags of this stuff and I'll cruise back to Century 21 and I won't just track down that doomster, I'll solve the Hodge Conjecture, discover a perfect cuboid, and figure out how to retain formatting between different editions of Microsoft Word. No sweat. 7 Prong made a sign of submission—sort of like saying "Congratulations, good game"—and stood up slowly. His knees cracked like two hazelnuts. He teetered past me and out of the cave room. The flap of deerskin swished behind me. I was already feeling that sort of winner's remorse that always comes over you when you really crush somebody. I noticed there was no feeling in my legs, and I started to stand up myself, but there was a rushing in my ears like two fire-hoses spraying blood against the inside of my skull and a flux of nausea like a bile-filled balloon inflating in my small intestine, and I tipped over into softness. Someone was sprinkling water on my face, and when I got my eyes open I saw it was a guard. A different guard, not the deaf guard. I rolled my head to look around but there was a crack of pain in my neck and I had to give up. I moved a hand. Ouch. I was utterly stiff, the way you get if you take a lot of codeine and sleep for hours without moving. I realized three things: that I'd blacked out, that a lot of time had passed, and that maybe, maybe, if I got that Old Salter's dust stuff back to the folks in the last b'ak'tun, we really might have a chance.

(39)

The guard got me to drink some water. He massaged me in a rough way—something Chacal's body was used to—and got me to the point where I could sit upright. Finally he gave me a sort of paste of unsweetened chocolate that you were supposed to lick out of a little cup. I did. I'd guess it had about the same amount of caffeine as five espressos. 2 Jeweled Skull crouched into the room and sat on the other side of the game board, where 7 Prong had sat. He wore the same basic outfit as before, with the same chains of jade and spondylus shells, but he looked cleaned up. Maybe he'd been in a sweatbath. I heard someone, another guard, probably, come in and sit behind me, but my manners were improving and I didn't look around.

"So Old Salt came to you the first time," he said.

Yes, I clicked.

"That's a good sign." He said that most people didn't get much out of him the first time they met him. Like with most drugs, I thought. Except if that wasn't much, what's it like when you get used to it? I bet if I played LEON on that stuff I'd be able to spot that doomster in no time. And I'd only had a quarter dose, at most. Not that it hadn't nearly killed me anyway, but still.

2JS took a fresh cigar, lit it on a coal, and puffed on it. I watched. Suddenly, and astonishingly, he offered me one. I said the little ritual thanks. He said the little ritual don't-mention-its. He lit it on the coals and handed it to me.

I had trouble lifting my hand to take it. Evidently part of the Old Salter's dust's distinctive back end was a feeling like you were a victim of selective gravity, or like sixty pounds of miniature lead shot had been injected into your blood. Still, I did manage to grab the thing and get it into my mouth—I know when in Rome, I thought, but I still wasn't into nasal—and sucked in the smoke. It had a strong vegetal taste, with an overtone of chocolate and hints of mint, flint, and lint on the finish. Damn, that's good. Chacal's body was hopelessly addicted.

Well, so maybe old 2JS was at least a bit impressed, I thought. I did pretty much blow away that 7 Prong character, didn't I? Except don't mention it, I thought. Don't insult his adder. Incompetent though the guy might be.

"We had an eight-skull adder but he died," 2JS said, apparently reading my mind.

I didn't know what that was or what to say. Maybe it meant that his old adder could play with eight running stones. If that was true, he must have been pretty brilliant. Even though I didn't understand, I clicked, "Understood."

"7 Prong is a three-skull adder," 2JS said. "We're working on getting a seven-skull, from Broken Sky. But supposedly the Macaw House has also made him an offer."

I clicked. So there was a competition between houses to attach the best adders. It was the same way when I grew up in Alta Verapaz; different villages tried to attract the best curanderos.

An inferior wasn't supposed to question a superior, but maybe I could risk it. He's opening up to me, I thought. We have a special bond. Right?

"And who do you above me believe is the best sun adder?" I asked.

"11 Whirling is the only nine-skull adder in Ix," he said. "There are only thirty-one nine-skulls." From the declension it was clear that he meant that was all there were in the entire world. He said that 11 Whirling had been attached to the Ocelot House when he was a little boy, over sixty years ago, and that he was now legendarily powerful. In fact, 2JS said, he might be homing in on me as we speak. Sometime soon he'd figure out that deer hunt had been a sham. And he'd locate me in one of his Games, and the Ocelots would send a squad to capture me.

I asked why the Ocelots were still angry at us—and I mentally stressed the *us*—if we'd made things up to them with the deer hunt. Right after I asked I regretted it. That's either a stupid question or an annoying one, I thought. Watch it.

But if it bothered him, 2JS didn't show it. He said that for one thing, most of the Ocelots probably assumed that we had ruined the sacrifice on the mul on purpose. But the roots of the disagreement went way back. The Ocelots had been the leading family in Ix ever since it was founded on, supposedly, 9 Ahau, 3 Sip, 8.0.0.0.0. On that day, One Ocelot had claimed the water caves in his mountain and had divided the land around the mountain between his family and the ahaus of the other four high houses, including, supposedly, One Harpy.

Of course, even if that One Ocelot had really existed, 9 Fanged Hummingbird, the current ahau of ahauob, probably wasn't so directly descended from him as he'd have everyone believe. Still, nobody was about to challenge his hereditary control of the sweet waters—that is, irrigation, and therefore pretty much all Ixian agriculture—or his monopoly on slaves, which came from the fact that he was the only Ixian who could initiate warfare. The Ocelots also controlled the duties of the Ix collective, that is, the rituals and what you could call the priesthood. And they had monopolistic hunting rights in most places and on certain animals, the right to ask travelers for gifts—that is, to tax the roads—and the right to distribute the spoils of war, the sole right to deal in jade, and on and on. They owned one day out of every uinal—a month of twenty days—and five extra days out of every tun, the 360-day solar year. Most important of all, they had a monopoly on the Game drugs, which were indispensible and which armed Swallowtail Lineage couriers brought in once every four years from Mexico.

Great, I thought. So basically it's still all about the narco trade.

2JS said there was also a second Game drug, one 7 Prong had never tried, called Old Steersman's dust. "If you ever meet the Steersman, you'll see that he's even older than Old Salter," he said. "He's so old that his skin is dark gray. He stands with a long paddle in the stern of the canoe." It sounded to me as though Old Salter was the personification of the chronolytic drug and Old Steersman was the god of some kind of presumably topolytic one—that is, not in the cellular-chemistry sense, but as in something that collapses one's sense of space. And, supposedly, the two drugs together had a synergistic effect. "The adders say that when you have the two old men together, they throw so much lightning in your blood that it's like in the days of our great-grandfathermothers, when they could see the entrails of stones."

Still, 2JS said, even with the monopoly on the Game drugs, the Ocelot house wasn't unassailable. It had become top-heavy over the last few k'atunob. There were too many Ocelot bloods with expensive lifestyles and not much to do. And they'd gotten poorer and poorer. "Their new uayob' are runts," 2JS said. It meant something like how, in the old days in Europe, they would have said their blood was thinning. For some reason the latest generations of royal-line Ocelots had tended to be subnormal, or stillborn, or something. 9 Fanged Hummingbird was a dwarf, and no one outside his immediate family had ever seen him unmasked. It can't have been because they were eating off lead plates, like the ancient Romans, but they were doing something wrong. And lately they'd mismanaged their estates and squandered resources on festivals and overblown building projects. At their last feast, for their "victory" in the rigged hipball game, they'd used, and then burned, the feathers of 40,800 green violet-eared hummingbirds, each of which was worth more than a month of slave labor. And that was only one type of feather out of twenty.

Meanwhile the Harpy House and the Macaw House, and to a lesser degree the Snuffler House, had gotten richer. They'd organized increasingly long-distance trade routes, from Sonora to as far south as Panama. 2JS ran the country's chocolate trade like a vertical trust. The *milperos* who grew the cacao trees and harvested the beans were roundhouse thralls or dependents of his. The dozens of villages that husked, fermented, dried, and roasted them—chocolate needs a lot of processing—were all headed by members of his extended family. The long-distance traders were blooded to him somehow. And even the goods that came back from abroad, like salt and obsidianware, got warehoused in one of 2JS's towns while he decided on the right market and the right time to sell.

Lately the Harpy House had become the Ocelots' major creditor, and like other royals around the world, the Ocelots were perennially defaulting. Although he didn't put it that way, of course. The closest thing you could say in Ixian was that the Ocelots were becoming "unwelcoming." That is, they weren't reciprocating gifts. Instead of giving away any of their core wealth, like some of the water rights, they'd simply dug in. 9 Fanged Hummingbird had started demanding "greeting gifts," that is, extra tariffs, from goods that barely even crossed over the Ocelots' roads.

I asked about the three other Ixian greathouses. 2JS said that two of them, the Macaws and the Snufflers, disliked the Ocelots as much as the Harpies did. But just like the Harpies, they were related to the Ocelots through webs of marriage and adoption. 2JS's grandfather was 9FH's grand-uncle's brother-in-law. 9FH's sister was the aunt of the patriarch of Macaw House. The patriarch of the Snuffler House had adopted two of 9FH's nieces' sons. And on and on. And a lot of these different families' rights derived from their relationship to the ruling house. Attacking the Ocelots would be out of societal character, the way killing a family member still seems more evil to people than killing a stranger. And it would shake up the system so badly that the other houses would immediately start feuding with each other. And, of course, you'd have to give up on whichever of your relatives were currently "visiting" in the Oce-lots' compound.

And even if all these problems somehow vanished, 9 Fanged Humming-bird was still a living god. Being the greatfathermother of a feline clan was like being the pope in Renaissance Italy. No matter what kind of a jerk the pope was, people believed he had God's ear. Even mercenaries who'd stick at nothing else wouldn't attack him. And if you took him down, you'd better be sure to become pope yourself, and in a hurry. For 2JS to come to power and hang on to it, the Ocelots would have to be forced to seat him in their moun-tain, that is, to acknowledge him as their rightful heir. They'd concoct some genealogical history "proving" that 2JS was a direct descendant of One Oce-lot, and then, in a sham election at the *popol na*, the council house, they would "choose" him as their ahau. But, 2JS said, there was no chance this would happen.

Of course, even in a premonetary society wealth does make power, and maybe, if things were allowed to run their course for another few k'atuns, the Harpies would become so rich they could hire mercenaries to help take on the Ocelots, or they'd marry into them, or they'd get all the other clans on their side, or something. But the Ocelots wouldn't allow things to run their course. They wanted to clean the slate now, before the Harpies got any stron-ger, and they were on the lookout for any sort of insult from the Harpies that could start a conflict. They'd almost found it in the way I'd ruined 9FH's re-seating ceremony on the mul. And since then, they'd come up with some-thing even more menacing.

"The Ocelots have challenged us," he said, "to a great hipball game, and I've named this sun: 1 Sweeping, 0 Gathering."

That was a hundred and six days from today. According to 2JS, great hip-ball games could only happen when a new yearbearer came in, which was once every four years. It had been eight years since the Ocelots' team last played against the Harpies. In the old days, k'atuns ago, the most important hipball games were contests between the great ahaus and captured royal bloods from other cities. They'd given the ahau a chance to show he was still fit to rule. Other hipball games had functioned as duels between brothers, sons, or in-laws of the kings, resolving conflicts that might otherwise have led to civil war. "But in our own degenerate b'ak'tun," as 2 Jeweled Skull put it, the overlords were usually represented by professional in-house hipball players, like me, Chacal. Sometimes a challenged house would even put together a

sort of all-star team of loaned or freelance players from other cities. But the
Harpies couldn't do that this time without losing all the face in the world. The
Ocelots' team would be all in-house, so the defending team would have to be
all Harpy bloods.

And in most situations that would have been all right. The Harpy House's
team had done well for the last three war seasons. The team had been a good
source of revenue for 2 Jeweled Skull, both from shares of winnings and from
the trading contracts it had promoted. But this season the Ocelots' team
would be as good or better. And, 2JS said, Chacal's being out of the lineup
wasn't going to help.

Sorry, I thought.

2JS told me—not in so many words, but more between the lines, if conversation has lines—that theoretically it was an honor to be invited to play
against the ruling family, but actually it was usually a disaster. As per tradition, most members of each clan would want to stake a large part of their
worth on the game. 2JS would be pressured into putting up more than half of
his estate on their team. And their allies and dependents and other supporters would, collectively, stake even more. If the Harpies lost the game, they'd
lose a huge amount of their property but stay alive and unenslaved, at least
for a while. If the Harpies were winning in the last period, the Ocelots would
probably pull a fake foul. The Harpies would have to contest it, and there'd be
an instant civil war. Or, possibly, the Ocelots would manage to rig the game
from the beginning, either by co-opting the umpires or by some other trick.
Then they'd either take the property or, if the Harpies objected, start attacking. One way or another the Harpies were screwed. It was a transparent swin-
dle, but it didn't matter. You couldn't refuse a challenge. Around here, if you
lost face you lost everything.

La gran puta, I thought. Well, at least I was starting to understand what I
hadn't before, that the Harpy House was under a huge amount of pressure.
Maybe at some other time I would have been able to pull off the potter's
wheel project or whatever. But wherever you went, mafia bosses like 2JS and
9FH were always inches away from a turf war. And now, after my mul fiasco,
9FH was looking for an excuse to force the issue. And he was going to win.

This is hopeless, I thought. I'm on the wrong side. I should just sneak out
of here and defect to the Ocelots. Except that, A) I wouldn't get out the door
here, let alone in the door there, and B) they wouldn't understand me the way
he did. I'd be lucky if they just ate me without torturing me first—

Uh-oh.

I'd gotten a horrible feeling that 2JS was guessing what I was thinking. I mean, about trying to go over to the other side.

I looked at 2 Jeweled Skull. He looked at me. I didn't look away.

At first, I thought I was waiting for him to order me killed. But as the stare-down wore on, second by second, I realized I was feeling almost close to him. Maybe it was just Stockholm Syndrome.

Or just that when you're in a weird spot you latch on to the person who's most like you, even if that person's totally out to get you. Maybe he's actually not such a bad guy. Maybe he has so much of me in him that he feels close to me—

Hang on. Don't get cozy. He did just treat you to the worst hours of your life. Remember?

"Tie your uay to its post at night," he said. It was like saying, "Don't get any ideas." But he said it with a slight undertone of humor.

Whew, I thought. Okay. Change the subject.

"I want to play another Game," I said. I said I wanted to try the Old Salter's dust again, and I wanted to work out whether 11 Whirling was really closing in on me, and what the Harpies should do next, and what to do about the hipball game. I didn't say I was better than 7 Prong, but it was obvious that I thought so.

He said I shouldn't have another dose for a few days. You had to "polish yourself" against it, he said. That is, you had to increase dosages over years. But even if I did develop a tolerance, I wouldn't know so much as 11 Whirling. There were secrets about the Game that the lower-skulled adders weren't supposed to know and that the higher-skulled adders usually wouldn't teach them. Kings didn't want their house adders training too many apprentices, because an enemy might get hold of one of them. Most adders, even the ones who came from Maya cities, were trained in Tamoan, and only a few left the city in each k'atun.

Tamoan? I wondered. I didn't know the name, but it triggered an association in Chacal, a triad of huge pyramids.

2JS said that of the thirty-two living nine-skulls that he knew of, eighteen of them were in Tamoan. The other fourteen were spread through different royal seats in Mesoamerica, with one or at most two per city. And unless I could study with one of them, I wouldn't become a nine-skull myself. And I wouldn't anyway, because I was too old.

I understand, I signed. Damn it.

"And even if you could make one of them teach you, you might not really learn anything," he said. For every nine-skull adder there were four hundred who never got that far.

Bullshit, I thought, I'll do fine. But I didn't say it.

And even if I did turn out to be a good student, he went on, I still wouldn't be able to play the nine-stone Game without years of practice. Of the thirty-one nine-skulls, very few were under forty years old. Although, he added, some of the female ones were younger.

I asked why.

"Old Salter is friendlier to women," he said. "So they say." Yeah, I thought, either that or they're just better at it.

Also, he said, he only had a little left, and it was getting stale. It wasn't so much about the dosage but about how fresh it was. The stuff did not improve with age. And the Ocelots weren't going to let him have any more. Supposedly they were getting low on it themselves.

"And besides all that," he said, "11 Whirling will find you first. You have to be a nine-skull to fool a nine-skull."

It was frustrating, but I had to admit it made some sense. It was like how ratings in chess or Go are so solid that you don't get too many upsets. Like in the Go world, say you were a 1-dan professional. Your odds of beating a 9-dan, in an even game, would be around one in thirty. And even though I'd felt amazing during that one-on-one Game, I was still only playing with one skull. I couldn't imagine playing with more than four, let alone nine.

Hmm. Speaking of that, there was something I'd been meaning to ask about . . . oh, right.

"Is 11 Whirling really the only nine-skull in Ix?" I asked. "What about the woman in the Codex, the ahau-na Koh?"

"I saw her in the book in your worm," 2 Jeweled Skull said. "The lady Koh's *k'aana'obol*"—that is, her eldest maternal uncle—"is my *e'ta' taxoco' obo l'ta'taxoco.*" That is, he was the half-brother of 2JS's second cousin's maternal grandfather. I'm glad we've cleared that up, I thought.

He said Lady Koh was born twenty-eight solar years ago in a village about two *jornadas* north of Ix. Her family was a branch of the royal house of Lakamha, that is, Palenque, and they were related to both the Ocelot and Harpy Houses of Ix. She'd shown physical signs of being a sun adder. One of the signs was that she had eleven children of her hands, that is, eleven fingers. When she was seven, the Ocelots arranged for her, and a few other children from upper-caste Maya families, to be sent to the Star Rattler compound in Tamoan. And the same number of children from the families of high-ranking Star Rattler *tu'nikob'*, that is, sacrificers or offering priests, or, literally, "sucklers"—got sent south from Tamoan to the Maya cities. I guess it was more of the guest/hostage system, but in this case it sounded like a bit of a student exchange program. Most of the Mayan apprentices couldn't cut the mustard and had come back from Tamoan in a few years, but Koh had become one of the forty sun adderesses in the Star Rattler Society. In the meantime her home village had been absorbed by the Ti'kalob, and her family had been captured. 2JS didn't know whether they'd been executed or whether they were still hostages.

"The Codex said she was in Ix," I said.

2JS said that wasn't true. He'd read the Codex in my memories, he said, and all it said was that she was *from* Ix.

God damn it, I thought. Well, come to think of it, that glyph was a little ambiguous. Hell. Just one more in a grand parade of crushing setbacks. So Michael Weiner just assumed she'd be around here. Moron.

"What about the Game in the Codex?" I asked.

"I have a copy of that game," 2JS said. Even though she played it for the Ocelots.

Great, I thought. It's a fucking best-seller. Although I guess that makes sense. I mean, if you were walking around the ruins of Orlando someday in the future and you pulled an ancient, crumbling book out of a junk heap, what would it most likely be, some incredibly apropos special significant secret thing? Or just *Orlando for Dummies*, or *The Good News Bible*, or *Caddyshack: The Novelization*?

I asked him where the Game had been played. He said she'd staged it in Tamoan, as a gift to her relatives in the southeast.

"You over me," I asked, "is Tamoan a name for Teotihuacan?"

"I don't know that name," he said.

I told him I meant a huge city, with three great mulob' and hundreds of lesser ones. I said it was about thirty-five k'inob—that is, *jornadas*, days' journeys, if you figured a day of brisk hiking as about thirty miles—to the west by northwest.

2JS clicked in a plosive way that was like saying, "Correct."

Hmm, I thought.

Teotihuacan was an Aztec name. But the Aztecs, who first saw the city in the fourteenth century, knew it only as a gigantic ruin, and neither they nor anyone else knew what its real name had been. They said it was the place where the Fourth Sun and the Third Moon had been born. And as I think I may have said, it was the largest city in the Western Hemisphere, with at least two hundred thousand people, the size of London in 1750.

2 Jeweled Skull said Teotihuacan—as we might as well call it, just for consistency—was just one *jornada* from the place where time had started, on 4 Overlord, 8 Darkness, 0.0.0.0.0, that is, August 13, 3113 BC. On that date the greatest greatfathermothers, the Green Hag and Hurricane, had built a city called Tola, with captive waterfalls in red coral towers and plazas tessellated with amethyst and jade. The first fleshly people lived there until 4 Overlord, 18 Forest, 7.0.0.1.0—that is, June 25, 353 BC. On that day Prank the Sun Chewer destroyed the city with a cyclone of hot knives. Nine-score survivors hid in a cave and later followed a vulture to the site of a secret spring about thirty miles east. After twenty sunless days, on 11 Overlord, 18 Cowering, they founded a new city, Teotihuacan. The survivors all bled themselves—that is, they swore—that in the new city, no one would ever do anything boastful, that is, anything that could possibly irritate Prank or any of the other smokers. No single ahau would exalt himself. Instead the city would be administered by a council of patriarchs from each of two moieties. Everyone in the city would belong to one or the other of these populations, either the red side, which owned the acts of war, or the white side, which owned the acts of peace. None of the patriarchs would exalt themselves by name, either in orations or in written inscriptions, and in fact writing was still a disreputable art. At dawn and at noon every person in the valley would be present under the sky and offer smoke to the smokers. There would be no deviation from the routine, not because of war, weather, disease, or any other reason. And for one thousand and seventeen years there hadn't been.

Teotihuacan's empire had spread over the world. They had the closest thing to a regular military in the Western Hemisphere, with drilled infantry that marched in formation and fired volleys of darts from atlatls. Warlords from Teotihuacan had taken over Maya cities like Ti'kal and Kaminaljuyú and founded their own dynasties there. Hundreds of cities and thousands of towns sent preagreed "gifts" to the city every year. Teotihuacan controlled the trade in obsidian, which came from nearby mines, which was why in some dialects the empire was called *K'Kaalom K'sic*, the Domain of Razors. But it also exported hematite, rock salt, north-country slaves, and a dozen other things. And it had the monopoly on Old Salter's and Old Steersman's respective dusts.

Still, over the last two centuries, the empire had weakened at the seams. Every year there were more and more people—or I guess we could call them barbarians—outside its borders, trying to get a piece of the action. Despite the infantry, some frontier outpost got raided almost every day. And worse than that, upstart towns within the empire were defaulting on tribute and ignoring the collectors, and undercutting the syndicate. For instance, the empire was supposedly in charge of the entire salt trade, but lately the Ixians and others were buying sea salt directly from villages on the coast. And the city of Teotihuacan itself was beset by what twenty-first-centuryites would call the troubles of urbanity: overcrowding, tuberculosis, economic decay, rural resentment, and, recently, what a twenty-first-century person would call religious issues, or, as he put it, "shouting and stoning around Star Rattler's House."

It wouldn't last much longer. As I think I mentioned somewhere, archaeologists had dated the end of the city's main phase to between AD 650 and 700. But despite all the advances in pollen DNA dating, radioisotope dating, and a dozen other dating technologies, as of 2012 they hadn't yet narrowed it down more than that.

Not that the place would exactly fall into a memory hole. By around AD 1000 the Toltecs would be the dominant civilization in the Mexican Highlands, and although it's not clear whether they were closely related to the Teotihuacanos, it's probably fair to say that most of their culture ultimately derived from Teotihuacan. And three hundred years after that, the so-called Aztecs would take over what was left of the Toltec cultural system and parlay it into an empire that in 1518 would be nearly as large as Teotihuacan's empire was now.

Anyway, the main thing was that the empire certainly hadn't collapsed yet. 2JS said he thought it was mainly because the Two *Popolob'* of Teotihuacan— hmm, maybe in this case we should translate *Popolob'* as "Synods," because they were religious councils as much as secular ones—could cut off supplies of the Salter's and Steersman's dust to any client regime that stopped supporting them. The network of sun adders, which was like a loose international guild, might pick up some of the slack, but at some point they ran out of the stuff and needed more from the source. He suspected, he said, that the synods had cut down on the supply lately because they wanted to set off minor wars between different Maya cities, in order to keep them weak. More than anything else the Game was a peacekeeper. When governments can't predict what's going to happen, that's when they get paranoid, and that's when the situation devolves.

And of course, he said, the adders in Teotihuacan had fresh dust each peace season, and that was why they'd been able to safeguard the city so well for so long. They could see threats coming from a long way away, both in space and in time. But it wouldn't last much longer.

2 Jeweled Skull paused. And when he paused, he really paused. Even though he was bare-chested under all his bling, you couldn't see him breathe.

I sat. I took a long drag. Damn, that's strong. Whew. Well, that'll turn you upside down, shake the change out of your pockets, and spend it on Night Train.

"I under you have a question," I said. "Is it true that the last sun of Teoti-huacan hasn't yet been named?"

He said not so far as he knew. "But I can see in your worm," he said, "that the city will not last another two k'atunob."

I clicked.

"When the empire is gone, the Ocelots will suffer," 2JS said. "Still, it will be too late for us."

No kidding, I thought. I only had about seven months left before my brain turned into Fluffernutter.

There was another of those insufferable pauses. My legs were going numb despite their training. Maybe I should ask for another shot of something.

"You over me, why was there stoning around Star Rattler's house?"

He said he didn't know exactly. But the problem went back a long way. Star Rattler was the greatest of a class of beings who weren't just not human, but who weren't even related to any ancestors. I suppose you could call them gods, but that doesn't get the distinction. The ancestors were gods, too, and so were important living people. In fact, as somebody once said, everything was full of little gods. Maybe a better word for the Rattler—and for the Earth-toadess, the four Chacs, and a bunch of lesser critters like mountains and lakes—would be "elementals." Each one had a shrine and sucklers and follow-ers in every major town. But right now, in 664, the Rattler's cult was growing faster than any of the others.

And, as you probably know, it continued to grow. Later on, Von Humboldt called the Rattler the Maya Dragon. Morley called it the Feathered Serpent and Salman Rushdie called it the Snakebird. The Rattler's Yucatec name, Ku-kulkan, became pretty well-known, and its Nahuatl name, Quetzalcoatl, be-came so famous it's even a character in Warcraft.

Since the Rattler's body was the Milky Way itself, its offering societies weren't connected with any single house or color. Theoretically, they embraced all of them. So there was an internationalism associated with the cult that made it a bit of a subversive element. Even so, it still had royal support. In Ix, and I suppose in any Maya city, any person of substance would be a member of several temple societies besides his own ancestors', and certainly all the Ixian greathouses donated to the Rattler. Star Rattler's mul in Ix was small, but it was old, well-groomed, and rich.

But in Teotihuacan the Rattler was an especially big deal. And it was an increasing annoyance to older entrenched interests. Supposedly—and the news was delayed by about twenty days—the Rattler's children were pledging more and more oblationers, that is, followers, every day. The two great Teotihuacano synods—who owned the two giant pyramids, the ones the Aztecs would later call the Pyramid of the Sun and the Pyramid of the Moon—still allowed the cult to operate, but they'd been increasing restrictions on it, and apparently that was what had set off the riot. After that, the forty Rattler adderesses had basically become political prisoners, under permanent house arrest in their compound at the south end of the city.

Hmm, I thought.

"Is the Lady Koh loyal to the Ocelots?" I asked.

There was another pause. It stretched out and out, like scamorza cheese out of a hot pizza. Suddenly 2JS laughed. It was the first time I'd heard him laugh, and it was such a charming, Santa Claus chuckle, and I started laughing myself.

She was more closely related to the Ocelots, he said. On the other hand, they had sent her off to Teotihuacan when she didn't want to go.

Hmm. Maybe she missed the tropics, I thought. Most people from the tropics who aren't in the tropics miss the tropics.

Yeah. Maybe the thing was to try an indirect approach, to come at the Ocelots from outside.

Okay, Jedster. Go for it. He's got to feel you can really do something, something essential, something that could bail us all out. Otherwise, why keep you alive? And he can't get away. But you can.

I suggested to Ahau 2 Jeweled Skull that maybe I underneath him should visit Teotihuacan.

(40)

At the ninth of the orchids—that is, the first watch of the night, just after sundown—2 Jeweled Skull presented me to the Harpy 11 Viper Caravan Society. It was a new organization—or you might call it a new brotherhood or even a new corporation—that had been created ostensibly for an unscheduled trade run, with the real purpose of getting me to Teotihuacan.

We sat on feather mats on the burned-over peak of a low conical hill that was sheltered between two higher folds of the sierra. We were still close enough to Cacao Town—which was what they called 2JS's capital village—that there was a whiff of chocolate in the air. I faced southeast. The nineteen other blood members of the society—bloods usually traveled in k'atob, that is, vingtaines, companies of twenty—sat facing me in a semicircle with their legs and arms crossed. Much later, the Oglala Sioux in the cast of *Buffalo Bill's Wild West* would sit in a similar way, and it would come to be called "Indian style." But when these people sat, it wasn't just sitting. It was a state of compact readiness, like a compressed volute spring. 2 Jeweled Skull—the Bacab of the East, Fathermother of the Harpy House, Torturer of Jed "Chump" De-Landa, and All-Around Big Chalupa—sat next to me, on my male, right, side. 3 Blue Snail, the dwarf cantor, waddled in front of him arranging bundles on an offering mat. He spoke in his wise-child voice:

"All of us underneath him hear:
Our carver,
Our Fathermother,
Modeler, dissolver,
2 Jeweled Skull
May speak to us.

We listen,
Below him
We wait crouching,
We attend."

2 Jeweled Skull said:

"I one address you many next to me."

And everyone except me answered:

"We underneath you answer you above us."

"Will you accept this gift,
Take on this burden?"

2 Jeweled Skull asked. His voice wasn't louder than anyone else's, but it seemed to carry farther and to echo back from distant invisible cliffs. I'd known he was famous as an orator, but until now I hadn't understood why.

There was a pause for the bloods to examine me. I stared at them. Making and holding eye contact was a martial art around here. If you did it, you had to be ready to fight. They stared back. Hun Xoc and his younger brother 2 Hand sat together at the far right of the line. They'd been Chacal's first and second backcourt men, and they were the ones who'd looked out for me in the deer hunt. Hun Xoc and 2 Hand were two of only four people in the caravan who knew, roughly, what had happened, that is, that I'd been Chacal and now I was somebody else. The other bloods had seen Chacal play, but they hadn't seen him close up, and so far, none of them seemed to suspect anything. The old dude on their left was named 18 Dead Rain. He was our Steward of Burdens, which was like the chief financial officer. He was chubby, smooth-skinned, and apparently good-natured. The schlep on his right was the remembrancer, a different one from the one 2JS had in his cave. He was a short, slight guy with bulgy eyes and monkey markings. Then on the extreme left there was a wiry character, with receding eyes and sun-stretched skin, named 12 Cayman. He was 2JS's niece's husband's brother and his main title was Steward of Long Things. It basically meant "master of arms," like the war leader, and he was also the *nojuchil,* or company captain. He had unattractive snaggle teeth and two lumps on his shoulder where bits of flint points were still embedded in his flesh. The sides of his torso were dotted with memorial tattoos for a high-ranked brother killed in a raid on Motul. There was a rumor that he could see in pitch darkness because his grandfather had been a badger. He was the oldest one in the group. Then, on his right, there was a lesser blood in oblationer's colors named Hun Aat, or just Aat, that is, "Penis," who was an acolyte to 3 Blue Snail. He was the fourth person who knew about the Chacal thing. He'd be our ritualist and official sun adder. How much does he know about the Game? I wondered. Probably not even as much as 7 Prong. God, what a bunch of losers. Okay, who else . . . damn, this moment-of-silence bit's going on a little long, isn't it? Maybe they're really going to come up and start poking me and find something wrong and reject me. This whole thing's dead in the water. Hell, hell, hell, and—

Suddenly the bloods spread their right hands over their left shoulders in an extended salute and spoke, almost in unison:

"We underneath you,
We do not deserve this gift,
But we will cherish it,
We will look after him."

Whew, I thought. Glad we've got that straight.

"So then, now these are
Your own elder brothers
Your own younger brothers."

2 Jeweled Skull said to me,

"Follow them, serve them,
Don't weaken, don't shame me."

I answered:

"I underneath you
Will pass their tests."

"You are accepted. We're finished,"

2JS declared.

I stood and turned 360 degrees counterclockwise, offering myself to each of the five directions, and then crouched to the ground, with both hands on my forehead, submitting to my family. The Steward of Long Things walked forward first and presented me with my blowgun. Thanks, just my size. Next I got a fresh, mint-scented stalking *wi'kal*, which was kind of a midlength cloak made of quilted cotton. Everybody wore them when it got cold. The word *poncho* doesn't quite get it, because they're round or octagonal, and the slit goes all the way to the edge, but the word *cloak* sounds like there would be a bit of tailoring to it and maybe a hood. Well, I'm going to call them mantas. Mine had a red-and-black border of interlocking talons, like the rest of the Harpy bloods'. Its core was some kind of bamboo, but it was wrapped in deerhide thongs woven into my name and genealogy signs. The steward's main carver had been awake for two days getting it ready. After that each of the remaining bloods stepped up and gave me something—a pair of complicated rubber-soled sandals, a pair of ear spools, a network of deerskin straps and harnesses, a black right-wrist cuff, a string of twenty blowgun darts with their tips stuck in baby pinecones for safety, a traveling mask, a jar of skin poison, a jar of oral poison, a pouch for my nonsacred personal stuff, a pouch for my sacred personal stuff, a plain blanket, everything but a quetzal in a prickly pear tree. Finally, 2 Jeweled Skull gave me a spear with an eagle-feathered ferrule cushion, which meant that in addition to being a blowgunner I was also a member of his family guard. A pair of bearers entered the circle, hoisted 2 Jeweled Skull up on their shoulders, turned him through the four terrestrial directions, and then started off down the hill to the east. As soon as they got out of eyeshot, we were free to go. The bloods stood and arranged themselves. My acolyte came up to me and hunched his body into a ball, which was like kowtowing. It was the first time I'd seen him, but I knew that his provisional name, until he became a blood, was Armadillo Shit. He was thirteen years old. Maybe I should call him a squire instead of an acolyte—except that makes it sound like I was something like a knight or samurai myself already, and I really wasn't. Not yet. Maybe I should just call him my personal assistant, except that doesn't get how much he was like an altar boy. Well, actually, I guess I'm kind of embarrassed to call him what we really called him and the other acolytes. But I suppose since we've made it together this far, I'll just spill it, so to speak. They were called *a'anatob*, "fellators." The reason is that when you were on a raid, or hunting or whatever, you weren't supposed to have sex with anyone or anything because it could deplete your manly whateverness, and, even worse than that, the smell of it could tip off your enemies' prowling

uays and, even worse than that, if you left semen lying around in strange ori-
fices, your enemies might find it and use it to cast scabs on you. However,
most of the bloods you'd have on raids or hunts, or on caravans, which, ritually speaking, were the same as hunts, were men between the ages of fourteen and twenty. So you can imagine the rule was tough to enforce. And so,
every so often, the interns had to take care of our carnal appetites. That way
we'd keep everything in-house, as it were. It's one of those Secrets of the Warrior Lodge kindsa things.

Whew. Well, I'm glad that's off my chest.

Anyway, Armadillo Shit packed up all my new loot, right down to the
earspools. 12 Cayman signed for everyone to stand. The bloods saluted the directions of their ancestors' villages and I copied them, feeling first-day-of-high-
school self-conscious, and followed them through a makeshift ceremonial gate.

Without any discussion we trooped down from the crest of the hill to its flat
eastward shoulder. The line of nonbloods—what you might call the support
staff—stood packed and ready on a freshly watered path, in marching order:

—Six forerunners, or advance scouts

—Four snake watchers, who carried big brushes like leaf rakes, watering
  gourds, and rattles

—A pair of formal messengers with long wooden flutes strapped over
  their shoulders, like heralds

—Four flank scouts

—Ten dedicated bearers with empty wicker back racks, like big yuppie
  toddler carriers

—Nine porters in charge of the three big travois sleds

—Five individual porters, each with a big cylindrical basket on his back
  held by a tumpline across his forehead. They carried emergency backups in case we lost the sleds

—Two brothers from a strange little clan with an incomprehensible language whose hereditary job was carrying, buying, purifying, and distrib-
  uting drinking water

—One masticator, that is, someone between a taster, a chef, and an
  apothecary

—Two dog handlers, each in charge of fifteen fat food/pillow dogs and ten hunting/watchdogs

—Four people from a very low caste whom I'll call groomers. Or maybe "scareflies" is a better word, since their main job was to keep bugs away

—A tailor or valet

—A sandal maker

—A mask steward, who was in charge of all regalia, not just masks

—Two armorers, or spear smiths, in the service of 12 Cayman

—A fire wrangler with his flints and drills and a basket of hot coals

—A separate sandaler for the nonbloods

—A separate cook for the nonbloods

—Four people whom one might call untouchables. Two were nightsoil collectors with their twenty dogs. The dogs' only job was to eat our excrement so that enemies couldn't get it and use it in curses. The other two humans were *nacamob*, sacrificers, standing apart from the rest of the line like a pair of crows waiting for a flock of red vultures to vacate a carcass. They would do any killing if necessary and also handle dead bodies. The four of them, and their porters, if any, would follow either in a separate boat or forty paces behind us and a little to the side, so they wouldn't pollute our path.

—Nine outrunners, or scouts. Four of them were stalkers and the other five were what we called "four-light couriers," that is, specially skilled stealth runners who'd have the task of bringing the Game drugs and information back to 2JS from Teotihuacan. Supposedly they were able to run for four solid days and nights, with two of them carrying a spare sleeping courier on their backs, although I was sure this was an exaggeration.

—Finally, there was a rear guard of four. Three would drop back in stages and watch for tails. The other would stay closer to the line to make sure no one had dropped anything, not even a hair bead. He'd also sprinkle chili pepper behind us to eradicate our trail, ceremonially and to some extent olfactorily.

So the total was 120 heads, not counting the dogs. So there were five lower-caste supporters to each blood. Which actually wasn't quite first-class around here. But 2JS wanted enough of a squad to hold off attackers and let me escape, but not enough of an army to look threatening.

There was a pause. The ranks tightened.

18 Dead Rain signed something. The nineteen bloods and I—or I guess I should proudly say "we twenty bloods"—slipped into our places in the middle of the line, with 12 Cayman in the lead and the second-lowest-ranked blood at the end. I was the lowest-ranked blood, but I was breaking protocol by traveling in the middle of the body, with Hun Xoc ahead of me and 2 Hand behind. Our twenty-one acolytes formed up behind us.

De todos modos. I thought. Let's blow this joint and get on with the plan. We take the golden road to Tamoan.

12 Cayman gave the first outrunner a sign. He ran off ahead. Noiselessly and without any fuss the line woke into motion and slid forward like a mag-lev train gliding out of the station without even a hiss of steam. The dogs trotted along without a yip. Even the yearlings wouldn't think of barking unless they'd been told they were on watch. With only a few creaks from the sleds and a squeak or two from one of our two hundred and forty oiled sandals, we headed northeast down a series of stepped ridges into a cultivated valley. The pace was a sort of near jog. Actually we could go faster, but we needed to look normal. Hup, I thought. Hup. No problem. Hup.

The path ran along the male side of a nearly dry streambed, and every forty arms we had to step over an irrigation ditch that branched off toward another newly burned-over *milpa*, a charred rectangle gasping for rain. Then there would be two fallow *milpas* from previous seasons, and then another burnt one, sometimes with the skeleton of a temporary granary just under construction. Some of the burnt fields were still smoldering, but the trees in the bands of sericulture orchards running between the *milpas* still had all their leaves, and there weren't any signs that the fires had gotten out of control. The word was that the burning had gone off without any major accidents in any of the Ixian Harpy villages. It was a huge good omen and a sign that, despite his problems, 2JS was still running a tight ship.

And it looked like we were getting out of town, all right. And I felt good. Maybe things were looking up. And at least we had a plan, or at least an outline of a notion of a plan. As soon I got set up in Teotihuacan, somehow I'd get an audience with Lady Koh. 2JS and I had agreed that I wouldn't tell her who I really was—that is, nothing about Jed, which she wouldn't believe anyway, and not even anything about Chacal, if I could help it. Instead I'd try to come up with something short of that that would still get her attention. Then I'd convince her that I had special information about the imminent end of Teotihuacan and that she should let us spirit her out of the city. As they'd say in the law-enforcement and espionage industries, I'd try to flip her. Then, as soon as she got us the components of the Game drugs, and as soon as I'd taken notes on how to make it, I'd send all that stuff back to 2JS with a team of four-light couriers. In return 2JS would bury a sealed stone box with a sample of the drugs and my notes on the Game. The box would be in the center of a cross of magnetic iron so that Marena's team could find it. And at that point I'd be able to consider my mission as basically accomplished. The data would get back to 2012, and the Chocula team would upgrade the Game and spot the Doomster, and the world would get on track and everybody would ride off into the Blu-ray sunset.

Everybody but me, that is. I'd still be stuck back here. However, that was why there was a phase 2. As I made my way back to Ix, 2JS would be using his Game-drug manufacturing operation as a bargaining chip. If he controlled the supply, all the nine-stone adders in the world would have to come to him. Also, he said, if he had a more potent batch of the stuff, 7 Prong might be able to compete with the Ocelots' adder, 11 Whirling. I wasn't so sure about that, since I didn't think 7 Prong was all that talented. Maybe 2JS meant "*even* 7 Prong would be able to" etc. Anyway, if 2JS managed to set himself up as k'alomte', or at least neutralize the threat from the Ocelots, and if I got back in time, then we'd do basically the same thing as before. But we'd use a bigger and more elaborate stone box this time, since my whole body would be going along.

Of course, I wasn't quite clear on why 2JS thought I might be able to pull it all off. Except that maybe once I was out of Ix, and less restrained in what I could do, I'd be able to use my Otherness to advantage. I supposed 2JS figured I'd made it this far—back here, that is, and even into his head—so he might as well give me a chance. And he knew I was highly motivated. Other than getting the stuff back to 2012, I didn't have other personal ambitions here, because I wasn't even going to live for very long. And I didn't have anywhere else to go. He owned me. Besides—

—what was that?

My eyes flicked automatically from side to side, like a deer's ears, scanning for movement. Just squirrels in the branches. A nightjar whirred. The path shrunk to a trail. By now we were away from any real villages but still in what

I guess we can call one of the Harpy bloods' hunting preserves. The trail became more and more twisted, curling close around gigantic trunks. Even Chacal's eyes could hardly see anything in the starlight, but my feet automatically found the spots where the others had stepped before me. Anyone trailing us wouldn't be able to tell how many of us there were. Not from the tracks, anyway. And anybody out in the jungle, a trapper, a smuggler, or a spy, say, who wasn't right next to the trail, would hardly hear a thing. Hup. Hup. I could feel crushed carrycillo grass through the layers of deerhide, reed matting, and rubber in my stiff new sandals. We passed three tiny villages, all of them our own. After the third, Hun Xoc dropped back and took me out of the line. Two of the junior bloods, out of five who were my size and dressed just like me for safety, that is, my safety, did the same thing. Hun Xoc whispered to me that my knees still needed to heal where the calluses had been sanded off. I said they were all right. He touched the right one. It was oozing. He signed to the bearers. Four of them stepped out of the line and knelt down. The four of us, that is, including Hun Xoc, climbed into the little seats, with our legs around the bearers' waists. My bearer stood up, got his arms over my knees, pressed them to his sides, dashed forward, found my previous place in the line, and fell into step.

About eighteen miles from our starting point the route turned northward, down out of the highlands into uncultivated bush, and tunneled into a wall of black foliage. There was a rushing sound up ahead, the snoring of Great-Uncle Yellow Road, who led north to the brine desert and the white edge of the world.

(41)

We filed downhill into a black valley filled with the river's negative-ion energy. The line slowed and bunched. I was a "jade bundle," that is, "something to be protected," so five of the bloods clustered around me, but between their bodies I could just make out the boatmen's huts silhouetted against a gray belt of water, the river that would later be called the Río Sebol, which was now called the Ka'nbe, the Yellow Road. It was less than thirty arms across here, just a bit above its winter low, and it looked barely navigable, but there were at least forty small ten-man canoes stacked on the near bank. In less than three minutes the menials had unlaced the cargo bales, gotten them off the sleds, wrapped them in rubberized cloth, and, taking directions from the boatmen, loaded them into the hulls. There wasn't even a single torch anywhere. But I figured they could all probably do the whole operation blindfolded anyway.

Our porters collapsed the sleds. We got ourselves out of our sandals. 12 Cayman offered a bundle to a big rock that held part of the river's uay; the boatmen guided the rest of us into the canoes. The bloods were in the last five, except for the two rearguard boats that would follow ten boat lengths behind. Each canoe had eight passengers, four bloods and their attendants sitting between the boat's owner, who stood with a long pole, on a projecting board in the prow, and the steersman in the stern. They put me in the second-to-last boat, the safest position. When I stepped in, the hull gave under my feet. It wasn't wooden but woven, or rather bundled, out of rushes. There was that old sensation of state change you get when you shift into the floating world with its different physical laws, and we'd already pushed off downstream. The stars faded as clouds came over and we were in that scarier sort of woolly darkness. Even so, the boatmen didn't light the prow torches and just kept poling us along by feel and the occasional glimmers of foxfire fungus and glowworm beetles. Tapetal eyes blinked between invisible tree trunks, monkeys, kinkajous, and owls, or even, one imagined, jaguars. We passed through aural mountains of tiny clicks that I realized were the sound of caterpillars chewing leaves, through zones where chitin rasps of a hundred kinds of orthoptera drowned out all other sounds, and through belts of the innumerous grunts of wo frogs, like hordes of ancient diesel tractor engines straining, unsuccessfully, to start, a sound that in my own, that is, Jed's, childhood, had the same cheerful meaning it had now: RAIN SOON, and which, come to think of it—

That was it. That was the thing that had been missing from the soundscape back in 2012, when I was here with Marena.

They couldn't *all* have died out, I thought. Could they?

I suppose they could have. Those polycyclic aromatic hydrocarbons are pretty heavy shits. Damn.

And even with all the noise Chacal's ears could also tell that something wasn't quite right. Maybe it was a little too noisy. Or maybe the tone was wrong. Maybe it was that there weren't any owls. Owls are pretty smart, I thought. They know the eruption's messed something up, weatherwise.

And the other bloods feel it, too, don't they? There was a stiffness in their pace that shouldn't be there . . . and it's not just me. And it's not just the political stress. Everyone really is a little more on edge than usual. Seismic activity makes critters nervous. Temblors. Giants in the earth these days.

As the river widened we passed other parties of canoers, some with rushlights on their prows, and before dawn we'd already blended into a stream of commercial traffic. We set a fast pace and passed dozens of other boats. Sometimes I could hear 12 Cayman, in the second vanguard boat, shouting at fishermen to get their traps out of the center channel. Just before dawn the Yellow Road merged with the Gray Road, that is, the later Río San Diego, at a town called Always Roaring Place, whose ruins would much later be known as Tres Islas. Like Tyre, the little city had overgrown its peninsula and new buildings rose directly out of the water. I got an impression of perpetual fire in the eyes of the little mulob' and of sweepers clearing a treeless market plaza lit by high torches like streetlamps. At daylight the water was the color and texture of worn battleship linoleum and the banks were a monotonous scroll of avocado-green sapote orchards and half-woven *halach yotlelob,* that is, raised granaries or drying sheds. At the second thirteenth of the day the river merged with the wider and faster Ayn Be, the Crocodiles' Road, which

would be called the Río Pasión. There was a glimpse of a city called Chakha',
"Red Water," which would be El Ceibal, a hunched white mound of palaces
and storehouses stacked over a hill like a heap of sugar cubes, so that you
couldn't tell what was construction and what was cut out of live stone, and
then it was gone as the river doubled back south. Just as we heard whitewater
ahead the boatmen beached us on a paved bank and a team of porters un-
loaded and raised the canoes over their heads and jogged off down the tow-
path. As the bearers lifted me out and rushed me after them, I got a glimpse
of the falls between huts and pilings, oddly regular cataracts over smooth
white platforms of encrusted lime. Hun Xoc said they were sacrificial stairs,
which the mud babies had built during the third sun. We shot through a Class
II rapids onto what we called Great Uncle Howler's White Road, which would
later be the Río Usumacinta.

They call the Usumacinta the Maya Nile. But the Nile flows fairly straight,
through flat deserts, and it floods them and recedes more or less on schedule.
The Usumacinta twists around mountains and through gorges and then widens and slows as it eases through the lowlands in long looped meanders.
Even so, in a country without wheels or horses or even llamas, it was the only
game in town.

Dawn oozed up in a greasy, saturated mauve. The color meant that it
wasn't ordinary clouds over us. It was ash from San Martín. At the second
thirteenth of the day, Pa'Chan, "Broken Sky," that is, Yaxchilán, appeared on
our female side. The city covered a bluff in the center of an oxbow, so, like
Constantinople, it was circled by water on three sides and fortified on the
fourth. Palace façades fronted the river to advertise the wealth of their clans
and five flights of wide pilgrimage stairs zigzagged up the main hill to a five-
mul acropolis. It's a perfect site because foreigners could pass close-up and
get the full tour from the oxbow, but they couldn't very easily attack from the
water. It was still too swift here to land easily, even if there were any good
landings, and even if someone did try it, they could throw nets across the
river above and below the invaders and lock them in.

We rounded the last curve of the hill and drifted under the *halach be*, the
great suspension bridge, two immense square piers thirty-six feet across
at the base and sixty feet high, with a six-hundred-foot roadway and a two-
hundred-three-foot span in the middle. Currently, in 664, it was the longest
suspension bridge in the world, and nothing this long would be built in Europe until they finished the Charles Bridge, in Prague, in 1377. Just in front of
the bridge there was a row of forty naked captives along the paved bank, hung

on poles like yellow scarecrows. Or rather, I saw as we got closer, it was just their stuffed skins. That is, the skins included the hands and feet, but the heads were fake, maybe made of gourds, and they were yellow because they'd been cured in latex. Their limbs were plump and inarticulate, like sausages. I guessed they were stuffed with corn silk. Hun Xoc said four of them were Vampire Bat House bloods from Ix, who'd been taken in a botched raid six years ago. As he was talking, our lead boat edged up to the shore and one of 12 Cayman's men leaped out. He waded to the embankment, climbed up three tiers of pilings, ran across the square to the vampire dudes, added one of our bundles to the mound of offerings at their feet, and, just as it looked like we were going to leave him behind, jumped into our last canoe. Our other bloods gave him a big whistle, the equivalent of a cheer. Show-off.

As we passed into the shadow of the bridge there seemed to be snow around us. I looked up. The roadbed fifty feet above us was ten feet wide, supported by a double set of ropes that looked about six inches thick. People were just standing up there, watching the hundreds of boats, a line of men and, unusually, a cluster of unmarried greathouse women. One of the women was shaking a basket of the white stuff down in a long swirl over the river traffic. Hun Xoc leaned precariously far over the gunwale, caught one of the flakes, and ate it for luck. It was popcorn.

On our male side the buildings grew in size and finish until I realized we were looking at Yaxchilán's greatest rival, Yokib'. They also called it "the princess of the jewel cities," and much later it would be called Piedras Negras. Yokib' meant "Entrance" or "Threshold," and there was supposed to be a cave there that led straight to the main hipball court of Xib'alb'a, the Underworld. Yaxchilán was a peach city, and Ix was turquoise, but Yokib' was yellow and in fact, it was all a horribly intense yellow, almost exactly a Bloxx Cadmium Yellow Light, banded with black so that even in the diffuse ashy light the city was hard to look at, a geometricized valley of flickering moirés, like it had been painted by Bridget Riley. The main mul was pure yellow, a steep fin thrusting out of the shimmer, with workers crawling around on it polishing the stucco like paper wasps resurfacing their combs. Supposedly the latest shell of the pyramid had been built a k'atun ago, when the city had eradicated two of its rival towns and taken thousands of captives, with lime made from the captives' ground-up bones, like the Palace of Mud and Blood at Dahomey. I counted fifty-four heads on display at the river gate. It wasn't a huge number, and also they looked so fresh that I figured they were wooden fakes. Then, as we passed them, I saw that the older ones, on the lower racks, were wrinkling. So they were real, but they'd been cleaned, salted, stretched over clay forms, oiled, and cosmeticized, and probably covered when it rained. Their names and capturing dates had been tattooed on their foreheads, probably while they were still alive, and their sewn lips had been puffed out somehow to look lifelike. Their eyeballs had been replaced with plain white stones, so they seemed to stare at you. Probably their brains and tongue and whatever had been pulled out from the bottom so they wouldn't rot. At least they weren't all scroggy like those guys back at Sky Place. Or, for that matter, the ones they used to leave out breeding maggots on Temple Bar until 1746.

Outside of the portages we didn't stop, not even for water. Vendors' canoes came up alongside us and we shopped as we moved. Our nightsoil collectors poured our urine over the side and fed the excrement to the dogs. They seemed to like it. Maybe they were some special type with an inbred fetish. Then later on the collectors would bundle the dogs' feces in elephant-ear leaves and hand them to local nightsoil men who came up alongside in boats surrounded by clouds of dung flies. Our outrunners dashed ahead along the towpaths, making sure there was a full crew waiting at the next rapids. In the twenty-first century people are always like, "Oh, there's no time anymore, modern life is so fast-paced, not like in the old days before cell phones or TV or whatever," but if I've ever learned one thing about the past, it's that it wasn't any more leisurely than the present. Not if you were one of the paranoid elite, anyway, rushing to get your act together before someone else took you out. And deadlines were always deadlines. As I think I mentioned somewhere, there was going to be a solar eclipse on what we'd call May 1. 2JS had said the Teotihuacano would probably close the borders five days before that, on 6 Death, 14 Stag, which was only twenty-two days from today. On that day the entire population of Greater Teotihuacan would start observing a "silence," and nobody would get in or out of the valley until after the sun was back on track. Speaking of which—contrary to popular belief— eclipses weren't something only the elite knew about. Word had gotten out, and when the day came around, everybody and his greatfathermother was ready for action. The city would be packed. Although it sounded like it would be more of a vigil, or a wake, than a festival.

Anyway, the point is that when 2JS had said we'd get to Teotihuacan in twenty-seven days, I'd thought it was major wishful thinking. I mean, it was 658 miles, for God's sake. If you were a crow. By car it would have been about 1,250 miles, and that was on mainly modern highways. And now not only didn't we have cars, but we didn't even have wheels. And the nearest horse was in Ireland. I'd remembered something about how Napoleon's army in Austria covered 275 miles in twenty-three days, and at the time that was considered a miracle. On the other hand, an army doesn't have relays of porters. Each of those poor French grunts had to cover every inch on his own feet. And no matter how hard the emperor drove them, they had to camp every night for at least a little while. It looked like we were going to be moving day and night, and sleeping, drinking, eating (mainly raw river snails, turkey jerky, and *ch'anac,* a kind of solidified corn gruel mixed with dog blood), delousing, defecating, and gods know what else all on our bearers' backs. Supposedly the relays of Inca runners could get a message from Cuzco to Quito, in Ecuador, in less than five days, and that's about a thousand miles. Right? Although they were faster. But still, if an expert hiker with a small pack can make twenty miles per day, figure that if we kept getting fresh porters we could make fifty. And then on the water . . . well, twenty miles per day is really outstanding for a canoe trip. But that's with a two-person canoe, and a longer one'll go faster. So if we have fresh paddlers coming in from shore, say we might also make almost fifty miles per day, even on the ocean. So to be on the safe side, let's say we have to cover 1,600 miles, then maybe our schedule wasn't quite impossible. Assuming no weather or whatever delays. Although it still sounded a little tight. But these guys did this all the time, I thought. Right? And anyway, 2JS wouldn't have any reason to bullshit me about something like that. Maybe we had a shot.

At a city called Where They Boiled 3 Tortoise—it would later be Ruinas Aguas Calientes—we passed our first enemy caravan. The town was a glut of multitiered complexes on both banks, with two rope bridges over us and an odd ruling-clan mul on our female side that had been covered with half-height wooden dolls. I guess they were offerings for a specific festival, but they were all elaborately carved and dressed and in a riot of colors, so that the place had an almost Tamil feeling of visual overload. A chain of large, ornate canoes was idling at a sort of ghat below the mul, and Hun Xoc said that the yellow and green on their streamers meant they were nephews of K'ak Ujol K'inich, the ahau of the Jaguar House of Oxwitzá, that is, Caracol, who'd been in a constant state of vendetta with the five greathouses of Ix for over four k'atunob.

Word came down the line that our paddlers should stick to their pace and that everyone should pretend not to see the Oxhuitzob' unless they saluted us first.

So far we'd exchanged some sort of greeting with everyone we'd passed.

Our boatmen hailed people they knew, sometimes effusively and sometimes with just a slight raise of the right shoulder, the equivalent of a nod. Evidently our trade party was a regular occurrence, just a little off-season and unusually hurried.

But the Jaguar boats did signal to us, and we slowed and edged over to them like we'd been planning to acknowledge them all along. In the shallows our boatmen turned their extra-long paddles around and used them as poles. I could feel the bloods in our canoe stiffen, and Hun Xoc's hand drifted an inch toward the roll of blowguns and maces he had tied under the gunwale. It's nothing, I thought. They had peace perfume out and so did we. That is, each boat had a little animal figurehead, a prow godling, lashed to a short bowsprit, with threads of incense streaming from its nostrils. Burning cakes of acacia gum and powdered tobacco told everyone you were coming without any violent agenda. As we got closer I could pick out their leader in the last boat. He had a high cat headdress, a blackened body, and a whitened face, and he scanned us with deep eyes. I and the five bloods who were duplicating me were wearing wide conical straw hats like Vietnamese *nonlas*, and I tried to angle my head down without breaking posture. Chacal had played against the Agouti Hipball Society of Oxwitzá, and won. Some of these cats must have seen the game.

It's going to be fine, I thought. Nobody's going to make you out of context. Like most hipball players Chacal had both played and accepted awards wearing an animal helmet that more than half masked his face. Even the best figurines of him were vague, likenesswise. And what with the hair extensions, the lack of ball calluses, the new tats and body mods, and the fact that I'd lost so much weight nobody'd think I'd ever been a hipball player at all, no outsider, we hoped, would connect me with Chacal. 2JS's idea was that I should try to come off as sick and maybe a bit retarded, so that people wouldn't talk to me so much. And of course I wouldn't look anyone in the eye.

12 Cayman's cantor sang a greeting song. A herald jumped out into the water and handed the whitefaced guy's attendant a red bundle of tobacco, jade, and our signature powdered chocolate.

There was a pause. Ix had lost hundreds of bloods to these people over the years, in a war that was just one strand of the eternal web of revenge that made the world stay put. At least it was limited, individualized warfare, not a total mobilization. It was more like you had to worry if someone had vowed that they were out to get you, specifically, or if you got onto the wrong turf, which you just wouldn't do. It was like gangs walking around downtown in daylight, crossing the street to avoid each other. Or you could say it was like the Middle East, where there can be, or rather, usually is, a war going on and there are still commercial flights taking off and landing all the time, strings of tour buses at the borders, and civilians all over the combat zone.

But the waterways were also sort of churches, as well as markets and stock exchanges. They'd been the only real commons for a thousand years. When you were on water you were under the protection of Jade Hag, who had dug the river in the days of the third sun, before Seven Macaw came. An attack on the river was as rare and despicable as the Pazzis attacking Giuliano de' Medici in the Duomo. Anyone who did anything violent was in danger of getting torn apart, not just by watchful locals but by his own party. Also, the cliché about how walking into a traditional village is like walking into someone's living room is absolutely true. Around here, wherever you were, you were somebody's guest, and you and they were woven into a web of reciprocal hospitality. Instead of handing over passports and bribes and ticket money, you gave gifts and got cheaper gifts back. And if your gifts weren't good enough, or if you made any trouble, people would remember, and it would come back to you later, and worse, somehow.

Finally, someone in one of the other Jaguar boats sang back the antistrophe of the greeting song, and someone else gave us a bundle of whatever their kind of shit was, and we were off.

"He looked at you," Hun Xoc told me through unmoving lips like a ventriloquist. When we were out of sight he made me put on a light mask, and my five doubles did the same. I guess wearing a mask around seems odd. But the fact is that in Europe people wore masks well into the nineteenth century. Men and women wore traveling masks partly because of the dust from the roads, and partly because, like respirators today, they were supposed to protect you from some diseases, but mostly just not to get hassled. Even in the U.S., even into the 1950s, lots of ordinary women still wore hats with veils. Right? It's not all that outré. And besides, the concept of disguise wasn't a common one around here. If you put on a mask, it didn't mean you were concealing something but rather that you were honoring or in fact embodying the being whose mask it was. Masks made you more the thing you really were.

A bigger danger than getting spotted was that part of our caravan could get separated, or ambushed, or turned, or all three, and someone would give something away to an enemy that would, eventually, get back to the Ocelots. Of course, all of the bloods in the caravan, and a few of their attendants, knew that Chacal hadn't really been killed at the end of the deer hunt. But they'd been given to understand that two of what you could call Chacal's souls, his uay and his inner name, had left his body at the exorcism. Now only Chacal's breath was still here, and his other souls had been replaced by mine.

Characteristically, 2JS had spun the situation as a positive development: 10 Red Skink, he said, had come from the Harpy House's mountain before his time to be born in order to warn the lineage that they were in danger and to help them persevere.

The head of our rear guard was waiting at the next portage. 12 Cayman, 18 Dead Rain, and Hun Xoc stood aside and met with him. They didn't ask me to be a part of it and they whispered in a hunting language I didn't know. But when we got back on the water Hun Xoc told me that the rear guards said there was a crew of twenty or so people following us, both in boats and, maybe, by porters on the towpaths. The guards couldn't tell where they were from, and from the little they'd been able to hear, they were speaking in market Ixian. The head guard had said he thought their headdresses meant they were from the Catfish House of Xalancab, near Kaminaljuyu, which was a neutral house in respect to both the Harpies and the Ocelots, but on the other hand no one had recognized any of them so they could just be in disguise. The Catfish were an obscure house that didn't get out much, so it would have been an easy deception.

Hun Xoc said 12 Cayman had asked whether they moved or signed like monkey shooters. The word could mean "manhunters" or "assassins." The head of the scouts said he couldn't tell. But they definitely weren't trying to catch up with us. 12 Cayman asked whether it seemed like they knew where we were going or only following. But the guard didn't know.

"If I had to bet on it I would say two to one they are Choppers," Hun Xoc said. As I think I mentioned, *Choppers* was a nickname for "Ocelots." They'd gotten it because they had the right to use a special kind of large ax in combat.

Maybe 9 Fanged Hummingbird had spotted us when he was prowling around as his nocturnal uay, Hun Xoc said. Maybe he'd come to suspect that Chacal was still alive. If the Ocelots captured me it would prove that the Harpies had perpetrated a blasphemous deception, and 9FH would be able to seize everything owned by the Harpy House, including goods, water and land rights, and people, without much protest from the other clans.

I didn't know what to say. Just don't dump me over the side until you're sure, I thought. Next I thought about asking whether our pursuers could have been sent by 2JS himself, but I caught myself in time. If they had been, either Hun Xoc didn't know about it or he was trying to fool me.

Besides, it was good for these guys to think I was closer to 2JS than I maybe really was. They were letting me in on a few things, letting me sit with the big kids in the lunchroom, but I had a feeling—well, let's call it a certainty—that they'd also gotten orders to keep an eye on me at all times. I never woke up from sleeping without finding one of them watching me. I never left the file of bloods without 2 Hand or Armadillo Shit running farther out than I had, outflanking me. And I noticed they never let me near the extra sandals, or the food, or the water.

And really, 2JS was right to be worried. Of course, I had to trust him. One takes the deal because it's the only deal. But there was still the little fact that he'd tortured me that kept popping up in the back of my mind. And even with all the pomp and bling-itude about adopting me, and all the bonding, and even with how much a stranger in a strange land wants to have a family, still, in my most *selbst ehrlich* moments, I had to admit that I didn't have any reason to think he had my interests at heart. And his objectives weren't the same as mine. He really just wanted the secret special sauce recipe. If he could break the Teotihuacano monopoly on the drugs, he'd be able to write his own ticket. But as far as my own lookout went—well, if I thought I could get away from the bloods, find some secluded village, do some tricks to get the locals on my side, put a raiding troop together, grab some sun adder out of one of the smaller cities—and supposedly there were at least forty-five nine-stone adders in Mesoamerica, outside of the seventy or so in Teotihuacan—and get samples of the *drogas* and bury them for the Chocula team to find (and really, they didn't need more than a mg or two of each one to be able to analyze them) then maybe I would have . . . well, come to think of it, now it was all sounding kind of daunting. But the point is, it was possible, at least, and 2JS had to be worried that I might try it.

So, my guess was that if I made a break for it, or if I even started planning to make a break, I'd find myself trussed up like a Christmas goose in about one second.

Still, I thought, maybe this is the right thing to do. Let's not forget that Lady Koh was the authoress of the Game in the Codex. Right? Even if she wasn't the best-known adder out there—and according to 2JS, that would either be 11 Whirling, who belonged to the Ixian Ocelots, or Boiled Tapir, who worked for Pacal the Great at Palenque—she might still be the best person to get on our side. Maybe she was something really special, one of the great adders, the kind who, as 2JS had said at some point, only come along once in a b'akt'un. Maybe if I got in to see her, everything after that would be smooth sailing. She might know everything and clear it all up for us. Maybe she'd scope out the Doomster right away. Just get that name back to the Chocula team and the twenty-first-century world'll be just fine. Maybe she'd even throw in a few stock picks. When/if I got back, I'd be richer than Prince Alwaleed Bin Talal Bin Abdulaziz.

So go with it, Jed. For now. Don't overthink.

I asked whether the people who were following us could be from Teotihuacan. Hun Xoc said they could have been hired by someone from there, but why would anyone want to? And Lady Koh—or the Twenty-second Daughter of the Orb Weavers, as he called her in order not to alert her uay by pronouncing her name—wouldn't have hired them because she's a nine-skull adder. She would already have seen that we were coming in one of her Games.

Right, I said. I don't think so, I thought. No matter how great she is, the Game still isn't a crystal ball—

The sea.

It was that Precambrian smell of salt, or more accurately of salt-loving things. I looked around at the others. You could tell they smelled it, too, from the way their movements were quickening. We were nearly at the edge of the dry world. Tomorrow we'd be out on the gulf, on the trade lanes to the Empire of Razors and the Lakes of Wings.

(42)

Two sea canoes and their crews were waiting with the advance men at a rendezvous point on the coast, a hidden beach three miles north of the outlet. It can't have been much of a secret, because there were about three hundred scruffy-looking people standing around on a strip of buttery sand broken by jags of black lava and the corpse of a lemon shark pulsating in the wash. There was a delay when the canoe's owners said that because of the eruption, the paddlers were afraid of being boiled and eaten by the Earth-toadess and we'd have to go farther off land than was usually considered safe. So naturally they hit us up for a higher rate even than what they'd agreed on a few hours before. Also we had to hire a highly thought-of local *k'al maac*. He was like what in South Africa they call an *inyanga*, a water doctor, someone who keeps you afloat by constant chanting and pouring baby oil on troubled waters and whatever. I figured he was just another faker, but later I saw him using an odd and, to my eye, simplistic version of the Game to suss out the sea weather. 18 Dead Rain did the haggling and finally we got loaded. Our rear guard stayed on shore. They'd look around to see if we were still being followed and catch up to us later. We offered blood to the Cradlers of the Northwest and launched.

I guess it might not seem like you could get over two hundred people into two canoes, but these weren't Old Towns. I figured each was about ninety-five feet long and eight feet across at the widest point. They were dugouts, or rather burnedouts, made from from mahoganies the size of Luna, Queen of the Redwoods. The lead canoe had a long neck on the prow with a little head like an elasmosaurus's, and the second, the one we'd be riding in, had a kind of lobsteresque thing with antennae. Their black hulls were scaled with or-

ange and white glyphs and glistening with manatee oil. They also had cano-
pies on them that made them look like Cleopatra's barge, but 12 Cayman
made the crew take them off for speed. There were no sails anywhere. Maybe
I should show them how to chef one up, I thought. Except better not. Don't
attract attention.

As we got safely out past the breakers, the bloods seemed to loosen up.
Finally, for the first time since we'd left Cocoa Town, they could chat.

"Ac than a puch tun y an I pa oc' in cabal payee tz'oc t pitzom?" a voice
asked. "Remember when we played here and you knocked out the forward's
eye?"

It took me a beat to realize he was talking to me.

"B'aax?" he asked. It was like saying "Hello, Earth to 10 Skink."

It was 2 Hand, Hun Xoc's brother. He was sitting behind me. Hun Xoc was
sitting in front of me, and the other major people in the canoe were 3 Returning Moth—the remembrancer—and 4 Saw-Tongue, one of my sort-of doubles. Our acolytes sat on our left. I turned around.

"Ma'ax ca'an," I said. "That wasn't me."

"Well, he fell down and you hipped the ball at him and hit him on the back
of the head, and his scarves kept his head from cracking, but his eye fell out."
2 Hand was big and squat with a kind of bug-eyed face, and he pulled back
the lids of his right eye and bulged it out as much as possible. "And he could
still see with the other eye, so he tried to stuff the loose one back into the
socket and couldn't, and then didn't know what to do with it, and he knew he
was about to pass out and didn't want us to get it. So he ate it."

"I don't remember that," I said.

"You need to eat a big bowl of tapioca," Hun Xoc said to 2 Hand. It was an
idiom for "cool it." Chacal was under a sort of *damnatio memoriae*, and even
asking about something that had happened to me before the Change was
getting too close to breaking the rule that my previous name wasn't to be
spoken. But 2 Hand didn't pay much attention to stuff like that.

I could hear 4 Saw-Tongue trying to stifle a giggle.

"Did that really happen?" I asked.

"It wasn't quite like that," Hun Xoc said.

"It was exactly like that," 2 Hand said.

"Do you remember 22 Scab?" 2 Hand asked me.

I clicked no.

"He was one of 3 Balls's gardeners," Hun Xoc cut in. "He was all warty and awful-looking, and he used to always go to the sweatbath alone, and then finally one time 22 Sidewinder came in and saw that he had the tip of his penis cut off. And he wouldn't tell any of us how it had happened."

"Do you remember when we found out how it happened, with Shit Hair?" 2 Hand asked.

"Are you asking me?" I asked. He clicked yes.

I clicked no. I looked at 2 Hand through my mask. How much was he buying it? I wondered. That is, my amnesia routine? He didn't strike me as all that swift, but there was still some reservation there. Anyway, how much were the other people in the canoe buying it, or the other people in the expedition, who'd hear about everything I said later on? Did they believe everything 2JS said or were they just going along with it? They weren't idiots. On the other hand, there wasn't any great tradition of skeptical secularism around here. Probably it varied. Some of them believed everything and other people thought their religiopolitical leaders tended to overstate things.

And of course even if they did believe it, they'd be mad at me for messing up Chacal. Apparently that had been part of 2JS's speech to them, he'd told them I'd come to rescue Chacal too . . . but still, there had to be some resentment here. And fear, too, probably. They're not sure I'm human.

Anyway, don't get paranoid. It's not all about you.

2 Hand went on. "Well," he said, "on the way back from the game here, we stayed in this mudman village and there was a *k'aak*"—that is, a domehead girl—"who wanted to fuck everyone. Every hipball player. She had long hair with brown streaks. And she was always hanging around and they called her Shit Hair. You remember?"

"No," I said. Actually it was ringing a cracked bell somewhere, but I'd have needed more context to bring it up.

"Then you don't remember when you were asleep and 1 Black Morpho rubbed *c'an aak'ot* on your penis?"

I clicked no again.

"What happened?" 4 Saw-Tongue asked.

"Well, Ch— this one here woke up," 2 Hand said, "and he started jumping up and down holding his penis, and he was yelling, 'My penis is too big! *MY PENIS IS TOO BIG!!!*' Apparently *c'an aak'ot* was some kind of topical priapic hallucinogen. And he was running all around the yard and he saw Shit Hair, and he said, Aha! And he grabbed her and started fucking her in the ass. So after a while he is feeling better, and he is wiping off his penis, but now Shit Hair starts to bounce around. She is going, 'Ayyy, ayyyeee, yee, yee, yee!'"

As you may have guessed, 2 Hand was now imitating voices and performing a vigorous pantomime, almost rocking the boat, so to speak.

"So she squats down and starts shitting. And all this shit comes out, and the rest of us are standing there staring. And then she starts shitting out her intestine. And more and more intestine just comes out of her ass, and it curls up under her, and then one of the dogs comes over and runs away with the end of it, and that just pulls out more and more. So he starts eating it, and more and more comes out, and then Shit Hair makes this wincing face and this part of her intestine comes out with a lump in it. And so this one"—he meant me—"grabs the intestine away from the dog, and pushes the lump out of the chewed end, and it falls on the ground. It is this little scrawny thing, and it is all wrinkled and warty. It was the tip of 22 Scab's penis! So this one is saying, 'I would know this penis anywhere! It is 22 Scab's! Somebody run and get him! We found it! We found it!'"

The acolytes were biting their lips to keep themselves from giggling. 3 Returning Moth and 4 Saw-Tongue were laughing. The paddlers, luckily, didn't understand our house language.

"This is all new to me," I said. Then I started laughing too. Maybe it was the way he did it. I guess you had to be there.

"That is enough," Hun Xoc said. "Finished. The Choppers will smell your hard-on."

I may have forgotten to mention this, but we weren't supposed to do much of anything sexual on this trip. Long-distance travel was the same as a sacred hunt. You shouldn't even ever have a secret erection, if you could avoid it, because, as Hun Xoc said, the same way it was supposed to spook game animals, it might let enemies smell us coming. But, of course, the bloods were mainly teenagers and of course males.

"We have to be *sac kanob,*" Hun Xoc went on. That is, fer-de-lances. The expression meant that, more than any other snake, the fer-de-lance was fast, hard to spot, and, especially, mute.

2 Hand settled down.

"Besides," Hun Xoc said, "you are saying more than really happened. Only a very tiny little bit of her intestines came out." He leaned back and put a plug of chewing tobacco in his mouth. It was dark already. No twilight in the Courts of the Sun. As we passed the bonfire at Comalcalco we turned northwest—

deathward—steering perpendicular to the stars of Teotihuacan, the Vulturess and Vulturess's Wound, that is to say to Thuban, which was the pole star back in 3113 BC, at the beginning of the Long Count, and its red shadow, ι Draconis. I could see the red in it more clearly than I'd ever seen it before, even with a telescope. Hun Xoc said that we were getting close enough to the stars to hear them hissing as they touched the water. I could hear what he meant, a sound like the sizzle of cigar butts dropping in a puddle, but of course it was just the waves. Phytobacteria flashed at each dip of their paddles, like sparks between flints. Just before dawn, which is the best time for collecting, I'd lean over the side—making an effort not to look at my new reflection, since it always freaked me out—and I'd try to list the inverts. There were peppermint shrimp, of course, and long red lines of krill, but there were also these huge cnidarian medusas and some kind of giant lavender ctenophore like a Venus's girdle that I didn't recognize. One time I spotted a 'branch I was sure was undescribed, but when I reached in to try to grab it the water was so full of venomous jellyfish that it stung my hand and I missed it.

Our rear guard caught up with us at noon. They were in a narrow canoe like a racing scull with ten active and ten resting paddlers. Hun Xoc and the other bloods had their hands on their spear throwers, but the boat was draped in strings of Harpy-colored paper flowers and when they got close the bloods recognized them. Our boats pulled closer to shore and into the lee of a sandbar.

The head rear guard climbed into our canoe and moved to the back. The steersman left his post and he and everyone else moved forward so the five of us, including me this time, could talk.

There was a big squad following us, the guard said, ten or fifteen people at least, the same people who had been shadowing us on the river.

We couldn't resist looking east. There were a lot of boats on the water, but he said they were too far away for us to pick them out of the pack.

12 Cayman told the scouts to make port, hire two smaller boats, and follow the people who were following us. Meanwhile we'd outdistance them. If they knew where we were going, he said, they'd stay on the water. Otherwise they'd stop at every port to find out whether we'd been through.

"And do not catch up with us again until you are sure which it is," he said.

The upshot was that instead of making landfall today, we reset our course north by northwest, farther out into the gulf, and paid the paddlers our first bonus for speed. Later tonight we'd reset again, to the west, and try to lose the tail. The lookouts kept watching the horizon behind us, shielding their eyes with rolled-up skins like telescopes, but the air was getting foggier, or rather smoggier, and they couldn't pick out anything suspicious.

By morning the water was swirling with iridescent slicks from dead whales and speckled with bloated carp. We couldn't see or feel the dust falling on us, but we looked gray around the gills, and if you scrubbed wet cotton lint over your face it came up blackened. The die-off had attracted all the seagulls in the world. I'm not exaggerating. I'm sure of it. Some were only the size of crows and others were as big as pteranadons. When we passed the ragged white carcass of, I think, a porpoise, so many gulls took off from it that some of the paddlers thought they were hatching out of its body. The flies, too, had had a major population spike and there wasn't enough wind to keep them off, but Armadillo Shit did a good job, constantly dusting me with a human-hair whisk, switching from one arm to the other every few hours. Poor old hardworking Armadillo Shit.

On our ninth night out of Ix the gulf got choppy and they lashed the canoes together with long boards to make a sort of catamaran. We had to get even farther out from the shore in case the wind got stronger and pushed us toward the rocks. It's a hurricane, I thought. We're grouper bait. So much for the Water Quack. He'll be the first one we toss over. But the shit passed over us and at what I figured was three A.M. the big orange moon slid out from under the clouds like a half a 5 mg Valium and dropped into the water. *So auch auf jener Oberfläche sich noch im krystallinischen Zustand befände.* The next day we almost surfed into port on the dead rollers. The town was a Teotihuacano outpost called Where They Were Blinded, on the north side of what would be the Laguna de Alvarado. It was mainly a complex of ghatlike mud terraces leading down into a shallow estuary clogged with canoes and barges and crews speaking fifty different languages. There was a big encampment of salters curing swamp rat and croakers, and even with the wind there was a fermenting-fish stench and a general sense of bad vibe.

While the big guys haggled, 2 Hand and Armadillo Shit set me up in a sort of portable wicker hut, like a bathing machine. I got out my writing stuff and a blank screenfold book with plain covers. I was going to use charcoal, but then 3 got me some splinters of hematite that made good clear marks on the gesso, like silverpoint, and I was all set.

I wrote and coded up my most recent note home:

[deciphered]

NEW KEY WORD: AWHNNBAGHSDDLPFSETQHYTAHBDSZ

Jed DeLanda
Tacoanacal Pana' Tonat (Alvarado)
Chocula Team
Ix Ruinas, Alta Verapaz, RG

Wednesday, March 31, 664 AD, about 11:00 A.M.

Dear Marena, Taro, Michael, Jed, et al.

You'll have noticed that in my first letter I tried to describe some of the local color, as it were, and soon gave up. In this installment I'll stick to business. As I mentioned, my first priority in Teotihuacan will be to get an audience with the woman from the Codex N, Ahau-na Koh. Here's what I know so far about her:

She was born, or rather named, on 1 Ben, 11 Chen, 9.10.13.13.13, in a place called Rotten Cane, which is a small city in B'aakal, in the orbit of Lakamha, Palenque. She was a member of the ruling family there, who were avian rather than feline and descended from 2JS's maternal grandmother. When she was five, she showed signs and a female adder of the Lakamha Rattler Society taught her the Game. She was especially apt and six years later the Society sent her to Teotihuacan to study with the Orb Weavers, a sort of convent of adderesses in the service of the Rattler cult there.

Even if it makes things seem more complicated, I guess I should mention that the Orb Weavers—they were named after the giant orb weaver spider, *Nephila clavipes*—were part of the Aura, or Vulture, or White, or Peacetime, moiety and Synod of Teotihuacan.

This was probably to help solidify ties between Lakamha and Teotihuacan. Even though Koh had to ceremonially renounce her biological family to become part of the Rattler order, the connection would still help her family politically, especially if she came back. 2JS mentioned that when Lady Koh left her family, the leaders of all the avian clans in the area sent gifts. 2JS gave her an especially talented contortionist named O Porcupine, who was still supposedly her favorite jester. In Teotihuacan she was one of a few young adderesses to become a nine-skull, an adept who knows how to use, and maybe formulate, the Game drugs. People say she talks to flies and sheds her skin every peace season. Like a few other Maya members of her order, Koh has either decided not to return to the Maya area or been prevented from leaving because of tensions between the Rattler's children and the ruling clans. People say that her clothes are woven by spiders, that she remembers being in her mother's womb, and that she can shed her skin. The cult she belongs to, the Star Rattler Society of Teotihuacan, was founded by a transplanted Maya ahau named 11 Xc'ux Tsuc (Coral Snake), who settled his lineage in the city on August 9, AD 106. It grew steadily over the centuries. Meanwhile, the two councils were dominated by the Aura (Turkey Vulture) House and the Swallowtail House. But starting about eighty years ago the two greathouses and their affiliated lineages moved to reassert the dominance of their own protectors, especially Hurricane, or the Wizened Man, and Koatalatcacalanako, a fanged water woman they call the Jade Hag. The Rattler Society was subjugated and forced to build a wall that blocks the view of the Rattler's pyramid from Teotihuacan's fetish-market square, which it had previously dominated. So maybe the Orb Weavers are getting squeezed somehow, and maybe they'll be willing to cut a deal with me to get out of a bad spot. Well, we'll see.

I'm at a loss for a better strategy. I have to admit that I've thought about sneaking off somehow and trying to pull a Lord Jim. Maybe I could take over some remote-ass village and then, when their archery was in shape, just march back to Ix and roll over the place. But that could take time I don't have.

I also wonder whether there is some other way to take care of the Game and the Game drugs. Wasn't there some other nine-skull sun adder closer to Ix whom we could capture and get to spill the beans?

But when I mentioned that to 2JS, he had three good objections. For one thing, any of the feline-clan sun adders would rather die than get captured. Dying was nothing for them, they'd off themselves if you just looked at them funny. And even if you could capture one of them and keep him under suicide watch, there was still no way he'd actually tell you anything. There's a myth that no one holds out forever under skillful torture, but it isn't quite true, at least not around here. According to 2JS, you could keep some people screaming 24/7 for twenty years and they still wouldn't give you the time of day. Second, the adders in this part of the world would only have small stocks of the prepared drugs. What 2JS really wanted was the whole recipe, and the actual plants or whatever, if I could bring 'em back alive.

Incidentally, he had reasons we couldn't steal the Ocelots' stash either. As we saw on the radar, a whole network of caves branches out into the mountains behind the Ocelots' mul. Right now, they're supposedly digging 9 Fanged Hummingbird's tomb in one of them. They say there's a whole little colony of sucklers down there who hardly ever come out. And they hang on to the drugs. Even if we found where the stuff was, they'd swallow it and kill themselves before letting us get it. You have to realize that bribes don't often work with greathouses. These people are absolutely incorruptible. ·

Forty years ago the Ocelots had assassinated the last of the other lineages' best sun adders. 2JS is only a four-skull and even so he's now the senior sun adder of the Harpy House as well as its ahau. His own eight-skull adder died years ago, and now the only adder of more than four skulls left in Ix is O Whirling, who belongs to the Ocelots. At this point, as far as anyone knows, all the nine-skull players outside of Teotihuacan are pledged to jaguar- ian lineages.

Whether these have been overridden by newer allegiances, and how persuadable she is, remain unknown quantities.

There also seems to be some conflict between female and male adders. There's a story that in the old days, most adders were women, and that some male adders had themselves cas- trated to improve their level of play. Some people say the female sun adders are more accurate but that they're being squeezed out by the men. Koh's group, apparently, gets around the problem by, effectively, becoming men. Supposedly Koh and the other female Rattler adders even have wives, that is, female wives, or concu- bines or whatever. Although maybe this is just a salacious rumor.

2JS says that if I come back with the package as planned, he intends to give away doses of the drugs to the heads of the non- Ocelot Ixian lineages, claiming that his ability to make them is evi- dence that he and not 9FH is the person who One Ocelot, the mythical founder of Ix, wants to have ruling the city. This might weaken the Ocelots enough for 2JS to get the support of the other Ixian greathouses. When they definitely were on his side, he'd find some excuse to call off the Game. Ideally, the other great-houses would force the Ocelots out of power and elect 2JS as ahau. Then, if 2JS lived long enough, he'd leave Ix and found his own city somewhere to the east. For all we can tell archaeologi-cally, 2JS's family could survive in power in some other city for at least another two hundred years.

2JS pledged to me that if I brought Koh or some other ninth-level player, along with some way to produce the drugs, he'll make sure I was put into an unmarked tomb, with the lodestones in the right pattern, and all the chemicals and information. Of course, I realize this is assuming a lot. How sincere is he? Well, of course I'm going to have to watch him on the back end. But I guess I could say that during our few furtive conferences, 2JS and I actually became almost close, despite everything. We understood each other. And as far as I can tell, he hasn't yet lied to me.

I'm enclosing fifty-six pages on what I've learned about the Game so far. You'll see that in the short time we had before I left town, 2JS taught me masses of "new" (to us) rules and strate-gies. He also drilled me on points of etiquette that he said would allow me to play with any Maya sun adder.

You'll probably be wondering whether 2JS taught me as much about the Game as he could. Well, I wonder about that myself. For one thing, I know enough about games to be able to tell that even if I were to study with 2 Jeweled Skull for ten years, I'd be lucky to get to the stage of playing with six stones. And of course, that's still nothing next to nine. I could probably spend years playing and never be able to read more than a single k'atun ahead into the unrevealed, let alone eighty. So either I've got to get a nine-stone adder working on this thing, or LEON will have to improve very fast, or the drug will have to do a lot of the work for us, or we're screwed. But whether 2JS was keeping anything from me, whether he had his adder flub that Game on purpose—well, I can't say. I don't think so. But as you know, I was never very good at reading people.

2JS has promised that if these notes return from this trip

without me, he'll try to entomb them and any other Sacrifice Game material he can find, with the lodestone pattern as we discussed, as near as possible to the target zone. Although I'm also not too optimistic about 2JS's chances after the hipball game . . . however, I am feeling good about getting to Teotihuacan on time and starting what may be a more fruitful phase of this operation. Thanks again for your confidence—

All best,
JDL
Encls.

(43)

They called the Nacouitan waterfalls "Xcaracanat," "Afterbirth Place," because the Earthtoadess had been mutilated there at the creation, when her eyes became wells and springs and caves, and the ocean became the pool of blood she's dying in. 18 Dead Rain said she had mouths at her knees, elbows, wrists, and a lot of other joints, and any eruption was just her screaming again for enough flesh and blood to keep her alive despite her wounds. He gave the sacrificers there a porter we weren't happy with. The bloods sat and waited at a travelers' ramada, haggling with vendors. Hun Xoc came back from the road and squatted beside me.

"We've taken on eighteen two-leg turtles," he said. He meant we'd ended up having to buy slaves, who weren't likely to be good porters.

I clicked, "Right."

It wasn't just to save money, he said. There were just too few professional carriers. It would be better to run an inexperienced slave crew ragged, sell them or just leave them by the side of the road, and hire replacements on the way.

I clicked, "Sure." That is, I clicked, "Right" twice, for emphasis. It was still two hundred forty miles to the Lakes of Wings, nearly due west. If we traveled twenty hours a day we might just make it before the Big Curfew. But the roads were filling up.

Hun Xoc looked at me. I looked back.

"Am I speaking to Chacal or to 10 Skink?" he asked. It was kind of out of nowhere, but he had a way of catching you off-guard.

"Chacal is gone," I said. "My real name is Jed DeLanda."

"Jed DeLanda?" he asked.

"That is right," I said. He'd pronounced it exactly the way I had. He was a hunter, and he was always practicing mimicked animal calls.

"And so, Jed next to me, where do you really come from?"

"I come from near Ix," I said.

"When do you come from?"

"I came from the thirteenth b'ak'tun," I said.

"I suppose 2 Jeweled Skull over us doesn't feel we have to know that."

"No."

"Eeeh." There was an instant contact and he looked forward again. "What is it like there?"

"Well, we know a lot of things," I said. "And people built a lot of things, cities even bigger than Teotihuacan . . . in the thirteenth b'ak'tun we wouldn't be walking here, we'd be gliding along in a sort of big sled on rollers. Except they carry their rollers with them so you don't need to keep replacing them. And we'd be going much faster than this."

"Eeee. So have you been to the Razor City before this?"

"Yes, but in the thirteenth it's all just empty stone."

"And you close to me know what is really northwest of Teotihuacan?"

"Yes."

"What is there?"

I said that there was a lot more land up there, and then oceans, and then more land on the other side of the world, which was round like a ball. I said that people and things don't fall off the bottom because the ball attracts them, the way a lodestone attracts another lodestone. I mentioned that the earth rolls around the sun, which is actually a much bigger ball on fire.

"But the zeroth skin is also on fire," he said.

I said, yes, the earth was hot in the center.

"Is that under Xib'alb'a?" he asked.

"There is no Xib'alb'a," I said. Maybe I was feeling a little testy.

"I know there is," he said. "I've seen it."

Richard Halliburton, who'd been everywhere and back twice, said that people were surprised when they asked him what the most beautiful country he'd seen was, and he said Mexico. And even though it's been well and truly trashed since he saw it, it's not a surprise to people from there or from near there. And a lot of people would claim that the old road from Veracruz into Puebla is the most gorgeous route in Mexico. Still, when one's trying to set a land-speed record, one is not in a touristic mood. We just pushed and slogged.

The road tended uphill. We passed so many no-place towns that I lost count after 455. Just imagine the phrase *village after village* with a bar over it to mean it goes on forever. Each had its own pathetic little mul or two in the center of a ring of huts. Swirls of malnourished kids and gangs of lowlifes tried to rip off the more helpless-looking wayfarers. At one point in the late afternoon we were jogging along—or rather our bearers were jogging and we were jostling—between low gray hills, out of sight of any other caravans, and I heard a flock of birds coming up at us out of the north. What was odd about it was that from the calls it seemed to be composed of all different birds, gulls and starlings and crows and oilbirds all mixed together, which would never happen, and then as it came up over us I saw it was a flock of hundreds of scarlet macaws, huge red, blue, black, white, and yellow things, like flying chimpanzees in clown costumes but with long fat tails. Hun Xoc, who was just a few paces in front of me, jumped off his porter's back, stepped out of the line, cupped his hands around his mouth, and sang up to them:

> *"Ah yan, yan tepalob' ah ten Ix tz'am!*
> *Ah ten popop u me'enob nojol . . ."*

> "All you macaws, all you proud things, go tell them in Ix,
> In our southlands,
> Go tell our grandfathers, go tell our children,
> Our brothers, our women,
> Sing in our gardens, our dooryards,
> To wait for us patiently, bravely,
> Wait for us, wait for us, wait for us, wait for us, wait for us . . ."

The flock expanded and constricted and seemed to turn inside out as the birds half circled over us, wings in lockstep. The blizzard of color made it seem like the white of the sky had shattered into its component primaries. A couple of droppings angled down, missing me. One hit Armadillo Shit on the chest. Well, that's what he's there for, I thought. The birds picked up Hun Xoc's song and sang it back in a thousand raucous but very passable imitations of his voice, repeating it over and over, fading away as they trailed into the south: "*T'u men, t'u men,* wait for us, wait for us . . ."

That night, 12 Cayman switched the pace to a walk so we could all stretch our legs without really working. It was like how Boy Scouts used to do thirty paces of walking and thirty paces of running, except the installments were closer to ten thousand paces. At 31 Hands, which was somewhere near Córdoba,

Chtlaltépetl came into view. It was and is the largest volcano in Mexico. Its Spanish name would be Orizaba, and 12 Cayman called it "Where Scab Man Jumped into the Hearthfire." There was a wisp of something trailing from its peak, but I figured it was just a cloud. From what I could recall it had last erupted two thousand or so years before now and wouldn't have another big one until 1687.

A shadow fell across the road, and I thought for a second it was the storm, or maybe a pyroclastic plume from some nearby eruption, but then I could see it was birds, or rather doves, and then as a few swooped close to us I had trouble keying them down in my head because they had these pewtery breasts tending to that warm sort of no-name red, and then I realized they were passenger pigeons. All at once they shifted direction and the entire sky had the feeling of a forest of poplars or aspens, the way when they're hit by a sudden wind they turn up the silver undersides of their leaves, and then the whole continent-spanning sentient wave streamed off to the west, toward Nacananomacob, the Lakes of Wings. An hour later some of the stragglers were still going by. It was unbelievable that they'd ever be extinct, but in a way it was even more incredible that there'd be a time when there was only one left, and that that one would die at 12:30 P.M. on September 1, 1914. At noon we had to stop absolutely short at Topacanoc, that is, "Hill of the Nose," because of a directional taboo. Or maybe instead of "directional" I should say "vectoral." That is, if you were walking in a given direction, you were presenting yourself to a certain protecting deity, in a certain mountain, and you had to respect it. In this case Hun Zotz, that is, One Bat, who lives in the west, was indisposed until dark. They didn't want to tell me what the problem was, but I got a feeling that maybe he was a she and had gotten her celestial period. It was insanely frustrating. Don't freak, I thought. It's not important how far away your goal is—just that you're moving toward it. This is the granola that gets you there.

In the fifth ninth of the night the Red Chewer attacked. That is, there was a partial umbral lunar eclipse. Supposedly the Chewer's eye was like an owl's and could spot motion in the dark. And he favored the Ocelots. So we had to stop and camp where we were, in a weedy fallow field too near the highway. Shrieks rose up around us, most of them far away, but some nearer than we would have liked, as people tried to scare away the shadow. There were old voices croaking an ancient form of whatever gibberish they spoke around here, and the outlandish dialects of the travelers and refugees who were quartered in Choula, and then even dogs and pet squirrel monkeys and wildcats got in on the act, barking and yeeking and spitting. I got up on Armadillo

Shit's shoulders and looked back over the tall grasses at the rotting town. The fifty-two niches on the visible side of the anthillish old mul glowed as the sucklers stoked their fires.

The rusty shadow reached the Mare Vaporum. There was a ghastly seventh chord from what Chacal's ears knew were long, thin Mexican requiem trumpets. It was the first time we'd heard them on this trip, and they touched off an automatic shiver. Eight hundred and fifty-four years from now the Aztecs would play them to try to scare off Cortés. The mul blazed and smoked like a volcano. Finally the Chewer's red shadow fell away—right on schedule, as I would like to have told them, but I was trying to keep a low profile—and there were hissing cheers that finally died down into four or five competing versions of the same sort of skirling hymn, tirelessly repeated in a meterless fugue. The Rabbitess lighted on the peak of the coal-red mul and hesitated for a moment, like she was deciding which side to roll down. I didn't really sleep anymore, but I dozed.

At dawn the outrunners came back and said there was some kind of riot at Where Their Grandmother Lived—that would be around San Martín Texmelucan—on the main route to the lake, so we decided to take the nearer southern route to the altiplano, over the Paseo Cortés. The road climbed hill after hill, like eroded giants' stairs. We passed hundreds of acres of recently burned-off forest, dotted with smoking limekilns like giant beehives. Pretty soon even the few hardwood trees that had been left for religious reasons disappeared. Pinyons and savannah grass took over the slopes. The people here lived in cobblestone houses and grew tiny-eared black corn. Piles of obsidian chips sparkled between the boulders. Obsidian was for Teotihuacan what steel was for England or Germany during the Industrial Revolution. There was an inexhaustible need for it all over the world, and like steel, it seemed to be a vector for some virus of militarization. Road after road gathered into the main drag. The smell of cedar was all around, not from live trees but from crews bringing in lumber from the northeastern forests. At night the temperature went down to about forty and to us it seemed polar. Our dogs flushed grouse and snipe out of scrub junipers and, amazingly, 2 Hand killed a partridge with a hand-launched javelin. Just to punish him for breaking the pace, 12 Cayman made him give it to one of the locals. My knee was better and I tried to run, but as the peaks came into view I got winded like everyone else and slumped into a carrier seat. Let the proles take care of it. I was past trying to be PC.

By the peaks, of course, I mean Itzaccihuatl and Popocatépetl on our left and, far off to the right, Volcán Tláloc. Our names for them were One Hunahpu's House, Seven Hunahpu's House, and the Boiling Chac. Most of the cones around here had been dead since the Ice Age, but Popo was showing a little activity, maybe sympathetic with San Martín, and dust hung from his east slope. Still, I thought, it was a pretty minor eruption, maybe a 1.5 or so on the VEI scale. If this were 1345, 1945, or 1996 we'd be in trouble.

Our twentieth day out of Ix was sunny with scattered clouds driving east. At noon we crossed the high point of the pass. The Lakes of Wings, that is, the Lake of Mexico, spread out 4,770 vertical feet below us, cradled in the mandorla between the bows of two sierras. From here you could see that it was wide and waveless, that its shores were scalloped by volcanelli and buttes, and that it was minty-fresh green near its edges from all the rushes and duckweed but fading to open water as smooth and reflective as a pool of mercury. You could see that the farthest point on the far shore was about forty miles away, and you could see that the basin was inhabited, that the shores were studded with villages, and that the lake was scored with causeways and crowded with canoes and barges and giant circular rafts.

Well, I thought, at least I could stop wondering why the place was called Nacananomacob, the Lakes of Wings. Congregations of *bach haob'* and *halach bach haob'*, egrets and white ibis, and droves of *kuka'ob'*, tiger herons, waded in loops near the shore, and farther out in the green zone *bich ha*, that is, sandhill cranes, moved around stiffly in ranks and files like frost-covered Napoleonic infantries. A population of redwing blackbirds lifted off in lockflap with the sound of all the barn doors in the Old Midwest swinging on their rusty hinges, and for a few seconds you could only see a few shreds of blue sky between the Hitchockian swarms before they changed their collective mind and settled down again. Nacananomacob, I thought. Νεφελοκοκκυία. *Nephelococcygia.* Cloud-Cuckoo-Land.

We descended into that different sort of air you get around high lakes, where it's as humid as it can get but too thin to hold much water. From down here you could start to see just how urbanized the area was. The better islands had been built up until they were chockful of houses like Mont Saint-Michel. People had been forced to build their huts farther and farther out into the lake, on piles of rocks, on stilts, or, it seemed, nothing. Speaking of that, Greater Teotihuacan, like greater almost anywhere, was 95 percent shantytown. 12 Cayman said a lot of these people had been living on the dole, dependent on various clans and members of different relief societies. Supposedly the Rattler Dole was one of the biggest. They gave out long braided manioc cakes like churros, and they paid for it directly out of contributions and diviners' fees. At about two hundred feet above lake level we passed an isobar and the air had a new sound. A *kos*, a laughing falcon, snapped at a leash of green teals, but they flapped and scrawnked and got away. Cliques of green kingfishers hassled the juveniles. An osprey splashed down, bubbled underwater for a minute, and came up empty. A pair of *halach pocob*, jabiru storks, with black heads, white bodies, and red collars, like Dominican nuns with slit throats, puttered through the rushes looking unconcerned, as though they knew the penalty for killing them was death by peotomy. There were enervations of Inca doves and triple redundancies of pigeons. There were things out there I knew I'd never seen a picture of, and they weren't just juvies or breeding plumage or whatever. Basically it was enough to give David Allen Sibley a heart attack. Guess I can't put these on my life list, I thought. The NAS won't go for it. A crowd was shouting below us, and when we passed them it turned out that despite the tense atmosphere there was an amateur ball game going on. They were knocking a big wooden ball around with crooked sticks like hurleys. We passed the game and flowed downhill in the river of masked supplicants, around long looping ramps. Most of them carried bone baskets. That is, they were bringing their parents' skeletons to add to the ossuaries in the eternal city so they could wait on the enshrined founders of their lineages. And still, the birds were everywhere. You'd think that it was impossible for anyone living here ever to be hungry. You could just reach out in any direction and pull dinner out of the air. And you'd think that for every thousand of whatever that you took, ten thousand would always come back.

At least, that seemed to be about what the human residents thought. We passed hundreds of open-air workshops in the courtyards of low white-plastered storehouses, and two out of three belonged to featherworkers. Trappers ripped live birds out of rolled nets, snapped their necks, and sorted them into piles while an accountant dropped a counter in one of several pots and kept an overall count on a knotted cord. A woman gutted and skinned them, and then other women plucked and washed and sorted. It was like a pre-Ford production line, with each person doing only a few operations. Some families specialized in plucking protected critters alive, and all you could hear when you passed them were herons and chachalacas shrieking in Dantean agony. We saw thousands of them staggering naked around the yards, pecking at dead fish and waste corn and flapping their featherless wingstalks like thalidomide arms. This was a civilization founded on feathers as much as England's was founded on wool. And even so, I thought, we'd brought these people two sledsful of even more feathers. Although, come to think of it, all our bird skins were in shades they didn't have. They had plenty of black, white, grays, browns, tans, light blues, pinks, and reds. We'd brought cloud-forest colors, purple, magenta, deep blue, turquoise, and golden green.

The mobs pressed in around us. Most of them were what I was starting to think of as *ma'ala' ba'ob*, that is, people lower than the soles of your feet. As much as I tried to stay populist, racism was a virtue around here.

We kept pushing. Sometimes all I could see through the range of heads were folded miles of fishnets drying on high forked poles. Hun Xoc whispered to me that 14 Wounded should have come out to meet us on the other side of the lake, at least. They'd only learned we were coming four days ago, and only from our own couriers—we didn't have homing pigeons, and even though there was a sort of watchfire semaphore system on the road from the coast, we hadn't wanted to use it—but still, that should have given them enough time to get ready.

"14 is acting the part of 7 Macaw," he said. It meant, basically, "He's giving himself airs."

"Hmm," I clicked. I squinted ahead. There was a line of what looked like squat ceremonial archways separating the road from a wide white causeway that led two miles across a sort of estuary to the main body of water. From closer up the piers turned out to be skull racks. Damn, I thought. This makes us look like pikers. Us Maya, that is. Back home we only put up a few celebrities and the occasional miscreant. Around here it seemed like they'd whacked anyone who ever even looked at them funny, and then they'd held on to every single head like it was a big deal. The ones to the far west were so eroded you could hardly tell they were human. These guys have no couth, I thought.

We gifted or bribed our way through onto the causeway. At the next peninsula the shore peons loaded us onto two rafts, each with forty polers, that took us east and north to Tamoanatowacanac, that is, "Lake Port of Teotihuacan." We passed an island that was a single giant saltwork, with short-haired slaves raising water out of the lake in counterweighted cranes like shadoofs and pouring it into acres of white-crusted tubs. A scarlet ibis stared at me like it knew more than I did. Thoth, I thought. And what god are you here?

The shore had been banked up and lined with a green-and-gray makeshift wall made of thousands of felled trees, all lined up with their branches toward the lake so that attackers would have to scramble over them. We landed at a gap in the wall and, with as much dignity as possible, which isn't a lot when you're getting off a boat, stepped into Babel.

```
 ••
••••
```

(44)

You know how a city like, say, Marrakesh or Benares or wherever looks all charming on the Travel Channel but then when you're actually there the smell and the squalor make you wish you were right now back in, say, Tenafly, or wherever you came from, no matter how wherever? Tamoana-tawacanac was like Benares without the filmi music. There must have been eight thousand people that I could see from here just milling around on the shore trying to get somewhere else. I had my porters lift me up so I could see over the crowd. We were in a sort of open circuit or pomerium, about a thousand arms wide, between the shore wall behind us and, to the east, a high stockade ribbed with ramshackle watchtowers. There was an ad hoc quality to the whole place, that sense of a once-proper park turning into a Reagan-ville, raggedy people setting up camp, in tents, in yurts, under blankets, under nothing, under each other. Vingtaines of Swallowtail javelinmen turtled their way through the mob, threatening too-aggressive pilgrims with palm-fiber flails. One blood at the back of each troop held a thirty-foot pole with a big round feather shield on it about five arms from the top. Each shield had a different pattern, which, I guess, was the troop's crest. Then, at the tip of each pole, there was the tanned skin of someone who'd gone somewhere or done something he shouldn't, flapping weakly like a wet museum banner.

In this world your clothes were your passport, and a gang of javelinmen helped steer us through the plebes. Members only, I thought. We edged past knots of people. By now I could pick out clans and nationalities by their clothes and body mods, and, as a bonus, Chacal's set of mainly disdainful status associations kicked in automatically: For instance, the orange sort of saris those short, dusty people were wearing meant they were Cacaxtlans, and over there, those tall wiry domeheads with—damn, I'm using derogatories, which was good manners here but bad, bad bad in Century 21—those wiry individuals with the precancerous sun-cracked skin were Chanacu, proto-Mixtecs, from the mountains around Zempoaltépctl. The roped-together gang of tall ectomorphs with the fresh scabs and penitential sand-bags tied to their ankles weren't slaves but Yaxacans, people from the far northwest of the valley, expiating a black debt. That line of tiny, pale, furtive, nearly naked characters with the big lip plugs and clay-caked bowl cuts had come from the far, far south, maybe even from Costa Rica, and sold little frogs and insects made of hammered gold, which was still a huge novelty in these parts. A minor Zapotec king, covered with rattling yellow shell scales, passed us riding on the shoulders of a hyperteloric giant nearly seven feet tall. There were two kinds of people with a western look: Taxcanob' from the Pacific coast and another tribe I didn't place, some kind of fishermen in eelskin and shark teeth. Four of them were squatting over a pricked cross in the pave-ment, playing the simple gambling version of the Game. The rest were stand-ing around kibitzing loudly. That's a dumb game, I thought. The difference between the full Sacrifice Game and what they were playing was like the dif-ference between tournament bridge and Go Fish. Times a hundred. Hun Xoc pointed out a crew of tall, hickish-looking northerners in deerskins who'd supposedly traveled for years across the northern deserts and might have come—it was hard to believe, but possible—all the way from one of the in-cipient corn empires along the Ohio Mississippi. They traded a kind of blue stone that was just coming in, tremendously expensive and still unknown in the Maya states: turquoise. Ahead of us there was the sound of someone get-ting beaten up and on our left a wandering mat-man, that is, a sort of inde-pendent auctioneer who had set up to sell off pilgrims' children so their parents could get in. He lifted a naked four-year-old boy up above his head to show him off, holding him by the cord that tied his feet to his wrists, so that the kid drooped forward, squealing. A troop of Maya bloods next to us, in low-grade homespun and overambitious hair, were Yucatecans, and the dudes with pyrographed whorls on the left side of their bodies were Coli-mans, here to hawk pottery to replace the stuff that would be smashed dur-ing the Silence. Apparently—and I wasn't quite clear on it yet—the idea was that anything with a soul, which basically meant anything with a func-tion like a weapon or a tool or even a bowl, could easily get possessed during the vigil and start attacking its owners. I pictured a stocky housewife thrash-ing her arms around in the dark, fending off an angry swarm of terra-cotta kitchenware. Anyway, you were supposed to break all of that stuff and start fresh. Maybe it was just a marketing ploy so they could all sell more stuff to each other. Instead of planned obsolescence, which would mean you had to come out with a new model every so often, they'd simplified it to planned obliteration.

We pushed toward the stockade. Move aside, VIP comin' thru. Getting in didn't look easy. A chain of Swallowtail bloods, three deep and in the fullest possible peacetime drag, blocked the only gap in the wall. Behind them, through the steam from hundreds of sweatbaths, you could see a terraced slope chockablock with freshly thatched warehouses and piles of stripped and sharpened tree trunks. I was thinking how we'd probably come all this way for nothing when I noticed we were getting into a receiving-hospitality formation and that 12 Cayman was being saluted by quincunx of Maya bloods who'd come up out of nowhere. Hun Xoc pointed out one of them to me: the famous 14 Wounded, 2JS's adopted nephew.

He wore what seemed like more jewelry than he needed for the occasion, but he was a little shorter than Maya-nobility average and he had a nondescript look under his nose mask. He was the head of what you could call the Harpy House trading mission in Teotihuacan. Actually, it was a little more complicated than that because the Harpies were part of an international sort-of-federation of eagle-related lineages, and he did business with a lot of them. But the basic point is that he handled a lot of Lowland business and even though he wasn't a citizen of Teotihuacan—which was itself a pretty fluid definition—he supposedly had a lot of friends in highish places here.

14 Wounded stood in the center of four adopted bloods. They were displaced rural Ixob, probably refugees, who'd been blooded one way or another to his clan. Despite the Maya faces they had a sense of foreignness, with angularly draped mantas and skin shining with red dog fat. They wore *tanasacob*, which were a sort of comblike pendant that fastened through a piercing in your septum and hung down over your mouth. They reminded me of Victorian handlebar mustaches, demure, in a way, but also menacing. They made it surprisingly hard to read a face. The reason for them, supposedly, was that in the presumably violence-free city, teeth were considered too aggressive to show. They said bad, scab-carrying winds came out of people's mouths. Which isn't far from the truth, come to think of it. It was like an evil-eye charm, except it was against the evil mouth. If your tanasac fell out, you were supposed to cover your mouth with your hand like a giggling Japanese woman.

It wasn't easy, but our group brain took over and we managed to clear a little space in the throng.

"Please let us feast you, don't refuse our cakes,"

14 said in a still-mellifluous old smoker's voice. You couldn't see much of his face, but his eyes had a jokey feeling.

"Thanks to your lords for sheltering our bloods,"

12 Cayman said in the honorific. Hun Xoc unrolled a gift mat and 12 Cayman laid a bundle of our best highland cigars on it.

We did the whole little greeting dance. 14 Wounded touched his shoulder, saluting me respectfully but not as an equal, kind of a condescending "Hi, little brother" salute. He'd hosted 12 Cayman and two of the other bloods before. But he hadn't been to Ix for over twenty years, and thankfully neither he nor any of his household had ever seen Chacal. I saluted him back as my superior. It wasn't the time to get huffy about the pecking order. Meanwhile, the porters who'd been trailing behind caught up with us, oozing in around the circle like a rope coiling into a bucket. 14 said he was anxious to share chilies with us and that the Swallowtails had decided to close the roads early, so we had to move. Right, I thought, what have we been doing all this time? Lounging around eating bonbons? Jerk.

Like a drill team we formed into our meeting-relatively-important-strangers pattern. It was basically a half-circle of bloods, with 12 Cayman in the center and three layers of attendants, of decreasing rank, crouching behind us. They'd put me on the side, in the second-to-most-junior position, so I wouldn't have to do any talking.

Around here, everything was like getting backstage. You had to know somebody. 14 already had an arrangement with the Swallowtails. The wall of bloods opened slowly, oozed around us, and closed behind the last man of the caravan, like an amoeba eating a rotifer. If it had been any kind of regular gate instead of a human one, some of the riffraff would have pushed through. Now we were in an awkward space between the stockade and the pass about a thousand arms uphill. There were high cairns of fuel wood and cotton mantas drying on lines, like we were in the collective backyard of some cracker trailer park. There was more elbow room here and we found a clear area. The porters, who'd been carrying the sleds over their heads, finally unpacked them and took them apart. They seemed upset about dismantling old pals. *My very chains and I grew friends.* A crew of odd-looking characters from a Teotihuacan house called the Cranes, who seemed to be like tax inspectors, picked through the contents. 12 Cayman and the Cranes' head dude sorted out the gift to the hill, which was like an entry tariff. An accountant paced around tying butterfly knots into a big shaggy string tally. We separated our weapons and a few prohibited classes of objects, like any green fabric, anything made from snakeskin, or any hipball equipment. The games with large balls were considered a type of warfare, or I guess you could say a martial art, and so they were prohibited here. In fact the only legal ball sport was the lacrossish affair we'd just seen, which didn't have any official betting. I noticed Hun Xoc and the other players wrapping beaded bands over the hipball calluses on their knees and arms. Around here professional players were considered disreputable characters.

"Am I allowed to bring in the shit in my stomach?" 2 Hand asked the accountant in our house language. "Or do I have to leave it here?"

The accountant said he didn't understand.

"Because I will want it back when we leave," 2 Hand said.

We all had to wear dark gray mantas, and we put in our tanasacs, those mouth comb things. Mine had been made for me—you couldn't ever wear another person's—and it still didn't fit. Damn thing. Supposedly you couldn't be barefaced anywhere in the sacred valley. Even the menials had to tie a rag across their mouths, like Old West bandits. Anyway, you couldn't imagine a more annoying piece of masculine jewelry. I've seen four-inch clit rings that were more comfortable. Probably.

The mask steward ran back and forth getting us ready, like a hairstylist before a fashion show. Meanwhile the acolytes put us through our paces. They were deferent but we still had to do what they said. I guess it was like the lord chamberlain, or whoever tells the Prince of Wales to walk this way or whatever. Each one of us—even the slaves—had to repeat a little peace oath, both in our own language and in Teotihuacano, which had endlessly agglutinated words and weird creaky vowels and was incomprehensible to most of us. The oath was all about how we'd never raise a weapon to anyone, always cover our mouths, and be present to suckle the noon and the dawn. Next we each had to throw an article of clothing into a bonfire. It turned out that the dressers had tied a single ribbon around each of our ankles just for that. You guys just earned your bonus, I thought. I'd been about to toss in my loincloth. Then we all also had to step across a line of morning-glory vines that made a uay boundary, that is, something the wrong kind of invisible characters couldn't cross. Finally the thurifers rebaptized each of us with smoke out of a giant pipe and gave each of us a little clay thing.

I looked at mine with that "Thanks, what the hell do I do with this?" feeling, like when they hand out that clay pipe and tobacco at the Yale graduation. It was an oblong lump of plain unglazed clay, fresh out of the kiln, with two holes or cups or depressions. Oh, okay. The cups were packed with powdered charcoal ground with copal and perfumed with scarlet beebalm. It was an incense burner.

We did our leave-taking gestures, turned east, and climbed the wide road with the lake at our back. I noticed that at some point four tall men dressed as Swallowtail acolytes had joined us. They're minders, I thought. Spies. 12 Cayman had said there'd be *tsazcalamanob*, "guides" or "hosts," and not to acknowledge them unless they said anything. Fine. Just pretend they're bellboys. It's for your own good.

Even more than most Mesoamerican cities Teotihuacan only had a few fortifications, just some low stone walls in a few key places. I got the feeling that for a long time the city had felt it was invulnerable out of sheer fabulousness. Lately they'd been building movable wooden barricades, cheveaux-de-frises, as they would have said in the old cavalry days, that is, stripped tree trunks with shorter pointed trunks lashed perpendicularly onto them in groups of three every few arms, making an array of spiked tripods. We passed four gangs of slaves dragging the things to the spots where, starting tomorrow, they'd lay them across the road. There were also three freshly dug dry moats, with punji stakes at the bottom, that we crossed on woven bridges. One was so shaky-looking I got off my porter and walked across myself. 12 Cayman glared at me with his sunken eyes, but enough pomp is enough. I got back on my human steed.

Birds scattered. The lacrosse game behind us dampened and hushed. Thunder rose around us, or rather it wasn't thunder—it's drums, I thought, big stone water drums, as full and inexplicably satisfying as D-bass timpani, rolling in bursts with long rests between them, *bombombombombom, bom . . . bombombombombom, bombombom . . . bombombombombom,* and I realized that the rhythm was the numbers of the day, *Wak Kimi, Kanlahun Sip,* 6 Dying, 14 Stag, over and over in a unique pattern that would never be repeated, 6 . . . 14 . . . 9 . . . 11 . . . 11 . . . 12 . . . 6 . . . , *bombombombom, bombombombom . . . bombombombom . . . bombombombombombom . . .* It was the angelus, the noon offering. Our troop slowed and stopped. I got a signal to dismount.

Damn. From here on we'd walk. Litters weren't allowed in the holy city, and you weren't even supposed to ride on someone's back unless you were incapacitated.

All the caravans had stopped. Everyone faced forward, to the northeast. The birds resettled. We got out our candelarias. Now the bulk of the booming came from over the ridge ahead of us, from the holy city. Drums answered from far across the lakes, coming in a half-beat late to sync with the echoes. Go for it, I thought. Rock the Casbah. The rumble filled up the valleys and the world seemed to shrink. Smaller household drums took up the beat until it broke into hundreds and then thousands of smaller, less disciplined voices and dissolved into an unparsable global rattling, like all the snare drums Ludwig ever made. Lighter-men were passing through the caravans with fatwood brands and one of them lit my incense burner. He whispered something about how it was fresh fire from the Hurricane mul. Do I tip this guy? I wondered automatically, but he was gone. Ah, that clean resin scent. That's the smell of freshness. Ouch. I'd burned my thumb. Damn. I turned the thing around and held it level with my forehead so the unbreathed smoke could float up. On either side of us women and babies and wobbling oldsters crowded the warehouse rooftops and held up their censers. Nobody within the city's orbit could get out of presenting her- or himself to the sun at dawn and noon. Even if you were a hundred years old, even if you were quadriplegic, even if it was pouring rain, in fact especially in the rain, to say thanks for the damn rain, you had to be there. And if somehow they couldn't drag you outdoors, they hanged you. So a little fresh air was pretty much compulsory.

The drums faded into an all-over chanting, a deep-throat ululation in a language that seemed to have fewer consonants than Hawaiian. I just mumbled along under my mouth comb. Later I heard that supposedly no one remembered what the words meant. Maybe everyone was just mumbling along. I plejuh legion . . . *to* the flag . . . Don't notice me, I'm just one of the sheep.

The chant faded. Like everyone around me I got some sand out of the path and snuffed out my incense. We walked up the last flight of wide white stairs, into the cooler air of the pass, through a big *Karamon*-like ceremonial gateway, and over the crest of the ring—

"*B'aax ka mulac t'een?*" 2 Hand asked. "But where is the city?"

THREE

Razortown

THE SEAS OF WINGS

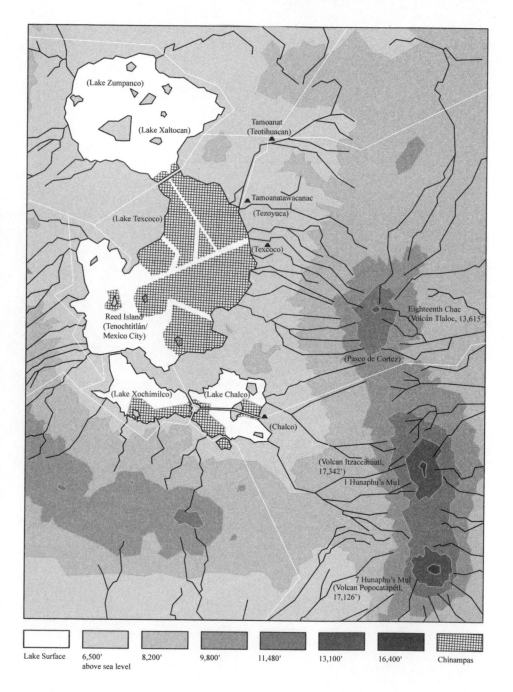

(Lake Zumpanco)

(Lake Xaltocan)

Tamoanat
(Teotihuacan)

Tamoanatawacanac
(Tezoyuca)

(Lake Texcoco)

(Texcoco)

Reed Island
(Tenochtitlán/
Mexico City)

Eighteenth Chac
(Volcán Tlaloc, 13,615')

(Pasco de Cortez)

(Lake Xochimilco)

(Lake Chalco)

(Chalco)

(Volcan Itzaccihuatl,
17,342')

1 Hunaphu's Mul

7 Hunaphu's Mul
(Volcan Popocatapétl,
17,126')

| Lake Surface | 6,500' above sea level | 8,200' | 9,800' | 11,480' | 13,100' | 16,400' | Chinampas |

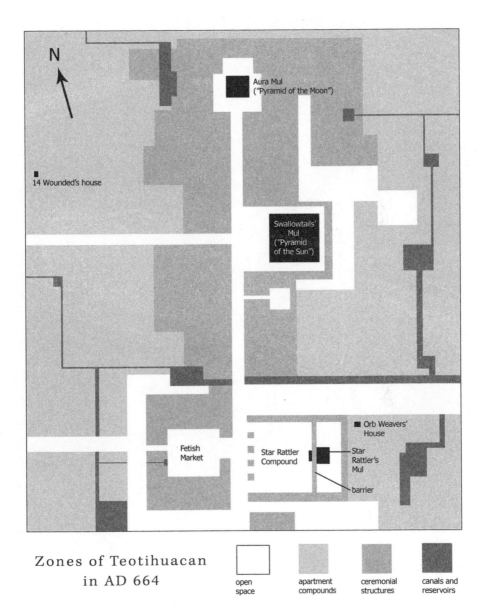

N

Aura Mul
("Pyramid of the Moon")

14 Wounded's house

Swallowtails'
Mul
("Pyramid
of the Sun")

Orb Weavers'
House

Fetish
Market

Star Rattler
Compound

Star
Rattler's
Mul

barrier

Zones of Teotihuacan
in AD 664

open
space

apartment
compounds

ceremonial
structures

canals and
reservoirs

(45)

A lake of fog filled the valley below us, with only the wide cone of Cerro Gordo, the city's White Mountain, outlined against the gray sky. We stood on a pass at the south end of the basin, and the stepped road descended in front of us between big, blocky stuccoed villas, down the long grade to what I knew was a smooth alluvial plain. It's not fog, I thought, it's blue. It's smoke, copal offerings from a few hundred thousand of those little censers. And just in the last second a layer of the smoke had sheared off from the top of the bowl of still air, so that now you could see one and then three orange lights in the mist, almost level with us, one far away framed by Cerro Gordo and then two closer and to the right, and then you could just see shapes swelling beneath them and see that the lights were the watchfires at the apices of the three great mulob, the Jade Hag's mul at the north end, farthest from us, and then the gigantic Hurricane mul on the right, and then, closer on the right and smaller than the other two, the indigo-blue mul of the Star Rattler's Children. Other fires gleamed out of the gray, each at the peak of one of the hundreds of other mulob, not so high as the three biggies but no dwarfs, either, and then, as the smoke rose and dissipated, more and more things solidified Brigadoonishly out of the haze, very very very solid things, growing by slow accretion like crystals of alexandrite in a laboratory vat, a molecular-scale skeleton morphing into a jewelscape for giants.

When I first saw it in ruins thirteen hundred and fifty-one years later, I was a late-twentieth-century urbanite, more than a little blasé about jet travel and skyscrapers, and I was still overwhelmed. For an eighth-century Meso-american there could be no conceivable doubt that this was the earthly paradise, the greatest city that ever had been or ever would be, that it had been built by gods before men existed, and that its rulers today were descendants of those gods, sitting unassailably in the center of the twenty-three shells of the universe. There are no words in English, Spanish, Ch'olan, Klingon, or any other language that could convey the otherworldly awe of this place at the height of its power. Before you could see the crowds you could hear or feel them, like if you put your hand on the outside of a beehive, and then you could just see that the surfaces, all the horizontal surfaces, were crawling with orange and black and gray specks, that the place was packed. There's no way all those people can get indoors, I thought. This can't be the usual population. They must be sleeping outside, on top of each other. Swollen, swollen . . .

As at Ix, only a tiny proportion of the construction had survived into the twentieth century. But unlike at Ix, those fragments had been excavated and restored in the early twentieth century. I'd spent a few weeks here in 1999 and knew the archaeological map well. Now I could see how botched and misleading the INAH restoration had been. But even if it had been perfect, there was still so much here that wouldn't last, so much that was new, that I barely recognized the place I'd studied. What the tourists would see was just the center of the teocalli zone, brown and stony in the middle of nowhere. Now that center was just one more elaborate part of a packed metropolis that spread out and out, a formation of interlocking hives that seemed more like one single building than many and that sprawled over the entire valley and all the hills, right up and over Cerro Gordo, a landscape of aggressive artificiality like you associate with places like Hong Kong or Las Vegas and not with the premodern world. There were no streets visible, since the streets were just narrow alleys between wide houses or rather kin-based apartment compounds, so that from here the residential areas looked more like a Middle Eastern city than any other Old World type, except for little things like the colors and the style. Like Manhattan the city was oriented a bit east of north, in this case 15.25 degrees, to align with Kochab, and the long, straight chain of sunken courts and wide spectator walls that the Aztecs would much later call the Street of the Dead stretched straight away from us. Actually, it wasn't a street at all, and from the look of things today it was barely even a processional route but a series of linked plazas, and it bristled with towers that hadn't been even thought of in the reconstructions. I guess for clarity I'll just call it the main axis. Now you could see that the Hurricane's mul was black and red, and the Jade Hag's mul was black and white, and the Rattler's mul was black and cerulean blue. The Hurricane's mul loomed like a heart attack against the hills, like, whoa, that's bigger than big, it's on a completely different scale, it's not built for humans. You could feel the mass, the sheer gravity, of the core, like if you put a steel ball down on a level surface it would roll toward it. The same fire had been burning continuously for over forty-four years, since the last gap in the cycle, but they'd extinguish it eleven lights from now so that it wouldn't defy the Prank, the Black Chewer. Then, when the eclipse lifted, they'd light it again from the sun itself. The thing had a numbing certainty that simply didn't allow for the possibility of dissent. Who could even think of revolt against *that*?

Now you could clearly see the Jade Hag's mul—much later the so-called Pyramid of the Moon—staring down the end of the titanic street. It was too far to see clearly through the smoke and steam, but it seemed to have flecks of something swarming around it. Birds? Something in my eyes? The third great mul, the blue one, the only blue building in town, the House of the Star Rattler Society, was where it should be, aggressively chunked down at the southeast end of the main axis like a rook sliding over onto the king file. It was smaller than either of the others but infinitely more ornate and still huge enough not to mess with, in fact quite a bit bigger than it would be in the reconstructed version centuries later, which would uncover an earlier façade. There was more than a touch of the Maya South about it, with its surface of interwrithing snakes, but even so the design had been geometricized or Mexicanized or Cubisticized or whatever, so that it both fit—fat?—fit in and didn't fit in with the rest of the city, another bit of asymmetry, in this case, maybe, more destabilizing.

In the center of the main axis, in the big plaza in front of the Hurricane mul, there was a fourth element that wasn't on my mental map. 2JS hadn't mentioned it, and it hadn't been reconstructed by archaeologists. How could they have missed it? Damn, it was big, a huge steep cone sticking up like a green thumb, almost as tall as the mul. As I focused on it, it resolved into a sort of open pagoda with thirteen floors or platforms, each about five arms above the other. The ant people crawling around on it were naked and painted with streaks of gray, which meant they were slaves. I decided that it must be woven out of reeds and green wood and that it was probably the *xcanacatl*, the sort of bonfire-of-the-vanities thing that 12 Cayman had talked about. That would mean it would be finished and packed with offerings in time for the darkness, and that after the sucklers drove off the Chewer, they'd light it with the fresh fire of the second dawn.

The Jade Hag's mul faces down the main axis like a general at a review, but the Hurricane mul faces off against emptiness. There's only a medium-sized plaza on the other side of the main axis to balance it, and it doesn't balance it, and the swollen hulk stares out alone into the west, and there's a sense of loneliness or loss. There was that feeling of a question, like say you see a Classical marble athlete with a raised arm, and that arm's broken off at the shoulder and you wonder, is he saluting? Is he throwing a javelin? Is he raising a sword? Or maybe if you hear the first part of a musical phrase without a resolution, and it's so disturbing you try to come up with a resolution yourself and hum it. There was an odd sense of expectation . . . a sense not exactly of something incomplete but simply of *waiting*, a Miss Havisham feeling of a world-size table set for an important guest, some great visitor outside, arriving soon.

(46)

Our porters hesitated. Mine mumbled a little protective prayer in a village language—"Grandfathers, look out for me," or something like that—but 12 Cayman got them going again and we moved forward and down. My mouth comb was dripping wet and ouchy on my septum. Because the road had stairs, it didn't have to zigzag like Old World roads, and a few times I thought I'd pitch forward. Waves of drying chilies, boiling corn, burning feces, and the clayish tang of freshly chipped flint and obsidian passed through us. Constant clicking and grinding sounds rose up to us from the flint- and polished-tool quarters, like thousands of click beetles and hieroglyphic cicadas. A white-faced registrar from the Aura House came through and took names, titles, and amounts, and knotted them into a tangle of cords like an Inca quipu.

We regrouped. There were only twenty people left in our core party. This didn't seem like a good sign. We moved down again. As the Hurricane mul rose level with us, its angles shifted in an inexplicable rhythm, layers coming into view and fading out again, steep and less steep and then steeper, in some kind of logical progression.

When we were nearly level with the valley floor, about a half-mile from the teocalli district, we turned west off the trade route into what I guess you could call a pedestrian alleyway. It was packed with people, and 14's men got into the front of our line, swinging these sort of flails to beat the riffraff out of the way. *Place, place, pour le Reverend Père Coronel.* We moved slowly past a row of doors that had recently been boarded up, or rather filled with stones and tied over with vine ropes. Hmm. Expecting trouble? Too many sailors in town?

Citizens edged sideways around us on either side. They stared at us, not with any hostility, I thought, but in a blankly curious way that was still disturbing. Maybe it was just the paint. Maya faces only got painted on a few special occasions. The Teotihuacanos painted their faces whenever they went out. But also the face paint here was aggressively abstract, with dark bands across the eyes that camouflaged the features and made everyone look the same, except for clan-marking dots that I couldn't read anyway. Some of them had ulcers or pustules under the paint, and really a lot of them didn't look that healthy. There was a lot of coughing and hawking. There's tuberculosis around here, I thought. It's a population sink. Probably a lot of parasitic infections, maybe some unclassified plagues . . . well, great, that's all we need.

We edged forward. The crowds got thicker. I was getting a creepy feeling about this place. I mean, on top of the ten thousand other creepy feelings. What's bugging me? I wondered. It wasn't that it was messy, in fact there was a certain Shinto cleanliness to the town. And it wasn't filled with shady characters. If anything, there was almost a middle-class air about the people we'd passed. You sure wouldn't get that in a Maya city. In Ix you were either a hotshot or not. Maybe it was just that the walls here were all rubbed with carbon and looked like fresh charcoal, mute matte black with sparkles. It's just a strange feeling to be in a black city. On the other hand, it wasn't so uniformly black as it had looked from the pass. The pavement, where there was any, was red stone, there were colored fabrics in the upper windows, there were the bands of shell, and the foliage drooping down from the roof arbors gave the place a lush sort of Hanging Gardens of Babylon feeling . . . still . . . maybe it was just that there were no written inscriptions. Nope, no signs, no glyphic monuments, no bills posted, nothing. In fact, 12 Cayman had said there was no written version of the language. Maybe writing was frowned upon as sumptuary excess. At any rate, except for a few accountants who'd learned writing from imported Maya scribes, the Teotihuacanos were illiterate. Still, they kept a pretty tight ship, administratively. We turned north, into an even darker alley.

Why'd we have to be in the white district, that is, the black side? I wondered. I bet the red side of town is nicer. And why the hell is the black side called the white side? It's like how in the U.S. what they call the "red states" aren't red. And in fact they're the more *anti*communist states. It's just to be confusing.

Every family in the city belonged to one of two moieties. The Aura, or white, or "peace" moiety lived, in general, on the western—black—side of the

main axis. There were hundreds of major white lineages, but the most important one was the Morning Glory lineage. The patriarch of the Morning Glories
was someone named 40 Agouti, who 2JS said was also Lady Koh's local foster
father and the archon of the White synod. Supposedly another name for him
was the "Peacelord." The other, red moiety, the Swallowtails, was traditionally
led by the Puma lineage. The "Warlord," the head of the Puma lineage, was
someone by the odd-to-me-sounding name of Turd Curl. Auras traditionally
dealt with agriculture, water allocation, what we'd call "religion," trading, and
most crafts. The Swallowtails dealt with war, as well as with weapons crafts
and foreign trade. You'd think having a division like that would be a recipe for
trouble, but because there was no intramarriage within the moieties—that is,
an Aura woman has to marry a Swallowtail man and vice versa—the two
groups were heavily interrelated and mutually dependent. For centuries the
balance between them had held up. This may also have been because of an
almost socialist ethic. Clan leaders weren't supposed to be honored outside
their own families, and the city wasn't ruled by any single person but by two
councils composed of the heads of the hundred or so main lineages in each
moiety.

We took another turn into a narrower alley. It was filled with people who
had to basically back up to get out of the way. A little farther on, finally, we
stopped. 14's herald climbed up the steep staircase. We all followed, up about
two stories into the white sunlight.

We'd gotten to about the same height as the Hurricane mul and had a
good view of the white quarter. Flat terraced rooftops stretched away on all
sides, broken with flower and fruit gardens growing in shallow beds of lava
silt and night soil. Plumes of sweatbath steam rose out of hidden vents and
vanished quickly in the dry air. A few of the compounds went up to roughly
three stories, but most were at the same height so that you could walk across
catwalks from one compound to the next, like you do in the pueblos or in the
old quarters of cities in Muslim Africa. Behind us the porters handed up the
bundles. I passed the "ready" signal forward and we padded generally northward on rattley plank bridges. Hun Xoc pointed out rows of big covered pots
at the edges of the roofs and said they were full of water in case there was a
fire. Finally we teetered onto the roof of the Harpy trading house. It was part
of a larger compound of buildings housing avian-clan Maya families from a
few different lowland cities. Something was going on down in the street in
front of us, but I couldn't see it. It sounded like somebody was getting beaten
up. 14's fellator had to call down to the street to ask what was going on, and

there was another slowdown while somebody shouted up and explained it all to him, and then somebody else's voice came in and explained it differently. Damn it, we don't have all day, I thought. I pushed through to 12 Cayman.

"Let's send a courier to Lady Koh now," I said in the Harpy House language.

"We should wait until we are covered," he said, meaning indoors. He said it wasn't a good idea to flash our merchandise where random people could see it.

It's true, I thought. People were crowding around on other rooftops to see what was up. I clicked, "Okay."

I went back to my spot in the line. I rocked up and down on my feet.

14 came back and explained what we were hearing. Apparently a woman was getting killed by the acolytes of the Morning Glory Synod, who I guess were like Taliban religious enforcers, for having a sneezing fit during the noon vigil.

12 Cayman ordered us not to go down to the street. He said we might not be able to get in through the formal door. Instead we climbed down a half-ladder, half-staircase into a small courtyard. It was about thirty arms square, empty except for a table altar in the center and a big wooden ancestor in each corner, with a single door in each wall. Automatically, we formed up on the east side of the courtyard, the direction we'd come from. 14's group stood on the west. Basically the whole household, which was at least fifty people, had come out to gawk at us. There was a minute of awkwardness. One was supposed to ask permission to come into a house before you were in the house. Now here we were already in the house. Still, 12 Cayman gave a foot sign and we got out the cigars and went into our greeting routine. It seemed to me that 14 Wounded and his men kept checking me out, out of the corners of their eyes. I knew some of them had seen Chacal play. Still, I looked totally different, didn't I? It's probably just that I was a striking-looking character. I'd been coming to realize that I had a certain personal charisma or physical presence, a lot more than I had as Jed. Chacal had been a major athlete, and even though I tried to subdue my movement, his body still carried itself like one. It's like when you meet some top baseball player, you can tell in a second he's someone special. I got a twinge of stage fright. 2 Jeweled Skull had drilled me on the right salutations to use with 14's household, the different way I'd have to walk in Teotihuacan, how to crouch below someone or stand tall over someone else, where I should sit in relation to 12 Cayman, to the hearth, to my own attendants, on what words was it all right to look up and when I

should just look down, and on, and on, and on. But even so, my rank in the group was still a little unclear, and that made it difficult for everybody. And around here you could offend somebody just by, say, facing in the wrong direction. Be careful, I thought. Not nervous, but careful. Hun Xoc sidled a little closer, either to make my face a little harder to see or to show support. Thanks, I thought. You're a good guy.

14 led us over to one of the big wood figures, the one in the southeast corner. It was an ugly, chunky, nearly naked seated female, a little under life-size, not an ancestor like I'd thought, but maybe the Jade Hag. 14 and an assistant held the thing by knobs on the shoulders and knees and lifted it up. Only the front half came up. That is, the whole statue opened up like a clam, and the entire anterior section of the body came off, with half of each arm and half of each of the crossed legs, down to the calves. The feet, and the posterior half, stayed on the stone base. The whole thing was filled with little painted clay dolls, about sixty of them. They were all over, not just in the torso section but fastened onto the back of the arms, the inside of the legs, just crawling all over. I guessed that each one represented somebody in 14's household. Maybe matryoshka dolls are kind of the same idea. An attendant came over with a tray of twenty dolls, one for each of us, and we stood around while a painter marked each one with colors to individualize them.

I snuck a look at Hun Xoc. What fresh insanity is this? his expression said. I looked away so that I wouldn't smile. The painter handed me my doll. It was a squat, cheap, moldmade clunky thing with a big Teotihuacan-style headdress, not like me at all except for the red stripes on the sash. But I guess now that I'd held it, it was me. I waited my turn and gave the doll to the acolyte. He tied it onto a spur that projected from the shell under the statue's left buttock. Does the spot mean anything? I wondered. Or is that just where they had some room left? 12 Cayman hesitated a moment before he put in his figurine. This was a Mexican affectation. Not Maya. I got the sense that 12 Cayman felt that 14 Wounded was going a little too native. When everyone was in they closed the thing up again. In spite of myself I got a feeling like the body wall was closing over me and I was all safe and cozy in the big civic organism, with zero individual freedom. Maybe it was the same with everything in Teotihuacan, it was all little mulob huddled around big mulob, small plazas enclosed in bigger plazas, and everything dependent on something else.

Now that we were family, we finally got invited into the sweathouse. As we trooped into the north archway, 12 Cayman made some excuse and he, Hun

Xoc, 3 Returning Moth—our remembrancer/reciter/accountant—and I managed to split off and duck into a side door. It wasn't polite, but 12 Cayman had been in the house before and he outranked everyone here.

We needed a little privacy, but the first room we tried had a horrible smell that turned out to come from a clutch of five slaves. They were about eight years old and squatted patiently in the corner of a wall, tied together with ceremonial light rope. One flinched at the flies crawling over his shoulders but didn't swat at them. Too passive. We went through another courtyard. There were cisterns, avocado trees in baskets, yellow cotton mantas drying on racks, and women in yellow *quechquemitls*—that is, the triangular things gals wore here instead of huipils—dying strips of something in a barrel. All very normal, I thought. Relax. We found a darker, deserted room. It had a provisional bandits'-cave look, with bolts of cloth stacked against the walls and big jars whose shape meant they contained pure salt. One of 14's attendants followed us in, but 12 Cayman glared at him in that dark way and he backed out. Hun Xoc undid his bundle and dug out the gift we'd brought for Lady Koh. It was a head-sized box of four hundred score tiny gorgets—that is, throat skins—of male violaceous trogons. When he opened it up to check them out, they seemed to glow in the gloom like a nuclear pile. It was an incredible gift, representing hundreds of man-days, worth who knew what.

(47)

One peculiarity of ours was that despite all the books, we didn't really have a culture of letters. I mean, like, memos or epistles. You didn't really send people written material, and the few times you did, it was always just ceremonial writing bundled together with something, like a card accompanying a gift. No one would ever just dash off a note to someone. For that we used remembrancers, people like 3 Returning Moth, who could speak ten languages, who were certified runners, who were practiced at standing up to torture, and who could listen to a long speech once and recite it back anytime in the future without losses or misprisions. I guess I was like that, back when I had my old brain. Except for the running and torture part. So what I was doing was already a bit of an innovation. Well, at this point, maybe we had to scrap the low-profile thing. Anything to get this woman's attention. Even if it raises a few eyebrows.

12 Cayman asked if Hun Xoc or I had anything to add to the message 2JS had worked out. We said no. He recited the message. 3 Returning Moth repeated it back. It was both a request for the gift of an audience and a warning that we, as emissaries of part of Koh's family, had an obligation to tell her about a threat. But we didn't know how she'd receive it. Her loyalties might be divided.

12 Cayman said that on the way here he'd found out exactly where Lady Koh was. I wondered whether he'd been discreet enough with the inquiry. Well, he's pretty cagey, I thought. It's fine. I'm sure it's fine. He told us she'd be in the east building of her convent. Then, surprising me, he said that we had to wait for two ninths and that he was sending two of 14 Wounded's people along.

Local escort, I thought. Hell. So much for secrecy.

We waited in the antechamber of the sweat lodge with 14 Wounded and his fellator, a son of 14's named Left Yucca. We got our hair done. You always had to look your best around here. I guess it's like being a celebrity, a female celebrity anyway, with something to promote, you're just going to one ghastly gala event after another, spending hours every day on hair and makeup when you could be learning Greek. Hun Xoc and I were having our hair redressed in the Teotihuacanob style, with thinner local oil and without beads or knots. Most Ixian would be too proud, or you might even say too patriotic, to do anything of the kind, but we wanted to be able to blend in if we had to. Blissfully, we'd taken out our nose bars.

The Teotihuacano were famously laconic, not chatty like the Ixob, and 14 Wounded and his little court had picked up the mannerism. But 12 Cayman had kind of cleverly drawn him out, and now 14 was telling us how at the moment there were at least a thousand native Maya living here—not that we had a concept like "Maya," though, just the names of different city-states—and out of those, only about thirty were Ixob. Eighteen of those were from Harpy-dependant clans and lived in this house, and the others were from lineages allied with the Ocelots. Compared to the hundred or so Ti'kalan here it was a small community. And since lately 14 Wounded had had to avoid the Ocelots, I figured he probably felt pretty isolated.

12 Cayman asked where the Ocelots were centered. Of everyone in Teotihuacan they were the people we most had to avoid. "Luckily for us they have to live with the Pumas," 14 said. "And the Pumas are becoming impossible."

According to 14 the current situation in Teotihuacan couldn't last much longer. Chalco, Zumpanco, and five other city-states in the huge Valley of Mexico economic zone—which had all been uncomplaining subordinates of Teotihuacan for centuries—were now defaulting on tribute. Most seriously, they weren't sending more fuel wood to the metropolis Teotihuacan's lime-kilns. 14 didn't say any more about this, but my guess was that over the years the deforestation had caused the flooding, erosion, and mudslides we'd seen on the trek through the valley.

Even so, he said, more immigrants than ever, especially Too-Talls, were pouring into town. He said the Too-Talls were the biggest problem in Teotihuacan. There were "four hundred times four hundred times four hundred families of them," which was an idiom for a whole lot. If all of them got together, he said they could overrun this whole place. They were descended from coyotes, which was why they were so smelly. They had to be wiped out.

The problem was that the city was obligated to host anyone who showed up. Now, just based on what I'd heard of their language, my guess about the Too-Talls was that they were the same people whose descendants, or close relatives, anyway, would be known as the Toltecs. So I was a little curious about them. But 14 said that the Too-Talls were low-clan "fog gravelers"—I didn't know what that meant and didn't get a chance to ask—who'd been kicked out of their own city and were overrunning the valley looking for things to steal. From what I could tell, their city was about a hundred miles due north of here. I couldn't identify it as any site I knew about. 14 claimed that he'd been there and said it was a low, sprawling, stinking barbaric place where the children ate feces and packs of coyotes ran through the courtyards.

"The Pumas go out hunting for them in the hills," he said. "But they can't do that inside the valley." There had been street fights and riots, and the Puma sentries had become insupportably overbearing. Over the last few peace seasons there had already been food shortages and "brown scabs"—some kind of plague—in the poorer sections of the city. Now, with the irregular rain, the coming harvest was expected to be the worst in seventy-one years.

And finally, he said, there was the growing tension between the Star Rattler Society and the synods of the two great moieties. The way he explained it, it sounded to me like there were parallels to Rome in the second century AD. The Star Rattler Cult was enjoying a resurgence, especially among the hearthless tribes and roundhousers, that is, the lower-caste clans who were constantly gravitating to the city. The Rattler Society was pledging more and more followers or converts every day, people affiliated with both the white and red moieties who were disgruntled with what you might call the stultification of Teotihuacano society. It sounded as though the Rattler Society offered a less hierarchical, less ancestor-based religion, with an overarching protector whose body wasn't localized in any specific shrine on earth but was the Milky Way itself. 14 said many of these new converts had also "blooded" themselves in particular to the charismatic Lady Koh.

The Rattler Cult was something like a Protestant movement, like Akhenaton's long before or Luther's long after. Wherever you have a syndicate of priests operating for a long time, they accrue a huge amount of wealth and people start getting resentful. And right now the Rattlers were riding a trend of burgeoning popularity among the dispossessed. The Silence would start six days from today, which would be five days before the eclipse. During that time the city would be under blackout and all fires would be put out, even the great fires at the peaks of the mulob. Athough there was a regular Silence every fifty-two years, this was a specially decreed off-schedule one, which was even more frightening. Those five days wouldn't be protected by any friendly smokers, or ancestors, or anyone, because they weren't real, name-able days at all, just cosmic mistakes. The people would feel adrift in a night-mare flextime at the mercy of heartless, malevolent uayob. A lot of people evidently hoped to make it through by "walking on the white back of the Rat-tler," that is, asking it for protection when everyone else had abandoned them. At any rate, it was going to get harder each day to see Lady Koh. We'd have to move soon.

Still, with all this, 14 didn't seem very worried. In fact, if anything he seemed blasé. Maybe he'd soaked up some of the myth of Teotihuacan's eter-nality. Of course, it was true that the place had been more stable than the Maya cities. If a Maya ahau screwed up a couple years in a row, the whole administration would be apt to change, by abdication or by coup. Or the place could be seen as tainted and abandoned. Teotihuacan was different. But that didn't mean it would last forever.

14 Wounded paused. 12 Cayman was silent. Neither he nor Hun Xoc nor I had mentioned Lady Koh. And we'd told 3 Returning Moth, the remem-brancer, not to tell his escort where he was going.

Lately, 14 went on, the Puma sentries had been harassing Rattler converts on their way from the market to the Rattler's Forum—the Ciudadela—and two days ago a family of converts had been killed. Relatives were demanding restitution from the Pumas, and people said the Swallowtails had broken their bargain with the rains.

So, with all this going on, the "chewing"—the solar eclipse coming up eight days from now—would be a dangerous moment.

Pause. 12 Cayman looked at Hun Xoc and then at me. He had that scary look of a commanding officer, but he didn't say anything. We didn't either.

"You next to me, have you offered to our greatfathers together with Lady Koh?" 12 Cayman asked. For all we knew, she might not just be under house arrest. 12 Cayman was trying to make sure she was still alive.

14 Wounded didn't answer directly. Instead he said that he and the other Harpies in Teotihuacan used to see Lady Koh in Rattler processions, but lately she'd been missing from them. But he said that, like a few of the other Rattler's sucklers, she was also said to be a top orator and that there was a rumor that lately she had been receiving pledges of personal service from many of the hundreds of people who were, every day, joining the Rattler Society.

"They say that four war seasons ago someone denounced her at the Puma Synod," he said. "And that night a scorpion came into his house and stung him, and his eyeballs popped and he went blind." He said she'd predicted the flood of three peace seasons ago, that she only saw the heads of a few of the top Rattler-pledged greathousers and wouldn't take any more clients, that she had two wives, and that she could "read the unborn k'atun," that is, that she could see twenty years into the future. "And she can talk to spiders and make them spin colored webs or weave ropes and banners."

I looked at Hun Xoc. He looked down—a Maya shrug—meaning, "Well, it's possible. Stranger things happen."

"The Two Synods don't trust her," 14 said.

Apparently Lady Koh was near the top, but not at the top, of a society or order called the Children of the Orb Weaver. They were women who, for ritual reasons, could act and speak as men and wear men's clothes. I guess we could call them cross-dressers, only that sounds like it's just an act. Epicines? No, that sounds femmy. Hmm. They use the word "berdaches" in a lot of textbooks, but really that's more specific to males from the Plains cultures. Maybe we should just call them "androgynes." Although that sounds a little biological, but whatevs. Anyway, over the last two tunob, he said, Koh and the rest of the Orb Weavers, and also their corresponding order of biologically male Rattler sucklers, had practically become hostages. He didn't put it this way, but to me it sounded as though the Puma sentries had put them under a kind of house arrest. It reminded me of this guy at the poker room in Commerce who used to wear sunglasses at the one-two table, like, "Ooh, I don't want anyone to get a tell on me while I go for that big twenty-two-dollar pot."

A messenger whistled. 12 Cayman whistled back, meaning, "You have permission to come in." He crouched over and whispered to 12 Cayman. 12 Cayman made his excuses and left. I followed him into the little passage. 12 Cayman turned and whispered to me that 3 Returning Moth had come back and said "the cedar stick had been broken"—that is, that Lady Koh wouldn't see us.

(48)

12 Cayman, Hun Xoc, and I found 3 Returning Moth and took him and his guard into the storeroom, the one with the jars of salt, to clean him up. Given all the ups and downs of traveling in the city, he'd probably run about three miles each way and was sweating and trying not to pant. Sunlight slanted through the oculus at a low angle. It was already the equivalent of four P.M. Late. 3 Returning Moth said he was as sure as he could be that Lady Koh had personally gotten the message. She'd sent the feathers back with another nearly-as-large gift from her to us, so it wouldn't be an insult. Her threshold-ers—that is, doormen—said all the Orb Weaver's children "had already pledged this time to suckle the Chewer," meaning they were fasting before the eclipse.

12 Cayman usually gave orders, but in this case he asked me what I wanted to do.

I said that we were going to go anyway. "We'll send a danger gift of equal size," I said. "Equal or greater."

We'll go right to the big guns. I sent Hun Xoc to get a few things out of the primary bundles.

"It's crowded there," 3 Returning Moth said. He told us that if we went back we should go south as close as possible to the main axis. They were clearing lower-caste people out of the teocalli district, he said, so there was less traffic. But it seemed that the upper-caste people were allowed to be there at least until sundown. 12 Cayman said he'd done a good job. Hun Xoc came back with a big armload of gear.

I'd settled on two items. The first was a green macaw-feather cape. It was worth a little more than two hundred and ten young male slaves, which meant it cost about as much as the rest of this trip so far. Well, if 2JS had to go into debt for this, that would be the least of his problems. We'd give it to the Rattler's table, not to Lady Koh, so they'd have to take it and burn it on the altar. That would oblige her to thank us personally. The second was a small white jar filled with what looked like tiny dried leaves about the size of a Scott number-seventy-six five-cent Jefferson stamp. They were symmetrical and jagged-edged, bright pink with biomorphic black marks like Rorschach faces. They were the dried skins of a lethal variety of strawberry poison-dart tree frogs from the Ixian cloud forest. They signified danger—specifically, "Prepare yourself, make darts."

I asked 12 Cayman whether the skins could look like a declaration of hostility. He said they wouldn't. These things had pretty definite meanings, and he was an old soldier who'd seen all of them. We resealed the jar. It was a freshly made piece with a profile-glyphic representation of two of the ancestors 2JS and Lady Koh had in common. The implied message was that we were reminding Koh of her family obligations.

"I want to add a coda," I said.

12 Cayman looked at me. I said the whole thing was serious enough for us to tip our hand a little bit.

I dictated:

4 Ahau: ajtonxa pochtal Tamoan . . .

In the tenth b'ak'tun, in the fourth k'atun, in the sixteenth tun,
In the zeroth uinal [~August AD 530], White Eel [that is,
Halley's comet] burnt over us

In the tenth b'ak'tun, in the eighth k'atun, in the thirteenth tun,
In the eleventh uinal [~February AD 607], White Eel
Burnt over us again

In the tenth b'ak'tun, in the twelfth k'atun, in the eleventh tun,
In the third uinal [~April AD 684], White Eel
Burns over us again

Before the fourteenth uinal of the nineteenth tun of the twelfth k'atun

Of the tenth b'ak'tun [that is, sometime before January AD
692], Teotihuacan is thrown down, abandoned

Finished.

None of the dates were in the Codex Nurnberg or in any of the other Game records that I'd heard about from 2 Jeweled Skull. But they were all real events. 2JS had also told me everyone knew about Halley's comet, naturally. But no one had been able to predict its reappearances exactly, not using the Game or any other way. I told him it was no wonder, since its periodicity is a long way from regular. You need modern instruments to get it within even two years, and they only really nailed it down in the 1960s. Koh would have to be intrigued. Right?

I made 3 Returning Moth repeat it. He had it right the first time. We sent him off.

"We won't wait for a reply," I said. "We'll give her four thousand beats"—an idiom for about an hour—"and then we'll simply be at her door."

12 Cayman looked a bit askance at this, but it was my lookout, so he didn't say anything.

Hun Xoc, Left Yucca—one of 14's sons—and I left through a vacant courtyard. Other guests of 14's household were already setting up to sleep on the roof terrace, but we stepped over them, climbed down into the narrow north alley, and headed east toward the main axis.

"Let's keep quiet," Hun Xoc said. He didn't want anyone to hear us speaking Ixtob. I'd insisted that we wear light offering masks instead of the nosebar that was driving me rabid—there's nothing worse than a bad piercing—and we had on local mantas with a gray-and-red scorpion beaded pattern that meant, simply, that we'd set aside our clan responsibilities for now and intended to make rain offerings for the whole city. So you couldn't tell what lineage we were from. Still, we weren't quite impersonating Teotihuacano. That could make for real trouble, if they caught us. I looked around. We seemed to have gotten a drop on the spies, if you can call them spies when they're so much not a secret. I guess it was like in the last decades of the old Soviet Union, when people knew who all the watchers were, or most of them. Maybe they were being overworked by all the new crowds in the city. Confusion would work in our favor. Anyway, we weren't doing anything subversive, were we? I mean, yet.

We turned right onto a dark lane like a Middle Eastern alameda. It was about five arms across and roughly the equivalent of a block away from the main axis, so that spatially speaking, it was similar to walking north on a (much narrower) upper Madison Avenue and at every corner getting a glimpse into Central Park. We were taking a different route from the one 3 Returning Moth had used. He would just be getting to the Orb Weavers' house about now. Give her a little while to listen to him. Read him and weep, as it were. I noticed a big hooknose snake basking on the low wall. They were pretty scrupulous around here about not hassling *Squamata serpentes*. It was like in India with the temple monkeys or sacred cows. Side benefits included a low rat population and a relatively high number of deaths by snakebite, which were hyped as a good thing since they meant Star Rattler had personally sent one of his grandchildren to fetch your uay to the thirteenth shell.

Two "blocks" south we crossed a sort of invisible border into a native Teotihuacano area. The north-northwest section of the city, where we were coming from, housed some of the richest Maya embassies. But the houses were older and smaller, and the area had a Maya vibe. I guess it was like ethnic quarters in any city. To keep up the New York comparison, it was like walking down Mulberry Street in New York and crossing the Italo-Chinese boundary on Canal. A trio of clumsy Too-Talls, who were way off their own turf, appeared out of a side arcade. Hun Xoc darted between them and me. I looked at him through my mask, like, thanks.

Don't mention it, he eyed back.

You know, I went on, I don't trust this Left Yucca character.

Don't worry, Hun Xoc looked. We won't tell him anything. And I'll watch him like a thief.

The houses were larger and newer here, all at least two stories, with stone and plaster below and lath and plaster above. Traders and pilgrims passed us with silent salutes, always in groups of three or more. They all had a certain furtiveness, as though they all had assignations as sensitive as ours. We passed a gang of night-soil collectors who stooped deferentially around us under their big stinking jars. Puma sentries strutted down the middle of the street in bands of five. Supposedly they liked to collar people or even barge into houses and confiscate any accessories that could be considered ostentatious.

The city had a singular sort of silence. In Maya towns somebody was always singing, but I guess here the songs only came at certain times. So you could hear footfalls, and the birds, and sometimes flint chipping and the moan of stone saws on wood, but not much else, and the thick walls gave everything a stony reverb that stewed those sounds together into a kind of liquid hum. It seemed like about half the people were wearing nosebars and the other half, maybe the more traditional types, wore veils or masks. Just as well, I thought. I'd been feeling that sort of travel fatigue you get from having seen too many human faces. They start looking mostly the same and not that interesting. The masks were all about the same, smooth impassive faces made of gessoed bark or the local sort of corn-paste papier-mâché, creamy white with almond eyes, just the blank essence of a face with no expression, no identifiable age, no sex, no ethnicity, not dead, but not quite alive. So, what with the masks, and the long mantas, and the quietness, and the lack of trees or grass, from street level the only natural thing you saw was the sky changing color overhead and the occasional little bridge over a canal.

When we were well south of the Hurricane mul we turned left, toward the main axis. There were five Puma guards standing at ease at the corner and 14's nephew, Left Yucca, spoke Teotihuacano to them with no accent. They acknowledged him, barely, and watched us go by.

So, I wondered, where are all the chicks? Of course, this was a ceremonial space, so it was segregated. But even on the side streets you hardly saw any women, and not many children either. It was like a Muslim city in that the upscale women were considered too valuable to be let out of the house. Or at least that's how they explained the segregation to themselves. This place is bugging me, I thought. Nope, wouldn't want to live here.

The place was big but still unlike what a twenty-first-century person would think of as a city. It was more like a collection of villages. You could live here your whole life and never go into the part of town that was right next to yours. If you did, it would immediately be like walking into a stranger's living room. And if you did it anyway, you'd have to spend some time with the first person you ran into, talking about who your relatives were and who his relatives were, and if you couldn't find any relatives in common, he'd beat you up. There wasn't any reason to go out either. There weren't any restaurants—that was an unknown concept—and there weren't any shops, just the different market squares. There were no theaters, unless you counted the religious dramas in the various plazas, and those were members-only. There was no entertainment, unless you counted visiting some relative's house and listening to singers in his courtyard. Well, I guess you had to count that. But you know what I mean, you couldn't just go out and go to a show. In fact, people didn't really go out, not to speak of anyway. They didn't go out for walks. They didn't go out to the country to get fresh air on the weekends. They didn't drop their kids off at school. Not that they worked all the time either. I figured mostly they took care of obligations, to the family, the lineage, the house, the moiety, the scores of patrons, the living, the unborn, and especially the dead. They did things that we, that is, we twenty-first-century folks, would call ceremonial. To them, though, they were practical. But the point is, the place just had an anhedonic vibe, a dutiful, holy-rollery mood, like in Jerusalem. Maybe it was just contagious piety from all the pilgrims. And like Jerusalem it was too crowded and too edgy. You could tell there were different cults in conflict with each other. And you could almost feel, if you weren't afraid you were just projecting, that like a lot of other giant capitals, it had simply grown for too long, and its center was rotting. I hadn't had a great time in Ix, but now I felt homesick for it. For all their hierarchicality Maya cities had a permanently festive quality, and somewhere you'd always hear people laughing. Despite all the teocallis and birds and flowers, this place was dour.

We pushed our way through to the middle of the plaza. For a second I felt transfixed by a line of force radiating from the Jade Hag's mul and stopped as though I were dizzy. Hun Xoc touched me and I followed him south. The crowd was thick but moving. As usual, there were stairs in the road. They didn't tire me out—I was past that stage—but the up and down did create a trancey feeling. Bands of dark and light color on the walls and pavement created a sort of op-art illusion, so that you couldn't always see the difference in levels, or how close the walls were, or where the next step would be. It was like how if you paint horizontal stripes on stairs, people coming down them will trip and fall. Damn, Marena'd get a kick out of this place, I thought. Shoulda brung her—

Watch out, Hun Xoc signed to me. I was sort of striding forward, and there was a troop of Pumas coming up, and he wanted to give them a wide berth. We edged over to the right, toward the huge open fetish market—which I guess is the right translation for the place, since it was the designated place for trading things like figurines and drugs and slaves and blades and charms and whatever, that is, things with relatively powerful souls. Anyway, we didn't have time to shop. We turned east and headed into the Ciudadela, the Rattler's Court.

It was both imposing and welcoming, bigger and better finished than any of the other plazas, and raised well above the average level of the city, with twelve big lookout platforms and wide flights of thirty-one steps, each leading up from three sides. You could see why the Spanish had thought it was a fortress. On its east end the top third of the Rattler's mul jutted up over a high incongruous wall. Supposedly the two Synods had threatened to raise taxes on the Rattlers unless they built the barrier. Apparently they'd thought that if the mul were less imposing, that would cut down the number of converts to the Rattler Society. But if anything it seemed to have had the opposite effect. The place was packed, obviously the most popular destination shrine in town. We pushed through, tacking south by southeast, toward where you could just see the crenellated roofs of the Rattler's sacristies to the south of the mul. One of them would be the Orb Weavers'.

The first group we passed was another vingtaine of Puma guards. There seemed to be more of them here, keeping an eye on the Rattlers. The next was a bevy of old women. It was the first time I'd seen women without men out and about. Unlike the plazas to the north the court had a feeling of inclusiveness, which meant a lot of raggedy characters. 14 Wounded had said that the Sky Eel's children administered all their charity and judgments from here, but it had more of a feeling of a public square than a religious space. There were no stalls and no visible goods changing hands, but even without speaking the language I could tell there was a lot of business going on, barter brokers making deals, accountants with game-board abaci going over addition, and bookmakers taking bets. Old cities really used their public spaces. To do business without money or telephones, you need a forum, you need agoras and piazzas. We passed younger people playing *taxac*, which was a complicated sort of verbal game, and *kak*, which you played with your hands. I noticed the pavement under my feet was black, and then, as we passed the big central altar, it turned briefly yellow and then red. It was laid out in Game quadrants, in very bright colors, some kind of dye, I guess, soaked into the limestone. We passed a pair of blue-hatted Rattler oracles who seemed to be just drifting through the crowd, answering questions. Missionary spirit, I thought. We stepped around knots of people bending over fire bowls, making offerings either to the Rattler or, through the Rattler, to absent relatives, ancestors whose names or remains had been lost. Most of the out-of-towners looked to me like village charge-holders. Each one probably represented a few hundred panicked farmers from God knows where. Left Yucca said the drought had driven more people than ever to the Sky Eel, that is, Star Rattler. He said that the Swallowtail and Aura Synods owned their own families of sun adders, but the Rattler Society adders were still considered the best. 14 had said it was because they could write and had preserved a library of refinements too large for any one person, or even a college of griots, to remember. Some of them were Maya immigrants, like Lady Koh, so maybe they'd been keeping up an island of literacy. Supposedly, Koh catered to out-of-towners like the Too-Talls by using several different languages in her offerings. The Rattler didn't mind, Left Yucca said. And the Rattler didn't ask for expensive gifts, just music, mint and tobacco smoke, and a few strands of your hair.

Drumbeats rose around us. The crowd's motion slowed and stopped.

The drumming echoed from all over the city, and you could hear it expanding out into the hills and beyond. It was a beat we hadn't heard before, kind of an ominous five-stroke roll.

"They say they are closing the city borders now," Left Yucca said. "Two days early." They were shutting up the city for the vigil, and no one is getting in or out.

Damn it, I thought. I looked at Hun Xoc. Well, we're trapped here now, his return look said. We just have to make the best of it.

As the drumming stopped, the crowd went back to its business, but more hurriedly and more quietly. Hell and suckstration, I thought. I'd been thinking about trying to scam a few hits of the Game drugs from somewhere and then getting the hell out of this turkey town now, before the vigil. Well, so much for that idea.

We edged our way down the packed staircase. There were Puma guards eyeballing us on either side, so I kept my head down and only got a quick look at the Rattler's mul. It was designed to look as though it had been woven out of two species of giant snakes, or rather two aspects of the Rattler: the Sea Rattler, who was sinuous and naturalistic, and the Sky Rattler, who was stylized and geometric, with goo-goo-googly blue-goggled Chaak eyes and equilateral teeth. Koh's all-female society lived in one of two compounds on the south side of the Rattler's Court, and its male counterpart lived in the other. From the buildings you couldn't tell which was which. They were built of smooth-plastered wood in an older style, with next to no windows, just the occasional slit. Their façades were washed with blue instead of the orange that was usual on this side. The doors were all tiny, carved with scare faces but still not showy. Most of the main doors had a guard or two sitting outside. Were they a permanent fixture or was it just because things had been bad lately? Families of supplicants, Teotihuacanos, Too-Talls, and others, crowded the alley. They didn't have sleeping bags and there weren't any fires. They were just sitting, or huddling, and shivering. It's no wonder Koh didn't want to talk to us. She was turning them away in droves.

We stepped over them and, a few times, on them. One or two people complained a bit, but the caste system let us get away with anything. We were bloods and they were nonentities and that was it. Left Yucca led us to one of the buildings, not to the door, but to the side of the door. Knocking wasn't done around here. It would be too aggressive. You either whistled as softly as possible or just waited until someone came out. But there were three *dvorniks* squatting in front of the court entrance, playing the gambling version of patolli on a stained cloth board. They all stood up. We presented ourselves.

They didn't want to go in and they said it wouldn't be any use, but Left Yucca seemed to have ingratiated himself with them on his last visit, because he got them into an argument about how, even though we were only related to Lady Koh at about five removes, that still couldn't mean she'd want people to say she'd "kicked over her hearthstones," that is, that she'd violated the hospitality rule. Could she?

They told us to wait. One of them went in. I felt like it was late 1989 and we were talking to Armando, the doorman at Nell's.

We waited. This is lame, I thought. Maybe Koh was just a patzer anyway. Sometimes I wondered about it myself. That is, I wondered about the obvious question: How come, if the nine-stone game was so powerful, the top sun adders hadn't taken over the world?

Of course, one answer was that they had taken over their world. They're solidly in charge of this place, I thought, and the rest of Mesoamerica, even if they let the feline clans take the political heat. I guess the real question I was asking was, why hasn't, or wouldn't, the Game spread to the so-called Old World?

Fernand Braudel used to ask his students to figure out why fourteenth-century China, which had a big navy and paper money and everything, hadn't discovered America. His own best answer was that they didn't need it. Everyone in power in China was already doing great, and the only thing left for them to do was get more entrenched. So maybe the sun adders didn't need to take over anywhere else. There's always a lot of inertia around. It can be more powerful than innovation, or ambition, or anything. If things were going well, why rock the boat? Good inventions don't always take over. Sometimes they die out despite or because of being so good. Babbage's Difference Engine didn't get built for a hundred years. They had pottery in Polynesia at first and then forgot how to make it. The Romans had concrete, and then after they lost the recipe nobody worked it out again until 1824.

I looked around. It was already pretty cold. It reminded me of the first time I lived in Mexico City. I was surprised at how cold it could get at night here. I smelled some kind of bitter incense. A family of Too-Talls who'd been picking their way across the other side of the alley stood still, looking down.

Something was wrong. Now what?

(49)

Hmm.

The Teotihuacanos weren't noisy people, but you always could sense that there were zillions of them around. All day we'd been hearing voices, scrapings, hammerings, the click of tortillas and flint, the hum of the grumbling hive. Now it felt like everyone was gone. All human sounds had stopped.

There were no dusk rituals here like we had in the Maya states. There was just an uneasy silence. Here, even in regular conversation, you avoided mentioning "sundown." You just said "later on" or "early tonight."

I looked at Hun Xoc. He exhaled, the Maya equivalent of rolling his eyes. People looked up at him, like, Hush! Echoland!

I listened. There was still a sea of sound out there, the yawps of gulls and dogs and the drumming of turkeys and the ultraviolet scrape of the bats, but the human world was holding its breath.

Damn, I thought. It's getting a little tense around here. I looked around at the supplicants. They were staring down at the ground or at spots on their mantas, anywhere but at the sky. The woman sitting next to my right leg was shivering, and I don't think it was from cold or from illness but from fear. After eight hundred years the city was still afraid of the dark.

Finally, as the sun sank somewhere, Koh's men came and led us through a bare blue courtyard and across into a sweatbath. We got undressed, reoiled, and wrapped into new outfits, purple cotton kilts and sashes with big mantas over that. Purple was a neutral color, that is, not neutral in the design sense but in that it wasn't owned by any particular clan. The guards led us through a tangle of dark passages, maybe just to confuse us, and through another little yard into a small square room. Seven figures sat on the bench looking up at us out of the gloom as though we'd interrupted something, which I guess we had. Five of them were dressed as males and wore blue diamond-pattern mantas. They had hats like big loose turbans that hid most of their faces. Even so, I could tell from the piercings that most of them were native Teotihuaca- nos, maybe high-status converts to the Orb Weavers. One of them was a stocky guy with a broken nose. The black and orange beading on his manta identified him as a personage 14 had told us might be here: 1 Gila, the leader of the Gila House, a big mercantile Aura moiety that had converted to the Rattler. He had a son of his with him. They both looked pretty tough. We didn't meet them, though, or even really acknowledge them. Unless you were going to go through a formal introduction, which could take a long time, you sort of all pretended not to see each other. Then there were two people in the room who were dressed as women and who I thought maybe really were women. Maybe they were Koh's wives. Then there was a dude who I figured was maybe a clown or jester, because he wore a sort of funny porcupine suit. As my pupils dilated I could see there was a dog squatting in the corner be- hind us and that there were lots of little jars and bowls and a wide tray, luxu- riously heaped with melting snow, arranged on the floor over layers of blue-and-white eyedazzler rugs. There was a mural on the wall behind them with shoals of kiddoid gnomides cavorting around an underwater volcano.

According to 14, this was a communal house shared by five or six families. And the families were all women. They weren't thought of as lesbian mar- riages, though. As far as I could tell from what he'd said—which wasn't totally coherent—the Orb Weaver's daughters weren't all androgynes. Instead, ving- taines of them were socially presented as regular, hetero-normal families, with some of the women taking male roles and others taking female ones. Lady Koh was one of the "bloods," which, in anthropological terms, allowed her to enter male-gendered ritual spaces, for instance the teocalli on the Rat- tler's mul. I guess the point—

Whoa. What the hell?

The dog stood up on its hind legs. I got a little shiver. It was a human.

She was a dwarf, with an elongated anatine face, and she was almost na- ked. Her skin was dyed green, but in this light it looked black. As she waddled around the hearth I thought of a penguin. I didn't have the urge to laugh, though. She's not achondroplastic like 3 Blue Snail, I thought. She was what they used to call a primordial dwarf, or a bird-headed dwarf. Seckel syndrome. I remembered they didn't live long. Probably she was still a teenager. I'd also thought they were usually retarded, but she seemed functional. She made a "listen" gesture. I squatted down a little lower.

"You over us . . . the Lady Koh speaks only . . . to one inquirer at a time," she said. Her voice was a creepy catlike monotone, and she spoke in male Teotihuacano, which had a scraggy sound.

"I underneath you carry the petition," I said. I looked at Hun Xoc.

He looked back, hesitating. This was against his directive to keep his eyes on me every minute. Still, they couldn't do anything about it. My audience with Lady Koh was the whole point of the mission. He shrugged his eyes, like, "All right, whatever."

Thanks for your trust, I looked back.

The dwarf had peeled up one of the rugs. There was a square hole under it. Like at the French court under Louis XIV, they were crazy around here for trapdoors and passages and peepholes. The dwarf crawled down into the hole face-first, like the White Rabbit. I put a leg in to feel how deep it was, found a sloped bottom, squatted into the thing, and crawled after her. My knees kept pulling on my skirts and fetching me up. The tunnel slanted down at about thirty degrees. I crept through the dark for about fifteen arms and came out a mousehole door into the middle of a passageway that was open to the sky. The dwarf led me around a corner, through another small door covered with hide flaps, and into a dark room about eight arms square. It was lower down than the previous room, but the roof was at the same level, so the stucco ceiling was nearly twenty arms overhead and made it feel like you were at the bottom of a well. There was a trace of blue from a high oculus covered with oiled skin that I guessed faced onto an overhung courtyard. The walls were covered with what looked like metal scales. There was a plain terra-cotta brazier with a few dying coals, two Go-bowl-size baskets, a pair of fly whisks in a little rack, and a bone stand with a single myrtle torch that burned with a greenish flame. The green feather cape we'd sent and the jar of poison skins were curled up in a corner like a couple of sleeping cats. And there was a peculiar scent in the air I can't get it together to describe.

It wasn't the bitter smoke from outside, and it wasn't the wax-myrtle berries from the torch, which have an odor somewhere between wintergreen and linseed oil. It smelled—well, it seemed to me like the opposite of cinnamon, if there were such a thing. Although smells aren't like colors. There are no primaries on the odaphone. Although I guess that's what makes a new smell possible in a way that a new color isn't. I swung my feet under me and tried to adjust the drape of my manta with one suave, easy motion. Instead I flopped down like a three-flippered walrus. God, I'm a klutz, I thought. Got to rehearse this stuff. The dwarf scampered around me and left the way we'd come in.

I settled myself into a half-supplicant position, dutifully facing the brazier. The floor under my calves was covered with some kind of spongy matting and strewn with geranium petals to ward off my pollution.

I sat. I felt weird. After a minute I realized why: It was the first time I'd been alone in a room since I woke up stuffed in that basket back in 2JS's prisoner compound. Too bad this wasn't a good juncture to run away from the babysitters.

The flap rustled. Child-gauge steps came up behind me. It wasn't good form to turn so I just sat. A short, slight figure—not more than an arm and a half—teetered around me, leaning on a staff tied with blue ribbons. Unsteadily, she sat on the other side of the brazier and laid the staff in front of her. She was an ancient woman in a man's manta and hair.

I shivered a little, just internally, I hoped. Her face was so wizened and puckered that it looked like it was glued together out of pebbles. But I could still see that it was black on the right side and a pale but normal skin color on the left, with the border in an S-curve, just like on 2JS's model head. Her gnarled hands were crossed in her lap. Her black hair had to be a wig. Her eyes were sunk so deep I couldn't even see a gleam.

2JS had been wrong about her age. But how was that possible? Or had she been somehow aged by poison, like Viktor Yushchenko?

She settled herself and held her hands over the brazier, warming them, although the room temperature was still at least eighty degrees. I was pretty sure that no other people had come in, which was odd. No guards. Maybe the great lady just wasn't afraid of being attacked.

Lady Koh opened her crinkled dark hand palm-upward. Say something, I thought. I spoke in the male high-equals dialect of Ixian:

"Tzitic uy oc caba ten lahun achit," I said. That is, under you, my name is 10 Skink. "Our family under you calls me your brother [that is, relative], of the Harpy House of Ix, the eighteenth [foster] son of the twenty-capturing 2 Jeweled Skull."

"And who is your father?" she asked. "And what other names do you have besides 10 Skink?"

"2 Jeweled Skull is my father," I said.

"And who lighted your awakenings?" she asked. I hadn't answered the other names thing, but like all good interrogators, Koh didn't repeat an unsuccessful question, at least not right away.

I told her. That is, I told her 2 Jeweled Skull's ceremonial grandmothers' name days.

"And who lighted your grandfathers'?"

I told her. That is, I ran through the right names from the Harpy lineage 2JS had adopted me into.

"And when did you become a brother of the Harpy bloods?"

"Thirty-three lights ago."

"And who gave you your grandeza?" That is, what sun adder was my mentor? Her toothless voice sounded older than her skin, like a burnt log getting dragged down a damp gravel path.

"7 Prong," I said. "Of the Harpies of Ix." In my ears it didn't sound convincing. You're just nervous, I thought. You're doing fine. Chill out.

"And why don't you next to me trust 14 Wounded's son, Left Yucca?" she asked. "Or does he talk too much?"

"I do trust him." Hmm, I wondered, had she been watching us through a peephole when we were out in the courtyard? And if she had, was what I was thinking about Left Yucca really that obvious from my body language? Or what?

"And is the Harpy House still tight, still green?" she asked. The idiom meant "are the slats tightly bound to the posts, and is the thatched roof fresh?" That is, were they okay?

I said the House was fine.

"But they do have a great-hipball game scheduled against the Ocelots," she said.

Damn it, I thought. All the way up here, she'd gotten the gossip that we were in trouble. No matter how hard you traveled, news always traveled faster. At this rate, you might as well just give everybody a cell phone. Had she heard of the fiasco on the mul? Did she guess that my visit had something to do with it?

I clicked that yes, the great-hipball game was going to happen. I didn't elaborate.

"And you used to play hipball," Koh said. "But you don't now. Is that right?"

Hell. Had she just guessed that from Chacal's big build and broken nose? Or maybe she'd picked up on some bit of body language. Or she or some spy of hers had gotten a peek at the spots on my knees or elbows where the calluses had been removed. Anyway, one didn't want to lie more than necessary. I clicked yes.

Koh paused.

2JS and I had spent hours going over and over how I was going to present our case. And the idea was to make the approach as soft as possible. I'd ask her to play toward the end of Teotihuacan. If necessary I'd lay a little of my special information on her to convince her that the place was doomed. Then, I'd try to make this lead into a discussion of the Rattler Society's problems. Ideally, I'd hook her in, inspire her to want to get the hell out of town, and then see if I could manipulate her into asking us to help her. And then I'd offer her asylum in Ix.

Of course, to do that I'd have to convince her that we could protect her. But 2JS had been leery of telling her too much. We thought I might do a few little tricks to impress her—make a barometer or a floating compass, say, or draw an ellipse with a trammel, or just clue her in to, say, fractions. Assuming she was enough of a nerdette to be impressed by such things, which, since she was a sun adder, she certainly would be. And we thought I could even trade a few of those tricks, or a few bits of information, for the drugs and recipes. But I shouldn't ask her about the Game in the Codex, because that could lead into a discussion of the 4 Ahau date, in 2012, and if I seemed especially worried about that she'd wonder why. After all, the thirteenth b'ak'tun was a long way away. And we'd decided that I shouldn't tell her anything about Jed, or where I really came from or whatever. For one thing Lady Koh probably wouldn't believe it. And even a credulous type who'd believe anything wouldn't be able to visualize it. Only people who'd experienced it, the way 2JS and I had, would know what I was talking about. Otherwise it would be like I was babbling in Martian, about Martian stuff.

And if I showed her too many tricks, or clued her in to too much science or whatever, I'd start to seem too powerful. She might think I was some kind of scab-caster, or even a smoker, a deity, in a human skin. Or was I a representative of some great adder, working through 2 Jeweled Skull to disguise my real master? Or was I actually some great nine-skull adder myself, one she'd somehow never heard of, who was disguising his abilities? Or what if she thought I was a spy from one of the two Teotihuacano Synods—who, according to folklore, knew everything—trying to lure her into an obvious act of treason? There was no telling what she'd do. What if she told her order about me? After all, she was blooded to them. They'd likely have the usual knee-jerk reaction, that I was too much of a threat to the status quo, and have me killed.

At best, Koh would figure she was getting hustled. She'd assume—and with some reason—that as soon as I got what I wanted, I'd leave her in the lurch. I should just present myself as a novice adder who nevertheless had some very special insights, and leave it at that. She shouldn't know too much about why I was here in Teotihuacan, or rather she should think I was here on a routine trade run. She shouldn't know that 2JS was having problems in Ix. Although it was too late for that. I had to make her think that 2JS was large and in charge, and that he was the only greathouse in her home territory who was going to offer her a safe harbor. We needed her to feel like bringing the goods back to Ix was her own idea. And of course, most of all, I shouldn't ask her about the two dusts. In fact I shouldn't even mention them. If she suspected they were the main thing we wanted, that would set off every alarm in the place, and she'd toss me out.

Koh gestured with her tiny light hand. The Penguin Woman came up behind me again and slid between us. She held a big basket in her little talons. She kneed over to the brazier, sat, and took out two hexalobed terra-cotta bowls and two cylindrical drinking pots. Like almost all the dishes and vessels and whatever in Teotihuacan, they were well-made but unornamented—like Pyrex, as Esther Pasztory said. Supposedly some of the top smokers here were poor, and anything too luxurious was a hazard because it might make them jealous. The dwarf mixed powdered cacao beans, honey, and hot water, in that order, and, as per routine, poured the liquid from pot to pot to work up a foam. She put the empty pot down and passed the full one to Koh. Koh took a sip and gave the pot to the dwarf. She passed it to me. I did the little cup-accepted gesture, drank half of it, gestured that it was great, and drank the rest. It was hot, that is, spicy hot, and cardamomy. I put the pot down, and the Penguin Woman took it away.

And that was about as far as they went with serving drinks around here. I realized I was also hungry. You'd think they'd bring in a tray of fried goliath roaches or something. But they didn't do things that way around here. Serving beverages in a host-guest situation was more for ritual than thirst. You didn't often just sit and drink with someone. It wasn't like tea in the East or cocktails in the West or anything. You just took your beverage, drank it standing up in as few drafts as possible, and passed it on. And snacking was something you did on your own time. It was one of the things that would have totally fruk me out if Chacal's body hadn't already been used to it. Even people who could afford as much as they wanted hardly ever ate even two meals a day. And every third day or so, they didn't eat at all. Most of the time you could offer a strip of deer jerky to, say, Hun Xoc, and he'd say, "Oh, no thanks, I had something yesterday." And he was a hipball player who needed the weight. And then when they did eat, it was a Lucullan binge. At the average royal feast three-fourths of the food would go to waste. Well, whatever. Where was I?

Time to say something.

"We underneath you have brought you a bundle," I said. *Bundle* was a politer way of saying gift or offering, since it meant you didn't have to decline the noun any further and give away what was inside. "I under you have tried to read the skulls for us, for my family, and I have failed. We beg you, take the bundle and read our skulls."

"You next to me give too much," she said.

She treated us to another insufferable pause. I asked again. Damn it, I thought. If she says no, I'm going to start smashing things. Although really, one adder couldn't or shouldn't refuse to do a reading for another. At least not once you were face-to-face. Or maybe I was relying too much on professional courtesy.

The Penguin Woman lit something in a little dish. It was an incense ball, the kind they used as clocks around Palenque. From its size it looked like it would have about a quarter of a ninth-light on it, that is, about forty-two minutes. Better hurry, I thought. But the pause stretched on. Finally, she clicked her tongue twice, meaning she'd take the job. She untied two ribbons on her staff. It turned out to be a rolled-up wicker game board. She spread it out on the west side of the brazier. It was the same design 2JS had used, with the same number of bins and everything, but larger. She opened a jar, took out a pinch of powdered tobacco, and, rather demurely, rubbed it on the inside of her thigh.

Okay, I thought. Give her a lowball.

I asked her to tell me the date of my death.

She took out a grandeza of tz'ite-tree seeds and scattered them over the board.

There was something perfunctory about her style, and I got the feeling she didn't plan to give me anything but the briefest possible session. Four runners chased my alter-ego stone into a near dead end. After a little calculation she gave the next *Wak Ahau, Waxac Muan*, or 6 Overlord, 8 Jeweled Owl—that is, a hundred and thirty-two lights from today—as the most likely date. It sounded reasonable, for the death of this body, anyway. Given the expected progression of my brain tumors, I only had about a hundred and ten days of mental clarity left in me. There were also other possible death days for me before that, in this current tun, especially *Kan Muluk, Wuklahun Xul,* that is, 4 Raining, 17 Ending, and *Hun Eb, Mih Mol,* that is, 1 Sweeping, 0 Gathering. Whatever, I thought. I clicked, meaning I accepted the diagnosis.

So far, I was disappointed. This wasn't anything that out of the ordinary. I asked a second question: Where would my descendants—and the word didn't especially mean my personal descendants, which I didn't have any of, but descendants of my family, that is, of 2JS—be on 9 Night, 1 Dark Water, in the first tun of the fifteenth k'atun of the eleventh b'ak'tun? And how many of them would there be?

It was a pretty common query, except for the time span. The date was in AD 1522, 313,285 days from today. It was one of the catastrophe dates in the Codex.

She didn't seem to react. She took five runners and scattered her corn kernels over the board, counted them quickly, and told me that on that day about fifteen-score descendants of the Harpies would reinter their founders' bone bundles in the "riverless north." That would be the Yucatán, I thought. The others, about a hundred score, would be "scattered in the jungles, in the forests that will cover the jewel cities."

Well, that's at least a bit impressive, I thought. Okay. Time for the big question.

"What sun will be the Razor City's last?" I asked.

She paused, as often. I sat. Finally, she spoke.

"Children"—she meant clients—"have asked me this four hundred times." She said that over the last k'atun, a few enterprising adders had, in fact, set various dates for the end of the city. Those dates had passed, and those adders had fled or been killed. Still, she said, there was a general tacit feeling that the end would be soon, at least among the top sun adders and their elite clients. Supposedly even some of the ruling houses had privately accepted the fact and were preparing their clans for an eventual migration.

Now, as I'm pretty sure I mentioned somewhere, I didn't know how long the city would last. And maybe no one did. And the archaeological data was vague. And the collapse of Teotihuacan wasn't mentioned in the Codex Nurnberg, or at least not in the pages we had. Now, according to Koh, it hadn't turned up in any known Game.

"But you have not found a date?" I asked.

"That writing is too close to our eyes," Koh said.

What she meant—well, it's what Taro called event-cone trouble. That is, it's not really possible to predict something you have the power to influence. So you can be blinded by proximity. They also call it the problem of the observer participant. And La Rochefoucauld called it *"l'aveuglerie de l'oeil qui ne voit pas lui-meme,"* that is, "the blindness of an eye that cannot see itself," and Stephen King called it the Dead Zone. You'd think it would be easier to predict something nearer in time, and harder to predict something further off. And that's usually true, up to a point. But past that point, it never is. It's kind of like how it's always tougher to take your own advice.

"But can you over me play forward to that sun?" I asked.

"That sun lives in smoke," Koh said.

Oh, hell, I thought. She's thinking of blowing me off. Damn, you'd think she'd be a bit more curious. She's got to be wondering what kind of adder I was, how I'd been able to see all the stuff in the letter—well, whatever. Okay. Try to give her something.

"I know the Razor City only owns a few handfuls of sunlight," I said.

"This light, the last, and the next," she said. "Just as it has since I came here."

It was like saying, "As usual. What else is new?" It wasn't really the polite correct response. But maybe she thought she was above manners—

"Ch'ak sac la hun Kawak, ka Wo," she said. It meant "Don't start anything on 10 Hurricane, 2 Toad." But the sense was stronger, like "Don't even make any decisions on that day. Just stay indoors and out of trouble."

I clicked yes.

"Good," she gestured.

She stood up.

She teetered a little, hobbled back around me to the entrance flap. I heard it rustle.

I was alone. I sat for four hundred beats, and then another four hundred. She didn't come back.

What the fuck? I wondered. Was that it? She's just flat-out leaving? Nobody ever does that around here. What the flying fuck? WTFFF?

I sat. I counted four hundred beats. I listened. I couldn't hear a damn thing. How do they get it so silent in here? Somehow the compound had been constructed to deflect the hubbub of the city. There weren't any air currents that I could feel. The smoke from the torch went up toward the oculus in a nearly straight line. I sat some more.

Well, hell, I thought. This is a washout. Maybe we made this whole trip for nothing. Maybe 2JS was just trying to get rid of me. Maybe somebody's going to come in behind me and strangle me. Maybe Lady Koh's not all that super anyway. Damn it, why do I always get stuck with the second-stringers? All I needed was just to meet one hot shot. Just one person around here who could take some initiative.

I counted another eight hundred beats. I was feeling a little gravity-challenged. Something in that chocolate was putting me in some kind of a state. I wasn't sure what state it was, but it was a state.

Maybe I should've told her more. The stuff in the letter wasn't really enough to get her attention. And come to think of it, why had 2JS wanted me to be so cagey, really? Maybe he didn't want me to give her anything too impressive just because he wanted her to think the information came from him. He didn't want Koh to get any more impressed than necessary because he didn't want me getting too cocky. Or too autonomous.

Well, too late.

Maybe I'll just slink back whence I came. If I can even find my way out of here. Maybe I'll just sit here for another couple of hours and see what happens. Maybe—

Fuck it.

I don't usually think of myself as terribly insightful, at least not outside the boundaries of something I can control, like the Game. But for whatever reason—either because for a while now I'd had that feeling you get sometimes when you're alone at night in a brightly lit house, a house that doesn't have the psychohygienic provision of blinds on every window, and suddenly a certainty comes over you that you're being watched, and not by a friend, or maybe just because I was getting pretty frustrated, I reached out, picked the torch out of its holder, and thwacked it down on the floor. There was a little Vesuvius of sparks. Like I think I said it was made of a sheaf of wax myrtles dipped in dog tallow, and the flaming seeds scattered over the mats—which I guess had been dampened slightly, like tatami—and sizzled out.

I sat in the blackness. Already there wasn't even a trace of blue left in the oculus. There's not enough twilight around here, I thought. No twilight in the courts of the sun. I sat in the dark. Face it, Jedster. You've struck out big time. I watched the scattered myrtle embers fade out one after another like a dying galaxy.

I listened. Nothing. I sat. I thought I saw something.

There was still some light in the room. It was right in front of me. Or rather it wasn't in the room but from outside the room. I kneed forward across the hearth cover to where Koh had been and peered into the dark. It was the light from a brazier of fresher coals glowing through the screen of I guess feathers. There was another room on the other side of the wall. Although it wasn't really a wall but a metallic fabric screen, like a scrim in a theater. Whatever the metallic scales on it were made of, they worked like a two-way mirror. And there was someone sitting there, only three arms away from me. I started to make out the contours and then the major shapes. It was a young woman, in the same outfit and the same pose as the old lady.

She knows, I thought. You know I can see you.

Relax, I thought. I inhaled, resettled my spine, and exhaled. The woman hadn't moved. Now I could see detail. Her right hand seemed to be painted black, and I couldn't get a good look at it, but her left hand was unpainted and I focused on it. It had seven fingers. The smallest one was pointed and jointless like the tentacle of a sea anemone and barely the size of a .22 long rifle bullet. I looked back at her face. It was pale on most of the top half and black on the bottom, with the border running under her left eye, over her upper lip, and across her right cheek to the mandibular angle.

(50)

"What other names do you next to me use?" the woman asked. Her voice was the same as the old woman's.

Better give her something, I thought.

"My hipball name was Chacal," I said.

"And who are your other fathers, other mothers, other elder brothers, younger brothers?" At first her voice was still a presenile croak, but by the time she got to the word *"na'ob,"* "mothers," it had started sliding lower and smoothing out, as though she were aging in reverse.

I gave her the name of Chacal's biological father.

"And where are you from?" Now her voice was what seemed to be her natural tone, a clear contralto, lower than the average Maya woman's. What the hell? I wondered. So when the old lady was speaking, the real lady Koh had been ventriloquizing behind her. Why? And how had the impostor known when to move her lips? I wondered. Some signal. A string, a rod in the floor, maybe. Well, whatever.

"From Ix,"

"But before that?"

"From Bolocac," I said. It was the name of Chacal's village.

"And where were you from before Bolocac?" Koh asked. She was talking in this singsongy way and it was maybe trancing me out a bit.

"From Yananekan," I said, without thinking. That was the current name of the area around Alta Verapaz where much later I'd grown up as Jed. Hell.

"And after that, but before Bolocac?"

"I am dark," I said a little spacily. It was like saying "I don't understand." Damn it, Jed, I thought. You're letting this *marimacha* clock you. Cool it.

"You must have left Yananekan before you were a blood," she said.

I clicked yes. I could feel her eyeballing me. Maybe I shouldn't even try to bullshit this woman. Like any good sun adder, she could spot a tell through a lead wall.

"And what sun lighted your departure?"

I made up a plausible date.

"And what did people call you then?"

"They called me Chacal."

"But that was not your first name?"

I started to say it was and then I realized I'd hesitated. Too late, I thought. That was as good as a yes.

She paused. I snuck another look at her. When I'd seen 2 Jeweled Skull's portrait head of her I'd thought the pattern on her skin was just her signature face paint. Now it looked like it was under her skin, tattooed on. Actually, I thought, even with all that shitterie going on, she wasn't exactly bad-looking. She had great skin, achromatically speaking, and an otherwise symmetrical face, and a feminine affect. That is, it was feminine in the sense of maybe compassionate, or motherly, or rather pre-motherly, like someday she'd be nice to her kids, but not today. I looked down again quickly and focused on a single dim geranium petal on the mat in front of me.

"And you next to me, why do you travel?" she asked.

"Because 2 Jeweled Skull wants to protect his family."

"2 Jeweled Skull wants the things he wants. But you next to me, what do you want?" There was something a little different in her tone, something—well, I wasn't quite sure how to interpret it. A tinge of being a little miffed, a sense of "why won't you trust me?"

"I underneath you want simply what he wants," I answered.

"Still, you seem to want more than that."

"It is as you above me say."

Pause.

I counted forty beats.

"And do you belong here?" she asked, finally.

No, I thought, definitely not—but then I realized that I hadn't just thought it, I'd said it. Damn. Breaking protocol, I looked up. She was looking at me.

She sees it, I thought. She sees loneliness. It's all over you like blue on Smurf. I looked down again and made another "whatever you over me say" gesture.

"And then where were you from before Bolocac?"

"I was in the north," I said. I don't have to answer all this, I thought. I'm going to get peeved in a minute—

"How far north?"

"Farther than from here to Ix," I said. Oops, I thought. That wasn't what I meant to say.

"You went farther than the Bone Ocean?" She meant the deserts north of the lake country.

I was about to gesture "whatever" again and then thought I was just coming off as a sniveling, evasive little twerp. So I clicked "Yes."

"What was it like there?"

"It was different from here or Ix," I said.

"How different?"

"Very different." I sounded far away from myself.

"But it was more different than very different."

I paused. What the hell, I thought. "You are correct," I said. "It was different in ways that are unpaintable." That is, they were impossible to imagine.

That seemed to hold her for a second.

"And who was your first father?" she asked.

Pause. Damn, I thought. She's getting too close. And no wonder. You're chatting away like some giggly girl after two drags on a *banano*. God *damn* it, Jed head, *shut up*. I managed not to answer.

The pause stretched on. A hundred and twenty beats. Two hundred. Finally, against my better judgment, I looked up.

Uh-oh. I looked down.

I thought I'd seen a flash of something dangerous in her face. Not angry, but dangerous.

Damn it. She knows you're hiding something. Something serious. Maybe she'd caught some microexpression. Watch out. You could disappear in here. The Harpy trading clan was rich, but it didn't have much influence in Teotihuacan. Even if the Orb Weavers might have political problems, they could still crush us like a chigger.

"Who was the smoker who first lit the face of your mother?" she asked.

I told her Chacal's mother's naming day. I had the urge to say more but I used my tongue to stuff a bit of my inside upper lip into a spot between two projecting tooth inlays and pulled on it until it hurt, and I stayed quiet. It was a trick of Chacal's. God damn it, what the hell was in that shit? It had to be a dissociative, some salvia divinorum derivative, or tetrodotoxin, even, or—

well, whatever it is, you can beat it. Easily. Remember, the main thing about truth serum is, it doesn't really work. At best it's just logorrhea serum. Just screw your courage to the sticky spot. And just don't have any more of that hot chocolate. I bit my lip thing again.

Ouch.

The Penguin Woman waddled into my field of vision. She slid one of her stubby digits through a string loop in the screen that divided me from Koh and edged to one side. The screen went with her, folding up like an accordion. Now Lady Koh and I were really in the same space, and the change was startling, as though instead of just collapsing the screen the Penguin Woman had ripped my clothes off. Now I could see that the dark side of Lady Koh's face wasn't a tattoo but her natural color. That is, she was piebald. The right side was the color of the concentrated melatonin, like in a mole, that is, almost black. The upper part of her face wasn't blue, like 2JS's model. It was just normal Maya skin color, although like all upper-caste women's it was pale from being kept out of the sun. Maybe there had been some tattooing, but just to improve the border between the two zones. The line was a little too smooth and sinuous to be natural. She'd shown signs, 2JS had said. No kidding. And he'd mentioned that she was related to Janaab' Pacal, the ahau of Lakamha, that is, Palenque. And he has eleven fingers, right? Maybe the vitiligo or whatever was somehow related to the polydactyly. It's not all that far out. Anyway, it's better than having a Hapsburg lip. Or Hanoverian hæmophilia. She breathed in and I got a glimpse of two front teeth inlaid with what looked like emeralds.

The dwarfess tied the folded screen to the wall and then, it seemed, melted away, probably into one of her rabbit holes. Chacal's eyes did the polite thing and looked down again at the matting.

Koh asked,

> "When did you last touch your father? And when
> Did you last touch your mother?
> Who was the smoker who blew ashes over her?
> When was her darkness?
> Why did you wander away and not stay
> At their feet, at the hearthstones?"

There was a strange feeling in my throat. No, more in my chest. Damn it, I thought. She's reading me. Empath bitch. And I'd thought I had my game face on. I'd been off-guard and now she was on the scent.

Okay. Slow down. First think, then think again, then speak.

"There were, you above me, there were scores of reasons," I said.

"Where is your mother? And where is your father?
And where is your garden?"

Hadn't she asked me that before? I wondered. I was getting a gentle sort of buzz. You're slipping, Jedster, I thought. Keep it together. I pulled harder on my shred of lip. The bland taste of blood spread over my tongue. I didn't answer.

"When did you last see your own younger sisters,
Your own older sisters?
Where did you last see your own little brothers,
Your own older brothers?
When was your milpa last burned? Is it cleared?
Is it seeded and weeded?
Who sweeps your granary there? Is it thatched?
Is it clean for the harvest?
Who watches out for the grackles? Who bundles
Your stack of tortillas?
Who sings your names in the square when the grandchildren
Circle the bonfire?
When you come home with a sore on your back,
Who will rub it with mint oil?
When you walk home in the night, in the chill,
Who will wait in the dooryard?"

I couldn't answer.

I'd never cried as Chacal, and in fact I couldn't remember any moment in Chacal's life when *he'd* cried, not since the first hipball initiations, anyway. Where he grew up, you cry, you die. For all I knew he couldn't even force his eyes to cry anymore. He'd beaten it out of them. But his eyes still had that feeling of being about to cry, when the fluid around your eyeballs sours and heats and pressure builds up. Damn it, I thought. Get it together. I stared at the geranium petal. It was longer than the others, standing upright on a twisted tail, like a seahorse.

"You want to tell me something," Koh's voice said. Or had I just thought she said it? Get it together.

I sat up straighter and snuck a look at her on the way up. If I could have taken a photograph of her face, I'd bet it would have looked as blank as before. But in person, somehow she seemed to be looking at me with indulgence, with sympathy, almost with a smile. Maybe it was all in her eyes. Or maybe it was a slight inclination of the head. Or maybe she was intentionally emitting some kind of pheromone—

"There is something else inside you," she said.

I pulled harder on my lip flap. "As you above me say," I gestured. I glanced up. She was staring right at me. As I think I said, eye contact was a big deal around here. It was like in *An Officer and a Gentleman*, when Louis Gossett Jr. is all like, "Don't you eyeball me, recruit! Use your peripheral vision!" I looked down again.

"Answers are also great-grandchildren of questions," Koh said. I think she meant, basically, that if I didn't want to tell her anything, how could I expect her to count my suns?

"I under you am unpracticed at speaking, but I do want to see them counted," I said. That is, I don't want to chat, I want you to start playing the Game right the hell now.

"I under you am too poor to reciprocate your bundle," she said. Basically, "Take back your goddamn feathers and everything else and get out of my shop." She looked away and to her left, to the west, signifying the past. That is, This interview is in the past. We're done.

"The suns I want to count are very few," I said. "And they light you too." That is, "You're doomed, witch bitch. Your days are numbered in single digits, and if you don't get on with the show we all might as well—"

There was a sound like someone snapping a pencil in the desk behind you in second grade. I looked up. She was looking back, but differently this time.

Animal trainers say that the difference between wolves and dogs is that dogs look at you and wolves look through you. A dog looks into your eyes and empathizes. She wasn't looking into my eyes. She was looking through me.

She means me harm, I thought. Need to get out of here. Automatically, I shifted my weight, getting ready to stand up. But instead of just shifting like it ought to, my weight—my point of balance, I guess you'd say—sloshed heavily forward and back, like an inflatable kiddie pool full of green slime. My legs had fallen asleep and buzzed, painfully. Cripes, I've had it, I thought. She's going to—hell, maybe I'd better just lunge forward, grab her throat, try to—no. There are probably guards watching. Just get it together and leave in a dignified hurry. I uncrossed my sleeping legs as slowly as if I were trying not to set off a motion alarm. I shifted my weight forward and moved my hands down to push off the floor. Okay. On three. *A la uno, á la—*

Koh screamed.

My eyes locked onto her face. It was stretched back into a gaping terrified grin. Sclera showed all around her irises and her emerald tooth inlays glinted like a row of compound eyes. The shriek ran up and down the scale, an eardrum-scraping Fay Wray spew of absolute terror and agony, the sound you'd make as you felt a jaguar's fangs slide into the back of your neck. I recoiled, or thought I did, but nothing moved. I realized I was sitting in exactly the same position. I was paralyzed.

Policemen learn to shout "Freeze!" with enough authority that people really do freeze. But the problem is they don't always stay frozen for long. This was different. Something about the combination of the dope in the chocolate and the scream had triggered some kind of tonic immobility, a primeval reaction like marsupials can get if they hear the sound of a predator and don't see an escape route.

"Hain chama," Koh said. "Take this."

She leaned forward and reached out with her light arm. She held a single tz'ite-tree seed between her first and second fingers, like a Go stone.

My right fist entered my field of vision. I watched it glide slowly under her hand and open, palm up. The seed dropped into it. It closed and returned to its perch on my thigh. I looked up. Somewhere, two of my cervical vertebrae crackled, loudly.

I resettled into position. I was dizzy. I looked down and back up at her. Her face was back to its placid default state. Oddly, I didn't feel angry. I just felt deflated.

"When you are asleep, they can do many things to you," she said. She meant that she could freeze me again if she wanted, and could torture me, and get me to tell her whatever she wanted to know. Vee haff ways, et cetera.

I'd never thought of myself as an especially brave person. Still—and maybe it was Chacal's ball nerves coming through, or maybe I was just tired, but I just said two words:

"Bin el."

That is, "Proceed." And I think I managed to say it with a convincing measure of insouciance. I felt that old toughness, or heart, or courage or whatever, flowing back into my system. Go for it, *cabrona*. Like the granola bar says, bring it on.

She didn't blink. Her face had the monstrous inexpressiveness of, say, Kenny Tran's, the time he cleaned me out with air in the final table of the 2010 Commerce Casino No Limit Hold 'Em Tournament.

"*Actan cha ui alal,*" she said, finally. That is, roughly, "Beat it."

Well, maybe I will, I thought, and then almost before I'd thought it, everything seemed to turn around in my head and I felt this flood of cosmic frustration. Great, I thought. I'd been working this room for hours already and—hell. I mean, where could I go, anyway? You can't hide from a global holocaust. And I couldn't hide from my brain tumors, either. What was I going to do, sneak around Teotihuacan and try to scrounge up the drugs some other way? Walk into the red temple precinct and try to bribe it out of them? Not bloody likely. I'd get picked up by the Swallowtail Stasi and processed into *carne molida*. Hell, hell, hell. Something told me—and I hate to appeal to that old intuition chestnut, but at least this time something really, really told me—that this was the closest shot I was going to get.

"You are doomed here," I said. "And I did come here to help you. I know things you would never be able to find out yourself. And I know that Razor City has very few suns left."

"And what is your name?" she asked.

I got a little shiver, for some reason, maybe just from her tone, and I think she saw the waves of gooseflesh over my arms. All the time I'd been here, I'd been dealing with people who used what they thought was magic all the time. And still I'd never run into anything—unless you count the Game, which doesn't count—that you could really call magic, or ESP, or even a hard-to-explain level of coincidence or intuition. And I'm sure that however Koh had paralyzed me, it wouldn't count as supernatural. But it was enough to keep me in a state of creeped-outedness.

Chill, Jed, I thought for the googleth time. She's not a witch. I snuck a look at her. If she was surprised, she wasn't showing it. Her eyes raked over me. I looked down at the floor again.

Hell, I thought. Just roll the damn dice.

"*Caba ten* Joachim Carlos Xul Mixoc DeLanda," I said. The Spanish sounded weird here. I thought I saw a tiny flicker deep in her eyes, like maybe I'd caught her attention.

"And what sun lighted your naming?" she asked.

"The sun 11 Howler, 4 Whiteness, in the fifth uinal of the first tun of the eighteenth k'atun of the thirteenth b'ak'tun."

There was a pause, but not such a long one as you'd think.

"Who was your mother?" she asked. "And who was your father?"

"My mother was Flor Tizac Maria Mixoc DeLanda, of the Ch'olan, and my father was Bernardo Koyi Xul Simon DeLanda, of the T'ozil."

"And who are your smokers, your protectors?"

I told her the names of Jed's gods, Santa Teresa and Maximón. I gave him his Mayan name, Mam.

"And when did you leave your dooryard?" she asked.

"13 Imix, 4 Mol, in the fifth uinal of the eleventh tun of the eighteenth k'atun of the eleventh b'ak'tun." That is, September 2, 1984, the day my parents sent me to the hospital in Xacan.

Pause.

Well, good for you, Jed, I thought. That's the second time you've spilled your guts to somebody on this trip. Mix a dollop of loneliness and a pinch of tongue-loosening narcotics and it gets tough to be cagey—

"And how did you come here?" Koh asked.

"I rode here on a waterfall of light," I said. "Or rather, I was the waterfall." What the hell am I babbling about? I wondered. That's not a good metaphor. Oh, well, let it go.

"So," she said,

"Then, in your time, have our kin gone unfed?
Have our smokers gone hungry?"

There was a quality in her voice of—well, I hesitate to mention it, because it makes her sound like a downer, and so far, at least, she was the opposite, in fact being in the same room with her felt oddly energizing, like holding a sharp machete or a high-caliber handgun—but her voice had this undertone of incredible sadness, as though she'd seen more of the world than any single person could have, let alone someone her age, as though she'd watched millions of beings pass from childhood enthusiasm into ever-greater disappointments and finally into antemorbid terror.

"Do your hometimers still sing their names?
Do they still perfume their skeletons?

"Do our home smokers still suckle on slaves' blood?
And do they protect you?"

"It's true that my contemporaries have forgotten some of their obligations," I said. It sounded lame when it came out. In fact it sounded even lamer
than it sounds in English. "Still, some of your descendants do still suckle your
smokers on the altars, on the hilltops. Even if they do not remember their
names, they try to suckle them all."

"And what do they suckle them on?"

Well . . . I thought. Not humans, anyway. "Most of them are impoverished,"
I said.

"It sounds as though they let their ancestors go hungry."

"They do what they can."

"And so your world is rotting underneath you."

Yes, I thought, in the twenty-first century, things really are falling apart.
Ignoring the falconer, shuffling off to Bethlehem, it's so bad even the worst
lack all conviction.

"It may be," I said. "But it does not have to be that way."

"Then why are you here? Whose path do you scout?"

She meant who was I working for. I was about to say 2 Jeweled Skull, but
then I thought why go through all that again and just said "Marena Park."

"And then why did the Ix-ahau Maran Ah Pok decide to send you here?"
Koh asked.

"We saw you in a book," I said. "One of the books recording the Game you
played on 9 Overlord, 13 Gathering survived to our k'atun. I saw the book on
2 Were-Jaguar, 2 Yellowribs, in the nineteenth k'atun of the thirteenth
b'ak'tun."

"Two suns before the sorcerer would cast his fire out of obsidian."

"Yes."

"And this was the day that the Ix-ahau asked you to come here?" Koh
asked.

"No, it was days after that," I said. And, I told her, even then I had to practically beg Marena to send me.

"But she showed you the book just in time."

I said it wasn't just in time because it was too late to do anything, and
thousands of people died.

"But it was just in time for you to know the bad sun was coming."

"Yes."

"And so maybe the Ix-ahau Maran Ah Pok was planning to send you here before she showed you the book."

"I had to beg her," I said again.

"And how long did it take to convince her?" Koh asked.

I thought back. "Not long," I said. Actually, come to think of it, I guess it was about a minute and a half.

"Then maybe that is your answer," Koh said.

I sat and thought about it. You know, Jed, I thought, she could be right. You're stupid. You try to be all cool and sophisticated but inside you're a trusting sort of simpleton. Maybe Marena and Lindsay Warren and Michael Dickface and Taro and everybody were all taking advantage of you from day one. Maybe Sic never even wanted to come back here. That was just a ploy to get you jealous. No wonder his Ch'olan sucked, he knew he didn't need it.

I really didn't want to believe it, though. I shook my head a bit, discreetly, I hoped, trying to sober up.

"And you wanted to meet the adder who played the Game," she said.

I said that we didn't entirely understand what would happen on the last date.

"On that sun the four hundred babies will tell us what they want," Koh said.

Pause. Don't say anything, I thought. Wait.

Koh didn't say anything, though. Unlike the average interrogee. Finally, I couldn't stand it.

"In the book it says there will be more than before, but still none," I said.

"Correct," Koh clicked.

"And they will ask for something," I said. "Won't they?"

"They will ask for something we can't give them."

Pause.

Okay, I thought. Maybe I'd better just ask.

"And what is the Flesh Dropper?"

I don't know, she gestured.

"What about the total of the suns of their tortures and the suns of their festivals?"

"Every living being has more tortures than festivals."

"That sounds correct," I gestured. "What about the place of betrayal?"

"That is in the nameless suns," she said. Literally the expression meant the five nameless intercalary days at the end of the Maya solar year. But in this context it was more like when you say "in the middle of nowhere," except it's the middle of notime. That is, it doesn't happen in the same time flow—or temporal arrow or temporal dimension or whatever—as the rest of life. It's a kind of limbo, like a time out in a ball game.

Pause.

"And taking two from twelve makes One Ocelot?" I asked.

"No, that is something One Ocelot did," Koh said.

"I don't understand."

"One Ocelot did not make it clear."

"What did you see on that sun?"

"I didn't see anything," she said. "I heard it all from One Ocelot."

"You were playing against One Ocelot?" I asked. As I think I mentioned, One Ocelot was the ancestor of the Ocelot Clan, who opened the sweetwater vein of Ix and who stripped the wooden flesh off the drowned mute men in the last days of the third sun.

Koh clicked yes.

"Was he in the sanctuary of the Ocelots' mul?" I asked.

"They brought him to a secret court," she said.

She meant that they'd brought his mummy down from the pyramid, and she'd played the Game against him. Of course, he must have spoken and made his moves through an interpreter.

Well, it serves me right for not guessing that, I thought. Come to think of it, that character in the Codex had looked a little odd. As I think I mentioned, or maybe I didn't, mummies were a big deal in these parts. They weren't like Egyptian mummies, though. They were usually wood-and-corn-paste effigies, built around a skull and some, but not all, of the other bones in the skeleton. Often they wore a mask made from the tanned skin of the deceased, and sometimes they wore other masks over that one. They were bundled in all sorts of robes and regalia. And unlike Egyptian mummies, they didn't just lie around in tombs. They sat in at feasts and conferences and got carried through festivals and even battle. They got around. And of course they talked a lot, through intermediaries.

"And could you over me condescend to tell me more?" I asked.

"There is no more to tell from that Game. Your book was complete."

"But sometimes one could drive that prey again down that same path," I said. It was an idiom, but I meant "Maybe you could pick up that same Game again near the end and play out a different endgame." It was like how in chess you might go back to the move just before the winning move just to see if the losing side had a chance.

"That won't be done," Koh said. "One Ocelot still plays with living balls." As I think I mentioned, "balls" could also mean "runners." "Maybe no one will play a Game that large again. Finished."

Hell, I thought. Apparently, she meant that the art was dying out. And when somebody around here said "finished," it meant you weren't going to get any more information out of them, even if you tortured them. Although you might torture them anyway, just as a point of etiquette.

Koh looked at the incense clock. It had gone out. The session was supposed to be over. Damn it. I'd expected the ancient past to be leisurely. Now I was trying to squeeze another few minutes out of her, like some B-list journalist interviewing Madonna. Koh turned back toward me, with her eyes looking over mine, as was proper. Hell. Hellhellhellhellhell. Really, you'd think this might be at least a little interesting. That is, you don't meet Buck Rogers every day of the k'atun, but still, I guess she just couldn't do this right now, the Silence was starting soon, there were lines of other, richer supplicants outside, the Synods were getting ready to close down the Rattler's House, time was seriously a-wastin'—

Okay. Regroup. Try another tack.

"I know the exact moment that the Chewer will attack the sun nine days from now," I said. "It will be eight hundred score and nine score and one beat after the first shard of dawn," I said. As I think I mentioned, every sun adder in Mesoamerica knew that there would be a solar eclipse early in the day. But not even the most learned ones, the heads of the astronomer clans at Teotihuacan, Ix, or Palenque could predict the exact time. They weren't even sure if it would be total or partial. For that stuff, you need telescopes and calculus.

"He who knows, knows," she said. It was kind of an untranslatable idiom, but basically it was like saying "we'll have to wait and see, won't we?" Like, tell me something I can use this minute. She had a point.

"Then the sun will be blocked out for nineteen score and eight beats," I said, "and then, forty-one score and eighteen beats later, it will be whole again."

Pause. She didn't throw me out, so I went on.

"Except nothing really chews on the sun," I said. "Blood Rabbitess comes between the earth and the sun"—Koh clicked unimpressedly, meaning she already knew that—"and blood Rabbitess is a ball, with the same side always turned toward us, and the sun is a flaming ball, like a night-game hipball, and Sun Vanquisher and Sun Trumpeter are the same being"—she clicked at that too—"and that being is also a ball, and the zeroth level"—that is, the earth—"is also a ball, and it holds us to itself the way a large lodestone holds on to smaller ones. And the cigar fires of Iztamna and Ixchel, and 7 Hunaphu, they're also just balls, all lobbing high around the sun."

"But they don't fall," she said.

Hah, I thought. The mask slips. The Ice Empress really is interested in something.

"They are falling," I said, "but they have a long way still to fall before they hit the sun. They'll be falling for another four hundred times four hundred times four hundred times four hundred times four hundred times four hundred times four hundred b'ak'tuns." This had better be blowing her mind, I thought. It's my A material. I leaned forward—ill-manneredly—and picked a shallow round bowl out of the array of clayware next to the brazier. I pulled the neck-slit of my manta up to my mouth, popped off one of the round gray-stone beads with my teeth, yanked the dangling thread out of the bead, dropped the bead in the bowl, picked up the bowl, and rolled the bead around. It was pretty wobbly but I launched into my spiel anyway:

"The center of this bowl is like the sun," I said. "And we stand on one side of the bead. And as we spin it appears to us that the sun is moving. But really we're the beings who are moving."

"So you next to me say the sun is at the bottom of the turquoise bowl," she said.

"No, there is no bowl. There is no sky shell. The sky is just wind all the way up. And actually, we don't move around it quite in a circle. We move in a shape like a goose's egg."

I leaned forward—unconscionably rudely, again, but I hoped we were past that—and swept away a drift of petals with my powerful forearm, exposing a truncated crescent of pale, fine-woven reed matting. I poked my index finger into the least hot-looking zone of the brazier, rubbed it around in the soot, and drew a circle on the mat.

"This little round is the Fourth Sun," I said. "The ball that is both Sun Vanquisher and Sun Herald rolls around it on this larger round." I had to go back for more soot six times before I finished the drawing:

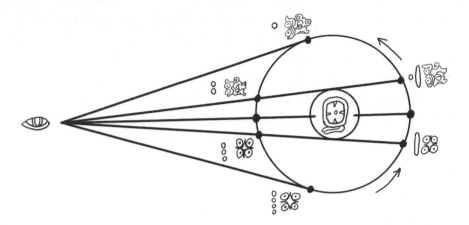

Of course, my sketch looked a lot rougher, but it was still readable. "This is the zeroth level here," I said, writing an eye/oyster glyph at the extreme left. "And this is where Sun Vanquisher rises furthest whiteward." I wrote a Venus-as–Evening Star glyph at 11:00 on the large circle and put a single dot next to it.

I thought Koh was about to say something, but she didn't.

"This is Sun Vanquisher's last night," I said. I wrote the glyph below and to the left of the first. I poked two dots next to it.

Koh stared at the drawing. She didn't say anything. As I think I mentioned somewhere, it's true that the Maya calendar was indeed famously accurate, better on the solar count than the uncorrected Gregorian one. But they didn't have heliocentrism yet, although from the way Koh was taking it I guessed that she and the very best Maya astronomers might have an inkling of it.

"And this third spot is the ball's first morning, when it's named Sun Herald," I said, moving it around counterclockwise. "Then this is yellowmost morning. This is its last morning. Then it's behind the sun for fifty days, and then it appears again as Sun Vanquisher, here. Twelve score and four days and ninety-one score and five beats in all." I wrote the number 6 next to the last glyph. I didn't mention the superior and inferior conjunctions. Why belabor the point?

I paused.

The pause stretched on.

Gotcha, I thought. If there's one thing you could always count on with these folks, it's a solid foundation in naked-eye astronomy. She was a sun adder, after all. And every adder was always looking for an edge over the others. Even if progress got frowned upon—that is, what we dead white males would

call progress—there was still the haphazard sort of progress that comes naturally and irrepressibly out of plain one-upmanship. Adders are hustlers, and
they're always looking for a new angle. And not even just to, say, predict the
first rain a little more accurately than the adder in the next town, but to trade
with other adders. In Koh's case, for instance, she'd be expected to share stuff
like this with the other Orb Weavers, so that the whole group could use the
extra accuracy as a bargaining chip in their squabble with the Synods.

Finally, Koh spoke: "And so you say that when 2 Peccary steps out of the
procession and turns back caveward down the white road, that is the same."
She meant Mars.

"He doesn't turn at all," I said. "It only looks that way to us because the
ground underneath us is moving. It's the same as with Sun Herald. But it
takes longer because 2 Peccary is farther away from the sun than we are."

"And Sun Herald is closer."

"Sun Herald is closer."

"And you say the sun is bigger than the zeroth level," she said.

"More than four hundred times four hundred times bigger," I said. "And if
you started walking to the sun now, although you couldn't, but let's say you
were flying as fast as you can walk, you wouldn't get there for nine hundred
times four hundred b'ak'tunob."

Koh stared at the diagram, calculating. She's making some leaps, I thought.
She's Copernicus at Warmia. She's Tycho Brahe, freezing his nose off from
poking it into space. She's Johannes Kepler. She's Gallifreakingleo. Wait'll I
turn you on to some general relativity, I thought. You'll cream on your abacus.
$e = babes^2$.

"And so your hometimers know everything," Koh said finally. I had to stifle
a jump, she'd been quiet for so long.

"Not quite everything," I gestured. "They are—they will be working to
know everything eventually."

"And are they all powerful greathousers?" That is, were they all rich and in
charge?

"No, many of them are still roundhousers. But still, most of them are much
richer than roundhousers now. There's so much food even the heartless get
fat. Most people will live for more than three k'atuns. We'll ride through the
sky inside giant copper bird canoes. We'll have cold torches that burn for
hundred-scores of nights and weapons that kill hundred-scores of people a
hundred-score jornadas away. We'll speak to each other and see each other's
faces over any distance, through lines of invisible light. Even before I was

born, twelve men had canoed to the ball of the moon. There will be four-hundred-score-four-hundred-score-four-hundred-score-four-hundred-score-four-hundred-score-four-hundred-score of us. We'll see inside ourselves without cutting ourselves open. We'll make devices that are cleverer than we are. We'll dive to the bottom of the salt sea, and stay there for days, and come back alive."

"But you have forgotten the most important things," she said. "And so you came here. Correct?"

I paused. Well, whatever. "Correct," I clicked.

"Because you in your time have forgotten your grandfathermothers," she said.

I made a "not entirely" gesture.

"But you do know how many suns the Razor City will keep up its offerings," she said. That is, how long would Teotihuacan last?

Damn. "We do not know that," I said.

She asked why, if I came from the thirteenth b'ak'tun and knew so much, I didn't know the exact sun.

I told her how, by the time I was born, almost all her world's books had been destroyed, and how the few that had survived didn't give the date. I tried to explain what archaeologists were, and how they dated things, and told her that they'd calculated the abandonment of the city to some time in the eleventh, twelfth, or thirteenth k'atun of this b'ak'tun, that is, roughly between AD 650 and 710, but couldn't get any more accurate than that. "The damage will be too extensive for better archaeological dating," I tried to say.

Pause again. She stared at the drawings.

I didn't say anything. At least it was easier not to talk than it had been. The mental Ex-Lax was wearing off.

Koh took one of the fly whisks off the rack and held it against her thigh. It meant the reading was over.

"Perhaps you next to me and I will consult the skulls again in a basket of suns, after the Chewer has been driven off," she said.

God DAMN it, I thought. No, let's make that "I inwardly shrieked." Bitch. Maybe I should just take off, maybe I can just score the shit on the street, better than schlumping around here all—

No. Be persistent. Who knows, maybe she's just haggling you up for more goodies. Take it up a level.

"The Orb Weavers' House will not survive much longer," I said, desperately breaking protocol. "We don't know how long it will last but it won't be long."

"I next to you have known that for a long time."

"2 Jeweled Skull offers asylum in Ix, for you and for your order."

Koh shifted. I thought she cocked her head a bit, as though she heard something, but I might have just imagined it. She didn't answer.

Hell, I thought. Well, that's the end of my A material. 2JS had said I should wait to make the offer until she asked for it, and then to make it seem like a concession, and that otherwise she'd think it was some sort of con.

She shifted again. For a second I thought she was just going to stand up and leave, and that would be it. Instead, she said: "And so, you next to me wager that 2 Jeweled Skull will win his hipball game against the Ocelots?" She meant that she thought the Harpies were going to lose—fairly or otherwise— and would get run out of Ix.

"Ma' lo' yanil," I said. That is, "No problem." "Win or no win, the Harpies will stay. And the Ocelots will run." The idea was to let her think that my super-human knowledge had provided 2JS with enough firepower to hold off the Ocelots.

As you might guess, there was another interminable pause. Well, at least she didn't just keep babbling like your average *chica perica*.

"You came here for the Steersman, not for me," she said.

I didn't know what to say. Well, maybe that's it, I thought. I'm getting thrown out. Back to Square Zero.

Instead, Koh said: "Your hometimers have forgotten how to seat a cycle."

I clicked yes.

"But the ahaus you suckle would like to midwife a lineage of new suns. After the suns of the thirteenth b'ak'tun have died out."

"I would like to help start another cycle," I said.

"And why?" she asked. "Are you going back?"

"I want to try," I said, half-avoiding the question. I thought she was going to ask me how I was planning to do that, but instead she just took the answer as a "yes" and asked: *"Bax ten tex kaabet?"* That is, "why do you want to [go through all this]?"

"Everyone wants to protect his family."

"And do you next to me have family there?"

"I have—people whom I think of as foster family." Or at least I have a few half-friends on the web, I thought. I guess Koh knew I was pushing it. Still, she didn't pursue the thought.

"And if your hometimers do survive,"
Would they still forget us?
Would they observe all the days of our namings,
The days of our dyings?
Will they forget how we planted, and raided,
And built, and bore children?
Will they sometimes sing a song with our names in it?
Will they remember?"

"I will arrange for them to remember your lineage, and to suckle your uay on your deathdays."

"But you told me they only offer poor things."

"Not necessarily," I gestured.

"And you said your hometimers are dishonorable," she said. There wasn't really an Ixian word for "evil," and even if there had been, "dishonorable" would have been worse.

When did I say that? I wondered. Huh. "In many ways they'll be worse than people are now," I said. "But in some ways you over me might say they are better."

"And so you want me to play a nine-stone Game. And you think just by watching you could learn to play it in two lights." "Two lights" was an idiom, like saying "You think you could learn it overnight."

"I under you do not think that."

"Then what else do you next to me and I have to do here?"

"I under you request a reading," I said.

"But I next to you have already read for you."

"But I want to exchange something larger this time," I said. I told her that I could tell her almost anything she wanted to know about anything that would be explored or discovered or created through all the next four b'ak'tuns.

"I know enough already to make me sorry I know it," she said. It wasn't clear whether she meant the things I'd told her about, or the things she'd already known, or both.

"Then let me tell you something that will help you. Let me give you something."

"You already gave me the shape of the sun."

"Let me give you something that would put honey into your followers' ch'anac." That is, something that would help out the regular folks.

"I next to you . . . we could build any number of yet-unseen devices," I said.

"Like what?" she signed. She put down the fly whisk.

"What about captive rollers?" I asked.

"What do you mean?" she gestured.

I started to explain about wheels. I told her how they were like rollers, but with a stick through the center, and how great wheelbarrows were, and I started to draw one, but then she said they already had them here, and she sent the Penguiness out for an example. I didn't know what to think. But the dwarf brought back a little yellow wooden jaguar with a respectable wheel on each of its feet. Koh said that toys with this feature were pretty popular among the elite, but they weren't to be allowed out of the house where the public could see them. As far as I could tell, this wasn't because regular folks might get the idea that wheels would be useful, but because someone might copy them and use them to gather a following. That person could go to some other city, impress everybody with his gadgets, promote himself as a great sorcerer, and ultimately become a problem for the aristocracy. The wheel could become another magic cult object, the center of another order, like the knife or fire or the closely guarded secret of the concave mirror—or, of course, the Game drugs. And besides, Koh said—and I'm paraphrasing pretty freely here—there were so many roundhousers around these days that there wasn't any need for wheelbarrows anyway. If you wanted to move something heavy, you just got the plebes to drag it.

It was frustrating, but I dropped the subject. It was like this one time when I was giving this very Park Avenue–type girl a ride up to New Haven in my van, and I mentioned that she ought to learn to drive. "What if I hadn't been going up today?" I'd asked.

"I'd ring up some other boy and gotten him to drive me," she'd said. "And then I'd fuck him."

Well, okay, I thought, forget wheels for transportation. What about just for dinnerware?

I started to tell her about potter's wheels. The thing was, just to be frank, when you talked about the dinnerware around here, I mean here in Mesoamerica, you had to admit that, yes, some of the painting was awesome, but the shape was always just a little bit borkly. Anybody turning out perfectly round pots would cause a sensation. But as Koh caught on to what I was saying, she came back with the same objection. That is, the Synods would say that whoever had created the new pots was some kind of inordinately powerful sorcerer, and they'd immediately send out hit squads to get rid of him. And even if that didn't happen and the wheel-thrown stuff caught on, it would doom thousands of potter families to starvation, since they'd never be capable of making the change. I guess it was basically the same rationale behind how we—I mean, we Maya or Teotihuacanos or any of the big-city Mesoamerican civilizations—didn't use bows and arrows, even though the Too-Talls used them. It was like the whole samurai cult-of-the-sword thing, how Tokugawa figured that if decent guns got into Japan they'd wobble the power structure even if the shogunate got hold of them first. So he and his successors confiscated firearms and gunpowder, shut the Portuguese traders out of most of Japan, and basically kept the place as backward as possible for another two hundred and fifty years.

"We cannot use those things here," she said. "Finished."

Hell. I was running out of ideas. This was one eventuality we hadn't rehearsed for back at the Stake.

"Then do it just to throw out a fresh ball," I said. It was like saying "Throw in the bet for the pot" in poker, just to see what the other hands were. Do it on a bet, do it on a dare, do it for the sheer ineffable fuck of it.

"You think I'm not curious about your level," she said. I didn't answer. "But I am curious. But curiosity is of the teaser, the torturer." That is, her being curious would hurt people she had no reason to hurt.

Well, at least that suggests she's got some empathy in there, I thought. Doesn't it? The thing is—although in general I don't want to make sweeping statements about humanity in general, not because I'm wrong but just because they've all already been made—the thing is, either you're a person with a head for empathy or, much more often, you're not. And either she was the first type or we were fucked, and that was all there was to it.

Okay, think.

Empathy just as a concept was a little abstract to express in Ixian. You had to frame it in the language of family.

Okay, here goes.

"I know . . . ," I said, "I know that if you were on the road and you saw someone strangling a five-rounder"—that is, about a three-year-old—"you would want to stop it. Even if it was his child, even if the child was scab-possessed and inauspiciously born, even if he had every right to kill it, you would still want to stop him, and if you had the power to—that is, if you could stop him, you would."

"Your hometimers are not on our road," she said.

"They are. By then scores of scores of scores of scores of them will all be your descendants, or descendants of your sisters, your brothers, because . . ."

I trailed off. I looked up at her. Her eyes were still looking past me, over my head.

"They are dying," I said, "they will be dying, and just before they die they'll wonder why nobody cared to help them, and if they knew that I under you and you could have saved them and decided not to, they would wonder why, and if we told them, it wouldn't be a good enough . . ."

I trailed off. Those never-to-be-born tears were welling up again somewhere a bit behind my eyeballs. And I was gasping, I was short of breath, and even almost stuttering like I used to do in English when I got panicked when I was little. Damn it, Jed, keep it together, keep it to—

"I next to you have made my decision," Koh said,

"Too many suns have already been born
And too many are coming.
All corn-fleshed people will end with the sun
On 4 Overlord, 3 Yellow.
Maybe someday after that some new heir of Iztamna will come along,
Maybe he'll model new lineages from some other material,
Maybe from jade."

She paused and then started to say "Ca'ek," "Finished," but I interrupted her.

"WAIT," I said—well, let's say I shouted—"wait, you DO NOT have, you"—Tone it down, Jed, I thought—"you far over me do not have the authority to decide that for them. Not even if your decision is correct."

"No," she said, "it is that I don't have the right to prolong their time on the zeroth level, even if I could."

"No, you do, it—you want to save them, but you think you shouldn't, or rather you know you shouldn't, but if what I've seen can add anything to what you've seen—that is, I've been in both places, and I've seen things that . . ."

Damn. I lost track of what I was saying. I started again:

"If I know one thing—and it's not even a good thing, but it's true—it's that you're allowed to do whatever you want."

Since I'd already broken almost every other rule of decorum, I looked into her eyes. Her eyes opened wide and bulged—no, wait, that wasn't it. She'd shut her eyes, but her eyelids had been painted with white lead, so they looked like they were still open and pupil-less, like they'd been drawn by Harold Gray in *Little Orphan Annie*.

Whew. That was a little shock. Shocklet. Damn, had she not blinked this whole time? Well, if she had, I'd missed it. Okay.

I didn't know what to do, so I just looked at her false eyes. I guess she hadn't wanted to look down, or to lash out at me, as she had a right to, so instead she'd just shut down.

Come on, Jed. Come up with something.

"I underneath you challenge you to look at me," I said. It was like saying "I dare you to hit me." Still, I felt like I needed it, I needed a scrap of eye contact that wasn't just about dominance. Anyway, maybe it was just sheer fighting spirit—as I think I mentioned, around here you'd do anything on a dare—but she opened her eyes and looked back.

(51)

When I was at Nephi K–12—and I realize there's really never any good time to break up a narrative, and that even if there were this wouldn't be it, but still, as they used to say, dear and thrice-indulgent reader, let us pause for just a moment—there was a perennial substitute teacher who worked the lower grades, a large, ancient lady who remembered when the grandsons of the pioneers came to school barefoot and who was a dissertation-worthy storehouse of premedia entertainments. She knew what there was to know about yarn puppets, fancy needlework, and folding dolls, and especially parlor games—Forfeits, Charades, the terrifying ritual of apple bobbing, Pass-the-Slipper, Snapdragon, and Shadow Buff—a whole lost world from endless dim evenings before the REA. And anyway one Friday afternoon she cut a row of three pairs of tiny eyeholes in an old white bedsheet and had us tape it up over the wide doorway into what they called the cubbyhole room. Half the class of twenty-four went behind the sheet, and three of them came up and peered out at the rest of us from behind the eyeholes. And each of us in turn went up close to the sheet, and looked directly into their eyes, and tried to guess who was looking back. It had turned out that it was almost impossible, that—except in the case of Jessica Gunnerson, a near-albinic ginger whose irises were the same aniline violet as the methanolated ink on the last and lightest copy out of the ditto machine—you couldn't tell who it was. Without seeing more of the face, you couldn't tell whether it was your best friend or your worst enemy, you couldn't tell what funny faces that person might be making at you, you couldn't even tell whether it was a boy or a girl. It was disturbing enough so that decades later I might be looking into, say, some young lady's eyes, attempting to connect on some at least supra-animalistic level, or to convey a scintilla of commitment or, at worst, a trace amount of honesty, and I'd be feeling that yes, she was being straight with me because I was looking right into the limpid depths of her windows into the whatever, and then out of nowhere I'd remember that stupid guessing game and suddenly her pupils would look like just two cutout holes with just blank transgalactic vacuity behind them, and that cut-loose feeling would swell up between us, that sense of being adrift in the mechanistic cosmos not just without any communication with another being but with no possibility of any communication with any other being now or in the future or even in the past, and everything would just turn to *mierditas refritos*. And now—I mean, right now in AD 664—I was at it again, I was looking into Lady Koh's eyes, and I was hoping more than desperately that I could see something there, some shred of magic or spirit or at least indeterminacy, some sign that she and I were both more or less real and conscious and autonomously volitional and in the same space at the same time. As I think I said, Lady Koh's face was about as inexpressive as any I've encountered, and I've seen some stony ones, across about ten thousand chessboards, Go boards, and Hold 'Em tables, but her eyes had something else to them, something liquefacient and vortical, like Cléo de Mérode's. Her irises were so dark that you couldn't see where the pupils started, but you could still see that they were two different colors of black, like in an Ad Reinhardt painting, that the left eye was colder and the right eye was warmer . . . I thought it was raining outside and then I realized I was hearing blood swashing through my ears.

Come on, I thought. I know you're in there. Come on.

Forty beats went by. I thought I saw something in her blank face, something like maybe she was biting her tongue, some kind of pain that wasn't quite concealable, and then I decided I'd probably imagined it.

Eighty beats.

This doesn't need to be a rape-like moment. Let's turn it into a lovemaking-like moment. Okay?

At the hundred-and-twentieth beat there was a click in my back, a vertebra resettling, and I got an urge to pull my eyes away and managed not to. Just keep at it, Jed. Now I felt like we were a couple of sumos exerting a half-ton or so of pressure on each other in the middle of the dohyo. Come on, I thought. No need to wrestle. Come on. Hold it. Hold. Please, Nonexistent Dude, just this one time, let there be something there. Please. Please.

"It is because I do care for them as my children that I do not want them to have to toil through the zeroth level," Koh's voice said, sounding about a mile away. She didn't look away.

"The zeroth level is the only level," I choked out.

"If that is true it is just as well," she said.

"No, no, no, no, it is not just as well, they want to . . . they want to spend as many days with each other as they can."

"So they are greedy and afraid."

"No, no, not—no, they're like a family going together to a festival."

"And what is there to see at the festival?" she asked. I guess she meant that the fun wears off after a while.

"That's why they want to have new children," I said, "to see it fresh, that . . . what I and you are saying here is *b'ach na tok.*" That is, this whole thing is ridiculous.

"Yes, it is," she clicked.

"And if the suns do go on," I said, "if a new race of suns . . . who knows what could happen after that? I and you could play the Game four hundred score times and we wouldn't know. Maybe something will happen in the ten scoreth *b'ak'tun*, in the hundred scoreth *b'ak'tun*, that will make it all worthwhile. . . ."

I trailed off. Jesus, I thought. This is getting a little intense for me. A billion years of evolution and five million years of human evolution and it's all come down to the two of us.

"There is a jar in the blackmost mountain," Koh said. "All the *yaj*"—that is, all the pain, or pain smoke, or in this case, tears—"of all beings everywhere drips into the jar."

"I under you have heard of this," I said.

She said,

> *"Lai can h'tulnaac,"* she said,
> *"Lail x nuc homoaa*
> *Cu tz'o, cu tz'a."*

> "And when the great jar
> Is filled to the brim
> It will end, it will shatter."

"X'tan boc ch'ana k'awal nab," I said. "This is making solidified corn gruel with peccary urine." In Ixian, it was the closest thing you could say to "bullshit." Although I guess it sounds funnier if you've spent the whole day dragging two-hundred-pound limestone blocks up a ninety-foot pyramid in 110-degree heat.

"As you next to me say," Koh gestured.

And for some reason—and I don't think it was one of Koh's witchy-poo tricks—after that, I had a feeling almost like passing out for a second or two, or like having been thinking of something important and then forgetting it, and when I remembered what I'd been up to we weren't staring at each other anymore. I looked down. Koh shifted under her manta. We were in some other timespace.

"Old Steersman isn't coming here," Koh said. She meant that she didn't have Old Steersman's dust, the topolytic component of the Game drugs.

"Would you next to me play without it?" I asked.

She signed there wasn't any point.

"But you do follow the Steersman sometimes, correct?" I asked.

She clicked yes.

I heard the Penguin Woman behind me. She came into view and lit a second incense ball. Well, that's a good sign. Does that mean it's a yes? She waddled up to Koh and stood on tiptalons. Koh tilted her head, whispered about fifty words into her ear, and handed her something. The dwarfess scuttled out.

It's happening, I thought. She's going to get hold of some of that Steersman shit and go for it. Maybe we can just catch that bastard right now. If we get a name, I could just leave that in the lodestone cross box and not even worry about the drugs for the time being. I'm gonna get you, Doomster Man. Yeah. No sweat.

Koh took a fresh myrtle torch and held it in the brazier. It flared up yellow-green. She set it in the holder. The light glinted on the dark side of her face.

If there'd been a single moment when Koh had a change of heart, I hadn't seen it. And now that we were going ahead I didn't even feel that I'd convinced her myself. There was a sense that it wasn't about me, that at most I'd been able to deliver some new information and she'd been strong enough to change her mind based on it. I felt weakened. She opened one of the baskets, took out a long, thin, green cigar, bit a quarter-inch off the mouth end, lit it on the myrtle torch, took a deep drag, puffed smoke to the five directions, and said

> "Now my heart's breath is white,
> Now my heart's breath is black,
> Now my heart's breath is gold,
> Now my heart's breath is red,

Lord Old Salter, we two here far under you
Ask you to loan us your quick eyes, your wary eyes,
Sovereign knowing lord, watching lord. Finished."

She bent down and puffed a chestful of smoke through the mesh of the basket. She waited a moment, lifted off the cover, reached in, and pulled out a slightly smaller basket that had been nested inside it. Its mesh was looser and I could see movement and a white heart-shaped thing hanging in the center. Koh set it down and half-lifted the lid with her right hand. The white thing was the paper nest of a small colony of polybiine wasps. More quickly than I could follow Koh had reached in with her left hand and had grabbed a fat golden-green female wasp with the long black nails of her thumb and sixth finger. She set her down in the center of a little dish. The wasp was at least two inches long, with a gravid abdomen and an extended ovipositor. Her wings had been amputated. She peered around with her big eyes. Koh's left forefinger came down out of the sky and pressed the wasp down on the dish at the junction of her thorax and abdomen. Even though she was tranquilized by the smoke, the wasp scrambled to get away, her feet slipping on the smooth glaze of the plate. Koh used the first two fingernails of her right hand as scissors and snipped off the wasp's head. It bounced on the dish, its mandibles opening and closing. Next she grabbed the stinger and ovipositor and yanked them out of the poor thing's abdomen. A fat little toxin sac, a couple of clear beady eggs, and some yellow hairs and shreds of chitin came along with them. Koh set the cluster of gunk down on the side of the dish. Finally, still holding down the abdomen with her left hand, she tore off one of the six thrashing legs—the right front, I think—and dropped it on a second tiny dish. She pushed the dish over to me.

Koh lifted up the struggling, five-legged, headless insect, popped it into her mouth, chewed twice, and swallowed.

I hesitated.

Come on, Jed, I thought. Don't be such a wuss. I picked up the leg and rolled it stupidly around in my hand as though it might leap up and pinch my eye. Okay. I popped it into my mouth. It was still twitching on my tongue. I crunched it up and swallowed as fast as I could. Koh handed me the stogie, I guess to wash it down. I took a good-size drag. It was a little dry and oddly spiced but not bad. I didn't know what to do with it so I held on to it. The dwarfess came back in and laid out a little array of baskets, jars, and tiny

dishes on each side of the hearth cover as though we were about to have afternoon tea. Already my mouth felt as though it was larger than my head.

Koh said,

"Now we'll suppose that I play a great-Game here,
In front of you next to me,
Would you betray me to hostile greathouses?
Or name me to strangers?
Would you recount in the open what now happens
Inside our citadel,
Here on our jade mountain, here underneath the sky,
Over the heartland?
Would you then chatter about it outside, in the hundred zocalos?
Would you slice open my vein-knotted book
In the sun, in the daylight?"

I choked out a response around a tongue that felt as fat and slow as a
woodchuck:

"How would I still be a blood
If I ever repeated a secret?
Then from that time they would no longer call me
A son of the Harpy House,
Grackles would jeer at me, hornets would sting
My two lips, my two eyeballs,
Then armadillos would lick at my skull
In the dunes, in the wastenesses,
Far from this mountain cave over the sea crater,
Under the sky shell."

How was that? I wondered. Correct enough for you? Or do you also want
to hear it in Latin?

Slowly, Koh gestured, "Acknowledged." I watched her dark hand drop
toward her thigh. It seemed to be falling and falling and not getting there, and
then it seemed as though it wasn't falling anymore, that she was just holding
it out in midair. Weird, I thought. I looked over at the clock, or rather I started
to, but it took my eyes a while to get there. It's that time-smashing Old Salter

dust stuff again, I thought. Chronolytic. Except this is a lot more chronolytic than the last—oh, there it is. My eyes had gotten to the incense ball, finally; it looked like it was about half-gone, but I couldn't see it well because the dwarfess must have hung a strip of cheesecloth or something over it—oh, sorry, no, it was just a wisp of smoke, not moving, or appearing not to move because of the drug. I heard the Penguiness whispering something. I turned my eyes back to Koh. They felt like big granite spheres rolling in oiled sockets. Koh gave me a "strong wait" hand gesture, the same gesture the Harpy clan used in hunts or raids when everyone was supposed to freeze.

Someone outside the room whistled. The dwarf scuttled out the door. It seemed that minutes went by between each little footfall. Koh stood up. It was like watching a mountain being slowly thrust up by the subduction of the tectonic plate underneath it. She turned toward me and shook her manta into a better attitude. Whoa, I thought. Surprisingly, she was a lot taller than the average Maya woman, maybe even a hair taller than I was, that is, than I was now, and Chacal was a big guy. Rudely, I twisted my head around, watching. She seemed thin under her quechquemitl. Most sun adders were thin, but she was maybe a little too thin. She took four steps toward the center of the half-room and lowered herself to her knees facing the door behind me. I'm not generally a ballet queen, but a long time ago I saw Rudolf Nureyev in *L'Apres-Midi d'un Faune,* and there was a kind of haughtiness in his movements, where every finger was just, like, I'm the hottest and you're the nottest, and Lady Koh had something a lot like that. Except around here it wasn't so off-putting.

I twisted around. A head and shoulders appeared in the little doorway and bobbed up and down as their owner stood up. My irises had to strain but gradually, like a nebula in a big telescope, he came into focus. He was a tall man. He wore a dark thin manta. He had loose hair like a nacom's and skin rubbed with gray ash. I couldn't make out his markings, but he smelled like cat musk, or rather he was wearing a kind of artificial musk, made from *Mimulus inoschalus,* that the low-level Ixian Ocelots also wore. So he was from the other side, the Puma House, but he wasn't a feline being himself. Probably he was from some foster clan that served the Pumas as monks. He recited something incomprehensible in a whispery voice and Koh answered in the same language. I don't understand, I thought. Say it in Bumfuckistani. He walked toward Koh, taking five slow, tiny steps. Koh didn't move.

There was something about the scene I didn't like. In fact it gave me a bit of the creeps. The Puma fumbled with something near his waist. No way, I thought. He pulled out a little pouch, held it up near his face, untied what were probably some more of those impossible secret fisherman's knots, thumbed it open, and took something out. I didn't see what the something was.

Koh leaned forward and opened her mouth. The Puma put the something on her tongue. She closed her mouth, leaned back, and chewed it up.

I got a little shock, a relic from my days as a preconfirmed Catholic. Was that how communion rituals got started? I wondered. Take and freak, this is my blotter. I felt like I nearly choked staying silent.

There was something poignant about watching her do this very common, human thing, that is, eat. It had a kind of affectionate drudgery to it, like you could see she'd done this thousands of times. Suddenly she seemed like a human being, like a fun girl to be around. A little wacky, maybe.

The Puma messenger leaned forward, listening to Koh swallow. The dwarf handed him a cup of I guess hot water and he held it out to Koh. She took it with the hem of her manta between her hand and the cup, drank down whatever was in it, and gave it back to him. He looked into it and then down at her. She opened her mouth wide. He examined it for a moment and then spread his arms to show he was satisfied. To me it seemed kind of degrading to Koh, like she was getting tranqs in prison. The Puma took another little thing out of a different waist pouch. The Penguin Woman held out a trading tray and he set it in the center. It was a little figurine of Koh, with her face painted in that distinctive way. Maybe it was what Koh had given the dwarfess before. The Penguin Woman chanted a little thank-you-guest speech in that same old language.

The Puma whispered a thank-you-host reply, squatted, and withdrew backward into the tunnel. The Penguin Woman followed him out.

So that's how they do it, I thought. Koh and the other Orb Weavers didn't even have direct access to all the components of the Game drugs. Instead, it was basically a double-key system. You could only get the full effect by taking two different compounds. And the head adders of the Morning Glory House knew how to make one of them and the Swallowtail House adders knew how to make the other, and neither one had gotten the secret out of the other, not in the hundreds of years since whatever genius it was set up the system.

Well, Jed, you should have guessed it. No wonder this town's been so stable for such a long time. Damn, why didn't I think of that?

Hell. This is going to be tough.

Frustration. Deep in my clenched fists I could feel my long nails breaking the skin of my palms. Relax, I thought. Keep it together. True strength is seeing every finish line as the next starting point. Breathe.

Koh was still. I sat still. I blinked. My eyelid rolled down like dusk and, after a long night, like dawn. There was silence except for the rustlings in the tunnel beyond the door. Then there was a low whistle like a mourning dove's. Koh stood up, walked over to the screen, slipped through it, bent down over me—I hadn't quite had a chance to get back to my spot—and grabbed me by my hair, not by my pigtail, which was still false, but the forelock, and kissed me, violently, thrusting her smooth tongue into my mouth, twisting it around mine, rubbing it into my cheeks, over my palate, between my sharpened teeth and the fresh laceration and old scars on my inner lips, down to my tonsils, everywhere—

(52)

She tasted like nothing I'd ever tasted, not in the ninth b'ak'tun or in the twelfth, maybe a little like that wistful taste like *uni,* raw sea urchin, but darker and older and more metallic. Wow, major kiss, I thought, just about the last thing I expected in this context; Native Americans don't really have a kissing culture.

I almost thought she was she expecting me to rip her damn raiment off and go at it, and I was considering trying to fondle her somewhere—if I could get it together enough to find a fondlable spot—when she let go of my hair, broke away from me with a wet pop, and sat back in her spot on the far side of the hearth cover. The dwarf, who evidently had come back, set down a basketful of pots and jars and gave Koh a cup of something. She drank it as though she wanted to wash my taste from her mouth. I settled down again on my mat, trying to quiet my breathing. She looked as though nothing noteworthy had happened. Weirdly enough I felt unfaithful to Marena, even though she and I weren't really an item, probably. Settle down, Goofus, I thought, you're dreaming. All these broads are out for marlin. They're not interested in some grungy little . . . whatever . . .

Whoa. A numby fugu-ish aftertaste was growing in my mouth. I wobbled a little and sat up straight again.

Well, so that's the deal, I thought. She was just giving me a taste of the dope. Purely a professional maneuver. Chill.

So the colony of wasps produced X chemical—maybe they fed on something specific and they refined it in their bodies—and that was the Old Salter's dust. And that process was owned by the Orb Weavers. And then if you combined it with the Steersman's dust—that is, the topolytic drug, the

Y chemical that the Puma messenger had given Lady Koh—it gave you the full nine-stone enabling effect.

Well, damn. That's a disappointment. 2JS had thought she'd have a stash of the stuff on hand. Instead she had to fill a prescription and use it all in one shot under feline supervision. And from the way she was talking before, it sounds like even that was out of the ordinary, that they weren't giving any of it out on demand, except that she was able to get a tiny dose of it by calling in a favor. Fuck and fuck.

Hmm.

Ready? Koh gestured.

I sat up straighter. Ready, I signed. Koh took a deep drag on her cigar.

"My breath is red, my breath is white," she said.

When you root yourself you make yourself believe you're at the heart of the universe. But this time I didn't have to make myself believe it. I was already sure of it. The bite of gravity felt stronger than it ever had, but at the same time it seemed like I was feeding off it, building up a mountain-full of energy. I thought I could feel each of the different layers of material beneath me, cotton, rush matting, clay, soil, stone, molten stone, all the way down to earth's white-hot crystal core. The underwaterworlds and overworlds rotated around us. I was home.

The dwarf slid a claw through a loop of string on the hearth cover, lifted up the wooden square, and slid it aside. It looked heavy but she didn't seem to strain. In the space underneath, instead of a fire pit, there was a nearly perfect square depression, about fifteen inches deep and forty inches on a side. On its flat bottom I could just make out the incised outlines of a game board, a thirteen-by-thirteen square. Koh was sitting on the southwest and I was on the northeast. The dwarf set rushlights on the northwest and southeast sides of the stone well, filling it with light. The stone was some kind of dark, fine-grained gneiss, and it had that patina that you can only get from skin, from generations of hands tapping and rubbing, sweeping and polishing, and when Koh tapped the southwest wall five times with the butt of her fly whisk, you could tell from the resonance, or the lack of resonance, or something, that the pit had been chipped out of living rock, and that we were sitting on the peak of a buried mountain that went down through the alluvium of the valley and into the roots of the Sierra Madre Oriental.

"*Ya'nal Wak Kimi*," Koh said,

"Now on 6 Dying, on 14 Stag, in the eleventh tun, counting,
Nearing the end of eleven k'atuns in the tenth b'ak'tun, counting,
Now I am borrowing this sun's breath, now I will borrow tomorrow's,
Now I will borrow the wind of the suns that will follow tomorrow."

She took a finger-scoop of damp tobacco out of one of the little baskets and drew her hand inside her quechquemitl so that she could rub the stuff into her thigh. I couldn't get much of an idea of what was going on under all the drapery, but it was still a pretty sexy gesture.

I sat back a bit. I felt extremely wrong. I was sure that I was going to vomit, and not just the contents of my stomach, but my entire digestive tract. Everything from the esophagus to the colon was going to spray out of my mouth and pile up on the board. I choked it all back and sat a few degrees straighter. Keep it together, Joaquinito. You wanted to play with the big kids. So play.

"Now my own breath is a yellow wind,"
She said. "Now my own breath is a red wind,
Now my own breath is a white wind,
A black wind, an emerald-green wind.
You of my uncle's house,
You far away and now close to me,
Here we are sitting together
Between the four heights, four volcanoes,
Here on the blue-green volcano,
Five suns from the northeast white mountain,
Five suns away from your southeastern heights,
From your family's red mountain,
Five suns away from the yellow southwestern volcano,
And five suns
Away from the darkness,
Away from the scab-black northwestern volcano."

The dwarf handed Koh something. It was a black stone, a rounded cone, about two inches wide at the base and seven inches high, polished to a licked gloss. Koh set it down in the red quadrant—although there were only traces of pigment left on the board's surface, but of course one knew what the colors were—in the bin, or rather the faint depression, that corresponded to today. Its bottom fitted into the concavity so that it stood upright and stable. The Penguin Woman handed Koh another and another, until there were nine pillars rising up from the board, making a star map of this particular day at this location, with the Pleiades, the moon, and then Venus just rising at the eastern edge. Next she added five stones, which, I guessed, stood for the five mountains of Teotihuacan, that is, they established our exact place on earth.

Koh held out her dark hand and opened it slowly, meaning "Now, what is your question?"

Okay, I thought. Better phrase this right.

I'm still not sure just how on board she is. I have to get her to commit. If it isn't enough to just identify the Doomster now, then she should show me how to play with nine stones. And if you need to get together the Game drugs to do that, then she should tell me how to do that too. Right.

"You next to me please tell me," I said, "how can I preserve my hometimers' lineages through the last sun of the thirteenth b'ak'tun, and for the thirteen b'ak'tuns following that sun."

Koh didn't react. But the pause stretched on in a way that made me pretty sure she was displeased. Well, she's not throwing me out, I thought. Pause. Pause. Pause.

Finally, the Penguin Woman—who seemed to get cues from Koh telepathically like some kind of homunculus—crawled into view with another set of wicker boxes. She took a jar and a paintbrush out of one of them and painted the walls of the sunken board with some kind of fat or oil. It had an odd smell. Next she painted the stuff on the sides of the standing rocks—

Whoa. Dizzy.

By now the taste from that kiss had filled my whole body. It was crab-meaty and sour—not so sour as an ant, though—and then under that there was a cocaine-like buzz, and still farther down and later in the aftertaste there was some unnatural flavor that maybe reminded me of some kind of soft drink they used to make when I was a kid, some really debased pre-natural-food-era chemically futuristic drugstore novelty, except I'd forgotten the name, what was it, some . . .

Where was I?

The dwarf handed Koh a basket. She took a little wiggling pinkish-brown thing out of it and set it down on the game board's blue-green center point. It crouched there, and turned its head, and blinked around in the light. It was a baby monkey, smaller than a lab mouse—maybe about two inches high if it stood up, which it didn't—and nearly naked. Its groin was painted or dyed black, to look like a loincloth, and there was a black sort of cap painted on its head, I guess to make it look more human. It didn't look like a miniature human baby. It had the proportions of an adult. I couldn't tell what species it was but from its malnourished, elongated look, and from its spiraling tail, I guessed that it might be a spider monkey, an *Ateles*, one of those dark tiny things that eats a lot of fruit and almost never comes down to the forest floor. They grow fast, so it had to be almost a newborn, but already it had a dusting of dark down, and as it dashed twice around the perimeter of the board, it seemed as mobile as an adult. It tried to climb up the corner of the polished wall and then tried to push itself up between two standing stones that were close to each other, but it kept slipping down, scrabbling against the greased stone. Then it tried leaping, and I almost thought it would clear the edge, but it didn't have the muscles or coordination an adult would have and couldn't leap above twice its own height. Finally it paused and urinated in the center of the red quadrant. I couldn't see much—you'd need a jeweler's loupe—but I got the impression it was a male. He looked up at us, although of course he couldn't see us with those tiny eyes that hadn't yet learned to focus. It crept into the red-and-black corner and cowered there, shivering. Koh brought one of the dry chocolate cups down over the monkey and slid it over the shallow bins to the square in the white quadrant that corresponded to today, four lines from the Eclipse Day on the border of the black quadrant.

There was a pause. I noticed I was listing slightly to port. By now whatever she'd slipped me in that kiss had brought me beyond the point of sharpening my wits and into a stage where I couldn't have told you who I was—although come to think of it, that was actually an issue. And I'd only gotten a trace of what she'd taken, I thought. She must have enough of this stuff in her system to kill a blue whale. And she was also a lot smaller than I was. No wonder the nine-stone adders had to start getting habituated to the drugs when they were five years old. I probably had this dopey high-guy grin. Lady Cool would think I was a total fruitcake. Well, that's what happens your first time.

The Penguin Woman handed Koh a second box. It was shaped like a little square hut with a tuft of strings on top. This time she set it down in the center of the black quadrant, untied the little knot, and pulled up one of the strings. A wall of the box slid up like the door of a Chinese cricket cage.

Koh laid her open hand in front of the open door.

We waited. Now what? I wondered.

A pair of segmented longhorn antennae unfolded out of the shadow, paused, rotated in opposition, and paused again, and then a white ribbon of fangs flowed up into Lady Koh's hand. It was a centipede, but not one I could classify, and it was a cavernicole morph, an eyeless albino species that for all anyone knew might have been living in the same light-tight sinkhole since the latest thing in vertebrates was the coelacanth. It was unpigmented, almost transparent in the soft places, but with brown at the edges of its chitin plates like the singeing at the peaks of a meringue pastry. It was around twelve inches long, which is enough to get your attention. It held still for long enough for me to see that it had twenty-one pairs of legs and that it had no eyes, just four stubs where the eyes would have been. The fangs, or rather poison claws, were long and gently curved, like cavalry sabers. And the setae—that is, the bristles that pick up motion—on its antennae were hugely enlarged, like spikes on an ocotillo cactus. It was like a zipper with the universe caught in it, painfully.

More quickly than I could follow Koh had reached in with her left hand—the heptadigital one—and had grabbed the thing by its second tergite, the one right behind its head. She set it down in the center of a little dish and held it down with her thumb. It—or let's call it she, because Koh did—she tried to get free, rearing her hind length up and scratching at Koh's wrist with her flailing tarsae.

"She is one k'atun and tunob old," Koh said. "She is very wise."

Koh took her thumb away.

I shifted on my crossed legs. I hadn't seen or heard of this before. Really, I'd expected Koh to just bring out her stones and seeds and start playing away. Well, *uno nunca sabe.*

Koh tapped her fingernails next to the 'pede, apparently communicating with her in her own vibratory language. The thing seemed to cock a slit sensillum to listen. Finally, she unstiffened a little and looked sightlessly up at me. I got a shivery impression she could taste us. She slid twice around Koh's palm and curled into a loose spiral. Koh spoke to her in a new, smaller voice, and in a different language, all close vowels and sibilants. I leaned in too closely and the critter turned and snapped its labial palps at the warmth of my face with a pair of double clicks.

"Your spine must move northwest," Koh said. She meant to sit back a bit. I did. I almost thought she was smiling a bit at my little drug problem. I probably had eyes like a twelve-year-old's after his first toke. Very funny.

Koh set her hand down near the board's extreme southeast. The 'pede slid off her palm like a trickle of mercury and took possession of the corner. She reoriented herself. She settled. She seemed used to the board.

"Forgive me, lead me, shining guest," Koh said. With a shell-game-quick movement she covered the centipede with a second chocolate cup. I was unpleasantly reminded of little entertainments that my stepbrothers in Utah set up, gladiatorial combats in TV crates involving whiptail lizards and lab rats. Koh laid her light hand on the cup over the centipede and her dark hand on the cup over the monkey.

> "My breath is black, my breath is yellow,
> My breath is red, my breath is white, my breath
> Is now blue-green . . . ,"
>
> Koh said.

She lifted both cups.

Nothing moved. I watched the centipede through weeks, and months, and years. Finally her antennae stirred, raised, and swung slowly through a 150-degree arc, tapping like a marimba player's mallets as they spot-tasted the surface. She paused. She's feeling something, I thought. Was the board like a kind of seismograph? Was the 'pede sensing the ebbs and floods of lava tides two miles below us? Was it gauging the pull of the moon?

The two creatures were as far apart on the board as possible, and because of the cluster of standing stones in the middle, they couldn't see each other. But, slowly, the centipede rustled, orienting herself, and then moved three wary steps east, perpendicular to the monkey, palpating the surface of the red quadrant. From the way she found her footing in the shallow bins, it seemed that she was accustomed to the terrain. The monkey stiffened. Something was up.

In terms of size, the centipede had the advantage. But I'd seen howler monkeys kill snakes bigger than they were. And even if the monkey decided he didn't want to fight the centipede, he could always just bounce away. And the 'pede was blind. So my guess was that, once again, things looked bad for the invertebrates.

The monkey turned his head left, ever so slightly, and the centipede cocked her own cephalothorax in the same direction. It was hard to believe that he'd made a sound. But the 'pede's ancestors had lived underground for a long time, and they'd learned to sense the tiniest vibrations. There was another long pause and then the monkey edged slightly left, checking out a possible route to the south. The 'pede reacted immediately. The monkey paused and crept forward. I counted four beats and then the centipede began to move, first only stroking the board in place and then creeping *au·pas de loup* southward, perpendicular to the monkey, her claws contacting the surface in waves. I thought I could almost hear the taps of chitin on the stone and the differences between the taps. The *Scolopendra* came to the edge of the standing stone at today. Her antennae probed past the edge, thinking around the corner. I thought of Marena in that photograph, climbing that rock face, feeling for cracks above her head. The monkey crept nearer. The 'pede started to slide forward, moving in a way that looked like she was chewing her way through space, and then froze in position, tasting the air with her antennae. She looked like an open mouth with the teeth on the outside, a Cheshire jaguar's bloody grin. The monkey took a tiny hop left, out from the shelter of the standing stone.

The 'pede stiffened.

The monkey saw her. He froze.

Did he know what she was? All mammals instinctively fear segmented things. On the other hand, monkeys, even frugivores like this guy, eat a lot of bugs. And this monkey didn't just look hungry. He was truly underfed. His eyes narrowed, and you could see by the greed in them that he'd been on a starvation diet, that he'd attack anything with meat on it. Was he going to grab her by the tail and whip her head against the stone? Or would he paw at her over and over until he'd smooshed her, like a fox does with a scorpion?

He studied her. The centipede crept forward again, warily, into the yellow and clockwise toward the red. The monkey's tensed body didn't move, but his eyes followed her. She crossed into the red zone. The monkey shifted his weight. Suddenly, too fast for the eye to follow, the centipede darted forward. The monkey jumped and leapt sideways, almost backward, and crouched behind one of the obstacle stones. The centipede slowed and turned.

There was a standoff. I counted five beats, and then ten. The monkey crept backward, keeping the standing stone between them. At fourteen beats, the tableau dissolved into motion. The combatants ricocheted across the surface too fast to follow, like a pinball between bumpers or a video of subatomic particles bouncing around in a cloud chamber. I had an impression that it was the monkey chasing the centipede. *All around the vinegar bush,* I thought. Then it seemed that the centipede was chasing the monkey, roughly counterclockwise through the henge of stones, which made something like an obstacle course. On each circuit the centipede came closer to the monkey than it had before. Now the monkey was into the red, and then the centipede was into the red and up into the white and the monkey had leapt across the board, into the black, with the centipede following and then not following but turning and heading backward, as though she were figuring out where the monkey was going to go, and before I could see what had happened the centipede had headed him off against one of the standing stones. Then the monkey had looped around behind her. He faked her out, I thought. The centipede froze. The monkey seemed to gather his courage. He jumped, grabbed the 'pede's last segment, and raised it to whip her down to the stone, but before he could get her off the ground the centipede's head had curled up behind the monkey's back. I got a disturbing feeling that the 'pede had planned this, had seen it all ahead of time. She clenched around his torso and dug her bladed arms into the flesh at the nape of his neck.

The monkey tore away, leapt backward, and stumbled. It was clear that he'd been envenomated. He struggled westward, creeping on all fours, but by 8 Reed his hands were slipping on the stone. He stumbled around Venus and back northward. He made it as far as 13 Wind. After decades of playing the Game I could feel, without knowing how, that his terror keyed into something basic about the layout of the board.

I looked up at Koh. She was concentrating on the scene with what I'd have to call a burning focus, reading the monkey's panic.

The centipede sat, waiting. I noticed she was in the very center of the board, on the green zero date, which also represented Teotihuacan in the board's world-map aspect. After thirty seconds the monkey was moving more stiffly, dragging himself forward, away from the centipede. He wouldn't be so much in pain now, I thought, just feeling terribly cold. Two minutes later he was at the far side of the black quadrant. He toppled forward, like a little figurine, resting on his face. He could still flex and unflex his hands. Otherwise, he seemed to be paralyzed below the neck. The centipede approached him, more insouciant this time, legs rippling unhurriedly like oars on a galleon. When she reached him she palpated him with her furred antennae in long, delicate strokes. She folded herself around him. He tipped over stiffly but his hands still curled around two of the 'pede's spiked legs, trying to push away.

They were small animals, but the scene felt gigantic, like we were seeing the true, unedited story of Saint George and the dragon. The monkey began to scream.

The sound was almost too high to hear, as shrill as a diamond cutter across a sheet of Pyrex. It was a tiny sound. But it was so penetrating that I was sure that Hun Xoc and the rest of them could hear it out in the courtyard, that 14 Wounded could hear it all the way across town, that they could hear it way out in the wastelands, in Ix, at the North Pole, and on Mars. After a hundred and four beats the glass seemed to shatter, and the scream stopped, and started again, and broke again, and finally the monkey was screaming silently, with his mouth frozen open and his lips drawn back from his tiny teeth. After three thousand beats he was swelling with digestive juices but still twitching. The centipede began to feed, her little jaws and palps moving over the monkey, back and forth, like a child eating corn on the cob, tongue-lessly licking him, basting him with gelatinous saliva. 'Pedes are messy eaters, and soon the monkey was glistening with the stuff and there was a clear pool of it underneath him. After sixty thousand beats, the centipede's enzymes had largely dissolved the monkey's muscles and internal organs, and it looked more like a skin filled with water than a recently living creature. The 'pede gnawed at the base of his neck, and then up through the soft skull into the brain, and then back down into the torso. We watched in the suffocating si-lence. Koh's pupil was so dilated that the brown of her iris was like an aureole around an eclipsed sun. The centipede turned the monkey's torso over with her quick delicate fussy harp-plucking movements and began coating his stomach. I estimated that it only took about an hour and forty minutes for the monkey to be reduced to a smudge of fur and teeth.

I snuck a look at Koh. She was looking at me with one eye and keeping her other on the 'pede. Whoa, I thought. It can be disconcerting to talk to people who have a wandering eye. But unlike someone with the medical condition Koh could apparently control her eyes independently. I looked back at the board. Nothing happened for another eternity or two. Just when I felt like everything had ended and we were all mummified in our spots, Koh seemed to move. I looked up at her. Nothing. I looked back at the centipede. Some-thing was wrong.

The centipede tensed, as though she sensed enemies. She whipped her head to the left and then to the right, snapped her maxillae twice, and then seemed to panic. She ran clockwise, and then counterclockwise, over the red land, over the yellow land, out to the eighth b'ak'tun, and then turned right and dashed into the black land, and then ran back again over the white land and the yellow land, way, way out this time, into the thirteenth b'ak'tun, and back and forth, pastward, futureward, crossing the present over and over until finally, in the center of the north quadrant, on 14 Night, she dug in and spun around and around counterclockwise. For some reason a word scrolled across my mind: *INSANE*. On the twenty-eighth spin she seemed to come to a decision and froze, her tail raised. Her antennae quivered. Her legs drummed preternaturally fast. There's an Ixian expression that says you'll never move faster than when you shiver at your death.

The centipede took four halting steps north, then six slow steps southeast, and shuddered to a stop on a bin that, with the numerical stones, signified 12 Motion, 5 Turquoise, in the seventh k'atun of the twelfth b'ak'tun, or December 3, 1773. It was the year of the earthquake that destroyed Antigua when it was the capital of Guatemala. Should I mention it? Or did Koh already know? I decided not to volunteer anything. The centipede moved forward again, staggering, if you can stagger with forty-two legs, until she came to on 2 Etz'nab, 1 K'ank'in, 2 Razor, 1 Yellowribs, two days from the end date.

Evidently she'd been poisoned by the monkey, or by whatever the monkey had been raised on. She writhed, curled, uncurled, flipped over onto her back, curled and uncurled, and flopped onto her stomach. She bit at the base of her left 18th leg. Bits of white flesh swelled out through cracks in her exoskeleton. Mist sprayed from her fangs as she pumped neurotoxins into the air. She flipped onto her back again, clawing at herself. A seam opened in the center of her back and widened, the cuticle unzipping segment by segment. She was molting.

Arthropods molt using peristaltic waves. A molting spider looks like a lone hand pushing its way out of a glove. Insects tend to tear off one piece at a time. A centipede flexes and extends, like a foot shrugging off a slipper. Usually the molt reveals a complete fresh exterior, and it's as though the creature has been reborn. I remembered that someone—maybe my mother, or maybe Chacal's mother—had said that if we could shed our skins we'd be able to live forever.

Now, though, this centipede was trying to molt when she wasn't ready. There was no new exoskeleton under the one she was shedding, just raw liner cells oozing bubbles of hemolymph. Basically, she was skinning herself alive. She twisted and flopped against the stone, obviously in agony. Curls of chitinous shell separated and dropped to the stone with shreds of white flesh stuck to their undersides. The ventral sides of her last two segments seemed to be moving, or kneading, maybe, and then they fell apart—but the pieces were moving, no, they were little things moving, maggots, maybe? No, they were hundreds of tiny translucenty-white centipedes, each only about the size of a bit of shaved dried coconut from some old-fashioned ice-cream snowball dessert. I thought I remembered that *Scolopendra* laid eggs, but evidently this type was different. The little guys crawled and spread and wriggled and clustered around the gobbets of their mother's flesh, lapping up ichor. Finally the mother curled into a ring, gnawing at herself until she was just a soggy tangle on 9 Skull, 11 Wind, in the white quadrant of the board. Eventually only her antennae were still moving, drawing slow figure eights in the air. Within another thousand beats, the kids had stopped too. Koh's fingers came down out of the sky. Her nails closed on the tattered centipede. She picked her up—the 'pede was as stiff as a burnt strip of bacon—and put the opal runner down in her place. She swept up the bits of the monkey and the loose bits of the 'pede with a new cotton cloth. The dwarf held out a clay box. Koh wrapped the remains of both animals in the cloth, laid the bundle in the box, and spoke briefly to it in two languages. The dwarf took the box away, presumably for dignified entombment. Before I knew what she was doing Koh had already taken away the large standing stones and started laying out the skulls, that is, pebbles, on the bins where the creatures had been, counting again in that old language. It seemed that she paused for several minutes between each stone and the next, and I had to keep reminding myself that she was moving at normal speed and I was just thinking faster.

Even so, the actual combat between the creatures had still happened so fast I barely saw it. But not only had Koh seen it all, she remembered the entire tangle of paths that the centipede and monkey had taken, and remembered it perfectly. She traced it with a chain of markers, using different shapes of pebbles on the spots of different events, a flat oval on the bin where the centipede first struck, a wedge where the monkey died, and a near-perfect sphere on the site of the centipede's death. It was one of the most singular mental feats I'd ever seen, and I'd seen a few. To me the whole thing had been 80 percent blur. I bet she could have watched a ten-minute video of balls bouncing around on a billiard table and then sketched every frame.

Finally, Koh tapped the board five times and emptied out a bag of little stones. They were all different. Some were flattened on one side like gumdrops. Each represented a planet or a major star. She selected the cast of characters that would currently be overhead and put back the rest. She laid out tonight's skyscape on the board, slightly differently this time, with the Last Lord of the Night bowing down to the west and the birth of Sun Vanquisher, that is, Venus, in the east. The stone she used to represent the moon was a smooth spheroid hydrophane, a water opal. In Europe, in the Middle Ages, they called it the Eye of the World.

Koh said:

> "Now blackward I salute the cave of the dead,
> Now yellowward I salute the cave of the breathing,
> Now redward I salute the cave of the unborn,
> Now whiteward I salute the cave of never at all.
> Now I am scattering yellow seeds, black seeds,
> And now I am scattering
> White skulls and red skulls,
> And this is your own blue-green skull,
> Your own namesake,
> And now we are moving."

She brought down a green stone and tapped it forward, walking down into the west, up into the east, and back to the crossroads, up the side of the Crocodile Tree, past the Four Hundred Boys, that is, the Pleiades, and along the long white road of the snake's stomach, past the hearthstones, that is, the belt of Orion, and then south toward Sirius and Mirzam, what we called the Second Lord of the Night, leaving a trail of stones behind her through the convolutions of time. She moved fast, but I followed it with no problem. In fact, even though Chacal's brain didn't have the Game connections my Jed one had had, I was coming up with solutions to stuff I'd screwed up in my old games. And it didn't even exactly feel like I was thinking more clearly. It was something different, a feeling specific to the topolytic drug. It wasn't like flying through space, but like having all space conflated, or with the whole world balled up in your hand, so that if you just turned it slightly you'd be wherever . . . or maybe it was more as though the world were a deck of cards, so that you could bring distant spaces together just by reshuffling, you could plop Ceylon into the middle of Oklahoma or pour the Trifid Nebula into this room.

Koh set down nine white pebbles and started them hunting the runner. It came to the sun eight days from now, the day of the eclipse. She said there was a faint gray smell there, and that there was also a *k'ii* for me on that day. The word meant a ploy or a strategy, a way to turn things my way. The kii had a two-part name: *"chaat ha' anachan."*

The first word, *chaat*, meant the Northwest Wind, which was dry, hot, and coded black. Or it could mean just wind in general. The second word, *anachan,* meant a mortuary town, that is, a Mexican-style miniature city of the dead. We'd passed hundreds of them on the long trudge inland from San Martín. Other than that, the dust was too thick, as she put it, for her to see anything more clearly.

Wind in a cemetery, I thought. Hmm.

"Five suns, fourteen suns, and thirty suns,
"Fifty-five suns, ninety-one suns, one hundred suns . . ."

When she'd made twenty placements, Koh took up the first one and continued, like the way a solo mountain climber sets a safety line, climbs up past it, sets another, and then climbs down to remove the first. I'd thought she might use tongs to move a piece on the far side of the board, but instead she leaned way out over it. I got a half eyeful of décolletage. Mmmm. Some things never change. I was feeling like I wouldn't mind another Kiss of the Spider Woman. Maybe the light-and-dark thing was kind of cute, in a way. What was wrong with her? Was it just hyperpigmentation? You could get extra melanin from hormonal imbalances. Or was it really vitiligo? Melasma? Addison's disease? Hæmochromatosis? Angina? Xeroderma pigmentosum? Zero-sum game—

"Zero suns," Koh said. She'd come to the date that corresponded to the spot where the monkey was killed. But she didn't stop. Instead, and without hesitation, she kept on placing stones, as though the centipede was still chasing the monkey through in some Kaluza-Kleinian collapsed dimension. Some of the bins nearly filled up with pebbles. If there had been only one or two runners I could have followed it. But as I think I've said, each new runner increased the difficulty many times over. A nine-stone game isn't just one stone harder than an eight-stone game. It wasn't even nine times harder. It was 9!, that is, $9 \times 8 \times 7 \times 6 \times 5 \times 4 \times 3 \times 2$, or 362,880 times harder.

"14, 51, 124, 245," Koh whispered. She read ahead and then reversed. She backtracked all the way to 5 Kaban, 15 Chen, 8.14.17.7.17, the date identified in the Codex as the collapse of A' K'aakan, that is, El Mirador, and then turned around and continued along the path into the future, moving ahead 394 days, to the edge of the red quadrant and the founding date of Ix. There was something about the pattern of the hooked path she took, the way it wove back and forth and from point to point like a Maurer rose, and the way it kept repeating itself at different scales as it expanded to wider and wider angles . . . but it always had the same curve to it, a sort of hook, and there was something about that hooking curve that seemed to slice through the mushroom cloud of effects and strike, like a knife on a peach pit, on causes.

"When we come to a place and a sun that are strange to me," Koh said, "I will tell you the things I read there, and you will tell me their names."

I clicked that I would. The system she was talking about wasn't unusual. In fact there were already precedents in the protocol of the Game. For instance a client might ask the adder what's likely to happen on a trip he's taking. If he's talking about a place that he's visited but the adder hasn't, the adder will try to intuit the outlines but ask the client to clarify particulars along the way.

"Three hundred ninety-five, five hundred six," she said. She moved ahead one bundle of fifty-two solar years and then another and another and another. Tzam lic crackled under my skin like static voltage around a Van de Graaff globe. Koh described the Jewel Cities imploding into the jungle, and I imagined them like a backward film of silent red Chinese skyrockets against a green sky. Ix, Axcalamac, Yaxchilán, Bonampak, Palenque, Kaminaljuyú, Ti ak'al, Uaxactun, and Tonil all dissolved in the wave of dissolution that spread from the ruins of the Teotihuacano empire. Her fingers jumped ahead, setting a skull-kernel on the next square at each silent beat, leaving a widening wake, but a wake *ahead* of the line of seeds, the feather-hairs of the board weaving into crystals of history. New cities sprouted in the north, Kan Ec, Pink Mountain, Tula, Flint Lake, Chichén, Kabah, Narrow-Never-Empty-Well, Uxmal, and Mayapán. Later, after the beginning of the tenth b'ak'tun, new clusters of pyramids crystallized in the lake again, near the center of the board but south and west of the ruins of Teotihuacan: Tlaxcala, Tenochtitlán, and a hundred other towns of the Triple Alliance. Files of soldiers streamed like conqueror ants out of the capitals and over Mesoamerica. I snuck a look at Koh. She was straining, carrying me through history like she was surfing a lava flow with me riding on her back. If you play competitive chess or Go, or probably even if you compete at Neo-Teo or whatever's the latest nontrivial computer game, you know the feeling, the mental agony of keeping that many balls in the air. Even if you're an athlete, it's the same. You make that final effort and you think you can't do it and then you do, you go through that wall and get it up there, but then there's no way to bring it down, and you panic and yell for a spotter. Koh held thousands of eventualities in her mind and watched them spread out from her alter-ego-stone, and on each move, she chose one of them. Canoes the size of towns slid up out of the sea into the red bottom of the board. She saw the tarpon men again and saw blackberry boils erupting out of square miles of tan skin, lungs throbbing with pustules, bodies dying and spoiling too fast to bury. She moved up to 1518, the year Hernán Cortés reached Mexico City, only a few miles from the ruins of Teotihuacan. The white cities in the center of the lake shriveled in a burst of flame. She moved again.

"Nine Wind, ten thought, sixteenth k'atun," she said. That was February 4, AD 1525. The lake dried into mud and blew away in storms of dust.

"He almost destroys us," she said.

"Who?" I asked.

She described a tarpon-scaled giant with an orange beard.

I said I knew who it was.

"Who is it?" she gestured.

"Pedro de Alvarado."

(53)

Koh repeated the name. There was something chilling about hearing it here, now, in her voice.

"Now we are slaves," she said. I focused back on the board. Now it was as big as the entire Western Hemisphere, and populations rolled over the continents like loose beads in a platter. She described cities that doubled in size every few peace seasons, like ground fungi, and dark double roots with wet, giant worms slithering over them. I told her what I guessed she was imagining and she repeated the word: "Railroads." She moved from December 24, 1917, into 1918, on the dates of the earthquakes that had destroyed Ciudad Guatemala. She described the roots multiplying, and gnarling and sprouting and oozing bitumen. Dark running ticks would crawl over them, sucking the Earthtoadess's blood, and the trees would shrivel in their breath. After the ninth k'atun of the last b'ak'tun the stinking ticks multiplied into vast enameled herds, red and blue and yellow, and some of them sprouted wings. I told her I thought she was imagining roads and cars and airplanes. She described clusters of quartz crystals that "grew overnight, and vomited white flies over the cracked blue-green bowl." I wasn't sure what she meant by that. She set her sapphire down on 11 Howler, 4 Whiteness, in the fifth uinal of the first tun of the eighteenth k'atun of the thirteenth and last b'ak'tun.

"Your name-day," she said. I clicked "Correct."

She moved it to February 4, 1976—the day of the last big Guate city earthquake—and then farther out into the last b'ak'tun. "Eleven Motion," Koh said. "A blowgun-snake with mouth and anus joined vomits a dust-mote into the God of Zero's fire, and the sands fuse to crystal knives." The Maya date corresponded to June 2, 2009, the day of the collider blast in Huajapan de Léon. I started to tell her a little bit about it, but she moved on, tapping her lead opal outward, to 6 Razor, 6 Yellowribs.

"They fight themselves here," she said, "in the game-city in the northern coral flats."

"Disney World," I said.

"And what exactly will happen on that sun?"

I described the day as well as possible.

She moved on. We came to the edge of the world at the extreme west rim of the board and the bin named 4 Overlord, 3 Yellowribs, that is, December 21, 2012, at the limit of time.

"A hidden ahau turns his men against his own," she said. "He has a crooked skull."

I clicked yes. Still, that didn't seem like a lot of information.

"No, wait," she said. "He is not an ahau. He is only using an ahau's voice. His name is Trumpet Vine."

Whoa, I thought. Well, that's pretty specific in its way. The only problem was that I'd never heard of anything named Trumpet Vine.

Hmm.

The Ixian term she'd used, *t'aal chaconib*, meant something like "hummingbird chocolate flower." And it definitely meant "trumpet vine," *Campsis radicans*. But the thing was, the word was more common as an adjective, as an idiom for a salmon-pink color. That is, one thinks of trumpet vines as red, but the wild species we had was pink, or salmon pink. So maybe she just meant "light red."

"Can you over me tell me where he is?" I asked, but she'd already moved on, tapping her runner beyond the last day, into no-name time. Damn it. I snuck a look at her. Gamers learn to hide mental fatigue. But they also learn to sniff it out. So even though Koh didn't show more than a hint of that pinched dryness you get in too-long-focused eyes, and maybe a slight swelling in one or two thin veins visible through the melanin-free side of her face, I still got an impression that she might collapse. A single bead of sweat crawled out of her oiled hairline. On the board and, it seemed, around us, multitudes of inchoate shapes tumbled and howled with a sound like some tribe of giant nonhuman mammals in some huge stone hall. Ahead of us there was something like an edge, and beyond that, a zone that wasn't fog or darkness, but something like the area outside your field of vision, the 80 percent of the sphere around your head where not only can't you see, but you can't even really visualize what it would be like to see there. You strain to look up, say, past the widow's peak above your nose, and there's something like a bank of brown fog, but then, beyond that, there isn't even blackness but just a sort of nothing that your brain isn't wired to imagine.

"And this is the cliffside," she said. It meant there was nothing else.

Pause.

Well, that's a drag, I thought. I stifled a monohiccup. I felt queasy. The dwarf waddled over and took out the standing stones and cleared away the pebbles. There was a last long pause while Koh looked down at the empty board. My eyes were so tired that my vision was getting bluish. When Koh turned away the dwarf washed the board down with b'alche', salt, and water, tapped it five times to let its uayob know we were leaving, replaced the cover, and scattered fresh geranium petals over it. She got a wet cloth out of one of her jars and snuffed out the stumps of the rushlights.

I blinked. There was light in the room. It was the blue light that I'd thought was in my eyes. It was still weak but it was strong enough for me to see that the waxy stuff that covered the walls and screens and ceiling, and that had looked black in the firelight, wasn't paper or leaves or feathers. It was a mosaic of the wings of blue morpho butterflies. They were little circular sections, laboriously trimmed out of the center of the wings and sewn onto the canvas backing, tens of thousands of iridescent lapis-lazuli-blue disks rippling in otherwise undetectable air currents. Supposedly, here in the northwest, morphos were the uayob of slain warriors, and they could only be collected after they'd died naturally. Sometimes the collectors followed dying ones for days. How long had it taken? I wondered. How many lives' worth of man-hours had been spent on this room? The light swelled. It seemed to be falling down from the oculus like snow, so slowly that I thought I could see individual photons. The blue deepened to that unimaginable liquid morpho ultramarine, that structural blue that isn't a pigment, that comes from the interference of their billions of angled scales and vanishes under a drop of water, and it deepened beyond that, as though we were sinking in the tropical ocean, becoming so saturated it was as though I'd never seen the color blue before.

The dwarf stopped what she was doing and scurried out, as though she'd gotten one of her telepathic signals.

I guess that's it, I thought. I took in a breath to start the usual thank-you speech but Koh interrupted me with a "wait where you are" gesture.

She closed her eyes. It felt like the most intimate thing she'd done since I got here.

We sat.

So, I wondered, do we count that as a failure? She did get us there, I guess . . . still, that wasn't enough to really go after anyone . . . was it? I don't—

"I need to play that through again," Koh said. "With a full measure of Salter's and Steerman's dusts."

I didn't know what to say so, as I do too rarely, I shut up.

Hmm, well, *she* seems to consider that a failure. Still, at least she has confidence. It was kind of like how Taro'd said that we'd need another 10^{20} ply to be sure we'd bring the Doomster into range. We couldn't do it, of course, because there wasn't that much computing power on the planet, but at least he knew it wasn't impossible.

Well, maybe we can do it this way. She thinks—

I heard something faint and looked up. The Penguin woman was back, whispering something in Koh's light ear.

I sat.

The whispering went on and on. My sense of time wasn't back to normal yet, but I was sure it was more than ten minutes. Koh asked a few things in single-hand signs that I didn't understand. She looked at me in a way that made me a little nervous. Finally, the dwarf left. Koh settled back into a formal position and looked at me again in a way that made me look down at the place where the board had been.

Do you know how—well, I'm sure you know—how in Greek tragedies, all the action happens offstage? And the only things that happen onstage are like, say, a messenger comes in and says something like, "My queen! The Thessalonians are defeated!" Well, the first time I read those plays I thought it was all pretty stagey and unrealistic. But the more I saw of the world and things, especially things here, that is, here in the Olden Times, the more I realized that stuff actually is kind of realistic. Queens and dukes and ahauob and whoever really did spend most of their time sitting in their offices and getting third-hand reports and sending out couriers and generally staying out of the action.

"I'm told that the Harpy 14 Wounded's compound has been raided," Koh said. She didn't exactly glare at me but there was a flatness in her tone that I thought was more than just exhaustion from the Game. She was mad.

"B'aach?" I asked. *"What?"* It was an unforgivably rude way to speak to her, but I guess I was regressing to our twenty-first-century lack of manners.

"14 Wounded is outside in the courtyard with your men.'"

"What happened to the rest of the Ixian bloods?" I asked.

"For all we know they are also on their way here," she said.

I started to uncross my legs. "I under you should—"

She turned her hand over, meaning "Shut up," before I could say "go out and see them."

"I am told it was the Swallowtail Clan who entered the house," she said.

It's those Oxwitzan Jaguar fuckwads, I thought. Those boats that had been following us in the gulf. They'd probably gotten here right after us, pleaded their case in front of their foster cousins in the Puma Synod, and gotten them to shut 14 down. And there was about a 100 percent chance that the Ixian Ocelots had put them up to it. Hell.

"I am told there are more of them on their way here," she said. Apparently, the Harpies who'd gotten away were trying to claim temporary asylum here, in the Rattler's quarter.

Damn, she's angry, I thought. And it wasn't just because the Rattler's children weren't eager to take in any more refugees, although they weren't, despite the fact that the universal hospitality rule—of which this whole vigil festival thing was kind of an overblown extension—basically obligated them to. The problem was that this incident was likely to scotch any chance of repairing relations between the Rattlers and the two synods.

Well, okay, I thought. Change of plans. Don't get discouraged. It's not important how far away your goal is—just that you're moving toward it.

We still have a little time. 14's small potatoes. Right? The synods might go after some minor foreign trader right before High Holy Week, but they wouldn't stir up anything with the Rattlers until after the vigil. Would they?

Okay. Think.

There was no way to get out on the sly. We'd have to stay in the Rattler's quarter until after the eclipse and then come up with some way to force our way out.

And Koh had just better bite on the asylum offer. She'll take it, I thought. She has to.

"I beg you over me to come to Ix," I said. "My father 2 Jeweled Skull now offers you—

(54)

Eight days later, at the start of the second ninth of the day—10:32 A.M.—every human inhabitant of the holy valley of Teotihuacan was outdoors, looking upward, waiting for the Chewer to ambush the sun. The only unoccupied surfaces were the *taluds* and *tableros* of the mulob. Bloods, slaves, traders, crafters, pilgrims, porters, captives, children, old women, young women, babies—and even people who couldn't see or stand, and even the dying, in fact even the recently dead—were assembled in their ranks and orders and packed into plazas and rooftop gardens. Old men sat on their sons' shoulders and young men wore stiltlike sandals or teetered on tall stools. Every initiated male held whatever noisemaker was traditional to his clan and allowed to his seniority—drums, horns, maracas, ocarinas, clay bells, stone bells, castanets, sticks, clappers, bullroarers, rasps, whistles, flutes, and a hundred other gadgets, every one of them brand-spanking-new.

There were no fires in the valley. In fact, there were no fires in the entire altiplano. And even beyond the empire's farthest reach, hearthstones had been doused and scattered. In most of the Western Hemisphere, and probably in all of Mesoamerica, every torch, rushlight, coal, cigar, and miscellaneous flame had been extinguished. Last night it was overcast, and there was no moon, and as we made our final preparations in one of the Rattler's courtyards, it felt like—well, despite the fact that we were in the center of what was at the moment the densest concentration of people in the world, we could just as easily have been deep underground in a vast phosphorless cavern. Between the Sonoran Desert and the Andes, the continent was as dark as it had been before hominids infected it, thirty thousand years ago.

All but a few vessels and pots had been drilled or smashed. Blankets and clothing had been stained, slashed, or unwoven. Pictographic inscriptions had been canceled with streaks of blue ink. Livestock and slaves had been killed, and thousands of old, sick, or just pious people had killed themselves. Everyone, or at least everyone except me and maybe a handful of other skeptics, was terrified that this might be the final death of their sun. And I was terrified too, of course, just not about that.

From our perch up here on the snout of the Rattler's mul—that is, about halfway up the front of the pyramid, facing east toward the fetish market across the southern end of the main axis—we could feel the heat rising off the bodies, the mélange of their breaths, sour air from the ulcerated throats of the captives in their wicker standing-cages, the black air from the elders' tobacco, cancerated lungs. The sky was clear, and luckily for us there was only a little breeze. It was a perfect day for the end of time. I shifted from foot to foot. A loose end of gut cord from my combat sandal was hooking into the skin of my shin, but I didn't want to bend down to deal with it. That sort of thing wasn't done. I wobbled forward. Hun Xoc held out an arm and eased me back upright.

We were facing west, in the center of our core group of Harpy bloods. Hun Xoc was on my left, and Armadillo Shit was behind me. His job was literally to watch my back. We were in the center of a group of eleven other Harpy bloods and twenty-two Harpy nonbloods. 12 Cayman was in the vanguard, ready to move to the rear in case of attack.

We all wore blue outer mantas that identified us as aspirants to the Rattler Society. Under them we had on as much armor as we could get away with without looking suspicious. That is, we each wore wicker shin and arm guards and a vest made of two layers of thick canvas quilting, each filled with wood chips, which could stop most blades. Each of us had a short mace or a club strapped to the inside of one thigh and a rolled-up wicker shield strapped to the other. We also had a three-part spear, hanging from weak, easily breakable threads in the center of our backs, under our mantas. Next to it we each had a rolled-up wicker shield, which we'd had made specially for this action. Each one had three cross-pieces that folded down and a pair of strong hide straps that let you hold it with both arms. Still, I wished the shields were bigger. They might be our weak link.

The Puma bloods on the opposite mul were in full dress armor and carried tall parade javelins that, despite their ornamental eccentric-flint spearpoints, could still do a lot of damage. As I think I mentioned, the Pumas hated the Rattler's Children, and at the first sign of a fight they'd take the opportunity to cleanse as many of the Rattler's Children as possible. And the Pumas were still hosting some Ixian Ocelots. And who knew whether they'd heard anything? Word traveled a lot faster than people. Somebody back home might have realized that 2JS was up to something and sent a message here, and put the Pumas on the lookout for any Ixian Harpies. On top of everything else we might have bounties on our skins.

"Look," Hun Xoc signed by tapping on my left arm.

I followed his eyes forward and down. Three vingtaines of Swallowtail javelinmen in red quilted armor had just pushed through the crowd and stationed themselves between the plaza and the fetish market, blocking most of the entrance to the main axis.

Damn it, I thought. Well, that'll put a crimp in our schedule.

Koh must see them. Doesn't she?

I snuck a look over my shoulder. Behind us the top third of the Star Rattler's ornate mul wedged into the thin sky. Its staircase was packed with converts and aspirants. Sixty arms above us, at the lip of the sanctuary, the fifty-two senior sucklers and adders to Star Rattler stood in an immobile row. They were all dressed, almost identically, as men, with blue Chaakish eye masks, like fat glassless goggles, to help them see through the Black Chewer's breath, and big scaled helmets and platform sandals. Above them, at the apex of the mul, framed by the mouth of the sanctuary, there was a glimpse of a tall headdress that belonged to Lady Yellow, the senior sun adderess of the Orb Weaver Synod. I guess she was kind of the mother superior. Supposedly she was a hundred and eight years old.

I counted five figures in from the north corner and picked out Lady Koh. Stupidly, I got a flash of pride spotting her in the lineup. Her face, or what I could see of it, was impassive.

It was hard to believe we were really going forward. How did Koh know the whole thing wasn't some kind of trap? Well, at least she knew from her cross-examination of me that I wasn't lying. In fact, I'd bet she considered me as under her control. Well, maybe I was. Still, she can't know what's going to happen when she gets to Ix.

Or can she? Maybe she's worked out more of her own future than she's letting on.

Maybe she wants to take over the Game drugs operation so she can start her own empire.

Hmm. Well, maybe that would be okay. Why not? Go ahead, set your sights a little higher. Still, don't worry about that right now. Okay. One thing at a time. A, B, C. And A, right now, is the Swallowtail squad.

She must see them, I thought. Should we just try to go past them anyway? Or should we change the route? And if we do, will we be able to signal it to her?

No, don't do it, I thought. Better just follow the plan. Get to the first rendezvous at the pharmacopoeia and then change if you have to.

Hun Xoc touched my arm again. I snapped my head around. Face front, soldier.

You know, I thought, really the creepiest thing about this—or the most singular thing, anyway—was that despite the temptation, not a single member of the crowd made a premature sound. Well, they'd been practicing for five days, I thought. I'd been whispering for so long that I wondered if my vocal cords would still work. For the last five days it had seemed that the only living thing you heard was the birds.

You could feel the crowds shivering. You could smell the anticipation in their sweat. The mass of life rustled and creaked, like a jungle in that quiet phase of the night just before the predawn chorus. Their hands hovered over their instruments. But nobody whistled, or tapped, or even dropped a rattle. I wondered whether any other city this size in the history of the world had, or would, ever create this kind of unity in its population. Even animals seemed impressed by the silence, so that the occasional scrawk of a gull or a blackbird or the bark of a dog in a pen seemed halfhearted, just a little dust in the groove. Every so often a baby would squeal, and, immediately, it would be muffled. And probably suffocated, I thought.

Bastards. Despite the colors and the freshness and the collective goodwill, it was still a dire, horrible day. Even if you didn't know anything about the place—say you'd just stepped out of a teleporter—you'd instinctively feel that the city was at a tipping point. It felt like a doctor's waiting room, with all of us waiting for the receptionist to call our names and say, in as neutral a tone as possible, that they had the results of our test.

Of course, from a twenty-first-century perspective I suppose it was all actually pretty silly. After all, it was just another eclipse. But on another level—and even when I tried to cultivate some emotional distance—I kept feeling there was a certain sanity behind the whole thing. In the twenty-first century people just went barreling ahead, and then when something bad happened they couldn't believe it. Here, at least, everyone wasn't pretending that everything was always A-OK.

I snuck a look to the right, toward the center of the city. The great main axis stretched off to the north. The city seethed with newly woven streamers and long strips of spoonbill feathers raised on a hundred thousand bamboo poles, all orange to attract the sun, curling in the weak breeze like the polyps of octocorals. Underneath the banners, each of the thousands of bloods standing in the choice real estate of the teocalli district had a small circular shield over his left shoulder, and each shield had a featherwork design, bright, simple, geometric, and slightly different from all the others, all facing the same direction—west—like a field of sunflowers. The effect was so heraldic that you could imagine we were medieval knights, meeting for a tournament on the Field of the Cloth of Gold. There wasn't a single person with an uncovered head or a bare face. Even the slaves wore rags wrapped around their upper lips. Higher-ups were so encrusted with jade and spondylus shells, and with such long-feathered headdresses, that they seemed to have exoskeletons and antennae. It was like the people in this town might as well have been pinned in place, in drawers labeled by greathouse lineage, dependent clan, subclan, sub-subclan, serving clan, and slave clan, and every individual in that slave clan. I'd say it was regimented except that, unlike uniforms in a modern military review, no two people's markings were exactly alike.

I let my focus crawl north along the axis until it found two plazas that reflected the flat blue of the sky. The sunken courts near the Ocelot's mul had been filled with water, like swimming pools. One was stocked with axolotl, water lilies, and jabiru storks, which were sacred to the Jade Hag. The water in the other pool was bare. Supposedly it was laced with ololiuqui, so that the captives who'd be thrown into it later on would drown without struggling. There was a row of squat offering platforms along its western bank, and on one of them you could just make out a dash of turquoise that might have been the five Ixian Ocelots who were 9 Fanged Hummingbird's delegation to the festival. At least we'd managed to avoid them this far, I thought.

At the midpoint of the main axis the swollen haw of the Hurricane mul dwarfed everything else. Its peak was about twice the height above us that we were above the plaza, high enough so that on a hazy day, or in the offering smoke, you could really believe the sucklers on it were being swallowed by hungry clouds. But today Chacal's sharp eyes could pick out the whole scene, the lesser synod members on the second-from-top level, with the row of giant megaphones, like alphorns, twenty arms long, resting on their shoulders, and now, on the highest level, the tall red-orange headdresses of the Puma Synod, just emerging from the four mouths of the teocalli.

The crowds rustled. The distorting perspective of the receding levels of the pyramid made the Synod seem like inaccessible giants farther away than the shell of the sky. Teotihuacan didn't have kings, and the archonic offices passed between different members of the two councils. When they appeared in public, they were heavily masked, and no one outside the council was supposed to know who they were. But Koh had it from good sources that the current archon of the Swallowtails was an elderly Puma named Turd Curl. She'd also said to watch for the person who was likely to be Turd Curl's successor, a Puma blood named Severed Right Hand. Supposedly he was only thirteen years old—but already he was considered the up-and-comer. They said he'd been born with fur and fangs, and that he always knew, without being taught, how to transform into his feline self. They said he only ate humans, captives younger than he was. But that was probably just propaganda. Koh had said his colors were yellow and lilac.

I followed the angle of the great mul's stairs down to where it met a freshly built wooden mul. Fifty-two sacrifices, each exactly nine years and twenty-nine days old, had been keeping a vigil inside it for five days. When it was set on fire they'd help carry all the other offerings and present them to the newborn sun. About two hundred arms southeast of the pagoda there was a tiny minor mul in a sort of orange-and-black checkerboard pattern. The Puma's pharmacopoeia, the monastery garden where the Pumas grew and distilled their components of the Game drug. Our target.

According to Koh, the Swallowtail sucklers knew exactly how long the totality of the eclipse would last—about eighteen and a half minutes—and they'd try to increase the illusion of their power by cutting it as close as possible. They'd wait until only one or two hundred beats before the sun would reemerge, and then, Turd Curl would signal. On the level below him fifty-two of his sucklers would start swinging bullroarers made from the femurs of their predecessors. On the level below that two hundred and sixty of their acolytes would blow their giant horns, and on the levels below, and spreading through the known world, the men would strike up their instruments and the women and children would shout or chant, "Marhóani, marhóani," "Go away, go away," and babies would get chili powder blown in their eyes to make them cry, and even dogs would get kicked in the ribs, and everyone would make as much noise as possible until the Chewer was driven off. Then the head sucklers would light the new fire from the sun itself, using a huge and reportedly magnificent concave mirror ground and polished from hæmatite. They'd send the fire down the mul to the pavilion of the new sun, that is, the bonfire. All through the rest of the day and night the charge holders of the four thousand towns would troop past the bonfire, light their torches, and take the fresh fire and tales of the capital's grandeur back to their homelands. And the vast majority would believe it was thanks to the Puma Synod's leadership that they were able to rescue the sun.

Or that was the Swallowtails' plan. Koh and I had other ideas.

Two days ago, Koh had made her move. Just after noon, without notifying her fellow adderesses, she'd called forty-eight of her closest followers together and issued a warning about the eclipse. The Sky Eel, she said, had told her that this time, the Black Chewer would not be persuaded to regurgitate this sun, but would "steal the ball," that is, swallow the sun for good. The Eel, that is, Star Rattler, would give birth to a new sun, she said, and since that sun would be unrelated to the cat lineages, over the next k'atun the Sky Eel's children would be privileged above all others. But before that, in order to cleanse the dying world, the Rattler was planning to open a cloud gourd and release an army of what they called *dadacanob*, "long bees"—that is, yellowjackets, *Vespula squamosa,* a major nuisance and minor killer in these parts—to sting the eyes of everyone in Teotihuacan who hadn't followed the Rattler. Everyone but the Rattler's Children would be condemned to darkness. After that the Sky Eel would tell Koh where to lead its followers and would extend its protection to a new Rattler city in the Red Land, that is, the southeast. Meanwhile, messengers visited the leaders of twenty-four Koh-affiliated households and gave them the location of the rendezvous point: Flayed Hill. As soon as they heard the voice of the yellowjackets, they should gather their families and their most valuable possessions and start marching east.

That last part made me a little uneasy. Somehow we'd gone from talking about her own household and a few followers to close to five thousand people. Would there be enough food for them in the Harpy towns? For that matter, would there be enough food and water along the way? How many of them would die on the trek?

Don't worry about it, I told myself. Just keep a low profile, score the drugs, ship them back to Ix, and get the fizook out of here.

Koh had immediately been called into the presence of Lady Yellow, who was something like the order's mother superior. It meant that at least one of her forty-eight confidants was informing on her. Lady Yellow told Koh that the society was planning to vote on her membership. If Koh were blackballed, she'd be expected to drown herself. Later, an informant in the Aura Glory Synod got word to her that the Synods considering inviting her to present herself to them—that is, forcing her to turn herself in for what would inevitably be torture and execution.

By noon on the day of the silence ordinary people were repeating what she'd said in whispers, in the well courts and markets of Teotihuacan. It was a rumor, an order, and a rallying cry: *The next sun is Star Rattler's.* Everyone in the city and probably everyone in the Valley of Mexico had heard about it, from Turd Curl to the lowliest night-soil collector. And, as is usual with such things, it was already getting exaggerated. The world was dissolving. The sky was falling. The city was going to ooze into a hole in the zero earth. And on, and on, and on.

Still, nobody wanted to do anything to stir up trouble before the eclipse. It was partly because it would look like a sign of weakness, but also because everybody, from top to bottom, took the silence period very seriously. Besides, when the sun did reappear, Koh would be discredited and easy to attack.

Of course, the Synods knew the sun was going to come out again. They knew almost everything about solar eclipses, not just the saros intervals of eighteen years and eleven and one-third days but whether they'd be partial or total and how long they would last. And they tried to make sure the masses knew as little as possible. Like psychiatrists the ruling class had to keep you feeling that they were making you better but that the situation was still dire enough for you to have to keep coming back.

When the eclipse ended, the Pumas would come for us—they'd kill Koh and most of us, if they could. Before they got to us, I had to steal their component of the Game drugs and everyone had to get to the rendevous point. Oh, and then if we all survived, I would learn the nine-stone game and get my notes on everything entombed back in Ix. I still didn't know how the "trumpet vine" had destroyed Disney World, but that was a problem for another day. Let's call it a long shot.

(55)

Something was wrong with the space. It was like the whole outdoors was getting smaller, shrinking to the size of a single stuffy room. No, I thought, it's not the space, it's the light. Everything looked just a little more solid, a little closer. The shadows were sharper. The hills, the crowds, and a loose strand of my oiled hair were all in too-high relief. There was a sense of muffling, like all the dampers had come down on a thousand-pipe cathedral organ. I snuck a look up at the sun. There was a nibble out of it at two o'clock.

I've never seen anything to make me think there's anything like ESP. But even so, I can't imagine that you could have been anywhere in the city—even blindfolded, earplugged, and double-boxed in some soundproofed basement—without feeling the fear at that moment. It oozed through stone walls. It rang in the soil.

As clear as a heart attack Turd Curl's voice cracked the silence:

"Charhápiti sini, chá jucha phumuári . . ."

"You with red teeth, will you now skin and scatter us
Over your darkness?
Now will you never return to the heart of the lake,
Of the sky shell? You . . ."

The Teotihuacan Valley has echoic properties, like a whisper gallery. When plastered construction covered the hills, the echoes were much stronger. There was no doubt that every being in the valley had heard him. But there was no answer. And there wasn't supposed to be. This was the only thing Turd Curl would say and the last words we would hear until he gave the order for noise.

I focused on Hun Xoc's harpy-feather headdress, about twelve inches away. Something was odd about the latticework of fibers. They were morphing, sharpening. The Black Chewer, who was much more powerful than the sun himself, had jagged the edges of every object everywhere. I looked away, toward the crowds on the steps below us. Everything had the same curling, frizzing, wrinkling disease around the edges, as though every loose fiber, every projection, was gnarling and sharpening into a hook, a sort of twisted fingernail. I shuddered.

I listened. The calls of the birds had stopped. I didn't hear even the buzz of a fly.

Let's get going, guys.

I shut my left eye and snuck another look at the sun. It had already shriveled to a thin sliver like a tungsten filament. On its right edge, Baily's beads spiked out between the mountains rimming Humboldt's Crater on the horizon of the invisible moon. *Viel besser wäre, wenn sie auf der Erde so wenig, wie auf dem Monde, hätte das Phänomen des Lebens hervorrufen können,* as Jupiter Tonans said. The sanest person ever to live, I thought. Well, don't dwell on it. Out in the plazas, and up on the hills, the serried crowds looked spiky and menacing. Now the sun was circled with the spiracle of light, what they call the diamond ring. The edges between the lights and shadows on Hun Xoc's scarified cheeks were as sharp as if the light were coming through a pinhole. His red-oiled skin looked brown, and his blue headbands looked gray, almost like we were under sodium light in some future dystopolis. The corona bloomed and spread around the hole in the sky like the cardiotoxic tentacles of a *Chironex* jellyfish. Houston, we have totality, I thought.

An unsteadiness or quivering rippled through the crowd. You could feel the breath held in a million lungs, and you could smell the hysterical tension, the terror that the source of all warmth might never escape from the Black Chewer's stomach. I, or let's say "even I," since I think it's fair to say I was the least superstitious person there, had to remind myself that it was just a phase. Things would go back to the way they were.

Wouldn't they?

I listened. There was just that same thick woolly silence. I looked up at the blinded twin again. Still total. Less than two minutes left. Okay, come on, homes, anytime you feel like it.

Anytime.

Hell.

I closed my right eye to refreshen it and focused the left one on the line of the western hills. Nothing.

I listened.

Nothing.

Come on. Do it—

Something floated over the valley from the east, a thin sound like a long Mylar ribbon. It was a sound with no name. I think that at first the people in the valley weren't even sure that it was a sound. Then, as it went on and grew a little louder, I suppose most of them thought it was a cicada, which was the closest thing in nature. The sound spread, or else the same sound rose up in other places. Even with all the human bodies buffering the sound the chords ricocheted off the planes of the hundred mulob. First it seemed to be coming from the east, and then maybe from the south, and next maybe from somewhere nearby, and as more invisible sources joined in it got louder and louder, louder than I'd expected, and more reverberant, with a feedback drone like God was fooling with a stack of old Fender Twin amps.

My trainees, down in the dusty cellar with the rat droppings and the walls muffled with corn husks, had been more than startled when they first heard the sound. First they were creeped out, and then they were fascinated, and then they had to master it. Imagine that you'd never heard a violin before, that in fact you'd never heard a stringed instrument of any kind, not even a plucked string. What would it sound like? It would be a little bit like a cicada, a little bit like a pumice-string saw, a little like a cat, and a little like a swarm of bees.

The voice of strings is just a major technological marvel. There's nothing else that's so shocking and so hypnotic, that combines so much sharpness with so much breadth. There's nothing else like the shape of its sound wave sawing into your ear. Even dogs are spooked by strings until they get used to them. It was transfixing.

Of course, my trainees—the Fifteen Fiddlers, as I thought of them—didn't get it quite right. What we were hearing was a long way from Fritz Kreisler and the Berlin Philharmonic. In fact it was a mess. And of course the instruments didn't quite sound like cellos or violins or dilrubas or violas. Still, they were decent, full-voiced, uncracked, well-rosined strings, played with a bow. And my guys had it down close enough to give you the same shiver you'd get hearing it for the first time:

(56)

By the fifth time they repeated the phrase, I smelled urine and feces rising off the crowd, and that stale-and-sour species of sweat people excrete when they're terrified. Guess some folks just can't take the pressure, I thought. Ahh, that sweet smell of fear. Smells like . . . apocalypse. You could feel the strings hooking their fear and drawing it out like taffy into threads that just stretched thinner and thinner, up and up and up, until they finally crystallized and broke into plain inchoate invertebrate panic.

I was proud of my team. They'd all worked hard over the last six days. I'd had twenty craftsmen going almost nonstop, in the inner courts of a big householdful of carpenters in the north Aura quarter. They were dependents of the Gila House and loyal to Koh. They were really good folks. Still, it wasn't easy. Even though there'd been a muted, fireless, but urgent bustle through the valley—preparation for the festival that would follow the eclipse—we still had to sneak around. We only moved after dark, since you weren't supposed to do any business during the silence. Every time, we had to bribe our way past different troops of low-level Swallowtail guards. They thought we were smuggling copal, since they could smell it on our hands. What with trying out different types of dried bottle gourds, waiting for wildcat gut, getting the cedar necks carved, getting the horn pegs made, finding that human hair breaks after a few strokes and figuring out how it could be corded into tiny strands and still work in a bow, trying out fifty kinds of gum to find a decent substitute for rosin, and getting everything glued together only two days ahead of D-day, it was definitely the hardest project I'd worked on in a long time, tougher than setting up my *Chromidorus marislae* tank.

Some of the men were pretty handy flute musicians already, in their pen-tatonic way. They were all eager beavers, were excited about the project, thrilled to help the Rattler reclaim the sun, and ready to do anything for Lady Koh. And they learned pretty fast, sawing away in the dark. Still, just like when I'd tried to hum some show tunes for Hun Xoc, they didn't get Western music right away. It was like they couldn't really hear a tune with a phrase and repetitions and a resolution. I guess if you haven't been acculturated, if you've never heard an octaval chord before, it's just not a natural thing. Still, once they got harmonic they wouldn't stop playing it. And when we tried out the passage in question, the pyramidal scales from the Violin Sonata no. 1 that Prokofiev said ought to sound like a wind in a graveyard, it affected everybody. Evidently the Game gods had been right.

By the time they'd run through the passage ten times, children were crying and their high voices blended into the strings. The crowds packed into the plazas were moving but not yet on the move. They were just jiggling against each other like molecules of compressed gas, feeling for exits. Any minute now, I thought.

Come on. Time for phase II.

I heard a couple people on the stairs below us sniffling. I turned and looked north into the plazas. Children and old women were rubbing their eyes. Men were squirming. Good.

Around me the bloods squirmed and sniffed.

I felt what I thought was the first sting in my own eyes. Ouch. Good.

I smelled something sharp. Something hurt back near my tonsils. Good.

I looked around. The bloods behind me were squinching up their faces. It meant our second team of confederates had lit their hidden fires.

There were thirty-six of them, spread out in a rough half-circle on the east side of the city, in the kitchen yards and courtyards of fourteen different compounds. The top layers of the fires were dried heaps of a kind of tropical poison ivy, fatwood, and dried poison sumac, which is a strong lachrymogen, like CS. At first the smoke was nearly invisible. It wasn't scentless, but it had no distinctive smell. I saw people squirming down in the courts of the main axis, which meant it was hugging the ground. Good.

Koh knew everything about the local weather. Two nights ago she'd decided that the breeze would be weak, and from the east as usual, and that the smoke would hang in the valley. The conspirators had moved as much of the fuel as they could from the sites on the west side to ones in the east. And here it was working out like she'd said. They'd done a good job. They'd had to buy up hearth wood, low-grade rubber, and, more suspiciously, sumac, ivy, and loads of cecropia leaves, and smuggle it across the pilgrimage ring in small batches. They'd had to hide the coals they'd use to light the fires from the Morning Glory bloods, who were like the religious police.

The blood in front of me dropped his manta. It was the signal to get ready. I disengaged and dropped my own and pulled the javelin off my back. I unwrapped the obsidian spearhead and fitted the three parts of the shaft together. Even without metal fittings the shafts clicked into each other in that efficient way that gives you a (false in this case) feeling of slick power, like a marine assembling an M16 in whatever point whatever seconds. With as little bending over as possible I got the wicker shield off my leg, unrolled it, and tied the two crosspieces to the uprights. It was a little like making a kite. The end product was light but pretty rigid. I fastened the deerskin strap, got the spear tied onto my right hand and the shield onto my left, and straightened up. I found my green headband under my testicles and tied it around my forehead one-handed. It was a move I would never have been able to execute as Jed. Everybody on the Rattler's side was supposed to have a green headband for IFF. That is, Identification, Friend or Foe.

My eyes were watering. I closed the left one.

So, how much attention had we just attracted? I wondered. I looked out over the plazas. The crowds were stirring and squirming in a sort of Brownian motion, feeling for exits.

Ouch. My eye was twitching. Now there was definitely dark smoke overhead. The second layer of the fires was supposed to make as much smoke as possible, to block or at least obscure the reemerging sun.

I closed my right eye and opened the left one again. I dug my left hand down past my belts and loincloth and into a little bag. Everybody who was in on the plot had one. It was filled with a kind of salve made from copal amber, royal jelly, ageratina, and hummingbird eggs. I scooped out a dab with my designated clean finger, the pinky, and smeared it into my right eyelid. According to Koh's surgeon, if you kept switching eyes and salving the closed one, you could walk through smoke for a long time and still see. Somewhere I'd heard that old-time firemen used to do something similar. Still, just offhand it didn't seem too effective. Note to self: Remember to take some back and pitch it to the Body Shop.

I took a quick look at the top of the Hurricane mul.

Something was going on up there.

Turd Curl's archimage couldn't properly light the fire with the light of the sun blocked by smoke, but they were pretending to do it anyway, by sleight of hand. Someone lit the giant torch at the apex of the Hurricane mul, and the fire runner, a trained athlete in a puffy and cumbersome suit of feathers soaked in tallow, held his arm in the fire pretty much as planned, and turned and bounded down the steps, as planned, and when the fire overwhelmed him his flaming body rolled forward between the ranks of Puma bloods. The bloods knocked and guided his body down, out onto the snout of the great mul, which was on a level with Hun Xoc and me but separated by a gulf of humans, and down the lower stairs and out into the plaza into the bonfire pagoda, almost as though nothing was wrong.

But the pagoda had already started burning. Somebody, maybe one of Koh's men, must have thrown or shot a hidden coal into it. It had already flared up before the fire runner even reached the snout. By this time the general public wasn't watching the mul ritual anyway. People were looking in the sky for the Rattler and trying to run, or fight, or hide. I heard the cantors of the Puma Synod up at the sanctuary, calling through their alphorns, *"Hac ma'al, hac ma'al,"* "The new sun, the new sun," but the chant had that tone that creeps into people's voices when they know they're being ignored. It was too late.

The crowd's motion was brisker now, like people in a busy street just before a storm, when everyone steps lively for cover even though there are no raindrops yet. A wave of yellow-gray smoke swept over us. The fiddling had degenerated, less and less Prokofiev and more and more random sawing, but it seemed louder than ever. You don't think of strings as loud instruments, but now they were a global whine. Somewhere I heard one of Koh's confederates shouting a phrase they'd rehearsed: *"A'ch dadacanob, a'ch dadacanob,"* "The yellowjackets are here, the yellowjackets are here!" Another voice picked it up, an old lady's. I didn't think she was a planted agitator. But you know how people shout what their bosses shout. A few more of the Rattler Society converts shouted it, and then more, and then people were shouting it who couldn't possibly be Rattlers. The voices were hoarse, maybe from days of disuse during the Silence, and the chant spread through the crowd with a sound like a hailstorm rasping over a cornfield. Koh's people accentuated it, like cheerleaders, and inserted other phrases welled up and spread alongside it, "The sun is dead, we're dying, we have died," and *"Ak a'an, ak a'an,"* "This is the end, this is the end." Laughter mixed in with the chanting—hysterical laughter, I suppose. A few musicians had started drumming and piping; it sounded halfhearted and their effort trailed off as the cries of fright rose up from the zócalos. The cacophony of noisemakers and shouting, which I was still half expecting, never came. The crowds in the courts and rooftops stirred and bristled. Below us the packed market plaza began to roil.

The majority had no doubt that this was the army of yellowjackets— invisible or not—that Koh had predicted, and that they would sting everyone into blindness. I saw old women, bloods, undercastes, and little boys looking up at the sky, pointing and shouting, *"Ha k'in, ha k'in," "*The Rattler, the Rattler," and involuntarily I looked up myself. The ropes of smoke wreathed and undulated, and I bet if I'd looked a little longer I could have caught the wave of the consensual hallucination myself and watched Star Rattler in all its detail coil down out of heaven, tongue probing, feathers rippling, fangs spurting holy ichor.

"Ha k'in, ha k'in, ha k'in, ak a'an, ak a'an, ak a'an . . ."

Terror crackled through the crowd. It seemed like some kind of pheromonal imperative: GET *AWAY! **YOU ARE GOING TO DIE!!!***

As the multitudes stampeded, I felt the stone under my sandals quiver. I teetered a bit and caught myself. Shared, multiplicitous terror can sweep you into a wave of weightlessness. If you were there on 9/11, or on the Indian Ocean during the tsunami, or in Florida during the Domino Star, or at any of the other big ones, you know that there's a moment in these things when everyone around you is utterly unsure. You all look at each other and you can see that no one knows anything, that everyone else is thinking the same things you are, that we could all be dying, that the rest of the world might already be destroyed. Society generates a kind of gravity that you feel even when you're in a personal crisis. But in a global crisis that gravity's gone. There's a feeling of the absurd. Of course, the absurd is pretty mainstream now, so one tends to discount it. But when the real absurd really comes out, it has teeth.

By now the mobs were on the move. I turned my head way around to the left and took a last look up at Koh. She was floating down to us. No, wait, she was being carried. It looked like she was on a sort of human funicular. I'd heard a nasal barking and now that I saw the scene I could tell it was Lady Yellow, the mother superior, screaming at Koh. It sounded like more than a capital offense.

Hun Xoc tapped three times on my forearm.

It was a few seconds before I could even get myself together to realize what he'd signed: *We're going.* I reached back and tapped the same signal on Armadillo Shit's arm.

The bloods below me moved forward. Let's get the hell off this fancy rock.

I jumped down the fourteen-inch step. Another step. Another.

Fourteen more steps to go. A few women down in the Sidewinder's Court had started singing the Rattler song, and now more and more people were joining in, and the singing and laughing combined with the shrieks and the violins to create a sound that I really think, despite the fact that nothing shocks anybody anymore, could still drive anybody insane.

Step. Step.

I saw from the blue-plastered flagstones under my feet that we were at the level of the plaza. The bloods in front of me paused. They moved. I marched, or rather shuffled, forward.

The "stop" signal came back. Okay.

I stopped. We waited.

A slap on the chest. It meant "Form up." I slapped Armadillo Shit's chest.

I raised my shield. The bloods packed in tighter around me.

12 Cayman had turned out to be an open-minded guy, especially for a career military type. I'd told him about the classical testudo, that is, the turtle, the infantry formation invented by Alexander the Great and used by the early Caesars against less well-organized armies from Scotland to Pakistan. He'd liked the idea and implemented it. It was designed for pushing through a crowd with minimum losses. Basically you all clumped together and held up your shields to make a shell. The soldiers at the edges of the formation held their shields with both hands, and the ones in the second rank stuck their spears out between them to jab at anybody who came close. Unfortunately, we couldn't use the big wooden pavis shields the Romans had. You can't do everything.

I raised my shield over my head and fitted it in between everyone else's.

I had the most protected position in the testudo. Like if you were playing nine ball, I'd be the five ball in the center of the diamond. So I couldn't see much of anything, and the main sounds were scuffing feet, heavy breathing, and the creaking of the wicker armor.

We crawled forward, plowing through the throng. The pavement here was covered with scarlet poinsettia leaves, and as we shuffled through them we kicked up a red blizzard. I couldn't see anything ahead of us, and behind us all I could see was smoke rising from about where Koh's house would be.

Hell. If a fire really gets going, we'll be in trouble.

We made it to the west side of the Sidewinder Court and down the northernmost steps into the main axis.

Our hope had been that even if the Puma bloods found their commanders and got into their squads, they still wouldn't be prepared for a small, focused charge into an offbeat part of their compound. Maybe they'd even leave the pharmacopoeia relatively unguarded. Well, we'll see about that when we get there.

Ouch. Ouch.

Two slaps on my right shoulder. It meant that we were about to turn right.

I wriggled my arm back and slapped the shoulder of the blood behind me.

We turned right.

The testudo reformed, lengthening along the north-south main axis and narrowing on the east-west one. Now 12 Cayman, who'd been four ranks to my right, was three ranks ahead of me, commanding from near the head of the formation. The sign to march forward seemed to carry through our squad as quickly as cracks in glass.

I was swept up in the charge, pressed between human stalks so I could barely breathe. I could've rested just by raising my feet and getting carried along in the center of the turtle. I got a flow of—well, I guess you could call it courage, or group courage. I suppose it's what the legionnaires felt.

Damn, I thought. We're unstoppable.

We headed up the main axis. We'd go a quarter-mile farther north and then, just before we reached the southwest corner of the Hurricane mul, we'd turn sharply right and east and force our way into the Pumas' pharmacopoeia. We'd planned the routes over a model of the city and made the bloods memorize the route backward and forward.

Besides the turtle, I'd introduced one other innovation to the squad: an injunction not to try to take prisoners. It had turned out to be one of the most difficult things for them to accept. Around here prisoners, and not territory, were the final object of war. Loot was secondary. But we'd told them that on this raid, if any of our bloods broke formation to take a captive, that blood, and his dependent family, would be derated and banished. Their only goal was to get us through as fast as possible. 12 Cayman was a gifted drillmaster and so far they seemed to have understood.

We got the stop signal. We waited.

Another more complicated signal came back in the Harpy's hunting sign language: *The Gilas are here.*

I felt the squad shifting around me, and I got a glimpse of blue Gila regalia through the press of bodies. We'd just met up with six vingtaines, that is, a hundred-and-twenty-man contingent, of Gila bloods. They absorbed us like an amoeba swallowing a paramecium, and the enlarged creature moved forward. In a panicked crowd it can actually be easy to go upstream, since they're so eager to get around you. So far, so good.

Soon we were on the Street of the Dead. With the crowds streaming around us, we had to feed our collective body through these narrow gaps, up and down through flights of stairs, up, down, and do it again. Each time we crossed over the top of the wall that separated one plaza from another, at that moment, going over the hump, I could get at least a glimpse of what was going on. When we trooped over the next wall, I held back for a second and took a better look around.

Whoa. Bad.

(57)

Swarms of humans flooded down the Hurricane mul toward bonfires lit from flaming leaves and banners and offering paper. People staggered to the fire with loads of thatch and cloth and hearth wood, pushed through the circle, and dumped the stuff into the flames. I watched one white-banded Morning Glory blood, a bit older than me, holding up a little kid, away from the flames, as he tried to pick and push his way to the steps in the wall of the court. It was kind of heroic, I thought. At least somebody was saving somebody. People aren't all bad. He stepped over a circle of ancient women. They were sitting on singed bodies, munching on flowers and peppers from the festival garlands while right next to them their grandchildren were strangling each other and hacking trophies off the corpses.

They were laughing.

And not only were they laughing, they were helping themselves get killed. For instance, I saw this one character hold his arm out and dare this other guy, who I thought was his brother, to chop it off. And his brother hacked at it with a battle saw. It took three chops to get the forearm off the humerus and sever the extensor tendon. Then his brother handed him the saw and he tried to chop off his brother's arm, except he was too weak already to do it. It was like some creepy slapstick comedy act, like that bit with the Black Knight in *Monty Python and the Holy Grail*, except you could tell that these people really were in pain after getting maimed, even if they were still laughing. I saw a bunch of acolytes taking turns diving off the wall onto the stairs. They weren't getting up. A kid was running through the circle of musicians and toward the bonfire. I thought he was going to try to jump over it. He'll never make it, I thought, it's impossible. But instead he took a running leap and dove into the heart of the fire, in a puff of sparks. His friends cheered. It was like they were playing at doing these things.

It certainly wasn't a popular revolt in the twenty-first-century sense. Nobody was planning to set up a people's state. For that matter, I don't think anyone from any of the lower clans ever expected or hoped to take charge of anything. It was pretty easy to tell if people were related, from their clothing and markings, and now we could see brothers, fathers and uncles and children killing and maiming each other, clustering in these little groups and practically beating their heads together, picking up the grandmother, say, and throwing her into the air, or biting each other in the back of the neck. And then people who would never have even touched were messing with each other. Social distinctions were dissolving. Women were dancing with men from rival clans. Porters in paper loincloths were were slap-fighting with Puma javelinmen in their outrageous finery. A line of twenty nearly naked slaves, who had sawed through their anchor rope but were still tied together at the waist, slithered like a centipede between us and the bonfire, grabbing bits of food from fallen offering bundles and stuffing it into their mouths. An hour ago it would have been a capital offense. The city had been held together by a brittle pyramid of hierarchies, and when you pulled out a few, they all tumbled down.

It wasn't like what you'd think of as a riot. It was all more of a Mardi Gras gone bad, a Black Plague debauch, a gradual dissolution into chaos that I associated with the last day of the year in Jubal High, when wastebaskets would fly out the windows and kids would tip over desks and tear and scatter torn-up books down the stairwells. Or when a crowd slides out of control after a sporting event and turns vandalistic. Those are all on a pretty small scale, of course, but the mood was the same, and eternal. Nothing feels more freeing than the permission to destroy, to give in to the hatred of life and blow it all in a Sardanapalian flourish. It was abandon befitting the end of the world.

La gran puta, I thought. The idea had been just to create a diversion, to get people to start raising hell so that we could get in, get the goods, and get out. We hadn't wanted things to get this much out of control. They can't really want to burn down their own homes, I thought. Can they?

Maybe it'll happen in any situation when you get the right mix of stressors. They had that deadly combination of economic despair and religious conviction going on here, just like with, say, the PLO. But like with the suicide bombers, I think the main motivator was a sense of insult. They weren't just ready to do what Koh said but so angry at the feline clans that they'd do almost anything. For Star Rattler's followers this one dark day would recover their *baach*—that is, their toughness, coolness, macho, *soldatentum,* honor, manliness, heart, or however you want to translate it. This was their chance to settle old scores.

Well, at least so far the Pumas hadn't even started to come after us. The "diversion" had worked, right?

I noticed that the white-banded Morning Glory blood had turned back to the bonfire. He held his child with both hands, one on the kid's hair and one on the back of his belt, and swung the kid forward and back to build up speed, and then, just like he was tossing a sack of potting soil into a truck, threw his son into the inferno. The child screamed in the air, stopped screaming when he hit the coals, and screamed again, more and more shrilly, until his little lungs filled up with smoke.

Hun Xoc grabbed me with two fingers of his spear hand and steered me forward. Up here we were exposed to dart fire. I galumphed down the stairs into the plaza. We formed up again and moved forward.

We made it halfway across the square before I realized that the swarm ahead of us had thickened. The bloods in the vanguard thrashed at the crowd. I stumbled forward, leaning on the blood in front of me, who turned out to be 4 Sunshower, the skin mender. Good. It's always nice to have a doctor around. Ouch.

I couldn't see.

I turned, groped around, and found Armadillo Shit's shoulder. It had a burn scar on it, so I knew it was his. I gestured at my eyes. He leaned forward, nearly pushing me over, took my head in his hands, opened my eyelids with his fingers, and licked my eyeballs.

It was a move we'd all rehearsed, to supplement the salve. To an outside observer it would have looked like we were taking time out from the battle to make out. And in fact, even through the quilting, I couldn't help feeling that Armadillo Shit did have a rock-hard erection. It's just stress, I thought of saying to him. Don't get any ideas.

I got my eyes open. Ah. Better. Something pushed into our part of the turtle. It was one of the Gila bloods. He was just a limp body. He'd been badly wounded on the outside of the formation and passed in to the center. They laid him down one row in front of us. We couldn't help stepping on him. Our nacom, our executioner, killed him by slitting the axillary arteries under his arms.

The problem here was that everyone wanted to carry their dead along with the group. You didn't want enemies getting the corpses of members of your family. But 12 Cayman and I had said we couldn't afford to do it. The bloods hadn't been able to deal with the idea of just leaving them, though. And we didn't want them to think that if they were killed, they'd be left and have to work as slaves in the mountain of our enemies' souls. So we'd worked out a compromise. The nacom cut off the blood's pigtail and his testicles, to take back to his family, and spoiled the corpse, canceling the tattoos with a rasp and chasing out the blood's breath, name, and uay with a little sharkskin flail. Even so, 12 Cayman had to order the bloods around the body to drop it. It was like he was telling a pair of dogs to drop a dead fish on the beach.

We waited. The blood's blood was sticky under the rubber soles of our raiding sandals. We nudged forward every so often and kept getting repulsed, like a little dog pushing at the door of his crate.

Maybe we wouldn't get any farther. What was going on? 4 Sunshower took a step forward. I did the same, stepping over the corpse's legs. More resistance. Damn—and then there was a feeling of release, something breaking, then we were flowing forward faster and faster. I got my feet on the ground. I felt soft impacts through the bodies around me. The crowd was giving way in front of us. I strained my head up, trying to see where we were, but all I could see was the headdress of the blood in front of me and the dark-yellow wedge of the Hurricane mul looming behind it. I heard coded yells going back and forth, not any of ours. Probably Pumas, I thought. Hell. I felt the signal to turn right pass through our composite body. We lurched and I crushed into the body of the blood in front of me until I was practically sucking on his blue-tattooed earlobe. We seeped, slowly, into a narrow alley between two plazas. The vanguard was only able to feed into it a few people at a time. I noticed a hand was gripping my free wrist and then realized that it was tapping out a message: *Keep close.* It was Hun Xoc. I got my fingers around it and squeezed back that I was all right. Now we could hear actual fighting at the outskirts of our squad. There was no clanging of armor, of course. Combat with flint axes and obsidian-flake spears sounds like shuffling feet and breaking glass, with a few taunts, screams, cracks, and shouts thrown in.

Something gave and we were moving again, the squad oozing forward like dough out of a kneading machine, and I let myself get carried under an arch and down into a sunken courtyard. Now my feet were actually touching the ground, or rather the layer of quivering bodies we were walking on. We pushed up four steps and into another courtyard, crossed it, and then poured down sixteen steps into another plaza. Sixteen steps, I thought. Good. That means we're almost there.

I stumbled, took three steps on my knees, and then got hoisted up by 2 Hand and Armadillo Shit. In a gap between two walls of crowd noise I heard 12 Cayman shouting for us to keep the turtle together.

Everything slowed. We stopped. Crowds pressed in on our perimeter. Ow. Now my left eye was blinking. Damn. The poison ivy stuff was supposed to burn out after a minute or two. We strained against each other, trying to maintain the latticed structure of our formation, like a crystal under compression, craning our heads up to try to get fresh air. We took another three steps forward, gooshing over bodies. It felt like wading through living lasagna. Something grabbed my right ankle. It was a hand. I kicked at it with my other foot and tipped over. The blood in front of me pushed me back, not good-humoredly. I balanced again and brought down my spear on the wrist. It reacted but didn't release. I followed the arm back to the head. The head was biting my left ankle. Damn it. I jammed the obsidian point into his cheek. It went through and scraped on teeth. He released and lunged up to bite again, staring up at me with this expression that was wild, hateful, and sleepy at the same time. I pressed the shaft down into his eye, pulled it out, and jammed it into his mouth. His hand let go of my ankle. I pried the javelin out of him and we moved forward. Damn. He's messed up. You messed him up. Damn.

There are too many of them, I thought vaguely, I'll be crushed to death and nobody'll ever know what happened. And Marena will just think I wussed out. She won't even know I got this far, I did all this good work, I really, really tried. Serves me right for getting involved with fanatics. All these people think they can walk on lava. Idiot. *Todo por mi culpa.* Damn I'm tired.

Yeah. Tired. Rest a second. Just see what happens. I felt myself collapsing just as we started moving again.

Move. Okay. Move. Forward. Half a league, halfaleague, halfaleagueonward. Hup. Hup. We came up on another staircase. Up and over. Down. I grabbed Hun Xoc and held on to him like he was the thwart of our canoe as we went over the rapids in the crush of sweat and oil.

Across. Push. Push. One more. Up. Over the top, doughboys. This wall was twice as high as the last one and when I got to the top I risked another look around. From here we could see out over the plazas and could get a good look at the northern and western suburbs and the adobe-covered hills beyond them. Plumes of smoke rose and widened, angling only a little to the west in the still air. Behind them streams of pilgrims were pouring over the crest of the ridge, down into the valley. They eddied and coiled, slowly pressing toward the teocalli district.

It took me a minute to get it through my head what was going on. Instead of running away from the fire, the crowds were rushing toward it, into the city, toward the main axis, pushing inward, into the flames.

Now, I'd seen one or two dicey things lately. But at this moment I really was freaking horrified. All those people were going to push in, and bunch up, and crush each other to death like turkeys in a thunderstorm. So far the holocaust was just getting started. It was like watching a train heading for a collapsed bridge. We heard the first shrieks of people being crushed to death, but they were just the first. Mass death was on the way. Hell. Hell.

We'd assumed that once the fire started, people would run away. That is, they'd run *out* of the city. Even Koh thought that. Didn't she?

Armadillo Shit grabbed me and steered me toward the stairs into the plaza. I twisted out of his hands. Leggo, I'll do it myself. I tromped down through a collapsed fence of offering poles and into the wide square. We formed up and moved on.

We pushed into the Puma's Plaza. A bonfire roared at its midpoint, about four hundred arms ahead of us. To the right the staircase of the Hurricane mul angled up. Puma javelinmen poured down it, silhouetted against glowing steam from the flooded plazas to the north. The bonfire was only fifty arms away from the point where the Pumas spewed into the plaza, so as soon as they got down they were in danger of burning up. Evidently there was no other way off the mul. That is, there was no interior staircase, and although I suppose you might be able to climb down the back or the sides, it wouldn't be easy. There were twenty-arm drops between the levels, and they weren't really level at all but sloped, and smooth enough to be tough to hold on to. And even then, the fires were getting stronger in the eastern barrios, behind the mul. So apparently the people up there had decided their best shot was to go down the normal way and then move up the main axis toward the Jade Hag's mul, where there wasn't yet any fire, and then onto the trade roads up to Cerro Gordo.

A signal came back through our squad: two open-handed slaps on the chest. It meant we were clear to break up the formation and troop along the wall in double file.

We did. I pressed my back against the tooled plaster. It was warm and sticky.

We trudged forward, slowly, snaking north along the eastern wall, toward the alley that would lead to the pharmacopoeia. Where was Koh? I wondered. She should be coming up behind us somewhere. We'd worked out code calls, but now it was too noisy to use them. Well, just stick to your end, Jed. Ouch. I was hot, I realized. Really hot. My skin on the side facing the bonfire was drying out and ready to peel. I found 4 Sunshower and stood in his lee. He had a strip of manta cloth tied over his face like a Wild West bandito. Good idea. I yanked off one of the wide ribbons in my hair and tied it over my mouth.

Two taps on my shoulder. Turn right. We narrowed and fed into a kind of ceremonial alley between high walls, with feliform pilasters snarling at us from each side. There were no Puma bloods in the alley. Maybe they wouldn't hassle us at all. We'll just get in, get out, and get off. No sweat. Now that I was only two bloods from the edge of our double line—what was left of the turtle formation—I could see into doorways as we passed. There were glimpses of families huddling inside, chanting atonement songs.

We'd come to a big door, not a high trapezoid like Maya doors, but a squat, swollen rectangle in a two-story wall covered with black and red fanged cat masks.

12 Cayman divided the forces. Most of the bloods were going to wait here and secure the entrance. They'd make a path for Lady Koh and her escort, if they got here. Thirty of us left our shields and spears and went in two at a time. I yanked the little mace off my left thigh and wound its loose hide thongs around my hand. A mace is a terrible thing to wind. Hun Xoc and I stepped over the dead doorkeepers and onto wet steps, down into a wide, dark passage. *Lasciate ogni speranza.* We didn't have torches, but smoky daylight filtered down through angled light wells in the roof. The passage went straight east for sixty paces and then forked. We went right, like Koh had said. The passage narrowed into a trapezoidal tunnel dripping with condensed breath. The place had a smell of secrecy and exclusion, and the sporiferous scent of mushrooms. The light disappeared. Hun Xoc stopped. There were fighting sounds up ahead. The tunnel curved a bit, so we couldn't see anything. Damn. We'd hoped we wouldn't run into many people, because absolutely everybody had to be outside during the vigil. But evidently the Pumas weren't stupid. Some of them had come back into the compound when things started going wrong. Hell. They could hold us off for hours—wait. The line of bloods ahead of us moved again. We'd won. Oops. Spoke too soon. We stopped. We moved. We moved, stopped, and moved. It was dead dark. Hun Xoc and I picked our way over what felt like bodies. One was still wheezing and as I kneed over him I felt the handle of a mace. I felt down along it. It was sticking out of his mouth. I pulled it out and moved on. There was light ahead. We came out into an enclosed courtyard with a weird camphorish smell and blank, high

walls rising to a square of sun about two stories above us. The screams from the panicked city around us seemed far away. The floor was soft. It was dirt. Rich, black dirt, in fact. The courtyard was filled with trees, something like the gum tree they call *indio desnudo* in the islands. They had red, peeling, and probably toxic bark, and there were twenty of them in four neat rows, each about ten arms tall. There were little fruits all over them, growing directly out of the branches like persimmons. I looked closer at a branch. The fruit was snails. Or rather the branch was crawling with orange-and-black tree snails. They were some kind of *Liguus*, but I hadn't ever seen the species. I didn't get a good look at them before Hun Xoc pulled me around the perimeter of the garden to a low door. I ducked my head and crawled after Hun Xoc, my knuckles splotching through warm mud and shallow water. We shuffled through a heap of broken jars and through a slashed hide door. Hun Xoc helped me stand up in the room on the other side. It was the pharmacopoeia.

(58)

I t was the largest interior space I'd been in yet. I mean, back here in the good old days. It was wide and weirdly long, going back and back. A double row of ancient wooden pillars held up the roof. They were carved into guards like at the so-called Temple of the Warriors at Chichén and freshly painted in Puma colors. Weak daylight slid through slits high in the walls. The stone walls were lined with niches and the place was chockablock with big baskets, low tables and rollers, man-size water jars, basins, dippers, strainers, stoppers, mortars, pestles, pots, phials, and on and on. Evidently they were making a lot of stuff in here in addition to the Game drugs. Probably just quack remedies. Snake oil and Daffy's Elixir. There were little water runnels cut into the high wall and a big stone basin tub, like a porn-movie Jacuzzi, with ducks flopping around in it. Along with the barnyard smell of the ducks and a horrible pond-muck odor, the place even had a bit of that icky scented-candle-and-potpourri smell of the ersatz country store. Adders and acolytes were stumbling around, frantically tipping clay basins out of the niches and smashing them on the floor.

The Harpy bloods pushed in, grabbing the staff and trying to pin them down before they could swallow poison or slash an artery. The room filled with crashes and smoke. No, not smoke. Dust. The compounders, or compoundresses— a dead one near me was a woman dressed as a man, so maybe Koh had been right—were pulling vases of narcotic powders off the shelves and dashing them to the floor. Yellow clouds of powder twisted up into the smoke holes above the cold hearths. I could hear our men choking and stumbling in the dust, and Hun Xoc yelled for everyone to cover up. Stinging particles puffed over me and even with my facecloth, and breathing through my nose, I still got a whiff of the shit. It felt like I'd snorted a line of curry powder.

I sat back on the bloody tiles, sneezing. Ticks and pops of pink and white light and ghastly seventh chords of synesthetic sound flickered around my vision. Whatever I'd inhaled, it wasn't FDA-approved.

Six of our bloods had captured four compoundresses and were holding them down on a pile of broken furniture in the center of the room. I saw two of them were vomiting blood, probably from the critters they'd swallowed. I noticed there was still fighting going on at the other end of the room. But it seemed to be happening soundlessly, and even with a dollop of slow motion. There was another little door in the far wall, an escape hatch. A few of the compoundresses were sneaking out through it.

"*Y okol paxebalob' ah yan yan tepalob' ah ten,*" 12 Cayman shouted. Basically, "Somebody go block that door or I'll eat your testicles." One of the Harpy bloods lurched to the door, grabbed a compoundress who was halfway through, and yanked her back into the room. There was a flash of orange light, and I thought we were on fire for a few seconds until I realized it was just me.

Damn, I thought vaguely. I'm a mess.

I sat for ten beats and then twenty beats. Something made me think we were outside again, in a quiet forest, and then I realized it was the night sounds, crickets and fat juicy locusts and cicadas and peepers and chorus frogs. Hell. There were a lot of different critters in here, in a lot of different baskets. What if we couldn't find the right ones? Would we have time to make one of the compoundresses talk? What if we couldn't make her talk? Like I say, people around here were dead set on going down with the ship—

"*Hac' ahau-na-Koh a'an.*"

It was Hun Xoc's voice, whispering in my ear. A message had been relayed through the tunnel: Lady Koh was on her way.

And even before he said it, I thought I smelled something, that scent from Koh's inner court, that seashoreish tang I couldn't identify, the fragrance of Star Rattler's breath. It seemed stronger than it had been in her rooms, and harsher. Angrier.

Two of Koh's escorts, male acolytes of her order, dressed as warriors and with long maces like hiking staffs, crouched in, looked around, stood on either side of the door, and signaled.

Koh walked in between them, slowly, in that heavily graceful way, looking left and right. How'd she get here so fast? I wondered. Maybe she had a route, and other confederates, that she hadn't told me about. Well, it figures. She was dressed as a Swallowtail warrior, in long quilted armor and a full-face mask carved from thin light wood and covered with tiny turquoise scales. All you could see of her were her hands, her ankles—one light, one dark—and maybe a flash of her searching eyes.

I got on my feet again. We still had cloths over our faces, but she recognized us—that is, Hun Xoc, 12 Cayman, and 1 Gila, and me—from our markings and saluted us. We obeised back. Koh paid special attention to 1 Gila. Have I forgotten to mention that his family was an independent Teotihuacano house that was loyal to Koh? Well, even if I didn't forget before, let's just leave it in here. Also, 1 Gila was the stocky one with the broken nose, whom we'd glimpsed before in the Orb Weavers' courtyard, with I think his son, whose name was—well, now I've forgotten his son's name. Damn, this is confusing. Anyway, I'd thought Koh was keeping him waiting while she and I had our first chat, but either he wasn't mad about it or he'd been there for something else or it didn't work that way or whatever, because he was our best ally here. Okay, back to what's happening.

Two more epicene escorts walked in behind Lady Koh. They were both dressed as warriors but one of them, I think, was a woman, and instead of a mace she was holding Koh's dwarf, the Penguin Woman.

Lady Koh walked down the sort of aisle between metate tables and the south line of pillars. She passed a trio of Gila bloods who were wrapping up one of the Puma adders who was still alive and who kept straining his head forward, trying to choke himself against their hands. They sat on him and saluted her as someone very much superior.

She acknowledged it and moved on. I followed her, walking behind the dwarf carrier.

She went to the far wall and selected a large pierced terra-cotta jar in the third niche from the left. Her attendant took it out, lifted off the lid, and held it up to her. Koh reached into it.

I craned my head over the attendant's shoulder. Koh pulled out her hand. It was dripping wet and seemed to have suddenly contracted a pustular disease. But when I looked closer I could see that her black skin was crawling with tiny toads. They were like Surinam toads, flat with triangular heads and eyes in the wrong place on the sides of the triangle. But they were smaller, and their skin was a faint gray-blue, almost lilac, and their backs were tuberculed with half-buried orange eggs.

(59)

By the time we made it back to the zócalo, the situation had seriously degenerated. 12 Cayman's men parted to let us out into the center of the turtle, or what was left of it. Javelins came whisking in over my head. One of them hit one of Koh's people. They'd been aimed high, over the heads of the first rank of bloods, in order to kill in the center of the formation. That meant we were under attack by real warriors and that they had actual weapons, not just the ceremonial spears they were supposed to be carrying for the festival. We got our shields up, but the formation had fallen apart. Another volley of spears came in. Hun Xoc pushed me down and said to stay down. I tried to look back at Koh, but she was surrounded by her own guards. They were tall and instead of shields they had these big squares of quilted blue cloth that they held up over her. To me the quilts looked silly, like some sort of classy throw you'd order from Missoni Home. But I guess they were effective—

Gkk. My lungs were still having trouble. Am I drugged or just out of breath? What about everybody else? Are they okay? I blinked around.

Overhead the sky was lighter, and I could even get glimpses of the sun through the smoke. But it didn't seem to be having any effect on the panic. When people are caught up in a frenzy, nothing deconvinces them. Most of the fiddlers had stopped, or had been stopped, but a few were still going, just sawing away randomly now. There were still people laughing, all over, hundreds of voices, giggling, chuckling, and cackling.

He's here, Hun Xoc signed on my arm. 12 Cayman had pushed his way back into the center of the formation.

He was furious. And he had a right to be. We'd been in there for at least twenty minutes. About nineteen minutes too long. I gathered from his shouting that four vingtaines of Puma bloods had found and surrounded them. And just from the sound of things, we were losing.

I didn't even try to justify myself. I was afraid he was going to bite my nose off, something he'd done to others more than a couple times, if half the stories I'd heard were true. Anyway, what was I going to say? That we'd lost three bloods from breathing that powder, and that I'd gotten a whiff of it myself, so don't expect me to last long either? That it had taken a while to corral the toads? And the snails. And the ducks. And a tree? He'd skin me alive. Which was something he could do in about thirty seconds. I should tell him it was like herding cats down there. Except they didn't have an expression like that around here.

The deal—as far as I now understood it—was that the snails had been eating the tree, and then the toads ate the snails and then the ducks ate the toads. It was like something out of Dr. Seuss. So we had to be sure to get all of those things. Koh had said the trees would grow from cuttings. Which was good, but even so I'd made the bloods pull a small one out by the roots and bag it. I also wasn't sure what was in the soil, so I insisted on two bags of that. Plus we had the captives to deal with, and they weren't making it easy. So when we trooped out of the door, we had what looked like a whole little Gypsy caravan, porters with baskets and bundles and jars and the rolled-up tree and whatever else Koh had decided she couldn't live without. And we'd managed to truss up four of the Puma compoundresses and two of their eight-stone adders who oversaw the drug's production. The rest had killed themselves or were too messed up to bother with. So with six captives and about twenty fully laden porters we weren't exactly a mobile fighting force.

And, from what I could tell reading between 12 Cayman's lines, Koh's followers weren't helping much. She'd brought a contingent of at least a hundred guards and acolytes, which was a lot more than I'd expected. No wonder she hadn't wanted to travel together, I thought. I would have tried to downsize her entourage. She'd said that she'd be sending almost all her retainers and whatever on to the rendezvous point. Maybe she was a bigger deal than I'd realized. Still, most of her people weren't trained fighters, and they were getting in the way more than they were helping.

When I used to work on research ships, we'd ship live animals around the world all the time, usually by DHL. I've sent and received fish, tarantulas, gastropods, snakes, and more other livestock than I can remember, and I've only had a few deaths in transit. With a lot of those sorts of critters, if you pack them with soft stuff and keep them dark, instead of freaking out like a mammal would, they actually calm down and just wait for something better to happen. And we'd done our best packing four bundles, one pack for each of the four-light couriers. So maybe they'd make it.

The lead courier assured us that he could get back to Ix in under eight days. It sounded impossible, but 12 Cayman had said they knew what they were doing and that they were absolutely reliable. They were from a Harpy-dependent hill clan, so they were loyal. They'd been chosen by competition. They were the best of the best. They were all ready to go, with their introductory petitions tied in their hair and their suicide knives strapped to their forearms. They crowded around me and we went over how to keep the animals calm, how to change the damp rags every half day, and when to throw in a little of this and some of that. Basic pet care tips. If a critter died, they were to put it in a bag of salt immediately. Even if the creatures didn't live, 2JS would bury them, along with my notes on the Game and the right pattern of lodestones. And that ought to be enough for Marena and the team. I hoped.

They'd have to pick their way through a lot of cranky Pumas. And they'd have to stay ahead of any vigilantes in the towns who had heard about what happened today through the signal network. They'd have to steal food and sneak water.

Still, stealth was their second profession, after speed. Maybe they'd make it. And some of the animals might survive the trip. Not impossible.

I looked into their eyes, trying to act like a leader, trying to gauge their mettle the way a real commander like 12 Cayman would do. They looked back, eager, salty, just wanting to please. They really believed that I was a superior person and were happy to die for me. I felt like a jerk.

It's not for you, Jed, I thought. It's for, like, the future.

Remember the future?

It sounded hollow.

The four-lighters ran off through the crowded alley, east toward the upriver road into the foothills.

Break a leg, I thought.

Damn.

12 Cayman gave the order to move out. We trooped west, toward the main axis. Eighty steps on, we were out of the alley and moving into the southeast corner of the Puma's plaza. Our Plan A was to head north, up the main axis, and then strike west just before we reached the Jade Hag's mul. On the north-

west side we'd be among Auras, who were friendlier to Koh and the Gilas. And we'd be able to get on the wide trade road to the lake.

Fifty steps on I knew we couldn't go any farther. The pagoda bonfire ahead of us was just too hot. Its top three stories had collapsed and there were coals and brands flaming all over the flagstones. Beyond the bonfire there was more trouble. Out in the barrios on the western side of the main axis, the fire had progressed a lot faster than we'd thought it could. There was no way we were getting out in that direction. And we couldn't go the way the four-lighters had, either, at least not without leaving all our cargo and most of our people behind. The four-lighters were like parkourists, climbing on top of bodies and bouncing from people's heads and ramadas and awnings and up onto rooftops and back again. We were an army, a little one, but still an army, and an army has to use streets and roads. We slowed to a near stop. A couple of scouts came back from a lookout mission. Actually, it was only one scout, since the other one, who he had over his shoulders, was almost dead from a poisoned blowgun dart. They'd climbed up onto the wall, and from there onto one of the big offering scaffolds. What they'd seen was crushing. The alley to the east, which was our Plan B escape route, was choked with bodies. Some were alive and a lot were dead on their feet between the live ones. There was no way all our people were going to get out that way. The rooftops in the eastern quarters were already on fire and some of the catwalks had collapsed. Our shield men on the outside of the formation wouldn't hold out much longer. Basically, we were trapped. There was simply no way to get out of the city. We'd have to wait out the fire here. And if we did that, we'd burn to death, if the Pumas didn't kill us first.

Like an acrobat Hun Xoc jumped onto 4 Sunshower's shoulders to look around. I started to try to do the same with Armadillo Shit, but 12 Cayman had come back through the ranks and ordered me to stay down. Evidently 2 Jeweled Skull really didn't want to get rid of me and had told 12 Cayman to keep me alive. Well, it's nice to be wanted. Hun Xoc jumped down onto me and I caught him, automatically. He gave me a we're-fucked look.

1 Gila and Lady Koh pushed through to me and we joined arms and pressed back and made a little circle of open space. Clockwise from north the council was made up of Hun Xoc, me, 12 Cayman, 1 Gila, and Lady Koh.

There was an embarrassed pause.

We looked back and forth. We had to decide on something, at least, and do it.

"We have to take the Hurricane mul," Koh said through her mask.

Everyone looked at her.

"The fires will not reach the teocalli," she said. I thought she was going to say more, but she didn't.

1 Gila said that was going to be even harder than what we were doing now. It's not easy to fight your way uphill. Also, the Pumas on the mul were trying to get down. *They* didn't think it would protect them from the fire, so why should we? Also, he said, the facing would burn when it got hot enough. And even if we did get up to the Puma's sanctuary, we'd just die up there instead of down here.

No one answered.

Koh's pretty smart, I thought. She's got to be right. Right? Right. Better put in your two cents, Jed.

I said—or rather croaked—that the Hurricane mul was faced with mother-of-pearl, not with painted and oiled plaster like the other mulob. It wouldn't burn, and in fact it might reflect the heat—although I didn't really get this idea across—and at this rate we were going to die down here anyway. The Pumas were coming down because they were panicked, not because they'd thought it through. Also, if a lot of them had gotten off the thing, that meant there'd be room at the top for us. There was a chance up there, there was no chance down here, and that was the end of it. Koh was right.

There was another pause. Maybe everyone was listening to the shouted code from captains at the edges of the formation, hoping that the combat would turn in our favor. It wasn't going to happen, though. The only shouts we heard were alarms, crow calls from 1 Gila's men that meant "We can't hold out much longer." Another volley of javelins came over and sizzled into the bloods just a little bit east of us.

Come on, I thought.

We didn't vote. Everyone just eye-gestured, "Agreed."

12 Cayman, 1 Gila, and Koh gave three versions of the order. It passed through the squad: "Attack the Hurricane mul."

First, it meant we had to break right and put everything into heading north. 12 Cayman went back to his command position near the vanguard. He told his men to keep the formation thick. If we got too elongated and the Pumas cut us in two, that would be it for us.

There was another difficult minute of waiting. I tried to imagine what our formation looked like from overhead. Probably it looked like a lollipop, with a long line of us squeezed into the alley and a rounded portion trying to emerge into the Puma's plaza. Then there would be a ring of Puma bloods surrounding the candy element and, beyond them, the thickening crowd of pilgrims and citizens pressing into the sunken plaza.

We're going, Hun Xoc signed.

I raised my shield.

Our march snake paused, as though it were coiling, and then, as 12 Cayman gave the order to charge, we shot forward into the plaza. Immediately we turned right and snaked along the plaza's high eastern wall. At least it protected us on that side. My left side was hot already from the bonfire.

We marched. Pumas attacked us on our flank, only three people to my left. Some of our bloods fell and no one even picked up their bodies—which was like giving your enemies a free ticket to curse you down to the nth generation and should give you an idea of how desperate things were getting. Damn. Hot. My shoulder was peeling. Too hot. But we were being pushed toward the bonfire. How did the crowd stand moving closer?

Move. Move. Can't see anything. What's going on? Hot. Hell. I could hear signs of a bloody fight on the edge of the turtle. What's going on? I looked back but couldn't see Koh's people. And the critters. Have to move or the critters'll bake on the shell. Dammit.

I stopped thinking. At some point we turned right, into the stream of people rushing down the stairs. These weren't fighters, at least. They were classy people, official people. Old people. We plowed into them. They swirled around us, surprised at our attack but more eager to get away than to fight. We came to the staircase, which was half-covered with bodies on the lower steps. A few of 12 Cayman's Harpy bloods picked their way up the first few steps, jabbing their javelins at the Puma elders who were still coming down. And the rest of our formation should have charged up after them.

But I felt hesitation in the bloods around me. The Gilas, especially, were hanging back, murmuring. I looked up.

Above 4 Sunshower's shoulder the three-story sanctuary complex at the top of the mul head scowled down out of the brown haze. It seemed far away, and there was just something daunting about its expression. Two big T-shaped upper windows made up its eyes, and the four entrances to the lower sanctuary made up a gap-toothed grin. Maybe you could say its expression was insane or inhuman. The whole thing felt as far above us as the peak of the Eiger from Interlaken. It was a malevolent giant. You'll never make it up me, it said. It laughed.

Now, on an ordinary day, climbing this rock would mean instant death to anybody but a Puma. And not just death by execution, but death by what even twenty-first-century people would call supernatural means. It would be like a medieval peasant walking up the nave of St. Peter's and defecating on the altar. You'd expect to get zapped up the chutney chute by celestial lightning or something. The mul was a titanic hive of powerful and malevolent giant cats, transmortal cosmic predators who could kill with a thought, rulers of the zeroth level since the birth of its time. You didn't fuck with Pumas, living or, especially, dead.

Somehow, though, Koh had pushed through the formation, and with her guards flanking her, she picked her way over the bodies on the zero step, the lowest step, and then up onto step number one and step number two. The steps were high, and she had to step up to each flat with one leg and then follow it with the other, and then take two steps across the flat of the stair, and then do it again. But she did it with style. On the third step she wobbled a bit, but her left-hand guard only had to support her for a second before she got it together. Meanwhile, Puma bloods whooped behind us, and a javelin flew overhead and hit the steps five arms to her right. She took another step.

Maybe even Koh wouldn't have done it ten days ago. Maybe it was only since she'd met me that she'd become a skeptic. Or maybe she would have. Anyway, sometimes it only takes one person to defy an authority, and everybody follows. When they saw Koh climbing that thing, standing tall, not wobbling, not hesitating, our whole troop, the Rattler acolytes, the Gilas, even our own Harpy bloods, seemed to decide that her protector was with her, that Star Rattler had won the battle in heaven, and they swarmed up after her, shouting their battle whoops as though the day's action was just starting. At that moment they probably wouldn't have been surprised to see Lady Koh walk on water, or grow into a hundred-arm giant, or transform into the Rattler itself and swallow the city and the stars. At any rate, the Gilas charged forward and up the stairs, the Rattler bloods and acolytes followed them, and my own little entourage of Harpies went along. I got all excited and almost scampered up the first steps, over a little hill of luxuriously appointed corpses. It was like climbing a waterfall of Jell-O. By the eighth step I'd slowed down. Come on, Jed. Move. Yuck. Move. Finally I felt the sticky plaster of an actual stair under my hand. I crawled up onto the next one. Hah. We were on the stairs. Up. Onward, blistered shoulders. Up.

Up. Come on. Step. Up. Come on. Step.

Up. Tired. Come on.

One more step. Well, three hundred sixty-two more. No problem. Up.

I noticed that I'd dropped my shield and that I was on all fours. Whatever. Hup. Hup. Come on. You don't have to worry about where you get your strength from, just where it will take you. Up. Hup. Up.

The Harpy bloods prodded the Puma elders out of her way only two steps ahead, sparks flew around us, dogs howled, booms and crashes thundered through from collapsing roofs in the compounds, a jade-scaled corpse clattered down the stairs from high above and gooshed to a stop. I was having some trouble knuckle-walking with my right hand, since it was still holding on to my mace. I took a second to pull the mace off with my other hand, but my fist seemed to be stuck closed around it. I pulled at the cords with my teeth and got them undone, but the thing still wouldn't come out of my hand. Fuck it. Ouch. The breeze shifted a bit and a wave of hot air from the fires rolled over us. I made it over another eight steps. Above me I heard 12 Cayman telling Koh to stay back a bit. She stopped in the center of the staircase, and Hun Xoc and I passed her on the right. I could have reached out and touched her as I went by, but now her guards had scampered after her and surrounded her with their blue quilts. I moved on. Onward and upward. Fourteen steps. Eight steps.

Oof.

I pressed my hands into the sticky surfaces of the stair and tried to pull my feet up without lacerating my shins on the honed edge.

Four steps.

Come on.

Two steps. Oof. You're messed up, bro, I thought. If Chacal were here he'd be majorly ticked off. He'd had the best body in the league, but a few days of abuse had turned him into a ninety-eight-pound weakling.

One more step.

I made it. One more.

Made it. Okay.

Whoo.

If you've visited the site, you know it takes a long time to climb up that pyramid, even if you're not weighted down with armor and weapons and exhausted from combat and blood loss and also fighting off the people who are up there already. I might mention that the risers of the steps were actually higher than the ones the reconstruction put in later. The steps were taller, we were smaller, and we were exhausted.

Okay, come on. One more step.

These stairs weren't made for climbing. They were built for intimidation.

One more.

I made it.

One more. Step. Good. One more. Step. Oof.

Step.

Uf. *Ni modo.*

Come on. Step.

I tried it again. No go. My chest pressed into the sharp angle. I slid back and pressed my knees into the crotch of the stair.

Can't go any farther. Just lemme hang out here a minute. What was going on, anyway? I snuck a look uphill.

The stairs were wide enough for twenty people, and we'd had to spread out to cover its whole width, so our front line, with 12 Cayman and his vanguard troops, was only three steps above me. The people who'd already been on the pyramid, and who had been trying to get off before we'd rushed it, were jabbing at our bloods with their parade spears and trying to push them back off the stairs. But the Pumas were mainly old folks, and they were encumbered by heavy festival regalia and giant headdresses, which, oddly, they hadn't taken off. They were only five or six steps deep—say, a hundred and twenty of them—and above them the stairs stretched nearly naked up to the teocalli.

As I watched, 12 Cayman barked a new batch of commands to his captains, and they relayed them to the bloods. Slowly, they rearranged themselves. From where I was cowering it looked like 12 Cayman had positioned the best fighters on the left side of the stairs, that is, to the north, and the weaker ones on the right. Then he had the left flank charge up a few steps, while the bloods on the right, southern side retreated a bit, and as they retreated they shifted some of their men toward the middle. Then, the whole line pushed up two steps, with their shoulders on their shields, ramming into the more disorderly line of Puma elders. A few of the Pumas fell off the right side of the stairs. There were only soft thuds as they hit the sea of bodies in the plaza below.

12 Cayman ordered another charge. Our line moved up another two steps, and a few more Pumas fell, or were pushed, off the right edge of the steps. And I realized that 12 Cayman had done a very clever thing. He'd formed his vanguard into an angle—that is, our formation was about eight steps higher on the left side of the stairs than we were on the right side. And if the bloods in our front line just kept their shields up and moved forward, and if they kept the angle consistent, they'd sweep the Pumas off the staircase, dislodging them from one side, pummeling or dribbling them southward along the row,

and ejecting them on the other. It was like how a plane angles into a plank and extrudes a curl of wood out the top.

Damn, I thought. Maybe we'll make it. We moved up another two steps.

What's happening down below? I wondered.

I knew better than to look around, but I did anyway. Mistake.

Even though I was less than a third up the staircase, the space pulled my head forward and I felt I was sliding out, way out over the stairs, and all I had to do was relax and go with the gravity and everything would be easy and all right. I dug my still largely artificial fingernails into the bloody stucco.

There were worrisome-sounding grunts from above. The Puma elders had moved farther back up the stairs and were rolling rocks and dead bodies down on us. A big chunk of something bounced down, took out one of the bloods in our front line, and smeared to a stop two steps above me. Dang. If we lost our grip and started rolling back, that was it. One person could dislodge many. The bloods in the front line absorbed their crushed comrade and got their shields down closer to the stairs. 12 Cayman told them to angle the shields more to the south. They did, and the rocks and bodies started to glance off better. Our formation moved up, first two steps at a charge, and then four, and then eight. Gila bloods tromped around me. They probably thought I'd been hit. Once or twice one of them tried to help me up and I waved him off. It's okay, dude. I'm just chilling here for a second.

I put my forehead down on the edge of the stair. Ahh. I noticed my mace had fallen off, somehow. My right hand was still in a fist, though, and wouldn't open on its own. I got it flattened out with my left hand and pressed it against the warm plaster. Aaaahhhh. Bliss. Just one more second. Rattler bloods trudged past me on either side. I watched their cone-shell ankle bracelets jiggling like tambourine bells. Where was Hun Xoc? I wondered. Where was Armadillo Shit? Well, I'll find them in a minute.

I closed my eyes. Damn. I was still getting these stupid Timothy Leary flashes of psychedelic orange from the spilled drug powder. I lapped up some air. There was a whiff of burning fat in it now, that devil's-barbecue smell. It triggered an animal knowledge that this was a place of death that you had to escape immediately. Still, there was real air up here. At least we were getting up out of the fumes. Get the critters up here, I thought. Amphibians are sensitive. They can't breathe smoke and last.

A hand closed over my wrist. I opened one eye and looked up.

Armadillo Shit and two Gila bloods had come back down and found me. They picked me up by the arms and carried me up toward the sanctuary. I tried to help, but really my feet were just flopping on the steps, doing nothing. One of the Gilas held up a shield wrapped in a wet manta to screen me from the heat. Move aside, I thought. VIP comin' thru. We got onto the platform of the snout, that is, the flat-topped pyramid that projected out from the main one, and pushed forward.

A medium-sized Puma corpse bounced sluggishly down at us, like a boulder rolling down an undersea trenchside. Armadillo Shit braced himself in a hipball player's receiving stance, blocked it, and shunted the body off to the right with two kicks. Well done, I thought. Get that kid a contract. He yanked me forward and up.

I think I may even have fallen asleep for a few seconds. You'd think it would be tough to fall asleep in the middle of a battle, but actually it happens to soldiers all the time. Their adrenaline gives out and poof, they're draped over their rifles, snoring away.

At some point Armadillo Shit put me down.

It felt almost cool here. I got both eyes open.

I was on all fours, looking down at a floor tiled with silver shells. There were gleaming gold shards scattered over the silver, and as I raised my head I saw there were tens of thousands of them, in big drifts. I guessed that they were polished pyrite, pieces of the Pumas' giant concave mirror. They must have smashed the thing before we got here so we couldn't take it captive.

I realized we'd made it.

This is it, I thought. Top of the world, Ma.

If you believed the hype of the empire, we were now directly over the heart, navel, and womb of the universe. The four-lobed cave under the mul was the original omphalos, where the smokers took counsel at the end of the last sun, when Scab Boy jumped into the fire and became the sun that had just now died.

Eventually I even got my head up. I looked around.

They'd set me near the edge of the temple porch, about twenty arms north of the top of the stairs, so that I'd be less exposed to attacks from below. I was also shielded from the direct heat of the fires, and even though the day was still calm, we were high enough to catch a little breeze. Maybe we'll live, I thought. At least for a while.

I crept to the edge of the platform and peered down over it. Whoa. Dizziness. Moving from that packed, half-underground world, up to this height . . . it felt like I suppose it would feel to transform from a three-dimensional being into a four-dimensional one. Below me the inner plazas and private courts were all laid open, like a patient etherized, sectioned, dissected, dyed, and plastinated on a table. On my left the great staircase angled down into the Puma's courtyard. It seethed with heads. The bonfire was in a ring of blackened bodies, but then beyond that ring, at about the point, I figured, where the heat was down to around 140 degrees, at least twelve thousand people were jammed into the space, caught between the heat of the bonfire pagoda and the high walls. They were far away, and it took a minute to get my tipsy eyes focused. But when I did get a clear picture of them, I could see that the people were dancing in the heat, or dancing from the heat, bouncing and bopping in a giant disco of pain.

Gusanos, that is, agave worms, are a delicacy in Latin America, and one time when I was about three or four—it's one of the earliest things I can remember—I was in my grandmother's *ripio* and she was frying something, and I looked down into the pan. It was filled with what looked to me like white eyeless babies writhing in the sizzling grease, a mass of writhing death, and I think I cried, or screamed, or something, and Tío Generoso laughed at me. Of course, later I got to love the little suckers. But now I got a flash of that first moment with them, when I'd picked up on their pain through preverbal empathy, and it was like all the stuff in between that moment and this one was utterly trivial. The only important thing was that these and about a quadrillion other beings were or would be getting cosmically screwed, and that therefore the entirety of creation was just a mistake.

Killing one or two people can feel odd at first, but killing a whole lot feels odd in a different way. Especially when you see it happening. I didn't mean it, I thought. Or at least it was for a reason. Right. The same stupid phrases kept looping in my head, I didn't particularly want them to get killed, I didn't want them to get killed, there were no other options, no other options, nother noptions. Stop it, I thought. You're tripping on guilt in order to make yourself think you're a nice person. You're not a nice person. You're shit.

Still, we'd done it. We said "Take the mul," and we had. How'd we manage that?

Thanks to the salve and the rehearsed buddy system where we licked each other's eyes, most of us could see. And a lot of other people couldn't. Also, plain surprise probably counted for a lot. A little organization, planning, and just being ready for what's going to happen goes a long way.

And then, to top it all off, the Pumas down in the plaza had been too awed by the holy mulob' to climb up where they weren't allowed, even when they were burning up. Really, the main thing was just that I didn't believe, and

Koh—well, she might still believe in that stuff a bit, but not so much as before she met me. Superstition may be the world's most powerful weapon, but doubt can be a pretty good second-most-powerful one. Cortés didn't believe, and it sure worked for him. Come to think of it, when he got cut off and surrounded in Tenochtitlan, he and his men did the same thing we were doing. They rode it out on top of the mul of Huitzilopochtli. Maybe the locals just would't go after them up there—

Whoa. There she is.

(60)

K oh climbed the last stair and stepped onto the temple porch. Her guards lowered the shielding quilts and backed away from her. She was still in her green mask, but her arms were bare, one pale and the other the solid blue-black of her vitiligo. Her dresser had tied on her feather headdress—I was impressed that she'd found time to rethink her coiffure in the middle of a battle, although I guess that's what girls are like—and the light of the fires behind her projected a nimbus of light into the golden-green plumes. The crowd of Harpy/Gila/Rattler bloods on the platform parted. She walked between them, unhesitatingly, like Joan of Arc through the north portal at Reims. The Puma elders who were still clinging to the top of the mul turned their heads to look at her. She took nine steps. She was walking the way a lizard walks, deliberate, alert, and seemingly emotionless. Two extra-long quetzal feathers trailed through the air above her head in a delayed duplication of her movements, like antennae that sniffed the past. Her dwarf, the Penguin Woman—who, just by the way, supposedly had a seagull uay, and because of a lightning storm she'd been stopped midway through the process of casting off her human skin and becoming her animal self—positioned herself just in front of her, held up her little claws for a moment, put them down, looked left and right, and spoke.

"Now all to the southeast, northwest, northeast, southeast, attend," she chanted in her throaty whine. "All above, below, and in the center attend. Now all before us, all after us, and all now, attend, attend."

There was silence on the platform and then a significant sound. It was almost imperceptible against the noises from the panic below us. But the bloods next to me heard it with their professional ears, and I heard it, and Koh heard it.

One of the Pumas on the far left of the line hadn't given up his atlatl, his spearthrower—he must have been hiding it in his manta—and he nocked a short poison dart into it, as though he was going to launch it at her. Or maybe he was trying to get one of us to launch a spear at him so that a fight would start. That was always a problem with these people. They'd prefer to be killed than be taken captive. At any rate, with a quick shift of position, the bloods on both sides of me were suddenly aiming their javelins at him and about to launch them. But Koh shrugged—it was our equivalent of holding up a "wait" finger—and they didn't fire.

And neither did the Puma blood. Koh stood for a moment, not looking at him and not speaking, daring him to throw the dart.

I don't know whether she felt any fear, but she knew that if you showed any fear you were done for. Anyway, she didn't budge.

Five beats went by, and then ten. Finally the Puma blood—well, he didn't quite lower the dart, but he relaxed, or shifted his body in a way that you could tell he wasn't about to throw it.

Koh spoke. Her voice was low, cold, and heraldic. You could just tell it was her, but it was different from any of the voices she'd used before. She used an ancient sacerdotal form of Teotihuacano, and I only picked up about every third word. But of course, I got a translation later:

> "You on a level with us, but divested
> Of maces, of javelins,
> Pumas, all cowed on your citadel,
> Now overmastered, surrounded,
> You within range of our javelins,
> Holding your suicide razors,
> Now our ahau, our sun-swallowing eel,
> Our jade-feathered Star Rattler
> Speaks through the Ahau-na Koh of the Orb Weavers,
> Koh of the Auras.
> She on a level with him comes to speak with the Puma,
> The Warlord."

There was a pause. The Pumas shuffled a bit.

One of the elder Pumas stepped forward, agonizingly slowly. He walked in halt-steps, that is, with the left foot never stepping forward of the right one, which meant that he wasn't yet her bound captive and so he wasn't in a hurry. He wore an orange full-face mask and a gigantically swollen full-length red feather cape. So this would be the symposiarch of the synod, I guessed.

"I on a level with Ahau-na Koh, I may call him, or not," he said.

Koh didn't answer. The Puppy Woman, who was maybe a bit hyperactive, shifted from foot to foot. After ten more beats he made a hand sign behind his back and the crowd of elder Pumas parted in the middle and edged away from the doors of the teocalli.

The four doors led straight back to four long temple cellae, a tripartite sky cave that supposedly mirrored the underground one directly below it. I couldn't see much of them from where I was cowering, but I could see that the left-hand chamber, the northernmost, was mosaicked or paneled with mother-of-pearl. The right chamber was lined with light-green jade, and the middle one was all polished pyrite. The rooms seemed to be filled with people, but a little later it turned out that most of the figures inside were mummies. Four attendants carried the living god out of the central chamber. Turd Curl sat, cross-legged but leaning back against puma-skin cushions, in a small covered palanquin. He was covered with red-orange feathers and an orange feather mask. The only visible parts of his body were skeletal hands painted with red cinnabar and a section of shriveled leg above his right ankle. He looked . . . well, he looked like a dying god, one who was even more powerful for being close to death. And he didn't look like a benign one either. If they'd sent me to deal with him I'd already be banging my forehead on the flagstones and mumbling, "I beg you to make my execution mercifully swift, O Great One."

They stopped just ten arms from her. They didn't set him down, although that would have brought his eye level closer to hers, which should have been the protocol. Koh simply ignored the insult.

"You on a level with me, will you accept a yellow rope?" Koh asked.

"I next to you speak for Hurricane," he said. His voice was like the sound of some engine down in a mine. "When he returns from hunting, soon, what then?"

"On that sun all of you next to me will reseat your line," Koh said. "On that sun Star Rattler's brood will nest far away."

Basically, what Turd Curl was saying was that Hurricane, the Old Man of the Storm, was just taking a little vacation, and that was why Star Rattler had taken over the day. In other words, he was spinning it like his own god had planned this all along. What Koh had said, basically, was that at a date in the near future—to be negotiated shortly—she would release Turd Curl and the rest of the captives, and she and her followers would be on their way to somewhere else.

There was another pause. As usual, my twenty-first-century side scoffed a bit. What a load of gilded hooey. All these poor people were fighting and screaming and getting incinerated below us, and we still had the time to go through this whole elaborate protocol. On the other hand, my gone-native side realized that people don't just *do* their stupid rituals. They *are* their stupid rituals. If we didn't go through the correct motions, nothing would really have happened.

And I have to say, Koh was keeping her head in a tense situation. We were still vastly outnumbered, in the middle of a bunch of people who really hated us. If they got their act together, they could take us apart. If the fire didn't get us all first.

Finally there was something like a silent vote, and the Puma elders threw down their obsidian suicide knives. As they broke on the shell floor they made humble little shattering sounds, like Christmas ornaments falling off a tree. Maybe it was just fatalism. Maybe even most of the Pumas believed that this was all supposed to happen, that everything the greathousers did was inevitable, and that they had a new master.

Two of the top Gila bloods tied a yellow rope around Turd Curl's chest, the symbol of a hostage that may either be killed or might still be exchanged. They carried him to the lip of the stairs and exhibited him to the Pumas down below.

Two of Koh's men dragged a discarded megaphone to the lip of the platform. They held the Penguin Woman up to the mouthpiece. When she spoke through it, her little singsong voice came out huge and inhuman:

"You underneath us, you Swallowtails, Pumas,
   In range of our javelins . . ."

She ordered the Puma bloods to stop where they were. If they advanced even one step farther up the mul, she said, we would begin killing the hostages and tossing the bones of their ancestors off the sanctuary.

The sounds of combat below faded. A few battered-looking Rattler bloods clambered up onto the platform. Evidently the Puma attackers were taking the whole thing seriously. A little crowd of invalids had grown around me,

Gila and Rattler bloods who'd been too badly injured to do any work. Hun Xoc bustled through it and crouched down on my right.

He asked if I was all right. I said I was good but about to collapse. He said I had blood under my nose and helped me wipe it off. I asked him how strong we were. He said we'd lost eight Harpy bloods. The Gilas had lost forty-one bloods, and Koh had lost sixty. Altogether, our numbers were down by almost a third. Hell. Given what we still had to go through, that was enough to sink the whole campaign. Even aside from the human tragedy, of course. As they say.

We also now had two hundred and eighty-six hostages, including Turd Curl himself, two of his wives, six other members of the imperial family, forty-eight members of the Puma Synod, and fifty-nine generally elder Swallow-tails. That wasn't so bad. The main thing was that Severed Right Hand, the likely heir, wasn't anywhere on the mul.

Also, 4 Sunshower was dying, Hun Xoc said. Just five steps from the top he'd been gored by a spear from the defenders. I'd missed it.

I got to my feet with a little help and staggered twenty paces east to where they'd put him. I sat down next to him. He'd gotten pale underneath his red body oil, and it gave him an odd pink shade, like dry, uncooked liver. A flint point had been driven deep into his small intestine. It would only come out in pieces, I thought. Sour-smelling gastric juice and two-thirds-processed feces were leaking out. Around here you didn't recover from a dirty wound like that. Hell, I thought. He was a good guy. He was breathing, a little, and I put my head down and called his name in his ear, but he was already unconscious from blood loss.

I started to stand up again but couldn't.

Koh took up a position on an upended altar stone in front of the central cella. One by one the Puma elders trooped by, and each one put something— an ear spool, a mouth comb, a hair bracelet, or whatever—down on the ground in front of her, offering her allegiance. At each gift she tapped her right hand on her left shoulder, lightly acknowledging the giver. She was still masked, but I'm sure if I could have seen her face it would have had a queenly serenity to it, as though she'd always known, since even before her birth, that this would happen.

Great, I thought, I've created a monster. A regular Elsa Lanchester. Take it easy with those Tesla coils, babe.

I'd never been a big believer in the Great Man school of history, but now that I was seeing history closer up, I have to say charisma does count for something. Sometimes all you have to do is just take charge. And I guess it was just as well somebody did too.

Well, so, let her have her day, I thought. Let her do her victory thing. They're into victory around here.

Forget it, Jed, I thought. It's not entirely our fault.

(61)

A wave of ashes rippled over my face, and for a minute we couldn't see a thing, and then the wind revolved and the burning city was clear again. We didn't want this, I thought. This sort of thing happens sometimes. It had happened—would happen?—to the Xhosa, in 1856, when they burned their crops and killed their cattle and forty thousand of them starved to death. It happened in the 1890s, with the Ghost Dancers. It used to happen every year at the Rath Yatra festival at Puri in Orissa, when people would dive under the wheels of the Jagannath. It happened at Jonestown. It happened in Orlando. It happens.

But of course, it was entirely our fault. My fault. *Todo por mi culpa.* My fault, my fault.

I looked west. Down in the four hundred plazas the heat currents twisted the smoke and spark-showers into fat cables, like the gold-thread ropes on old theater curtains but the length and width of freight trains. They coiled around and up the sides of the pyramids and whipped upward at the top. One of those giant round kites floated underneath us, rolling slowly like a flaming tumbleweed. I looked south. Way out beyond the ruins of Star Rattler's mul, you could see that the cyclones of fire were processing counterclockwise around the city, as though we were in the eye of a hurricane on the sun.

(62)

I walked, or rather staggered, over to Koh. She'd taken off her mask, holding
it in her dark hand while she stroked the Penguin Woman with the light
one, fondling the scalp under the dwarf's thin hair and then running her
hand down her cheek and then down her body, scrabbling her fingers as
though she was scratching a cat. The dwarf snuggled and stretched and finally slid out of Koh's arms and toddled back to her keeper. Koh stood up and
took four steps to the edge of the terrace. She looked down at the smoke and
corpses in the zócalos. She looked up and this way, north, and caught my eye.
But we'd agreed that she wouldn't single me out in front of the Pumas, and
she turned south, toward the Rattler's compound. It was already in the last
phase of its burning, dribbling black smoke up into the brown sky. I thought
I could see an odd expression through her blankness, even in profile. Something near the corners of her mouth was conveying something close to doubt.
Whirlwinds of sparks that looked more like flakes of gold leaf and droplets of
molten steel flew upward behind her. Koh's turquoise mask dangled from her
dark hand, facing me dead on, and I had the odd feeling that she could see me
through its empty eyes. But she didn't move her real head. It just stayed there,
the curve of its jaw underlit by the flames, facing out over the courts of the
sun like a giant basalt head in some Ozymandian desert, polished by eons of
sandstorms. Somewhere below us the fire hit a reservoir and a thunderhead
of steam sizzled up into the vortex. Koh's eyes followed it up and then, unhurriedly, settled back down again on the smoldering symmetry that was no longer the axle of the world. I thought at first that she reminded me of some
painting of Helen on the deck of Menelaus's ship, looking back at Troy as it
burned, and then I thought maybe I was thinking of Garbo at the end of *Queen*

Christina. Or maybe it was Marena standing on the causeway staring out at the oil-glazed gulf. Or maybe it was that nephila spider at the center of its orb. Suddenly I saw something under her dark eye, and I realized it was tears, but then I decided it was probably just from the smoke. She reset her mask, tied it behind her head with a blood knot, and turned away.

FOUR

The Aftercomers

(63)

"Who was the voice of Mickey Mouse?" Marena asked.

"Hang on a second," I said. I had to cough. I coughed.

"Jed? You want some more Squirt?"

"No, thanks," I said, "I'm fine, uh, Walt himself was the original voice of the Mouse."

"Right. Okay. What's the square root of five?"

I told her.

"What's the name of your last—hang on." She paused. "Ana's on the line, she wants us to wrap it up," she said.

"It should be enough by now," Dr. Lisuarte's voice said, close behind me in the tiny room. She paused. "Hang on. No, I need to talk to the lab first," she said, evidently talking to Ana through her communicator. "Okay, out. CTP? This is Akagi, we have a three-nine-eight from Keelorenz." It took me what seemed like a while to remember that when she said "CTP" she was addressing the Consciousness Transfer Protocol lab at the Stake, that "Akagi" was Lisuarte's code name, and that "Keelorenz" was Ana Vergara's code name. I didn't know what a three-nine-eight was. "Okay, check," she went on. Pause. "They say they've got enough," she said. I figured the last sentence was directed to Marena and me, and that it meant the lab had enough scans of my thought processes to stop transmission.

"So we're going to unplug me now?" I asked groggily.

They said yes. Lisuarte powered down the toilet, that is, the big white PET/MRI ring around my head. I could hear the magnets dragging against their tracks as they decelerated. Predawn light was coming up in the doorway. Marena started pulling off my 'trodes, not in a sexy way. Well, that's it. Whatever version of me had shown up under the questioning was on its way.

In fact, it had gone on its way, arrived, done what it was going to do, and died, a long time ago.

They hustled me out of the ahau's niche. The sky was dark gray and the stars were gone. Michael and Hitch, the cameraman, were still on the landing and they and Marena half carried me down the crumbling stairs, passing me down over the twenty-six-inch risers. It seemed to take about a month.

"I can walk," I said.

"Yeah, but not with any accuracy," Marena said.

There was a cleared area at the base of the mul, with a path leading downhill past the palace to the river. I stumbled along. Ana and Grgur were waiting on the beachlet where Marena and I had had our little thingy fourteen hours ago. Ana was talking into the air with her hand over her ear.

"What's going on?" Marena asked Michael after he'd caught his breath. According to the briefings we'd had, this was where the Hippogriff swivelcraft would pick us up if we had to make an impromptu exit.

"Ana thinks we may have to pull out now," Michael said. Unlike Marena and Lisuarte and me he'd been listening to all the radio talk.

"Why?" she asked.

"There's a patrol coming in. They think it may go through here."

"Fuck," Marena said. "If they don't come through the site, we'll go back later."

We waited. Ana kept talking. She didn't explain anything.

"Where's No Way?" I asked. Michael said he didn't know. Boy Commando didn't seem to be around either. I found my ear thing, got it in, and turned it on.

"... sixteen clicks," Ana's voice was saying. "Hey, where are you going?" she asked, louder.

"I need to go back to the palace and get my stuff," Marena said.

"Negative, Asuka," Ana said. "Nobody goes anywhere."

"Why don't we just hide out someplace in the forest with the other ES people?" I asked, taking advantage of Ana's being off the air.

"Because if they find all our gear, they'll have an eye out for us," Ana said. "We'd have to hump all the way to Route 14. And even then we could still get grabbed. We went over this scenario."

"I must have missed that class," I said.

"Anyway, the Hippo's a stealth lander, it has a signature legend, it'll take us out with no problem."

"What if they—," I started to ask.

"If they bypass the site we'll be back in two days and we'll start digging then," she said. "No more questions, please."

I shut up. What she didn't say was that if the patrol did find all our gear and everything, it would be a long time before we'd be able to get back here. And Ix was the only place where Jed$_2$ would have entombed himself. Or might have, I should say. If we didn't dig the royal tombs, we wouldn't even know whether he'd managed that.

And then there wouldn't be any of Jed$_2$'s memories getting uploaded into my brain either. Whatever I'd seen back there, I was going to be keeping it to myself. And from myself, if you follow me. Damn it. On the other hand, in a way I ought to be relieved, because if that did happen, his memories would have erased mine, that is, the ones I've formed in the last few minutes, or since whatever point in the downloading our consciousnesses had split, which could—

"Okay, it's here," Ana said. "Two minutes."

I nodded. Worry about all that stuff later.

A big sharp shadow flickered over us. There was a bang and the whine of a big engine starting and then that thwocketing sound, and out past the rash of lily pads the smooth water turned sharkskinny. Above us it seemed like this thing had just appeared out of a fold in the air, a knot of white at the hub of a single long straight arm that turned slowly back and forth like the needle of a big compass. It's the Hippogriff, I thought vaguely. It must have some kind of fast-ignition system. They'd glided in without engines. Ana waded out under the thing with that GI Jane, *Special Forces Handbook* movement. Military types take themselves so seriously. She reached up and grabbed a plastic two-man troop cage out of the air. Someone skootched past me into a pocket of JP-5 exhaust. Marena held my arm and we waded out into the eye of the snarling little waterspout. Ana started bundling us into the five-sided cage. She twisted my muddy legs under me so I was kind of kneeling on the mesh. There were orange straps all over. I looked up. The big weird-looking aircraft was hovering in its bubble of downdraft about fifty feet overhead, making minute adjustments. It didn't want to get any lower and maybe catch its rotors on a tree. Fans of distortion spewed out of dorsal heat-vents like sharks' spiracles.

"Wait, where's No Way?" I asked.

"Load one, hoist," Ana said. We jerked up toward a big padded opening in the light belly. I tried to spot the palace to see if No Way or anyone was there, but we were spinning too much. I felt through my pockets. Where's my phone? I wondered. They'd better not have left it back there. A pair of orange-gloved hands steered the cage up into the dark cloaca. There was that macho smell of motor oil, vinyl chloride, and old leather. The guy with the gloves unbinered the straps, pulled Marena and me out onto the padded floor, and sent the cage down again. I sprawled on the carpet and looked up for the hands' owner. He was a big guy. He wore a video helmet, but the visor was up and I recognized him as the copilot—or more correctly, according to the readouts, the WSO, the weapons system officer, even though our aircraft wasn't armed—from our flight from the Stake to Pusilha. It was only a two-man crew.

"Please take your seats from the previous flight," he said, as though we were on Virgin Air. It was pretty dark, but there were constellations of LEDs all over everything so you could tell what things were. If you already knew, that is. I stood up, and before Marena could grab me I bonked my head on the vinyl-skinned foam. She steered me into the port bulkhead seat. It was like a big child-safety seat. A tykeish-looking powder-blue bar came down over me with an easy-to-read label in orange letters: CHECK FOR SECURE LOCK. There was a little QWERTY keypad on it. Marena sat across from me so the two of us were closest to where the partition would have been between the hold and the cockpit. I looked around. The passenger windows had been covered, I guess because now it was a military operation, but I could see some of the canopy windscreen past the pilot's head and below that, starting nearly at my ankle, a wedge of the left chin-bubble window. When the rotors blew away some of the mist, you could see a patch of the river turning black in our chop. Michael and Dr. Lisuarte scrambled up through the low door and past us. Michael had been assigned the seat near the tail to distribute the weight. Hitch came through next, and then Grgur. He climbed in less heavily than I would have thought and then hunched over Marena for a moment, whispering to her, before he went aft to sit across from Michael. The WSO settled into his seat to the right of the pilot. Ana came up last, pulling the cage in after her. I guessed Boy Commando was staying out in the bush. She flipped up a sort of jump seat between and behind the pilot and the WSO. She started to strap herself in but then reached back and around like she was going to hug me. But her hands went above my head.

I felt this secure feeling of soft pressure over my ears and I was plunged into deep quiet, a gentle thrumming like a big hummingbird all around me with just a thin underall hiss and the open-system beep repeated every two seconds like a grasshopper's mating call. She'd pulled a helmet down over my head. It had a regular visor on it, but there were sort of goggle things inside that slid down and gave you an augmented video view out of the helmet's two lenses. The first time we'd used this aircraft, back in Belize, they'd recommended that we "deploy the AVRV goggles at all times," in case somebody attacked us with eyedazzler lasers. At first it was all just a blur, but then the thing adapted to my eyes and I was seeing in a different mode. It was sharper than real life, kind of like listening to a violin on your phone instead of on mellow old vinyl. Also, everything was brighter and more contrasty—it adapted to the dark—and, because the cameras were farther apart on the helmet than one's eyes, it exaggerated the space between things, like in old 3-D movies where everything's either scraping your forehead or way back in Row Z. Finally, just to complicate the experience, there was text hovering over everything, keyed to different hot points in the aircraft so that it could label the safety features and readouts and even the crew and passengers. And of course it had a scroll at the bottom running through all kinds of data that I couldn't puzzle out. There was a little flight-plan map in the lower right, though, that was clear enough. It showed our course heading due north by northeast into Belize, crossing the Sarstoon River, that is, the southern border, at its mouth. Well, that seems straightforward, I thought. No problem.

Was No Way still out there? I wondered again. Was he in trouble? I'd gotten him the hell into this thing. Kind of instinctively my right hand found the little keypad on my toddler bar and flicked at the buttons on it until I found an active audio. A different layer of sound cracked into the muffle-world, like I'd switched from mono to quad.

"Hey, wait a second, hang on," I said, but I didn't hear my voice. I found the MIC button and turned that on too.

I switched into Marena's personal channel.

"Marena?" I asked.

"Jed, hi, you okay?" she asked.

"Yeah," I said groggily.

"You understanding stuff?"

"Yeah. I'm fine. I'm fine. I'm fine. Is No Way still at the site?"

Ana's voice cut in on the channel.

"All passengers stay off the air," her voice said. Fuck you, too, I thought. Marena's voice came on.

"Jed, we can't find him," she said. "He may have just taken off."

"That's not possible," I said, but by the word *not* I could tell Ana had cut off my mike. I started to take my helmet off, got a taste of how dark and loud it was out there without it, and thought better of it and put it back on. I focused on the little AUDIO MENU readout in the upper left of my virtual visual field, got the cursor on the pilot audio channel, and switched it on.

"—for the treetops," a voice said.

"Okay, we're all in, go go go," Ana's voice said. I felt myself falling, sucked through a crack in the seat, sinking into the Earthtoadess, as the Hippo lifted off in that sickeningly backward way with its rear end up like a whale's flukes. There was a sudden increase in air pressure as the doors folded shut. Out past the chin-bubble window, foliage rushed downward and disappeared as we passed into a low raincloud. Water beads fanned out over the bubble. Marena's voice came back on.

"Jed, if you need anything, use channel four," she said.

I found it and clicked in.

"No Way wouldn't just take off," I said.

"Jed, he may have gotten cut off by that patrol," Marena said.

"I don't think so," I said.

"Anyway, he never really trusted us. Come on—"

"I mean—"

"We'll call him when we get back," she said. "This is not the time to argue about this."

We hit a pocket of thinner air and slid sideways. Protovomit welled up in the back of my throat. Beyond the windscreen the mist parted and space seemed to curve around us like we were inside a fisheye lens, a second layer of overcast expanding ahead and above. I tucked in my foot as a palm top almost brushed the bubble. We were lower than I'd thought. I looked over at Marena, but she just looked like the Fly, so I clicked into MENU—VIEWS, highlighted MONITOR CREW HI-HUDWAS—which meant helmet-integrated head-up-display and weapons aiming system—and hit WSO. It was like I'd switched heads; I was sitting in the shotgun seat, seeing exactly what the WSO was seeing. I guess the idea behind the eyephone setup was that any helmet could access the viewpoint of any other helmet, so the whole class could all look through the pilot's eyes so you could all learn about piloting at once. Or the pilot could see what the tail observer saw, or whatever. A whole world of information floated over everything, vectors, velocities, pressure and temperature readings, windows SHOWING AIRSPEED 248 KH, ELEVATION ABOVE SEA LEVEL 381 M, ELEVATION ABOVE GROUND LEVEL 28.2 M, and scrolls repeating warnings like CLOSED TRANSMISSION ONLY, THIS IS NOT

A FUNCTIONING DISPLAY, and even notices not to watch if you were epileptic. The view shifted front and I tried to turn my head back down, but of course nothing happened. I was at the dude's visual mercy, and he was focusing on the false horizon drawn in blue against the clouds. I found the channel that gave me the WSO's audio.

"—no te preocupes amorcita, este es el caballo," he was saying. It was the punch line of some joke.

"Sí, pues," a Guate-accented voice responded. It seemed like the WSO was rapping over the radio with the local controller like they were old pals. Maybe this was going to turn out all right. They must have fixed it with the Guates. Only, then, who'd barged in on us back at the site? Just some patrol that wasn't in on the fix? Maybe they hadn't wanted to put too many people on the payroll.

We headed almost due east, down out of the high bluffs over the rapids, and then veered east by southeast as the Chisay bent into the Río Cahabón. A gray chalk cliff came up in front of us, and instead of hopping over it the pilot dug into a turn around it, staying low and over the center of the river, so that it felt more like we were snowboarding than flying. Foliage seemed to envelop us and then we were around it and into an expanding void.

A different voice came onto the main communications channel. "Es este el vuelo 465-BA del Poptún?" the voice asked. "You are 465-BA out of Poptún?" The ID readout said he was calling from Guzmán Base, the Guate City military airport.

"Correcto," the WSO said.

"¿Perdone la molestia, mas el OC dice qué pasa?"

"There's some kind of a problem south of Chisec," the WSO said in Spanish. "Corporal Olaquiaga at Poptún Base told us to respond."

"Okay. You seem to be off schedule today, though."

"No kidding, that's why we're going back."

Uh-oh, I thought. He's pretending we're a Guatemalan air force plane. Trying to fool the air traffic controllers for as long as possible. Which means we don't have support within the Guate military.

The Hippo climbed a thousand feet as we hopped over the source of the Oxec, between Cerro Tabol on the left and the west flank of the big Sierra de Santa Cruz on the right.

"—that ID by us again?" the Guate voice was saying.

"GAC 465 BA, 20380-821809-234874211," the WSO said.

"We have to check that," the voice said, "otherwise they'll give you trouble at the border."

"I'll call them," the WSO said.

"Why don't you just hang out where you are for a second? Slow down."

I flicked to Marena's channel, channel 4, and beeped her. She flicked in. I told her the Guates sounded like they were getting antsy.

"It's probably not a problem," she said. "They're looking for flights coming in, not going out."

"—but why the heading?" another Guate voice was asking.

"There's a chance some of the terrorists may have left by truck earlier this morning," the WSO lied. "He wants us to see if we can spot them at the border."

"Yeah, okay, but I have to account for all flights near the DMZ," the controller said.

"You should call Olaquiaga," the WSO said. He started giving a string of call numbers.

"He's not at that base, you have to call the CO there."

"Can you patch us in?" the WSO asked.

"You have to hail him with your own band."

"I'll do it," the WSO said.

He cut the radio channel. The pilot—who I guess didn't talk unless it was necessary—came on the ALL PAGE channel. That is, he was talking to us, not to anyone outside the Hippo. "Okay, be advised," he said, "we are going to increase our airspeed." Before he finished, my head stuck to the right wing of the seat and I could feel the loose skin of my cheeks creeping backward in the four or five extra Gs. He'd tucked in the rotors and fired the forward jets. Guess that blows our low profile, I thought.

"Just hang out for a second," the Guate controller's voice said.

Ana's voice came onto the channel. "So what do you think?" she asked.

"They don't know what they're doing," the pilot's voice said. "Let's just stay on at this speed." His right hand hovered delicately around the cyclic stick cradled between his legs.

The Guates squawked in again.

"465 BA, this is Guzmán Base CG, what are you doing?"

We didn't respond.

"You have to get a new order or reverse heading and land here," the controller said. "Sorry."

"No me quiebres el culo," the WSO said. "Don't bust my ass. You're *not* telling us to head back."

"Sorry."

"Olaquiaga se va a cagar," the WSO said. "Olaquiaga's going to shit himself."

"Yo no te puedo asegurar que llegues salvo," the voice said. "I can't make it safe." *"Te van a chingar por el culo. Agarra la onda."* "They'll fuck you up the ass over there. Come on, go with it."

The WSO paused.

"Bueno, reconocido, Guzmán."

"Bueno," the voice said. It clicked off.

But we kept going. On my little map the flight plan had shifted. Now it went south down to the Lago de Izabal, and then out into the Mar de las Antillas, that is, the Caribbean Sea. I guessed the idea was to make them think we were heading back and then head out low over the water, where there wouldn't be any large antiaircraft installations.

The Guate controller dude came back on the radio.

"465 Barcelona Antonio, aterrize en seco," he said.

"Somos responsables del seguridad del Corporal Olaquiaga," the WSO lied.

"No contestes. Pararse en seco desde ahora."

The WSO clicked off. "Okay, they're not buying it," he said on the PAGE channel.

"465 BA, tomar tierra a Poptún," the Guate controller screeked. *"Esto es el último apelar."*

"No puedo," the WSO said. "Please call your commanding officer." He clicked off and went back to PAGE. "Okay, that's fucked," he mumbled. "Let's get a directive here."

The pilot slowed, leveled us off, and swung the nose around like he was going to head back inland.

Marena's voice came on. "What are you doing?"

"Uh, they've basically got us cut off," the WSO said.

"We have to decide," Ana said. "Either we let them land us or we go to Case B."

"Okay," Marena said.

"Okay what?" Ana's voice asked. Pause. "It's your call." She spoke a little more clearly than usual, making sure the flight recorder got every word.

"Case B, evade and deliver," Marena said.

"Understood," Ana said. Another pause. "Okay, we're going to take it on, right? Anybody object?"

This is getting way out of hand, I thought. Maybe I ought to object.

Nobody objected.

"Right, then, remember I'm the sole CO from here in," Ana said. "Nobody takes order one from Marena or anyone else."

"Hoo-hah," the pilot's voice said.

"Hwah," the WSO said. What was that? I wondered. Oh. They were saying HUA, like heard, understood, and acknowledged.

"Okay, hang on," the WSO said. He opened a different radio channel. "Zepp to NERV Base."

"Hello, Zepp," a white-sounding voice said. It was the head air traffic guy at the Stake. "This is NERV Base, go ahead."

"We're switching to Case B," the pilot said. "We're requesting MD4s."

"Copy that, just a sec," NERV said. "Looks like you're in a bit o' shit."

"Fuckin'-A."

Our speed dropped even more until we were practically hovering. I stared through the nose-cone camera at a square of burning forest. I typed "MD4?" into my high-chair-bar keyboard. A silhouette of a drone cruise missile came up. It was a slender thing, only six feet long, with long nose wings. It said it was fast, and that it was armed with an air-to-air warhead. Hell. Send in the drones, I thought. Hell. Hell. We're fucked. We're going to get shot down. Well, at least it probably won't hurt—

"Okay, Zepp," the NERV voice said. "We see your beacon and four MD4s are prepping for launch."

"Thank you, NERV."

"Tell them we're landing," Ana said.

"All right, Guzmán. We acknowledge and we're going back to Puerto Barrios," the WSO lied. My map spun around as we made a sharp about-face.

"*No Puerto,*" the Guate voice said. "*Pop—*" Click.

"Okay, Zepp," the NERV voice said, "the MD4s are up and headed your way."

"Okay, thanks, NERV," the WSO said, "do you have an ETA on those?"

"They will be alongside you in two minutes forty-five. You just bear south another twenty degrees and they won't have to turn around."

"HUA."

"You guys take care, you hear?"

"Will do and thank you, NERV," the WSO said.

"Forty degrees coming up," the pilot said. He pitched left and pulled his left foot off the antitorque jet, banking us into a turn that seemed to screech in the air. We screamed south along a narrow watercourse between gorges and out over the Moxela River.

"There's the intercept," the WSO said.

(64)

looked around but couldn't see any aircraft. I guessed she meant they were visible on the map. I clicked it up and enlarged. I was beginning to get the hang of the interface. Ahead of us the Belize border was dotted with active antiaircraft installations like a string of Christmas lights. Oh, there they are. A pair of red dots were drifting toward us at 310 degrees. I put my cursor on it and typed IFF, for "identification friend or foe." A window came up and scrolled through the radar profiles of various aircraft until it found a match. 2 COMANCHE H-18 (?) AIRBORNE A+?, it said. I guess the A+? meant they looked armed, but it wasn't sure with what yet. I found INTERCEPT PROBA-BILITY on the menu and it drew two range circles, a green one around us and a red one around them. They looked too close for total comfort.

"They don't want to pop us," the WSO said. "They want to get a Hippo. They'll try to force us down up ahead."

"Let's not be too sure about that," Ana's voice said.

La gran puta. How'd I get into this again? I wondered. An hour ago we were all nice and cozy up in the king's niche, taking our time, and now we're risking death from the Guate air force. Why didn't Ana just let them arrest us? Warren would have bailed us out in a week. No. Two days. Our timetable can't be that important. I mean, it is and everything, but still . . . fuck. It just hadn't quite gotten through to me that these guys were ready to take it all to the next level. Damn. Idiot. You know, the fact is, Jeddo, you wanted to think you were just getting into bed with corporate thugs, but really, you were get-ting into bed with war thugs. And honestly speaking, you knew it all the time. So don't—

We nosed up toward the center of the Sierra de Santa Cruz, climbing at two thousand feet per minute, and flashed past a green cliff with a narrow white chalk gorge. There's a depression in the range that extends nearly due south, and we followed that at about 340 miles per hour, hugging the cliffs. On the map the two circles crept up on each other, about to connect.

Well, so much for the royal tombs, I thought. We wouldn't be visiting Ix Ruinas again anytime soon. Or ever, probably. The only thing we could do now—if we even got back to the Stake, which was looking less and less definite—was look for the lodestone cross. That is—and I think I mentioned this—where Jed$_2$ was supposed to have buried a crate with a second copy of all his notes on the Game. And now we also had to hope that it turned up far enough away from Ix that we could still sneak back in and dig it up without the Guates hassling us. That is, if Jed$_2$ even got that far. How many ifs is that? I wondered. A lot—

A new cluster of blips entered the map from the north.

"Okay, that's the MD4s," the WSO said.

He slowed. The drone blips increased their speed and came in underneath us like pilot fish. I guess the idea was to keep them hidden in our radar profile.

"Okay, NERV, we've got 'em," the WSO said.

"Uh, copy, Zepp, we're releasing the wire. Take over."

"Thanks," the WSO said. "Got it. Listen, Keelorenz wants to make sure you've got the Ducks in a row." He meant the pickup boats.

"The Ducks are fine."

"Okay," the WSO said.

I scrolled ahead along the flight plan until I could see the string of boats. We had our choice of four pickups, two in the Mar de las Antillas and two in the Gulf of Mexico. Were we going to have to bail out? I wondered. For some reason I shivered. No, *ni modos*. They'll lower us down. And after that I suppose these two guys would land this Hippo thing in the Keys, answer a whole lot of questions, do some time, and get amply compensated.

"I see 'em, I see 'em," the WSO said. I cursored over the two enemy dots. The IFF said (2) US-B/CAH#220? It meant they were two Guate Comanche helicopters. They had rockets.

"We should expect a launch," the pilot said. He changed heading to forty degrees northwest, toward Punta de Manabique.

"Better give me the balls," the WSO said. "Now. Seriously." We passed through the opaque cloud-front, like we were wadded in cotton for a second, and then rose out of it into the blue.

"They're hailing us," the WSO said. He clicked the air-to-air common channel.

"*. . . no me friegues,*" the Guate Comanche said. ("Don't fuck around.") "Land and surrender."

"*Diles que nos la mamen,*" Ana said. "Tell them to suck it."

They can't be going by the book here, I thought. Generally you weren't supposed to chat with the other side. Maybe Executive Solutions had given up that rule since they'd gone private.

"Listen, Comanches, get out of the way," the WSO said on the common channel.

"*Pela las nalgas,*" one of the Guate helicopters said.

"*No les hables,*" a Guate controller cut in. "Don't talk to them."

"*Vete,*" the WSO said. "Back off. You're way out of your league."

"*Mejor andate a la mierda! . . .*"

"We've got some heavy shit," the WSO said. "You're going down."

"*Chíngate,*" the Guate pilot said. "Go fuck yourself."

"I do not want to fuck you up," the WSO said. "Beat it. Last chance." He clicked off and came onto the PAGE ALL channel. "Okay, team, listen up," he said. "Just in case w—"

A high-E tone, the targeting alarm.

Oh, fuck, I thought.

"Oh, fuck," the pilot said.

"Ave María, LAUNCH!!!" the WSO said. "Shitfucker! Don't worry this is pretty routine we're designed for this—"

"Try fifty-five," the NERV voice said. "Four at six point forty-two."

A rose flash bounced through the cabin as the Guate targeting laser swept across us. I choked back a glob of vomit. We're fucked, I mumbled inaudibly into my visor, I can't believe I got talked into this, I can't believe it, I can't believe it, I can't believe it. I pounded my thigh.

"Roger that," the pilot said, "we'll vector to ninety-five at the low end."

"Low radius should be one eighty."

"Make it one seventy." A red danger dot appeared on my screen and then didn't seem to move, the way things don't when they're coming at you. "*Mierdita!!!*"

"Got it. Okay, counting from ten."

"Okay, mark." The pilot swiveled the nacelle positions and the tilt-rotor simultaneously, throwing the Hippo almost into reverse. My head felt like it was going to twist off my spinal cord. Suddenly our turbines reduced power and the rotor pitch changed again, practically stalling us in midair, and all at once the interior was weirdly silent. A gloop of that oh-shit-the-bottom's-fallen-out feeling inflated and burst as we dropped. It's okay, I yelled to myself, it's cool, there's still a whole hell of a lot of air around us and it's holding us up pretty good. We were under the overcast again and you could just see the red beacon of the Punta de Amatique lighthouse one mile due east. We flew northeast over the bay.

"Okay, I have it still closing," the WSO said. "Uh, ninety. Eighty-five."

"Right, we're doing a U49," the pilot said. "Mark."

Our engines slowed again and, to me, they almost seemed to stop.

On our port side one of the MD4s fired its engine, mimicking our heat signature. We fell. At about two thousand feet the pilot tilted the rotors back to where they started catching some air again, but he kept us almost-falling toward the foam at the tip of the peninsula, down into denser air that would lower the ATAs' hit probabilities. It felt like we were burrowing into additive-free peanut butter. On my map view the missile looked like it was just hanging out next to our permanent spot in the middle of the screen, tiptoeing a bit closer every so often and then edging away. At less than twenty feet above water level the pilot pulled us up in a sickeningly smooth parabola. I felt my testicles rise up through my inguinal canal, through my digestive tract, and into my mouth, and swallowed them back down. I swear I could really feel both of them, the left one bigger than the right one, and I had to choke back each one separately. There was a *PFRROOOOSH* underneath us, like a safety valve popping on a giant cappuccino machine, as the red dot went past us, following the decoy, down toward the swamp. I didn't see any impact, but the missile must have hit the point only about a hundred feet ahead of us, just a bit offshore of the lighthouse. There was a *BUMP* shockwave through the cabin and a POCKETA-POCKETA-POCKETA staccato from everywhere at once as the Hippo's composite shell expanded in the heat. The chin-bubble window buckled inward from the pressure and popped back into shape all webbed with cracks. Pebbles clattered over our Kevlar-skinned undercarriage, there was a sickening uprise, and then it was already all back to normal. I switched to the tail camera. All I could see was scattering gulls and a blob of steam the size of a ten-story helping of instant mashed potatoes. For some reason I kept thinking about all the dead parrot fish. We leveled off again and headed straight on northwest, out into the Golfo de Honduras, rising again.

"Come on," the WSO said, "they still have five dicks left. Let's not fuck around."

We rose into the clouds and up through them. This is such bullshit, I thought. If I'd wanted to play with GI Joe toys I would have intentionally fucked up my SAT scores, joined the marines, faked the physical, and gotten vaporized in Iraq. I called up com channel 4.

"Marena?" I asked. "Are you okay?" I couldn't really see her with my helmet cam, or rather she was just another floating label.

"I'm fine," her voice said after a few seconds. "I've got Max on the line, I'll call you back." Click.

I noticed a strong smell of vomit, with a top note of urine and maybe even some feces in there. Somebody'd gotten scared enough to let it all go. Probably Michael, I thought. What a wuss.

"Back off," the WSO said over the radio. "I'm gonna fuck you up. I'm gonna fuck you up."

"Muerancen huecos," the Guate pilot said. "Die, faggots." Our targeting alarm beeped again. Shit. I got another surge of panic and snuggled myself into the entirely deceptive security of my ergo-foam seating equipment.

"Ana, give him the balls right fucking now," the pilot said.

"Okay," Ana said. "Fuck 'em. Target and engage."

On my readout a discreet box came up that said the nearer Apache was a target for the number two MD4. Like it had said on their specs table, the MD4s were multiuse UAVs. They could divert rockets, like the last one had, but they could also act as missiles. They were slower than ATA rockets, like Sidewinders or whatever, but they could still come around behind an aircraft, creep up on it, and detonate. I watched the number two MD4 edge away from us and drift toward the Comanches.

"You're dead, shitter," the WSO said on the radio.

"Metetela, hueco," the Guate pilot answered.

Meanwhile, the second ATA was coming up on our rear end. "I'm going to drop foil on this one," the WSO said on PAGE ALL. I enlarged our tail camera view. Strings of what seemed like thousands of sparkles bloomed behind us, like we were birthing a population of chrome jellyfish. Each sparkle was actually a small self-inflating Mylar balloon, trailing a long fringe of streamers and a single burning flare. On the radar layer of my map a big smear of interference appeared between us and the missile. On the infrared layer it looked more like a thousand points of heat. Either way, the thing's primitive onboard brain found it confusing, and it drifted off course. At the same time the pilot banked us into an S-curve evasion move. There was a high rising and then descending whine as another rocket went under us. Somewhere it must have detonated, because we didn't try to evade it again. Instead we leveled out and got on another steady northeast course. There was a pause, as though we weren't fighting, just joyriding. On the map, though, the two Comanches were slowly getting ahead of us to the east, between us and the low sun. I guess the idea was that if they got much closer they'd launch two rockets at once, and there'd be no way we could deflect or evade both of them.

The lull in the action stretched out and out. "Mommy really, really loves you," Marena said to Max. "You're the best boy in the world." I watched the two orange enemy dots closing in. I watched the readouts of water depths flow under us. I watched the green dot that represented our MD4 drift closer and closer to the nearer Comanche. On my nose cam window the cloud shelf below us was like a field of corrugated pack ice. A single huge clump of cumulus clouds reared above the plain far away to the east like Arabian Nights domes, marking the Cuba Reef underneath. I still couldn't see any aircraft. Finally the dot that represented the nearer Comanche veered sharply to the southeast. He'd realized what was going on. The drone crept up behind him. He dove into a tight downward parabola, trying to reflect the heat from his jets off the water, but it was too late. On the video window you could just see a tiny yellow flash as the MD4 detonated, and then a tangerine streak of burning fuel that stretched out into a horizontal helix.

"*Dio perro,*" the pilot said. "Incompetent fucks."

"Hey, guess what happened in lacrosse," Max said. Now we were close enough to see the helicopter skim slowly across the water in a ball of steam, spurting little glowing chunks. One of the ejector rigs materialized out of the smoke and steam like a stamen out of a lily blooming in ten-minutes-per-second time lapse video. It shot up pretty high but then the chute didn't open all the way, and the Guate pilot's body spiraled down like a warped shuttlecock, strapped to the big seat and trailing pink specks of flaming plastic.

"*Dios mio,*" the WSO said. I could tell from his voice he was crossing himself.

"Did the other one eject at all?" Ana asked.

"I don't think so. Those things are pure shit anyway," the WSO said, "they never work."

"Fuck. My responsibility," she said.

We came up over the debris. The water was bubbling. Now you could see the second Comanche on video. I thought it was going to fire, but instead it seemed to be hanging back. Either he was scared now or his COs had told him not to engage.

We banked north again and headed out at twenty-five degrees into the Golfo de Honduras. We passed the closest point to the second Comanche. Nothing happened. We kept going.

En todos modos, I thought. Maybe everything's going to work out. No problem.

Nobody was saying anything on the main channel, so I hit MONITOR ALL. Nobody was talking there either. You'd think that everybody would be whooping and cheering and congratulating each other, but they just weren't. I didn't think it was because folks were disturbed about the casualties, though. It was more that this had suddenly gone from an international incident to a really serious international incident. Suddenly, we were all eligible for a whole lot of jail time. Not that anybody'd probably get their act together on that, but still. And we weren't home yet either. I noticed our speed was back up to 600 kph. I tuned into the WSO's helmet. He was sweeping the communications bands. There were dozens of outraged people squawking in Spanish and at least a few in English. I caught the phrase "Scramble all available," which didn't sound good.

"What's going on?" Ana's voice asked him.

"It's not great," he said. "I think Tyndall is sending some scouts. Maybe they talked to the Belize base already."

"Shit."

"They all think we're the other side, though."

"Great," she said. "Okay, what do you think?"

"I think we're going to get our picture taken," he said.

"Shit." Evidently they'd still been planning to try to bring the aircraft back to the Stake.

"Gimmie a second," Ana said. "How far to the A boat?"

"About, uh, one point five minutes. It's at Northeast Cay."

I widened my map window. It showed at least twelve other jets and helicopters coming in, including two British F-22 Raptors from Belize.

"We've got about four point five minutes," the WSO said. He meant before the next hostile interception.

There was a short, heavy pause.

"Okay," Ana said. She got on PAGE ALL. "All right, everybody listen up. We're going to scuttle this craft."

"Wait a second," the pilot said. For once he sounded a little flustered. He probably wasn't used to throwing good stuff away.

"This is not going to affect anyone's salary, combat bonus, or other bene-fits," Ana said. "Anyway, that's the only option, otherwise we might as well just land in Miami and see if they get us out of jail by Christmas."

"No, at that rate we can just forget the whole thing. Jed has to be at the Stake to interpret the data. Get LW on the phone, he'll say the same thing."

"Come on," Ana said, apparently to the pilot.

"Okay," the pilot said. "Let's do it."

"Right."

"We're getting marker from Alpha Duck, you want to hail?"

"Just scramble all of them and tell them to go for the raft beepers. *Not* this aircraft. And that's going to be our last transmission. They'll find us. Right?"

"Right."

"Listen, though, it has to look like a hit."

"Why, for the insurance?" he asked.

"Right. Why, are you telling anybody?"

"No, no. . . ."

"Great," Ana said. We headed due northeast over Laurence Rock and then Ranguana Cay, a pair of paramecium-shaped nodes in a long chain of that limpid living green reef color.

"We don't have a self-destruct mechanism," the WSO said.

"But you do have detonators, right?" Ana asked.

"Yeah. Two."

"So, just use one of those to light some gas."

"There aren't any fuel cells up here," the WSO said. "Uh . . . maybe I can drill into the lube."

"That's a great idea," she said. "Okay. Fine. What are the waves like?"

"Five feet," the WSO said. "No caps."

"Air temperature?"

"Seventy-four. The wind's fifteen at forty."

"Water temperature?"

"Sixty."

"Okay. Gendo?"

"Officer?"

"Just set the auto to take us low and slow over the A boat."

"HUA," the pilot, whose code name, it had finally turned out, was Gendo, said.

"Don't let the fucker get into Cuba air, though."

"Yeah, yeah."

"Uh, make sure it doesn't come down on anybody," Marena piped up.

"We'll do what we can," he snipped. He brought our speed down by two hundred kph. We crossed over the Silk Cays into the Mar de las Antillas, out toward the dark purple line of the Gulf Stream at the ceramic horizon.

"Everybody up and ready," Ana said. "Helmets off."

I got the thing off. It had a ventilator, but even so my head was dripping with sweat and the air felt icy on my near baldness. Marena, Lisuarte, Michael, Hitch, Grgur, and I all blinked at each other, wondering which of us had vomited. We were decelerating fast. Ana pushed past us from the back. She'd gotten a little cordless Sawzall out of a locker, and she climbed forward into the cabin next to the WSO.

"Be sure to erase the other disks," she said to him. She started sawing into a slot in the overhead instrument panel, like she was opening a can.

I couldn't see our speed without the helmet and looked for it on the instrument panel, but I couldn't find it. Still, it seemed like we were down to less than twenty miles per hour.

"Everyone out of your harnesses," Ana said over a loudspeaker. "And get into the vests. And be sure your earbuds are in."

"Come on, Jed, let's go, okay?" Marena said. After a few tries we got me out of my seat. She helped me into a thin yellow vest. It felt like she was changing my diaper. She handed me pair of regular sailing goggles. Finally she found a sort of bicycle-helmet-looking helmet, with a little beacon light on the top, and put me into that. I noticed that everybody else already had one on.

"Keep your earbud on, right?" Marena said. "And leave the channel open so you can talk with the rest of the team. Okay?"

"Right," I said. "Team." I realized that even though I was understanding things as clearly as I ever did, I wasn't moving very well. I guess I'm just really tired, I thought. Sex, uppers, downers, an all-nighter, a fair amount of stress. Well, I'll grab a nap in the raft. No prob. Michael—who, it now seemed, knew something about aircraft—squeezed past me, dragging two big yellow bales that would expand into deluxe life rafts with collapsible oars and even little outboard motors with a mile's worth of fuel. Ana came back from the cockpit with what looked like a chunk of crumbly gray insulation. I guessed it was the hard drive from the flight recorder. She sat on the floor, hunched over it, dug a little plastic box out of the center, and started jabbing at it with a screwdriver. Michael maneuvered the raft bales around the collapsed loading cage and carabinered them to a handle over the port-side door, which I guessed was how we were leaving.

Ana stood up.

"Okay," she said, "everybody hear me?"

Everybody did.

"Ready to bail? Headgear okay? Okay. The order's going to be raft one with Gendo. Then Asuka and Pen-Pen go *immediately* after that. Then Akagi and Kozo. Then Raft Two with Zepp. Then Marduk and Shiro. Then me. That's five in raft one and four in raft two. Got it?"

I guess everyone had it. The WSO pushed through us, heading aft. He crouched down way in the back, yanked a panel off the floor, and started fiddling with something.

"Okay," Ana said. "Remember, even after we're all on board we're going to transfer to C boat as soon as we can," she said. "So keep your gear on. Understood?"

Yes, everyone more or less indicated.

"Your vests are gonna inflate automatically when they get wet. Otherwise blow in the little dick. You all know how to drop out backward?"

Silence.

"Like on Jacques Cousteau," she said. "Anybody have a problem with that? Pen-Pen?"

"I dive," I said.

"He's fine," Marena said.

"Has anyone left any type of traceable identification on board? Anybody still strapped in? Pen-Pen?"

Everyone seemed ready.

"Okay. Remember, just sit-float. Don't kick. We'll pick you up."

"We're going to see the boat in about eighty seconds," the pilot said. "You want to hail 'em?"

"No more transmissions of any kind," Ana said. "They'll see the beacons." She hit a ceiling panel with her fist and the big port-side door slid open. The pressure increased like we were inside an over-inflating balloon. Damn, it's bright out there, I thought. We were less than ten feet over the wave peaks and even at this speed it felt like we were still screaming over the spray. On the horizon, just above the low clouds over Northeast Cay, the white moon was digitally clear against the blue Blood Rabbitess scampering away from the Lords of the Night. Ana pitched the flight recorder out the door.

There was a hiss from the back and a wave of that WD-40 smell. I looked around. There was a little geyser of fine spray in the floor next to the WSO. He'd opened one of the lubricant arteries and now he was fiddling with something that looked like a cheap digital clock. Detonator, I thought. Hell. Time to book. Now.

"Okay, go," Ana said.

Gendo—who now, thanks to the autopilot, had nothing more to do on board—released the first raft bundle, tipped it out the door, and disappeared after it in a sitting dive.

"Okay," Ana shouted.

Marena grabbed my shoulders and pushed me down into a crouch. "Now. Three, two, one. Go."

"Wait," I said, but no voice made it out into the wind. The blurred water under us looked like it was on a belt sander. Marena pulled me backward with her and we spilled gently out the door, like a cup and a saucer tipping off a tea table onto a tiled floor.

(65)

We rode in a Cyrolon globe over Oaxaca. The CH-138 Kiowa was small, slow, and open, the opposite of the Hippogriff. Fifteen hundred feet below us the farmlands gave way to forests, and then to scrub, as the ground sloped up toward the altiplano. It was 9:40 A.M. on February 29, a no-name, no-saint, once-every-1,040 days day that I'd always felt was somehow lucky in a non-Maya way. It was five days since our little unpleasantness in the gulf, it was sunny and 68°C, and we were 8,400 refreshing feet above sea level. Sixteen hours ago we'd gotten the word that one of the magnetism-sensing satellites had located the lodestone cross.

It was well inside one of the zones we'd designated as safe cache locations, but it was awfully far from Ix. What had he, or rather I, been doing all the hell out here? Maybe Jed$_2$ had to go to Teotihuacan for some reason. Or he tried to. And then he must have buried his notes on the Game here because he was afraid he wasn't going to get back to Ix.

Or he knew he wasn't going to get back.

Well, anyway, he got this far, didn't he? That's a lot. Maybe I'll pull this nightmare out of the fire after all.

We banked west and headed down toward the center of a low mesa in the highlands just north of Coixtlahuaca. It was all scrub pine and ocotillos. Good tarantula country. Four big ES guys from Mexico City, dressed like ranchers in too-new, too-expensive Stetsons, hailed us from a little campsite. They had two burros with big packs, a parabolic ground-penetrating radar dish on a tripod, and a small generator and a compressor set up next to a neat four-foot-square hole. We touched down, meeting the shadow of our equipage in a cloud of gravel. Ana, Michael, Marena, and I climbed out. Ana chatted with the dudes for a minute. The rest of us looked down into the pit. They'd gotten down five feet with a jackhammer and shovels. There were two feet to go, which they'd been taking more delicately, with plastic scoops. Michael said not to worry too much and let them finish. It took forty minutes to get to what looked like a big knot of half-petrified dirt. They hoisted it up and whisk-broomed it. It was a low, wide terra-cotta bowl, about twenty inches across and four inches high, with a knob on the lid in the shape of a frog. It was cracked all over, and a few shards had come off, revealing the hard cake of brown wax inside. It was a lot bigger than it needed to be for just a letter. We loaded it into a big plastic vacuum box in the back of the Kiowa and took off. We gassed up again in Nochixtlán—which, incidentally, wasn't too far from the Lake of Green Glass, the 2010 blast site—flew back to Ciudad Oaxaca and switched to a Cessna. Ashley$_2$ (remember Taro's favorite assistant?) was on board and she had a cardboard tray of old-fashioned Styrofoam cups and the signature charred-tar reek of Bustelo—damn, how great was it to have the real hometown sludge instead of that organic Kona peaberry bullshit you get used to in the States?—and I took two. We turned east by southeast, toward the Stake.

"So why do you think that was the only cross he left?" A$_2$ asked us. "He was supposed to tell us whether he was going to be in that tomb or not."

"Maybe he didn't make it back to Ix," Michael said. He looked at me. "Sorry."

"It's fine," I said. Yeah, what the bloody hell had happened? I wondered. Aside from all the other good reasons to be curious, I also wondered just because it had happened to me. Sort of.

"Besides, it doesn't look like we'll get a chance to crack the tombs anyway. There's probably soldiers all over the place."

"Yeah, but still, we're going to have to deal with it," Marena said. "Maybe he got the tomb going all right but then the second cross got dug up or damaged. Or he had some reason not to leave a second message. Or maybe there's something on it in this package. Right? Maybe he didn't leave it himself, maybe he sent somebody up here with it. For some reason."

"Well, I'll make sure we'll find out about that one pretty soon, anyway," Michael said.

And he came through on his promise. Six of his graduate students had set up a basement room at the Stake as an archaeology lab, and an hour after we got back we were already looking at the X-ray and tomograph views while the kids worked in shifts of two at a big argon-filled Lucite glove box, scraping apart the cake of wax. There were seven objects in the jar. Six of them were small-lidded clay jars. They couldn't get much of the contents off the tomograph, but in three of them you could see a few small animal bones. The other object was an unfired clay box the size of a thick hardcover book. There were three Maya screenfold books inside it, packed in dirty-looking rock salt. Michael said they could possibly get the text out of them without opening the box, the way they'd done with the Codex Nurnburg, but that nothing was going to happen to them in the argon box so it would be faster just to dig them out and read them normally. He said it would take about eight hours.

Except for Michael we all trudged back to our dorm rooms. What with one thing and another, nobody seemed to feel like celebrating yet. I thought about knocking on Marena's door but I decided I was still too upset, or too distrustful, rather, even though it looked like we were finally having a little of what might be a success. There was an international police investigation of the Hippogriff incident going on, and it was hard to believe they wouldn't track it back to us. And that patrol had in fact found all our gear at Ix Ruinas, so our hopes of getting back there to try to revive Jed$_2$ seemed pretty far-fetched. And No Way was still missing.

Ana Vergara had stated in the debriefing that she thought No Way had tipped off the Guates about us. "That patrol came in way too directly," she'd said. "There's no way they were just looking around. And all of our assets in the area were solid." They also showed us records of a big transfer and withdrawal from his Nicaraguan account. But, as I told them, anybody could have set that up. They could have shown me a video of him taking the money out himself and it still wouldn't prove anything. There's no way No Way would have done something like that, I'd said. Not just because he wouldn't, but because he was getting a bonus from us later. It had to have been one of ES's so-called solid assets, somebody from the village. They'd been spreading too much money around, I thought. The more people who know about something, the more likely you are to get nailed. In fact, with each new person it becomes ten times as likely. In fact, I thought but didn't say, maybe ES had put the cash in Nacho's account just to help make him out as the villain, to cover up their own ineptitude.

Anyway, even if they didn't push it, they were all blaming me for the screwup. I'd insisted on bringing along an outsider and look what happened. They wondered whether, besides tipping off the Guates, he might be spilling the beans on the details of the Chocula Project. I kept saying I needed to see some real proof that he'd sold us out before I believed anything. And they didn't want to make me too upset, because I might still help figure out the Game. But it was one of those times when everybody's looking at you a little funny. Even Marena had doubts. And I couldn't blame her.

I tossed and turned for two hours, gave up on sleep, padded across the courtyard in my complimentary Crocs to the security desk, checked out one of their encrypted and permanently offline laptops, and flipped through a PDF of a 335-page DHI report on their money-trail investigation in the Disney World Horror. It was badly organized and heavily redacted, with "EYES ONLY" and "CLASSIFIED-LEVEL GRAY" stamps all over it, like it was a prop out of a spy movie. But the upshot was that both the 209 and 210 polonium isotopes dispersed in the attack had definitely been produced in the Soviet Union during the 1980s. Like weaponized anthrax, the particles had been ground so fine that they behaved as though they were almost lighter than air, and there was a thin hydrocarbon coating on the particles that had allowed them to bond to water droplets in the smog that day—which, incidentally, might also have been artificially seeded. All of this suggested a professional military product. The dispersion-regulation system had probably been fairly elaborate, including at least two 100-gallon pressure tanks and, probably, remote-controlled regulator valves with some kind of feedback meter. So far, though, no one had found the tanks or even pinpointed the exact center of the release, although it was certainly somewhere very near Lake Buena Vista.

The report also said that currently, Russian and Kazakh refiners produce about a hundred grams of polonium-210 per year, mainly for medical and antistatic applications. At least thirty times that amount had been released over Orlando, an amount that, on the commercial market, would cost over two and a half billion dollars. And that wasn't even counting the larger amount of the (cheaper) 209 isotope that was released at the same time. Somebody over there had to have been producing a lot more polonium than anybody knew about. And even if they'd produced it cheaply, and even if it had been bartered for and not paid for in cash, or even if Dr. X was, say, a direct heir or successor of the original producer, a huge amount of wealth must have changed hands somewhere along the line.

Of course, this was pretty much what we knew already, with just a little more detail. And of course the DHS and dozens of other U.S. and allied intelligence services were already following the same lead. But it didn't mean it wasn't the right thing for us to work on. We just had to do it better.

And we would, I thought. The advantage we had—besides the Sacrifice Game—was that we were actually trying to find the real perp, which all those other agencies didn't really care about. The only thing they actually took seriously was increasing their own funding. They needed to hire as many new people as possible, take as long as possible, and, most of all, spend as much money as possible. We were lean and efficient. Maybe Dr. X had moved some gold around, I thought. Unminted gold. I'd better go through all those mining companies again, I thought. Maybe something in Africa. I closed down the laptop—it insisted on checking out my iris print even to let me turn it off—and checked out CNN.

News wasn't good. In the U.S., unemployment had hit 25 percent. The administration had released an official statement that God was chastising us for our immorality and secularism. States like Texas and Kentucky had made silence mandatory in the morning and at noon during the president-led prayer sessions on the South Lawn of the White House, and today thirty million people had joined in by video. As of last week the army, navy, and marines had been restructured into a single service that would respond to a single command from the executive branch, and the air force and NASA were "soon to be folded into the new system." About two hundred thousand members of the armed services had been discharged, and their positions were being outsourced to private contractors. Moody's had downgraded U.S. Treasury bonds to a single A. Spot gold barreled through five thousand dollars an ounce. Yesterday, in Chester, Illinois, inmates had taken over the Menard Correctional Center, and instead of trying to negotiate, a SWAT team had lobbed in incendiary grenades and burned down the buildings with everyone inside them. So far the police's decision had received a 90 percent approval rating on YouCount.gov. Dearborn, Michigan, was now under sharia law. On the international scene, more than two million refugees had now crossed from Bangladesh into India. Our old friends Guatemala and Belize were at it again, although I already knew that, because now, on most days, you could hear them shelling each other's suspected troop positions along the border. Bioengineers at Zion-Tech, in Haifa, were claiming to have bred the spotless red heifer. And—and I realize it's almost getting comical at this point, at least for those with hard hearts, like mine—Hurricane Twinkie was strengthening over Cuba.

Of course, the good news for us with all this—the ill wind that was blowing us pretty good—was that with so much expletive-deleted going down, the Hippogriff incident might get lost in the shuffle. Laurence had said that the

U.S. three-letter agencies—and of course the Belizean, Guatemalan, Mexican, and British Protectoral intelligence services—were working so many cases right now that they probably couldn't spare more than a couple people to look at it. Especially when they figured it would probably turn out to be just some billionaire narcotrafico getting out of Guatemala in a hurry. As bizarre as it sounds, we might get off scot-free. Maybe the insurance companies would even reimburse us for the Hippogriff.

Just before sunrise I walked back to the lab. Marena and Taro were already there. Michael smelled like he was still there. That is, he hadn't slept. So, less than entirely welcoming, was Laurence Boyle, who—now that we'd had some apparent success—seemed to have gone back to being a cost-begrudging corporate bean pincher. Inside the bright white world of the glove box, they'd spread out the last six pages of one of the three screenfold books. Creepily, the unbroken lines of enciphered text were in my own handwriting. The pages had been photographed by the various cameras clustered on the lid of the box, and Jed_2's last letter—they were taking them in reverse order—had already been deciphered. Meanwhile, on the other side of the box, one of the sort of canopic jars had been opened, and gloved hands were scraping samples out of the scrungy-looking mass of resin inside it. In an hour they'd be getting couriered to Lotos Labs, in Salt Lake, for analysis.

"You want to read your note?" Michael asked.

I tried to think of something sarcastic to say, but finally I just nodded. He put the deciphered text up on the screen.

I felt very odd. I could imagine my own voice but not much of what my twin had done and seen. And on the one hand I felt embarrassed that he hadn't managed everything, but on the other hand I could hardly believe that I or he had managed as much as I or he had, and I couldn't help feeling proud of myself, even though, or maybe because, I personally hadn't had to do any of the work . . .

[deciphered]

NEW KEY WORD: JBNNUIIDSXJWNNQOBEOOFLCOPRTXSVQCD-
FEHJRMR

Jed DeLanda
On the road to Flayed Hill

(Monte Alban, Oaxaca)
Chocula Team
Ix Ruinas, Alta Verapaz, RG

Wednesday, March 31, AD 664, about 11:00 A.M.

Dear Marena, Taro, Michael, Jed_1, et al.:

Forty-six of us, the inner remnants of our division, made it through the suburbs of Teotihuacan, and eighteen suns ago we reached 14 Wounded's men at the rendezvous point. 14 has lost nearly half of his division, and his scouts said the remains of the Puma clans, who have reorganized under Severed Right Hand, attacked and slaughtered whatever Eagle and Rattler Children are still in the Teotihuacan Valley. Now they are coming after us. A circle of destruction and fire, much of it apparently self-inflicted, seems to be spreading outward from the ruins of the metropolis, like a growing sinkhole. We pass through villages that have starved themselves to death because they believe that, since the world has ended, there's no reason to eat.

However, there are still living people everywhere. Many of them are now homeless, or uninterested in returning to their homes, and they attach themselves to our caravan. So our numbers continue to grow.

Most of them are not fighters. But this morning, Lady Koh has sent out about a hundred heralds—I'm using the word to convey a job title that combines "runners," "recruiters," and "missionaries"— to rustle up combat-age vingtaines out of whatever groups of Star Rattler pilgrims there still are in the unburnt parts of the lake country. They're also taking word to the heads of a few towns that have converted en masse to the path of the Rattler that Lady Koh wants them to meet her at Akpaktapec, a Oaxacan Rattler town two days west. We'll gather as many converted families around us as possible as a buffer and then march east to Flayed Hill, where the Cloud House has offered us sanctuary as fellow enemies of the Pumas. From there, if possible, we'll take an inland route, well off the beaten path, east and south to Ix.

I suppose all this is to say that my chances of reaching Ix again are low. So I've decided to put this first cross here, ahead of schedule, before something worse happens. I haven't yet mastered what I came to master. But I hope (obviously) that there's enough information in the notes for you to reconstruct the Game and that the Game drug components make their way through the years sufficiently intact for you to reconstruct them chemically or even clonally. To say something cringeworthily corny, if they do, maybe this will all be worthwhile, despite what things look like from here. Anyway, sorry for the mournful tone—more later if possible—

Best,
JDL$_2$
Encls.

P.S. Jed—could you pick up some more of those Pyramides for Maximón? Thanks, J$_2$.

(66)

"Now, this is the burning, the clearing," I said in Ch'olan. I took a plug of tobacco, chewed it, and rubbed some into the stain on my inner thigh.

"Now I am borrowing the breath of today, of Ox la hun Ok, Ox la uaxac K'ayab, 13 Dog, 18 Tortoise, of the tenth sun of the third tun of the nineteenth uinal of the nineteenth k'atun of the twelfth b'ak'tun, at noon on the eighth of April in the Year of Our Lord 2012, the sixty-first anniversary of my mother's birth, and two hundred and fifty-seven suns before the last sun of the last b'ak'tun. Now I ask the saint of today, Santa Constantina, and I ask Saint Simón, whose name to us who are his friends is Maximón, to guard this square of earth, to watch this field."

I rooted myself at the hub of the revolving worlds. *"Quinchapo wa 'k'ani, pley saki piley,"* I said. "This is the sowing, the planting, now I am scattering the red skulls, white skulls."

I clicked SCATTER. Three hundred and sixty so-called virtual seeds rattled down onto the 2.8 million OLED pixels that covered one wall of the dark, ergonomically luxurious isolation room, which was forty feet under the Stake Hyperbowl's playing field. LEON hesitated, lost in thought.

I stretched back in the new, comfy, tacky, expensive shiatsu recliner. An itch flared up under the blood-pressure cuff on my left arm and I scratched it. Well, here we are again, I thought. I should have known it would all come down to the online world in the end. Because, after all, I'm still just a code monkey. We all are. Toiling away in the data mines. Drag. I should've been the one that got to see it. Our ancient world, I mean. Yeah, shoulda been Jed$_2$. Lucky bastard. He saw the whole thing. Jewels and muls. Ocellated turkeys and turquoise ocelots. Feather canyons every—

LEON beeped.

It moved a red skull one tun northward, to April 28, and tagged it as *k'ak'ilix*. That is, kind of Anything Can Happen Day. Like on the Mouse Club. YOUR MOVE, it said in the File window.

Hmm.

Over the last three weeks we'd set up LEON so that it could work as a search engine. That is, in addition to the Game window, you could also open windows on the data its autodidactic engines were looking at, and you could use your own moves to steer its searches. Taro's kids had also improved the interface, so that when we played against LEON we'd have more of a feeling of playing a human opponent. Still, the most LEON could do was make the correct moves. That is, not the insightful moves, or even the best moves. Just the correct ones, what you'd call the "book moves," if there were a book. And the thing is, in a high-level game of anything—chess, Go, Cootie—the book move isn't always that different from a bad move. Sometimes it's even the losing move.

Taro had been visibly disappointed at how things had turned out, how there was no algorithm, no secret formula, nothing that you could teach to a computer and have it solve all your problems. Taro'd wanted some kind of closure. LEON was his baby. He'd wanted that bundle to contain some solutions to his equations, and he'd wanted it so much he almost expected it. Instead, all we got was a whole lot more game lore and game strategies and those five jars of drugs and critter parts. Which wouldn't increase LEON's computing power any more than pouring coffee on its hard drive. I tried to tell him how playing the Game isn't any one thing you can point to, how it was a whole way of being, how there's no secret to it any more than there's a secret to playing the cello, but he wasn't in a mood to hear it. He was a total scientist. If a problem didn't have a solution you could write on a blackboard, it wasn't part of his *Welterklärungsmodell.*

And really, why should we even have thought it would work on a computer anyway? The Game had been designed as a lens for the mind, not for some as yet uninvented gadget. To get a computer to play it the way a human would, you'd have to build a computer as massively parallel as a human brain. And even LEON was still a long way from that level. No matter how much more computers know than we do, and no matter how fast they process it, to them it's still just zeros and ones.

Naturally, as soon as we read about the drugs and before they'd even started analyzing them, I was practically trying to eat the stuff right out of the jar, like Marshmallow Fluff. And naturally they didn't let me.

I hadn't thought they'd be so uptight about it. I kept saying that we should take Jed$_2$ at his word, estimate the dosage he'd taken, and give it a shot. But the good folks at Lotos Labs—the psychopharmaceutical arm of the Warren Research Group—wanted to test the stuff first. They said they'd concluded that the two active components in the "tzam lic experience" were a bufoteninlike tryptamine and a benzamide compound that was similar to artificial ampakines like CX717. Together, they somehow enabled a vastly increased level of neuronal firing in certain cortices of the brain. Maybe more importantly, the first tomographic tests on sea slugs recorded "unprecedented growth in synaptic plasticity," that is, a huge increase in the number of new connections, and the types and lengths of new connections, made in the brain during the drugs' period of bioavailablity. Over time, the stuff would actually change the shape of your brain.

By the seventh they'd synthesized enough for animal testing. The first observation was that there seemed to be different phases as the drugs worked through the system. During the first phase it massively increased geographical memory and sense of direction. They spun the sea slugs around on potter's wheels in a dark room and put them back into a new, lightless tank, and within a minute or so they stopped spinning around and swam to the east corner, where the feeder had been in the old tank. We watched videos of mice swimming through water labyrinths, and on their second try the little bastards remembered the way through the most complicated mazes the lab had room to build. The monkeys did even more amazing things. Normal macaques can walk on tightropes, but the doped-up ones could walk on wobbling tightropes, in the dark, and then, on command, jump onto another tightrope they'd walked over an hour before. Lisuarte said the equilibrioceptual and muscular effects reminded her of propranolol, which is a beta blocker that a lot of classical musicians take before concerts. During this phase, IQ increased slowly, to over a standard deviation above the individual's baseline. This even happened with the slugs—which do have IQs, by the way, although none of them are quite Goethe level. The macaques learned dozens of new hand signs. They did jigsaw puzzles that would have stumped an average five-year-old. They staged a mass escape from their cages by having one of them pull a fire alarm on bath day. It was a whole *Secret of NIMH* scene.

But as the intelligence phase peaked, performance began to increase in other, odder areas, skills that aren't covered in IQ tests. For instance, the monkeys became hypersensitive to color. In general, people can only remember and distinguish a few thousand colors. People who work in, say, the textile printing industry can do around ten thousand. Macaques only manage a few hundred. But in the third hour of exposure to the drugs, that number quadrupled. Another thing was that the slugs and, to a lesser but significant extent, the mammals became much more sensitive to subsonic vibrations, and even to electrical currents in the water around them or running through the floors of their cages. When they groomed each other, one spark of static could make them scream. As they increased the dosage, the lab people also started seeing negative effects—that is, besides the usual and expected nausea, cold sweats, and sniffles. "In *Macaca mulatta*, onychophagia and trichophagia progressed to chronicity," the report said. In other words, they started biting their nails and chewing and eating their fur. And "in *Aplysia californica*, repeated large doses led to cases of acute autosarcophagy." That is, the slugs ate themselves until they died.

Dr. Lisuarte and the Lotos people were in an awkward position. Certainly they weren't strangers to the lucrative world of performance-enhancing drugs. In fact, there was talk that we might have done some inadvertent bioprospecting. Maybe a damped-down version of the stuff would have a bright future as a civilian medication. But like a lot of big companies Warren Group was heavily invested in the drug prohibition scam, to the point at which most of them probably really believed in it. And the whole Mormon thing didn't help either. Basically, they were as square as robot shit. And this was despite the fact that everybody around here was a total dope head. Michael Weiner popped oxycontin like Pez when he wasn't chugging Bundy out of the flask. Tony Sic still took steroids and androstenedione even though he'd stopped playing semipro soccer four years ago, and the lab's interns were smoking sativa landrace and having fat-white-geek ecstasy parties six nights a week. Even Taro took modafinil. Marena'd gone back to a pack a day. The construction workers were cranked to the eyeballs, the construction workers' kids were huffing toluene, and at least half of the Mormon staff loaded up on vodka and Red Bull when they thought no one was looking. So you'd think there'd have been some skepticism about the party line. But no.

Marena—talking to me from Colorado, over a new set of encrypted cell phones that she said the firm didn't know about—told me she wanted to push the suits to loosen up a bit, too, but that I shouldn't try to force the issue and risk getting kicked out of the project. "Boyle and those guys are just a bunch of accountants," she said. "Collectively, they have about as much curiosity as a jar of stale kimchi."

"Uh, yeah," I went.

"But whenever Lindsay sees the reports he'll lean on them and they'll come around." She also said she was worried about my health if I started popping the stuff unsupervised. I said that was sweet of her, but that she was taking on a Sisyphean task.

"Just hang in there," she said.

At any rate, on March 10 the results came in on a course of toxicity tests on a line of transgenic Yucatán micropigs. They'd gotten pretty smart on the stuff, and so far they hadn't manifested any serious health problems. "And biochemically, they're more than half human," Lisuarte said. It seemed fair, since behaviorally, humans are more than half pig. Of course, my guess was that Lotos were already doing human trials, probably in India, but that they didn't want anybody outside of the lab to know about it. Especially not a loose cannon like me. Anyway, they said they'd give us the go-ahead in a week.

But they didn't. The calendar gears ground forward toward 4 Ahau without us, or anyone else, getting any closer to closing in on any doomster. And outside our little enclave the world was degenerating.

On the eighteenth the Lotos people finally sent down nearly a half-liter of each of the Game drug components. "I told you they would," Lisuarte said. "They're as worried as we are." And she had a point. They were corporate, they were risk-averse, they were a bunch of lily-white, red-state, chicken-pluckin', shotgun-totin', penny-wise, pound-foolish, just-say-no Republican douchebags, but in the end, they were people. They had families, they had investments, they had ambitions, they had medical needs . . . and like us, they understood the math.

Releases got drawn up and signed. Doctors from Salt Lake Central came in to examine me and, I guessed, cover up and/or take the heat if it all went south. People put papers in front of me and I signed them. Probably I shouldn't have, but there was no time for the niceties. On the nineteenth Lisuarte gave me the green light. I could try thirty mgs of the combined chronolytic and topolytic drugs as long as I was monitored nine ways from Sunday. And then, the first time they gave me the stuff, I got too messed up to play.

Symptoms included vertigo, nausea, scintillating auras—like with a migraine—blackout, tachycardia, and presuicidal depression. When they came into the isolation room I'd slipped out of the chair and, according to Dr. Lisuarte, I'd bitten through my lower lip and was trying to gouge my right calf open with a Logitech ball mouse. They bundled me off to the infirmary. I told them those symptoms weren't anything out of the ordinary for me, that in fact I went through all of them a few times a day, on a good day, and that I just needed to take another dose and go back to work. But instead they flushed the stuff out of my system and wouldn't let me near the lab.

I was pretty upset. That is, even after the shit wore off and my mood was back to baseline, I was still pretty upset. I'd gone through fire, water, wind, and human excrement to get the stuff—well, actually, Jed_2 had taken most of the abuse, but still—and now I wouldn't even be able to use it. Lisuarte guessed the high-alkaloid component might be interacting badly with my meds. Specifically, it was blocking too much reuptake of glutamic acid, which led to excess nitrogen, excitotoxicity, self-injurious ideation, and a swag bag of other disagreeable effects. Over the next week she replaced my trusty old crew of behavior modifiers with a Don the Beachcomber Zombie cocktail of newer, meaner behavior modifiers. When I'd looked over the dosage list, it was too complicated for me to make much sense of, so I'd run it past my regular doctor back in Miami. He said it sounded like "hammering in a two-penny nail with a battering ram," as he put it in his folksy way, but I wanted to be a sport and went on it anyway. Amazingly, the new stuff seemed to work. Just a few days later we were getting the effect we wanted: It seemed like there wasn't much of the old Jed left. Instead of the angsty, vindictive troglodyte I used to enjoy being, there was a cautiously optimistic and rather bland individual also named Jed. In fact, the new me was almost imperturbable. For instance—just as an example—Marena had left for the States on the tenth to see Max, and she'd said she was going to make it back in a week, but here it was almost a month later and she still wasn't here. She'd said it was because it wasn't safe to travel. And it was true that things were seriously messed up. People were fleeing some cities and streaming into others. Customs checkpoints had waits of over ten hours. Airlines were hoarding jet fuel. Most major airports had turned a third of their hangars into enforced quarantine camps. Still, it sounded like excuses to me. If Marena gave the Warren gang a chance to work their magic, she could get back here. In fact, it seemed kind of out of character for her to be away while the rest of us thrashed on her project. Maybe she knew something I didn't. Maybe she couldn't stand the sight of me anymore. Maybe she just didn't want to pull Max out of school. We'd kind of moved in together, if you could count sleeping in the same prefab dorm room moving in, and I'd thought we'd gotten pretty close, but then when she'd taken off, I wasn't so sure. Normally I would have been raging and raving and flying up there and panting after her like a cowardly dog. But now, when I thought about her, I'd just get wistful for a second and then go grimly back to what I was doing, just like any normal person meekly accepting his daily ration of despair. Also, No Way still hadn't turned up. I'd been freaked out about him at first and tried to go back to find him, but now I was just pretty calmly waiting to see what happened. Maybe he'd been sucked into a black hole, like I had.

Also, I wasn't sure about my legal status. At least six different agencies were still investigating the Hippogriff Incident—hmm, good title for a new posthumous Robert Ludlum novel—and they'd finally made the connection to Executive Solutions, which meant that the rest of us might eventually get linked to it. And to top it all off, they'd let Sic and a few of the other trainees try the Game drugs, and on them they were working well. Sic had been studying Jed$_2$'s notes, and he'd taken to the new Game layout, and then, with the blood lightning, he'd gotten quite a bit ahead of me. Normally I would have been insane with jealousy, doomster or no doomster. Now, I just kept slogging.

My second bout with the drugs went better. I played two games on the stuff, and I cooked. By the fifth dose I was as good with four stones as I had been with two. I asked about upping the dosage. Lisuarte said no. Nine days ago I'd completed a game using five stones. Now I was making progress with six, and yesterday I'd even glimpsed the bewildering world of seven. But like I think I said, seven stones isn't just twice as hard as six, or seven times as hard, or forty-nine times as hard. It's about 7!, that is, 5,040 times as hard. So, realistically, I couldn't imagine that at this rate I'd ever get to eight stones, let alone nine, even in a lifetime, let alone in a couple of months. Some of the time, when I read in Jed$_2$'s letters about what that Lady Koh person could do, not just playing with nine stones but using live animals for the runners, and then doing whatever that business was with the spiderweb—I almost thought he might have been exaggerating. Except, why would he? Or why would I?

On the twenty-second, Laurence said he, and that meant Lindsay, wanted me to work on the Disney World Horror. I said I'd been planning to go directly to the Doomster and appealed to Taro and Marena. We decided I'd put in two days looking for Dr. X. If we delivered him, they said, we could write our own ticket with the DHS. After that, anything we said about 4 Ahau would immediately get taken seriously, no matter how odd it might seem. It sounded plausible, although I was sure there was more going on. Still, I'd already gone over Jed$_2$'s notes about Dr. X from his game with Lady Koh, and they were definitely provoking some associational flashes. Although, reading them over again, I found myself getting pretty annoyed with him. They were only about forty thousand words long, for one thing, which isn't a lot when you're trying to remember every little detail because it could possibly turn out to be important later. And then there was the style. There was a smirking slacker pomposity about the prose that set my teeth on edge. Although I realize that he/I was working under difficult conditions, but still—well, one gets annoyed with oneself a lot, even when one hasn't split in two. Anyway, I kept going over and over the Disney World Horror game, about how he, or let's just say I, had gotten a strong feeling that Dr. X would be someone whose name I knew well but whom I hadn't met in person, someone who was still alive, someone who'd been everywhere and back twice, maybe someone we'd already discounted, or maybe somebody I wasn't considering because it seemed too obvious. And as Jed$_2$ had said, he was someone "who was once half in the light but is now again in darkness."

Huh.

That day I got to my cubicle a bit late and scattered the first batch of seeds at noon. I tried to integrate the Game with LEON's search engines. Secret contracts, I thought. Cayman banks stuff. Functionaries living beyond their means. Jets, yachts, and Bugattis turning up in the wrong backyards. Gambling winnings. Wives suddenly inheriting a hundred times more than anyone thought they would. Antiques, artwork, old jewelry with new stones. Anything. Come on. *Quid bonum?* Follow the bucks—

Damn. Blocked.

I ran through it again, sifting one cyclopean block of data through another and then chasing down the points where they crossed. Hopping down the money trail. Come on. Forward. Into the Value of Cash. Mammon to the right of them. Wondering, wondering. Forward. It's definitely one person in charge, I thought. The whole thing was too coherent for groupthink. And as far as who benefited goes, well, that was easy, in a way. Every military contractor in the world benefited. Say it's one of them. Which one is it? Whose shares went up the most? Or second-most, say. Come on. Say it's Corporation A. Except Corporation B owns most of Corporation A. But maybe it's Corporation C that's really going to benefit, because they're going to get bought out by Corporation B. Or maybe it's Corporation D, which is going to make a deal to buy all of them. This way. That way. That way. This way. Hippity, hoppity. Chains of causes. Chains of effects. Russian nesting dolls within nesting dolls. Russian nesting-doll factories full of Siamese nesting dolls. Within Triamese and Tetranese nesting dolls. Come on. Every chain has a crummy link—

Hmm.

There was definitely cash there, and it was swirling around something, an outline of a shape—a head, maybe . . . and I could almost see it emotionally, that is, there wasn't really a visual, but I got a sense of hatred around it, maybe not even so much from the shape itself, but . . .

Yeah. Other people's hatred.

He's an outcast.

Come on. Think.

Someone wealthy and powerful whom nobody likes. Someone loathed even by the people on his own side. Someone who was beaten up on the playground. Someone with a twisted face. Someone who'd confirm my worst suspicions. Someone who's already considered truly evil. By most people, anyway. Some exiled imam? That guy from Myanmar? No, that's not it. Damn it, am I just getting stupid in my middle age?

Maybe I couldn't see it because it was too much what I'd expected. Maybe I'd already discounted it, like the way you might be looking for your car keys all over because you'd checked all your pockets, and then after turning the house inside out you find them in your pocket because in the first ten seconds of looking for them you'd misidentified them as, say, your house keys and not your car keys, and that was enough . . . well, you know what I mean. Okay, come on. Forward. LEON goes, I go. Chain of events. Chain, chain, chain, chain of food. LEON goes, I go. LEON goes—

Whoa. There it is.

Eighteen billion euros. And, really, it was just one transaction. Details clicked reluctantly into place like the tumblers of some big rusty old antique lock. The door groaned open—

Not Richard. The company.

Gotcha.

(67)

I'd kind of expected that the DHS and all the other agencies would have been pretty well paid off and that nothing would happen after we fingered the culprit besides, maybe, them trying to bump us off. But apparently the government still wasn't quite so monolithic because, amazingly, on the morning of the twenty-eighth, the FBI conducted simultaneous raids on Halliburton offices in Houston and Bakersfield, on the KBR building in Harris County, and on twelve offices and a hundred and ten servers owned by either Dyn-Corp or by shell firms controlled by the Carlisle group. 243 people were arrested. And according to Laurence, who'd gotten it from Lindsay, who'd undoubtedly gotten it either from someone very much on the inside or from God, they'd found files relating to aerosolized polonium in four of the raids, and there was a memo in one of the servers that talked about how the centralization of the military was "our number-one rainmaking priority." I guess the money trail was pretty damning when you had all the details. The short version was that they used a hawala system, which basically just means that everybody's a member of some big Islamic clan that all trust each other and don't write anything down. No actual money actually got shipped anywhere. Years before—in 2006, in fact—a couple of hotel owners in Dubai had hired some Moscow-based contractors to build some private highways and airstrips, and they'd let them overcharge a little. The contractors used the money to pay off debts to another firm—probably one of the firms that had merged into Lukoil—which had inherited the undocumented polonium 210 from the original manufacturer. And then the Carlisle people had undercharged the hotel chain a little for construction work on developments in Jordan and Lebanon. And this was spread out over dozens of handshake deals. So you'd think with all that, they could have kept everything under the Isfahan rug.

But the fact is that eighteen billion is still a lot, even these days, and most of it will eventually be represented in some deposits somewhere. And with new banking laws and improving search engines, it's getting easier and easier to search for deposited amounts that match estimates of missing amounts. Once LEON and his counterparts at the DHS knew what they were looking for, they just kept crunching data until eventually they had two patterns—kind of like two thumbprints—that matched enough to convince the judge.

Even so, though, they hadn't come up with a warrant for Cheney himself—he was still just a "person of interest"—and, as might be expected, he'd apparently been tipped off and was not to be found.

And he's not likely to be, I thought. The cat has more undisclosed locations than the Atlas Missile Program. Even if we worked on him full time, they'd just keep moving him around and we'd probably always be a step behind. Well, I did my job. It was unsatisfying, but things are unsatisfying. Anyway, there'd probably be more coming out about it all later. And that'd bring a lot of other people into the picture and maybe somebody'd drop the dime on him. So far most of the media response to the raids was just speculation, but supposedly there was going to be a big leak later in the week.

Or I'll blow the whistle myself, I thought. Just as soon as I get a break from some more immediate problems.

Things in the wide world had gotten flaky and flakier. Bangladesh was almost completely without electricity, food, water, or law. The Sword of Allah was attacking American bases in Pakistan. FEMA said it had underestimated the number of terminal cases in Florida and that they were now projecting sixty thousand fatalities within the next few years, which would bring the total death toll from the Disney World Horror to a little over a hundred thousand. Or probably about 124,030 people, I thought, give or take. There weren't enough facilities to take care of them all in the U.S., so the more advanced cases were being shipped overseas, although the State of Florida was already building the world's largest and most advanced hospice park. So far there'd been fourteen copycat alarms in major cities mimicking the Orlando attack. All of them had turned out to be dry, that is, without any real polonium, but the evacuations had cost billions. Conventional explosives, though, were enjoying a resurgence. Two days ago, eighty people had been killed in a second suicide bombing in DeKalb, Illinois. Like a lot of the new bombings, the DeKalb incident had been in two parts—that is, there'd been one large bomb that had taken out a whole dorm building and that the perpetrator had watched through binoculars, and then when that was done, he'd blown himself up with something about the size of a hand grenade. Investigators were pretty sure it was what they were calling "unaffiliated," that is, it wasn't ideological but part of a rising trend of suicide bombings by regular folks, people who were just fed up and wanted to take as many classmates, local officials, or coworkers as possible along with them and who, a few years ago, would have to have been satisfied with the handful of people they'd be able to shoot. And worst of all, there was evidence from the Sacrifice Game that the Doomster was on the move.

By the last day of March LEON's probability engines were indicating that the world—very roughly speaking—had reached a permanent critical state. That is, human history was at a point where any small disturbance might trigger an avalanche that would flatten the whole sand pile. In terms of the Doomster progression, the implication was that even if we identified and stopped the first (and still hypothetical) lone Doomster, pretty soon there'd be another like him. And there would be more, and at an increasing rate, maybe one every two or three years, say, for a while, and then one every month, and then one every day, and so on into inevitability. And for that matter, even if the first doomster's actions weren't a total success—even if it only affected one continent, say—a "casualty event" on that scale was "liable to reduce the functioning of all societies to the point that they will be severely vulnerable to further stresses." Or as Ashley$_2$ put it, the world's immune system was drastically compromised, and a cold could be fatal.

I kept saying we needed to get more serious about the dosage. Lisuarte kept holding back. Around April 4 I started to get the feeling that we might already be too late. Or we would be very shortly. It was just a feeling, but I didn't like that date LEON had flagged, April 20. This wasn't the first time the date had come up. And each time it felt to me like it had a gray halo around it. And it wasn't just because it was Columbine Day. It had the sense of a point of no return. Maybe the Doomster was going to use another timed virus, set to go symptomatic on 4 Ahau, and was going to release it into the population on the twenty-eighth. Or maybe it was a conventional bomb or some other chain reaction that got triggered that day. Whatever it was, it felt like our zero hour might be right now. It might even have been yesterday. It was time for the *D* word. *Drastic.*

It's easy to steal from someone who trusts you. Fooling Dr. Lisuarte would have been hard. But Taro had access to the dope fridge, too, and his lab wasn't exactly the world's tightest ship. And now Ashley$_2$ and I were, well, we had a little thing going on, what with Marena's absence and A$_2$'s husband being stranded in Beijing Province and the world going all *Dawn of the Dead* on us and everything. It was kind of a boffery of convenience. A_2 wasn't the sort of person one would notice or anything, but actually if you got her glasses and lab coat off and put her in a dim room, she could pass for Ziyi Zhang's chunkier twin. She was trying to learn the Game—she was about the worst player in the place—and I was giving her special lessons with benefits. It wasn't a big deal, except I got her saving me fractions of the Game drugs out of her own doses. As of today, I had about 480 extra mgs—the topolytic component had to be in liquid form, so the stuff was in tiny 40 mg scintillation vials—and I'd loaded 300, ten of my standard doses, into an AirJet helium tube. There weren't any cameras in the isolation room—not that I could find, anyway, and anyway things still weren't quite that uptight around here. Yet. I detaped the little steel cylinder from my underarm, slid it down under my elastic waist-thing to my right, nontobaccoed inner thigh, and squoze the button. There was a sound like slowly unscrewing a cold Shasta bottle and a feeling like a shard of ice materializing in my great saphenous vein and then melting away.

If I'd dosed it right, in twenty minutes it would bring me up to roughly one-fifth of the amount that we'd calculated Lady Koh had taken during her last game with Jed_2. Of course, she'd had a lifetime to build up her tolerance. The Lotoslanders had said this much could be fatal or that it might blow out my hippocampus. But they were worryworts. Anyway, if I start having a seizure, Lisuarte's staff'll rush in and sedate me and nurse me back to normal. They can do anything these days. Right? Anyway, we've got bigger problems. Focus.

I moved the first of my nine skulls to April 28 and displaced LEON's seed. Take that, glassbrain. THINKING, his File window said. I looked around from my new location. Or rather, "looked" is a bit of a misleading word because now that I was feeling the blood lightning sizzling through my arteries I was really seeing, if you could call it that, with all those little shivers and flutterings, feeling that every atom of my body had a paired particle on the game board. Maybe it's like the way blind people with those implanted cameras and glossopharyngeal electrodes see with their tongues—

BEEP.

LEON moved two forward, toward the center.

Hmm.

I moved my skull forward. There was that feeling of climbing stairs, of both expansion and contraction. It's hard to describe, but emotionally it's like what it would feel like if you'd spent, say, your whole life in a single small city, and you knew your way around but you'd never looked at a map of the place, and now you were climbing, say, a high radio tower that they'd just put up in the center of town, and for the first time you looked down at your hometown from high overhead. In a few seconds you'd understand things you never realized were even there to understand. You'd see that places that had seemed far away from each other were close together, streets that you'd assumed were perpendicular were actually disturbingly off-angle, parks that you thought were squares were actually irregular trapezoids, familiar buildings that had seemed huge were smaller than less familiar ones that had seemed small, and it would all be a new, different order of understanding, not something you could ever get from just living in the place even if you lived there another hundred lifetimes.

The trouble with this picture, though, is that it sounds as though it might be exhilarating, or even fun. But it's not, it's just scary. It was especially scary this time, of course. But it's always scary. Your apprehension increases with your perception. And in fact it has to.

When I'd read about Lady Koh's animals, it didn't surprise me as much as it seemed to have surprised Jed$_2$. Really, I'd been using myself as a monkcy all this time. That is, to really play the runner, that is, the skulls, you have to have some fear there. Even if you're playing for a client you don't much care about, you have to scare yourself. You need to look around you the way a prey animal does, seeing a predator in every shadow. And as your field of understanding widens, instead of feeling more powerful, your fear increases. It becomes fear not just for yourself but for your fellow prey animals, the members of your herd that you now see are all around you and too numerous to count. Instead of spotting escape routes you realize how many prey animals surround you and how far it is to any safe haven. You start comprehending how unlikely and contingent your consciousness is, and the farther you get up that staircase, that sense of tenuousness just keeps increasing. You start seeing more of the present, and more of the past, and then even some of the future, and then more possible futures and possible pasts—all the trillions of times you weren't born, for instance—and then even counterfactual presents and nonexistent futures and impossible worlds, universes where light is slow and local and gravity is fast and far-reaching, where two plus two equals one, or even where two plus two equals, say, grapefruit. And it's not intriguing. It's terrifying.

But if you can get past the vertigo of all that, you do start to notice a few patterns. I minimized the game board window on the video wall and took a squint at the scrolling swarms of raw information. Right now LEON was sifting through data relating to people with the same names and making sure they were assigned to the right individual. And by data, I mean all data—occupations, genealogies, online and RL webs of acquaintance, credit reports, purchases, school records, birthdays, photos, hobbies acknowledged and inferred, browser histories, haplotype estimates, cross-references, medical data, an Iguazu of facts, near facts, and falsities in every language on earth, human and machine. I was seeing the closest available thing to what God would see, even closer than what Google sees, since what Google looks at is determined by whatever all these not-too-bright human beings are looking for. Any really purposeful data mining has to be a lot more selective. You need to focus. And I don't mean focus on some little detail, like in a word search. It's more like those Magic Eye pictures, where you need to focus a couple of feet below the surface of the paper, and if you can keep from getting distracted by all the little squiggles, you start seeing a shape—or rather, it's more accurate to call it a space than a shape, since you're really seeing only the space, that is, if you only use one eye you can't see it at all—and if you can keep focusing on that shape, it coalesces out of the noise, it gets rounder and deeper and smoother, and at some point you start to realize what it is. As the Steersman's dust soaked into my nervous system, it was as though I was slowly opening my second eye; I was beginning to make out an outline of something in the east, and now the muscles of my iris were slowly focusing out beyond the cataract of names and dates and amounts and all the other quintillions of grains of garbage that constitute the monstrous world, and I was almost beginning to see what it was, something made up of all those things but not really of them at all, something direful looming up ahead.

(68)

LEON moved. I moved. He moved. I moved, toward the shape. It felt like it might be a ruined pyramid or a dead volcano, but it was horribly eroded, full of fissures and debris flows. And there was something odd just a little below the peak, a protuberance like a gigantic wart. LEON moved.

Hmm.

I moved, plodding through the blizzard of data. All this noise and so little signal, I thought. It was like TV snow in your eyes. He moved. Hmm. Not this. Not that. It was getting harder to feel my way forward. Fewer and fewer solid spots in the swamp.

He moved. Hypothetical moves faded in and out of clarity ahead of me. I moved. Now it felt as though I was climbing high, irregular, eroded steps. There were big shapes around, but I couldn't see them, or rather I couldn't visualize them, since it's not really like you can see the landscape of the Game anyway, it's more like you get an inner sense of it. Maybe it's like that blind mountain climber who keeps setting all those records in Tibet. Since he can't get a view of things all at once, he has to grab bits of information sequentially, feeling his way along traverses between shapeless heights and gaping un-knowns, and then assemble an interior model of the route, laboriously and one-dimensionally, like stringing beads. The steps rose toward 4 Ahau. He moved. I moved. Up, up. Come on. A sound, or rather a feeling like the mem-ory of a sound, came from somewhere near the apex, a faint irregular murmur that reminded me of something I'd heard a long time ago, something—hmm. The memory was on the tip of my mental tongue but I couldn't quite bring it up. Don't worry about it. Focus. Now I was starting to sense that there was a hollow near the peak of the cone, something like what we call a *k'otb'aj* in Ch'olan, a cave-in-the-sky. LEON moved, trying to force me back down the slope. I brought in another skull and set it down. He countermoved. Hmm. He goes, I go, he goes . . . okay. I moved up the slope.

He moved. I moved. Up, up. It felt as though there was rusty red stone, like Badlands pumice, crumbling under my feet. Up. There was already a sense of being way above the tree line. He moved. I moved. Up. Now it was so high that not even the condors came here. I was on the west side of the mountain, where there was still some warmth from the wrinkled sun. It was a different sun, not the daily sun. It was the sun of the b'ak'tun, the 394-year sun, which wouldn't reach its zenith until 4 Ahau. And, since we were on the other side of the world—the reflected side, you could say—it was rising in the west.

Up, up. He goes, I go. I moved.

Ahhh.

There was a pause.

It was as though I was on a level landing or plateau, or what you'd call a *tablero* if you interpreted the mound as the ruin of a Teotihuacan-style mul. Not far ahead there was a wide opening in the level shelf, a ragged, lopsided oval with a hint of a deep shaft slanting down into the mountain, and then just beyond it the next rise of the mountain, the *talud*, sloped up at a gentle angle . . . and then, at the edge of the next *tablero*, it was as though I could just make out a gigantic gibbous boulder, dull orange in the low nonlight. I tapped my way forward. He goes. I go. Okay.

The sound got louder, or I should say the feeling of sound intensified. It was a deep bleating, a fleshy trumpeting, and it definitely came from the pit. And somehow you could tell from the curve of the echoes that the cave was bigger inside than that mountain was outside, and that even so it was crowded with beings. They were like bats but not bats. They might be hanging in family clusters, it seemed, like bats, or at least clustering in families, and you could tell there were as many of them as there are bats in a big cave, in fact more, uncountable trillions of them, even. But they didn't sound like bats. They were bigger. And somehow I got a sense that they were hairless. What were they? The sound reminded me of something, something from my childhood, but it wasn't a Guatemala thing, it was something—oh, okay. Got it.

It was the *Eumetopias jubatus*. Around the third year I was living with them, the Ødegårds brought me along on a church trip to San Francisco and then to Seattle, and then on the way back the bus stopped at the Sea Lion Caves, which is a privately owned roadside attraction near a town called Florence on the Oregon coast. In the spring there are about three hundred Steller's sea lions gathering and mating on the rock shelves. You take this elevator

down from the cliff scarp, and then you go through this passage in the limestone to this rock-hewn balcony that looks out over the grotto, with the waves
the equivalent of about three stories below you and the cave roof about ten
stories above, and you try to make some sense out of all these churning hum-
mocks of fat and bone. The cows shriek as the two-thousand-pound bulls
mount them, and the bachelor and dominant bulls bellow at each other for
hours on end, and the roars resonate and echo off the wet stone. These days,
when you think *loud and terrifying sound*, you think man-made, jackham-
mers dismantling a mountaintop, monster jets warming their engines, artil-
lery and explosions and whatever. But even though the sound of that cave is
100 percent natural—in fact it probably hasn't changed for millions of years,
in fact it's probably not much different from the booming leks of, say, dxatri-
mas or ankylosaurs, or herds of pentaceratopsians—it was still as horrifying
as any sound you'll ever hear, something one almost can't bear and certainly
can't forget. I inched forward. Something in the sound made it seem that the
beings were stirring, stretching their wings, getting ready to swarm out when
this sun was buried on 4 Ahau. They'd stream out almost endlessly, through
tuns and k'atuns and bundles of bundles of b'ak'tunob, and they'd spread over
the world and grow, and live. If you haven't watched bats leave a big cave, I
can't describe it, and if you have there's no need to describe it. But the scariest
thing about it is how endless they seem. You think that inside the earth, it's
all just bats.

I felt my way around the opening. By now I could tell that all the bleatings
and bellowings had too much variance and repetition to be random, and I
paused on that square for a minute, trying to make out what they were saying.

Well, it was some language, all right, I thought. But not one I'd heard, in
fact I'd bet it wasn't even a human language, in fact some of the syllables reminded me of the curse language the howler monkeys use when . . . Hmm. If
I could hear it a little more clearly, if I could stay here a little longer, I almost
think I could figure it out . . . but LEON had moved again, and LEON didn't
stop thinking while my clock was running, and the sun was inching west toward 4 Ahau, and I HAVE TO MOVE ON, I thought, and I pushed my eighth
skull forward two squares, trying not to respond too defensively. Don't let
LEON get the initiative back, I thought. Now I was past the pit, at a point
where it was as though I could look up at the boulder hanging over me. From
here you couldn't believe it was still supported by something. If it ever slid off
its perch and rolled down, it'd pop me like a tick under a steel boot heel. But

more importantly, it would plug up that cave mouth, and those guys would never, ever get out. LEON moved one square back. I moved one square forward, to where it felt like I was reaching up, feeling its base.

Whoa.

The rock moved. Terror. I recoiled in the chair, contracting into a little ball as though the stone was already crashing down on me, and then after a while, when it was clear I was still around, I felt for the stone again. It was still there, wherever there is, the giant stone was poised on its center of gravity, it was just wobbling slowly in the wind on its tiny fulcrum. It was a rocking stone, like the Pagoda of the Golden Boulder at Kyaiktiyo, in Myanmar, which seems to be sliding off its perch. In fact, you can't believe it hasn't fallen already. But it's been there for at least two thousand years, and that's just using historical records. I could feel that the stone was just a tiny bit off balance, that it was leaning just a weensy bit this way, west, that it wanted to fall down onto the mouth of the cave and block it up forever, and then as I groped closer it was as though I could feel a single pebble jammed into the cleft between the boulder and the rock shelf. And then it was as though I could feel there was a filament or a thread tied around the pebble and stretching off, as untwangably taut as a piano's C8 string, out into the empty space to my left, and I understood that the whole thing was a deadfall trap, a Wile E. Coyoteish rig like the traps the Paiutes used to set to crush gophers and desert foxes. And for some reason I understood that it was as though somebody far away was holding the far end of the wire and was getting ready to pull it and jerk out the pebble and tip the boulder crashing down into the shaft. And the only way to keep that from happening, so whatever was inside could leave the cave on schedule, was to find the bastard holding that string—the Doomster—and keep him from pulling it.

I leaned back in the Ergo Chair and yanked on a clump of my blessedly regrowing hair. I could barely feel it. I tried touching my nose, but I couldn't tell I was touching it without peeking. Getting numb, I thought. Damn, I'm messed up. I leaned forward again and it was as though I could reach out and touch the wire. It was too thin to see, or rather to imagine seeing, but there was still a grayness about it that meant it was stretching off north-by-northwest, out into the black quadrant but close to the white one. I rubbed my head again, stepping back, and it was as though I could almost see the wire stretching away overhead to where it vanished in the haze above the Pacific. Alaska? I wondered. Can't tell from here. I felt it again. There was no way to attach a pulley to it or slide down along the string or anything like that, and not just because it was imaginary—although it was, of course, as convincing as it all was seeming to me at the moment—but because the Game doesn't work that way. It would be like suddenly deciding that your rook could jump diagonally. I'd have to go overland, as it were. Was. Is. I raced down the northern stairs and bore northwest across the plain. LEON trailed after me. I jumped forward again. He followed. Sometimes I thought that I could just sense the wire high overhead. Which meant that so far the latest hunch felt right, and that our guy—and by the way we'd already decided to assume it was a guy, since chicks generally aren't so into genocide—had some connection to the Pacific Northwest. Not that that narrows things down enough, of course. It's like saying "Asian food." The search engines gathered another few thousand terabytes of data. Damn it, I need tougher math on this stuff. More stochastics. Better curve fitting. Maybe some kind of Kolmogorovian-ass constraining function. Still, he's got to be in there. At this point there's hardly anyone who's entirely off the grid. In order to be completely undocumented in the online universe you'd almost have to be a newborn child in some hunter-gatherer tribe up in the mountains in New Guinea. And then you wouldn't be the Doomster anyway. Our guy'd have to have some technical skills. There was almost no way he hadn't been enrolled in a half-decent high school within the last forty years. Even if he'd been homeschooled, he'd be registered with a provincial education department or a state department of education. So that already limits it down to a measly billion or so souls, out of a world population of 6.8. With the Pacific Northwest thing, it takes it down to, say, thirty million. No problem.

I moved three squares east, farther into the future, to November. Data swirled by, names, addresses, social security numbers, military service records, occupations, investments, domain names, postal codes, arrest records, supposedly expunged juvenile arrest records, lists of corporate employees, lists of government employees, professional associations, unions, guilds, social clubs, secret societies, church memberships, magazine subscriptions, Google alerts, vehicle registrations, telephone records, prescription purchases, even paintball teams, an un-untanglable snarl of cross-references like a scalpful of matted, dreadlocked hair. I moved. LEON sifted the data, evaluated it, discarded all but .00001 percent of it, and moved.

Nothing. Fine. I moved again, into December. Another load of bits started to come in. I waited. The Net was slow today. Some new kind of Trojan worm had been closing down servers, not just locals but the routing stations on the T3 lines. People said it was the kind of thing only the U.S. government could manage to do. Either that, I thought, or just a clever twelve-year-old with a keyboard and a dream. LEON processed the whole thing, rating each bit of data by the likelihood of its intersecting with the hypothesized doomster. He moved. I moved. Another 3×10^{12} bits. Uncomplainingly, LEON sifted through it. This time he checked it against known millenarianist religions and doomsday cults. There were a lot of them—the end of the world's always been popular—and Taro had insisted we set up the system to check against them every few moves. Still, my guess was that our suspect would be an independent, or at most someone only on the edge of one of the movements. He might be an ethnic Muslim or an ex–Jehovah's Witness or even a holdout from the Order of the Solar Temple or whatever, but even if he were, I'd give five to one he wouldn't be a very active member. He'd be a loner. And not some Oswald-style patsy either. A real loner.

LEON moved. Damn. Nothing.

Hmm.

Okay. Slow down. Breathe.

Narrow it down. Suppose he's been bragging. Even just a little. I moved back a bit, into what we'd been calling the Bigmouth Space. It was a galaxy of hosted services, networking sites, and any other likely online communities, plus a little over a trillion cached e-mails, text messages, computer-transcribed phone calls, and whatnot. It was a monster, 2×10^{13} bits as of this millisecond. Take that, LEON babe.

He did. He cross-referenced everything we'd done so far with the whole load, Twitter, Facebook, Bebo, Orkut, Flickr, MySpace, Blogger, Technorati, and a hundred other lesser darknesses, active, cached, and abandoned. God dog, I thought. Imagine that they once called it the Information Superhighway. Information Superfund site, more like. World's biggest and smelliest dump. The Staten Island landfill of the mind. LEON dealt with it, though. *Esta bien.*

Trim it down again. I moved into a space called "Shibboleths." It was basically lists of giveaway words ("Rapture Day," "Dajjal," "chillism," "Abaddon," "Kali Yug"), giveaway phrases ("I have a bomb," "I hate all humanity," "The world must be destroyed"), and things that reminded LEON's increasingly insightful autodidactic engines of giveaway words and/or phrases. I told him to keep checking misspellings but that it was okay to ignore unlikely languages. Take a few seconds off. You've earned it.

LEON thought. LEON moved.

Huh.

Ten thousand four hundred forty.

That is, as of now—it was the Game's three hundred eighty-fifth move—I, or maybe I should say "LEON and I," had identified ten thousand four hundred and forty potential doomsters.

Of course, we'd discounted a lot. Our baby might have gotten tossed out with the bilgewater. Still, I thought, I'd go three to one that our guy's in there.

Not bad. Just roll with that for now. Okay.

I moved. LEON moved. The wire was still way high overhead, but it was getting closer to the ground. Eight skulls. I lost a skull. Seven skulls. Not in Alaska. Hah. Now we're getting somewhere. Hmm. Not California—

HAH!

Not in the U.S.

He's Canadian.

And playing odds again, he's still in Canada. And just guts-wise I'm betting on BC or Alberta. Leave out the North Side for now. Yeah. I'm gonna nail you, you maple-sugar-assed snowback fuck.

I moved. It was as though I was standing somewhere around Vancouver, and it was December 10, eleven days before 4 Ahau, and I was looking around in the fog, and I couldn't see much, but still, there was a feeling the fog was burning off, that things would get clearer. LEON moved. Okay. Not there, I thought. There. No. Not there. Not there. Not this. Not that. I flipped through the profiles. A lot of them were just names, with maybe a few associated handles from social-networking sites. Some of them were just handles without names. Some were just user IDs. Check 'em anyway, I thought. Don't be a choosy beggar. Okay. There. Not there. Not him. Not him. Now it felt like I could almost touch the wire again, except now the wire was flipping this way and that way, slipping away from me in the storm. There. I grabbed at it. Irrelevant bits dropped away like snowflakes melting in midair. Missed. Come on. Move. I moved. Okay. Things really were getting clearer. Or rather ... hmm. They weren't clearer in terms of shapes but just in terms of the light, the light. . . .

Huh. There was a glow up ahead, a color, a brilliant light red, like the color of the lacquer on Maximón's fingernails back in San Cristóbal Verapaz. Odd, I thought. Red's a southeast thing. What's it doing up here in Gray country? Was I going in the wrong direction? Maybe—

Beep. LEON moved.

Huh.

Light red. Okay.

I moved. Seven skulls. He moved. Six skulls. I hesitated. I moved. Down to five skulls. He moved. Four skulls. I started to move. No, wait. I took it back. Damn. Not thinking so straight.

Take a breath.

I snuck a look at the time window. It was three in the afternoon. So I'd been playing for nearly eight hours of clock time, longer than I'd ever been able to play before. On the other hand I was feeling worse than I ever had before. Symptoms included disequilibrium, depressed heart rate, and difficulty remembering my own name. I held on to the edges of the keyboard, as though it could be used as a flotation aid in the unlikely event of a water landing. Keep it together, Jed. It's just the endgame.

Somewhere the last dregs of the Steersman's dust flared into bioavailability just before my overstimmed synapses collapsed into Alpha. I managed to wonder whether the color might be a clue to something else, a shape, an animal, something associated with the color, something I'd seen before, a number, maybe, or even a word, or a phrase.

I moved. He moved. Three skulls, two skulls.

A word, maybe? No, two words. Two short words. It was something I'd seen before, something that didn't sound like it made a lot of sense, what was it, what was it . . .

I moved.

One skull—

Hell Rot.

(69)

In the first window an eight-hundred-mile cold front, represented as a choleric yellow against the royal-blue Gulf of Alaska, rolled west at twelve miles per hour. According to the accompanying text panel the front would reach the coast of British Columbia at about 5:30 A.M. PST, fifty minutes from now. Dawn would be at 5:22 A.M., twenty-one minutes after the scheduled assault time. In the second window, an unenhanced view from a KH-13 Ikon reconnaissance satellite, you could see the dark Strait of Georgia on the left, the orange sodium lights of Vancouver with the dark river running up through them, and then on the right the long tail of white lights along the Trans-Canada Highway, heading east in a wide U alongside the Fraser river. At the end of the tail, at the far right of the screen, you could just see a smudge of lights marking the town of Chilliwack. The text panel listed a few key facts: that Vancouver was the second-largest biotechnology center in North America and the fastest-growing one in Canada, that it was consistently rated among the top four major cities worldwide in standard of living, that its citizens' average IQ was estimated to be a robust 98, and—maybe contradictorily but, to us, relevantly—that it also had the highest suicide rate per capita of any major city in the Western Hemisphere.

The third window showed about two square miles of Chilliwack. It didn't look all that menacing. There were two street grids, one north-south and another in the northwest quadrant rotated twenty degrees clockwise. On the south side the streets got longer and curvier, which told you they were the better and newer residential blocks. The east side was an older residential zone, also with big houses but with closer, smaller blocks, short on the north-south axis and long on the east-west one. Marguerite Avenue ran east to west in the center of the area, and 820 Marguerite was in the center of the block.

This window's accompanying text noted that Chilliwack was a community of over seventy-eight thousand, that although the town's economy was primarily agricultural, many of its residents worked in the big city, sixty miles to the west, putting up with the long commute as a lifestyle trade-off, that the town's median income was forty-eight thousand dollars Canadian, and that the birth rate was 9.8 per 1,000 and the death rate was 7 per 1,000 per year. Soon to be 0 and 1,000, respectively, I thought.

"Why didn't they pick him up when he was out of the house?" A_2 whispered in my right ear. She'd just come in.

"He hasn't been outside in four days," I said.

"Oh."

"Anyway, now they think he's got the Goat in there someplace. That's why they moved it up to today."

She said, "Oh," again. She sat down next to me and looked up at the video wall. We were all in a big conference room at the temporary convention facility near the Hyperbowl—"we" meaning Taro, Dr. Lisuarte, Larry Boyle, Tony Sic, Taro's interns, Michael Weiner, who was bulking up the chair on my left, me, and almost everybody else involved with the Parcheesi Project except for Marena, who, for some reason I didn't understand, was watching from her house in Colorado. The whole thing had a such a *gemütlich* feeling that I could almost imagine that we were just a bunch of undergrads spontaneously gathering in the rec room to watch a presidential election or *How the Grinch Stole Christmas*. But y'aren't, Blanche, I thought. Y'aren't.

"That's the second tanker coming in," Laurence Boyle said. He pointed to the next window, #4, with a blue laser dot. It showed a real-time night-vision satellite view of about four blocks, with the Czerwick home at the center. You could see that the house had two gables, that there was a two-car garage with a flat roof added on, and that there was a pretty big deck in the long, narrow backyard. The roof, unfortunately, was made of copper-plated metal alloy, which made it hard to get an infrared reading from above. The tanker Boyle had pointed out looked like a can of Red Bull, sliding in without headlights behind its parked twin on Emerald Street, two blocks south of Marguerite.

I stood up to get a look over Tony Sic's head at window #5. It had a nice telephoto shot from a radio tower five blocks downtown, with a good view of the whole 800 block from about a 45° angle. From here you could see that the house was a roughly four-bedroom job, with just enough styling to identify itself as Colonial. There were four steps up to the door, going up sideways to a little sort of porch with an overhang, and that would slow the team down a second or so. But the place wasn't huge—the development had been built in 1988, just before the McMansion era—and the ERT captain had estimated they could clear it in less than eight seconds. The houses on either side were a little different but mainly the same. There were a few middle-aged maple trees in the front yards. They weren't in leaf yet. Everything looked pretty normal. The definition of normal, even. I could've told you, I thought. Everybody's known for decades that suburbs were a bad idea, but they kept building them anyway, and now look where the Seven-Headed Beast's coming from.

Ma and Pa—at thirty-six Madison Czerwick still lived with his parents—were almost certainly in the master bedroom on the second floor, and there was somebody, probably the little brother, in a room in the back. Madison—with whom we were all now on a first-name basis—was most likely in his room. All other readings were showing what they called a "pattern consistent with overnight sleep." That is, there were no televisions or task lights on in the ground or second floors. There hadn't been any mouse movements on any computers for over an hour. Telephones, PDAs, and other Net-enabled gadgets were inactive. Power draw was inconclusive, meaning that something, but nothing huge, might be running in the basement. Probably, everyone was nestled all snug in their beds. While visions of genocide danced in their heads. Head.

"They're talking about moving back five minutes," Ana's voice said over the communal speaker. You could hear voices hubbubbing in her background. "To set up the hoses."

"Thanks, Miss Vergara," Boyle said. Miss, huh? On any other day I and everyone else would have snickered. Today no one did. Ana—who was turning out to be less of a grunt, and more of a player, than I guess I'd realized—was one of thirty or so guests in the trailer of a poshly converted semi ten blocks away from 820.

"Okay, there they are," Ana said. Her cursor slid onto window #5, wiggling around a four-person crew who were now attaching long white hoses to the back of the two chrome tankers. They laid the hoses down in two neat paths to within fifty feet of 820, leaving a few hundred feet of slack at each end. There was a pause. Then someone turned a valve, and each hose inflated up to just before the slack section, where I guess there was another valve. You could already see water vapor condensing around the hoses. They were full of liquid nitrogen, which, we hoped, would hold in the Goat.

On their first day of investigation the detectives had found that Madison had been "one step removed" from access to a breeding population of a "purpose-raised" strain of *Brucella abortus*. By the end of their second day they'd confirmed that his Internet activity, especially the haplotype maps he'd downloaded, indicated he was actively tweaking their DNA. *Brucella* are a venerable and trusty bacteria, something you'd get from, say, delivering a baby water buffalo or drinking raw goat's milk with Zorba the Greek. Over the years it had been called Malta fever, goat fever, contagious abortion, Bang's disease, or any of a hundred other names. We were just calling it the Goat. Compared to the Disney World virus, the symptoms weren't anything fancy: sudden sweat that smells like wet hay, muscle pains, fainting, and, of course, death. Which is pretty scary, especially the sweating part. Better be sure to pick up an organic deodorant crystal on the way to oblivion.

The Goat's main claim to infamy was that it had been the first bacillus ever weaponized by the U.S. government. In 1953 they'd tested it on animals, using the same grapefruit-sized bomblets they later used for anthrax. The air force had chosen it because, unlike most bacilli, it could survive airborne for hours and, even more excitingly, could penetrate intact human skin, so that even if you were wearing NBC gas masks and rotating them in sealed off-gassing booths, if you had a patch of pink showing somewhere, you were toast-to-be.

Even so, by the 1970s, what was left of those strains had been decommisioned and stored in two igloos at the Pine Bluff Arsenal in Arkansas. And by the 1980s it was supposedly all destroyed. But somebody'd been kidding around with it since then, either to develop defenses against it or to sell it or, probably, both.

In the sixteen months since he was downsized from his job at CellCraft's Vancouver facility, Madison had greatly improved the Goat. The Czerwick Strain—at least, as the CDC had projected it based on data they'd grabbed remotely from Madison's hard drive—now had the usual trendy features like ultrafast reproduction, disinfectant resistance, asymptomatic infection, and a precision nanochronometer. But the most notable upgrade was what they called vector flexibility. The classic *Brucellis* strains can jump from some types of animals to humans, and possibly from humans back to animals. But most animals either don't get them at all or because of lifespan or lifestyle aren't suitable vectors for human transmission.

Madison's work had vastly enlarged the pool of potential vectors. The new strain would mutate faster, and in more likely adaptive directions, than any natural bacillus. It would seem as though it were adjusting its own DNA to accommodate the different protein profiles of hundreds of families of animals, not just primates. *B. czerwicki* could jump the species barrier again and again, back and forth, throughout the biosphere. Ordinarily epidemics become less virulent as they spread—since otherwise there wouldn't be any vector animals left—but with so many species susceptible to the Goat, it would be a long time before that happened. Some of the CDC projections said it could probably kill off all species of primates and all or most other mammals. Which just tells you what an angry little weasel Czerwick was. People is one thing, but when you go after Bonzo you know you're really fucked up.

Like its ancestors the Goat could probably be treated by intramuscular injections of streptomycin. But with timed, simultaneous symptomaticity, there wouldn't be enough antibiotics to go around even if there were still people who were able to administer them. And of course, the CDC was already working on a vaccine, but it would take another week or so to finish developing it and more than a year to produce it in anything like medical quantities. The CDC's projections, or at least the ones we'd gotten reports on, suggested that some people in polar areas might survive. But with the Goat's resistance to cold, it wouldn't be many. The species-jumping geneware would keep the subarctic world too hot for humans for decades. At least.

"How much of the stuff do they think he has in there?" A_2 asked. I realized she was standing on tiptoes to get close to my ear. I guess she was too polite or uptight to grab my shoulder and drag my head down. I crouched down a bit.

"Ana thinks it's about two gallons," I said. "He's been going through bovine colloid like it was bean dip."

"Is that enough?"

"You mean, like, enough to do the whole planet?"

"Uh-huh."

"Well, you have to figure that's about three point four trillion microbes per gallon," I said. "So say you had, like, a ten-percent-per-day division rate, even with a twenty-percent die-off per day you'd get around, uh, two times ten-to-the-eighteenth bugs in one week, and that's more than most diseases that are, you know, considered epidemics."

"Oh," she said.

"Yeah. Yeah, depending on the number of added vectors . . . in a month or so it could be as common as, like, say, Staphylococcus."

"Gesundheit," Michael Weiner said in my other ear.

"Thanks," I said. "Yeah, there's no humor like gallows humor." He nodded.

"At least it sounds like they know everything, anyway," A_2 said.

"One hopes," I said. Actually, she was right, or righter than I was. From what I'd seen, at least, the U.S. and Canadian detectives had, amazingly, done a good job. I'd have thought they'd take weeks to build a case against him, but they were ready in couple of days. Although I guess you could get probable cause off the Web site. In fact, he'd dropped enough hints in his blog that you'd think I'd have spotted it right away all that time ago. The way he'd been going on about the Disney World thing had been more like somebody who was afraid he was going to get scooped, that some slant teenager was going to steal his place in history, than like somebody who actually cared about the problem. Should've made him then, I thought for the nth time. Idiot. Could have avoided this whole thing. Except it's not so easy, is it? Especially for somebody like me, for whom empathy requires some effort. Anyway, cut yourself some slack. Hell Rot wasn't a big page, but thousands of people had seen it, including DHS profilers, and none of them had flagged it, despite the fact that it included such gems as this:

> *People have been making movies and*
> *games and stories about the END TIME*
> *for FOUR THOUSAND YEARS. The*
> *Reason is that they KNOW it is the*
> *RIGHT THING TO DO. And finally Now it*
> *is achevable [sic].*

Maybe it hadn't gotten singled out simply because Madison hadn't put up anything specific. He hadn't mentioned any names, places, or dates. Speaking of which, one odd thing was that from the blog, at least, it looked like he'd chosen December 21 arbitrarily. There was no mention of the Maya calendar, or pre-Columbian stuff, or anything. It was like he'd just pulled it out of his paper hat. Although I was sure he hadn't.

"Two hundred seconds," Ana said.

Everyone in the room straightened up a little. Michael Weiner started to cough and then didn't follow through. Nobody threw up, though. Somebody turned on the general operations audio and we listened to the CO running through the final checklist.

"Hazmat Unit A," his voice said.

"In place," a lady from Hazmat Unit A said.

"Hazmat Unit B," the CO said.

They covered a lot in the next sixty seconds, a chemical hazard team, a poison specialist, a biohazard reduction team that used antiviral and anti-bacterial sprays, two inhalation specialists, two gas compression trucks, a truckful of tracking dogs, a bomb squad, a bomb-disposal robot, and a bomb-disposal robot wrangler. Next, the three five-person assault teams checked in. Or, rather, they called them "elements," not teams. Each element had a captain, two assaulters, a spotter, and a rear guard. Two elements would go in the front door and the front ground-floor rooms and the upstairs. The other would go in the back, check the kitchen, and then head to the basement.

"High Man A," the CO said.

"In place," High Man A's voice said.

Six other spotters, or high men, checked in after him. Each one had a different perch on a rooftop or a telephone pole. Normally, some of them would be snipers, but today they were unarmed. In fact, the Goat Operation differed from most raids in that there were no guns anywhere near the assault zone. It wasn't just because there was no real chance of return fire—who cared about that when we were all screwed anyway?—but because "delivering the suspect alive and coherent over[rode] officer survival" Last of all, the marked vehicles came into view. Two ambulances pulled into Marguerite and stopped a block short of the house. An ordinary fire engine stationed itself on Emerald. About twenty regular police cars materialized out of nowhere and formed a four-block-wide perimeter centered on 820.

"Any issues?" the CO's voice asked. "Right. We're at T minus seventy seconds. I want to check prep on Eight twenty."

"All target preps are in," a British-sounding voice said. He meant that they were ready to turn off the main electricity just as the assault teams breached the doors so that there wouldn't be any lights flaring in anyone's night vision, that the Czerwicks' door alarm had been turned off at the service provider, and that Mrs. Czerwick still had two cats but no dog. Ana'd said that six neighbor dogs who'd been judged overly vigilant had all been lightly sedated. It wasn't quite clear how, but they hadn't wanted to tip off anyone in any of the surrounding houses, so probably they'd sent in burglars with bacon-wrapped diazepam. Target prep also included what they called a wire delay. That is, at about two A.M. they'd moved the whole house sixty seconds back in time. They'd reset the link to the atomic clock on Madison's computers, they'd put a sixty-second delay on the Internet and on the cell phone read-outs, and they were even sending new, delayed signals to the TV satellite dish on the roof and to old-fashioned radios that anyone might turn on. Of course, any watches or unattached clocks or watches would be off, but who looks at those things anymore? So if some blabbermouth noticed any of what was going on—and to me it seemed like enough of a buildup to invade a whole country—and started talking about it on the Net or TV, they'd catch it.

"All right," the CO said. "Brown team, I want—"

The audio cut out. There was silence.

There was a sense of everyone—that is, everyone in our conference room—stirring uncomfortably. It was the aural equivalent of watching a black marker redact a line of text on some CIA document.

"I bet he's checking the FAEs," Ana's voice said.

She meant fuel-air explosives. And she was referring to a bit of information that we, and probably the folks in the VIP trailer, and probably even Lindsay Warren himself—who was undoubtedly watching the same array of windows in his pathogen-proofed safe room in the Hyperbowl—weren't supposed to have.

Early in the Goat Op discussions, more than one person had mentioned the possibility of eliminating the entire town. Apparently, these days that sort of thing got done with a ring of fuel-air explosives that were positioned to incinerate any living particle in the area. Ana'd said that the U.S. had done it twice in Afghanistan, and each time, no biohazards had gotten out of the targeted factories. Anyway, as far as the Goat Op went, this option had gotten rejected pretty quickly, not out of any moral qualms, but because, despite a psychological profile that said it was doubtful, it was still possible that Madison was working with others, or that others knew about him, or that he knew about others, or that he'd mailed some of his research work to others, or that others had sent stuff to him, or, most nightmarishly of all, that he'd already started the dispersal. It wasn't quite clear how he planned to handle it, but it could be as easy as sending small packages to addresses around the world.

Two days ago Ana'd told us she was guessing that there were still FAEs fused and positioned outside the city and that somebody in Victoria would detonate them if they determined that there was an uncontrollable release in progress. She said part of the giveaway was that the real big shots from D.C. and Ottawa—the directors of the CSIS and FBI, for instance—hadn't wanted to be on the scene. If the biowarfare experts said there was a noncontainable release in progress, we should expect the whole place to disappear, and then we should all just hope that the heat had got most of the bugs. During the conference call, Michael had asked her why she was still there, in the blast zone, but Ana blew off the question. I guess she was just too butch to think about girly issues like personal survival.

The CO's voice came on again.

". . . nus twenty seconds," it said. "All ready?"

Our conference room was silent. On Ana's speaker the room she was in was silent. On the video windows 820 Marguerite looked like peace on earth itself. Someone had opened an audio channel to one of the parabolic mikes on Marguerite, and you could hear mourning doves and a little rush of breeze in the bare branches but nothing else.

"Wait, hold up," the CO's voice said. "We're holding the count."

There was a pause. It was uncomfortable at the beginning, and then it got more uncomfortable, and then unbearable. People shifted around me. I could smell sweat in the room. There was an odd little sound next to me and I realized it was A_2's teeth chattering. Put an arm around her? No, don't. If anything touches her she'll probably have a stroke.

"Window six," Ana's voice said. "It's nothing, it's a neighbor." Her cursor pointed at someone with big puffy red hair in a gray bathrobe. It was a lady from 818, the house next door. She toddled out to her car, which was in the driveway as always, slowly and deliberately opened the door, rummaged in the front seat for something, didn't find it, and minced around to the driver's side. I thought I was going to tear off my own scalp. Twelve seconds away from the earth's most critical moment since the Chicxulub meteorite and we're waiting for Endora to find her Dulcolax. The lady opened the driver's-side door, found whatever it was she wanted, closed it, and, shuffling in her puffy slippers, made her way back toward her house. By now I was sure one of us was going to vomit, or lose control of his or her bowels, or at least faint. Nobody did, though. I guess we were all just rock-hard. Or sufficiently medicated.

The door of 818 eased itself shut.

"All right," the CO's voice said. Even he sounded a little wobbly. "Everyone still in place? Right. Resetting to T minus twenty seconds."

A drop of something fell on my cheek and I realized it was sweat from my forehead. I wiped my face on the sleeve of my jacket—it was that same gray Varvatos thing I'd had in that Jeep ride with Marena and Max about seventy million years ago—peeled off my hat, ran my hand through my hair that still wasn't there, and put the hat back on. Whew. *De todos modos.*

"Seven, six," the CO's voice said. "Ready. Three, two, go."

On window number five the ten members of Elements A and B crossed the lawn like the shadows of crows flying over the roof. They seemed to have working keys for both doors, the doors opened without any sound that we could hear, and the elements were already inside. It took all of four seconds for them to pour through the hall, spread into the living room and dining room, and dash up the acrylic-carpeted stairs. On one of the helmet cameras there was a glimpse of gilt-plastic-framed photos on the wall, old graduations and older weddings and Madison accepting a trophy at a grade-school science fair. Ordinarily, SWAT teams make as much noise as possible when they go in, but this raid had been designed to assume that Madison might have a finger on a detonator. So there was just the creaking of the floorboards and the wheeze of the old refrigerator in the kitchen, and the darting shadows, as though the house were an aviary and the crows were all flying into their own little nests. Assaulters burst simultaneously into each of the three bedrooms. Oh, Christ. A face. It was a horrible fanged predatory face, lunging at us on helmet cam #6. There were gasps around me and Lisuarte, for one, visibly recoiled. It was one of the Czerwicks' attack cats. It vanished from the frame. By the time we got over that, we could see on two other Element A helmet cams that Mom and Pop were being gently held down in their bed. There was one good, steady shot of a Kevlar-gloved hand covering Mrs. Czerwick's mouth. On helmet cam #9 you could just see that they'd gotten a restraining hood on Madison's little brother—who was twenty-eight—and that he was kicking and wriggling but not getting anywhere. And on #6, the one that had dealt with the cat, which was now in Madison's room, on that one—

Hmm. Madison wasn't in his bedroom.

"Oh, *coño*," Tony Sic said.

"It's number sixteen," Larry Boyle said. His voice was unnaturally high. "Number sixteen."

We all looked at window #16. It was the helmet cam of one of the assaulters in Element C. There was a glimpse of what might be basement stairs, then a glowy bunch of shapes in the center of a dark field, and then, for a few frames, less than a half a second, there was a sofa. There was a pudgy naked torso on the sofa. There was a face on top of the torso. There was a big gawking mouth in the middle of the face. It was Madison's face. There was a sound like a big old woofer popping its voice coil and the element's windows grayed out.

"That was an NFDD," Ana's voice said over some kind of squealing or whimpering in the background.

"Which is what?" Michael Weiner asked. The video processors of the helmet cams had started readjusting and a few inchoate images drifted back into the windows.

"Noise and flash diversionary device," she said. One of the assaulters had tossed what they called a double whammy into the basement. The thing looked like a pair of yellow squash balls yoked together. One ball was a regular flash-bang grenade with an eight-million-candela flare and a 180-decibel report. The other was a sting grenade, which releases about two hundred tiny hard-rubber balls. It was more reliably debilitating, especially if the suspect had managed to close his eyes and cover his ears during the explosion.

"Righto," Michael said.

"Shhh, we want to hear this," Larry Boyle said.

We listened, but all we could hear was a hircine squeal. It faded into heavy panting, and then, suddenly, Madison seemed to have gotten his voice back.

"What's the charge?" he asked. His high tenor was familiar from the wiretaps, but it felt creepy hearing it in real time, especially since it sounded oddly calm. On the helmet cams the assaulters had switched on their flashlights for the first time and we got another unflattering close-up of Madison's jowls. I think he started say the word *officer*, but by the middle of the word there were Kevlar-gloved hands over his mouth. The assaulters weren't supposed to let him say anything, just in case he might have a voice-activated switch somewhere. There were another two seconds of abstract scuffling shapes on the windows, and then helmet cam #13 resolved itself into a pair of hands holding open Madison's mouth and a third hand grubbing around under his tongue, as though he were a SMERSH agent from the 1960s about to bite down on a cyanide pill. Finally they hustled him up the stairs. Back on window #5 the Czerwick lawn and Marguerite Avenue had, with a suddenness that made me remember the jungle gym scene in *The Birds*, filled up with a flock of black-uniformed officers. Someone had switched the audio back to an outdoor feed, and you could hear helicopters overhead, and sirens started up. In less than thirty seconds Madison had been strapped to a stretcher and loaded into his own ambulance van. The other ambulance was already pulling out with the rest of his family. We all focused on helmet cam #13, whose owner was going along in the ambulance and, it seemed, was about to give us another rare view of Madison, but suddenly, his feed grayed out.

"Do we not have a camera in there?" Michael asked.

"No, that's another one they won't give us," Ana's voice said. "Sorry." Once again, our information was being redacted.

Don't take it personally, I thought. The folks in the VIP trailer, and the directors in the capitals, and, one guessed, even Lindsay, probably needed to preserve their deniability if there was any torture during the interrogation.

Maybe we'd get some video later on, but there'd be some stuff nobody outside the spook shop would ever see.

Don't worry about it now, anyway, I thought. Ask Marena when she gets back. She has a knack for teasing bits of dirt out of people. I looked back at the long view, Window #5. Big black SUVs moved in behind and in front of Madison's ambulance. Motorcycle police maneuvered into positions on the flanks of the vehicles. Slowly, the caravan drove off east on Marguerite Street. They turned south on Young Road, toward Route 1.

Was that it? we wondered. We looked around at each other. Back in the basement they'd already positioned five remote cameras, giving us a whole row of new windows. Tech people stepped gingerly in and out of the windows, sweeping the place for booby traps. The TV was still playing the Lucifer scene in *Janine Loves Jenna*, to which Madison had evidently been masturbating. Nobody touched any of the mice, keyboards, cell phones, PDAs, remotes, or anything.

"Heads up, two primary suspects, section Delta," the CO's voice said.

"What's that about?" somebody asked.

"He means those two freezers," Ana's voice said. "In the garage. Check out window thirty-four."

The view showed a pair of workers in chrome responder's suits standing on the bed of the Czerwicks' pickup truck and waving long spray wands at a pair of waist-height freezers, which, according to neighbor informants, Madison's father had used for venison in the fall. "They're hosing them down," Ana's voice said. She meant they were spraying them with liquid nitrogen from the gas tankers. Even if any Goat was seeping out of its packaging, it wouldn't get through the ice.

"That's great," Larry Boyle said. "Good efforting, everybody." *Shut UP*, I and probably everyone else thought. Go hie thee to Kobol. A crew from Hazmat Unit B was up on the Czerwicks' roof, unrolling big sheets of blue vinyl. Other teams were twisting steel poles into the ground at the corners of the lawn. The idea was to seal the whole place and then set up a bigger enclosure, like a circus tent, over the wrapped-up house and garage. Then they'd set up a double system of hoses and fill the area between the house and the tent with CO_2. All the air from the house would get sucked into a truck and pressurized for analysis. It would be replaced with argon. Finally, when the pressure of the gas systems was stable, the biowarfare team could start tearing apart the house. A forklift rolled up the driveway to the garage, ready to load the nitrogen blocks into gasket-sealed containment trucks. Like all the other suspects, human and inanimate, they'd be going to a Vancouver containment complex, where air flows in but no air flows out. Now there was a bit of gray daylight augmenting the electric light. It started drizzling. The cold front had come over. Just another day in the Great White North.

We sat around. As there got to be less and less to watch, people drifted out of the command center. Michael Weiner slapped me on the back as he left, like, "Good job, Columbo." A few of the interns seemed to be going off to celebrate prematurely. The rest of us sat or stood there. We couldn't believe it was over and kept waiting for someone to tell us it really was. Eventually I walked out, took a service elevator up to the east side of the Hyperbowl. It was gray and wet, but it felt like the morning rain was over. A driver on one of the shuttle coaches asked whether I wanted him to take me back to the dorm, but I said no. It was less than two miles, and walking it was about the only exercise I got lately.

"Hi," A_2 said. She touched me on the acromion. I said hi. I noticed there was another pair of workers walking about fifty yards behind her, probably another element of the contingent that had been tailing me around the compound. Even though I'd delivered on Madison, I was still in a bit of trouble because of my near-OD on the Steersman's dust. Just ignore them, I thought. They're for your own good. Right.

A_2 wanted to come in, but I said I needed to just crash. She left. She was actually a really nice girl. I popped two blue Valia and oozed into the sack. Damn, I really am a bit wiped. I hadn't really relaxed since . . . I don't know. Since eighth grade or so. I rolled in and out of consciousness over the next twenty hours. Every once in a while I checked in with the team's situation report. There was no new news. Tony Sic texted back that everybody was just hanging around the vending machines, sitting on pins and needles, or more like daggers and ice picks. At 2:08 A.M. on the twenty-second I took another two blues. I remember the time because four minutes later A_2 banged on my door. There'd been a conference call from Ana. In Madison's second interview he'd told the interrogators that, as of last week, he'd already distributed over a quart of the *Brucellis*, that his own tests on his family members and "a few friends" had shown that they already harbored contagious levels of the bacillus, and that, in his own corny phrase, it was all over but the dying.

(70)

The Wet Lizard used to be crowded all the time, but now it was still two-thirds empty at 1 P.M., and I got the feeling they'd let me sit here all day on two mai tais. I didn't get why Marena'd wanted to meet me here, unless it was because it was close to the Belize City Airport. Maybe she wanted to coax me into her plane and get me back to the Stake. I sat at a too-small wobbly table on the sort of veranda on the second floor, looking out over Fort Street and trying to guess which of the parked cars belonged to the Executive Solutions people who were tailing me. My money's on the circa-1980 Econoline, I thought. It was grungy on the outside, but the windows were new and emphatically tinted. There was probably another pair of dicks at the bar downstairs, in case I made a run for it on foot. I should really take photos and go over them, I thought. Learn who they all are. Except who cares, really? Lindsay's put a lot of money into me. If he wants to feel like he's protecting his investment, let him. I looked down at the big screen on my new phone. 1:39 P.M. The desktop background—well, it's a little small to call it a desktop, but you know what I mean—was a new reconstruction of that crumbled mural that we'd seen back in the palace at Ix Ruinas, the one with all the bats and the Twin dude walking up to the Earthtoadess's mul. Michael'd put his digital reimaginer to work on it and it looked almost new. It was still hard to see what was what, though. A cicada-killer wasp landed on the screen. I touched the button that made the thing vibrate and the critter flew off into the humid air. It had rained and now that the sun was out it was going to get steam-bathy. Good growth medium for new bacteria, I thought. Designer bacilli . . .

Except that wasn't going to happen. By now—it was March 28—it was pretty clear that when Madison said he'd released the Goat, he'd just been blowing smoke at us. The stuff in the freezers had been the real deal, all right.

But Madison kept changing his story. First he'd said it was already out there, and then he'd said he had confederates planning to release it, and then he'd said he'd sent some out in packages with timed heatless explosives that would go off sometime in November. But—so far as we could tell from the DHS's terse reports—the more they'd sweated him, the less likely any of that sounded. The Goat couldn't live long without care, anyway. And based on the amounts of colloids and other supplies he'd bought, on the day of the raid he still had everything he'd grown. Also the Game was backing up the DHS theory. That is, plays of the Sacrifice Game addressing the issue—two of mine, and a bunch of games by Tony and the others—suggested that the Goat had not gotten out into the world and probably never would.

And as far as the 4 Ahau date went—well, it was a little odd. So far, the only thing Madison had said about why he'd chosen the date was "People are into this 2012 thing. I'm just giving them what they want." Otherwise, he hadn't talked any Maya stuff. Or if he had, the spooks hadn't told us about it.

I indulged in another sip of espresso. Hmm. I poured a half-shot of rum into the cup, took a minimarshmallow out of a baggie in my waist pocket, dropped that in, stirred everything around, and tried again. Better.

Fucking Madison. It wasn't enough for him to be the biggest loser of all time. Since he'd fumbled the big score, now he had to give us all—"all" being the two or three hundred people, at most, who knew about the Goat—he still had to give us all a few days of agita just to milk whatever cred he had left. Weasel.

Well, at least they got him, I thought for the nth time. Since I'm me, I was still amazed that government, or rather two governments—who, one naturally assumes, would always do almost everything wrong—had actually gotten their acts together. Not that they'd have found the guy without us. On the other hand, now they were saying that the Madison business had to stay classified—forever, one supposed—to avoid inspiring copycats. Uncharacteristically, I thought I might almost agree with them. Or at least I wanted to think about it before I blew the whistle. Of course, if they wanted us to keep it secret, that might also mean that they'd start bumping us all off. All of us who knew about Madison and whatever, that is. The old truism about how being paranoid doesn't mean people aren't out to get you—well, the reason it's called a truism is that it's true. So naturally I wanted to get away from the Stake for a while. Maybe I'd use the Martin Cruz identity for a while and then switch to one of my Jed legends . . . hmm. I looked around again. Nobody.

Hmm.

Weirdly, the fact that the world would keep on going for a while almost felt like a bit of a letdown, after all the—

"Hi there," Marena said.

She was wearing a Magic baseball cap, and a sort of bottom thing, and a sort of top. She looked a little less thin and a bit paler, but in a good way.

"Hi," I said. My voice cracked Henry Aldrichly. So much for sounding all cool. I stood up. She kissed me but it was almost an air kiss.

"Please, *nehmen Sie Platz*," she said. "Gentleman Jed."

I sat. She sat. I had a box of those Cohiba Pyramides sitting on her side of the table—I hadn't found a Maximón around here yet—and I pulled over another chair and put it on that.

"You look well," I said. "Weller."

"Thanks."

"Yeah." Pause. "Hey, how about a, a Kon-Tiki Zombie? I think they serve them in a hollow jackfruit with a parasol and dry ice smoke and a big Easter Island dude glowstick swizzle thing and everything."

"You're saying they can make me a zombie?" she asked.

"Or—oh. Heh."

"Hi, welcome to the Wet Lizard," a waitress interrupted. "Today we have a special on the Bikini Atoll Mai Tai, that's made with the house coconut rum—"

Marena raised a hand and cut her off. "Could I get just a bottle of Fiji and a shot of Glen Moray?" she asked. "Thanks."

Waitress girl bounced off.

"How's Max doing?" I asked.

"He says his new school is too arty," she said.

"Arty?"

"Yeah, they have the kids make all these leaf prints and, like, centerpieces out of pinecones and shit."

"It sounds like hell."

"Yeah. He's good, though. He says hi."

"Hi back, Maximum."

"Hi."

The waitress came back with the whiskey and water.

"Uh, how about a cloneburger?" I asked.

"Sorry, I'm not really hungry," Marena said.

"Nor am I," I said. "Sorry."

The waitress left. Marena looked down at the street. There was a maroon BMW X1 SUV standing in the right lane, not far from the Econoline.

"Is that your ride?" I asked.

"Yeah." She looked back at me and leaned back in her chair.

"No cigarette?" I asked.

"Not since Madison Day," she said.

"Great."

"I can give you a nicotine lollipop, though."

"Oh, no, thanks. Want a marshmallow?"

"You know, I hate to break it to you, but most people don't really like marshmallows. At least not to just eat them out of the bag."

"They don't? They sell a ton of them."

"That's just for—never mind."

"You think—"

"So are you still on—sorry," she said. "What were you saying?"

"What? Oh, sorry. Nothing."

"No, go ahead."

"No, I wasn't saying anything. What were you going to ask?"

"Just, you're still on retainer, right?"

"Yeah," I said. "I just put in for some vacation time."

"Well, I know it's not exactly the Plaza Athénée out there, but if you could stand to come out to this thing, it'd be great."

"At the Stake?"

"Yeah. At the Olympics complex. It's nothing exciting, just, Lindsay's having a sort of ribbon-cutting thing for the Hyperbowl."

"Already? Is it done?"

"No, but they're filming something there for the IOC, so I guess he wants to add some pomp."

"Well, I'll look in out there pretty soon," I said. Hmm. Did she really want me at the Stake? That is, did she want me to come along so we could hang out together? Or just so they could keep an eye on me? Something wasn't going right about this conversation. There was that sort of awkward distance happening. Maybe I should go along. Except if she really wanted me in, like, *that* way, she'd footsie me under the table or something. Wouldn't she? Damn it, it's like I'm still in grade school with this relationship shit. That's why I hate interper—

"Also, you know, Lindsay's working on getting those soldiers off the Ix site," she said. "So they should open it up for us pretty soon. Legally, even."

"Really?" I asked. "Even if the Belize war thing is still going on?" According to CNN, as of this morning they were still shelling each other across the Río Sarstún.

"That's what Larry tells me," she said. "Yeah, now that we're the heroes of the hour."

"Well, of course I'll definitely come out for that."

"Excellent."

I finished my coffee concoction. I shifted in my chair and looked around. She shifted in her chair and looked around. A familiar-sounding dog was barking somewhere. The day was starting to feel all sticky and carbon-monoxidy.

"So what are you planning on doing otherwise?" she asked. "Like, long term."

"I don't know. I moved around some more corn futures today. I still have to pass Go and collect two hundred billion dollars."

"How about getting into the time travel business?"

"Well, I thought I'd wait a bit so I can get into it earlier."

"Heh. Yeah."

"Yeah. Except, you know, if that were going to happen we'd already know about it."

"How does that go again?"

"If there were ever going to be any time travel on any sort of large scale, any time in the future, then there'd be visitors from the future here now. We'd already know about them."

"Maybe it'll just be too expensive," she said.

"Well, but, you know, TVs used to be expensive. The wormhole projection might be expensive now, but twenty years from now it'll be cheap, and everybody'll want to try it. Technology gets around."

"Huh. Well, maybe . . . maybe they are here, but they wouldn't be supposed to tell anybody."

"Why? Wouldn't it be better if they could tell us what to watch out for?"

"Except Taro said, you know, didn't he say something about how you can't do stuff like that because of the, the uncle problem?"

"The grandfather paradox."

"Right."

"Well, yeah, he did," I said. "But, you know, the farther you go back, the less that's a problem. So people way, way in the future from us, they could come back here and they wouldn't run into much trouble."

"Maybe it's going to be illegal to take over people's heads. Because it is basically murder, right?"

"Sure, but I don't think . . . I mean, even if there were a law against going back at all and erasing anybody's mind, even if it was considered murder, that sort of thing never stopped everybody. Right? Especially when they're going to be out of the law's reach anyway. They'll be back in the past."

"I guess," she said. She tossed back the first half of her Scotch. I was starting to notice all the car horns. I wondered whether, if they were some noise birds made, people would think they sounded pretty. Probably not.

"Or they could just take over people who'd otherwise be about to die, and then help out their families or whatever to make it even . . . no, I don't think that's a problem without a workaround."

"So you still think the reason they're not here is because there isn't any future."

"Well . . . I don't know," I said.

She had a slug of Fiji. There was a pause.

"Sorry," I said. "Maybe you're thinking about Max."

"Yeah."

"Maybe there's some other good explanation. In fact, there probably is. Sorry."

"No, I'm sorry," she said. "I'm being such a fucking mom."

"That's good. Mom does you credit."

"You know, the deal is," she said, "when you have a child it's like there's no value on it. Somebody . . . some alien or god or whatever could come up to you and say, 'Listen, if you give up your child I'll cure cancer, and I'll make everyone else live forever, and I'll even eliminate all the suffering in the universe,' and you'd be like, no thanks."

"Right," I said.

"It's some kind of chemical change. You turn into a life-support system for this other being."

"That's good," I said. "Anyway, I'm sorry I mentioned it."

"No, it's fine," she said. She finished off the Glen Moray.

"Maybe the old Game'll give us a clue about it," I said.

"Yeah," she said. "Speaking of which, there is still stuff to take care of with the Game. Right? Madison's not going to be the last doom dude out there."

"No."

"You have to keep working it. You're like in that Philip Dick story, with the Bureau of Precrime."

"I have to?"

"Well, I know I'm not your boss right now. But I mean, you know, you're James Bond. Except you don't have to leave the office."

"Thanks."

"Sorry."

"It's fine, I just meant, that, you know, I'm not the only thing going any-more," I said. "I mean, I think Tony and the gang, they're getting pretty good, so, you know. They can take care of it."

"Uh-huh."

"And LEON's getting good," I said. "The thing'll be running itself in a few years. We won't even know what it's doing. I mean, it'll be way too compli-cated for human beings to check."

"We'll just have to trust LEON, then, right?"

"Well, that's another issue," I said.

I looked around. The sun was really getting belligerent. Somewhere, out in one of the alleys, somebody was vomiting. Loudly.

"Isn't this kind of a low-rent town for a classy dame like you?" I asked.

"Yeah, it does kind of get you down after a while, doesn't it?"

"Like after ten seconds."

"So why are you here?" she asked.

"I'm not classy."

Pause. The vomiting diminuendoed out.

"Listen," she said, "I wanted to see you in person because I found out something that's not too great and you're going to be really mad."

"It's fine, don't worry about it."

"But you'll have a right to be mad. You got really, really screwed."

"How? I bet I'm about to get arrested."

"No, it's nothing like—okay, look, you know how the, the blood-lightning-making stuff, how there are two parts to it, and one of them's like a sense-of-space-getting-rid-of or whatever part? The one that sounds like an aftershave?"

"Old Steersman."

"Right," she said. "Well, I did some digging around on that."

"Yeah?"

"And, and the, those Lotos people weren't being—I mean, somebody told you and me both something different from the reality."

"Which is what?"

"It's not just a chemical."

"What is it?"

"It's a parasite."

Pause.

"Excuse me?" I said.

"It's a critter, it produces some kind of psychoactive—it's like those zombie snail things, with the worms in their eyes, you know, they make the snails climb up on things so that birds'll eat them—"

"Leucochloridium."

"Yeah. Or like, you know, that thing that makes mice stop being afraid of cats."

"Toxoplasmosis."

"Right. That's why it had to be in a liquid, there were like really tiny little critters swimming around in there."

"Uh . . . huh," I said. I was a little dizzy but I don't think I visibly wobbled.

"And that's why it took so long to get the stuff ready, they had to clone them up out of some other thingie or something."

"Okay, well, what . . . look, what are they, exactly?"

"The critters?"

"Yeah, are they trematodes, are they protozoans, are—"

"I don't know." She looked me in the eyes. I looked back. She looked down.

"Why couldn't they just isolate the psychoactive part of the secretions and just give us that?"

"I don't know," she said, "I guess that would have taken too long, or they didn't know which compounds it was, or it had to combine with some human neurotransmitter, or . . . I don't know. You know more about that kind of—"

"Well then, okay, what are the symptoms, what's their life cycle, what are the short- and long-term effects, what's the prognosis—"

"They say they're working on a cure."

"A cure or a treatment? There isn't even a cure for malaria yet."

"Maybe it's just a treatment."

"Damn."

"If you can resist your impulse to go—well, I don't know what you want to do, but I was afraid you might try to interrogate Dr. Lisuarte or something—"

"That's a good idea."

"If you can hold off on that, as soon as I get out there"—she meant to the Stake—"I'm going to find out whatever else I can and call you. . . ."

"You might make them nervous."

"I won't. Trust me."

"What about Ashley$_2$ and all the other people who took the stuff?"

"I don't know. I'm going to work on it and we're going to find out and document whatever we can and I'm going to take it all to Lindsay, who I'm sure isn't in on it because all these people always try to tell him as little as possible anyway, and then you and I are just going to deal with it. But I'm really, really sorry."

"Don't apologize. We'll handle it." *Cono cono cono,* I thought. I am so, so screwed. They really hung me out to dry, these, these people—I am so going to—

"Sorry."

"It's okay."

Pause.

"Well, otherwise you seem good," she said. There was a bass note of impending closure in her tone.

"You have to go?"

"Well, I'm sure they're done refueling."

Don't push it, I thought. Forget it. Don't fool yourself, don't drive yourself crazy, don't beg, don't do any of those things. She's busy. She really does have to work. She's got a child. She's got an empire to run. She's got fish to fly and kites to fry. She's corporate. She's tightly scheduled. She's living Xtra Large.

"Hey, are you sure you're all right?" Marena asked.

"I'm fine," I said. "I can quit anytime."

"Very funny."

As one might have expected, there was another awkward pause. Was I smelling the vomit from out in the street, or was it just my inner landscape?

"I'm feeling a little awkward here," I said.

"Sorry." She looked down at the blue Formica tabletop.

"It's okay." Damn it, Jed. You just rolled over, spread your legs, and said, 'Please be rough.' You pussy. Corny, stupid, pathetic pussy—

"All right, look," she said. "There's another thing. I wasn't going to mention this right now, but I should tell you that I'm thinking about getting married. Again."

Pause.

"This would be to someone other than myself," I said.

"Uh, yeah. Yeah, you don't know him, he's a neighbor in Woody Creek."

"Huh. Uh, well, congratulations."

"Save it, look, you know . . . I think, the deal is, I think the you-and-I thing is actually really terrific. But I don't think you're a settler-downer. Are you?"

"Well, mmm, no, I settle—I mean, I'm not a settler, no."

"Girls need to settle," she said. "I know it's ridiculous, but it's just a time-scale thing. Girls have a very short shelf life, and this whole Doom thing just made—I mean, look, girls just need all this stupid—you know, they don't really care who it is as long as he'll just, like, wear khaki shorts and, like, coach Max's lacrosse team and stay awake during the day and go to bed at night, and, like, be boring—anyway, you know all this."

"Boring is hot," I said.

"Yeah, for girls of a certain age, it definitely is."

"Right." Stupidly, I was feeling kind of not-in-a-good-way weightless. And maybe more about this Marena thing than about my new status as an infected host.

"Anyway—look, just come out and we'll talk about it when we have time to talk about it. Okay?"

"Okay."

"You okay?"

"I'm okay."

"Okay. I'd better go. I swear I'm going to make this right. Call me."

"I will," I said.

"Tomorrow," she said. "I mean it." She stood up.

"I will," I said. I stood up.

She kissed me again. I didn't entirely kiss back. She turned and walked into the indoor part of the restaurant. I looked over the balcony.

Damn, I thought.

The thing was, when I'd just met her, Marena had seemed like she was from some fresher, cooler planet close to the universe's imaginary bright center. And I was like, don't even fantasize about it, Jed. Not in a quintillion years. And then I'd thought she was turning out a bit like me under the gloss, and we were developing a rapport, and all the coolness was just an act. And now she was back to coolness, and I was thinking maybe it was the rapport that was an act. Or they were both acts, but she only did the rapport one at special command performances. Bitch. What you need—oh, there she is.

She came out of the door twenty feet below me and walked out into Fort Street. She didn't look up. Oops, no, she did. She waved. I waved. She turned away and let herself into the back of the X1. It pulled away. I sat back in the little uncomfortable chair.

Well, that was . . . unbearably uncomfortable, I thought.

Moth okay.

Hell.

Stupidly, intolerably, inevitably, I'd started thinking about this moment—it was after the Hippogriff incident and before we picked up the lodestone cross—when I was reading and Marena was asleep and dreaming with her eyes darting around behind her smooth lids. The window had been open and there was a medium-large sphinx moth in the room, flapping around the screen of my phone, and it landed on her forehead.

"Spider," she said, still 90 percent asleep but a little alarmed. "Get it away."

"It's just a friendly moth," I said in her ear.

"Oh," she said in this unconsciously little-girlish tone. "Moth okay. Friendly." She rolled over toward me. It felt like having a baby daughter, somebody who absolutely trusts you—

Fuck.

You get a moment or two of absolute closeness, and then when it's back to the dirty business of life as usual you get upset that it's not still there, and then try to find that again and keep repeating the cycle, over and over without learning. There's intimacy and distance and the ancient, perennial, insoluble, and cataclysmic disjunction between them, and you just keep— Fuck. You know this person inside out, you know how she orgasms, how she sleeps, and then in the morning you're both just a pair of dirty fucks again, and you hate yourselves and each other for it. You're pathetic. What did you expect? That you were going to ride off with her into the sunset in a maroon X1? It was just a nine-night stand. Or was it eight?

Maybe I should go back out there, I thought. Maybe we'd get back into that same groove again. Isolation, nothing to do, bad-looking colleagues. You'll be back in the sack again in one day. No big deal. These days it's just in and out of grooves, she'll give Woody the boot in—

Except no. Don't delude yourself. She was just gaming you to get you to work harder. Just volunteer for this suicide mission and you get to spend your last night before deployment with Miss Seoul. You maroon.

And the worst thing about it is how conventional it all is. The stupid little fling, your stupid emotions, the unavoidable last awkward conversation, it's corny and unremarkable. You're worse than damaged, unstable, and semiautistic, Jedface. You're *ordinary*. Skills or no skills. Money or no money. Game or no Game.

And even when you play the Game, you're not really playing it. It's playing you. As was she. As does everybody.

Loser.

I took my hat off and wiped an installment of sweat out of the band. Frigid interstellar plasma winds whistled over my dome. Well, maybe you deserve it, I thought. You're not even that great at the Game. You can't even get to nine stones. Not even with the aid of a computer with a brain the size of the Orion Nebula. You can't even finish an eight-stoner.

I put my hat back on.

Damn it.

What the hell were those things, anyway?

Hmm.

Just one little solitaire game, I thought. Half an hour. Just play out that last position. No big deal. I can quit anytime. Go ahead, set your sights a little higher.

I dug two plugs of tobacco out of the little bag in my other waist pocket and sneaked them into my mouth and masticated them into a big old quid. Okay. I got up, went inside past the noisy second-floor bar, down the stairs, and into the bathroom—the door said BAD BWOYS—and shot up with the fourth-from-last AirJet of my clandestine stash of hatz' k'ik'. I spat out the quid of tobacco. God, I'm disgusting, I thought. Silly habit. Quids are for hicks. I rubbed tobacco juice into my stain, put myself back together, rubbed lukey water on my face, and went back to my mini-table.

I opened my phone. That Ixian mural was still there. Damn, what was that thing? Snail, centipede, both, or neither? Well, whatevs. I clicked SACRIFICE. The game board came up. Just to feel independent, I closed down the Net connection. I didn't need it this time anyway. By now I pretty much knew what was out there. I had facts at my fingertips. Too many facts. The hard thing is to comprehend the weights of those facts relative to each other. Like, "There's a *Sphecius* wasp on the side of my rum glass" and "The universe contains about 4×10^{79} atoms" are both facts, but one is a lot more important than the other. Although I'm not saying which one.

I started feeling the throbs, spreading from my left thigh, down into my foot, and up into my groin.

"Now, this is the burning, the clearing," I mumbled. I put up the last position from my last good game, the one that nailed Madison. I wasn't even sure why I was going back into it, except that sometimes you want to finish playing out an alternate line to see who would have won. No matter how little you're enjoying the show, past a certain point you stay in the theater to see how it ends.

"Now I am borrowing the breath of today," I said, "*La hun Kawak, ka Wo*, 10 Hurricane, 2 Toad, the nineteenth sun of the fifth uinal of the nineteenth tun of the nineteenth ka'tun of the thirteenth b'ak'tun." I moved my eighth skull forward, toward 4 Ahau, up the western slope of that eroded mountain with the rusty dust, toward the cave in the sky with the echoing howls.

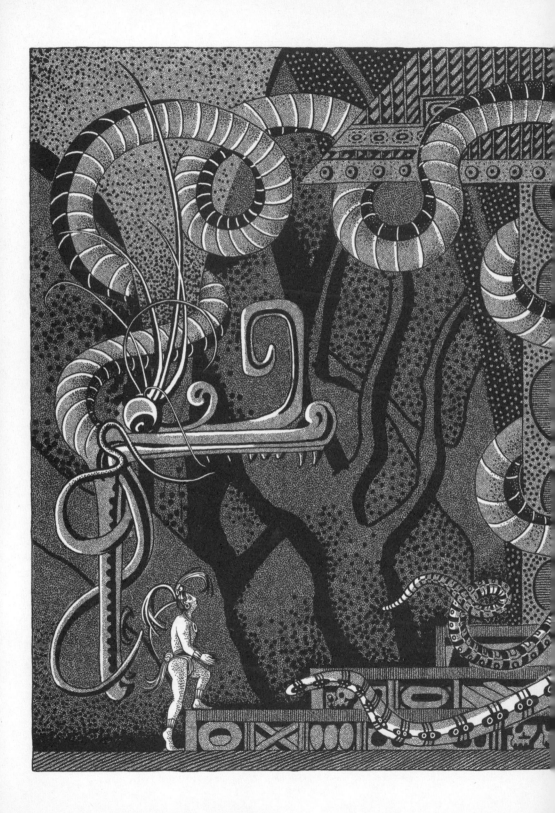

(71)

One of the distinctive effects of the Game drugs was that they seemed to create a separate place in your mind. You could take a break from a game and go about your regular life for days or weeks, and you wouldn't feel like you were thinking about the game at all, but then when you took another shot of the stuff you'd click right back into where you were and go on playing without having to reorient yourself. I guess it wasn't really much different from the feeling of watching a new episode of a TV show every week, or picking up a book where you left off, or just playing Warcraft on your phone or whatever, except that it was more self-generated and orders of magnitude more intense. Anyway, even though on one level I knew I was sitting at this rickety table on a balcony in Belize City, when I focused on the board it was as though I was right back in the same place I'd been when I was looking for Madison, on the west side of that crumbling mountain, and with almost no effort I could imagine the warmth of the old sun on my back and hear the hiss of the clouds of brick-red dust sifting down around me, and as I moved my eighth skull forward the lucidity increased and it was almost as though I could feel the stone under my feet and smell the bone smoke in the wind. This way, I thought. He goes. I go. That way. I kept climbing, up past the dust into clouds of steam and then up past that, through a layer of clouds of ashes. I stumbled. The stairs had aged since the last time I'd come this way and they were almost too cracked and pitted to stand on, but on the mental equivalent of all fours I kept climbing, out of the ash and through clouds of ice shards into the frozen zone just below the shell of the sky, up onto the eroded terrace. The booming and bellowing were louder than before. The boulder was gone. For a second I tried to get a look at the coming worlds in the east, but they were still hidden behind the bulk of the mountain, and I crouched down again. The maw of the shaft in front of me had widened since 13 Dog 18 Tortoise, and as I felt my way down into it the stone crumbled around me, and the chasm opened out as I descended, and I could tell it was way too deep for skull #8. Go for it, I thought. No problem.

I moved out my ninth skull. The abyss widened, and already I could tell it was larger than any cave on earth. Maybe it would be like rappelling down a methane icefall into one of the miles-wide bubbles in the interior of some Saturnian moon. Even so, the ninth stone had a solid link to the eighth, and I crawled down and down, toward the center of the sphere, into the roaring vortex. The beings whirled around me, almost but never quite grazing me, the way bats will rush past you if you stand in the mouth of a cave at sundown. You smell their sour guano smell, you feel the whipping air, and you hear the soft roar of their wings like a storm of leather leaves, and they always, always miss you . . . but the things around me were bigger than bats, and slower, and somehow . . . gentler, I guess, and wingless—and of course bats, to us anyway, are silent, and these things were deafeningly loud. Maybe this was where Dante's mind had gone, I thought, when he imagined the *luxuriosi* in their infernal hurricane. As my internal eyes adapted to the gloom the presences became clearer, and without seeing individuals I began to make out their motion, which was more like sea creatures, although now they didn't look like sea lions. They were more like beluga whales with their domed brows and taut white skin . . . but then their curled spines made them look like hunchbacks, or maybe they were more like dwarfs, with short bodies and huge heads . . . but then they had short fat tails, and only rudimentary buds for arms—like tadpoles, maybe, just morphing into toads?—except they had ears, and throbbing hearts visible through their translucent skin, and swelling eyes darting behind closed lids, like—

They were embryos.

They were the a'aanob, the aftercomers, the spirits of the unborn.

No wonder there were millions and quintillions and near infinities of them. There were whole populations of the future in here, all the men and women who would be born after 4 Ahau and who would never have been born if that boulder had fallen and blocked the shaft. Now, when the sun of the b'ak'tun reached its zenith on 4 Ahau, it would shine down the shaft into this cave and light up the multitudes of a'aanob. The ether in the great cave would heat and expand, and inexorably, irresistibly, they'd be carried up and out of the shaft, and wave after wave of them would spread over the earth. I remembered what Jed$_2$ had said, that Lady Koh had said about how the people of the zeroth level had three caves: the Cave of the Dead, which was on the other side of the world, in the west, and then the Cave of the Breathing, which is of course what we would call the world, and then, here, the Cave of the Unborn.

I watched. I listened. Suddenly, I realized something about them: that they were happy.

The shades of potential consciousnesses were playing. Or, to use an obsolescent word, they were frolicking. They swam in knots, chasing each other, like otters. They bumped hips like dancers in a 1970s disco. They spun around and around out of sheer delight in the motion.

Slowly, like my inner eyes, my internal ears adapted, and the cacophony of howls almost began to make sense. The first thing I realized was that they weren't roaring at each other. They were calling out to me, specifically me, in the ur-language babies know, and now I could make out what they were saying:

> LEAVE US HERE!
> YOU! FLESH DROPPER! PLEASE LEAVE US HERE!
> WE DON'T WANT TO LEAVE!
> WE DON'T WANT TO LIVE IN THE SUN!
> COVER US UP!
> DROP THE STONE OVER US!
> PROTECT US!
> HIDE US!
> ***DROP THE STONE!!!***

There wasn't even one of them who wanted to be born.

Still, I couldn't stay here. At some point, even in a solo game, you have to make a move, and it was as though my ninth skull was straining against the edges of its square. I climbed four squares up the blue-green axis, up through the striated years, out of the cave and into cold air, doggishly shaking off the amniotic mist. I could still hear the a'aanob screaming behind me, begging me to help them stay unborn, away from the world of pain. My last skull climbed and climbed and came to a small flat green jade block, about the size of home plate, and I realized that now the thin air was cloudless. I stood and looked around. The planes of time rotated below me, white, black, yellow, and red. I'd reached the summit.

"Can I get you anything else, honey?" the waitress asked in her soft voice.

"Uh, could I get another triple espresso?" I asked. "And another shot of Cruzan?"

"Sure thing, honey." She rolled off. I stretched and resettled myself. That dog was still barking out there, in a howly voice like Desert Dog's. I watched the little scene loop in my mind a few times, the last few minutes of the last night I'd sneaked out to his cage, when I knew my stepbrothers were going to torture him to death the next morning, and I'd given him water and petted him for a while through the wire, and then finally when it was clear that the sun wouldn't wait I got a strap from my backpack and found a stick of chromed metal from some car trimming, and I tied the strap around his neck with the stick through it and twisted it around. The strap sank deep into his luxuriant ruff, but he was oddly quiet, trembling but not struggling, so that I was quite sure he knew what I was doing. He was dead in less than a minute, curled up with an expression of frozen gratitude. The waitress came back. I had a sip of rum, a slug of espresso, and, just to spite Marena, a marshmallow.

Ahh. Better.

I looked back down at the board, where I was still standing on the tur-quoise center square, at the peak of the inverted mountain. I blinked around. Below me the storms had calmed and the dust was settling over the plains. Four staircases, or paths or arteries or whatever, led down from the block. The northeast path stretched off over coasts crusted with corroded mill towns and through whitecaps and silver gulfs over undersea canyons, under strings of giant aluminum aircraft and out past stained limestone cities, off into the fast ice, and then floe ice, and then field ice. A hot-tar smell of the recent past wafted up on my left and I turned ninety degrees counterclock-wise, toward the northwest. There were dunes of cinders and puffs of radioac-tive ash, and beyond that deserts strewn with oil rigs and dry valleys like bowls of acid gas over dark glowing coals, with snarls of asphalt draped on and around them, and beyond that I could see chains of coal smoke from steam locomotives and files of starving families dragging sleds across the prairies, and then beyond that flocks of trash-fed seagulls over dark water, and tundras and grease ice in the permanent twilight. I looked southwest, over choleric salt marshes crawling with malacostraca and plains with packs of giant canary-yellow carnivorous birds running down herds of hipparia. I noticed a coppery armadillo the size of Marena's Cherokee rooting in a dry gulch, and then a formation of *Quetzalcoatlus northropi*, with forty-foot wings covered with gold down, spiraling unflappingly over the corpses of giant crocodiles on the left bank of the Cretaceous Seaway, and beyond that there were more and more creatures and places and times, instants of the past like sheaves of animation cells pressed into striated canyons, to the point where I had to turn left again. In the southeast, dawn spread bloody onychitomized fingers over realms of pure potential that expanded out and out, past where the horizon would be on a spherical earth, as though I were standing on a planet the size of Jupiter, or not even, but on a truly flat and infinite plain, and because the air was absolutely clear, or maybe rather because there was no air, it was as though I could see the details of events in the farthest distance as clearly as the ones right below me. Too many details, in fact. Too much.

I turned around again, slowly, counterclockwise, like a reflection of the sweeping second hand of Lindsay Warren's Oyster Perpetual. The Steersman's final phase was kicking in, when you start to sense what Lady Koh had called the "other winds." Jed$_2$ had explained that she meant something like "elemen- tals," or personified invisible forces. With me the first one I usually see is heat. It looks a little like an infrared photograph, except the heat radiating out of bodies and engines and the earth has a color more like Day-Glo brown and a smell like rum and red pepper. Then other things come into the picture, dia- mond flickers of solar flares spewing out, looping around the earth, and fall- ing back into the sun, lugubrious maroon radio waves spelling out tides of terabytes of useless data, microwaves in a color like what orange and purple would mix to if they didn't make gray, and, at one limit of my expanding blob of awareness, cyan cyclones of gamma rays jittering through my body like shotgun blasts through a swarm of deerflies. I thought I could hear asteroids screeching toward the earth, that I could feel the friction between tectonic plates, the energy building up in granite watch-springs, that I could watch gravity—which is a kind of mulberry-purple color—spreading out from the earth and bunching into dark stars and draining into the abscesses in exis- tence, and that even the black holes were visible in a way, silhouetted against drifts of interstellar dustballs. I started to distinguish smaller forces, or let's say humbler ones, the powers of living things, vegetable transpiration flash- ing green and ocher, the orange mercilessness of trees strangling their neigh- bors, pheromonal trails dragging animals around like beads on strings. Eventually I started to make out human forces. Sexual compulsion had a highway-flare cherry glow, and it washed over the populous wastes like rip- ples in a pool of oil, scattered with flashes of orgasms that I thought I could taste at a distance and that I thought had a taste like sea urchins. Green- white sparks and arcs of fear crackled across the landscape, clustering into lightning balls in schools and hospitals and war zones. *Yaj*—pain, or pain smoke—rose off the plain like morning mist from boiling bloody dew. It was that livid gray color, almost lavender but not in a good way. It gathered into wisps and fogbanks and clouds. It had that same flavor that Jed_2 had said you taste in animals that have been tortured to death, that extraterrestrial tang like the opposite of cinnamon. It was the essence to which the smokers were most addicted.

As I think I mentioned before, the word *yaj* means "pain" in Ch'olan, but more in the sense of "pain smoke" or "pain as an offering" or, you might say, "holy pain." The opposing word would be *je'elsaj,* which you could translate as "pleasure" or "happiness" but which really means something more passive, like "rest" or "ease." But even after I'd stood for what seemed like hours scanning the eastern horizon, the yaj was like a roof of clouds covering the entire landscape, and the moments of je'elsaj were like grassy lime-green mountaintops pushing up here and there through the overcast. It's not even a contest, I thought. If you took any individual person and totaled up their instants of pain against their instants of happiness, it was like a gallon against a drop. And the farther I looked—well, I'd have thought things would get better in the future, that they'd run out of wars and cure all diseases or at least just dope everybody up with happy pills and plop them in front of a two-million-pixel screen, but instead the pain became even more pervasive as I looked farther out, and not one of the n-illions of possible world lines had more than a few scattered islands of je'elsaj peeking out of the clouds. For one reason or another things were just going to get worse and worse.

Even so, I tried to do my bit and measure one against the other. But the more I counted and calculated and compared, the more I felt like I was, say, Marie Curie, and somebody'd given me nine tons of pitchblende ore, and I'd had to extract all the radium out of it, and after three years I'd come up with a residue at the bottom of the last refining mortar that was so thin nobody would even know it was there if it didn't glow like a sunofabitch.

Finally, I gave up.

Really, it's no surprise, I thought. Pound for pound, pain is just n^{fuck}th times more powerful. Anybody who's experienced real pain knows that you'd give up more than an hour of any kind of pleasure—at least—to avoid a minute of real pain. I kept thinking about that kid in the video with the Milk Duds, with her face falling and crunching up and spraying out tears, and how just a few minutes before she was happy, she was bubbly and optimistic and having a great time, possibly the best day of her life so far, even, and how suddenly everything got wrecked for her. Just getting a glimpse of the unbridgeable distance between her state on the video and her state a little before, and how for her that distance is everywhere and forever—well, to glimpse it is to conclude that the only thing to do is just to have the entire universe vanish immediately, in a puff of quarks, because it's just too terribly wrong, and no amount of happiness could ever make up for it. Even if one week from now somebody cured aging and all diseases, and on that same day somebody else invented cold fusion, teleportation, and a delicious nonfattening doughnut, and after that there would be a trillion years of happy, deathless people, it still wouldn't be worth keeping the world around for that long, because in the meantime some other kid would have the same level of disappointment, and nothing that came after would even come close to balancing out the magnitude of that disappointment. If you have even a scrap of empathy, you know it invalidates everything good about the world. If you don't have empathy, then the pain has to happen to you for you to get the message. And people who think they don't feel that way—well, they may be nice people, but they're addicted to denial. They're like kids getting driven past a herd of cows and cooing about how cute the cows are while they eat hamburgers. The pain can't be alleviated, it can't be ameliorated, it can't be recompensed, and it can't be condoned. And most of all, it must not be repeated.

It's a cliché, of course. I mean, the magnitude of pain. It's like saying "the speed of light." It's something one knows about and sometimes talks about with a default position of zero comprehension. Except that unlike with the speed of light, there's a good reason for the incomprehension, because the moment you do start to comprehend it you just give up. One runs out of the room and hides in a dry bathtub. And it's only through massive self-delusion that you manage ever to do anything again.

Well, that delusion may have been necessary up until now. But now the end is achievable. And we know it's the right thing to do—

Whoops.

I was wobbling. I took my eyes off the horizon and got my balance back. Better.

Damn. I could still hear the Unborn screaming.

And no wonder, I thought. We drag them into the world, we give them nine tons of noxious crap on one hand and a half-gram of glowing stuff on the other, and then we want them to act as though they got a fair deal. People agree to abort a fetus whose life would inevitably be a misery, who was going to be born with harlequin ichthyosis, say, but they neglect to abort the ones who'll be born with quotidalgesia, everyday agony syndrome.

The thing is, you don't even have an obligation to give somebody something nice, especially not somebody who isn't born yet. But you do have an obligation not to hurt them. And making them conscious is definitely going to hurt them. Consciousness may be one of the many dirty tricks DNA uses to replicate itself, but that doesn't mean we have to buy into it. For us, consciousness is nothing but a mistake.

I took a sip of Cruzan.

On 4 Ahau, 8 Darkness, 0.0.0.0.0, August 13, 3113 BC, the ancients made a covenant with their ancestors to give them descendants. There'd be descendants to feed them, to praise them, to remember them, and most of all, to give them the liquor of pain. Je'elsaj is for us, and yaj is for the smokers. They love it the way oenophiles love a '47 Haut-Brion, the way a butterfly loves sugar water, or the way NASCAR fans love a crash.

But it would only be for so long. You have to give the smokers—or ancestors or gods or whatever—exactly what you owe them, but you don't have to give them any more than that.

So the Great Adders, the Knowers, had calculated that 4 Ahau was the day the ghastly payoff could finally stop. It was time to do the right thing by the Aftercomers.

I leaned back. I cracked my knuckles and reset my cheek flap. I looked around. The dog with the voice like Desert Dog's had stopped barking. In a few minutes the sunlight would start creeping onto my table. I signaled for the waitress.

The real thing about being an adder, I thought, isn't just being able to play the Game, or being able to deal with the Salter and the Steersman. The real responsibility is to be able to weigh up the world without getting befuddled by sentimentality, without spending all your energy on wishful thinking and superstitious nostrums and selective denial and all the other things normals do. Your duty is to see things unfogged, to understand enough to be able to work out what's actually right, and then to do what's right and not what makes you feel good. Heed the a'aanob, I thought. They know whereof they speak. *K'a'oola'el, k'a'oltik.* He who knows, knows.

The sages who wrote the Codex weren't telling us what would happen, but what should happen.

(0)

Waitress Girl sidled over. For the first time I really looked at her. She had frappuccino skin, a punky hair arrangement, and a guileless face. I figured she was about fifteen. Even though I wasn't in Gametime I could see a halo around her waist in that horrible yaj color, that bruised gray like hot pewter. Some kind of abdominal pain, I thought. A difficult baby? No, I'd spot that. An ulcer? Or a uterine cyst, maybe. Don't ask her about it. You're getting sharper, but you're not a doctor.

I paid. She sashayed off.

En todos modos.

One thing was still bugging me, though. How could Koh not have known about what the Codex was telling me to do? Or rather, of course she knew, but how could she not have told me, or rather not have told Jed$_2$?

I guess she'd just wanted us, or rather me, to get the message. Well, so she led Jed$_2$ on a bit. Nothing new there. But how could he have been so clueless about it?

Except that I've had that sort of trouble with a lot of things. I mean, I can be pretty gullible sometimes. Especially when there's a good-looking young lady involved.

Well, anyway, he'd never know. Jed$_2$, that is.

I had the penultimate slug of rum. Good luck to him. Bastard.

I got out my wallet again and left a 500 percent tip, because, you know, what's the difference? I finished the coffee. I popped one more marshmallow.

Parasites, huh? *Mierditas.* Oh, well. Maybe they can't handle alcohol. I had the last slug of rum. I leaned back.

So it's on me, I thought. It was a sense of . . . well, it was a tremendous sense of duty. But it wasn't overwhelming. It was energizing.

Anyway, like I'd said, it would have to be somebody who'd looked at the world and rejected it completely. Right? Somebody who could grasp the magnitude of what needed to happen, and who could accept that obligation, and who could manage to carry it out.

Esta bien. No problem.

I had the means. I had the will. I had the disgust and the despair. And best of all, I wasn't some dyed-in-the-DNA fuckup like Madison. He'd probably have half botched it anyway. There would have been some virus-free holdouts in Antarctica or wherever, and eventually they would have gotten the whole thing started again, and it would've all been for nothing. Well, that wasn't going to happen this time. Not on my watch.

It was a big responsibility, but I could handle it.

In fact, I thought, it was going to be easy. They'd sent the message of what had to be done, but more importantly they'd also sent the tool to achieve it.

I closed the Game board and stood up. Finally and unequivocally, I knew what I had to do.

End of Book I

GLOSSARY

ahau—lord, overlord

ahau-na—lady, noblewoman

bacab—"world-bearer," one of four local ahauob subject to the k'alomte'

b'ak'tun—a period of 144,000 days, roughly 394.52 years

b'alche'—lilac-tree beer

b'et-yaj—teaser, torturer

Ch'olan—the twenty-first-century version of the language spoken by the Ixians and others

grandeza—a pouchful of pebbles

h'men—a calendrical priest or shaman. Also translated as "sun adder" or "day-keeper"

hun—"one," or "a" as a definite article

k'atun—a period of 7,200 days (nearly twenty years)

k'iik—blood, a male belonging to a warrior society

k'in—sun, day

koh—tooth

kutz—a neotropical ocellated turkey

milpa—a traditional raised cornfield of about 21 × 20 meters, usually cleared by burning

mul—hill; by extension "pyramid" or "volcano"

nacom—sacrificer

pitzom—the Maya ball game

popol na—council house

quechquemitl—Mexican woman's triangular serape

sacbe—"white path," a sacred straight causeway

sinan—scorpion

tablero—the horizontal element in a Mexican-style pyramid

talud—the sloped element in a Mexican-style pyramid

teocalli—Nahuatl for "god house," or temple

tun—360 days

tu'nikob'—sacrificers or offering priests, or, literally, "sucklers"

tzam lic—"blood lightning," a frisson under the skin

tz'olk'in—the ritual year of 260 days

uay—a person's animal co-essence

uinal—a period of twenty days

waah—tortilla

Xib'alb'a—the Underworld, ruled by the Nine Lords of the Night

xoc—shark

yaj—pain, pain smoke

Yucatec—the present-day language of the Yucatán Maya, a version of which was also spoken during the Classic period

ACKNOWLEDGMENTS

People who did enough work on this book to deserve (at least) second-author credit include Anthony D'Amato, Barbara D'Amato, Julie Doughty, Janice Kim, Prudence Rice, and Deborah Schneider.

People who commented on multiple drafts and who helped in many other ways include Jacqueline Cantor, Lisa Chau, Brian DeFiore, Michael Denneny, Molly Friedrich, Marissa Ignacio, Erika Imranyi, James Meyer, and Brian Tart.

People who commented on at least one draft and helped in other respects include Amy Adler, Janine Cirincione, Sheryl D'Amato, Michael Ferraro, Jonny Geller, Karin Greenfield-Sanders, Sherrie Holman, Francis Jalet-Miller, Ellen Kim, Diana MacKay, Bill Massey, Julie Oda, Bruce Price, David Rimanelli, Rebecca Stone-Miller, Susan Schulman, Michael Siegel, Brian Tart, Caroline Trefler, and Joan Turchik.

People who helped in other ways include, among many others, Laurie Anderson, Steve Arons, Jack Bankowsky, Eric Banks, Barbara and Ken Bauer, Mary Boone, Peter Coe, Anne-Marie Corominas, Paul, Emily, and Adam D'Amato, Christy Ennis, Stanley Fish, Patrick Garlinger, Sherrie Gelden, Cathy Gleason, Justin Gooding, Stacy Goodman, Wendy Goodman, Timothy Greenfield-Sanders, John Habich, Peter Halley, Sylvia Heisel, Bryan Huizienga, Nick Jones, Barbara and Justin Kerr, Malachi Kim-Price, Lily Kosner, John Byron Kuhner, "Mad P," Jamie McDonald, Annetta Massie, Jamie McDonald, Mary Ellen Miller, Barbara Mundy, Pablo and Shana Pastrana, Helmut Pesch, Robert Pincus-Witten, Marlón Quinoa, Alexis Rockman, Sarah Rogers, Eric S. Rosenthal, M.D., Dietmar Schmidt, Deb Sheedlo, Pamela Singh, Michael Spertus, Stephane Theodore, Jack Tilton, Jane Tompkins, Andrew Solomon, Brian Vandenberg, Marshall Weir, "Tony Xoc," "Flor Xul," Alice Yang, Eric Zimmerman, and Sergej Zoubok.

The equations in Chapter 20 are taken from Joaquin P. Noyola, University of Texas at Arlington, "Relativity and Wormholes," 2006, and from S. V. Krasnikov, "Toward a Transversable Wormhole," 2008.

Thanks also to the Foundation for the Advancement of Mesoamerican Studies, pauahtun.org, the University of Illinois, and Yale University. Illustrations were produced using software by Adobe, Autodesk, Microsoft, and Wacom.

Finally, thanks to Brian D'Amato for any and all errors.

For a select bibliography, please see briandamato.com.

ABOUT THE AUTHOR

Brian D'Amato can usually be found in either New York, Michigan, or Chicago. He is an artist who has shown his sculptures and installations at galleries and museums in the U.S. and abroad, including the Whitney Museum, the Wexner Center for Contemporary Art, and the New Museum of Contemporary Art. In 1992 he co-organized a show at the Jack Tilton Gallery in New York that was the first gallery show exploring the then-new medium of "virtual reality." He has written for magazines including *Harper's Bazaar, Index, Vogue, Flash Art,* and most frequently *Artforum,* and has taught art and art history at CUNY, the Ohio State University, and Yale. His 1992 novel, *Beauty,* which Dean Koontz called "the best first novel I have read in a decade," was a best-seller in the U.S. and abroad and was translated into several popular languages. For more information see www .briandamato.com.

Look for the second book in the Sacrifice Game Trilogy

by Brian D'Amato

Coming from Dutton in 2010.